D-55-50

F
ER

SALVA

Ride Out the Storm

ROGER VERCEL

TRANSLATED FROM THE FRENCH

BY *Katherine Woods*

～～～～～～～～～～

Ride Out the Storm

G. P. PUTNAM'S SONS NEW YORK

To the Association of Ocean-going Captains of the Cape Horn Passage, its president, its governing board, its members; to all those "Men of the Cape" who have consented to live over again for me the heroic days of the deep-sea voyages of the great sailing-ships, and who have entrusted to me the recollections which give this book its entire value; and

To Madame H. Lelièvre, Madame M. Rose, Madame L. David, Madame L. Martin and the memory of her son, born at Cape Horn and dead on the field of honor; and to all the "Women of Cape Horn," in admiration and homage.

ROGER VERCEL

To Jean de Lestapis, who helped with the technical phrases of the sailing-ships; and

To Ina Telberg, who shared enjoyment of them.

KATHERINE WOODS

CONTENTS

Book One   THE SEAMAN

BOOK ONE

I

HIS hands in his pockets, Captain Le Gac was gazing at the three feet of water that separated his ship from the dock, with an intensity which he had never accorded to vaster horizons. He was a broad, thickset man whose short neck supported the face of a Roman pro-consul grown tired in far-off provinces, and whose coarse mustache might have been penciled in by some idle schoolboy. Frowning, his heavy jowls pulled down as if they were filled with buckshot, he was yielding to the pressure of an indignation which was, he knew, completely futile. The surface of the water between the ship's hull and the dock wall was paved with large pieces of puffed-up green-toned sea-biscuit, each touching the other like carefully laid flagstones: the army commissariat, during the night, had dumped bags and bags of damaged hardtack there.

Captain Le Gac was reckoning up the cost of this, and the shameless waste enraged him to the point of suffocation. One might have thought that the provisions had been snatched out of his storeroom, and that he was being presented with the bill. A little more, and he would have questioned all the men who, without so much as a glance at that scandalous stretch of water, were stepping from the dock to his ship: riggers, longshoremen, commission agents.

The drizzling rain had begun again and was blurring the belfry and roofs of Dunkerque, over toward the east. Behind the broad back of the captain, God's second-in-command, who gave no sign of paying any attention, the *Galatée*, a three-masted bark of eighteen hundred tons, with full to'gants'ls, was loading up. To the hiss of escaping steam and the clanging of metal, two cranes were taking up slings of boxes from the glistening quay and piling them up in the fore-and-aft gangway.

At this time—April, 1897—the great sea-going sailing-ships were still the masters of the ports. The steamships, with their boilers still spendthrift of coal and fresh water, could not get the best of them on the long voyages.

3

In the harbor waters of London and Antwerp, on the banks of the Clyde and the Mersey, in the tidal basins of Hamburg, at the wharves of Dunkerque, white or pale-gold forests of tall masts rose amid a confusion of yards wherever the tall ships reared their impressive structures toward the gray sky. Ship-builders then sought speed through beauty. The great four-masters of the French Bordes firm were rivals, in lithe elegance, to the vessels of the Laietz Company of Hamburg, known as "P ships" because all their names began with that letter. The square-rigged three-masters of London, Liverpool, and Glasgow set their sleek contours quarter to quarter alongside the slender clippers from Nantes, Bordeaux, Le Havre, and Dunkerque.

Like thoroughbred horses in their stalls before a race, the still-motionless vessels were maintaining a feverish activity on the part of their caretakers. Crews of riggers were bustling about in the rigging. The sails of incoming ships were being unbent, while sails were being bent on those preparing to depart. Coils of rope, paint, new sails, were being taken aboard. The great oceangoing vessels were themselves still at rest, but the docks beside them teemed with redoubled agitation and effort. Here, nitrates from Chile were being landed. There, cement, rails, and coal were being loaded for the Americas. Elsewhere, men were ballasting the slender clippers that, at New York, would take on drums of oil for Japan. New arrivals were throwing out the motley refuse from the last voyage.

This particular Dunkerque quay was echoing, too, under the weighty jog-trot of heavy draught horses and the steel-banded wheels of drays: brewers' trucks, wagons loaded with equipment, the wagons of the various "landladies," piled high with the decorated sea-chests of newly disembarked sailors or bringing to the ship those of their boarders who were on the point of departure. Open carriages, going in both directions, passed one another, bringing in or taking back the ships' captains, company representatives, ship-chandlers, and the "dealers in men," with their cargoes of sailors and their supporting forces of girls: a bare arm around a lad's neck and he could be had. . . .

The *Galatée* was about to sail from Number Two Freycinet Dock, loaded for Iquique, Chile, and for San Francisco. Beside her lay the *Cambronne,* of Nantes; and in front, the *Houguemont,* a sturdy ship from Liverpool, was moored at the quay. The *Galatée* was no longer in her youth, but her slender masts bore witness that she was a ship of class. Next to the heavy *Houguemont,* built to cut through the waves head down, one felt that she was made for swift dodging and tacking. Even the close proximity of the *Cambronne,* brand-new from the shipyards, did not put the *Galatée* to shame.

4

Monnard, the first mate, a notebook in his hand, was checking the coils of rope, the lines, all the stores that were being poured out of the ship-chandlers' trucks. Guézennec, the second mate, was directing the casks of salt pork and kegs of wine toward the steward's room where they were to be stored. Hervic, the bos'n, was stowing the sails in the lockers, the new ones at the bottom, the worn set on top, ready to be run up when they reached good weather.

The captain had turned back toward the quay. Outlines were blurred there by the thin wash of the rain shower. Three umbrellas were advancing in a line, but Le Gac did not notice them until they had changed their direction and the first one was already on the gangplank. Under it was a stout gentleman with graying hair and gold-rimmed eyeglasses, dressed in a well-cut suit of blue cheviot. His gait was more revealing than his stiff and expressionless face: a slow and measured step like a surveyor's, in which one sensed the mechanical habit of precision.

The woman who was sheltered under the second umbrella offered delicate and anxious-looking features to Captain Le Gac's inspection, with too-light eyes which at once encountered his gaze and became disconcerted.

Under the third mushroom there stretched forth a youth who was too long all over: legs, arms, neck. He had his mother's face, though narrower, with the same pale and very large eyes turning hither and yon in the bewildered search for something, some being, that would be reassuring. He became more terrified every second in not finding it. He wore bicyclist's knickerbockers, the fullness of which broke into accordion pleats on his skinny legs. His fair hair, though cut short, was standing up like a brush against the rim of his jockey cap. As a matter of fact, he himself seemed all on end.

The head of the family strutted as he accosted the captain. He was accustomed to do this whenever he felt the need of some extra assurance. The pink flesh of his neck swelled out so that it seemed like a sort of padding outside his collar, outside the "packing-box," as sailors would say.

"Captain, I am Monsieur Barquet. . . . Bérault has certainly put you in touch with the situation. . . ."

"Quite so."

Captain Le Gac took off his derby hat: Barquet, the cannery owner in Fécamp, to whom old man Bérault, the shipowner, had been obliged to appeal for financial aid after the recent wreck of his insufficiently insured ship, the *Saint Magloire*. Barquet, whose entrance into the picture made it necessary for Le Gac to accept

5

his son, for this voyage, as apprentice. It seemed obvious to the captain, nevertheless, from his first glance at the candidate, that there was only one thing for these parents to do: to take their son by the arm and lead him away wherever they might wish, anywhere, so long as it was not onto the deck of a ship!

"And is this the boy?" he asked, mildly.

"I wanted to bring him to you myself, so as to request you not to spare him anything," Monsieur Barquet explained, in the voice of a Spartan father. "They have not been able to make anything out of him in school. I decided that he was to go to sea, therefore, because in my opinion that is the best way of developing character in a man."

Le Gac acquiesced with a slight gesture which could just as well be an approval of the general axiom as of its application to his new apprentice. The latter was listening, overcome by shame, and by what Le Gac took to be fear, although it was really a loathing of this ship and of these men whom he had hardly glimpsed and yet had immediately detested. The captain, like most of his kind, had an understanding of human beings, elementary perhaps but swift and sound. He realized at once that the new majority stockholder was getting rid of an unsalable article by dumping it on him. For a year, Monsieur Barquet's eyes would be free of the sight of the son whose upbringing he had bungled. Perhaps, too, he genuinely believed in a possible training through the rough life aboardship. But about that, Le Gac was sure in advance, he was mistaken. . . .

"We will do our best," he promised, without conviction.

"You will look out for him, Captain?" the boy's mother put in.

"That is what I am here for, Madame," he answered. But as the gaze of her gray-blue eyes fastened itself upon him with a poignant fixity, he added, "Don't worry, Madame. We'll bring your son back to you, and, in any case, the fresh air will do him good. Now you shall see his cabin, and you can get him settled in it. Yes, Madame, he will eat in the officers' mess. . . ."

He submitted again, for the proper length of time, to the father's injunctions: "Whatever he has a right to, but nothing more. No favoritism." In conclusion Monsieur Barquet declared that his son would come back to the ship at the end of the afternoon, as soon as the train left for Fécamp.

"You will check on that, Captain."

"Certainly. . . . Excuse me, Monsieur Barquet, I see they are calling me, below. The eve of sailing, you understand. Everything must be in order tonight. Toupin"—he called a sailor—"you are to show the apprentice's cabin to this lady and gentleman."

6

Jean Barquet found the ship deserted when he came back on board.

He thought of the farewells at the station: his mother, dissolved in tears, being pushed into the train by his father with a "Come, come, this is ridiculous!"; himself, the apprentice, choking down a sob; his father, one foot on the step, turning around in indignation—"You're not going to cry?" In fury, he had cried out, "Oh, no!" and fled.

Then there had been the wet interminable streets of Dunkerque: rue Thiers, rue Alexandre III, rue de l'Église. He had gone down one after the other without any thought in his mind, his chest constricted as if in an iron corset. He wandered along the docks, from one tidal basin to another; and at last a customs officer put him on the right course and he reached the *Galatée* without having recognized her, because he had only seen her when she was stowed full of cargo, and noisy, and now she was silent and bare.

Sullenly he took a large and bulky key from his pocket and opened the square box that was his cabin: a box, made of pieces of planking, the same uneven planks for floor, walls, and ceiling. He fell into his bunk and rolled over and over in despair, that despair of the young.

The dinner hour, entering his consciousness with the yellower light that came through the porthole, drove him out of his narrow cavern. He was not hungry, but the habit of a meal always served promptly at seven o'clock in his father's house still operated in his distress. He was caught up by the old daily preoccupation with punctuality. Perhaps in some corner of this ship, as at home, there was a table where he ought to sit down, where they would be expecting him. The captain, informed in advance of his return to the ship—a return which he had to "check"—would no doubt have given orders.

Almost before he got to the deck, he felt again that sense of clumsy bulk that had struck him when he first saw the ship. Everything was rudely shaped, hewn out in the lump. The wood seemed scarcely to have ceased being a tree trunk, the iron kept the rudimentary marks of the anvil. The boy could not realize the resistance, the expenditure of force that the sea would demand of all these things; he still felt nothing in them but grossness.

He wandered into the fore-and-aft gangway, along by the hatches, under an unceasing drizzle of rain. Seeking shelter, he went for a moment into the galley, all full of the smell of soot, and crouched over the black range. Then he went out again, caught his foot in a chain, and tore his coat sleeve on the corner of a piece of sheet iron. His uneasiness increased as he traversed the ship. She seemed both deserted and full of traps. He went down a ladder, but with his first step in the hold a rat jumped at his legs. He stifled a cry as he climbed back. At the top of the ladder an old man with a beard, and wearing earrings, was waiting for him.

"What are you up to in here?" he demanded.

"I'm the new apprentice," Jean stammered.

"Oh, so you're the apprentice," the man said. "You pay to go to sea, you do. You've come to take the place of some boy who needs to earn his living."

The old fellow's stern eye fixed him, and young Barquet, stupefied by the revelation that he had stolen someone else's job, began to attempt a sorry smile before replying that he had had no choice in the matter—but the old man got ahead of him.

"Maybe you'll soon have more than your fill of it," he said. Then he went back to his question: "But what are you doing here? The crew won't be aboard until tomorrow."

Barquet explained that it had been arranged with the captain that he was to have dinner aboard ship.

There was a gleam of amusement in the other's yellow eye.

"Were you expecting the Old Man to open a bottle of champagne in your honor? That's not one of his habits, I'll tell you. . . . Since you have the cash, beat it; go get your dinner in town. You won't have another chance right away."

"But I can come back to sleep in my cabin?" the apprentice said.

Disarmed by such ingenuousness, the old man agreed.

"Oh, yes, if you want to. . . . But I've been at sea for thirty-five years and I've been on watch in port for ten years, and this is the first time I've ever seen such a thing!"

Barquet dined on two paper cones of fried potatoes, and then the rain-drenched city seemed to him even more sinister than the ship, and he went back on board, mulling over his sorrows until the monotony of repetition finally put him to sleep.

He was awakened next morning by the beat of a heavy footfall over his head, and going out, he ran into the captain. Le Gac looked at him as if he were a piano—a useless and cumbersome object, but expensive and complicated, which a whim of the ship's owner had constrained him to take aboard. For the maintenance of correct discipline, however, it was necessary to discover some semblance of work for him, and the captain proceeded to orders:

"You will give a hand to the second mate in the steward's cabin, to sort and range the stores coming in."

For provisions were being brought on board: fresh vegetables, bread, meat, sacks of potatoes, carrots, and onions. Guézennec, the second mate, was busy with all this. A Breton from Quimper, plum-cheeked and ruddy, he seemed for the moment happy to be alive and to see this abundance being poured into his domain. He too, with one glance, summed up the assistant that was sent him.

"You're the apprentice? I thought you'd fallen out of the bag of turnips. . . . Well, you'll see your mother again, all right. Now then, pick up the ones that are rolling **away.**"

He was referring to the potatoes that the provision-men were emptying out into the bins.

The new first mate, a tall gaunt man in a black jacket and a cap, whose spare visage was made sharper by a newly cut goatee, had just finished calling the ship's roll. Of twenty-two men, only ten were missing. That was something unhoped-for! To be sure, the bos'n in charge of the crew had himself answered to the names of six, who had had so much trouble getting into their bunks that they could not be got out of them.

A police sergeant and five of his men were waiting near the gangplank: maritime police in white pantaloons, with service cords and white epaulettes. The mate gave the list of the men who had not yet turned up to the sergeant, an official whose heavy silver stripes went up above his elbow, and whose heavy mustache raveled out at the ends and extended as far as his cheekbones.

"We sail at noon," the mate said, in a cool and measured voice. "You have two hours to bring them aboard, sergeant."

The policeman, accustomed to the rough outspokenness of officers in the foreign trade, looked with astonishment at this man, who was as austere and unyielding as a court magistrate. Vaguely intimidated, he assured him: "They will be here on time, sir."

A nod sent his men on their errands. He himself remained aboard with one subordinate, to register the arrivals and to keep those who were already there from going back to the pubs of the port. From this moment, the *Galatée's* delinquents would return to the ship under "square brace," that is, flanked by two official helmets cut in trapezoid form, like the tops'ls when they were square-braced. This would cost every latecomer three francs—three 1897 francs— the "premium for arrest." But it was the last game to be played before sailing, a final luxury to which they would treat themselves, a way of doing themselves the honors of the gangplank.

The first one was brought aboard at half-past ten, a swarthy little man, completely drunk but smiling, who gave a military salute as he stepped a little shamefacedly up the gangway.

"There's a queer bird for you!" one of the policemen said, wiping his forehead when they had shoved the man at last on deck. "He

9

didn't want to sail without Jean Bardt. We had a hell of a time, I'm telling you, getting him away from his statue!"

At a quarter to eleven three more arrived together, wearing women's hats and carrying parasols. Two policemen followed, with a fat brown-skinned woman in a white apron, the servant whose duty it was to retrieve the extra accessories.

Twenty minutes went by without bringing any more arrivals. The mate, Monsieur Monnard, pulled a stout silver watch out of his pocket and noted the time.

"Here comes another, sir."

The sergeant had stepped up to the officer and was pointing out two cocked hats advancing across the quay. But nobody was to be seen between them, and the sergeant frowned as he scrutinized their still-distant silhouettes, often blocked out by the cranes or the merchandise stowed high on the dock.

"Oh, I see," he said at last. "This one they're bringing in a wheelbarrow."

Soon, indeed, they were at the gangplank. With a final muscular effort a policeman pushed up the barrow, in which a man was lying in a heap, his head touching his knees, his arms hanging down to the ground.

"Who is it?" asked the mate.

"Névél," answered the policeman who accompanied the barrow-pusher.

"We never should have found him without Fortuné," declared the other, after he had got his breath. "He was snoring in the chicken coop!"

"We're only short five," announced the sergeant, who had just crossed Névél's name off his list.

The mate looked at his watch again.

"It's high time they were found. The tug will be here in forty-five minutes," he said.

"They take you in, with those tricks they pull on you," the sergeant apologized. And he began to go over his memories of sailings, the round-up of seamen carried on among the landladies and in all the cheap pubs of the port. There was no rancor in his recital, which was often enlightened by some droll recollection. It was a game of hide-and-seek that was played on sailing day between the "square braces" and the sailors: "It's up to you to find me—I pay for it. . . ." And they hid themselves well, the rascals! But as the only places where they could stow themselves away were with the landladies and in the pubs, the task of the policemen was simplified.

The sergeant was interrupted by Hervic, the bos'n, who was also watching the quay. Now he announced: "Here come Le Corre and Gouret."

These two were in no hurry. Le Corre, a square-chinned Breton from the Morbihan, was fast asleep as he walked, his head falling into his scarf with such rough jerks that it seemed as if his neck must be put out of joint. Gouret, his pal, a colossus with a shaven head whose blurred eyes were sunk beneath a flat forehead, was explaining something difficult, with the ample aid of wide flabby gestures, to the policeman on the right, who was laughing his agreement.

But at the moment of stepping on the gangplank the man had a recoil, the spring of an animal before the entrance to the slaughter-house; a hidden instinct of defense woke in the depths of his drunkenness. At sight of the vessel his bewildered eyes flamed with hatred; and as the policeman, startled, caught hold of his arm he gave an abrupt twist and jerked himself free. As he stood there for a moment motionless, fists clenched, on his guard against the ship whose menace had just struck him, the two policemen seized him at wrist and shoulder. On a gesture from the sergeant, the "square brace" who had remained on board ran up to lend them a strong hand. The three together hauled and shoved the sailor up the gangplank, in spite of his struggles. Then Hervic took hold of him and dragged him at arm's length toward the crew's quarters.

At the door of the steward's cabin Barquet, horror-stricken, was watching the embarkation of these men with whom he was about to live.

"How do we stand now, Monsieur Monnard?"

The captain asked the question without taking his eyes from the entrance to the inner harbor through which, in a few minutes, the tug would appear.

The mate, to whom the names of all the crew were new, consulted his list before answering.

"Three still missing, Captain: Morbecque, Mahé, and Rolland."

"Morbecque will come with Mahé," the Old Man averred. "He's his pal. But he's a Dunkerque man, and he'll make it a point of honor not to come aboard till the last minute. As for Rolland—"

He left his sentence unfinished because he had just caught sight of the curved bow of the tug, *Dunkerquois 6*, across the gray water. He made off in the direction of the hawse-hole, where the bos'n was assembling the mats and padding of old sailcloth that would protect the planking during the towing. The tug was already drawing close, at reduced speed, when the bos'n murmured, "Look at what's coming, Cap'n."

11

To distract the attention of Hervic, bos'n of the *Galatée*, from the *Dunkerquois 6* at this moment something extraordinary must have happened. The captain turned around and, on the dock where the passers-by—always curious about a ship's sailing—were already pausing, he saw Morbecque and Mahé. Each was giving one arm to a policeman, while he brandished a sword—the policeman's—in the other. The officers of the law were as drunk as the others, and the policemen and the sailors had exchanged their headgear. Mahé was wearing the cocked hat in the regulation way, but Morbecque had put on his *à l'amiral*, with the point in front. When they reached the gangplank, arresters and arrested broke their mutual hold, but only to fling their arms around each other's necks in the effusion of the final farewell.

Morbecque, a tall red-haired fellow who kept a girl's pure pink-and-white complexion even when he was completely squiffed, demanded solemnly: "You're not going to say you haven't been paid for your towing, square brace?"

No sailor run to earth by the police in the corner of some pub ever failed to offer a drink to his pursuers, but this pair had rather overdone it.

At the rail of the poop the sergeant was frowning, while his subordinates, putting on their hats again, were trying to recover a modicum of dignity. But when Morbecque, in crossing the gangplank, just missed going over the steel cable that formed the guardrail, Captain Le Gac gestured with his chin to the bos'n.

"Give them a kick in the pants and send them to bed. Sergeant!"

The police officer ran to him quickly, and they went back together toward the poop.

"Rolland is still not here," the captain said. "You'll have to find him and bring him to me in the roads." Then he added, as tradition required, "Stop by in the pantry for a tot of grog. Boy, go wait on the sergeant."

The policeman thanked him, briefly expressed his hopes for a good voyage, and hastened toward the pantry: the moments were numbered from now on.

"Ready up forward?"

"Ready!"

The slack tow-line was now linking the *Galatée* to the *Dunkerquois 6*.

"Let go, forward! Let go, aft!"

The hawsers were being underrun with that spirited movement which brings the cordage to life, and which is successfully achieved only by sailors and by women winding wool. The riggers went down

12

the gangplank behind the policemen. A crowd of spectators stood motionless on the quay.

"Go ahead!"

A sign to the tug, a blast from the whistle, a tow-line straining and vibrating, some fluttering handkerchiefs, some waving hands, and the vessel moved slowly away from the shore.

II

IT WAS two hours later, when the *Galatée* was anchored in the roadstead, that Hervic, who had for some time been watching an open boat dancing on the waves, announced to the first mate, "Here he comes—Rolland. The cops have got him."

The little boat came alongside, but nobody in it budged. One of the policemen, who was sitting in the stern, threw a glance at their prisoner, rammed between two of the thwarts at the bottom of the tender, and called out, "He won't be able to climb up. We had to put handcuffs on him, and our orders are not to take them off till he's aboard."

"We'll send you a chair," said the bos'n.

The "square braces" placed Rolland in a bos'n's chair—a small plank hung on four ropes—made him fast, and hauled him aboard. The policemen came up behind him and, once on deck, took off his handcuffs.

The sailor who had arrived thus ignominiously was a lad of about twenty, with firm and regular features. Blood had clotted in his chestnut hair and had sent two dark streaks, like tears, down the length of his right cheek. All the buttonholes of his jacket were torn. Freed from his bonds he stood straight and motionless, his brown eyes fixed on the deck planking, as if unwilling to acknowledge where he was.

Monnard looked him over in silence for several seconds, and then ordered: "Go change your clothes."

The level tone, as well as the brief order, seemed to surprise the sailor. He turned his head, cast a glance at the new first mate, and then, with a shrug of his shoulders, made his way toward the fo'c'sle. Not one of the men lounging about the deck appeared to notice that he was there. He had the savage expression of a man who is best left alone. The seamen were acquainted with one another's fits of rage, and they all realized that this one had reached the point of explosion, where a word, a look, would precipitate an outburst. Only Barquet, stationed in the fore-and-aft gangway, opened wide astonished eyes at the newcomer. With a movement of his shoulder as he passed, the sailor sent him tumbling against the rail. Then, pulling his jacket straight, he went on toward the crew's quarters without looking around.

Meanwhile the two policemen, on the poop, were reporting on their mission.

"We had a hell of a time getting him here," the older one was saying, as he handed the captain the voucher to sign. "We found him in a pub. Oh, he wasn't hiding, but when he saw us he came at us with a stool. That ought to be worth a little bonus, Captain: in one of his bad moods he hit my pal in the pit of the stomach."

"Agreed," said Le Gac. "Blows like that are always paid for. He'll pay for this one."

The policemen went back to their boat, and the captain joined the mate again.

"I am glad they brought him back. I had almost begun to go into mourning for him," he said. "Since he's still with us, I recommend him to you. He is resourceful, intelligent, beyond reproach in his work, but he's like a tops'l—if he's badly set there's no making him draw. And what a foul tongue! He tried to get the best of me. I warned him: 'Listen to my program,' I said. 'I'll let you pull off just one dirty trick. Then, very politely, I will call your attention to the fact that you are subject to the action of the law, and I will put your name on the disciplinary record. That means that at the first port of call I will hand you over to the consul, who will hand you over to the police.' He got it. . . . That is always the way I get rid of undesirables: push them along till they go too far; then, the record! That is my method, and it's a good one."

"That depends," Monnard replied.

The captain looked at him shrewdly and talked of nothing more but the work of the ship. He reminded him that the seagoing tug *Centaure* would take the *Galatée* in tow at seven o'clock the next morning. Whenever it was possible, he anchored like this in the roads. It took a good long night to clean out thoroughly all the surfeit of food and drink on board.

This time the first mate agreed; and when the captain had left him he began to pace up and down the poop.

No more than Le Gac did he ask himself questions about these sprees of the men. It was a tradition of a ship's departure that the

14

sailors should come aboard dead drunk. Monnard was not looking beyond that. At the end of a voyage, however, he had often heard the captain say to a man, "I've reckoned up your account—the gross amount coming to you is two hundred francs."

"Two hundred francs!" the man would echo. "I can't go home with that! Two hundred francs for a year's voyage—they wouldn't want to see me, I'll tell you!"

The easiest way was to go to a "landlady," to let oneself be taken in tow by one of the "hostesses" who hang around the docks, to put oneself in her hands to be cheated, but to find at once eight days of a good time for which she would furnish everything: board, room, spending-money, companions for the night. Then, one morning, she would look at a fellow with a face that had become grave and eyes that were no longer laughing.

"You owe me plenty," she would say. "I've found a good ship for you."

The poor Jack Tar would try hard, then, to argue about the bill. Dumbfounded over having devoured all his cargo, over having not a sou left from his three months' advances, he would break into torrents of profanity.

The landlady would say, "Now look, don't you remember? Last Tuesday you insisted on paying for dinner for the whole table, and Thursday, the twelfth, you stood drinks all round, twice. If I had listened to you, I'd even have brought in all the people that were going by in the street, so that you could pay for their drinks. And there's François and Jules, who haven't had a sober moment in the last three days, and you footing the bill. . . . I warned you, though, about those two . . ."

Dazed by these specific details, incapable of distinguishing anything in this alcohol-befogged passage that had been his sojourn on land, the sailor would fall silent, resigned if not convinced.

As an anesthetic, again, the landlady would supply the goodbye binge, and the poor bankrupt wretch would set out for a voyage of which he had already squandered the earnings.

All the first mate was thinking, as he watched the lights come out along the coast, was that getting drunk was not a solution. That only put off the bad moments, the moments that sooner or later one must ride out. Such a moment was beginning for him this evening, on this idle tied-up ship. He had left his wife six months pregnant, and with legs swollen with albumin. Her first confinement had been very hard, and she had been torn by the surgeon's instruments. In three months it would all start again. And unless a telegram could come in time to reach him in Chile, he would have to wait almost

15

a year before knowing anything, a year in which he would be asking himself every day whether his wife were still alive. His back was bent, this evening, under the weight of those days.

Then, too, he did not know anyone aboard this ship. The captain had the reputation of being close-fisted and crotchety, a good sailor, but one who had not ceased to resent his failure to be given a post as shipping executive. He wanted before all else voyages without incidents, either with the men or with the sea, and he "drove" his ship as he would "drive" a trolley car on a route that he knew by heart. He had welcomed his new "second captain" with some polite banalities and a defiant glance which meant, "We'll wait and see." The captain, like the men, would be trying him out. That was not worrying him; he had made his mark, elsewhere. But, by so much the more, it would prolong the period of his being a stranger on this ship. When he had made a place for himself the worst hours, no doubt, would be over; but he would have to go through them alone; that was inevitable.

He paused in his promenade and stood near the helm, gazing down mechanically at the black lines of the deck planking.

A step on the companionway made him turn around. In the dim light he recognized the apprentice by his gawkiness. The darkness, against which only his silhouette stood out, emphasized his crude and unpromising youth. He stepped up to the mate.

"Is there any work for me to do this evening, sir?" he asked.

"Why? Do you want to go into town?"

Under the officer's cold raillery the young man once more attempted the poor spiritless smile of which he had been making use all day to disarm ridicule.

"Go into town?" he echoed, in a tone which he tried to make easy and unself-conscious. "That would be difficult. No, I just wanted to know if I could make myself useful."

Monsieur Monnard considered this display of zeal untimely and childish.

"Well, then, go to bed," he said. "Starting from tomorrow morning, you won't be wanting to come asking for work."

The apprentice muttered a "Good night, sir," to which the officer responded with a gesture so slight that the lad did not notice it; and then he went below to his cabin again, bearing with him that threat of "tomorrow," like a lump of ice.

Daylight had come in through the portholes to the crew's quarters. But nothing entered except the light itself, a niggardly light dirtied by the thick muddy glass. The pure brilliance of the spring morning, the freshness of the air, the salt savor of the wind—all these re-

16

mained outside. In the enclosure, as in a chemical retort, the stenches of the night were fermenting, dreadfully: vomitings and breaths of alcohol, the barbarous smells of greased boots and sou'westers permeated with rancid oil. From all the tiers of bunks came the raucous and hissing sounds of open-mouthed snorings, so heavy one might have thought they were rattling the deck planks as they rattled the men's throats. Sea-chests, bags, and boots were piled on top of each other, pyramided on the benches and the big solid table. An empty quart bottle rolled back and forth across the cabin deck.

In the bunks, furnished with new straw ticks, the men were lying just as they had been thrown the day before, some of them with head and one arm thrust outside their cubbies, the whole body ready to slide out. Névél, the one the police had brought to the ship in a wheelbarrow, had tried at daybreak to go to the latrine, but he had fallen over the pile of bags and had gone to sleep again with his cheek against the table.

"Show a leg in there! Get up for watch!"

The bos'n's bulky form was framed in the open doorway. Hervic was so broad that he filled the entrance, and it was only above his shoulders that a little daylight got past. For a moment he stood lost in contemplation of the rows of bunks in which no one stirred, then he came into the room resolutely.

He seized the first man by the shoulder and shook him roughly.

"Get up!" he repeated.

The man's snoring was abruptly extinguished, as if a current had been cut. In other bunks, not reached so quickly by his voice, the bos'n found the men sunk into such deep wells of sleep that the awakening was sluggish. In such a case he would seize the man's jacket close to his throat, lift him into a sitting position, and then jam him down on the straw mattress. He shoved the men in the upper tiers down into their bunks; then, abruptly, he would seize one whose body was still limp, pull him out, and fling him down on deck. When he had emptied two more tiers, he paused to take another look around him. This time, arms were being stretched out everywhere. Their eyes flickering, their whole appearance stupid and besotted, the men were beginning to sit up. They were rubbing their heads with their thick hands and trying to recover a modicum of consciousness. Hervic did not leave until they were all standing up, and practically awake.

When he had slammed the door behind him, they did not speak immediately. Their eyes, still sunk in stupor, were slowly wandering about the narrow quarters.

"Say, Pierre, where are we?"

"On the *Galatée*."

17

"On the *Galatée,* good God! That damn cockroach Fortuné! I told him I didn't want to bring my bag to the *Galatée,* and that's where he's dumped it!"

As a good third of the men, among the eighteen who were there, were totally ignorant of the name of the ship for which the "landlady" had signed them up, a flood of curses and blasphemies was now poured forth.

"She's got the best of me again! I swear I'll kill her when I get back!"

"On the *Galatée,* with old Le Gac, the damn skinflint! I saw him at Melbourne. Listen—you could get a hundred apples for a penny, and he never handed you out one! Such grub!"

"If my poor mother could see me, on an old tub like this, when I've sailed on the Bordes line for five years. . . ."

Someone, a young sailor, called out, "Oh, well, to hell with it!" The cry that burst forth from the old nonchalance of the sea interrupted the imprecations. From one of the upper bunks Rolland, the only one of the men who had neither got up nor sat up, flung out disdainfully, "You'll work yourself to death here just as well as anywhere!"

"You're right, at that!" someone said.

Rolland jumped to his feet with a lithe muscular spring. It was only then that the others seemed to notice the little rills of clotted blood that made bizarre tattoo marks on his face.

"Well, say! The kid didn't scratch you; she bit you!"

He gave a quick smile, and went out. When he came back, a few minutes later, his face was clean and still damp, with a long diagonal cut showing across his forehead, and a lock of hair plastered down over a gash in his scalp.

The bos'n came in on his heels. "Everybody on deck!" he roared. "All hands, take in the tow-line!"

Feet dragging, they went along behind Hervic to the upper deck to take in the tow-line from the *Centaure,* the seagoing tug which was already puffing off the bow. When the cable had been made fast, the bos'n called out, "Man the windlass!"

They went off, grumpily, to take hold of the capstan bars.

"We've got a good captain: he's treating us to the merry-go-round," Nével announced as he picked up his.

But while the others, after fitting their spikes into the capstan, waited for the next order with the passivity of beasts of burden, eyes to the ground, Rolland sent his glance over the whole horizon— the sparkling sea, the coast stretching blue in the distance under a dust of light mist. And his mouth was warped with bitterness.

"Like all the other bitches," he muttered. "She smiles at you when you're leaving her."

Névél, who was waiting in front of him hunched over his bar, turned his head slightly. "Who does?" he asked.

"The land," Rolland said.

"Ready?" called the bos'n.

"Ready!"

"All together! Now, turn!"

They bent over the spikes on which their hands were clenched and stepped forward. A heavy grating noise sounded at once under their naked feet: the anchor chain rolling up on the windlass.

"Come on now, take up the slack!"

They did not have to put any effort into it now. The slack chain was rising to the hawse-hole without resistance, and the bos'n stepped up the pace. They did not run, however; it was still too soon for rapid movements. They merely walked a little faster, made still more stupid by this circular motion; and they really did, as Névél had suggested, resemble the resigned and sleepy-looking horses of a merry-go-round. The bos'n realized that roaring at them would have little effect, and that only for a few seconds. So he began to chant, in his most falsetto voice, which he only brought out on formal occasions:

"When the lame woman's off to the market—"

The men, all turning around together, gave him one look and broke into hearty laughter. Hervic himself smiled. It needed no more than this to put the sulky gang in a good humor, and Rolland was the first to take up the chantey:

"When the lame woman's off to the market,
With her basket on her arm,
Along comes a jolly sailor—"

The beat of the song kept time with the men's robust march. Little by little, the rough voices poured forth and swelled in the morning air:

"Oh, take two reefs in her apron,
And clew up her skirt so free—"

The ribald couplets rang out above the grinding of the anchor chain, which was gradually becoming stiffer, until lack of breath broke the rhythm of the last lines:

19

"O, what's she got now in her basket?
In less than ten months we'll all see:
A wee cabin boy launched in the shipyard—"

Then there was no more singing, but a series of dull grunts as several more turns pulled, link by link, at the chain.

Monnard, his tall body bent far over the side, straightened up and turned around.

"Anchor apeak!" he announced.

The chain was taut as a bar of iron now, between the vessel and the sea bottom, where the anchor was still biting.

The captain's voice sounded from the poop: "Nével to the wheel! Apprentice, take his place. It will give you some muscle."

Barquet came up to take the place left vacant at the windlass, in front of Rolland, and the captain called out: "Anchor aweigh!"

They arched their bodies over the bars, teeth clenched, straining their muscles to pull the anchor up. But it was as if a machine were jammed by a stone caught in the gears.

"Ho-ho. . . ."

The bos'n was cadencing their effort, both with his voice and with the forward movement of his body from the waist up. The men were flinging themselves against the spikes in rhythm, with great thrusts of their chests and shoulders that drew a kind of raucous moan from their throats. Once the apprentice pushed out of time, and Rolland, kicking out under his spike and without speaking a word, gave him a frightful blow with his knee, that fairly caved in the boy's back. At last the chain yielded: the anchor had just pulled itself out of its matrix of mud and was rising.

The first mate, still leaning over the side, called out astern, "The anchor is up!" Then he looked at the men, now standing straight and panting. "Who will cat the anchor?" he asked.

Rolland detached himself from the group of winded men, stepped over the stanchions, and let himself slide down the chain on the throat of the anchor. They let down the "cat," a hooked tackle which must catch the anchor in the middle of the shank in order to lift it horizontally and place it in position on deck. Rolland attached it and pulled himself back on board. The mate had not taken his eyes off him, but he had seen in his look and bearing only the indifference of someone who is thinking, Since it has to be done, I'll go to it and get it over.

After the call to rations, the novice had brought the kettle of coffee from the galley to the crew's quarters, and they were finishing soaking their hardtack in it when the mate and the bos'n came in.

20

"We'll make up the watches now," Hervic said.

The men got up, resigned but glum. Their trade was entering the fo'c'sle to gather them up one by one. Up to now they had remained lumped together in a kind of anonymity; but the watch meant the working team, a direct chief, and regular hours of duty, the first of which would be struck as soon as these two had chosen their men.

And the choice always made them anxious. Who would command whom? For the port side, this unknown first mate would fall to their lot; would he know how to carry out his trade by being sparing of their effort and suffering, or would he squander it, as unskillful or hesitant officers sometimes did? The men selected for the starboard team would have Hervic, the bos'n, as their "boss man," since the second mate had only just got his commission and this was his first voyage as an officer. The "boss man" was an old hand from the routes of the Capes, harsh as a nor'easter and with a bawl like a megaphone, but a man who knew how to smell out the weather. Under his guidance the little Guézennec would have a good schooling, and when he was on watch the men would not have to pay with their sufferings for his novitiate. This happened too often with young men who were getting their hand in, and who would shift course at the slightest change in the weather because they didn't know what it would do next.

But in addition to the officers there were also a man's fellow-workers.

Well-chosen watch crews did not separate one "home town" from another, nor one sailor from his pal. Otherwise, it was the end of all companionship: there would be one who slept while the other was on watch, one who went to take watch below, in the quarters, under shelter, at the very moment when his friend was leaving for the storm-drenched deck. The officers knew the sympathies that made ties among the men, and took account of them. Oh, not because of any sentiment! But because they understood that the fellows who get on together always do the best work; they are glad to lend a hand to one another; and the ship gains by it. The trouble, now, was just that the mate was new and wasn't acquainted with anyone. He would have had to find out about them. It was up to him to name the first man, and they were watching out with some apprehension to see whom he would call. Monsieur Monnard pulled out a notebook, in which he surely had his list all ready, but he did not open it.

"Rolland," he said.

The lad threw him a glance which at first showed surprise and then was enlivened by a gleam of amusement, quickly extinguished.

21

"Toublanc," called the bos'n.

This was doing honor to the ship's patriarch; that was as it should be.

"Névcl." Monsieur Monnard read the name, this time, from his notebook.

That young Breton had brought from Vannes a chubby countenance, a thickset body, long arms, and an optimism that even dared to accost Rolland in his black moods.

"Lhévéder," continued the bos'n.

This was an older man, like Toublanc his pal, and like him, disillusioned by more than thirty years at sea. Keeper of the ship's stores, and as punctilious at it as an Englishman, he would on this voyage as on the others make everyone who wanted to enter his domain leave his boots at the door.

"Le Corre."

"Cazabau."

"Gouret."

"Barigoul."

This was going the way it ought to: for the mate, Le Corre and Gouret, from the island of Arz, distant cousins who would be able to speak Breton to their hearts' content at the foot of the mast; for the bos'n, Cazabau and Barigoul, both from Arcachon, who would babble away in their crazy patois on their side of the ship.

The mate added to his crew the big fellow from Dunkerque, Morbecque, and his pal Mahé, the two who had been brought in together by the "square braces." He filled up his list with Zuyguedaël, a young sailor, and Gaborit, a novice. The bos'n chose Eustache, a smart Parisian lithe as a snake, and Nicolas, a slow and placid man from Fécamp, whose frame seemed built to serve him as a sort of padded armor, and who was able to absorb a rain of practical jokes and comical insults with the tranquillity of a pasture-lot. The young sailor Pëligon, a lively lad from Touraine, and Menut, the novice from Dol, were also named for the starboard watch.

Twelve able seamen, two young sailors, two novices: the watches were complete.

Obviously apart, in the middle of the ship's personnel, equidistant from the highest-grade seamen and the lowest-grade commissioned officers, there remained the men of petty officers' rank. To start with, there was "Big Pierre," Pierre Vidal, the ship's cook, who came from Rouen and who was about to be burdened with the redoubtable task of making the men swallow thick American salt pork, tinned beef, and beans for months on end. He had just left the *Armendral,* of the Bordes Company, on which he had made

22

four successive voyages with Captain Broniaud; and now, rather than re-enlist under Broniaud's successor, he had washed up on the *Galatée*. He was received with respect, for it was known that never in the worst weather off Cape Horn, immured in his galley as in a submarine, had he failed to prepare hot dishes, which—at arm's length, between two waves—he would pass out through the skylight to those who had enough appetite to come and get them.

Hervic, the "boss man," and the master-carpenter Francis Totten, from Sables d'Olonne, completed the petty officer's roster. Totten had never heard his real name spoken except at the Marine office. For everyone, and everywhere, it was Tonton, and that went well with his good shining face and chubby figure that made you think he had a breakfast bun under his leather apron.

With the captain, the apprentice, and the cabin boy—a youngster from the banks of the Rance, long and thin like a piece of string, who was nicknamed "Gee-Gee" because he was christened César, and César is a horse's name—that made five men, of the *Galatée's* twenty-four, who did not stand watch and who could claim nights of freedom.

It was of such nights, ruled out henceforth, that some of the men in the fo'c'sle were thinking dolefully—the older men especially—now that the watch crews had been assigned.

Then came the next routine order: "Those who know how to sew sails, give your names."

This was followed by the designation of the topmen. Rolland had the mainm'st.

"Port watch," Monsieur Monnard ordered, in his expressionless voice.

Then he went out, the bos'n at his heels.

The men turned, laughing, on Rolland, who was rolling a cigarette before leaving the sailors' quarters. "The new mate's taken a shine to you all right! He's put you at the head of the list!"

Rolland licked his cigarette paper to stick it together. He did not even seem to have heard.

Toward two in the afternoon, when Rolland's watch was on duty, the tug, a hundred yards ahead, blew its whistle and hoisted a signal: *Run up your canvas.* Hervic and his starboard crew were called as extra aids.

The weather continued to be fine, a smart breeze was blowing from the northeast; it was a day to put on full canvas and sail in state through the English Channel. The men of the port watch, with the mate, had to unfurl the jibs and dress the foremast. The bos'n and his starboard crew were to run up the sails on the main and mizzen. The mate, his head thrown back, was watching from under

23

his heavy eyelids. From the way the men looked at each other, waited for each other, he realized that since the weather was with them they were going to make a game of this business of getting under way. There was the play of emulation between the two watches as between two rival teams, to see which one would get the sails up first.

"Hoist the sails on the main and mizzen!"

In the naked rigging the triangular sails stretched out, four up forward, one 'midships and one aft, with the rapidity of swords unsheathed, of curtains drawn smoothly along their rods. As soon as they were run up, the breeze would swell them out, until they took on the sharp outlines of plowshares. The men were already scattering about on the yards and untying small lines that held the sails taut. They fell crumpled and flaccid, gone to sleep.

"Sheet the tops'ls!"

The command seemed to send a wave of life through the slack canvas. Under the rigging which was pulled tight from below, they stretched their white trapezoid forms, all together; then, braced, swelled out with the sound of a broad sigh. The two lower tops'ls, the storms'ls, those that are never furled, were beginning their stubborn effort to escape toward the bow. The men had come down from the yards.

"Haul up the upper tops'ls!"

This time it was no longer a matter of opening out canvas: this was a tree trunk that had to be hoisted, a yard that was twenty meters long, weighed three tons, and was as thick through as a man.

Rolland was the first to jump to the capstan. By instinct, this morning, he was putting forth all the strength of which he was capable. With an effort of bravado, he began to intone:

> *"Did you know Captain Lancelot—*
> *Goodbye, farewell—*
> *He gives a drop to his sailor-men*
> *As they turn the windlass well."*

The yard was slowly sliding upward, close to the mast, to the sound of shrieking sheaves. The men pushed round and round in their circle, with heavy steps. And the song went on:

> *"He eats meat, the bone's for you.*
> *He drinks wine, and what do you do?"*

The jeering verses were going the rounds too, beaten out in rough accents by every laborious step. Rolland gave a little thrust of his

24

head in Monnard's direction, as he passed him, to roar at the top of his voice:

"*And his first mate, who's a rotter,*
If you grumble, chucks you in the water. . . ."

The main upper tops'l went up easily enough in this favorable weather. Even to the last turns, which were the hardest, with the men's chests crushed against the bars, the song went on. It kept its strongest couplets for the final effort. It whipped a man on with gross obscenities which he spat out like oaths, with nothing but lightning-flash glimpses of their meaning.

Rolland was pushing furiously on the bar. He had taken it into his head that the fore upper tops'l should be hoisted before the main one.

"One more, boys! All together!"

There it was, finished: the tops'ls were set.

"We've got them," said Rolland, throwing a glance at the main upper tops'l.

The tow-rope was already slackening, and the *Centaure* whistled to give notice to cast it off.

At the order, the heavy steel hawser dropped into the sea, and for an instant the two vessels continued to be joined merely by the white trail of foam which it left there. Then the tug moved slowly away, with a great clatter of winches and hissings of escaping steam. As it went, it saluted with three blasts of its siren and ran up on its halyard, at the same time, the signal T O L:

WISHING YOU A GOOD VOYAGE!

III

THEY SAILED down the English Channel at a good speed, with a well-set breeze, the *Galatée* borne along by her canvas and not rolling. For two days they had kept within sight of the coast of England and its cliffs with their white damp plaster look; a safe coast, which pierced the darkness with lights so bright and clear that the eye could follow all its outlines.

On the way, they passed some steam freighters, and the men, very proud of leaving them in tow, apostrophized them:

"You good-for-nothing dog of a steamer! You stinking furnace, you damned crab, you smoke-pot! How would you like to go to sea on a thing like that, Pierre? I'd rather kick the bucket than throw my bag on that wheezy old drag-butt!"

Then one evening the breeze shifted to the northeast and grew stronger. They had to clew and reef their sails. And the boys' minds went back to the freighter they had just passed.

"Lucky devils on that ship! Just think of the easy life they have! A boiler that works by itself, with a roof over it! And never a bos'n at your backsides to make you brace and reef and bust your midriff! Once this jaunt's over, and I sign up for the next voyage, that's where I'm going to throw my bag—on a steamer! Let me tell you, I won't go on slaving myself to death on a wretched old tub like this!"

One night when Rolland was at the wheel, a liner bound for Southampton cut across the bows of the *Galatée*, and his eyes followed the three tiers of lighted decks for a long time. Like the others, when they passed the steam-propelled freighters, he felt a first impulse of scorn for this insolent parade of glaring lights. He had no envy of the rich who took their pleasure on the water. They had neither his strength, nor the pride that was his in holding firm under his hands, with a few spokes of the wheel, a solid ship and the wind that filled her sails. Yet he found himself gazing at this tall illuminated structure as it moved off, with a curiosity in which little by little his hostility melted away: to be in a position, one day, to step aboard, on equal terms with those whom the pursers welcomed with the bowings and scrapings of flunkeys, and to disdain to cross the gangplank! To become able to choose, and to remain of your own free will on a sailing-ship, where by necessity now, he was nailed down!

He shook off his dream and kept the course steady, his eyes on the lofty sails. Their whiteness, diffused thus in the dark, had suddenly made him think with a nightmare lucidity of his home in Erquy, the one room that was always rigged out with sheets hung up to dry. His mother was a laundress, and in the evening she would bring home armfuls of linen to be washed in the brook, winter and summer, and would hang them out in her own house. As a child, he used to walk underneath those sheets. They would drip down on his head and neck. As he grew bigger, they would hit him on the forehead, the face, the chest. The whole house, the whole of life, was invaded and taken over by this wet linen, their means of livelihood. It was only removed from the clotheslines to be piled up all over the table, the bench, the bed. Largely because of his loathing for all this other-people's-linen, he had left home. It was because of it now that whenever he went back he was always outdoors, so as not to receive the sudden shifting blow of a wet sheet or shirttail in his face.

Yet he remembered, with remorse, that he had never known how to push away all this beastly mess of washing, to discover his mother under it—little Mother Rolland, all bent over, her very flesh dissolved, so to speak, in strong soap. She existed for nothing but to turn soiled linen into clean linen, and he used often to be irritated with that, as with the acceptance of servitude. When she had cried, at his announcement that he was going to sea as a cabin boy, the tears had streamed from her along with the water she was wringing out of the day's wash. He had had forty francs a month allotted to her, out of his pay. But—how could he make enough money to throw all those sheets and shirts out of the mean little house once and for all, and force his old woman to take a rest!

At this point in his reflections Monsieur Monnard, the officer of the watch, approached him.

"You were told, full and by," he said. "Are you watching what you are doing?"

Rolland raised his eyes and turned as red as a hot coal: the mains'l was close to shivering. Hurriedly, he put the helm up.

The next morning they doubled Start Point. By noon, they were leaving the Channel. Papa Le Gac was humming softly on the poop, and the cabin boy reported that the officers had had a drink before luncheon. They were in the open sea!

The men immediately began to calculate how long it would be before they crossed the Equator.

"If these winds keep up even for four days . . . If we're not bogged down by foul winds from the southwest . . . If we have steady northeast trade winds . . . If . . . If . . . If . . ."

Today was Sunday. Each of the men had received his weekly twelve quarts of water to wash himself and his underclothes, and now they were pulling their boxes out on deck in the sunshine— those sea-chests of which so far they had had neither the time nor the wish to examine the contents. That was a pleasure held in reserve, the only one the land could still give them; and they needed plenty of time to savor it.

Their "landladies" had packed the chests and had them brought aboard. That was part of their professional duty, and they performed it with a commercial integrity with which the best of them sometimes mingled a little real compassion and tenderness for the individual sailor. Now the men were opening them and plunging their hands down among the woolens and well-folded underwear.

27

"Look, Jean! That confounded Célestine—you know she's not always a bitch! See—sweaters! She's put in four, and all good!"

"What's that you've got underneath there, Pierre?"

"Drawers."

"They're fine thick flannel! You're rigged out, all right!"

"Who did you stay with, Charles?"

"Mother Chandelle, you bet!"

"I'll bet she cheated you, the old girl!"

Charles Nével straightened up indignantly. "What do you mean, cheated me? Because she threw my bag aboard this ship? I'm telling you, I had my fun first, and you know it! Remember the night there were more than thirty of you there, and I came in and said, 'Drinks all round, and vintage stuff!'?"

Memories, so given a start, kept pouring forth. Looked at in the retrospect of almost a week at sea, the landladies who had fleeced them to the bone seemed like mothers to the sailors; they had coddled them, certainly, and had furnished them with pleasures on which distance was now setting a higher price.

They had also taken care of their money.

"To get hold of a penny, at Mother Chandelle's, you'd have to have a windlass! 'Just keep on talking, big boy!' she'd tell you. And it wasn't any use to say, 'When we're pitching about in a sou'-wester off Cape Horn, *then* we won't be able to drink up our money!' She'd get right back at you: 'When you first came, you told me I wasn't to listen to you when you were drunk. You wanted me to keep some of your advance pay for you to go off with. All right, I'm doing just what you told me to do.' You see, she was acting for your own good, that way."

And their thoughts took them all back to the cheap cafés of the rue Jean Bart, and the greasy tables with their sizzling platters of meat and their free-flowing bottles. The best man among them now was the one who had eaten and drunk the most, who had had the most extravagant love affairs. Memory was already transfiguring their miserable adventures. Le Corre, who had a birthmark above his right eye, declared that he had been loved for himself alone.

"An ugly louse like you!"

"Well, you just ought to have seen me—yes, me—with Armadine, the maid at Fortuné's! Isn't that so, Gouret?"

They were all puffed up with their own boasting, and the eight or ten days spent in the boarding houses became a Mohammed's paradise in their minds. But Rolland said nothing.

Yet he, too, was reliving that eight-day spree ashore, those sprawling torpors in the pubs, under the framed pictures of ships in full sail and the ships in bottles which the landlady used to beg from

the seamen and which they would give her, over and above everything else. But the only thing that came back to him intact now was
the disgust which had suddenly submerged him one evening, without any reason, and which was troubling him still.

Sitting alone at his table, he had had the sudden sense of being
shut up in an ignoble life, the very baseness of which was a stimulus,
like the repulsive ugliness of a woman-of-the-port who accosts a
man in the shadow and whom he looks at under a street lamp.
Through the fog of tobacco smoke he had gazed with horror, as at
zombies walking, at these drunken sailors, these dreary prostitutes.
To half-kill yourself on the ships in order to win a week of such
delights. . . .

A big red-haired girl had come up to lay siege to him. He had
repulsed her, without gentleness, and she had caught hold of him,
pressing against him with all her thick flesh. He had given her a terrible slap then, with the back of his hand, that had sent her sprawling full-length in the sawdust and given her a cut on the forehead
where she hit a table-leg. She had got up screaming and wiping the
blood from her face, and had begun to pelt him with insults. Behind the counter the hostess, outraged, was recalling him to the
proprieties.

"She was working at her trade, wasn't she? Yes, and you saw that!
Knocking a woman down! And the way you did it, without saying
a word! You're nothing but a dirty cheat, that's what you are!"

That was not at all what he was! He was someone who did not
like to be importuned, and who, when somebody refused to understand him, knew how to find the effective gesture. Yet he had left
the place: not from fear or from shame, but from boredom. At
random in the darkness he had followed one street after another,
and had come out in front of the theater just as the audience was
leaving.

As the crowd was thinning out, a young girl had paused at the
top of the steps, under the sheet of light that fell from the gas lamps
of the marquee, an opera cloak flung over her white chiffon dress.
Caught up short two yards away, he had gazed at her with an inner
turmoil which was further increased by his surprise in feeling it.
Was she pretty? Even today he would not have been able to make
up his mind about that. Up to now, he had paid no attention whatever to those daughters of the comfortably-well-off whom he used
to pass without seeing. When he was hardly fifteen—the age of
becoming a "novice" aboardship—he had been taken in hand for
matters of love by women of his own caste; and he had always submitted without regret to that obscure and profound social law which
puts couples into sailing trim in accordance with their social posi-

29

tion and their environment. But what had now pulled him up short before this unknown girl, with a suddenness and force that were alike peculiar, was the realization that she actually did belong to another world, as alien as the moon. Her tastes, her thoughts, were indecipherable to him, and he felt a raging scorn of himself on that account. She had sensed that she was being observed, and their glances had met. The girl's had turned away, indifferent, and then she had gone off between a man in a black coat and a woman in a feather boa—her parents, probably. Rolland had followed them with his eyes as far as the other end of the Square; then he had returned slowly to the Chile Tavern.

"Has your moonlight stroll calmed you down?" the proprietress had demanded sarcastically.

Without answering, he had beckoned to the girl he had slapped, who had been devouring him with her eyes since he came in. She had come to his call and had not left him until sailing time. But it was the image of the other that remained within him, like a splinter under the skin. That, and a phrase from Mother Chandelle—Madame Kandaël, his "landlady"—who had said to him, in what connection he no longer remembered, "You will never be satisfied with what you have, because you only think of what you haven't."

It was on this Sunday in the cabin that Monsieur Monnard, the first mate, and Monsieur Guézennec, the second mate, first became aware of the watchdog character which Captain Le Gac never took the trouble to conceal for long.

Guézennec had joined the *Galatée* immediately after leaving the Hydrographic Institute, with the rank of second mate—"lieutenant of the chicken-coops," as the sailors called these young officers who were in charge not only of the store and the distribution of supplies but also of the fowl and the pigs that were installed below decks.

The luncheon began in silence. Le Gac was eating, his heavy-jowled face very close to his plate, the brush of his gray hair very shaggy, when Guézennec, simply for the sake of saying something, announced, "I am very much afraid that before long we shall be running short of potatoes."

He made the statement as the most natural thing in the world. Old potatoes, dug up in October, would be rotting—that was normal. But Le Gac sat up straight in his chair, his eyes ready to start out of his head.

"Potatoes!" he echoed. "Good God, what's that you say?" A blow of his fist set the plates to dancing. "Listen to me!" he roared. "You are to take care of those potatoes, and sort them out one by one. Keep them aired, as they ought to be. And don't lose any of them!

I know you threw two baskets of them overboard today. . . ." Then he turned to the first mate. "Look what they send us! Apprentice seamen who haven't even got enough sense to conserve potatoes!"

Monnard seemed, at first, not to have heard. Without doubt, potatoes are a precious thing, the only fresh provisions for the long voyage. But to throw a fit about them! So the mate took his time about answering.

"If the mate threw away two baskets this morning," he remarked at last, in his impersonal voice, "it means that he had sorted them." Guézennec flung him a grateful glance which fell upon half-closed eyelids.

Le Gac yelled at his second-in-command: "I do not like my remarks to be questioned. You understand that?"

The first mate seemed more abstracted than ever. The captain swallowed his dessert in two spoonfuls, threw his napkin on the table, and left the cabin. Guézennec made sure that he had really vanished, before he muttered, "This is going to be a peculiar voyage!"

The first mate's answer was not what he expected.

"It wasn't two baskets that you should have thrown away, if you had sorted them conscientiously," Monnard said dryly. "It was four. I happened to take a look at them this morning: you left some in that were getting black, and, with the heat, they will spoil the rest. The captain was quite right: you have been negligent."

IV

THE DAYS went by, one after another. The ship was heading south, and the heat was already becoming burdensome. The routine of watches and duties was well established by now. The monotonous shipboard existence was regulated by the strokes of the bell, at the hand of the helmsman. They were reaching the zone of good weather, where they would take down the new sails they had run up and replace them by a worn set. Already, they were furbishing up the rigging, and the "middle watch"—the novices and young seamen, reinforced by the men who were not working either in the rigging or on the yards—had begun to chip rust in every nook and corner with two-edged hammers.

"The sailmakers to the sails!"

Four men from each watch—port and starboard—were to sew on the widths of canvas.

"Topmen to the masts!"

These would climb aloft with steel cable, marline, parceling line and a pot of tar.

"Running watch this way!" Then the orders for these "roving" workers: "Péligon and Menut, chip the rust up forward. Nicolas, Zuyguedaël, to the peak. Gaborit, wind up the ball of twine."

And Gaborit would spool miles of sail twine while the four others, with patient little strokes of their hammers, made the least little bit of ironwork shine again.

Four hours' work, four hours' rest—the "watch below decks"—except in the afternoon, when everyone was on duty. Four hours for sleep. Then a sailor would come bawling at the door of the crew's quarters: "What's wrong with you, you starboard men, you cuckolds, you bastards? Get up on watch!"

But often, too, the man would call out cheerfully, in order to brighten up the awakening: "It's good weather. There's a breeze. All sails up again."

But that would not appease the men who were being aroused. "So what! We're the ones who'll be stuck with hauling the royals in again soon enough!" They would pull themselves out of their bunks, grumbling, "What a hell of a trade! When am I going to have a free night to sleep in?"

In this fine weather the ship only really came alive at six in the morning, when she was washed: the deck, the poop, the quarter-decks flooded with water, scrubbed with brushwood brooms, by barefoot men in rolled-up trousers. Then when the Old Man got up, there would be the little game of stops. Each of the short lines fastened to the corners of the high sails was suspended at its loftiest reach by a yarn cord that must break when anybody pulled it from below. Every morning Le Gac would give himself the pleasure of pulling on the royal stops, as on a bell-lanyard, as he went by. Then he would call the cabin boy or one of the young sailors.

"Have you eyes in your head? Do you think we are going to let the royal buntlines wear out the canvas? Get a move on! Get aloft! You're not tired out yet, are you?"

And the lad would have to climb up the ratlines, strain his guts, and replace the bit of yarn that had just given way. If the cord resisted, the Old Man would only bawl the louder and would send someone up to change the too-sturdy line on the instant. So he would win the game every time.

A man couldn't look to his meals to bring any variety into his existence. There was coffee in the morning; salt pork every day at noon, with potatoes and hardtack; cod on Friday, and tinned meat on Sunday; beans every night; and over and above all this, half-a-quart of wine a day. The boys liked the salt pork better than their Sunday mess of canned stew.

In the evening, the captain would write in the log-book: *Fine weather, nice breeze from west-northwest. All canvas up. Smooth sea. Work in sailmaking and seamanship.*

Work in sailmaking: that was on deck, half-a-dozen men with nimble fingers, often the oldest of the sailors, pegging away with needle and sailor's palm to fit out the sails with leather at the points where they would be bearing down on the stays and the shrouds. They would line them further beneath the buntlines, and cut and sew the new sails. All this would spread out a huge sewing workroom on the deck: a workroom in which the work would never be finished, for with the first storm that hit them all these garments of the ship would split at the armholes. As for seamanship: that meant the detailed repairs and inch-by-inch reinforcement of the rigging—that monster spiderweb stretched out between the deck and the trucks of the masts, the lines to be bound with close turns of spun yarn, the blocks to be inspected, the footropes of the yards to be strengthened. Everything that was doing its work on the ship or that lay dormant waiting for its work to do, had to be checked incessantly: hemp, steel, wood, iron. . . .

That was the daily task of the topmen in the masts. Rolland loved it. He had a vanity about it, and a pride in it. He did not need to think, as the others thought, of the terrible chastisements with which the sea and the wind might punish any negligence; without that, he would finish off his knots and his fine points of cordage with an obscure instinct of artistry. And when the mate came down from the mainmast after one of his semiweekly tours of inspection, he would be waiting for him below with a sly gleam in his eye. Monsieur Monnard once again would not seem to see him at all and would walk away without any compliment, as without any criticism. Rolland, to be sure, was expecting neither the one nor the other. But this unfathomable first mate intrigued him, as he secretly irritated him, by being unlike anyone else.

Standing on the main royal footrope, which subtended the yard like a parenthesis, he would sometimes interrupt his packing of the ropes with the serving mallet, to look below and about him. Under his feet was the shining curve of the main to'gants'l, the broad bellying out of the tops'ls, the mains'l's harmonious canopy. Before him, the fores'l was pressing ahead, hollowed out and then distended like a powerful swell of the sea. Very far below, the ocean was opening up at the ship's prow, a bone in her teeth, rippling

33

back in a fringe of spray along the vessel and marking the course by its flat wake behind. There was nothing above him but the light and slender spire of the mast. There are three beautiful things in this world, they say in the officers' cabins: a lovely woman, a fine horse, and a ship in full sail.

But he was not at all sensitive to the harmonious magnificence of the sails, the airy lightness of their flight. He was delighting only in their power. The masts were quivering under the energy of the tremendous force that was harnessed to them, the tops'ls were pulling at the jack-stay with all their might, the blocks were whining, the yards were swaying back and forth in their flanges with the movements of monstrous shafts. And the lines were vibrating, the great even breath of the wind was blowing against his ears, the intoxication of space and height was buzzing in his temples. Up here the broad roll of the ship was not a cradling, as it was on deck: passed on through the interlocked yards and masts, the arc of its circle was broken into abrupt jerks, shocks, recoveries, in which the ship bore witness to her own life, her own way of reacting to the waves. All this was what Rolland was feeling so strongly, and his mind reached beyond it only to think of the coming violence of this passing wind, of the inevitable combats for which everything was being made ready.

Yet to have got into the northeast trade winds like this without being caught by a bout of bad weather—that was fine sailing! They had passed Madeira the evening before.

"In twenty years I've called there just once," old Toublanc had said. "But I tell you, that's the place for a man to retire to! Twelve months of spring! Sugar cane growing under the chestnut trees! And still they haven't enough flowers. All the good Sisters—there are some there—make them out of feathers and paper!"

To Cape Verde—that made twelve days at least of whipping along, scudding before the wind, almost without moving the helm. At night the men would bring up their mattresses and spread them out on the warm planks of the deck, and except for the man at the wheel and the man on look-out the whole watch would snore away until morning. Then the ship would wake up with the sounds of a farm; the roosters would crow under the little deck-house, the dog would bark, dashing off in pursuit of a rat. If it happened that there was a call to work the sheets during the night, all the men would wake up at once, and as none of them knew whether he was on duty or not they would go to get a close look at the officer who had called out the order.

"Oh, I'm not in his watch!" And half of the crew would go back to sleep. They only woke up again in time for the washing.

34

One morning the captain, smoking his pipe at the foot of the mainmast, directed Barquet the apprentice, who was coming up with the cabin boy, to clean out the chicken coop. The lad had the wild-eyed, and at the same time hopeless, look that had never left him since he came aboard. In spite of the fine weather he had been desperately seasick at first. For four days he had retched and gasped and hiccuped in his bunk, entirely emptied. Monnard had seen him turn green and run to the rail as soon as the canvas was up, and he had ordered, with an imperceptible shrug of his shoulders, "Go to bed!"

It was spoken as one would speak to a dog, but it did not have to be repeated. Barquet had collapsed on his bunk, his head aching horribly, his whole being given over to agony. The next morning he had tried hard to get up, but the hot mist of vertigo had swept up to his head and all he could do was grab hold of the guardplank of his bunk and haul himself back into it.

The captain had come to see him twice. The first time, he had cast a disapproving glance at his waxen countenance and said, "Well, what are you going to do in bad weather?"

The second time he had merely looked at him, without a word; and then, as he went out, he had remarked, "Really, you would have done better to stay where you were."

Following the captain, an eighteen-year-old boy had come into the cabin, with a greasy Basque beret pulled down over his eyes, and a turned-up nose.

"Do you want a mug of juice?" he asked.

"Juice" was coffee, and he had brought it with him, along with some slabs of sea-biscuit. He introduced himself: "My name's Menut. I'm the novice, and I'm from Dol. Me, I had it for two days on the first voyage. But the weather wasn't like this!"

Barquet had thrown up the coffee as soon as he had swallowed it, and had only been able to nibble at a biscuit.

The next morning, finding him still in bed and even more undone, Menut had looked at him scornfully: this was going beyond the limit that was allowed.

"My God, get up!" he said roughly. "There you stay and stew! Do we have to have a tackle to haul you out of your bunk?"

Barquet had obeyed, as he would have obeyed anything, without thinking. But as soon as he stood up he staggered, and the roll of the ship threw him down again, his body on the deck, his head and arms helpless and abandoned on the bunk. Menut had examined him for quite a while, with the look one fixes on someone one believes to be faking; then he went out and slammed the door.

All through these frightful hours Barquet's mind was filled with

35

one thought only: this would go on for weeks and months, as long as the voyage lasted, as long as the boat's indefatigable swaying motion endured. To that ceaseless swaying, this dreadful emptiness of his body would respond forever, with this nausea of his stomach and his soul. He was all alone among the impassive officers, the sailors who had appeared to him when he came aboard only as drunken, brutal faces.

He was one of those boys with whom an unhealthy childhood lingers. Thanks to his sickly appearance, his mother had succeeded in keeping him close to her side, and she exaggerated all his little ailments. Her son and her daughter had been the reward of a submissive marriage which had made a good business deal for the two fathers concerned, both manufacturers; and she clung to the boy. But one day, when Jean was fifteen, Monsieur Barquet—who used to boast of his squareness when he had just been hurting other people with his corners—had had an illumination.

"But, after all, he has never been sick!" he cried—and it was as if he had just learned that one of his bookkeepers was robbing him. "He is never sick!"

Things went as quickly then as an arrest. Immediately, school; and with that, three years of hateful reports: *A sluggish pupil. No attention, no effort. . . . Intelligent, but doesn't try. Some intermittent successes in the French language. . . . Efforts and results null in mathematics, science, and Latin. Incapable of meeting the baccalaureate examination.**

It was this last verdict which had precipitated him upon the ship, in spite of his mother's supplications and cries of rebellion.

"Oh, no!" his father had replied, curtly, to these. "You had him tied to your apronstrings for fifteen years, and you see the consequences! It's my turn now to take him in hand." And then, to his son: "Well, my boy, since you don't want to do anything in school—"

On the fourth day of his seasickness the cabin door had been kicked open to admit Menut the novice, his eyes ferocious.

"You damn lazy good-for-nothing!" he roared. "Do you think I'm going to go on feeding you out of a bottle like this, on top of everything I have to do? You wait, I'm going to empty you out, I am!"

Beside himself with rage, he had taken the apprentice by the shoulders and flung him out of his cabin. And that was the way Jean Barquet had made his true entrance upon the deck of the *Galatée*.

It must be acknowledged that within twenty-four hours his behavior there made everyone agree in their opinion of him. It was

* The baccalaureate, in France, is for entrance into college or university. Tr.

36

immediately evident, to the captain as to the cabin boy, that it would be impossible to discover, on any ocean-going ship, a being endowed with an equal talent for doing the precise opposite of what he ought to do. Toublanc the patriarch, the prince of good fellows, had tried against all odds to teach him the rudiments, the things that even a customs inspector is born knowing. It was impossible! He didn't know the difference between the upper tops'ls and the royals; and he would talk about "rope," a word that should never be spoken aboardship, any more than in the house of a man who has been hanged.

So he had been caught at once in the vortex of the crew's mockery and coarse joking, as in a whirlpool. The apprentice, the "Parisian," was always more or less a butt, but this one was made to order! Forever stumbling over his own too-long body, and the other men's legs, always at the worst moment; so clumsy that boots would fly out at his buttocks all by themselves. They had turned his name, Barquet, into "debarked," * and it really was as if he had been debarked, so little account was he on board.

At the beginning of the voyage they had sent him back and forth, from bow to stern, all over the ship, on April Fool errands which he would trustingly carry out; when he got on to them, he stubbornly refused to budge, even for bona fide orders that were shouted at him and that he was incapable of distinguishing from the others.

Rolland was the most merciless of them all. Barquet exasperated him. His presence aboard was an insult and an act of defiance. He cheapened everything he touched. The ship would always remain an incomprehensible object to him, and hostile. Every movement he made was an offense to something. He would not dare utter his disgust and his fear, but everything bore witness to them. Rolland saw no excuse for him. He was enraged at the sight of "that fellow" paying to go to sea, treated like an officer, with a cabin and the same food as the captain, while *he*—! And when the decks were being swabbed, there would be a bucket of water splashing up full in Barquet's face; a fine line would be stretched across a passage in front of him and trip him head over heels; last evening Rolland had daubed his face with tar, a swift and dexterous streak from ear to ear.

But, above all, he knew how to pierce that haggard indifference which the apprentice interposed like a shell between himself and the insults the men bawled at him. He himself would not insult him. Instead, he would say, "You make the others laugh. But as for me—do you realize that I sometimes want to murder you?"

* *Débarqué.* . . . Tr.

The wretched lad would look at him with wild eyes, for he felt that Rolland meant what he said.

At first he had essayed some tentative movements of revolt, immediately paralyzed by the sudden interest they had aroused.

"Jules, Marcellin, come see the silly chicken sticking up its comb!"

The bullying was not slow in coming, for indignation succeeded quickly to curiosity: a bundle of trash like this kid, with the nerve to try to put one over on them!

Swiftly humbled, he had given in: since his safeguard lay in being taken for an idiot, so be it! So he would repress his too-brief rebellions, his bitterness, his contempt, which, sometimes boiling up, would always be held down by the heavy lid of fear.

This morning the captain, who for the past ten days had seemed to be entirely ignorant of his existence, was watching his approach with eyes which filled him more and more with apprehension, the closer he came.

The Old Man spoke to a sailor: "Look here, Gouret, suppose you take this gentleman on a tour of the palm trees? He has long legs and long arms. That ought to help him play the monkey."

On reflection, Le Gac had decided that he must try something before relegating Barquet definitely and finally to the status of passenger; and as the ship was as steady as the palm of your hand—

Enticed by the prospect, the sailors gathered around, their faces wrinkled by amusement, to see the boy's bewildered air and to hear him stammer, "Captain. . . . But, Captain. . . ."

"Take off your jacket," Le Gac ordered. "You'll be easier that way."

"The others climb very well," added Monsieur Monnard, who had just come up. "You have to start sometime. You'll see that it's nothing at all."

But Barquet could not finish unbuttoning his jacket, with his limp and trembling fingers. It was Rolland who yanked it off him and went to throw it over a winch. In spite of the heat, the apprentice was shivering in his shirtsleeves. Mahé, though moved to pity by his panic, called out to him, "Go on up, you blooming marine! You've got to learn."

Gouret was not laughing. "Duffer that he is, he might take a tumble," he muttered.

"The main lower tops'l, to start with," said the captain. "There's a gasket hanging there. Have him see how it is gathered up."

"Go on ahead," Gouret ordered.

He pushed him into the shrouds and climbed behind him.

The boy went aloft by himself, first, in the wide ratlines. But the

38

steel ladder drew in with every rung, the hollow void was growing deeper on all sides. Barquet slowed down, stopped, clinging against the shrouds.

"Go on, sissy!"

The apprentice mastered a few more rungs, but now he was climbing chicken fashion, bringing one foot up beside the other on the wire ladder.

The men below, their heads raised to watch, were not laughing any more. Every one of them realized that anything might happen, that the boy was just as likely to let go and be crushed to death on the deck as to clamber up the last ratlines. They were obscurely satisfied in seeing Gouret take a firm hold of the seat of his pupil's pants and push him toward the main-top.

"Now what?" muttered Rolland, who was watching the climb with close attention.

Barquet reached the end of the main shrouds, under the futtock shrouds, those steel bars which support the top and which themselves slant outward, so that the man going up must climb as on the underside of a ladder, his back to the void below.

"Let go of your shroud," Gouret ordered, "and take hold of the futtock."

From below, they all heard the boy scream, "No! No!"

They saw him go down two rungs, in spite of Gouret's first trying to push him back with furious blows that set his muscles throbbing. Barquet was putting such a frenzy into this defense, indeed, that he actually came to grips with the sailor, clinging to him, deaf to his insults and impervious to the blows with which the heavy fist was pommeling his back.

"Nothing more to be done," the captain stated. And he called out, "Come down!" He was really afraid of an accident.

They were all waiting at the foot of the mast, given over again to good cheer. Only Rolland disdained to welcome the climbers. He strode off toward the stern, and, in passing, gave a kick to Barquet's coat. It slid along the deck, and the wallet fell out.

Rolland opened it as he picked it up. The corner of a photograph was sticking out. He pulled it all the way out, glanced at it, and put it in his pocket. Then he returned the wallet to its place.

In the evenings, leaning their backs against the big hatch, the men used to talk. They were tormented by the thought of women, on these warm tropic nights. But, as unskillful in speaking of them as in getting the best, on land, out of the pleasure they demanded from them, they reduced them all to a few brutal words of pillage which immediately drained their memories of content and made

39

them incapable of being turned to any account. Simple folk, they were brought up stubbornly against the terrifying simplicity of the act of love. Névél drew the general conclusion: "They're all alike!"

All alike: the women of Valparaiso, Tahiti, Yokohama. They knew it, they and only they; and they drew a certain pride from that knowledge, while at the same time they could not banish their feeling of disappointment in rediscovering, at all the ends of the earth, along with the uniformity of bodies, the banality of diversion which seemed to be imposed upon them by a convention that was worldwide.

As if in reply to Névél, Rolland pulled out of his pocket the photograph he had taken from Barquet's wallet.

"Have a squint at this one," he said.

They thought that he was confiding in them. To show a photograph—at sea as on land, that is like opening the door of one's house. Flattered, they broke out in exclamations of enthusiasm: "Oh, say, she *is* a winner! It's your girl?"

He let them look at the picture, without answering. It was a fluffy-haired blonde, with large wondering eyes and a rather wide mouth, and the men found her air of modesty somewhat disconcerting. The quality of the photography, too, was not exactly their style: the features scarcely emphasized, on a lusterless background of a uniform gray tone.

"It's the apprentice's sweetheart," Rolland explained at last.

They brightened up at once and became expansive. Everything fell into place again. That damn Barquet! Ashore, with his money, he would be treating himself to stylish girls, and photographs that weren't like other people's!

"Give it back to me," Rolland commanded.

When he had it in his hands again, he dipped a matchstick in tar and sketched the thick-limbed body of a naked woman over the light dress.

They broke into laughter: now they were getting hold of her!

The apprentice was wandering along the deck and was just then turning around a winch, his head down, his eyes fixed on the deck planking.

They called him. "Come on over, Barquet. We've got your best girl here."

Rolland held out the print. "Is this tart yours?"

Barquet stared, stupefied. The other was still holding out the photograph at arm's length. Suddenly the apprentice sprang forward, fists clenched, and flung himself upon the sailor. Rolland tottered under the unforeseen and impious assault. But he recovered himself at once, and with a swift reflex blow sent the boy rolling on the deck. They all heard the soft thud of his body against the hatch coaming.

Barquet picked himself up, however, all wild-eyed, and came back at Rolland, who had not deigned even to rise. This time the sailor's fist landed full in the apprentice's face and he staggered back, his hand pressed against his mouth with the gesture of a child who has been struck, that obscurely moved the men watching.

"What is going on here?"

Monsieur Monnard had suddenly sprung up behind them. In spite of their surprise, no one turned around.

The apprentice took down his hand. It was covered with blood.

"What is going on?" the first mate demanded again, still more coldly.

As Rolland made no reply, Gouret explained: "It's about a photograph."

"Give it to me."

Monnard took the picture and examined it.

"It's a photograph of my sister," Barquet hiccuped, wiping away both blood and tears with his handkerchief.

Monsieur Monnard's heavy gaze was brought to bear upon Rolland, who raised his head to look him in the eyes.

"Was it you who did this?"

"Yes."

"Well, that was cowardly."

This was a very unusual word, entirely new aboardship, where any officer whatever would have said, "You are a dirty beast."

Rolland's first reaction was one of savage pride. The big fellow had chosen a bourgeois insult for him, because he knew he would understand it. It was not until a moment later that he felt the sting of the word, which was far more deeply searing than any abuse spat out by a bos'n. He was deathly pale as he snarled, "Cowardly? I'm not a coward, and I never funk on anything—not even on watch, taking a snooze standing up, the way some people do."

They all realized that the retort was aimed at the mate, who during his hours on watch used to stand motionless on the poop, his eyes half-closed. Only Monsieur Monnard himself seemed not to have heard. He turned again toward Barquet, to give him back the photograph.

"You might try to clean it with benzine; the tar is still wet," he said. "But if I were in your place I should burn it."

Barquet, his handkerchief held like a plug against his nose, made energetic signs of agreement. So the mate took out his matches, set fire to the print, held it between his thumb and index finger until the flame was licking at his nails, and then threw the burned paper down on the deck and crushed it under his boot. The men avoided so much as a glance at each other when he had gone.

They were ruminating on this burned photograph. Each of them felt that an offense had somehow been committed against them, but except for Rolland, whose rage and shame were piling up so as almost to burst his skull, they did not clearly grasp either its meaning or its scope. What troubled them above all was that they were still unable to make out this first mate, the newcomer whom the good weather had made it impossible for anyone to test. There are three things on board that a man must know through and through, because from them may come danger and hardship: the weather, the ship, the officers. Now except for this Monnard everything was plain.

The Old Man himself would give them no surprises: hard, surly, as closefisted as they come—the whole man was there in his thick spatulate thumb, a thumb he was proud of and of which he used to say, "With this in the *moque* you'd save half a mug at every distribution." The *moque*—that was the measuring-cup for the wine ration, and all commissary officers knew how to stick their thumbs in it. . . . But apart from this, the Old Man was a good seaman, and he was just enough to think better of his rages if occasion required.

Monsieur Guézennec, the second mate, they didn't talk about at all; he was learning his trade, but he was intelligent, and he was not wanting in respect for his elders. Hervic the bos'n had a mouth and fists, which were what a bos'n needed. There remained, then, the first mate, with his tall slow-moving body which they had never yet been able to see grow tense or unbend in a shift of course in dangerous weather, his cold level voice which they had never yet had occasion to hear raised in a shout, and especially his heavy eyelids which seemed to scorn to be lifted on the routine tasks of the ship. Yet there was just now something new, something which might perhaps promise some good moments: Monnard had certainly understood the insolent allusion to himself, and he had shown no reaction to it.

They were by no means in a hurry to jump to any conclusion of a craven spirit, however, because the man didn't seem to be that sort, and because the photograph burned under their noses continued to plague them. One sure thing—the contest was on between Rolland and the mate. But they were still hesitant to mark up the first round in either one's favor.

42

V

"ARE THOSE damn filthy winds giving us the go-by already?"

The men, disturbed, realized that the trade winds were about to desert them. The breeze was slackening, and the sails were making more and more false starts: they would suddenly go empty and limp like a burst balloon, thresh about for a few seconds, then take hold again, but weakly. They were still rounded out under the flurries, but that was an appearance only and the canvas no longer gathered force. As for the men, the sultry storm-laden heat had stripped them of their clothes: they worked barefoot and with naked torsos, and their trousers were plastered to their thighs with broad streaks of sweat.

There were flying fish everywhere, and their swift darting movements were amazing on this apathetic sea. They would spurt out of the swell like wide-feathered silver arrows and glide above the water for some fifty meters, while the sun sent gleams of quicksilver over the transparent membrane of their rigid winglike fins. Then they would be swallowed up again. Sometimes they would touch the crest of a wave and take a new thrust from it that would fling them ahead farther, like a skipping stone.

The men would watch them but merely to see if one might fall on deck, for the officers' table: that was always good for a tot of grog. . . . They themselves were engrossed in the death struggles of the wind, the thought that they had come to the end of the great carrying breezes. It was the torment of the horseman who feels his exhausted mount faltering under him; the torment of all those who have been borne on their way by an external force, and who will have to make up for it by their own tremendous effort, when it has failed.

"Now we're in for a hard time!" the men were saying.

Mahé, after some ripe reflection, declared, "It's badly rigged, all the same."

"What is?" demanded Nével.

"Well, everything."

What he meant was the world, the universe—where there was

43

too much or not enough, but hardly ever just what there ought to be.

So it was that between the northeast and southeast trade winds —good winds when they got them—there was a sort of trough, an accursed zone of calms, of little changing breezes, with eddying storms, and rain: rain in drops as broad as the bottom of a bucket! It shouldn't have to be that way! It was as plain as the nose on your face that the two trade-wind zones should have been stretched out wide enough to meet. . . .

"Hey, fellows! Bonito!"

It was the man at the cathead who had called out to summon them. They ran forward, and about a quarter of a mile ahead they caught sight of a farandole of big fish, like thick nickel spindles, being tossed up by the sea and falling back into it, vertical as shrapnel shells: these were bonito, the big mackerel with striped bellies, brothers to the tuna fish. Their play seemed to be projected by the discharge of all the electricity suspended in the sultry air. Little by little, their saraband drew close to the ship; then some of them sprang up right under the stern. By this time the men had stationed themselves at the bow and were dangling baits of raveled-out white cotton threaded on weathercocks to the surface of the water. The bonito, in their leaps, took the bait for a flying fish. Rolland, the first to pull one in, slit it with one stroke of his knife from head to tail as soon as he got it to the deck. But instead of throwing the refuse overboard he kicked it under the rail.

When he saw Barquet coming up, lured by the new attraction, he made a motion with his chin to indicate the pile of offal.

"Throw that stuff overboard," he ordered.

The apprentice realized at once that this disgusting task had been carefully set aside for him; but there was nothing to do but carry it out, since it was part of his education. The others had turned around and were watching him with mocking faces.

He made up his mind to it, took the bloody mess in his hands, and dropped it with a start.

"It's moving!" he cried.

The others burst into laughter: this was what they had been waiting for. The bonito has an extraordinary vitality. Its flesh will still quiver when one pokes at it an hour after being gutted, and the heart, torn out, still beats.

Rolland was the only one who did not laugh. He threw a hard contemptuous glance at the boy and said, "Of course it is. That shows it has more life in its guts than you have, that's all."

"You will wash up this blood, Rolland. Dried blood eats into the paint."

44

Once more, the first mate's rejoinder had not been slow in coming; and, as always, it hit home.

It was the day after this that the wind became altogether irrational. Instead of the full and smooth trade wind that had seemed unfailing, gusts came from all points of the compass and made them tack all the time. Then even these capricious little winds abandoned them, and the *Galatée*, breathless, lay becalmed, sails hanging slack, on the oily sea. The men's arms hang as limp as the canvas. The sea had darkened. Clouds, so low as to graze the mastheads, were smudging the sky above them; the horizon was blocked off by walls of storm; and the men stifled in the heavy moisture that rose from the water, in the unstirring oven heat that lay over everything.

Suddenly the first rain burst upon them, gigantic drops that crashed down on the deck in broad glutinous splotches like broken eggs. The ship became practically invisible all of a sudden, slashed and scratched out by the downpour. It was no longer possible to see from stern to bow. Beaten down by the deluge, the men were being driven over to the shelter of the deck-house when Monsieur Monnard's voice caught up with them: "Haul down the tops'll!"

Dripping and impassive, the mate was standing erect at the rail of the poop. The men came forward, bent over, hesitating under the cataract of rain, but the bos'n began to drive them in his turn, and with knees, chest, and then fists forced them toward the lines. The first peal of thunder interrupted his barkings. It was the beginning of exhausting labors.

Dead calms, squalls, storms. . . . Naked men, their mouths held wide open, struggling to breathe in an air that was unbreathable, their lungs weighed down as if they had been emptied of air and all the burden of this opaque atmosphere were pressing upon them. There was no more rest for the crew on watch than for the horizon itself, which would suddenly grow black and be underscored by a white streak through which the squall spurted out like a stream of water under a floodgate. They braced, they clewed up, they set the sails again, with hands puckered up by these successive shiftings of the squall as by a laundress's lye bleaches. They were glued night and day to working the canvas. To lose one minute of a good wind was to lose a hundred yards on their course; but not to have reefed in time when they got one of those short and violent squalls that eddied with the stormwind—that was to lose a sail, or perhaps several.

Clew up, let out, furl, hoist. . . .

It had the air of a madman's cruel and stubborn joke. They loosed what they had just made fast, and did up again what they

45

had cast loose. The ship was dressed in its canvas only to be undressed again. And this went on without interruption day and night, nights like the tomb, in which beaten senseless by fatigue, their very brains hammered by the monstrous rain, they could only stumble on anywhere, into anything.

"He's breaking our bones in two, forever trimming sail," the men would groan. "There's no more wind than there is in my big bag."

What wind there might be, they could not feel. But the mate, who did not himself smoke, always had a lighted cigarette in his hand now, to watch for the slightest change of direction in the smoke.

The squalls were generally short. When they had passed, a band of blue sky the width of a handkerchief would appear between two clouds. Then everything would get black again as if someone had poured ink on it. And they had to brace, and brace again, and then counterbrace, to avoid being taken aback, which would have made it necessary to tack about and treat the ship to a complete turn before getting back on the course.

When that happened, a whole fireworks display of insults would rain from the deck upon the helmsman. He would try to excuse himself: "It's not my fault, fellows! The wind shifted more than four points all at once, before I had time to put the helm up."

But the others, grimly skeptical, would vie with one another in shouting: "You lie in your teeth, you damn caulker! The wind has only shifted one point! And here you've had us working the ship around for nothing, for more than an hour!"

And haul from one side, and haul from the other side, and run up sails, and trim them taut, and haul them down again!

The skin was peeling off their hands. They were no longer conscious of their wet feet, as sodden as if they were shod in blotting-paper. The officers stuck to your skin like horseflies. They were crazy. As if you'd lose the least gasp of this damn wind, that would leave you in the stew-pot in the middle of a calm, when it wasn't coming down on you like a firing-squad! They were crazy; even the Old Man, who wasn't sleeping any more and who would roar at you loudly enough to break the megaphone, as if the wind flurries you wanted were things he could pull out of his pocket; even little Guézennec, the nursling, who was learning to shout and bawl by shouting and bawling at you.

After four days of this existence, the barometer took a sudden plunge. Even for this latitude the weather had an ugly look, and the wind was blowing up.

46

"We will take in the small sails before dark, Monsieur Monnard," said the captain. "I don't like this weather at all."

Rolland had just left the wheel when the mate called the crew to action. They hauled down the tops'l, then the mizzen-top stays'l, and still he had not come back.

"Where is Rolland?" the mate asked.

"Probably down below," Névei answered.

"Go get him."

They were finishing clewing up the main royal when Rolland appeared, behind Névei.

"Furl!" Monsieur Monnard was ordering.

The novice and a young sailor were already going aloft, when the mate appeared to catch sight of Rolland. He looked at him, his eyes wide open this time, and with his raised hand, index finger stretched out, he pointed to the shrouds.

This was the supreme insult, the gesture of scorn and threat which is only directed toward the no-goods and the do-nothings, those who always hang back from climbing into the rigging and who only avoid reprimand by going up at the tail-end of the watch-crew, and with glue on the soles of their boots. It was, at the same time, a deliberate irritation: two men were amply sufficient to furl the high sail.

"Aren't they enough to furl a royal?" Rolland grumbled.

"I told you to go along."

"They're enough; I won't go."

The immediate and terrible blow he received laid him out on the deck. Anybody else—anybody, no matter who—would have emphasized it by an insult, or commented upon it by a sentence: "You needed a lesson, you've been waiting for it, now you've got it"; or, "I hope I make myself plain. . . ." But as if he had wholly effaced from his mind the man who was now rising to a sitting position on the deck planking—and doing it as weightily as if he were coming out of an anaesthetic—Monsieur Monnard turned his back and returned to the poop.

Nothing of this scene had been lost upon Captain Le Gac. He had immediately realized the profound impression which this first demonstration of authority, so patiently deferred and then accomplished at the opportune moment, had produced upon the crew. There was quite a new cordiality in his voice, as he announced: "We will take in the mains'l when the watch changes, Monsieur Monnard. The barometer is still falling. I believe we are going to be shaken up a bit."

The mate made a gesture of acquiescence and turned to the man at the wheel. "Call them at half-past seven."

Then, his eyes half-closed, he went back to that eternal sentry-duty which he carried out unmoving, arms fallen to his sides, and which had made the sailor accuse him of sleeping on watch.

At half-past seven, when the premature call to the watch echoed through the fo'c'sle, Rolland came out of his torpor. The blow he had received had given him a nose as heavy as lead, swollen painfully; he also had a black eye. But this was nothing beside the humiliation of having been so completely taken by surprise in a careless moment, so adroitly driven to bay in his mutiny, and then having been so tranquilly disdained once the punishment had been inflicted.

He realized more clearly than the men, even more clearly than the captain, the masterly perfection of the mate's counter-stroke. It left not one opening for a valid insult, a sarcasm with power to sting, a threat that would not be ridiculous. He was choking under it. All he could do was dull his brain by repeating over and over to himself, like some haunting litany, "The son-of-a-bitch, the son-of-a-bitch, the damn son-of-a-bitch. . . ."

"We're going to take in the mains'l," the man at the wheel added, after the call to the watch.

The announcement jerked the sailor to his feet. All right, he'd show him how to take in a mains'l, a fellow with a mouth like liver paste and eyes half-shut, the way his were!

"Bouse the weather clew! Come on now, bouse!"

The mate's voice carried without shouting. He gave his orders as if the thing were a matter of course, and not at all as if response demanded an effort that took all the strength a man had.

"Bouse the clew!"

The men, both hands clinging to the lines, hauled with rhythmic crouching movements, so quick and so far down that one would have said some enormous object was falling on them from above and crushing them. When the windward side had been clewed up, they crossed over to leeward, and when the bos'n saw them all in line, ready for the next effort, he hauled in the sheet. It was as if he had loosed a thunderbolt on their heads. The sail, half bundled up, whipped with the crackling of a cannonade, and the impact of the chain links against the drawing-wire of the clew sent sparks into the air.

"All together, boys!"

They were hauling, in a bunch, not with all their weight—their dead weight—but with all their guts, all their thighs, all the strength of their loins. Their muscles were hardening and stiffening, as in a seizure of lockjaw, and that gave them the faces of men in torture, teeth bared, eyes sticking out. Yet they only gained inch

48

by inch on the vast ballooning stretch of canvas that they were fighting over with the wind.

At last Hervic called out: "Chock-a-block!"

And the mate commanded, like an echo: "Furl!"

Rolland leaped furiously into the shrouds. In a few seconds he had reached his station as topman of the mast, but in the middle, where there was the biggest bundle to fit the gaskets to. There, it was an account to be settled between him and the sail, the mass at once hard and elusive, in hand-to-hand struggle with the heavy folds and the brutal excrescences of canvas that the strong wind was puffing out between the buntlines. Huge bubbles would suddenly rise up, to right and left, as if the sail were boiling. The topman beat them in with his fists, strangled them as if they were the throats of enemies. When, violently and with tremendous effort, he had pulled the last furling-line taut, he went down. Monsieur Monnard was waiting for him at the foot of the mast, and gestured to him to stop. Rolland would have liked to go right by, turn away from the odious compliment which the mate was no doubt about to inflict upon him. It was the look that brought him up short, by its gravity.

"Remember all this," Monsieur Monnard said simply, "if you are in command some day."

The small sails trussed up and the mains'l furled, they could look ahead more tranquilly to what might be coming. The night went by, however, in the weathering of dirty squalls. Hervic had had the fore to'gants'l furled. But Monsieur Monnard had it set again when the morning watch came on: the barometer had risen, the weather was clearing, the breeze was going slack once more. Then, by noon, those accursed winds were making them tack again; and rain, more rain!

The men, worn out, were hurling insults at the ship, now once more inert. "Damn filthy barge, worthless hulk of a lighter for the customs men! It's the devil's own luck, getting your bag thrown on a tub like this!"

Rolland was now the only one who was not talking. He might have said more than the others, if he had suspected that Monsieur Monnard was listening to his silences. The first mate was estimating these at their exact value: the sailor was not brooding on his punishment; that had been digested, as the officer realized. If the boy was keeping silent, it was because he had backbone.

There were two distinct breeds of men on a ship: those who obeyed, and who must be continually encouraged or threatened because they had no motive force within themselves and waited for a thrust from outside; and those who commanded, whose will must feed and foster that of the sailors. Rolland might be one of these last, the mate was thinking.

They dragged along for three days more through calms and rains, under the pallid gleams of light that filtered down between the clouds' dark swollen masses. The *Galatée* was like a wagon stuck in the mud of a sunken Breton lane, when men and beasts have to put forth prodigious effort for a quarter-turn of the wheel. It seemed as if the ship, unable to find any support in these irrational and fleeting breezes, would never get out of this stagnant water in which up to its middle it was bemired.

At last one morning they made out some sails far to the south that were moving away: another craft, then, had come upon some breezes and was whipping along under the trade winds it had found once more. They watched it vanish without even yelling insults at it; it was too far away! But they were such figures of dejection that the mate, coming up behind them, remarked as if to himself, "It's them today; it will be us tomorrow."

They turned around. Monsieur Monnard was walking along with his usual indifferent gait, his hands behind his back, as if he were no more than a passer-by on the ship's "main street." But the gaze that followed him was from different eyes.

Since they came into the Doldrums, they had changed their minds about him. They had vaguely scorned him at first as a man who did not know how to shout at them as the others did. And they had been irritated by his seeming to consider calms, squalls, exhausting tacking and working as negligible incidents, things to be taken for granted.

"It isn't bowels he's got inside him, like any Christian," they grumbled. "It's machinery!"

They actually had wondered whether he wasn't feeble-minded, whether he understood what was going on, and the orders he gave. But when they saw him impassive under the cloudbursts, his head raised toward a sail to be furled, taking the rain's furious pelting that was hard as a shower of stones; when they grasped the fact that all his curtly delivered commands, of which he required immediate and rapid execution, were fair and timely and provided a just distribution of effort, they realized that their labor, however toilsome, was in good hands, and that this man would not squander it. And because, this morning, he had guessed their bitterness of spirit and had known how to dispel it with a sentence, they stood gazing at his back in contentment, until he turned around and his stroll brought him back in their direction.

The next day, in fact, they did catch sight of a fixed rift in this

50

still-molting sky, a rift as narrow as an air-hole when they first saw it, but growing larger and giving them a glimpse of a band of blue that was not being diluted this time by mist. At the same time there came a light breeze from the southeast, a breath which was almost imperceptible but which did not die down, and which all their skin was anxiously on the alert for. On the poop, the Old Man had also felt the nascent wind and, his head raised, he seemed to be searching for it among the clouds.

It was Monsieur Monnard, however, who without interrupting his stroll gave a look at all the men of his watch as he passed them, eagerly on the look-out at the foot of the mainmast, and was the first to venture to say, in his most everyday voice, "There it is! We've caught them!"

He was pledging his responsibility there, gravely. Often, these light breaths that were forerunners of the trade winds died down, and you were bogged in calms and rains once more. The disappointment would be so cruel then that it would take all the starch out of your crew, and you would have all sorts of a time stiffening them up again.

That was what was keeping Le Gac, on his poop, from confirming the presence of this fragile breeze. But when he saw the men stirring about on deck, suddenly recovering even in this stifling heat the easy activity and natural movements of bracing weather, he realized that he had been outdistanced and, so as not to lag too far behind, he called out to the mate, who was coming up, "I think we've got them by the tail this time!"

Monsieur Monnard gave his usual nod of acquiescence.

The captain leaned over the poop-rail. "Trim all sails! Let out the royals, hoist the flying jib, the stays'ls, the tops'l!"

He flung the orders one upon another in a kind of frolic fashion, the genial way one hustles youngsters as they are leaving on their holidays. And the men responded with the shouts of pupils let out of school, egging each other on to get going at their jobs. The sails went up everywhere at once, and the ship glided along smoothly, close to the wind, tacking to port, all canvas up.

Like a convalescent taking her first airing, the *Galatée* moved slowly at first, making two or three knots an hour. By evening the breeze seemed settled.

At four in the morning the ship was once more becalmed, this time under a clear sky.

51

VI

IT WAS true that they still had the trade winds only by the tail. But, even so, the breezes were giving the crew a chance to breathe, after ten days of floundering in the Doldrums. Except for the helmsman and the look-out man, they were all sleeping the whole night now, and in the open air, on deck.

One morning they stopped Monsieur Guézennec with a question, as he was on his way forward to inspect his chicken-coops.

"We'll cross it in three days," he answered.

It was the second mate who was the liaison officer between the poop and the fo'c'sle. You couldn't count on the Old Man to whisper confidences to you about the voyage, and still less on the first mate. Guézennec, like all young men, was more talkative. That didn't mean that he wasn't on the defensive, like anyone else, in the steward's cabin; but the men liked him a lot, because he had a youngster's open face, was always ready for a good laugh, and was able all the same to preserve a marble calm under the abusive remarks the captain felt obliged to make to him as part of his education.

"Monsieur Guézennec, you brace as if you were dumping codfish!"

"Monsieur Guézennec, you don't know how to haul the stays'l sheets taut!"

"Monsieur Guézennec, your mains'l might have been tacked by a good sister in a convent!"

"Monsieur Guézennec" would go serenely on his way, have the sail in question hauled or tacked as if that had just occurred to him, and never seem to notice the glances of understanding and collusion that the men would dart at him on such occasions.

His popularity had shot up like an arrow among them; because of the rooster stunt. Overcome one day by a too-strong appetite for chicken, he had taken a sail needle and neatly buried it in the cranium of one of his boarders. Then he had gone back to the captain, to report that a rooster which had been giving him some anxiety for several days was going from bad to worse, and it was high time to wring its neck if they didn't want to let it die and have to throw it overboard. The skipper, who set as much store by his fowl as by his own two eyes, had at once gone with Guézennec to look at the invalid; he had found it lying on its side, and had been forced to consent to the execution.

"What are you giving them to eat, that they are starving to death?" the Old Man had grumbled.

"But look, Captain, he is good and plump," Guézennec had answered.

"Then you must be letting them die of indigestion. . . ."

It was the cabin boy, César, whom they called Gee-Gee, who had walked in on this scene and had told the men about it.

Now the second mate said they would cross "it" in four days. It was time to start getting ready! The ship became an unknown country they were prospecting for treasure. They would come back to the fo'c'sle from the steward's quarters, the stores, the hold, one with handfuls of oakum, one with a piece of sailcloth. It might have been thought they had just been seized with a feverish passion to build nests, like birds. The cook had to provide soot, the stores-man flour, and the chickens squawked as if they were having their throats cut when needed feathers were pulled out of their tails. In the fo'c'sle, the men sewed and carded and glued. The older sailors, custodians of tradition, were directing the work and rehearsing the roles. Some of these had been assigned by right of seniority, but others were still to be cast.

"Who'll do the imps?"

"Those parts belong to the young guys."

The two young sailors offered themselves, and were accepted.

"Who's to do Mother Equator?"

"Morbecque!" they shouted with one voice.

Morbecque, the big fellow from Dunkerque, smiled, flattered by being chosen. "Mother Equator" had to be someone of large breadth. Being given the physical attractions that must round her out, before and behind, her impersonator needed a chest and a backsides broad enough for them to expand on easily.

For the rest, Morbecque at once manifested the capricious perfectionism of a great coquette. He saw Mother Equator as a blonde, which necessitated an extra supply of tow for her wig. Then, God knows why, he could not conceive of her otherwise than in a plaid dress, and that meant an endless amount of painting on the sailcloth of which it was to be made. But Morbecque claimed to be sure of the effect.

"Rolland, you do the Postilion."

This personage had to go to the main top, with an oilskin hat, a megaphone big enough for the cabin boy to disappear under, wooden spurs as long as his boots were high, and his pockets stuffed with beans that were to imitate hailstones. It took an expert climber, a monkey of the first rank, to haul himself into the main top with all this impedimenta. The offer made to Rolland was, therefore, a compliment. Curtly, he declined it.

"You get on my nerves, with your stunts," he answered, when they asked him why, and went and sat down in the bow behind the chicken-coop, his eyes turned in upon himself, without a glance for the sea or the ship. What was the matter with him now, that these preparations for a masquerade should exasperate him so? He had crossed the Line three times, and he had enjoyed himself as much as any youngster; but not this time! It wasn't a pose. In the Doldrums, when they were stewing in what they called the "Black Pot," he had not given way for a second; yet now, when it was only a matter of having a good time, he was all upset. Their tow wigs, their dabs of paint, especially their heavy delight in getting ready for this carnival, had made him clench his fists there in the fo'c'sle a little while ago. He had been odious; he knew that. The dirtiest swine of a captain would not have made a gesture, or said a word, against the Equator Celebration, the only full day of merriment and pleasure that was allowed to men at sea. He had once had this merriment and pleasure within himself, like the others; now he had it no longer. How? Why? He had no idea. It was as if his home had been moved, something in his life changed, during an absence, and he had only just become aware of it.

He concluded that this was idiotic, since it was inexplicable, and that he would have to make an effort. So he went back, deliberately, to the crew's quarters, where they threw ugly looks at him, and stopped in front of Old Man Toublanc, who was presiding over the preparations.

"Who's going to do the Barber?" he asked.

They all understood that he had come to make his peace with them. Only, Toublanc made him wait a few seconds for his answer, so as to show the necessary reserve.

"You, if you will," he said.

"Good, I'll do that."

The celebration began with an attraction that was not on the regular program, and they missed the funniest part of it through not knowing about it in advance. The skipper used to go up to the poop about eight in the morning, by an inner stairway. He would go into the chart-house, look at the log-book and the barometer, wind up his chronometer, and then go out on the deck. This morning when he opened the door with his usual sweeping movement, he received the contents of a gallon bucket right on his head. Snorting, he burst out on deck, swearing so loudly that the loungers all gathered to listen.

"What dirty bastard—"

Monsieur Guézennec took a step forward and spoke in his most amiable tone: "There are two of us, Captain: tradition and I."

Le Gac, who was sponging his neck with his handkerchief, choked over this. "It was you? *You?*"

Imperturbably good-natured, very well satisfied, moreover, that his little mechanism had done its work so perfectly, Monsieur Guézennec sketched in the air with one hand and one shoulder a gesture of regret. "All my apologies, Captain; but honor to whom honor is due. . . ."

Old Toublanc's voice sounded from the first row of spectators on the deck: "That's right, Cap'n. Today, everybody has to get his baptism, no matter where it comes from."

Understanding broke upon Captain Le Gac. He realized, too, after a black look beneath his feet at the faces all wrinkled up with laughter, that he was making a show of himself for the benefit of the whole crew, and chewing on the imprecations that were still setting his jowls aquiver, he went back into his cabin to change his clothes.

When he came out again, he had recovered enough serenity to fill his role worthily in the ritual farce so often played, recounted, described, but always new for sailors, as Christmas is for children. Monsieur Monnard and the second mate had come up to take their places at his right and left, respectively, and were waiting for him.

A sonorous voice descended from the sky, magnified by the monumental megaphone: "Ship ahoy!"

"Ahoy!" responded the captain. But his "Ahoy!" was as short as a hiccup.

"You are at the frontier of the territories of the sovereign of the Equator," the voice went on. "Heave to, and make arrangements for him to board your ship."

"I shall be greatly honored to receive him," said Le Gac, with the same amount of warmth as if he had been asked to welcome the Minister of the Navy.

A hailstorm of beans clattered down on the deck, a vigorously rattled piece of sheet-iron produced long-drawn-out thunders, and then the Postilion, stumbling in his spurs, swearing behind his megaphone, let himself down into the shrouds, while the state procession of Father Equator was making its way up from the fo'c'sle.

The cortege paused long enough for the Postilion to alight from the rigging, and to take his place at its head. Behind him capered the two Imps, three-quarters nude, punctiliously coated with soot

55

and crowned with feather diadems. They were followed by the Barber and his assistant, the policemen in cocked hats of painted canvas, and finally Father Equator himself with wig and beard made of tow, and with his wife on his arm.

The sovereign and his escort made the tour of the deck three times. Every time the men would dash from one side of the ship to the other to see the procession again and to admire some detail— Father Equator's sextant, put together by Tonton the carpenter, and the size of a trestle; Mother Equator's plaid dress, which the paint-brushes had generously splashed with one colored square on top of another; her monstrous bosom; and the extraordinary bustle extended on a structure of stout wire. The men were contemplating all this with joyous bursts of laughter and the glowing eyes of children before a display of toys.

At last the escort paused at the poop-rail. Father Equator and his consort went up, alone, to join the officers' staff.

"Good morning, Cap'n! What is the name of your ship?"

"The *Galatée*."

"And what is your own name, Cap'n?"

"Le Gac."

"But I know you! You have already traveled across my kingdom a number of times. Sergeant, hand me my big book."

One of the policemen climbed up to the poop, his wooden saber rattling against the steps of the companionway. He held out a ledger.

"Well, now, let us look under the L's. . . . La Gâcheur, La Gadoue, La Gamelle, Le Godailleur, Le Groumeur, Le Gueulard, La Génisse,* Le Gac. . . . Here we are: Le Gac, Jean-Baptiste."

The captain had tried to achieve a smile during this litany, and he was schooling himself to keep it. But it was escaping him and turning into a somewhat wry grimace, while Névol, who had been chosen for the principal role because he would know how to slip some real digs into it, was pretending to follow the lines in the book with his finger:

"Le Gac, Jean Baptiste, a good seaman. . . . Voyages short, because he meets every gust of the wind with a hundred gusts from his jaw. . . . Oh, but listen to this! Weighs the rations with matchsticks, would as soon hand out a double wine ration as lose an eye, and gets up in the night to count the beans in the bags. . . . You will have to watch out for that, Cap'n, or else I won't allow you to cross my frontiers."

* These made-up names are part of the fun. They mean, in that order, *bungler, stinker, mess-tin, boozer, grumbler, bawler,* and *calf.* Even the everyday word for "mess-tin" or "mug" has a possible connotation of disastrous mistakes. Tr.

Having completed this balance-sheet, he seized his sextant.

"Wait a moment now while I take my elevation, so that I may give you the exact position."

The huge sextant carried a bottle in the place of a telescope. Father Equator raised it to his lips and drank it off in one gulp.

"Here we are," he said. "Latitude, twenty-two mugs of wine; longitude, twenty-two tots of grog. Your position is good, Cap'n, but only if you keep to that course!"

He turned to his spouse: "You remember, Mother Equator, the last time he came he left us thirsty. If that were to happen again he would be refused permission to pass."

"Monsieur Guézennec," said Le Gac, "you will hand out the double wine ration."

"Then I authorize you to continue on your way," said Nével majestically, "and to drink to my health before luncheon."

While the men below were already dashing to their quarters to get their canteens, Rolland was standing on the poop, his huge wooden razor in his hand, his face daubed with powdered red lead, awaiting the moment of the "baptism" in a state of dreary boredom. He felt as if he were taking part in a wretched little show on a country fair ground, a show repeated so many times already that he was no longer sensitive to anything in it except its ludicrous poverty. A mug of wine, a few ounces of brandy—it would have taken something besides that to make him entertained as his comrades were by this miserable assortment of rags and tags, this tow, this oakum, this wooden razor. He was seized, as the royal couple of "the Line" went down the poop companionway—one bogged up in his peplum, the other in that harlequin robe by an inordinate desire to get drunk. There it was, the succor that was always open to him, that mist of alcohol that could make a port prostitute seem desirable, and this mummery amusing. But this was worse than a sickness, to be looking today on things and on women that even yesterday had given him pleasure, with the eyes he had now, the eyes of a stranger, which saw them as they were.

He took a look at the officers standing near him. Le Gac, his hands behind his back, his chin sunk in his collar, was contemplating the hullabaloo on the deck with a spurious air of interest, the expression one sees on the faces of sub-prefects at farmers' meetings. The first mate was not even making an effort to seem attentive; one might have thought a tall lay-figure had been set down at the captain's right. Only little Guézennec was genuinely entertained.

"Take your places for the baptism," Father Equator ordered.

There were only two neophytes: Menut the novice, and the apprentice, Barquet. Even the young second mate had crossed the Line two years before. Now, with barbaric yells, the two Imps flung themselves upon the catechumens, and with the assistance of the policemen pushed them toward the poop-rail. Barquet was green in the face. For the last four days the men had been taking turns in giving him a foretaste of the terrors of this baptism. They had assured him that one of the victims had been held so long under the "baptismal font" that it had taken an hour of artificial respiration and a dose of ipecac as big as your fist to bring him to himself again and make him spit up all the water he had swallowed. . . .

A scudding sail, which is a square sail, had been installed horizontally between the hatch and the poop-rail, with its four corners pulled up parachute fashion, and they had used the fire pump to fill it with sea water. This was the baptismal font. There was a raised bench at the edge of it.

First they stripped the two victims as bare as the palm of your hand, and then Rolland, the Barber, began to perform his function. This consisted in smearing them over from head to foot with a mixture of strong ship's soap, soot, and grease. He began with the apprentice.

But when he saw the boy seated naked before him, his body too thin, his eyes closed, his mouth half-open, an expression of desperate resignation on his face, Rolland was obscurely moved, if not to pity at least to a kind of fellow-feeling. This chap was like himself: he wasn't having a good time, either! As he brandished his enormous brush he leaned over and whispered, "Close your mouth!"

Yet it was part of the game to fill the victim's mouth with "shaving soap" and enjoy his wry face and his frantic spitting. . . . Barquet closed his mouth, but he opened his eyes because he had been struck by the almost friendly tone of his executioner. He shut them again at the first stroke of the brush on his cheek, but he soon became aware that with the dexterity of a real barber Rolland was avoiding his lips, his nostrils, the corners of his eyes. When the lathering was finished, Rolland scraped him with the wooden razor, but this again with an extraordinarily light hand. He had hardly finished this when the Imps, picking up the bench on which the apprentice was sitting, capsized him from behind, head first into the sail full of water.

Their game was to roll him around in it, drag him under the surface, make him swallow big gulps. That was the rite. But Rolland noticed in his turn that under an exuberance of ferocious gestures and cannibal contortions they were disguising a concentration on making the victim drink as little of the salt water as possible. Their furious splashings, their spatterings, were adroitly covering up the fact that they were keeping his head almost constantly out of the water. It did not for one moment occur to Rolland that they too might have been seized with qualms.

He'll have promised them money, he thought.

He had the feeling that he had been taken in, and he was sorry he had not been harder on Barquet.

It was the fight that really exorcised his bad mood. This began immediately after the baptism of the novices, with a bucket of water majestically sent broadside, full in the captain's face. That was in the regular order of things, and Le Gac was now ready with his counter-attack. The battle was on, between the poop and the fo'c'sle. Rolland pitched into the first mate, but he was surprised by the rapidity of his dodges. The tall body would reverse its position in the split second necessary to avoid the other's stroke, and his counter-thrusts, after brief feints, would hit the sailor as directly as the flow from a pump.

"You've met your match," said Mahé in Rolland's ear.

"He's on top and I'm below."

The captain, the officers and the bos'n were avidly pursued, for when they ran out of "munitions" they too came down to fill their buckets from the baptismal font. Absorbed now in the sport, they were no longer trying to dodge but to return blow for blow.

The games were brought to an end by the midday meal, with a double wine ration and a dessert. In the afternoon there was Sunday duty. In the evening they sang. When darkness fell, they caught sight for the first time of the Southern Cross.

"It's foot is missing," said Mahé.

That was true. Three splendid stars formed the head and the arms, but the lower portion of the cross was lighted by a star of the third magnitude which was scarcely visible against the deep velvet blackness of the night.

"Yesterday, when I was at the wheel," said Nével, "the second mate was saying that we would see it today, with the other conglomerations of the south."

"Constellations," Mahé corrected.

"If you like. . . . And he called them, what do you suppose? The Clock, the Crane, the Compass, and the Stove!"

"The Stove, you blessed Nével! He wasn't looking at you when he talked about the stove, was he?" *

The bell sounded mealtime.

The southeast trade winds bore them along for several days more. Then they met with variable winds again, and scowls settled on their

* *Fourneau*, which means "stove" or "furnace," has the colloquial meaning of "nincompoop" or "silly ass," also. Tr.

faces. From now on they would have nothing good to hope for: the farther south they went the harder things would get. The good-weather set of sails had to come down now, to be replaced by a set that could ride out the heavy winds, and the men knew that they had not a minute to lose. The work began at sunrise, with the daylight watch, and the two watch-crews were rivals over which would get its task done more quickly.

The mast topmen ran from the parrel to the topping lift, minutely inspecting the rope-bands, footropes, ratlines, and roundings. Earings and clew lines were remounted one by one. Everything was examined, checked, and changed when necessary.

"You must be having a hell of a time with your mainm'st," old Lhévéder, the stores-man, said to Rolland. "What is all this spun-yarn and sennit you're making away with? You'd think you were putting new ratlines on all the shrouds!"

"I don't want to smash my face one of these days or make the others smash theirs," Rolland answered.

And he went on pestering the mate, to get everything replaced that did not offer a wide margin of security. Work, this work on the success of which they staked their lives, had at last brought him out of his own doldrums: those obscure and drifting thoughts, those gusts of anger without reason and without object, that had been beating, lately, through his brain.

When everything was in order, when the flying bridges had been installed from bow to stern—because a day might come when they would risk themselves on the flooded deck only for indispensable jobs—the two watches stopped working together, and the routine of one watch on duty and one watch below-decks was restored. In their quarters, the men took out of their sea-chests the little boats that some of them had been working on for years. They cut, scraped, and polished the ebony and *cajou* (mahogany). They would spend an afternoon chiseling out a tiny block from an albatross bone kept from the last voyage. Absorbed in their work, they worked in silence. After passing long hours in elementary exertions, after having been nothing but machines to heave and furl, they were obscurely tasting the delights of artists.

Rolland was painting. He had sandpapered his poplar chest until it was as white as snow. He had drawn on it with a carpenter's pencil complicated coils of scrolls and foliage. And now, surrounded by a circle of admirers, he was painting with all a primitive's atten-tion to detail. He had made his brushes himself, with bristles he had pulled out of the ship's pigs.

One evening, as it was growing dark, the fo'c'sle door opened sud-denly, as it opened only under the bos'n's fist.

"Everybody on deck! Take in the upper sails!"

They gathered up their treasures in indignant astonishment.

"What's that? Take in sail? With this fine weather?"

Rolland was putting the cover on his last paint-pot.

"It wouldn't be the pampero by any chance?" he suggested.

They fell silent. They had all sailed the southern seas, and they knew that when you come abeam of the Argentine pampas you have to be afraid of the terrible pampero, a brief but almost always extraordinarily violent cyclone that can raze the masts to the level of the deck.

"Clew the royals! Everybody aloft!"

The Old Man's barometer was certainly sounding the alarm. Far down on the western horizon there was already a black speck that was rapidly growing larger. Bronzed clouds were piling up, so metallic in appearance that one was surprised not to hear them go "Bing!" when they overtook each other. In the chart-house the captain was watching his barometer falling in a saw-tooth line that looked like the chart of a typhoid patient.

"Clew the mains'l! Furl!"

Which would win the race they were running: the ship, too confident, parading its three thousand square yards of canvas in the sun, or the whirling cloud that was swollen like a black balloon with all the winds gathered up around the Rio de la Plata?

"Clew the to'gants'ls! Haul down the main jib and the main stays'l! Come on, get a move on!"

Taking the clothes off a paralytic! That's what it was! And that's when a man realizes that a ship is a thing in chains, unable to help itself, that you have to do everything for it, tuck up its petticoats one by one and fasten them tight for fear it will let them fly off in the wind. The mates were on deck, shouting themselves breathless in the heavy calm, while the moments drew out. The bos'n was heard bawling:

"Hurry up! Look alive there, my God, and be smart about it! Are you sailors or pregnant women?"

Monsieur Monnard, who took on more of frozen calm as the others became more fidgety, threw out a recommendation as the men were dashing into the shrouds to take in the mains'l: "Take enough time to pass the gasket around it properly, boys!"

Rolland could not keep back a gesture of approval. What was the use of bawling? Everyone knew what a pampero was, and everyone knew they were going to get a taste of one. So what? No need to tell them to hurry!

Monkeys! It really was monkeys this time, climbing and running through the rigging on this calm and steady ship, with a suppleness and sureness that were actually simian. . . . Rolland got his footing, with a quick stiffening of his back muscles, on the to'gallant horse. In two leaps, ninety feet above the deck, he had made his way along the footrope to the end of the yard. He had no support except the grip of his body on the thick rounded surface. His two arms and his loins were alike laboring. It was a swift job to gather up that lifeless canvas, make a bundle of it, tie it together, and then go below again. The ship was made ready in record time. They brought her about on the starboard tack, head to the southwest, prepared to bear away under reduced sail.

"Now we can wait and see," said the captain, sponging his forehead—as if he were the one who had done all the work! "We're ready for the change of wind."

That wasn't slow in coming! The first stars were blotted out in a single stroke, and there was so much sizzling and crackling all around that you'd think the boat had been plungetd into a frying-pan. The cyclone was rushing upon them with the rumblings of an express train.

"Two men to the wheel! Hard a-port! Bear full around!" cried the captain, and added: "Lower the two upper tops'ls! And quick! We've got to hurry!"

Hardly were the words out of his mouth than, in the midst of a din like the end of the world, the *Galatée* went heeling over to port like a cow, sending Le Gac roughly against the ship's side where he might have been carried over the rail if Monsieur Monnard had not caught hold of him and pulled him back. Almost immediately the wind veered from northwest to southwest, blowing with still greater violence, as if it had taken on sudden force in the shift.

But the ship had already carried out its dodging movement successfully and had fallen off sufficiently to escape all danger of being caught aback. It was lying to, on the starboard tack, nose to the southeast, under the two lower tops'ls, the fores'l, the fore topm'st stays'l, and the mizzen topm'st stays'l.

Hove to thus, there was not another thing for anyone to do, except pray the good Lord that nothing would break till the dance was over. The darkness had come upon them suddenly, as if the pampero had sprayed it, furiously, over the whole sky. The men took shelter before the poop-rail, and, doing nothing and seeing nothing, they listened. The masts were crackling from keel to truck, a fusillade that ran along from the step of the masts to their highest point. The hull of the ship groaned as if it were being gutted. Hours were spent like this, in the darkness, listening to the ship suffering. Yet everyone was sure that it would weather the gale, since the captain had anticipated the first blow, the blow that might have leveled the masts, in time to parry it. A damn good smeller-out of weather, the Old Man!

"Stiffen the weather braces!"

It was Monsieur Monnard's voice that came to dislodge them from their retreat. Not one of them could see the mate, but it was better than if they actually were seeing him, so well could they picture him from that calm and level voice.

They went off like blind men, their arms thrust forward, feeling their way on the ship, butting against things everywhere and satisfied with their buttings, because that way you could catch hold of what had just hit you on the leg or the forehead, catch hold long enough to let the wave go by that was dashing up to your middle and might suck you down. Rallying where the voice called them, they reached the point at last where they could put their hands on the invisible line which they had to haul in or pull taut.

The wind went down gradually, and by morning the men could get on with clearing up the night's frightful mess. They went bustling about, in indignant haste, with the instinct of the housewife who hastens to set things to rights in the trail of a drunken husband. Rigging lay about on the deck; there were cracks in many of the portholes; the halyards and buntlines had gone slack and were banging along the masts; some ends torn from the racks were dragging.

"Ordinary damages, imposed by politeness," Guézennec summed up.

But the topmen on the masts, who were finding their gear all in disorder, and the sailmakers, who were obliged to sew patches on the slit seams of the sails, had no relish for this extra-curricular interlude.

Nor did it stand in the way of their going ahead at the same time with the customary preparations for rounding Cape Horn. The ship was being bolted and barred like a fortress before assault, doors boarded up and weatherstripped with sennet, hatches battened down with cross-pieces of heavy timber. The slings of the boats were likewise being reinforced with steel wire, and double sheets were attached to the lower sails.

One morning when the apprentice Barquet was nailing a strip of sennet along the edge of a door, a little piece of upholstery work that was really like fixing a piece of felt where it was needed to keep out a draft, someone struck him roughly on the shoulder. He gave a jump, then turned around. Rolland's hard gaze was fixed upon him.

"Well, you weren't around to get in our way much during the pampero. . . ."

The boy began to stammer.

"The captain said—"

"I know what he said—I didn't have to hear it," Rolland cut in. "He told you you were nothing but a cry-baby anyway, you might just as well blubber in your cabin and cry for your mother. At the other end of the ship there was the pig, that wasn't feeling well either. . . ."

"Leave him alone, poor kid," interposed Nével, who had been following the whole scene. "He's feeble. He'd have got himself carried away by the first wave."

Barquet had turned, automatically, toward this succor. Rolland snapped his attention back to himself, and his hard look.

"I'm the one who's talking to you! You are the apprentice. You have paid to come, you have paid to look on, you have paid to work. You oughtn't to lose your money, ought you? We fellows, we're paid, that's not so smart. . . . Now, you listen: at Cape Horn there aren't going to be any lazy loafers. Wherever you are, I'm coming after you. I'll take you where the rest of us are. And there you'll stay. I promise you that."

Barquet fixed his pallid gaze upon him.

"Why didn't you tell me sooner?" was all he said.

VII

THE MEN of the port watch were sitting on their sea-chests. The vessel was steady. Gaborit, one of the two novices—the "beaver," as they called the youngster who was not much better than a cabin boy and who did odd jobs—had lighted the little stove in the crew's quarters to dry out the dampness. It was one of the last "rest watches" that would be relatively peaceful before the battle of Cape Horn, which would last for weeks, during which the two watches, crowded together in a corner of the poop, would spend nobody knew how many nights on their feet, waiting for the orders that would launch them to all points of the beleaguered vessel.

They were drying out the fog which, for the past four hours, had been seeping into the very marrow of their bones; four hours of rolling about in air that had turned into water, a dirty and already icy water, so murky that it seemed to be soaking up everything. They felt the ship in its waddling gait, but they could hardly see it. After a few steps the men would become shadows shuffling along the sides,

64

then they would vanish entirely. The very sounds they made, the regulation of the bells from the wheel or the bow, the barking of the foghorn, were muffled, shivering, in the center of thick zones of silence, as if they were gagged with wet towels.

Other noises had haunted them during those hours of watch: whisperings, strange sighs, stifled cries in the air above them and in the drifting mist. Not one of them would have dared mutter, "Do you hear that?" For they all knew that these were really everyday noises, creakings of blocks or collars, snappings in a yard, breaths of the wind. But not one was recognizable. What they heard was no longer the voices of objects or of living creatures—at least, not beings of this world. And there was not one of those Breton sailors who would not have laughed, oh very loudly, if anyone had said aloud that he was trying with all his might not to think that this fog was peopled with presences, and that these were the lamentations of souls come back from the dead.

In the fo'c'sle, in the unambiguous warmth of the little stove framed by the solid lines of their tiers of bunks, they had relaxed, but they were still uneasy and disgruntled. The Horn was waiting in ambush behind these fogs, and when they could not see the route that was leading them to it, the course seemed to be growing the shorter for that. To be sure, they still had to go down along a bit of Patagonia, but the fog had soaked into their spirit, and the time of real suffering that was waiting at the end of the world was already pressing upon them harshly.

"I'd like to know what the Old Man is going to do this time," said Toublanc, who had been around Cape Horn thirty-two times and had been shipwrecked, in his youth, on Diego Ramirez, that dirty rock to the south.

"Oh, get out, with your 'knowing'!" said Mahé. "You make me think of those fellows that come along with their ideas moored fast in their heads. Did you know old Beuclerc, on the *Valparaiso*? That one, he'd bear down to the southwest as far as he could, until he had his nose in the ice-fields, without trying to stand in for the coast, and then he'd sail back again. He got away with that, until the day when he didn't sail back at all."

"And you have others," Nével took up the recital, "who want to keep veering along the shore, and who dash around like a bumble-bee on a windowpane trying to find a hole to get through. If the wind changes, they go on. They're betting on their luck. But we were stuck, waiting for it, thirty-two days, on the *Beaumanoir*."

"I can go you one better," said Morbecque. "It was forty-five days we hung around, on the *Aconcagua*, with Cap'n Legros."

"You're not in it!" exclaimed Mahé. "Me, it was fifty-six days, on the *La Fontaine,* before we could get around the Cape. And there were others caught like us—one of them waited three months! The night before we went ahead at last, I saw a three-master turning her stern about. Most likely she was going off by the Cape of Good Hope and Australia, but if she had waited two or three days, the half-day of wind we had from the southeast would have sent her through like a letter in the mail."

"We're getting there in the winter," Le Corre reminded them. "It'll be dark at three o'clock."

"Yes, but in winter the storms aren't so bad, and the wind is steadier."

"Where did you come across that? In your catechism?" Le Corre retorted. "That crazy weather is just as wild one time as another. You get through it all right or all wrong: that depends on your luck, and on the men who command you. . . ."

Rolland had been listening, up to this point, without saying anything. He had made only three voyages around the Horn, and he did not consider that this gave him enough weight to say anything: he would always lack the last word.

He spoke up now, however, to agree with Le Corre.

"In that case, we'll come through it pretty badly, because our Old Man isn't a real speeder, in spite of his head-wind mug. He'll make you take in sail the minute the weather gets dirty, and he won't put it up again until the barometer says it's all right. So what are you going to do, you and the ship, while you're waiting for the weather to clear? You'll be knocked to pieces, bit by bit, while you're hove to. The weather will crumble you away—see what I mean? And when you add up the account, you'll have lost three times as much as if you'd dared take the risk of going ahead."

The others, unconvinced, protested. The voices grew louder. The men became vehement in their indignation, not against the sailor, their comrade, but against the shameful doctrine he was venturing to defend, that of those dreaded captains who saw nothing but the object to be attained and who, to grasp it more quickly, would set at naught the sufferings of their men, their superhuman efforts, their mortal peril.

Rolland listened impassively, twirling a tiny splinter of wood between his fingers, and he went on with this occupation when they stopped speaking. They were waiting for his retort and, as they could not endure this silence, Mahé cried out to him: "Haven't you anything more to say?"

"Go ahead, talk!" cried someone else.

His only answer was to get up, walk over to his bunk, the top one on the port side, swing himself into it with a single bound, and stretch himself out on his straw mattress.

The fog did not lift until the next day. They had breathed it in all during the night watch, and it seemed like a crystallized fluid which was spreading out through their lungs and burning the very walls of their chests.

In the afternoon, when they were furling the fore to'gants'l, they caught sight of the first albatross. The birds were gliding up from the south, as if in a dream, with an incredible swiftness, and without any movement of their wings. They seemed to see nothing, and they were hastening northward with all their wing span outspread. After them came others, following the vast undulations of the sea swell with the same rigid wings, rising and descending, to graze the slope of colorless water with their wide claws.

Rolland, up in the yards and roughly jolted, threw a glance at them when he had hauled his last line taut. He would see them rise, veer, straighten their flight again, glide, without being able to detect anything but a slight banking of the points of their wings. Oh, they knew how to take the wind, those creatures, to hold it close beneath them, to settle down upon it! And he, who for the past hour had been wearing himself out struggling with this same wind for the mastery of a piece of canvas tied to a stick! He was swept by a jealousy of which elsewhere he was unmindful: the jealousy of primitive man, who compares his slowness and feebleness with an animal's swiftness and strength. The same wind, for them and for himself. . . .

One of the albatross—one of those that were called "admirals" because they were all white and had two rose-colored spots, like epaulettes, on each side of the neck—seemed suddenly to catch sight of the *Galatée* and came up on the wind right to the end of the yard on which the men were working. It hovered there, level with them, accompanying them in the ship's rollings, with no expenditure beyond a slight oscillation. A few yards from them, they saw his fleshy sheep's body,* his great white angel's wings, the sharp hook that was his beak. The bird was fixing them with his morose and piercing gaze and seemed to be surveying every movement they made.

"He's come to check the earings," Nicolas, who was working near Rolland, yelled to him. "That's a sign of damn bad weather!"

Rolland shrugged his shoulders again, and their work now finished, the men went below. They were reaching the last ratlines

* The albatross is also known as *mouton du Cap*. Tr.

when a wave swept the ship and drenched them from head to heels in an icy shock that plastered them against the shrouds.

The next morning they passed Staten Island, a few dark cliffs to starboard. Rolland gazed at the coast. Toublanc was beside him, suddenly grown old and shrunken by the approach to the Horn, which he was attacking for the thirty-third time.

"When a man sees Staten," he muttered, "he always asks himself, 'What are we going to find on the other side?' "

As a matter of fact, they had no more than rounded Staten Island than the hurricane from the west, no longer screened by any headland, struck them full force. That raging torrent of air which for thousands of years has hurled itself from the Pacific Ocean to the Atlantic—and which seems even to have twisted this end of the South American continent into strange shapes and fringed it out into islands—heeled the ship over on its port side, and the sea came tumbling across the rails.

The enormous swells of the southern ocean, slashed to bits by the monstrous wind, were like nothing so much as falls of earth, avalanches cut from moving crevasses and carrying along with them, like blocks of stone, enormous heavings of snow-packed water. The tempest was digging, hollowing out, dark caverns ready to swallow up the ship. At the same time the jagged gusts of the wind were gashing the crests of the waves into needles and curves like hooks, which the men saw loosed upon them, sixty feet above their heads, when they touched the ragged bottom of the sea's ravines.

They were still on the watch for each wave as it came. That was keeping them busy, since the captain had had the canvas taken in in plenty of time. Soon there would be no more question of meeting the waves one by one: the breakers would be sweeping over them in such a mass that they would simply take them, on their oilskins, without asking which was which. For the moment, it was still something new, and they were watching the waves rushing up, writhing, colliding, overlapping, in a seething eruption around them. Even the most seasoned mariners among them felt a tightening in the stomach at the plunges into what seemed to be a bottomless abyss. Then, when they had come up again as if some furious thrust had flung them back into the air, and when the *Galatée,* at the end of its strength, was helpless on its knees before the curving crest of the breaker, everyone's thought would rally to the ship, as in a lightning flash; and that thought would be so disseminated throughout the vessel that every man would receive, in his brain and in his heart, the blow that was striking it and under which it groaned and trembled.

And always there were those carrion creatures, the albatross, that

68

would shoot back and forth wherever they wanted to, up there above you, in a sure and inflexible arrow flight, with the comings and goings of easy saunterers, aerial regattas whose evolutions would intersect like the yachts at Dinard, all set to astonish a Minister!

Without knowing it, Rolland was already observing the sea and the ship with the eyes of an officer. He was obscurely irritated by feeling the vessel rigid and clumsy, incapable of adapting itself to the tremendous movement of the southern waters. He would so gladly have dreamed of it as articulated, flexible like a fish, whereas it was presenting itself in suspension on the crest of every wave, its bowsprit pointed toward the low clouds, only to fall back again, creaking, into an onrush of overwhelming water.

The sailor turned around suddenly, as if someone had called him. Behind him, the apprentice was looking out at the sea, too, his mouth half-open. His haggard face had the expression of one who doubts his own eyes.

Rolland called out to Morbecque: "Haven't you got a shovel, and a whiskbroom, and a little bucket, to gather him up, this one?"

Then he went up to Barquet, so close as to touch him.

"You're afraid, eh—afraid it'll be the end of you?"

The apprentice looked at him, a strange look; then he shook his head.

"No," he answered.

"No? You're not afraid?"

Again, more gravely, Barquet made the same gesture; and again Rolland stood disconcerted before him, without finding any reply. Yet he had to have an explanation, at any price; and at last one came to him.

"You're in such a poisonous funk that you don't even feel it any more, that's why," he growled.

He let him go and turned back toward the sea, never guessing that, alone among the men on board, Jean Barquet dared to think of death, that he believed it inevitable, and that he had come to accept it. . . .

The captain came out of the chart-house to sniff again at the weather. His jowls were drooping with the leaden weight of bad days. He cast a glance at the men at the helm, tied to it, laboring over it; one of them had stuck his knee under a haft, to wedge the wheel. Then Le Gac looked at the main upper tops'l, distended like the belly of a drowned man and streaming with spray. The men were watching him attentively: was he going to furl? The timid ones were wishing that he would, for fear of having to go aloft into the rigging later, when the task would be harder still, and when a man would be staking his life on the footropes, with a few chances less than now. . . . The skipper ordered only the tightening of the braces.

The night closed in on them at four o'clock, and the darkness was filled at once with eddies of snow and noisy spurts of hail. The men, boxed up in their streaming coats, were massed together like bundles on the poop, standing upright and motionless, offered to all the blows of sea and wind. The terrible southern cold was freezing their very guts, every intake of breath seemed to take form as a block of ice in their throats. The salt from the spindrift was searing the eyes that were strained wide in the effort to distinguish something in the terrifying invisibility in which they were immersed. Everything had vanished from their sight: the sea and the ship, so that only the soles of their boots still testified to the vessel's trembling, its vibrations like those of a maltreated drum.

The ear also reminded them that there was a forward and middle part to this object that was plunging and rearing beneath them, that sometimes emptied them out on the stern as a shovel tosses out a pile of refuse, and sometimes flung them ahead with the reflex of a catapult; for they heard the rest of the ship resounding under devastating blows. In this first night at the Horn, they were all thinking of the nights that would follow and that would be as bad as this, or worse; but fortunately their present misery was drugging them to a point where they did not fear those nights as they were fearing this one. "Monsieur Monnard, lower the fore upper tops'l."

Well, the Old Man had at last come to that decision. They recognized his voice. He was not sleeping. He had stayed on the poop to undergo the Cape's welcome with them. That was normal, but it reassured them: this attention, keeping watch. And then to hear him say "Monsieur" in weather like this!

They went off into the pitch-black night, huddled over, heavy-footed, chilled through and through. The waves knocked them down, struck them prone on the deck planks, and then, seizing them beneath the belly, rolled them over and bumped them against invisible objects at which they eagerly clutched. They would have been entirely alone, each of them, if it had not been for the voices; the hoarse voices of their companions who bawled as they spat, and the clear and courteous voice of the first mate, who had already made his way to the foot of the mast and was calling them.

Rolland, who was the first to lay hold of the ratlines, found them 50 per cent thicker: already, the ice! They were like rough sticks of candy, that tore first one's mittens and then one's hands. The wind flung him against the shrouds with so much force that he felt the "bars" pressing into his chest, his stomach, his thighs, like those of some huge grating under which he might have been caught.

The next instant there was a sudden lurch of the ship and his slippery boots almost lost their hold on the ratlines as he was whipped and stung by the rip of the swells. He clenched his teeth even harder than his fingers. Rage swept through him, luckily, and warmed him up: everything that was beating upon him became something living: the sea, the wind, the steel of the shrouds in which he was pulling himself up chicken fashion, as the apprentice had done on the day of the photograph. Where was he now, that measly pipsqueak?

Something hit his heel, the head of the fellow below him.

Those damn futtock shrouds! A swinging trapeze in a circus, and collapsing. . . . Were they going to let themselves be caught and mastered, the bastards?

At the moment when he seized them the ship heeled over, and he went backwards, hanging by his wrists above the void. He did succeed in crossing them, but it was as if he had just stepped over the ropes into a boxing-ring: a direct blow on the cheek filled his head with blood and his fingers with cotton. Holy Mary, Mother of God! Fortunately, the roll flattened him for two seconds against the main top. That was what had just given him the blow on the head. Strength flowed back, but slowly, oh so slowly, into the limp body. Would there be time for it to reach the ends of his fingers before the combined pitch and roll, multiplied by height, would have sent him to Davy Jones's locker?

"Hang on, aloft there!"

It was Monsieur Monnard's voice, shouting for the first time and surely to him, separated though they were by sixty feet of darkness, the darkness of the tomb. The shout went through him like an electric discharge. It was in vain that those demon-forces were pulling at him, to draw him downward; the lurches and lunges of the ship, the wind's buffetings. He had his hold again now, on the main top, and, on his knees, he drew a long breath. He had escaped; he had not taken that plunge! And when this thought goes through your body it warms you up, it makes you firm and taut for what's to come. The mast could ring bells in his ears if it wanted to, that wouldn't keep him from climbing to the upper tops'l, along the lower mains'l, which was rounded out, a wan resounding whiteness, in the night.

He had got hold of it at last, his tops'l! He had even put his nose into it, for with the pitching it had given way at the yard. The canvas, rigid with ice, was beating in the air like a dozen maddened albatross tied by the feet. The wind was blowing it out into great casks, as a series of little bulbs is blown by a glassblower. And it was by the strokes of his fist that he must stave them in: the strokes of one fist only, because the other hand was hooked into the jack-stay, so as to keep himself alive. Five fingers for him, five fingers for the ship-owner. . . .

While aloft, every lurch of the ship made Rolland feel as if he were hanging onto the branches of a falling tree, so long drawn out and inexorable was the swing to one side or the other. Volleys of spray, also, were rising from all this seething fury that grew white and exploded sixty feet below him, and they would have frozen him finally if the lashing of the hail were not giving him a drubbing that kept his blood flowing fast. For two hours he struggled with the tops'l, describing terrifying arcs in the air, stemming the buckings of the yard, with shocks that would dislodge you ten times over if there were no good God; his fingers were bleeding and his nails turned black, his head was ringing, his mouth was open and panting, open to all those eruptions that kept flying through the dark; and so far he hadn't trussed up a piece the size of a handkerchief! He would hardly have caught hold of a fold of the rigid canvas when the wind would snatch it away, and a little bit of his skin with it. It is at moments like this, when a man is alone on the footrope, that a slacker, a good-for-nothing, sometimes takes out his knife and cuts. . . . The sail is gone. Go and look for it! After that one can take it easy, at least.

But the guys on the *Galatée* went on fighting. . . . They didn't feel their hands any more. From the wrist out, there was no longer anything but chunks of frozen flesh, which still clutched, instinctively, on the canvas. Fatigue beat upon their temples, higher and harder than the wind and the hail. Sleep, that appalling sleep of utter exhaustion, was beating its own leaden hammer against the base of their brains. A little more, and they would have flopped down as at a café table when they were drunk, their head in their arms. But the beast was crouching, ready to spring still.

"Oh-h-h-h!"

They all heard the great wild cry and, leaning over the yard as over a balcony during an earthquake, they screamed into the darkness, at the bottom of which there was, after all, the deck:

"Somebody fell!"

Rolland had only cried out "Somebody—" Just at that moment, he felt a break in the storm, a few seconds' turning-aside of the wind, as if it had veered about to look somewhere else than at his labors. He had let go of his jack-stay to grasp the canvas with both hands. He was supporting himself only with the trunk of his own body now. At his right, in the wind, someone screamed "Who is it?"

Someone who was left, when a pal went down. . . .

"I don't know," he answered.

But he slid along the footrope until he could touch the man's elbow, so that he could say, in a broken voice, "They'll get him! Give me a hand here. It's almost finished."

VIII

IT WAS Cazabau, and he had gone overboard. The second mate had heard the splash in the water, to starboard. In weather like this there could be no question for an instant of lowering a boat.

They had learned the name of the man only when the tops'l had been furled, after the call. And to take in the sadness of this death they had had to wait until they had swallowed their tot of brandy; because for grief as for everything else it needs strength, and they had no more. . . .

At dawn, on the deck, water-swept and shaken to and fro as in a rinsing-bucket, they all had to get back to their posts. They did this half-walking and half-swimming, in the two or three hundred tons of water that were swishing about as if the place belonged to them, and that were playing a game of leap-frog with you, leaving you slobbering and spitting and cursing by the time you got through. It was only after this period of duty that they had leisure, on the poop, to speak of the dead man. Otherwise, they would have gathered their recollections together, to recapture him in detail: "You remember, he used to say this, he used to do that. . . ." But he was already so far away, behind them. Barigoul, who came from the same village, was shaking his head.

"I'm the one his wife will come to, to ask how it happened. What do you want me to tell her?"

At the end of the afternoon the *Galatée* had to "lie to running," that is, to lie to under the three lower tops'ls, the fores'l, the fore topm'st stays'l, and the mizzen stays'l. Even so, they were doing their four or five knots and were making slightly toward the west, in spite of the enormous seas that were buffeting them. On the poop, Captain Le Gac was reflecting on his worries.

"A man lost, poor beggar. . . . With this wild weather, I only hope there won't be another to follow him." He turned toward the helmsman. "How is the wheel?"

"All the way to starboard, Cap'n."

73

"Straighten it a little and keep the vessel steering. It will pick up speed and not drift so much."

"Aye, Cap'n."

But in the evening, when the wind was getting stronger still, with a tendency to veer forward, the skipper resigned himself to furling the fores'l and the mizzen stays'l. They took on less water then, but they were moving, crab fashion, to the southeast, precisely opposite to where they should be going. All the good headway they had made so laboriously—they were going to lose it again, and more, too!

The swift darkness fell once more. The men were huddled together in the shadow on the windward side, in the shelter of the weather-awning. They were asleep on their feet, and they could not have said how long it was before Monsieur Monnard called out the order: "Unfurl the main upper tops'l!"

Waking, they came to themselves with, at first, a sense of dejection: their heads, at once heavy and flabby; their bodies, chilled and black-and-blue; their worn-out legs, their bleeding fingers—here was the misery of the human frame, from which they had snatched a few minutes of unconsciousness. The realization of the ship, the weather, came back to them only after this. But from the first second they all felt that nothing around them had changed.

Yet here was the mate, taking advantage of being on watch to put up sail again! There were men like that who would boast of going around the world without lowering their tops'ls. The best of the watch crew approved of his wanting to get going on the course again. If you remain hove to too long, you may find yourself losing a week in a few hours. The other men, who saw nothing but the present moment, grumbled over going back into that icy bath, plunging into the water up to their middle on this deck which was awash from end to end—and to hoist a sail that would never ride out the wind!

"It's going to get away from him in a hurry, that tops'l!" someone grumbled. "You bet I'll split my sides when they gather up the pieces!"

It was Rolland who went up, with two others, to loose the small lines. When he came down, he had an ugly line across his forehead, the kind of line drawn by an ill-humor which is not for oneself alone.

"Where is the apprentice?" he asked.

A breathless voice answered, at the foot of the mast: "Here I am!"

For a moment, Barquet had really believed that Rolland was calling him because he needed him, and he had been swept by a

74

great wave of pride. But the topman came up to verify his presence, touch him, bring his face close to his.

"All right," he snarled. "You got it!"

Yet of the two, the one who did not "get it" was Rolland himself, believing only, as he did, in the effect of his threat. For it was not at all for fear of the sailor's retaliation that Barquet, tonight for the first time, had followed the watch up on deck; it was to compel his respect. He was one of those insignificant lads who, at school, become attached to a "big boy" whom they admire passionately, even—and especially—if he snubs them. Rolland's contempt seared him. Barquet was the only person, along with Monsieur Monnard, to have sensed that this sailor was different from the others, intelligent, of inborn quality, out of place like himself; like himself the victim of an injustice, but a victim in revolt. All that, he would tell him one day. But he must first acquire the right to speak. That was why he was here.

"Take your places at the windlass!" the mate ordered.

It needed the machine to hoist such a heavy weight.

They dragged the heavy, hard-line to the capstan, coiled it there, and gave it three turns, Gaborit, the novice, had hold of the free end so as to hold it in position. This would not be the moment to let it unwind!

They went to drive the bars into the capstan's drumhead, and Barquet was just in front of Rolland when a huge wave swept aboard and knocked them all head over heels. Above the tumult of those tons of water crashing down on and around them, above the howling of the wind, Rolland heard the apprentice's short gasp under the terrible icy seizure. He felt two clutching arms, the arms of a drowning man, knotting themselves around his neck. He thought, with perfect lucidity, When the ship rolls, and the water sweeps off, we will be swept off with it. But he did not make a move to free himself from this embrace: he had willed it. It was his own business that he was carrying out. He had demanded Barquet's presence on the deck. That imposed the obligation not to let go of him, even if it meant being washed over the rail.

His right arm, swimming, encountered a line end. He caught hold of it, twisted it around his wrist, then let himself be drawn along on his back by the wave's thrust, the other still body clinging to his. When the line pulled back, he stood upright again, roughly loosed the hold on his neck, and, taking Barquet's arm, led him back to the capstan.

The men pushed on the bars with the efforts of prisoners at forced labor. Above them, the canvas of the main lower tops'l was struggling like some gigantic bird, caught in the net of the rigging

75

and breaking everything to pieces in its effort to escape. The mast was trembling; the blocks, held captive in the ice, were refusing to turn. The men were pushing in the midst of water that came up to their thighs. Great masses of water were sweeping over the ship, without respite. They took them on their bent backs and bent only a little farther under each blow.

Once again a swell came dashing over the bow, with the hubbub of objects torn from their places and borne along in its rush. The men heard it coming, without seeing it. It passed over them, indifferent, frozen, crushing this little bunch of men after everything that it had crushed already. Once again they tumbled over on one another, like ninepins in a circle, tangled up, heads and boots together, so long submerged that their mouths, all out of breath through their struggles, had to open and drink in great gulps of sea water. Rolland, as he fell, had wound his legs around two slender legs that were thrashing to and fro. He did not loosen that embrace until the swell had passed over them and they were on the surface again.

Two wounded men were staggering back toward the poop, one blinded by the blood that streamed from a cut in his forehead, the other hanging onto his dislocated shoulder.

"All together here! Don't give way, boys!"

The mate was caught in harness as they were, suffering like them, his face lashed and cut like theirs by the rain and hail. But he had the surplus of strength, the second wind, to call out to them, to beat time for their effort:

"Hard ahead, boys—push on it—it's coming—haul it up!"

But everything seemed to be against them, and the windlass was resisting their efforts as if it had had to haul up a block of stone. Bruised and exhausted, they were breathing in shorter and shorter gasps now; and when a new breaker smashed them against the bars they took a long time to get up again, a long time to go back to the devastating round of their duty.

"Don't give way, boys! We'll get the best of it, the stinking muck!"

Actually, that! Monsieur Monnard, such a polite man, with a brother, they'd been told, who was a priest—Monsieur Monnard, beginning to talk sailors' talk to them, talking the way they did, getting close to them in this dung! Oh yes, by God, something was going to crack now, either their own guts or whatever it was that was keeping that god-damn tops'l from hoisting!

The bars creaked. Grasped in their bleeding fingers, at the end of their stiff arms, against their panting chests, they were forcing the windlass to yield a few turns.

76

"We've got him, boys! Don't give in! Heave hearty!"

Gasping, and by jerks, they raised the heavy yard, which made gestures like a madman as they were getting it fast alongside the mast. As the sail opened itself to the wind, it cannonaded with such violence that if they did not very quickly finish hoisting it and stretching it out they would be in danger of seeing it blown loose and going off in tatters. Rolland realized this at the same moment as the mate.

> *"There was a priest in Landevan*
> *Who didn't approve of flirting . . ."*

He called the old tacking song to his aid, the spiciest one of all, the one whose broad sallies were still able to reach a man and goad him to activity. They all took it up, with voices broken by the exhaustion of their labors, voices often choked by the ocean breakers; but the song made itself heard and felt, jerky and jagged as the creakings of the windlass. It turned with the capstan, forming a little circle of brightness in the dark inferno of the Cape.

"Hold!" cried the bos'n.

The tops'l was in place at last.

"Stopper and make fast!" Monsieur Monnard ordered.

He was now calling the men together.

"Haul in the mizzen tops'l!"

In a long ripple, puffing and exhausted, they flowed aft to the stern, with something of satisfaction in their hearts all the same.

"Splice the main brace!"—a landlubber would have taken that for an order, when what it really meant was to drink a tot of rum at last, one of those heavy-weather tots of rum that you don't feel when it's going down but which, once it's well swallowed, spreads a little warmth, just the same, all through your body. Barquet was dragging along at the tail-end of the watch, unable to find even enough strength, in the depths of his exhaustion, to hurry toward a haven as the others were doing; and Rolland once more caught hold of him. When the boy, gasping, begged to go back to his cabin, the sailor pushed him forward where the mate, in the glimmer of a lantern, had just begun to pass out the rum.

"For the apprentice," Rolland said.

This existence continued through every day and every night, according to the terrible law of the Horn, which permits no relaxation and which, hour after hour, drains the body of its strength. A few minutes of sleep, snatched here a little and there a little, squatting in a corner like a beggar on a railroad station bench;

77

and then, "Furl! Hoist!" They were sleeping as they walked, even Monsieur Monnard. When he did his sentry-go on the sixty feet of the poop, the mate would march back and forth with his eyes tight closed, but he would always stop short when he reached the edge. They used often to see him, during the day, go and plunge his head into the sea water at the forward pump, in the struggle he was waging against his heavy eyelids.

Sea-biscuit, a little stew, and a quarter-bottle of wine—this was what they had to fight on, against everything: against the ship that was dancing worse than a cork beneath a faucet, and diving into the sea under them like a dog drowning its fleas; against the snow and hail that would come dashing in flurries together, the better to rasp and saw at your face; against this stagnant and sinister twilight which at this season was the only light at the Horn—a light that made you think the sun was dead. The southern winter sharpened clusters of stalactites on the yards, and the ship was coated with them on every inch where they could take hold. On the bridge the men had to douse kettlefuls of boiling water over the blocks, so steeped in ice that not one of them would move.

They all had dirty faces, unshaven, rough with salt, and eyes red like albinos'. They had reached the point of wishing out loud, on the poop in front of the officers, for senseless blasts of wind so that they might heave to and drift wherever the devil might want to take them, just so they didn't have to do any more working and could get their sleep out at last.

Sometimes a sudden calm would fall upon them. The wind would cease altogether, as if it had been cut right off at its roots, and the canvas that was still up would hang as limp as in the dead calms around the Equator. But the sea, under the ferment of storms elsewhere, remained enormous. And then they would climb up to gather in sail quickly, for at the Cape the west wind's awakenings are too often terrible.

It was just as they were coming out of one of these calms that a link of the bob-stay broke. This chain, which subtended the boom and supported the stress of the masts, was the forward key to mast rigidity. As the boom was no longer rigid from below, it had slipped up several inches. This was enough to slacken everything, and to make the masts rake a trifle aft, one after the other. The captain had swung before the wind and squared the yards, so that the wind's action would thrust the mast forward again. Then he had looked around him, hesitating to ask a man to put a new link in the chain: to send a man down under the stem in this raging sea.

78

"I'll attend to it."

Monsieur Monnard beckoned to three or four of the men to follow him to the bow. When he reached the bowsprit, which was shaking with its chain dangling, he leaned over, examined the damage quickly, and turned back.

"Lash a hauling-line to the chain."

When that was done, he had a rope sling fastened under his arms and, so strapped, gave the order: "Let me down."

They looked at him, hesitating.

"Go to it!"

They lowered him cautiously, then, under the cutwater, and he began composedly to work at his first link. He was plunging with the ship, disappearing in the swell, coming up again, streaming, swung and shaken and whirling about like a jumping-jack on the end of its string. The recoil of the ship's pitching would fling him against the side, almost hard enough to stave in his ribs. Then he would fall back again to the end of his supporting line.

To the four men who were holding it, the impact of that tall body against the point of the stem brought a seizure of physical sickness every time it struck.

When he had finished mending the chain he signed to them to haul him up again, but when he got aboard he had to sit down for a few moments, exhausted, on the fo'c'sle. The men, leaning over him, were already preparing to pick him up and carry him to the stern, and Morbecque said, in his most respectful voice: "We're going to take you aft, sir."

He shook his head; then he got up, laboriously, and preceded them to the poop; but he staggered as if he had been drinking.

"I do not want to see you again until tomorrow, Monsieur Monnard," said Captain Le Gac, who was waiting for him. "I will take care of everything."

The men, around them, nodded their heads earnestly in approval.

"Thank you, Captain," the mate murmured, before he plunged into the companionway.

"Now you see what politeness is!" said old Toublanc to Gaborit, the novice, who was watching, open-mouthed.

And the wind, always raging, never stopped blowing from the west. . . .

"You can't do anything with it!"

That is what they would say, at home, about a willful child. . . .

Unable to make progress westward, they kept always driving a little farther to the south: so far down, now, that the thought of

79

the ice-fields, in addition to everything else, allowed them not a moment's peace, night or day. Every evening, the skipper would say to the officer of the watch:

"Above all, look out for icebergs. If you see anything shining, hard over the helm and work ship at once without any hesitation."

One night Rolland, on look-out, was staring ahead when he saw a wan brightness rising above the swells to the southwest.

"Ice ahead to starboard!" he called out. And, as an echo, he heard the mate's voice from the poop:

"Bear away! Haul down the mizzen tops'll!"

A few moments later, Monsieur Monnard came up beside him.

"What is it? What did you see?"

"An iceberg over there."

Just at the spot to which he was pointing, the moon emerged from the water: a washed-out, ghostly moon, daubed over with sulphur-toned clouds.

"There's your iceberg," said the mate.

For an instant he allowed confusion to sink into the boy and spread through him like a drop of vitriol; then he put his hand on his shoulder.

"You did right to warn me. I would rather be warned of the moon than not warned of an iceberg. And since we haven't seen the moon for some time, you were to be excused for not recognizing it."

The cold, next day, was enough to chill their souls. The thermometer had fallen to 14 degrees above zero. The snow was coming thick and fast, in horizontal sheets; and the ship, sheathed in ice from deck to truck, seemed to have turned to white marble. Blocks of ice as big as buckets were falling from the yards, while the waves kept striking their equally hard blows; and this would send the water from the deck—continually awash—splashing up as far as the yards. There was no longer any question of clewing up or furling the sails, which had become as thick and unyielding as the gates of a prison. They threw enormous slip-knots around them; making a throat halyard, which they hauled on the windlass. And it was galley-slave labor, with backs, arms, feet, to gain a few inches of this canvas that had turned to stone.

Barquet would always come forward to take his part in the activities; and Rolland assumed that of all the conflicting terrors in the boy's heart the one he had inspired remained the strongest. Yet it was no longer to him alone that the apprentice was offering the tribute of his shivering good will. As he had seen the vessel escaping, every day and every night, from a shipwreck which he believed inevitable, he had conceived for the men whose superhuman efforts

80

always staved off the disaster, an admiration which he concealed like a blemish. What amazement, and then what insults, he would have unleashed upon himself if he had allowed it to be seen!

And yet he believed himself to be, precisely because he was weak and timid, the only one aboard who was capable of taking these men's true measure—for him, the measure of giants. The officers were too accustomed to this everyday heroism to feel any astonishment at it. The apprentice still trembled whenever a sail was furled, but he was trembling more and more now for the crew. And it was to make himself less unworthy of them that he forced himself to follow the watch up to the foot of the mast, although he was convinced that, one day or another, he would be carried away. On his hands and knees, in a belly-flop on the deck, he prayed, in a frenzy.

No one had any suspicion of these struggles, these terror-stricken triumphs. The captain, however, convinced that the men were dragging him to workings by dint of threats, put his foot down!

"I am responsible for him. I don't want him to be lost, or injured."

Monsieur Monnard agreed with him on this. Insomuch as Barquet remained for the sailors a nuisance who got in the way of their work, and whom they would shove aside with knee or elbow when he tried to catch hold of a line, the mate had taken his own stand in the matter and had said to the apprentice, "You are to stay close to me, in case I might need you."

So he had kept him at his heels, and would find the semblance of occupation for him in the most sheltered corners.

One evening they were caught by a thunderstorm. The men were aloft taking in canvas when the ship heeled over, to the accompaniment of a monstrous crash, and a blinding stroke of lightning that rent the whole sky. Frightened, they returned to the deck. Flat on his stomach at the foot of the masts, Barquet listened to their outcry when they thought they were going to be thrown down, and that the ship, three-quarters under, with one rail in the water and the other standing up like a hilltop above their heads, had no further alternative but to turn turtle or to come out of it swept as clean as a float. But the onslaught ended as suddenly as it had begun. The vessel recovered itself, and, in an absolute and oppressive calm, the men did the same. And as if the passage of that frantic convulsion had drained all the air from the sky, they were panting, as they did after their worst efforts.

Suddenly the *Galatée* blazed forth with a supernatural flame. Arrows of fire darted along the stays, lines and yards. The rails, the circumference of the poop, the deck-houses, and the hatches were

81

outlined as with dazzling footlights. Streams of sparks flew aloft, reaching the trucks. The men, with an odd laughter that was meant to be swaggering, were stroking their hair with their hands to chase away the electric charges that were caught there, and that, no sooner than banished, would come back again.

"It's Saint Elmo's fires," the captain called out to them. These crests were giving him, like the others, a very devil's head of hair. But just so it didn't burn!

It quieted them down to know that this phenomenon had a name, and that one learned about it in books.

Suddenly the weather became absolutely clear again, and they were all looking at the sun, which they had not seen for days and days. It was on the verge of the horizon to the west: that west into which they must win their way, and in which the sun stood out before them like a target of flame. And it made them more sensitive to all the divergence of the course, which was turning away from the heavenly body and plunging deep into the south.

"It won't be tomorrow that it makes us sweat sitting down," the men said.

They watched the sun sink below the horizon, with a nostalgia never aroused in them by any shore that was fading from their sight. This was the first time that many of them had ever looked at a sunset. . . . When the last segment disappeared, a dazzling ray of green swept the sea, which for the fraction of a second was like a vast field of waving grass.

"It is more beautiful at Cape Horn than anywhere else in the world," came the voice of Monsieur Monnard behind them. Then, as if he realized how uncalled-for this comment of an enthusiast might sound, addressed to dog-tired men, he added, "This is where we ought to bring the Parisians!"

It was the first little pleasantry of which he had made them a present since the voyage began. They were eager to show that they appreciated it, and they turned around so that he should see them smile.

The next morning the men of the port watch cleaned up the deck, as was done every day. They were getting through the interminable session of getting things to rights with a larger stock of work than usual, because the squall of the evening before had tangled up some of the lines. The apprentice was working with them. It was Barquet's only opportunity to do something useful: to wind up a piece of "rope," as he continued to call it, that was his task! The roll of the ship would sometimes throw him between the men's legs, and they would free themselves without anger, as if he were a sack of something dragging at their heels. His zeal, which now made itself felt on every occasion, had ended by disarming them.

"He does what he can, but he can't do much!" old Toublanc had summed it up, with a wink.

They didn't even joke any more about his fur gloves, which had become completely waterlogged and were swollen out so that they looked like drowned kittens at the end of his arms.

Rolland, going by now on his way to relieve the helmsman, threw him a glance that held no gentleness.

"Don't you see that the end of your line is caught in the porthole?" he said. "And that you can always haul it up?"

The apprentice gave a start, as he always did when this hard voice struck him, and threw distracted glances all about; then he hurried to the rail, looking for the opening into which the end of his line had passed.

The sea was still rough, but not unduly so for this locality. One felt that the proximity of the ice-fields was putting a brake on it. The water was still washing over the deck, but not so heavily. Instead of rearing up and then crashing down on the ship, the waves were now taking it on the bias, running along the hull and then, with a great swell, tumbling over the bulwarks.

Barquet, still feeling the weight of that redoubtable gaze upon him, had leaned over, his stomach on the rail, his long arms outside it, to start untangling the hanks of hemp that had rammed into the porthole beneath. Suddenly there was a roundabout lurch of the ship. A wave dashed over him and swept him into the sea.

Going up the companionway to the poop, Rolland heard the cry from the men, and at the same time he saw the body washed abeam and flung up on the back of a swell. He sprang to one of the life-buoys placed to port and starboard on the poop, close by the officer of the watch, and threw it over. Whether by his accurate glance or by good fortune, it fell just above the head of the apprentice, who was still being held on the surface of the water by the oilskins that were fastened at wrists, neck, and waist, but who was rapidly being carried away in the wake of the ship.

"Luff," Monsieur Monnard ordered the helmsman, "and then keep the ship in the wind." Then, this time, he raised his voice: "The port watch, launch the dinghy. Starboard crew, work ship. And quick! Bouse the tacks and sheets of the lower sails, and counterbrace, without tightening too much."

The captain appeared from the inner stairway.

"Barquet overboard," the mate said.

The skipper opened his mouth wide in shocked amazement, that heavy mouth which nothing had ever set gaping. But as Monsieur

Monnard was running to the boat, he recovered himself and took charge of the ship's working.

"The buoy fell just above him, Cap'n," the helmsman said.

Already, Rolland and Morbecque had loosed the slings of the dinghy, taken off the tarpaulin, released the oars, driven in the thole-pins. With the help of the royal yard-line, the watch swung it out over the water. Rolland, Névol, and Morbecque lowered themselves into it. Monsieur Monnard hesitated for an instant. His place, on principle, was in the boat, which should always be under the command of a responsible officer. He glanced up at the poop. The captain was standing there alone. The second mate, no doubt bustling about in the depths of the steward's quarters, had heard nothing and, so far, was not making his appearance. But this was a question of seconds: the dinghy must put off; otherwise the man was going to be crushed under the tuck of the ship. He, Monnard, must before all else spot the shipwrecked body, recapture the sight of him before he should have disappeared.

"Rolland, take charge!" he cried.

Then he climbed into the tops'l shrouds to scan the sea, while the three men pushed away from the *Galatée* with the ends of their oars.

The dinghy slipped quickly along the side. Rolland, his back muscles strained for the shove-off, just missed being struck by the lurch of the vessel. Then the boat began its dance but without moving forward, because in a boat on a heavy sea the men cannot see more than thirty feet in front of them, and they must wait now to be given their course.

His eyes raised, Rolland at last caught sight of the mate, perched in the shrouds. His outstretched arm was pointing in a direction directly opposite to that which the sailor, left to himself, would have chosen; the ship, in heaving to under the tops'ls and the fores'l, had altered its course, and all the points of reference were confused.

The light boat rose on avalanches of gray water, to plunge down again with them. The rescuers were lashed by the spray. The tumult of the waters was booming in their ears as if two conch-shells were fastened to their heads. But they were living only through their watching eyes. The outline of the ship had been blotted out in the sooty sky. They were putting all the strength of both arms into their rowing, but blindly now; they would strain their necks when they reached the crest of a wave, to see nothing ahead but this rise of raging, empty water. . . .

And there was the weather getting dirty in the west. . . . A squall broke upon them, blinding them. Its eddying snow drowned

84

out, erased, the waves which they no longer perceived until the moment when they were bearing down upon them. The dinghy was shipping water badly, and Rolland, on his knees, had to bail with one hand while he held the tiller behind him with the other.

It's no use, he was thinking. He's gone down. . . . Yet at the same time he was vowing to himself, "I will not go back without him!"

He was seeing Barquet again as he hurried toward his porthole. It was because he had obeyed him, Rolland, too quickly that he had been swept away. . . .

The other two men, disturbed, were turning their heads toward him: should they go on?

A gesture of Rolland's chin pointed out to sea: they were to go on. . . .

In the water that was buffeting them more and more, they searched for a long time still. The two oarsmen were not yielding in their efforts; they were even redoubling them to ride out the weather, which was now altogether vile. Yet Rolland realized that they were discouraged, and that their movements had become mechanical. And he understood that Nével and Morbecque were only awaiting the word to veer about, while at the same time they were not allowing themselves to suggest it. He cried out to them wildly, "We've got to bring him back!"

He thought he saw Morbecque shrug his shoulders, but perhaps that was only in pulling at the oar. . . .

He caught hold of the buoy, he was thinking. This success, in having reached him at the first stroke, forbade him now to surrender. He had too much pride in his own good luck! That, and with it the horror of having the apprentice moored fast to him for the rest of his days, of saying over and over to himself, "I sent him down, by my own fault, when I forced him to come on deck against the captain's orders." No, no, he would bring him back, or he would stay here with him!

He had forgotten that he was not alone, that he had been made responsible for two others.

Suddenly he raised his head: a quarter of a mile off port bow three albatross were wheeling, very low, their necks stretched out toward an invisible prey. He leaned forward to strike the rowers' shoulders with his fist, to point out the birds to them. A few minutes later, Morbecque gave a bellow: he had been the first to catch sight of the body turning over on the crest of a swell.

They did not call out to him to hold on, they were coming; they were too certain that Barquet would not fail to make one of those fine maneuvers of which he had the secret, and that in gesticulating

85

he would sink. When they were right upon him, they saw that his teeth were bared, his eyes closed. He was floating on his back, hanging onto the buoy like a big round breakfast bun, pressing it against him, his nose inside. After they had pulled him aboard, unconscious, fishing him in with the boat's painter as a lasso, they had a hard time making him let go of the buoy that he still clung to with clenched arms.

"He only sails a straight course when he's asleep," was Morbecque's appraisal.

Was it the first mate or the captain who had handled the ship in this mess of a sea so as to come up close to them? In any case, when they had turned about, they saw the *Galatée* very near, struggling with its overtaxed masts in the storm and the snow.

"Have you got him?" someone called out to them as they came alongside.

"Would we have come back, if we hadn't?" Rolland answered.

They were beating about in the ice-fields now, among the flat-surfaced icebergs that come down from Graham Land. The ice blocks were higher than the masts. Looming up curiously straight upon the great swells, they blazoned forth the whiteness of the sepulcher beneath the dark sky. On one day of calm, the ship rode among three icebergs until evening: three alabaster cliffs which seemed to be luring one another, to be luring them. The wind only sprang up as they were on the point of collision with the largest one; they were already bringing up the boat-hooks to break the shock, although they knew that they would snap like glass rods. When the *Galatée* had taken on a little life, and the gleaming wall of ice was slipping away along the side, they went back to their places without saying anything, their boat-hooks slung on their shoulders, like farm workers coming back from the fields.

The next day they were running on the port tack, head to the northwest, without an iceberg in sight. The wind had changed in the night and was blowing now from the southwest. The captain had won out! He had gone far south in search of it, that wind of his, so far as to bump into the ice-fields; but he had hold of it and he was taking advantage of it. He had just had the fores'l put up, the sail that gives the most speed, and with the least belly, too. With that and the tops'ls, he was butting into the swell in a way to send everything popping, keeping his ship heeled over to starboard, the rail under water all the time. He was like that, the Old Man: shilly-shallying, fussy as a customs inspector, feeling his way right and left with his boom like a blind man with his cane, and

ways short of thread. For the rest, Valparaiso, like the other ports where the sailors did not set foot on land, was merged in his mind with the heavy toil of unloading.

Monsieur Monnard, since the day when he had shot the albatross, had made no further allusion to his offer of board, for Rolland, with his brother the priest. He waited, knowing that suspicion and pride were fighting in the boy against ambition, repugnance for the life of a common seaman, the lure of another sort of existence. Now, from the poop, he was observing Rolland, who was gazing at the shore. . . .

There had been coal at Valparaiso; now there was coal for Iquique, to be unloaded in a few days: fifty pounds on his shoulders, that would be his portion! And it would weigh all the more heavily since the other man, up there on the poop, had planted this impossible hope in his heart. Rolland threw an ugly glance at him, then went deliberately up the companionway and accosted the mate.

"I have thought over what you said to me the other day, sir, and I see that it would not be possible."

Monsieur Monnard merely raised his eyebrows imperceptibly and waited.

"First," Rolland went on, "so far as your brother is concerned, I must tell you that I have never been very strong for priests."

The mate gave a slow shake to his head. "That has nothing to do with it," he stated.

"And then," Rolland added, "supposing your brother would take me on credit, there would still be the years at school to pay for, after that. It can't be done."

"I have thought of that," said the mate. "If I could, I would advance you the money myself, but I am not able to do that. The only thing is, I believe I could get you a loan."

"I don't like to go into debt," the sailor muttered.

"So much the better! You will get out of it more quickly."

Rolland's mistrust was redoubled by hearing him answer back so patly like this, like a man who is in a hurry to carry his point.

"What I should like to know," he said, with a note of defiance in his voice, "is how you got the idea of taking an interest in me. This is the third voyage I have made with Captain Le Gac. He has never spoken to me about anything like this. And you, in less than three months— All the more as I have done nothing to— It isn't as if you could have any feeling of sympathy for me."

"There is no question of a feeling of sympathy, in this," Monsieur Monnard interrupted coldly. "It is my opinion that you would be able to render more service in the chart-house than in the fo'c'sle. It is my duty to urge this upon you, just as it is my duty this morning

91

to hoist all the canvas this ship can carry. So there it is! As for the captain—perhaps it is because he has known you too long that unpleasant memories keep him from seeing exactly what you can do. I, who have only judged you at work and have not had to trouble myself about your past behavior, may perhaps be able to see you more clearly. In any case, you will not be indebted to me."

Rolland turned red, and that made him look strangely young, even childlike.

"It isn't for you I have been speaking, sir," he said. "No, it's just the other way. I will do whatever you wish."

Monsieur Monnard's nod registered his acceptance of this.

"Do you know what an angle is?" he asked.

He beckoned him into the chart-house and, pencil in hand, began to explain the way the ship's bearings were taken. . . .

When the mate spoke to the captain about his project, at lunch, the latter seemed surprised at first; then he said, "Oh, if the fellow wants it . . . But watch out, when we get to Frisco! I know him: going ashore sets him crazy. He's always all to pieces when he comes back. That is why I have never thought he could be anything better than a common seaman. But you can always try. . . ."

It was when they were off Taltal, the first nitrate port as they came up from the south, that Barquet reappeared on deck. He was so thin and so pale, he bared such long teeth behind such white lips in such a pitiful smile, that they were touched, and they all gathered around him.

"Well, Débarqué, you've weathered it after all!"

"We thought we'd lost you! You've been making the voyage on your back!"

"Seems you've given yourself a double ration, with pleurisy!"

"Now you're going to run straight ahead; all you have to do is to get fat, kid!"

They would have administered all the hearty slaps that are due a convalescent, but they did not dare touch him for fear of knocking him down, such a wraith he was, there on the deck. He himself, very happy, responded with little waggings and forward thrusts of his head, but his eyes were searching beyond the circle around him and paused when they fell upon Rolland, who had remained at one side and was apparently absorbed in knotting two lines together.

Barquet gestured to the men to move a little; the group opened up, and the apprentice, his steps dragging, made his way toward the sailor. Rolland did not look at him at all as he approached, but his cheek was quivering.

Barquet's voice was low and grave, as it had not been before he came back from death's door.

"It was you who saved me. Thank you," he said simply.

Nobody was laughing. Rolland had to swallow twice before he could answer:

"No more I than the others. There were three of us in the dinghy."

"It was you who threw the buoy."

"Oh, that was just luck!"

"You don't want to shake hands with me?" Barquet asked, in the same deep voice.

As Rolland was silent and did not move, Gouret burst out for them all, "Aren't you going to shake hands with him, damn it? You bet you'll shake hands with him, you mutt!"

And he flung himself upon them, caught hold of them, pushed them against one another.

"You're going to put your arms around him, that kid!" he roared at Rolland. "Perhaps you think he hasn't deserved it, eh?"

And it was because he felt that Barquet had, indeed, deserved it— but how, and why?—that Rolland finally put his arms around him and touched his cheek to his.

When the *Galatée* drew closer to the coast, after passing Tocopilla, the winds died down. The ship dragged its way for eight days, along gigantic cliff walls, and rocks calcined by the burning sun. Guano was spread out on them in wide patches, like veneer. Monsieur Monnard was teaching Rolland how to pick up the slightest indentations in the cliffs, the beaches where the green waves of the Pacific were rolling in with their thunder or where a few tumble-down Chilean hovels were squatting on a tongue of sand at the foot of the precipitous hill.

At last, at the base of a high chain of steep and rugged mountains whose recesses were sometimes like rough sketches of gigantic elephants' foreheads and trunks, they caught sight of a low flat town, all its lines horizontal except for the upward thrust of a slender church tower. This was Iquique, crushed under the mass of the Taracapa. The roadstead, level and with a more brilliant sheen than an iceberg, was full of ships drawn up in strict ranks. Their bare masts were standing up like a dead forest: All that was possible, it seemed, in the lunar aridity of this coast where not a lichen, not an insect, could live. It was only men that could subsist here in the chemical sterility of the sulphates, the chlorides, the nitrates, and could draw riches from it. Old Toublanc, who, just once in his life,

93

had climbed up to the nitrate pampa, remembered the astonishment with which he had seen the bodies of dead mules, dried by the salts and still standing upright, all black on the white soil. . . . On the metallic surface of the harbor waters, pot-bellied barges and little square-sailed Spanish boats were crawling along between the sailing-ships, and were bringing them this dust which they had come all this way to seek, through the hurricanes of Cape Horn.

In the early morning, the tug took the *Galatée* in tow and conducted it to the third row of ships, reckoning from the sea, and to the third place as reckoned from the town. The ship was moored there broadside on, with two anchors forward and a spring at the stern; and then the unloading of coal began.

On the *Galatée* this was still done by hand winches; four men to heave at the capstan, one on the platform-deck to sling the gantline, another to turn the toggle on the pin and pay out; in the hold, eight men would be filling the bags.

They would begin at six in the morning, work until noon, take an hour off for lunch. Then the bos'n would call out, "Every man to his post!" and they would not stop work again until six in the evening. Then the deck had to be watered and swabbed. At night, each of them still had to stand watch for an hour.

After the waterlogged inferno of the Horn, there was now the aridity of the desert, the coal dust that burned a man's eyes and throat, mixed with this ash of saltpeter that one breathed in the scorched air. When the bell struck the end of the day's work, they would flop down on deck, as black as demons, and invoke the night, with the sudden freshness that descended on them from the savage mountain.

The sea gulls would fall silent, at the same time as the creaking winches and the shouting men. Only a few seals out hunting would be splashing along by the boat, and the plaintive voices of penguins fringed the bay like the croaking of frogs around the rim of a pond. Suddenly a song would rise from some ship's fo'c'sle, rounded out by the echo from the mountain, and, clear and powerful, would reach even the vessels that were farthest away:

"When darkness falls on the waste land. . . ."

In the bow of another ship another singer would answer, and the men, stretched out on the decks, would listen with a mournful pleasure until some facetious fellow somewhere would break in with a ribald ditty which would bring them back to reality, still numbed as they were by dream.

94

"Boatmen, to the boats!"

Every evening, after work, the bos'n would call out the order, and Rolland and Gouret, who would have eaten before the others, would go off in the dinghy. It was Monsieur Monnard who had named them as boatmen. As for the captain, he was spending almost all of every day on land, with the agents and brokers, not to mention the short stops in pleasant nooks with fellow-captains.

Halfway between the ship and the landing-stage, the boatmen would have to pass between a line of reefs and a pyramid of rocks cut into sharp ridges. The channel was so narrow that on entering it, well in the middle, one could touch the rock on each side with one's oars. On these rocks pelicans, nibbled at by lice and gorged with fish, would be sleeping with their heads tucked under their wings; not one would budge as the boats went by. Sometimes the men would step ashore on their domain, to amuse themselves by kicking them on the behind and making them scamper; but they never killed one of them, for their flesh was tough and they were under police protection. They were the scavengers of the harbor, as the black vultures were of the town.

When the swell from the open sea reached the roadstead, augmented by one of those tidal waves that the Pacific so often belches forth, the bar of Iquique became dangerous. But it kept its cadence, like a clock or the revolving gleam of a lighthouse: three waves, one space; three waves, one space. And the boatmen would pull hard on the oars, then, so as to go through in the calm between the onrushes of the breakers and not be overtaken by the charges already surging upon them from behind. Rolland and Gouret, who had been selected because they were at once strong and skillful, were clever at this sport. Then when the bar was crossed, they had only to row calmly through the seething water, which, however, very quickly quieted down.

Captain Le Gac, just as punctual as the bar itself, in his tan duck suit and straw hat, would be waiting for them at the landing-stage, which was built in tiers like an amphitheater and covered with red sheet-iron. When the dinghy came alongside, he would inspect both the men and the boat with the same keen glance. It was for him, Le Gac, to stand worthy comparison with the captains of the great four-masters of the Bordes Company and the fine clippers of the Laietz firm.

These captains, indeed, would come ashore and go away again in elegant lifeboats with four oars, which sped through the water like arrows under the long rhythmic stroke of the strapping fellows who were rowing. Automatically, when two boats found themselves abreast, they would race, and the *Galatée's* dinghy, though weighed down at the stern by the captain's eighty-seven kilos, would often ride out the frisky lifeboats.

The skipper, who would have been running around all day with varying success, visiting his agents or his supply men, would ring changes on affability when he came on the boat. On bad days, he commented only upon failures. One evening when a German boat, manned by four blond Herculeses, shot past them with no answering exertion from his own men, he groaned bitterly that he was in the hands of bunglers who let everybody in the roadstead get ahead of them. Gouret went as red as a live coal and muttered, "If there were a double ration of grog once in a while at the end of the trip, that might make our arms stronger!"

Rolland did not utter a word.

Since his conversation with Monsieur Monnard, he had found himself constantly embarrassed by being, so to speak, sandwiched between the fo'c'sle and the chart-house. He still belonged to the one, but he had already been singled out for the other. The day before, for instance, big Morbecque had asserted that with these duds of boatmen there was no danger of the *Pisco* upsetting any-one's stomach. On all ships, in spite of the thunderous blasts of the captains, the boatmen—the only ones who could go ashore—would bring back supplies for their ships. This time, again, Rolland had made no reply. He had merely eaten more slowly, watching for the first allusion that would permit him to get up and raise a row. But nothing had followed, except a long and oppressive silence.

Rolland knew, from having seen it elsewhere, what it cost to be marked out for attention by an officer, to be set apart from the others, not to join any longer in the chorus of their complaints and criticisms. One came very quickly, so, to be regarded as a lickspittle and a climber; and then a void would open around the turncoat. He was waiting for that void and hoping for it, since he had made his choice. He would drive back the words with blows of his fists as soon as they were spoken; but that was known, and the chances were that they would not be spoken at all. . . .

It was the working hours that he liked best now. He was expend-ing upon them that easy activity which one brings to tasks of which one knows one must soon let go. He was endlessly repeating to him-self what the mate had said to him, and, from a distance, his thoughts were revolving about that new life to which the way had just been opened up.

Monsieur Monnard, however, had not spoken to him since the ship came into the roadstead. Rolland knew in advance that on the return voyage the mate would be harder on him than on anyone

96

else, that he would demand of him twice as much as he asked of the rest. That was in the natural order of things, and all intelligent officers acted in the same way when they wished to push a young man, so as to outweigh the mistrust of the crew. As for the captain, he continued to behave as if he knew nothing. Only Monsieur Guézennec, the second mate, would talk to Rolland, when the sailors were not around to hear him, more freely than to the others, a little as if he were talking to a future colleague.

If the crew never set foot on land, the officers did, generally on Sunday. Before re-embarking at the wharf they would tell each other about the day's joy-rides. Sometimes it would be a trip on the "cabbage stand," as they had nicknamed the little steamer which brought supplies of fresh vegetables and fruit, and even fresh water, to the desert of Iquique and its treeless plain. The officers would try to buy batches of vegetables, which they would divide among themselves. They were not always successful; but on the other hand they had all they wanted to drink on the steamboat. And, again, there were stopovers in all the dusty little cafés and other resorts of the town, the good little nooks pointed out by the skippers long since: notably Mother Valéry's, the *refugium peccatorium*, with the Chilean girls who had nothing in their heads except their eyes, but what eyes!

The boatmen, attending on their officers, would listen without seeming to. They did not need to strain their ears, moreover, because the well-warmed voices rang out loudly over the landing-stage. Through these recitals, Rolland would enter the forbidden city, go to the Place Candell and into its shuttered cafés—La Grandina, El Triunfo. He would follow the officers, on streetcars drawn by mules, through the straight streets with their wooden houses so often shaken by earthquakes—the Calle de Bolivar, the Avenida Cavancha —bordered by scrawny palm trees like whiskbrooms planted in cement pots filled with made earth. And he would listen with a tranquil ear to the captains recounting the pleasures of the day: it was a bill-of-fare which one could read without impatience, because one knew one's turn was coming, to be served. . . .

The *Galatée* was only unloading coal at Iquique; it did not have to take on a cargo of saltpeter, like most of the other vessels in the roads. Captain Le Gac's three-master was to make its way in ballast from Iquique to San Francisco to load its cargo of grain there.

The ship's bell rang next evening at nightfall, and immediately the "Southern Cross" rose at the fores'l stay: two red lanterns, two white lanterns, fastened to spokes of the capstan in the form of a cross.

97

"Good luck and a good voyage to the captain of the *Antonin,* his officers and his crew! Hip, hip, hurrah!"

The men of the *Galatée* were calling out in chorus, all turned toward the *Antonin,* the ship farthest away in the first row. Their colleague's bell answered at once, and the good wishes shouted by its crew reached the *Galatée* clearly, in spite of the distance, above the booming of the bar that sent its waves breaking without cessation on the reefs and the sandy shore. These angelus ringings of bells and these shouts were carried from one end of the roadstead to the other on the echoing night air; and the mountain wall behind the city was an amplifier for their resonance.

After the *Antonin* it was the turn of an English boat, then another French four-master from the Bordes Company, then a German craft, to respond to their bell and their shouts. It was like the versicles and responses of vast complines sent back and forth from ship to ship, under the twinkling of the stars that shone so close above them. Rolland and Gouret, on their last trip ashore, had left the *Galatée* earlier than usual and had passed between the rows of vessels, picking up their names and calling out to them, at the same time, that this evening they would be bidding them farewell. Thus Rolland found himself quite naturally the leader of the choir. With a piece of paper in his hand, he was leaning down to read, by the glimmer of a lantern, the name of each ship to be saluted. . . .

"To the *Emilie,* the *Margaret,* the *Faithful,* to the *Reine Blanche,* to the *Gerda*—"

French, English, German, they would all answer in the same spirit, but the last-named more as a single voice.

That night, when it was his turn to be on watch and he was alone, standing guard over the ship, Rolland went to haul a crate of oranges out from under a coil of rope. He had smuggled it on the dock the evening before and had brought it aboard in the dinghy with the provisions the captain had had loaded on the ship. He groped his way to Barquet's cabin, where the apprentice was fast asleep, put the crate down beside the bunk, and tapped the boy on the shoulder. Barquet gave a start and sat up, bewildered.

"It's oranges," Rolland said. "They're for you. Hide them."

Then, without waiting for the other to understand what he was talking about, he went back on deck.

It was neither remorse nor compassion that had impelled him, he thought; it was only that he continued to feel responsible for the boy. If he had caught his death of cold, it would always have been for having obeyed him, Rolland; and that put the sailor under an obligation, created a duty. . . .

98

The next morning the other captains, Le Gac's friends, came to empty a glass of champagne on the *Galatée* just before it sailed. After a last wish for a good voyage, and as they were about to pull away in their boats, several of them kissed Le Gac on both his heavy cheeks: the Frenchman takes pleasure in being expansive when he is far from home.

When the tug had towed the *Galatée* out of the roadstead, when they had passed the line of ships where the men on the decks interrupted their scrubbing for a last friendly gesture, Barquet appeared on deck. They were finishing putting on sail. He waited for Rolland, therefore, at the foot of the mainmast.

"It was you, last night?" he murmured. "I recognized you by your voice. Nobody had thought of such a thing. . . ."

"It's just because nobody had thought of it that it was up to me," Rolland replied crossly. "If you have nothing fresh to eat, you're going to be in a bad way again; and you'll have cracked up before Frisco. There's not a whole lot left of you to lose. Where did you put them?"

"In my box, under my clothes."

"And the crate?"

"But they are in the crate."

Rolland raised his eyes to heaven, as if to call it to witness to such obtuseness.

"It didn't occur to you that they would take up less room and keep better if you stuck them in among your shirts? Well, run along and put them there. And then break up the crate into little pieces that you can put in your pockets and heave overboard when the captain's looking somewhere else. You get me?"

As Barquet was trotting off obediently, he called him back:

"And then don't go leaving the skins lying around. . . . And start with the ripest ones."

The young man paused, made a movement as if he would grasp the other's hand, and gazed at him with eyes all imbued with gratitude and friendliness. Rolland encountered this look, and his own face hardened. He clenched his teeth. This was what he hated, what he scorned, more than anything else in the world! A man, a woman, who fastened onto you when you didn't want him, or her. . . . He had thrust away with a blow of his fist, just like that, hands which were reaching out to seize him. . . .

"Clear out!" he commanded, in that low voice that everyone on board knew, and that was a forewarning of one of his terrible rages. "You make me sick! More than ever. . . . Get out of my sight!"

X

HE WHEELED around several times, his arms whipping the darkness, before he fell, head first, on something hard and cold. There was a clangor of bells in his brain and then, at once, the band, the mechanical piano, the trombones with their long-drawn-out moanings, the horns' excited cries. Lying prone, his cheek against another cheek of chilly stone, he thought he had dreamed all this that was bursting out of his whirling head: the red plush settee where he had been sitting between two girls, a Spanish girl made out of rolls of pink flesh, and a tall muscular German. No, no French girls: never any French girls for him, except in France. . . . That would be as if one anchored in the roadstead among foreigners with a fouled and worthless boat, a boat one would have brought from so far away just to show that it was fouled and worthless, to have people say, "It's a French boat, and it's no good." No, that was impossible.

Well then, this band? The coarse mechanical piano? The girls' sour-smelling dresses were whirling above him now with motlings of light, blue and red, on their bare shoulders. Since he was lying here, it must be that he had got into a fight again and had been drinking. Why? How? There had been glasses of beer in the story, great thick glasses with faceted surfaces. Faceted surfaces, yes, he was sure of those; he was still seeing the play of the shifting light on the heavy cuttings of the glass.

He continued to lie there on his side without trying to get up, because at the moment nothing was working except his head, at the end of a leaden body. All his effort was concentrated there, inside him, to get his bearings, to remember, to understand.

The wind was dead now.

A wave of memories lifted him up, but without bringing him to a place where he could get a foothold, where he could at last understand where he was, why he was there, what was happening and what had happened to him. Bonito. . . . Yes, he had made the bonito jump, even some dorade, and big ones! Even some squid. . . . Fine weather, smooth sea. . . . And Gouret coming cluttering down from the mast and crying, "Sea serpent off the port bow!"

A head stretching up, a head of a conger eel cross-bred with a seal, the size of two hogsheads, twenty to thirty feet of black body out of the water and falling back with a terrific splash. . . . Was he dreaming that, too? That he had seen the Sea Serpent off the coast of Mexico? No, because Barquet, all his yellow teeth showing, had shrieked, "Sea Ser—!"

Barquet! Good God, Barquet! Holland raised himself on his forearm and looked straight ahead of him with eyes that were beginning to see.

Paving-stones were slipping away, there in front of him. They still seemed to be moving between their curbings, but they really were paving-stones, gleaming from a recent rain. Then it was in a street that he had keeled over. But it was only a moment that his mind stayed there: he was back now on the deck of the *Galatée,* alongside of Guézennec, the second mate. It was not his watch, and he was taking advantage of that to look out at the approach to San Francisco. He had never seen San Francisco. The only place he knew in this part of the world was Portland, Oregon, with its Columbia River, a mournful stream with pine forests along its banks and with its mechanized salmon fisheries. He had seen them, those salmon, swallowed up between the reed fences that narrowed down around them and flung them on a great overshot wheel, the wheel would pick them up and deposit them on a platform, where they were scooped in helter-skelter. That's how a man runs aground, even when he believes himself to be sure of his course. . . . But it wasn't the salmon this business had to do with. He was losing his way, running after them. It was the deck he must get back to, beside the second mate.

The point was that Guézennec had already been to Frisco, when he was an apprentice. In his quality as officer he had taken it into his head—he, as well as Monnard—to have a hand in Rolland's education, and now, like a schoolteacher, he was explaining the coast to him, and the roadstead, and the port. That cut in the hill was the Golden Gate. You might say it was narrow, that Golden Gate, but it was actually a wide and deep passage. To the north, there, was the Punta Bonita, and to the south Point Lobos, where the water was alive with sea calves. In the north, again, was the mouth of the Sacramento River. And the roadstead, one of the most beautiful in the world, was furrowed through with ferry-boats from which the American girls, as poised as statues in the public squares, would wave their handkerchiefs to you in greeting. They would anchor just off the city itself, a magnificent city on the flank of a hill, lighted throughout with electricity. It was intersected by Market Street, with its buildings, its carriages, its policemen in green uniforms, its Hotel San Francisco, where the captains went to lunch. . . .

From Market Street Guézennec now slipped over to the right, into Pine Street and Bush Street, the "red light district." There were far too many French girls in the houses there. He himself hadn't felt that he must speak English; French was enough. And he concluded with what was certainly true: "In France we go to extremes: we export the best and the worst—missionaries and tarts."

It was at this moment—yes, at this very moment—that someone spoke behind them: "Do you know where the hospital is, Monsieur Guézennec?"

They turned around, struck dumb with astonishment. It was Barquet—a Barquet lost in his big overcoat, thin as a strand of hemp and yellow as rancid pork fat—who was asking the question. There seemed to be nothing in his head but eyes; but they were eyes that were alight with joy. The Old Man had decided to put him ashore, to bundle him into the hospital; infusions and concoctions were awaiting him, and he was fair licking his lips in anticipation. . . .

Guézennec, who had recovered his aplomb, and who never lost an opportunity to pull Barquet's leg, answered, after a pause: "The hospital? It's in Chinatown. They'll feed you turtle cooked in tar water, pepper preserves, and penguins' eggs ready to hatch out, all on lacquer trays. In a week that will have made a new man of you!"

He walked off. Barquet laughed.

Then he came up so close that he was breathing his sick breath right under Rolland's nose and, quite serenely, he said unbearably dreadful things to him, things that were resounding so loudly now at the bottom of the pit into which he had fallen that for several moments he did not even hear the pounding of the mechanical organ any more.

"There is something I want to say to you. . . . I know that you would like to become an officer. As soon as I am at home again, I will speak about it to Papa. He will attend to everything. Oh, that is the least he can do!"

Rolland had gripped the rail with both hands, his nails boring into the wood. When he turned around Barquet had vanished, tactfully, his errand done. . . .

So, then, that was why he was here, on his knees on the Bush Street pavement; that was why he had drunk so many whiskies just now—one after the other—that the big German girl, lolling back on the settee, had counted them. "*Acht, neun, zehn* . . ." Then she had stopped counting, because at the next table they had just made note of the last one and were laughing over it: "*Elf!*"

As for himself, he hadn't counted either; he hadn't counted how many there were of them, those sailors from the Laietz boat who were guzzling their beer while they made fun of him. He had sprung at their beer glasses, seized one in each hand, and brought them down on two of the fellows' heads. Then he, in turn, had staggered, the nape of his neck struck by a fist blow that stunned him like the blow of a hammer. He had a momentary sense of two gigantic Negroes in the group that was beating him on the head; it was they who had taken hold of him and thrown him out on this street, where he was now pulling himself up from the sidewalk.

He passed his hand over his head: hair soaked with blood, as always after a fight, blood that was running down into his ear; an atrocious pain that shot through his head whenever he moved it, and the whisky that was still throbbing against his temples in great muffled beats like the blows of a rubber truncheon.

In spite of everything, pride was awakening again within him, a somber satisfaction was warming his spirit anew. Wasn't that once more enough for him, to be an ordinary able seaman? That he was and that he would remain, all through his rotten life, rather than owe one mouthful of bread to that little hunk of stable-litter that he would have been ashamed to be seen speaking to in the street, a misbegotten runt to whom Monnard—another fine stinker, that one!—had gone begging for bits of cash for him, for *him,* Rolland! His "loan"—so that was it! To touch Barquet's father for money, make him pay for the rescue of his son. And as soon as he was an officer, the other, that young skinned animal, would be coming to look at him with the eyes of a dead eel and bleat, "You owe it to me. . . ." Good God in heaven, what did they take him for, the lot of them?

He was standing up, by this time, holding himself upright. Strength was slowly returning, flowing through him again. He looked at the door he had been tossed out of: it was yellow, thick, studded with heavy nails; one of those doors that close on life. . . . Savagely, he flung himself at it, struck it with all his force, kicked it, while the Salvation Army band, on fixed post in these streets of sinners, attacked Hymn Number Ten with all its brasses: "Nineveh and Babylon, tremble before the Lord."

"How many have you, Robert?"
"Four."
"And you, Le Gac?"
"Two."
"Well, I have five," declared Captain Rozier, of the *Duchesse Anne.* "So I win. Then we'll go and get them?"

103

It was Monday morning, and every Monday the captains of the ocean-going ships would become anxious about retrieving the men who had not come back aboardship Sunday night. This was ordinarily easy, for in San Francisco the drunks, like others, were quickly centralized. Through the main thoroughfares, already feverishly active, the three colleagues went, therefore, to police headquarters, where the cop* on sentry duty stopped them. Captain Robert explained, in English, that they had come to identify their seamen and, if they so decided, put up the bond required to free them.

"Very well."

An elevator took them to the eighth floor of the building. There another policeman, this one with gold stripes from cuff to elbow, conducted them to the "Lions' Den."

This was a vast rotunda surrounded with iron bars, a circular cage in which the men were spontaneously adopting the attitudes of captive beasts. And appalling animal odors, as from a badly kept cage, were arising from the "den."

There were all sorts here: ragged hoboes, glassy-eyed, their lifeless faces stamped with the terrible American abasement that can suck a man's soul from his body, down to the last trace; and gay roisterers in dress suits and capes lined with white satin, picked up by the cops with the same impartial indifference because they were drunk like the rest. But the sailors were specially numerous, from all the ships, from all countries. And among them there would be a sudden eddy of movement, and the shuffle of men elbowing their way to the railing, when the captains came in and were recognized. At once, hoarse voices would call out:

"This way, Cap'n! Here I am, Cap'n!"

Rozier was the first to spot one of his men, a fellow with one empurpled eye entirely closed, who addressed him with an amiable and toothless smile: "Me, Cap'n!"

"No."

And Rozier walked on, while the sailor shot a murderous look at him out of the one eye he had left and then stepped back, muttering imprecations on the lousy captains who would let their good guys down, and whom they would let down—and how!—when their turn came. . . .

Release from the Lions' Den was, in fact, a matter of selection. To free a prisoner on the spot, a "guarantee" of two dollars must be paid. For the really "good guys," the captains would make the payment and then subtract the amount from their fifty francs† a month. But there were some who were better left to stew in their

* The word in the original French manuscript. Tr.
† Approximately ten dollars. Tr.

104

own juices. These, the old offenders, the insubordinates, the big-mouths, the shirkers, the captains would leave to the magistrate, who would come by in the afternoon to clear out the lot. They would be let off with three days in the Martinez prison, three days on a diet of spoiled rice, after which they would be off to the steward's quarters at a gallop.

As for Le Gac, he was hailed by Morbecque, but a Morbecque who had got himself up very strangely. He had had his hair clipped close on the right side of his head and, by way of balance, had had his mustache shaved off on the left side. Robert and Rozier had already paused in contemplation of this spectacle, and as he was not one of their men they were frankly finding him amusing. His sailor's success cheered up the skipper, and he made a sign to the cop who accompanied them: he was disposed to bail out this one!

It was only after some searching that he caught sight of Rolland, standing at the back with his hands in his pockets, looking at him. In his turn, Captain Le Gac fixed upon Monnard's protégé, re-lapsed now into debauchery, a gaze which was at once reproachful and satisfied. He had given the mate enough warning that as soon as the fellow set foot on land he would become again the head-strong incorrigible, the brawler, that he had always been; a man whom three glasses of *pisco* or whisky would transform into a bat-tering-ram. And this was what the mate wanted to make an officer out of! The idea had never come to him, Le Gac, and for good reason!

He was about to say this, in no uncertain voice, to the person concerned, when Rolland smiled a smile of such sheer insolence that the captain's thick lips moved up and down as if he were chewing on tough grass. He controlled himself before the others, however, and lowering his massive head, turned his back.

It was not until five days later, around ten o'clock in the morn-ing, that Rolland returned to his ship. Everyone was hard at work. The *Galatée,* half unballasted, was standing high in the water. The carpenter and a sailor were on a punt moored along the hull, scraping it as far as they could reach because the ship had been fouled in the warm seas. She was plastered with thick and close-clinging sea-weeds, and that cut down her speed. Others of the crew were chipping at the surface of the hull and putting on red lead. In the ship, down below, they were finishing work on the "gran-ary," a double inside hold made of boards covered with sacking, in which the cargo of grain was to be stored. Already, they were setting up the moving belt which was to bring in the first bags.

Rolland slipped across the gangplank without deigning to see any of this activity and went straight to the crew's quarters, deserted at this hour. He came out five minutes later dragging his bag, that big black canvas bag, so crammed full that it came up above his middle. The bag, to a sailor, is so much a part of the man that to throw it over his shoulder as he was now doing and carry it toward the gangplank, in broad daylight and in sight of all the crew—who had stopped dead in their work and were watching him—that was to say to their face, to all of them, "I am deserting."

"Where are you going?"

The first mate had come up with his customary measured gait, his hands behind his back. He challenged the rebel in his every-day voice, without even a lift of his heavy eyelids; and Rolland, stopped for a moment, did not find his eyes as he answered, "I'm going where I please."

He started off again, at the very moment when Monsieur Monnard was making a swift gesture, with his chin, to the bos'n.

The bos'n of a sailing ship—the crew-master—must always be a man who can pull off two things at the same time: one with each hand. Hervic knew how to do that. He knew also, as the captain did, that Rolland lost his head completely on contact with the land. And in the depths of his heart he was not sorry that the mate's protégé should have got himself in wrong. He flung himself upon Rolland, encircled him with his muscular arms and, with a hard pull, yanked him off his feet.

"To the sail locker," Monsieur Monnard ordered.

Hervic threw him there, through the open hatchway, and at once fastened it down on his head, with the bolt pushed across.

"All right, bos'n, we'll leave him to calm down."

Then the mate called Gouret and pointed to the sailor's bag, that had rolled across the deck. "Take that to the saloon."

Monsieur Monnard himself remained standing beside the closed-up sail locker. First there shook and sounded from it the leaps and bounds of a wild creature fallen into a trap, thrusts of shoulder and back that made the timbers tremble. Then came the abusive language, spewed out by the mouthful, coming up through the heavy hatches; but these were only insults, with nothing in them that could tell the officer what he wanted to know.

The captain, as usual, returned to the ship for luncheon.

"Well, it seems your pupil has come back?" he said. "Do you want my opinion? You can shut him up forever, you won't keep him from getting himself shanghaied, since that is what he wants."

And Le Gac seized this opportunity to set forth his theory of shanghaiing. In the beginning he, like everyone else, had been all against those "dealers in men" who would skim the cream off his crews. He had sometimes made them pay dear, in "blood money," the dollars they would cash in on as a shipping bonus when, having stolen a man from his ship, they would sell him again to another vessel.

Monsieur Monnard was listening with only one ear. He, too, knew the shanghaiers. If he was absolutely certain that Rolland, at the very instant when he had stopped him, had been on his way to fling himself right into the arms of a trader in men, he was just as sure that the sailor had not bitten at any of the shanghaiers' usual baits. In his case there was no drugged beer, no night escape from the bow of the ship in a rowboat with muffled oars; nor had he any fear here of one of those dens in which they lock up a man and stupefy him with alcohol so as to throw him, dead drunk, onto the deck of a boat as it is leaving. There was not even the lure of America and its placer mines. A sailor, such as this man was, does not dream of digging in the earth, even to find gold there. Rolland was leaving in broad daylight. He wanted to change ships at any price, because he had suddenly conceived a hatred of the one he was on. Why? At that point, the mate became lost in conjecture.

In the afternoon, on the wharf, he noticed a well-got-up fellow in a light suit, with a panama hat pushed back on his head. The man never stopped smoking his cigar as he scrutinized the *Galatée*, and attentively examined the men who were at work there. Accustomed to seeing everything without seeming to look at anything, the mate took care to ignore the inquisitive stranger, who, after an hour on watch and inspection, took himself off without having identified the man he was looking for, among the crew.

It was only then that Monsieur Monnard had the door to the sail locker unbolted.

When he had the hatch raised, something long and white shot up in his face, a sort of soft fusee, like a strip of fabric. It was so unexpected that he took a step backward. At his feet there now lay a piece of canvas carefully cut to ribbons. And the mate was seized with a veritable terror: he had shut the man up in the sail locker without taking away his knife! All the ship's sails, all the rolls of canvas, must be in shreds. . . . A monstrous vengeance, whose very enormity must have fascinated the rebel. . . .

"Don't make such a face about it! There's no more to come, and it's an old piece!"

The jeering voice rang out in the depths of the dark hole and was amplified by the sound-box created by the hollow holds that surrounded the locker. The mate went red to the roots of his scanty

107

hair. The men saw him lean over, fists clenched, as if drawn by the cavity below.

He's going to jump down and kill him, they all thought.

Rolland, watching from beneath with upraised head, thought so too, for the face strained toward him was terrible. He did not stir a step, but he unconsciously drew his head and shoulders back a little, and that prevented, for both of them, a clash that might have been serious. Monnard felt that he had come out on top in this confrontation, and he was strong enough to be satisfied with that. He took a backward step, drew a deep breath and then, turning around, he went down the ladder, opened the sail-locker door wide, and commanded: "Come out!"

Rolland obeyed, but he kept to one side, on guard, ready for attack. As the stage of physical blows had definitely been passed, Monsieur Monnard felt scornful of the seaman's failure to realize this, and that completed the restoration of his own calm.

He led the prisoner into the saloon, a room furnished with a sofa in imitation leather, a built-in chest of drawers, and a square center table fastened down and covered with a red cloth. Rolland threw a glance, as he came in, at his bag standing upright in a corner. The mate took up once more that eternal pacing back and forth which, since Dunkerque, he had carried on in every part of this ship where he had never been seen sitting down.

"Why should you want to leave the ship?"

The voice was again level, unassailable. Rolland looked at him, impressed. He had expected that the anger controlled before the men would burst out in this well-closed room. That was the regular thing, when the officers had an account to settle with a sailor: to shut themselves up with him, like this, with no witnesses. He was himself flattened out, now, by the swift mastery of that fury which had blazed with the arrested desire for murder in the thunderbolts of the mate's eyes, just a few moments ago.

He was scared by shame, in appearing, to this man so perfectly master of himself, nothing but an elemental brute irresistibly impelled by instinct. To escape from this fear, as from this shame, he went straight to the heart of the matter and muttered, with sick disgust, "You told Barquet I wanted to become an officer. . . . You asked him for the money!"

Monsieur Monnard paused, looked at him attentively, then shook his head.

"Ah," he murmured, "so that was it!"

Having said everything, Rolland was silent.

"You are mistaken," the mate went on then. "I have never spoken to Barquet about your plans. But there was no secret about them, for anyone. There is nothing surprising in his having known. And he offered you money?"

"Yes."

"For your schooling?"

"Yes, and all that—"

Monsieur Monnard stopped him with a sharp gesture.

"Even if he was clumsy, he meant well. Only, you have never understood anything about this boy, not even so much as the others have. That is nothing for you to be proud of. . . . In any case, what he said to you was his own idea. What I had been thinking of was an honorary loan from our Hydrographic Institute Alumni Association. That is done, sometimes."

He repeated—and this time he looked straight into Rolland's eyes, "An honorary loan. . . ."

Then he turned around and looked at the black bag, as if he had not yet seen it.

Rolland, not moving at all, was waiting for what must now be said.

"Now," the mate concluded, "you know how things stand. Have you decided again to have a try? But I want a definite answer, *Yes* or *No*."

He pronounced these two words with such severity that Rolland winced under their lashing. But he said, in a low voice, "Yes, sir."

Monsieur Monnard paused again in his walk, as if he wanted to let the two words sink into his mind without disturbing their progress by even the slightest physical movement; then he registered them by a slow, deep inclination of his head. He took three further steps, paused once more, looked at Rolland, and spoke in his poop-deck voice: that slow voice which dropped to earnest notes whenever the order was peremptory and difficult to carry out.

"In that case, no going ashore before we leave: punishment and study. We are agreed on that?"

Rolland bowed his head; and as the officer remained silent he understood that he must go away without any expression of thanks. This was not the time. . . .

"You can take your bag back with you," said Monsieur Monnard as he went out of the door.

XI

THE *Galatée* had just cast off the tow-line and was finishing the last few yards of the voyage. The men standing at the rail had no more than their feet on the ship now. Neither the eyes already sweeping the quay, nor the ears deaf to the final orders, not the voices hailing the women ashore, nor the arms that responded to their gestures—nothing of them was really still aboard.

The return trip had been long delayed by calms. First there was the calm off Chile, when Monsieur Monnard had manufactured multiple hooks for them, with big codfish bait, so that they could fish at night for huge squid. Big Pierre, in his galley, would have to pound them for hours to smash their tendons and make them edible; but it kept the watch busy, and the men, entertained by the fishing, were less irritable and upset. Then at last they had turned south again, doubled Cape Horn once more, but in the right direction, with the inflexible western storm wind behind them this time. That wind could rush you along at ten knots under a single goosewing the size of a handkerchief. After that, they had come up rather quickly through the bad-weather zone, and had picked up the southeast trade winds again. Then they had had to sample anew the tepid downpours of the Doldrums, and to haul the lines taut, to trim the sails, to brace the yards, with muscles like tow, so as to gather into the canvas only the dirty cotton of the low clouds.

When they got out of that, they had hugged the northeast trade winds as closely as possible. But hardly were they off the Azores when the calms had emptied the sails once more: eleven days in a sea of oil, gazing at the tops'ls, slack and sagging like the breasts of a woman a hundred years old!

There was no more tobacco. For the past two months there had been no more potatoes; there were no more onions; the wine was running short; the hardtack was full of worms and weevils. Every morning, in the cook's galley, Gaborit, the "beaver," would conscientiously skim off, with his dirty hand, the top of the coffee kettle where maggots, their bellies in the air, would be swimming along with the soaked sea-biscuit. There would still be some left. . . .

"It's a good thing their bones aren't too hard," the men would say. "With all this time we've been chewing at them, they'd have broken our teeth!"

And then there was the Old Man, coming out of his den twenty times a day, all bristling like a demon.

"Monsieur Guézennec, have you got a bug in your eye, or are you asleep? Don't you see the breeze down there?"

Monsieur Guézennec would look at the point indicated, without perceiving the slightest wrinkle that would forecast a little freshening.

"We are ready for it, Cap'n," he would reply, in the best manner.

Le Gac would wait around a few minutes for his breeze, then he would go in again, growling, "Well, watch out for the least flurry, and call me."

At last, one morning, he was called. The waves were rippling in the offing. A breath of air woke the dog-vane, the sails swelled out, the exasperating lament of the canvas beating against the masts was no longer to be heard. A week of carrying winds, and they were off Dunkerque.

The men were now pointing out to each other the faces of people they knew, there in the front rank of the spectators attracted by the ship's arrival and fixed in smiles of welcome that could be read like a flying ensign.

"There's Mother Miche!"

"Get an eyeful of old Kuche, with his mug like a lantern to port! I'll bet he hasn't been sober since we sailed!"

"And there's that big bastard Fortuné! Hi, Fortuné!"

The "landladies," male and female—the same word is used for both sexes by the men of the ocean-going ships—had dropped everything to come and wait for them, as soon as they were signaled. And there they were, all ready for them, and happy as could be to see them again! Six months of wages to be cashed in, plus three months of advance pay for the next voyage—that was something to make the women show their teeth in a fine smile! For the women predominated. And as they alone counted, on a dock, for a sailor, Fortuné, old Kuche, and Célestin were flanked for the occasion by their most attractive and agreeable serving-maids.

Névél, Gouret, and Le Corre, however, were looking beyond this group which, with the completion of the final maneuvers, was dashing to the edge of the quay and entering on conversations from one end of the ship to the other. And at last the three seamen saw a stout red-faced woman emerging from the crowd; she was sponging her face as she advanced, and her flower-trimmed hat swayed back and forth in rhythm with her steps.

"There she is! What was I telling you, Charles? Look at her at the end of the quay, and isn't she speeding!"

Charles Névél seemed relieved of an anxiety.

"I was saying to myself, My God, how does it happen that she isn't here yet?" he said.

The new arrival forced her way into the front row, with some emphatic digs of her elbow. The men called out, together: "Hullo, Mother Chandelle!"

"Hullo, Louis; hullo, Charles; hullo, Marcellin!" she called back. "Things all right with you? Had a good voyage? Not too bad a time? Well, I'm to take your chests, eh? And who else's?"

"There's big Léon, and little Paulo, and then perhaps Jules."

This was the land: a place where they only called you by your first name. . . .

"Where are they?" Mother Chandelle asked.

They hailed them.

"How about it, Léon, Paulo, you coming with us?"

The two sailors had had time to cast an eye over Mother Chandelle, about whom they had listened to so many recitals, and they found that she corresponded to what they had heard. They acquiesced readily.

"Of course. We've told you that already."

With a glance of her eye, a nod of her head, the "landlady" adopted them.

"Which are your chests? I know Louis's and the others that come to me, but you'll have to show me yours. Who else is coming? Oh, here is Jules'. I'm to take your chest, Jules? Where is it?"

Jules, satisfied like his comrades to be in such good hands, at once pointed out his sea-chest, on the deck. Mother Chandelle dug into her pocket and dug out a stout handbag, as bulging as she was.

"Here's a hundred sous for all of you. But try to get to the house in time for supper. We don't ring for rations thirty-six times, at our place."

She was already picking out her boarders' luggage when Névél asked, "Tell me, Mother Chandelle: is Maria still there?"

"Of course; and little Léonie, too. . . . Hurry up and tell them about your voyage. I'm paying for a round of drinks, and it'll be a good one, I'm telling you."

"Well, it won't be too much of a good thing," Névél said. "It's a long time since we've had a chance at the scuttle-butt, on that damn ship with the old man cheating us on his tots of grog and

112

mugs of wine! Now we'll squirt something down our speaking-tube, eh, Marcellin?"

These men would be drunk an hour after the ship docked. Women would be drinking with them, so that the process would be quick and thorough. After that, the women would have only to entertain them until they sailed again, and nobody would have been swindled, since the men looked for nothing more than this, on land.

Already, Mother Chandelle was having their things loaded on a hand truck: the sea-chests, the oilskins, the little ship models so carefully packed, the ships in bottles, the albatross heads. Suddenly she turned back to Névél: "And Pierre?"

The sailor smiled jeeringly. "He's at confession."

Mother Chandelle received this without good humor.

"You can joke as much as you like at the house, but here I have no time to waste," she said.

"In that case, don't waste any on Rolland," Le Corre put in. "He's going to the Seamen's House."

"The Seamen's House!" And Mother Chandelle stood staring, open-mouthed. "Pierre!"

"I'll say! It was the mate picked out that place for him to anchor. He's his pet."

"We'll see to that," the landlady declared.

Just at this moment Captain Le Gac appeared on the deck and called out, off-stage so to speak: "To the office Thursday morning at nine o'clock!"

To the Marine Office, to get their pay. . . . The announcement struck the suddenly attentive "landladies" motionless for several seconds. On that day, they would all go with the sailors to the Maritime Registry. They would all wait at the door, to fall upon them again as they came out, and to lead them affectionately and post-haste back to the fold. As soon as they reached the house, as soon as they had been offered a round of drinks by the proprietor —man or woman—they would be relieved of their money: "You'd have it stolen from you, my poor fellow!"

And the best of it was that some few of the "hostesses" were sincere: like Mother Chandelle who, while she feathered her own nest generously, would handle the men's earnings in such a way that the sailor would have something to rig himself up with, suitably, for the next sailing.

"How-do-you-do, Cap'n!"

"How-do-you-do, Madame Kandael. How-do-you-do, Madame Miche. How-do-you-do, Monsieur Fortuné. How-do-you-do, Papa Kuche. Take note that I said Thursday at nine o'clock, won't you?"

Mother Chandelle promised, as spokesman: "They'll all be there, Cap'n, and sobered up."

"I count on you, Madame Kandael."

The old denizen of Dunkerque stepped up close to Le Gac.

"Have I ever gone back on you, Cap'n? I've always given you my best boys: Charles Nével there, and Louis Le Corre, and Marcellin Gouret, and Yvon Mahé. It's at least six years that they've been coming to me, and they can tell you, those and the others, my man, that they're always got up in grand shape for sailing again. Fortuné's fellows aren't got up like that."

Le Gac let her run on, entertained by her fluency.

It was not for the captains as it was for the sailors: the arrival in port did not necessarily transport them to seventh heaven. It was only the conclusion of a voyage of which they must render account. Now on this voyage as on the others there had been both good and bad. Cazabau lost, Nicolas put in confinement; yet the good predominated. The captain had just been figuring it out, roughly, in his cabin. So he punctuated Mother Chandelle's defense with nods that were as amiable as he could make them, when she concluded:

"So it grieves my heart, Cap'n, when your first mate, who does not even know me, gets one of my boys away from me—Pierre Rolland, who has been coming to me for four years—and to send him to the Seamen's House!"

Monsieur Monnard was just coming down from the poop-deck companionway, a Monnard relaxed and happy. He had just been handed a letter which announced the birth of a son. He had a seven-months-old boy, just like that, in a few seconds; one of those fine turn-abouts of fortune that the sea holds in store for its own!

The captain made a quarter-turn toward him, and with a glance, pointed him out to the "landlady."

"Talk it over with him, Madame Kandael. That's he, coming."

And he went off to shake hands with Fortuné and old man Kuche, who were also supervising the transfer of their boarders' sea-chests. For Captain Le Gac dealt with the "landladies" of France as he did with the "slavers" of Frisco. "It is thanks to them, after all," he would explain, "that the men bring the indispensable duds with them when they sail. Otherwise, they'd be just as likely to come aboard stark naked!"

Mother Chandelle, meanwhile, had purposefully accosted the first mate.

"So," she said, her eye dark and her hat to windward, "it is you who are keeping Pierre from staying with me?"

114

"Since you are acquainted with him," Monsieur Monnard replied blandly, "you must know that he only does what he wants to do."

Mother Chandelle was silent, impressed. It was true, what this tall man was saying. She had had to come up against it, too. Then what was this Nével had been telling her? Rolland shut up in a room, a seminary student forbidden to keep bad company. . . . When she spoke again it was in a different tone.

"Yes, I'm acquainted with him all right, and I've kept him from more than one piece of silliness. But you, you aren't acquainted with me. You haven't heard what the boys on the ship say, when they go through their chests: 'She's taken good care of us again, the old girl! But with her you're always sure of having everything!' That's what they say. You're wrong, not to trust me."

Monsieur Monnard looked at her.

"Indeed I was not acquainted with you, Madame. But I am convinced now that with you Rolland would be in good hands. If he is not going to you this time, it is not because he would have anything to reproach you with, but because he is not sailing again. He has to leave Dunkerque on Thursday, to go home. He has to stay ashore, to prepare for the officers' examinations."

It was Mother Chandelle's turn to look closely at Monsieur Monnard.

"It certainly is you, sir, who have urged him on to that. Captain Le Gac never thought of it. Suppose I told you I've had the idea myself, for a long time? But I never said anything to him about it. . . . To become a captain . . . yes, he can do that. But will he be any happier? With his disposition . . . you tell me that! He hankers for what he hasn't got; he's bored by what he has. . . . But if you want him to go back home, that's one more reason for his coming to me. At the Seamen's House, he's going to be so fed up that he'll run away from it the way he would from a barracks. And with the money he'll have been paid, you can be sure he'll miss his train! If he stays with me, I give you my word he'll make it, because I'll take him to the station myself."

She had taken him there at eleven o'clock Thursday morning, straight from the Maritime Office.

"It's not worth while for you to go back to the house," she said. "I've brought you something to eat on the train. The others will be drinking in a steady stream, and when that starts you don't know when it will stop. I shan't be satisfied until you're on your way."

And when the train started she sent him a fluttering little wave of the hand, which might equally well mean, "A good trip!" or, "Good riddance!"

He had let himself be pushed into the compartment, as if the journey were someone else's affair. He seemed to be living in a world turned upside down, in which "landladies" kept a man from drinking, in which he was going to sleep among priests, and in which the aim was to shut himself up within four walls and live sitting down. It was because he felt himself so completely alien to this life that he was allowing himself to be guided so docilely in it.

"You will go to see your mother at Erquy, but as the school term has already begun you will not stay there long," the mate had said to him. "Arrange to be at Trézel Sunday, and to see Papa Rémy that same day. In that way, you will be able to start in on Monday."

He had followed the program step by step. His mother, more dissolved in clouds of moisture than when he had sailed in the first place, had said merely,

"It will make a very long time without being paid anything. But if it's what you have in your mind—"

He did not see her at all while she was speaking, because she was standing on the other side of a line on which towels were hung out to dry. He had thrown a look of hatred at the linen spread out between them.

"If it can only mean that you will be through with this filthy mess!" he cried.

And the invisible voice answered firmly: "You are a very good boy, but as long as I have my strength I am not willing to be a burden to you."

Then she had come out from her corridor of washing, to go to the fireplace, troubled.

"I wasn't expecting you. I haven't any meat to give you today. But tomorrow I'll have a fricasseed rabbit."

They had eaten it together at noon, next day, and during the meal his mother's torturing anxiety had returned. She had never stopped worrying over all the money those courses would cost.

"How much will the priest take from you? And the teacher? And when you are in the school? You are making a good living—and, besides, you aren't used to studying."

At this, he had laid down his fork.

"Listen: would you rather I went back to the ship?" he demanded.

If she had said yes, he would have left once more for Dunkerque, so out of patience was he at finding the road blocked with discouragement at the very first steps. But she had answered, "Since your chiefs are urging you to it, they must think you can get there."

"Very well, then!"

"In any case," the good woman had added calmly, "I haven't touched the allowance you've made me. You take it along. With my day's work, I have more than enough for myself."

He had got up and put his arms around her, in tenderness and wrath.

"So you've sworn that you'll work yourself to death? Haven't you earned some rest?"

She had set her Breton headdress to rights.

"Shan't I rest in Paradise?" she retorted.

That afternoon he had walked to Lamballe, and had taken the train there for Dinard, where he had slept in a small hotel near the station. Then the next morning he had set out, still on foot, for Trézel. It was about seven and a half miles, but he said to himself, "I have plenty of time; he has to get back from Mass— and I'm not going to drop in on him just in time for luncheon!" As a matter of fact, the nearer the moment came for shutting himself up with this priest, the more the prospect oppressed him.

The day was mild, though it was the middle of November. The trees had already lost their leaves—save for the oaks, that kept their bronzed foliage longer than any of the others. Over the ploughed fields—purple-toned, rich-soiled—the ravens were swooping down by the hundreds, pecking at the autumn seeds. None of this interested Rolland. To give himself something to think about, he would change his valise from one hand to the other at each yard and would keep on the look-out for the little granite markings in the grass beside the road. He paused to eat a snack on the edge of an embankment, swallowed some coffee and soup in wayside inns, and at two o'clock rang at the door of the rectory by pulling on a bell-rope made of a piece of wire threaded through an empty spool at the end.

When the door opened, he had to keep from jumping. It was the mate of the *Galatée* who was framed in the doorway—the mate in a black bodice and a velvet headdress: the same tall gaunt body, the same immobile countenance, the same eyelids slow to lift on men and things. And it was still the same voice, gentler to be sure, yet sadder, when the old lady said to him, after he had given her his name, "We were expecting you for luncheon."

They crossed a little gravel court. Two linden trees stood at one end, and across from one fork to the other there was an iron beam from which hung a child's swing. Then there was a threshold with three steps, and another door; and they were in a tiled entryway at the end of which rose a flight of stairs.

"But you were expected for luncheon!"

Here at last was a warm and vigorous voice that fell on him from above and made him raise his head toward the second story, from which Father Monnard was descending to welcome him. The entryway, badly lighted through a narrow transom, left the stair-well in shadow. At first Rolland could distinguish nothing more than a dark silhouette, a dim gray face that became lighter and clearer with each downward step, and then, on the last stairs, a priest of an appearance so young that the sailor was completely taken aback by it. But when he came over to him, on the black-and-white tiles of the hallway, Rolland realized that this effect of youth was due to the extreme fragility of the body that seemed lost under the priest's cassock. One might have said that a boy had grown too fast, with those thin wrists, that too-long neck to which the round collar seemed to have been fixed like a handle. But the newcomer was at once fascinated by the sparkling gaze which the priest fixed upon him, a gaze of happy, and almost admiring, surprise. Father Monnard was smiling, and the smile made rounded wrinkles in his lean cheeks, uncovered the too-long teeth and the too-pale gums; yet this smile was so affectionate, and at the same time so joyous, that Rolland felt embarrassed, as if it had been directed toward him by mistake. The priest took his hands in his own warm hands—moist, and with long sinewy fingers.

"First of all, have you had luncheon?"

"Yes."

"That's just what I have to reproach you for!"

The stroke of a bell came to their ears, followed, after a long interval, by another. The clumsy jingling went on, broken by mis-fires, never quite getting the cadence.

"The catechism class," said Father Monnard. "It's the children who ring the bell, and they wrangle over the bell-rope. That goes without saying. . . . But I have time to show you your room, all the same."

He preceded Rolland up the stairs, and the sailor had a feeling of astonishment in going up like this, behind that fluttering cassock, to what was to be his "home."

It was a whitewashed room, with walls of rough plaster and a floor of wide boards, freshly scrubbed; there was an iron bed with brass knobs, a cherry bureau, a white pine table that was really white because it too had just been washed and scrubbed, a little stand for the water pitcher, and near the door, three or four clothes-hooks behind a curtain. A crucifix hacked out of a branch of dry boxwood had been nailed up at the head of the bed, and a little porcelain Virgin stretched out her hands from a bracket.

The priest crossed the room without pausing on the threshold as landlords did, to invite their tenants to take an inventory of the room in one glance. He went straight to the window and opened it.

A broad slope of meadow swept down to meet a line of willows and elders that marked the course of an invisible stream. Then the land rose again, under woods and ploughed fields, to a hilltop where the view was cut off by a curtain of pine trees.

"You will not have the feeling of being too much shut in. But when you do feel that way—"

He made Rolland lean out the window to catch sight of a latticed hen-house just underneath, as he finished his sentence:

"You will think of yourself as already the junior officer in charge of the chicken-coop."

He left him with the same happy smile; and this time Rolland answered it.

But when he was alone he turned away from the window, and his eyes made a tour of the room. He was going to live here for months, in isolation: he who had lived up to now only as a member of a crew. The simplicity of the objects by which he was surrounded frightened him. Instead of the complexity of the masts, the precise entanglement of the rigging, the sea's surprises and the wind's caprice, there were these bare walls and this table! For peopling the endless hours that awaited him here, he would have to find all his resources within himself, poor and empty as he felt himself to be. "You aren't used to it," his mother had said. Oh, no!

He opened his valise, put his underclothes neatly away in the chest of drawers, hung his outer clothing on the hooks. There, he had finished! He might search forever—he would never find anything else to do in this room.

He made up his mind to go at once to Saint-Sylvère, to present himself to "Papa Rémy." Perhaps that would dispel this crushing sense of futility, of idleness. The teacher would at least talk to him about the labors that lay ahead.

He went out. His room opened on a rather dark corridor; at the end there was a step he did not see, and he stumbled. He swore in an undertone, and someone spoke immediately from the stairway:

"Did you hurt yourself? It is my fault. I should have warned you."

It was the priest, going downstairs with a box of diagrams and pictures he was just bringing from his room. Confused, Rolland stammered, "But no . . . I'm the one to beg your pardon. . . ."

The priest made a gesture with his hand.

"Oh, I think a sailor's oaths are about the same thing as a devout woman's 'My God,' which means nothing more than 'Dear me!' No doubt you are on your way to see Monsieur Rémy? In that case, will you do me a favor—one I shall ask you to repeat every day? It is to take my bicycle to go to Saint-Sylvère. I don't use it any more, and you will keep it from rusting. That is, if you are not ashamed to push a woman's bike? No? Then all you have to do is get on it."

As he pedaled toward Saint-Sylvère, Rolland made an effort to straighten out, after a fashion, the tangle of his impressions. He knew that kindness was part of the strategy of priests. When he was a little boy the rectors used to pat him affectionately on the cheek, and he had always felt that that was a mere gesture. Instinctively, now, beneath Father Monnard's welcome and the cordiality of his words he had assumed an intention, however distant, to bring him into the fold. That was a priest's trade.

Nevertheless he was convinced that Father Monnard had felt something of satisfaction in seeing him enter his house, something of pleasure in opening his home to him. Beyond that, his understanding did not go. He had thought of this boarding in a rectory as a species of military service, or like a voyage with a cantankerous captain: a few glum months to which he would have to resign himself, since this was the only place where he could board on credit. All he could say now was that it didn't look so bad as he had feared. He was even having to struggle against the liking with which, at first glance—in spite of being got up like a grappling-anchor in a sack—this priest had inspired him. Watch out, wait and see, my boy! A priest is smart! He doesn't tell you what he's thinking or what he wants, out of the northwest side of his mouth, the way a bos'n does!

"Now for the other one," he said, aloud.

About the other one, Papa Rémy, the mate had had plenty to say. Rolland knew that he was the son of a poor sabot-maker in the forest; that he had studied all by himself, at night, after driving his drills into the hard beechwood all day; and that his father used to cuff him over the head when he went to sleep at his lesson and let the lamp go on burning uselessly. It was the kind of thing one reads about in prize books. . . . Then Rémy had won a scholarship, got his certificate, and after various teaching positions had been appointed to Saint-Sylvère.

That little Breton market-town had been filled with lads like himself, Rolland: lads who would be hauling at the canvas as long as they lived, when with a little education they might have scaled the poop to command with more quickness and ability than many sons of the bourgeoisie. The new teacher had taken three or four of these boys for study in the evening, and then he had opened a real preparatory course for the Hydrographic Institute, in addition to his regular classes and outside of school hours, beginning at five o'clock in the morning in summer and continuing until nine at night. The course had been for the local boys at first, but little by little his fame as a "maker of captains" had spread; pupils came to him from other places, sometimes from far away. And as this had been going on for twenty years there were captains, mates, and junior officers on a good number of sailing-ships in the foreign trade, who swore by no one but Papa Rémy and venerated him as they did God.

"Hard on himself and hard on others," Monsieur Monnard had concluded. "I have seen fellows that no captain had been able to take down, stammering and trembling like children before him."

As to that, he would see!

For on the day when the first mate, in the chart-house, had spoken in this way of Papa Rémy, Rolland had had the impression —truly extraordinary in connection with this gentleman—that he was carried away by enthusiasm, that he was adding to the good man's stature without sound cause. And that had displeased him: to hear exaggeration from this man who was as exact as a chronometer—a chronometer that might have gone off on a few minutes' notice! When, after this, Monsieur Monnard came to speak of his brother, the priest, he had spoken only two words, but they were two words a fellow had no use for: "You will love him." Love, my eye!

He was coming into Saint-Sylvère now: a square, with a drugstore; in a narrow street, some rectangular dwellings set back behind bare gardens or guarded by hedges of palm and cypress; the school, a building like all other schools, flanked on the right by a two-story structure of gray granite: the house of residence.

XII

HERE HE WAS. . . . He opened a barred wooden gate, leaned his bicycle against the low wall, and rang at a green door. "Might I see Monsieur Rémy? I come from Monsieur Monnard."

"Monsieur Rolland? Come in, sir; Papa has been expecting you."

A double surprise. . . . First, he was expected here, as at Trézel. This was decidedly as it had been aboardship: wherever the first mate passed by, everything would be found to be in readiness. But it was also a surprise to happen on a pretty girl, when he was looking for an old schoolmaster. For she was pretty, with her fresh color, her fluffy hair, her brown eyes: pretty in spite of her Breton nose, that was a trifle broad. She went ahead of him now and led him into a dining room where paintings of ships, running before the wind with all sails set, hung, framed, on the walls; unquestionably, these were presents from former pupils who now were captains.

"How-do-you-do? You are Monsieur Rolland. Sit down."

The words followed one another in the same carefully articulated voice, the voice of classroom dictation. Here, again, Rolland had not imagined him like this: small, ruddy, and as if kept warm by a perpetual wrath, with a long nose on which rode a pair of steel spectacles: a face one might have said had been hacked out in broad strokes by the paternal adze. He was wearing a black lounge coat that showed green where the light struck it, and a very high collar, dazzling white. Seated opposite Rolland, he bent upon him the sharp and penetrating gaze of an old physician who has made up his mind to take plenty of time in examining his patient.

"Monsieur Monnard has written me about you," he said, in the same formal voice. "He assures me that you have good stuff in you, and that you will behave well here, because, up to now, you have behaved badly ashore. That happens. . . . The contrary also. . . . But, insomuch as you are here, you must have made your own choice. . . . You have your school certificate?"

"Yes."

"And since then? No individual studies, no reading?"

"I've read—some novels."

"Yes—dime novels the 'landladies' lent you. I know them. . . . And going around the world without being able to find Calcutta in an atlas. . . . In a word, zero for everything since you left school, at the age of thirteen."

A doctor, a terrible doctor; with merciless sureness he was putting his finger on those spots where his pressure would reveal a sensitiveness under which one would cry out. And a fear woke in Rolland in response: precisely that fear of the doctor who, in three words, makes a gravely sick man out of a fellow who's assured he's perfectly well. As soon as he became aware of this, self-contempt awoke also, to action: was he going to sit there and say nothing! For shame!

"Monsieur Monnard taught me to take observations, on the return voyage. He explained to me how to take approximate bearings, and the meridian altitude."

Papa Rémy did not reply at once. He was studying, over his spectacles, the reaction he had just aroused.

"Yes," he said, at last. "You will owe a great deal to Monsieur Monnard, whom I am proud to have had as a pupil, and who has not the position he deserves, because he will not consent to ask for it. He has made himself responsible for you, to me. You are boarding with his brother, I believe?"

"Yes."

"I trust that you will be capable of appreciating your good fortune. Father Monnard is an admirable man, and a saint. Since he has agreed to receive you, I could not do less. That is what decided me." He pinched the end of his big nose and concluded: "I accept you, then, as a student here. Only, I repeat, you have years of aimless drifting from which to get back to the course; I assume that you realize what arduous effort that will demand of you. You will have to relearn everything, and then to start learning; not to speak of the months you have missed since the classes began. Be here tomorrow morning at six."

He got up and opened the door, but in the entryway he stopped his caller with a movement of his hand.

"Just a moment. . . . Monsieur Monnard had a package of books left here for you. Madeleine!"

A door opened behind Rolland, and he turned around. The girl who had welcomed him was standing on the threshold, and she looked at him before she looked at her father.

"The books Monsieur Monnard sent here for Monsieur Pierre Rolland," the schoolmaster said.

She went to get the package, came back, and handed it to him with a smile.

As soon as he was outside the town, Rolland stopped and opened the bundle which he had tied on the luggage-rack: *Theoretical Arithmetic, Algebra, Geometry, Trigonometry, Cosmography, Elements of Theoretical Navigation. . . .*

He opened the *Geometry* first: diagrams where lines were combined without converging in any familiar form: an arbitrary and sterile complexity. He read: *In similar polygons, the areas are proportional to the squares of the homologous dimensions.* Discouraged, he closed the book.

The *Algebra* offered him pages of formulas on which the slender-shanked letters seem to swarm like colonies of insects. He flung himself back upon the treatise on Navigation: the same sea-wrack of formulas, the same crazy drawings. But this was entitled "Method of

Coast Navigation," or, "The Effect of the Wind on the Sails. . . ." The effect of the wind on the sails! He used to think he knew it, all the same, when he was hauling at the canvas sixty feet above deck, on a wild yard, or when he was holding a headstrong ship, with the grasp of his two hands, exactly on the given course. But tomorrow the old man would say to him, "Zero for that; zero for that as for all the rest. It is with lines and circumferences that one must learn it."

He swore at the schoolmaster out loud, tied the package angrily to the bicycle once more, and, pushing as hard as he could on the pedals, dashed off toward Trézel, determined to throw everything overboard, fasten up his valise, and start back to Dunkerque that very night.

As he turned into the village square he saw Father Monnard coming out of the church, at the end of the evening service, behind several good women who looked at the sailor with curiosity. The priest went ahead of him to open the rectory gate, then he stepped out of the way so that Rolland could bring in the bicycle. But as soon as the gate was closed again, he took his arm.

"Ah, it's not going well, this time!"

"No."

"What is the matter?"

Rolland turned away before he answered, as if he were afraid to meet that too-wide gaze— Oh, this one didn't use his eyelids as carriage-curtains!

"The matter is that I want to go away," he said. "I want to go back where I came from."

"Yes? Come up to my study and tell me about it."

He had kept hold of Rolland's arm, and he did not let it go until he had pushed him into his own room and made him sit down in an armchair. Then he lighted the lamp and closed the shutters, while his guest threw a surly glance around him. Books were overflowing the white pine shelves, papers were crowding each other off the table, a small model of a four-masted ship was enthroned upon the desk, and the gilded figure of a young girl was holding out brass flowers on top of the clock, between two candelabra in sconces. On the night table, near the bed with its faded rep curtains, he noticed a bottle of medicine and a spoon.

"It gets cool quickly," the priest murmured.

He struck another match; the fire, already laid, flamed up, crackling. Then he pulled a package of cigarettes from the bottom of a drawer, offered one to Rolland, and sat down beside the table, against the pink paper lampshade that lent a tinge of color to his pale cheeks.

124

"Monsieur Rémy didn't receive you well?" he said. "I have seen him, and found him excellently disposed toward you. André had written to him."

André—that was the mate, the man who had shoved him into this hornet's nest. Rolland shrugged his shoulders.

"Neither well nor badly," he answered. "He told me I had a great many lost years to catch up on. . . . During those years, I've been making my living!"

"Did he say 'lost'?"

"That is what he meant."

"I don't think so. In any case, he accepted you for his study course?"

"Yes. . . ."

"Then he considers that the delay can be made up for. You won't be the first one he's got into the saddle again. I've seen fellows twenty-five years old working with him. When you know him, you will find out that he has too much heart, and that he hides it. But there is something else troubling you."

Rolland threw a dark glance toward the door, as if an adversary was threatening to enter.

"Your brother had sent him some books for me. I have looked at them. . . ."

"Now we have it!" the priest said. "And as they were all Hebrew to you, you want to leave them to me as a souvenir?"

Rolland scowled again. He was only sitting on the edge of the armchair, not consenting to abandon himself to it.

"I shall never be able to stick that rigmarole," he declared.

"Oh, yes, you will," the priest said gently. "Because you will very soon realize that it is not a matter of just tracing out some lines or other, arbitrarily muddled up by professors to discourage poor candidates. A pencil stroke applied here may save a ship, and men, out there. To take only one example: what is more dry and dull than a triangle? But when that becomes two anchors that have been put out and a ship that is making an effort to raise them? If that triangle were not accurately calculated in Papa Rémy's classroom, you would drag the anchors and run aground. Don't think I found this out all by myself," he added. "I have heard him say it, many a time, to my brother, and I have been impressed by it. I have also heard him say he could imagine nothing more dreadful for a ship's commander than to be unable to meet a situation because he had neglected to study the point which was now actually presenting itself. . . . But André told me, too, that nothing would ever get you down from a yard, in the worst storms, until you had finished what

125

you had to do there. And here you'd give up before you'd even tried?"

He rose, and took Rolland's arm again.

"Come to dinner. Mama had surpassed herself at noon, in honor of your arrival. You'll get even now by eating cold chicken."

It was a strange dinner, which Rolland was never to forget. Apropos of Papa Rémy and his courses, the priest had embarked with furious energy upon his own college memories. He evoked the figures of professors, sometimes comic, sometimes crossgrained; told stories of pranks and scrimmages; and filled his guest's wine glass to the brim the while. But Rolland soon noticed that he himself only moistened his lips in some reddened water, and that, while he served him plentifully, he scarcely picked at the piece of white meat on his own plate. His mother, listening with a fixed and constrained smile, would sometimes throw a distressed glance at the good food that was being disdained. But the priest, stimulated, his cheeks rosy, talked on and on. Suddenly he was interrupted by a severe fit of coughing, at once smothered in his napkin. He got up, with the apologetic gesture of someone who has just choked. Madame Monnard, her face aghast, had already risen. But her son, his hand on her shoulder, forced her back into her chair and left the room, his napkin still at his lips. The old lady's eyes were on the door, and her face was anguished; then she recovered herself, and, in her turn, mechanically filled Rolland's glass to the brim.

"He isn't well?" Rolland murmured.

"He is very tired," was all she said.

. . . Father Monnard came back, smiling, but terribly pale. Rolland noticed that he no longer had his napkin.

"A bite that went down the wrong way," he explained, as he sat down again.

Then he struck the table with both hands, palms down, to serve notice that the incident was closed, and in the voice of a gourmand he said, "Now, little Mother, you are going to make us a good cup of coffee."

Madame Monnard rushed to the kitchen as if she were fleeing to refuge there.

The priest looked closely at Rolland: that gaze of grave admiration which the sailor had surprised on his face at their first meeting.

"It is a pleasure to look at you," he said gently. "Health is such a beautiful thing, such a great grace!"

At five minutes to six the next morning, after the nocturnal journey across a stretch of country that had surprised him by its

126

ruts and pebbles, Rolland entered the classroom, which was badly lighted by three copper lamps suspended from the ceiling. Some ten youths were already waiting, some of them talking in low voices, others seated and hurriedly going over a lesson. So, he was going to have to sit on one of these little benches, pull his big legs together under these tables meant for kids! He'd look well there! This thought did not give him a particularly amiable attitude with which to accost his new comrades. Yet in one quick look he had sorted out and set apart those in the group who had been to sea, and who, like himself, came here from the crew's quarters. They were the first to whom he held out his hand, though his face was still reserved and expressionless. Then there were two others who came in, and after a hasty nod of greeting all round, went to sit down at their table.

On the stroke of six, an approaching clatter of wooden shoes was heard, and all these big boys' noses were glued to their books as Papa Rémy entered. Then they all rose. The teacher seated himself at his desk on the little wooden dais.

"Sit down, gentlemen. First of all, I bid welcome to our new comrade, Monsieur Rolland. He has sailed more than many of you, and in such a fashion as to win the esteem of the best of his chiefs, who have sent him to me. It is altogether natural, Monsieur Rolland, that you should not understand the theorems which are to be explained this morning. Take comfort in telling yourself that you are not the only one. Monsieur Nollier, will you come to the blackboard?"

Nollier, a broad-shouldered lad of nineteen, left his bench, his head down, the nape of his neck offered, as it were, to the guillotine's downward stroke, and took his place resolutely before the board. He had got in from the "Little Billy Assembly" at two in the morning, and he had been asleep at his desk when the blessed old boy had picked him up, as if with compasses, the very first thing!

"Will you please explain to us, sir, the second proposition on the equality of right-angled triangles."

Nollier began in a muffled voice which gave notice of the approaching breakdown:

"If two right-angled triangles have the hypotenuse equal—"

Then he began to outline his figures, with chalk; rubbed them out; blocked them in again. . . .

"What are you doing there, sir?"

"I am constructing two adjacent triangles."

"On what principle?"

Papa Rémy was watching this shipwreck over the spectacles that sat astride the end of his long nose, and he allowed the unfortunate victim to struggle for several minutes before he remarked, "This is Monday, sir. Your Sunday evening has been extended just as unfortunately as your line AB."

Nollier took the eraser again and wiped out the extension of the line AB.

The door connecting the school with the dwelling house opened, and Nollier threw a glance at it as if he were hoping for the arrival of some succor. What came in was only shame. Madeleine Rémy was bringing her father his breakfast, as she did every morning: a bowl of coffee with a piece of bread soaked in it. Usually she would cast a look of amusement or pity, as the case might be, at the current victim. This morning she ran her eyes swiftly over the class and caught sight of Rolland seated on the back bench; when the door closed again, he thought he saw her healthy red lips sending him the brief suggestion of a smile.

When she had gone, Papa Rémy began his breakfast. He ate slowly, as he spoke, and he would sometimes interrupt himself to gaze attentively at the blackboard, now black again. Under this gaze, the unhappy Nollier essayed several more triangles, but he did not even get so far as the ends of their sides. He tried in vain to recover some fragments of the demonstration.

"I knew of only three examples of the equality of triangles," the teacher commented, "and here we have a fourth! Have it patented, sir. That will be the only patent* you can count on getting." He drank the last of his coffee serenely, then said, "Return to your place. You parents will be informed that you are robbing them."

No one had laughed during the execution. Papa Rémy selected another pupil, who made his way practically without hindrance all the way to Q.E.D.

At eight o'clock, the entrance of the regular schoolboys drove out the class of candidates. But Papa Rémy held Rolland back as he was going out of the door.

"Monsieur Rolland, the lessons will begin again at eleven o'clock. I do not wish to oblige you to take the trip to Trézel and back. That would be wasting time. And I have thought that you might install yourself here in the dining room. For this morning's task there, you will learn the definitions of lines and angles. Come."

He led him to the door at the farther end of the room and opened it. Rolland found himself again in the entryway into which Madeleine Rémy had conducted him the day before. Her father— still keeping a watchful eye on the youngsters who were climbing over the benches—called, "Anna!"

* The pun is on the word *brevet*, which means both "patent" and "certificate." Tr.

At the end of the wide corridor the kitchen door opened, and a tall thin girl, her hair tightly drawn back, presented herself.

"Make Monsieur Rolland comfortable in the dining room. Give him a pen and ink, and some paper."

When she had set before him a glass inkwell, a school pen, and two double sheets of lined paper, she asked, "Have you everything you need?"

Then she left him alone. Resigned, he opened his geometry book and read: *The idea of the point is given by very small bodies (grains of sand): an imperfect image, for the geometric point has no thickness in any direction.* He shook his head: here it was at the first shot, just as preposterous as he had feared. . . .

What impressed him and then filled him with a vague respect, at the end of that first day, was the crushing effort it had demanded of the old schoolmaster. He didn't have a watch below-decks often, that one! From six to eight, the special class; from eight to eleven, the regular courses; from eleven to twelve, the special class; at one, the regular courses again until four; from four to eight, the special class. . . .

"And in the summer," Rolland was told by Savinat, who had been on the *Antoinette* and had remained very much the sailor, with his turtle-neck sweater and broad freckled face, "we begin at five o'clock, and finish at nine! The only time he keeps for himself is Thursday afternoon, when he goes for a walk in the country. And that has lasted for twenty years! On Sunday he plays the organ in church, and he is still the town secretary. Fortunately, Anna helps him."

"Anna—that's the older daughter?"

"Yes. She's a good girl, but she isn't pretty like Madeleine," he said, twisting his lips like an old gourmet.

Rolland made a slight effort in asking, with a smile at the corner of his mouth, "And you are all running after her—Madeleine—aren't you?"

Savinat winked.

"You think so? Well, try it and see! Oh, there are those who would like to! But, believe it or not, nobody has dared go to the old man and ask for her: to hear him say, 'Sir, return to your place!'"

The new life developed as a rowboat glides with the current. Rolland was by no means aware, at first, that the rhythm of the schoolwork was bearing him away, and that he would no longer recognize—so far had he come from them—the attitudes he had had when he arrived. Papa Rémy kept him half an hour after the others, every evening, in order to make up for that famous "drifting," and during this half-hour he fastened himself to him like a bos'n who drags from you all the effort you are capable of, without ever once letting up. Father Monnard, on his part, had insisted that Rolland work in his room, the only one that was heated. These sessions of work were held in the afternoon and also in the evening; for the priest, though he did not say so, dreaded the sleepless nights and their torment of suffocation, and used to stretch out the evenings very late.

It was geometry that had been the first to yield. Rolland had quickly learned his way about in the jargon of the demonstrations: superpositions, reversals, constructions. You always had to haul the line tight at the finish, after several passages as in splicing, or turns one upon another as in a stopper knot. It was seamanship, in a word, and there he excelled.

As for algebra, he had at first stubbornly refused to accept its conventions. That the product of less by less should equal more—that he would not stand! The little tricks of geometry were at least inoffensive; but this absurdity, this calm dishonesty! It was in vain that the priest said to him, over and over, "But it is only a play of symbols, for convenience in calculating."

"I tell you it's a shanghaier's racket," he would declare. "They take off a man here and a man there, and when it's all reckoned up, all these men less, that makes more dollars in their pockets."

The priest would laugh.

"Well, you see, you've hit the bull's eye!"

Often they would work and talk until midnight, but it was not always Father Monnard who did the talking. Little by little, with limitless dexterity, he had led Rolland to tell him of his life aboardship, his voyages.

"So many chatterers who talk without saying anything; and you who have magnificent memories—"

So the sailor, flattered, recalled the Capes, only three of which have a right to the capital letter: Cape Horn, the Cape of Good Hope, and the South Cape in Tasmania. He spoke of a ship fleeing before the storm, a mast torn away, the fores'l furled; of life aboard when they were caught in the tempest that they called "the devil's skin"; of his own bird-flight stunts on the "coconut palms" of the masts, under the burning sun of the tropics. . . . And the priest would listen avidly, his mouth half-open as if to breathe inexhaustible wind that blew through these violent recitals. He would only interrupt the narrator when the ship touched at a port.

"Let us not go ashore. I would be in your way there. . . ."

Yet one evening he himself was quite explicit:

"I believe that God must be very indulgent toward the sprees of sailors. They are like Noah when the ark came to land at last: wine

130

slips up on them. Now the Bible has not one word of blame for Noah. . . . And to be quite frank with you, I am afraid that Saint Peter, your patron, who was also a sailor, might perhaps not always have been beyond reproach in the matter of temperance. One day when he was preaching with the eleven, to a multitude that had come from all quarters of the land, and when everyone heard the preaching in his own tongue, some people were saying, 'They are full of new wine.' And—I am telling you the reflection of someone who went by—Saint Peter cried out, 'What! Drunk at nine o'clock in the morning!' "

Rolland laughed. But he commented: "This is the first time that you have spoken to me of religion. And you do it in your own way!"

The priest shook his head, and there was a mischievous gleam in his eyes.

"I speak to you of religion every Sunday, since you are so kind as to come to Mass—solely, I know, to please me and to avoid shocking my good parishioners. Can't you hear them?" he said. " 'The sailor who is staying with the rector, and who doesn't so much as set foot in the church!' Besides, what is the use of speaking, if the time has not come when the paths of the heart are open? That time will come. For the moment, simply recall a very beautiful phrase which is to be found right at the beginning of the Book of Genesis, the first Book that the Holy Spirit inspired: 'The spirit of God moved upon the face of the waters.' Like a ship. . . . It is always there! Sooner or later you will meet it, on a night when you are alone. . . . But we have come a long way from the *Pons Asinorum!* Monsieur Rémy must be turning over in his bed!"

In the morning, when he was studying at Saint-Sylvère, Madeleine would sometimes come into the room on some pretext. She would merely make an appearance, smile, say good morning, delve swiftly into a drawer, and exchange two or three words with him about the rain or the cold; but Rolland used to feel that she would have been glad to stay longer, if she had not heard Anna poking about in the kitchen, or, perhaps, if he had tried to keep her.

But he had sworn that he was not going to waste his time—time so limited and so filled—in running around after girls. Now that he felt he was on the road, nothing counted but the goal. Without effort, he was treating himself as if he were a ship being driven toward port, and kept strictly on the designated course.

XIII

IT GREW COLD a few days before Christmas. One morning when Rolland went into the dining room at Saint-Sylvère, he found a fire in the fireplace. Madeleine came in a moment later.

"Is it going all right?" she asked, glancing at the burning logs. "I was thinking that you were like me: I can't work when I'm freezing! And then if Papa finds you turned into an icicle, I'm the one he'll hold responsible."

He thanked her.

"I've given you extra work," he said.

"I don't mind."

Without seeming to have heard her, he got up and went over to the hearth.

"The wood is dry," he said, as one delivering judgment. "And then oak burns well."

As he remained standing with his back to her, and seemed to be absorbed in contemplation of the flame, she went out.

"You will be more comfortable," she murmured, as she left the room.

When she had closed the door behind her, he gave an impatient shrug to one shoulder. Oh, yes, she was a nice girl! Agreed! Only, if she was beginning to get herself worked up— Since that could lead nowhere—

On Christmas Eve, when he got back to Trézel at half-past nine— for Papa Rémy had not given his evening class a holiday—Rolland found Madame Monnard waiting for him in the entryway. In the glimmer of the lamp she looked more than ever like her older son. But on the ship Rolland had never seen the first mate so distraught, with such grief and anxiety in his heavy-lidded eyes.

"He is not at all well," she murmured. "He had to go to bed at six o'clock; he is burning with fever. I have found one of his handkerchiefs, all soaked with blood. And he is absolutely determined to say the midnight Mass! He doesn't realize the state he's in. That is fortunate, my God! But if he goes out in this cold it will kill him. So then, Monsieur Pierre, you will have to go back to Saint-Sylvère and explain this to the rector there; then you will bring the curate back with you, to say the Mass."

"No, Pierre."

The priest had just appeared at the turn of the stairs, wrapped in a quilted robe which he had thrown over his nightshirt, and the edge of which he was clutching tight.

"No, Pierre," he repeated, in a voice of authority. "I forbid you to go." And he added, breathlessly, "It will be much better. I shan't get up until time for Mass. But I insist on saying it. . . . Come now, be reasonable."

Reasonable! Madame Monnard flung a desperate glance at Rolland. He was silent. He had sensed the fact that an argument would do nothing but use up, to no purpose, what life-force this man had left. The priest, leaning against the banister, was merely waiting for him to give in.

"Go back to bed, at least!" Rolland said.

It was a solemn entreaty, but it rang out like an order. And Father Monnard responded docilely. "Right away."

And then he vanished.

That Mass! Rolland had seated himself, as usual, at the back of the church. The little nave, full of the shuffling sound of wooden shoes, remained in shadow. Only the altar was gleaming under its tiers of candlesticks. At the stroke of midnight, the priest came out of the sacristy, behind the four acolytes and the two choristers. Rolland was immediately anxious, seeing his tense pace, his rigidity. As he moved up toward the altar, he stumbled at the second step, and the sailor thought he was going to fall.

He himself sprang forward, ran around from the back, mounted the stone steps of the sacristy in two leaps, and opened the door so abruptly that he knocked against one of the acolytes and his censer, and sent the live coals rolling on the floor. Rolland picked them up without even feeling them burn him. Then he stationed himself by the open door that led to the choir. There, if the priest were to collapse, he would be ready to jump forward to carry him out.

He remained there, standing, until the end of the service, which, with an unceasing poignant effort, Father Monnard succeeded in wrenching from himself, clinging to the altar for support, his eyes closed, at moments when his knees gave way under him, or when the apse of the church began to whirl about him with the ruthlessness of a fly-wheel. Little by little, throughout the church, the people became aware of the condition of the celebrant, and no one took his eyes off him. The old women were watching him anxiously over their spectacles, and the men, so prompt to sit down, remained standing all through the offertory. An agonized silence hovered over the nave; but when, bathed in perspiration, the priest staggered back into the sacristy, all the men and women, as they streamed toward the door, broke into loud-voiced comments on the dramatic service.

They did not scatter over the little square, in spite of the cold. They waited for their rector. When they saw him coming, lost in his big overcoat with its turned-up collar, and supported by Rolland, they crowded around him.

"This is not reasonable, Father."

"Oh, you gave us a great fright!"

"You aren't going to start it again at high Mass?"

The priest had paused to answer, to thank them, to shake their hands.

"Let him get home."

Rolland gave the order in a voice which struck them all to silence. The little crowd opened up before the brusque gesture with which the sailor was clearing the path. When he had shut the door again behind the priest, a girl said, in an undertone, "He doesn't seem very agreeable, that fellow!"

"He doesn't talk to anyone," another remarked, in a sour-toned echo.

An old woman, who would have shown a sharp eye in the daylight, turned on them.

"That may be, but he's a handsome fellow!" she said.

January, February. . . . The months went by with the monotonous rapidity of a voyage that has no history. When the first difficulties of adjustment had been surmounted, when the mathematical vocabulary had become as familiar as the words applied to the ship's gear, and when he had caught, so to speak, the tricks of the trade, Rolland worked easily and well. Papa Rémy was now citing him as a model.

"Monsieur Rolland shows you how far one can go with an unflagging will," he would say. "That is very good, sir."

It was only his spelling which remained very bad, and which humiliated him cruelly. There was nothing he could take hold of there, get his fists into. "Usage"—and that he lacked. He knew that this was throwing him back into the caste which he had made up his mind to get out of, and that made him furious.

Father Monnard, like Papa Rémy, promised him, "That will come by itself with time."

In spite of these assurances, he would keep right on making mistakes at the daily dictation exercises in the evening classes, and he would plunge his hands into his pockets so that he could clench his fists.

There was that.

There was, further, the feeling that, though he was hewing out his path, he moved between two dangers whose menace was drawing close: Madeleine Rémy, and Father Monnard. . . .

When Madeleine came into the dining room now, it was with a sorry, disappointed face, a self-consciousness which found it difficult to support the weight of the simplest words. As for himself, he responded in monosyllables, with the cold politeness of a person who has been interrupted and is trying not to show it too plainly. But as soon as the door had closed behind her, his resentment would express itself in growls. He did not want to marry, that was simple and clear! Not now! Not for years! . . . When he was a captain. . . . Well, then, let her keep out of his way and let him work! True enough, she was pretty, serious-minded, a good housekeeper; but he would find all that again when the right time came. He was not going to saddle himself with a wife and kids, when he was only on shore in order to make himself a better seaman! He felt a resentment against her for her mute reproaches, her sadness, as against all the women from whose arms he had extricated himself at sailing time. As if it amused him, today any more than yesterday, to have someone weeping into his woolen jumper!

Then, too, to be Papa Rémy's son-in-law? No! He would have the sense of spending all his life at school, especially with someone like the old man, who actually made a point of creating such impressions!

Yesterday, when Rolland had given a brilliant resolution of some difficult equations, Papa Rémy had said to him—to him, Rolland—"Well done, dear boy."

"Dear boy!" It was enough to topple over the walls that had never heard such words! And the fond gaze with which the old fellow had followed him back to his seat afterward! It was the other fellows' turn to laugh now! Savinat had scribbled *Congratulations! When is the wedding to be?* on a scrap of paper which he had pushed across under his nose.

As they left the classroom they were all there together, ready to begin their gibing again; but as he got on his woman's bicycle—a bicycle at which no one had dared to smile—he had looked them all over from head to foot.

"Madeleine?" he said. "If anyone of you wants her, he has only to tell me and I will deliver the message to her tomorrow morning."

And as they all realized that he would do just as he said, not one of them dared turn a hair. They watched in silence as he went down the hill.

At Trézel it was quite another thing. The priest was sinking, gently, with respites and relapses, as in zones of dead calm where from time to time a flurry of wind will make you think you are going to get away, and then will die down, abandoning you to fever and sweat. He was only out of bed, now, for a few hours each day. He spoke very little, but he would gaze at Rolland for long minutes, with a very sweet smile to which the sailor had learned, timidly, to respond. If anyone had told him this—that he would make pretty faces before a little country priest, and that it would grip his heart every time! . . .

Otherwise, when Father Monnard did talk, especially when his mother was present, it was to make plans. There was the mission—not for this coming Lent, for the next—but it was better to think about it a year ahead of time. This mission would exhaust a good part of the church's reserve funds; he would have to wait another year to do over the choir stalls. But, when that was done, what a beautiful little church he would have! His eyes glowed in anticipation.

The curate from Saint-Sylvère was now taking his place for Sunday Mass, catechism class, and the visits to the sick. He was a well-set-up priest, with a ringing voice, and Rolland felt a resentment against him for his rosy-cheeked and confident health, and for those clarion tones that never became soft enough to be right for the invalid's bedside. As for Father Monnard, when his mother brought the curate to see him, he would be profuse in apologies and thanks.

"May it soon be good weather again," he would greet the visitor, in his short-breathed voice, "so that I can free you from all this burden of extra work!"

One evening, as the curate and Madame Monnard were on their way downstairs after the usual session of smiles and encouragements, leaving Rolland alone with the sick man, the priest murmured, "Fortunately, it will be over soon."

Rolland, arrested, turned back from his table, where he had begun to write.

The priest looked at him with a gentle mockery in his eyes.

"You have been taken in yourself, Pierre—thinking I didn't know! But for the last two years I have been watching God come closer to me step by step. His approach has been much more rapid since you came, my poor Pierre, and that is the only thing that saddens me—to have imposed the company of an invalid on you. It isn't cheerful, and you need cheerfulness, more than most people do. It was so as not to add to all that is depressing, here, that I let you believe I didn't 'see how things were,' as they say. Only, now, our time is getting short, and I must talk with you: not as a priest—not yet—but as a friend; the things that are said between friends . when one of them is going away. . . . Yes, I shall perhaps observe

136

Lent here, but I hope with all my heart that I shall celebrate Easter elsewhere."

He fell silent, for he heard his mother coming upstairs again; and Rolland marveled that he could so quickly assume the confident visage that he wore in her presence. And during the days that followed he spoke very little, for he was emphatic on one point: "The examination is coming soon, and that is all that matters."

Lately he had insisted that Rolland work in "Monseigneur's room," which was in its humble way a state chamber, with a velours armchair, a canopy bed, and rep curtains, and in which a fire was made; but the anguished spasms of coughing pursued the sailor even here, and if he did not hear Madame Monnard hurrying to the sickroom, he himself would go to raise the pillows gently, lift the invalid to a sitting position, and support him while he laboriously got his breath again.

One evening the priest's moist fingers held him beside the bed, as he expressed his thanks for what his coming had meant: he had experienced the proud rejoicing of a delicate child, he declared, in the protective strength of a comrade. Rolland was moved, as he listened. Could he not have surmised that another had already felt the attraction of that strength?

"That is an atmosphere which is wanting among sick people," the priest was saying, "and it came in, full blast, with you! The day you lifted the cupboard in the dining room, it was like a little miracle. When one has always been a poor shrimp of a creature, it is a happiness to live beside someone to whom nothing is a burden, and who is never tired."

Another evening, when Rolland had dexterously made him swallow a spoonful of medicine, he said, "André had written me that you were rough and violent. But he was not troubled about that, nor was I. We were right. The proof—" His glance went to the empty spoon. But his tone changed immediately, and it was an anxious gaze that he fixed upon Rolland. "The danger I fear for you much more, my dear Pierre, is hardness. I should be the last to point that out to you, after all you have done for me; but I am afraid of being the only one to find mercy from you. I am sure that you are irritated by everything that is ill-favored or weak."

Rolland stiffened a little.

"Your brother talked to you about Barquet?" he asked.

"The boy whose life you saved?"

Rolland raised one shoulder.

"I didn't save him. It would be better to say that I pushed him into the water—because he was exactly as you just said."

The priest shook his head.

"No, André only told me how you went after him and brought him back. But you will not be able to bring them all back, my dear Pierre. And that is what frightens me, for them and for you. They take a terrible revenge, like all fragile things and people: simply in letting themselves be broken. And afterward it is irreparable."

The day before mid-Lent, Papa Rémy kept Rolland for a few minutes after the youngsters came in at eight o'clock.

It was becoming more and more frequent, this "Monsieur Rolland, a moment—which would stop him just as he was going out of the door. It belonged among the privileges reserved for the model pupil, to whom the teacher had said a few days before, "You have the stuff in you to be head of your class." Called back now, Rolland went to the desk, where the schoolmaster was carefully arranging a stack of notebooks he had just taken out of his drawer.

"Are you free tomorrow afternoon?" Papa Rémy asked.

Rolland supposed that he meant to set aside the sacrosanct hours of his country walk for a last consultation and review before the examination.

"Yes, sir," he said.

"Then give us the pleasure of joining us for a little collation, to celebrate mid-Lent. We shall expect you at three o'clock."

And Papa Rémy screwed up his face in a smile that half-closed his eyes.

Until the next day came, Rolland cudgeled his brains to discover the exact meaning of the invitation: was it a special distinction accorded to the most promising candidate for scholastic honors, or was it the first snare laid by a father with daughters to be married off? His preoccupation did not escape Father Monnard.

"There's something bothering you, Pierre."

"Oh, no."

Next morning, during the class, Papa Rémy announced: "As we are ahead in our schedule, we will have no session this evening. But in celebrating mid-Lent, gentlemen, remember that it is in the choice of diversions that a good education makes itself known."

Rolland, on his bench, had stiffened all over. This unexpected holiday was, by all evidence, intended for him. It could only tend to prolong the "collation."

At eight o'clock he stepped into the hallway of the Rémys' house, as usual, for his morning study period. The doors were closed and everything was quiet, though ordinarily he would be hearing the two girls bustling about in the kitchen. He opened the door of the dining room and was surprised to see a notebook lying on the table.

Moving it aside to settle himself for his work, he found a letter underneath, and opened it. . . . With the first lines, he was struck motionless: that tense immobility which came over him aboardship when he first sensed the menace of storm.

It was a letter such as can only be written by very quiet and modest girls, who know, better than others do, the dangers of repression and silence. The time had come, Madeleine said, to decide about the future. She did not believe it was right for her to drag out her uncertainty for the sake of obedience to convention; and she was writing to him because she did not dare to speak. He had surely become aware of her sentiments, and must know his own; if he had not shown this, perhaps it was because of her father. . . . In any case, she wanted to know how she stood, even if that meant periencing the greatest disappointment of her life. She under-
he might not wish to enter into an engagement
s ready to wait as long a time as was right for
ng, after the little party, when she took him
uld ask him for his answer. Her father knew
e had confided in no one but Father Monnard.
he tore the paper to bits, stuffed them into his pocket,
ent out, slamming the door behind him with a brutal crash that echoed through the silent house—where he felt that people were silent only for better listening. The letter told him one thing and one thing only: that the priest had betrayed him. They were all the same: this one was merely more artful. . . . He had never preached to him: he was throwing a "Christian girl" at his throat instead; with that, he'd have him hard and fast! He flung a savage accusation at the priest's nearness to death: he knew he was going, so he had to act quickly, to hand him over to old Rémy; with that one's fist he would still be pulling on the wheel! Fortunately, the girl had gone ahead too soon: she thought she had him already signed up and on board!

He jumped on his bicycle and pushed off at top speed toward Saint Servan. Father Monnard used to insist on his going out every Sunday, and for the rest, had remarked, with an air of light mockery: "Saint-Sylvère is on the outskirts of Trézel. You are there what you are here—'the rector's sailor.' That enrolls you among the clergy, my poor Pierre! So, when you want to dance, go as far as Saint Servan: my cassock will be less in your way."

He had gone there, on three or four Sundays, with Huet and Savinat. He had danced at Florine's, a bar with a mechanical piano, in a little street that looked out on the harbor. He had not been back for several weeks, because he had become acquainted with a fisherman and had been going out with him in his boat every

Sunday afternoon. But Savinat had remarked on several occasions, "Florine has asked again for news of you. It looks as if you'd thawed her out!"

Florine was a widow in her thirties, a former barmaid who had got herself married to her employer, a man fifteen years older than she. He had died, twenty months before, of cirrhosis of the liver; and since then Florine, a tall brunette with a cold face and regular features, had seemed to be interested in nothing but her business. She never joked with her customers; and on Sunday afternoons she would wait on the dancers with the systematic rapidity, the indifference to the noise and movement about her, of the women who collect the ticket money on a country merry-go-round when it is in full swing.

"She's well-keeled, with a fine pair of bows, ———d to sa "But watch out for the ice, boy!"

With the facility of youth, he found it sin reserved woman who never seemed to notic each other in her bar. As for Rolland, he l Florine's gaze fixed upon him and immediate had taken the position of not appearing to be aware of t attention. But when his companions had told him that asked about him, on the Sundays following, he had been only half-surprised.

When he went into the café, at ten o'clock in the morning, she was standing behind the bar, and she could not keep from flushing—yet more from surprise than emotion—when she saw him. She recovered herself at once, however, and said, in her even tones, "You make yourself as scarce as sunny days."

"I'm working hard," he apologized, as he sat down.

"I know. . . . And today you have a holiday?"

"Yes. That is, I'm taking it. . . . I've left my bike at the gate; couldn't I bring it inside?"

She did not seem to be surprised by this request, which nevertheless meant that he was counting on staying for some time.

"Of course," she said.

She followed him to the street, opened the gate of a passage adjoining the café, and led him into a little yard.

"It's quite safe there," she said. And then, when he had come back and seated himself again at his table, she asked, "What am I to serve you?"

"It doesn't matter," he answered. "A pernod."

She returned with the blue-green bottle and leaned over to pour the drink. He had sunk back on the settee, his head tilted backward and raised toward her. Although she kept her eyes on the glass she was filling, she was disturbed by the brutal gaze which she felt crashing down upon her, and she spilled the liquid.

"You are trembling," he said.

She looked at him, with a tense smile. Everything had been said. He took the bottle from her hands, set it down on the marble-topped table, seized her wrists and raised them to his lips.

When he released her, he went over to the door and pushed in the bolt. She let him do it, submissively, without a word. It was two o'clock in the afternoon when he drew it back again.

"Your friends are coming," she informed him. "They told me they were."

"That doesn't bother me."

Four of them, in fact, came in a moment later: Savinat, Huet, Trévéder, and Baud... They all stopped short, amazed at the sight of him s... at ... table. Savinat was the first to recover himself.

"W... ... ... of finding you here!"

"I'... ... re si... ... ten o'clock," he replied calmly.

"We ... ... ght you might be sick," Trévéder explained. "But Papa Rémy was afraid something must have happened to the rector, and he sent me to Trézel. . ."

Rolland's face clouded over. Florine was listening with the greatest attention.

". . . And they told you I wasn't there," Rolland finished the sentence, curtly. "No, I was here."

The tables filled up, one by one. The piano ground out the first polka. Soon the dancers, thirsty, began to crowd up to the bar. Rolland stepped behind the counter, beside Florine.

"Wait, I'm going to help you," he said.

He began to unstopper the beer, and poured it out so naturally that everybody, after the first start of astonishment, seemed to accept the situation.

At seven o'clock, when darkness had fallen and the café began to empty, Rolland beckoned to Savinat.

"Would it put you out to pop over to Trézel on the bike and tell them not to expect me?"

Savinat did not take his cigarette out of his mouth, and that made his enunciation none too clear.

"When should I say you'll be back?" he asked.

"I don't know. I've found a first-class 'landlady.' "

Florine's rapid smile flashed across her face, but she did not look at them. It was impossible to guess whether she was dissatisfied or pleased to be thus ticketed in front of her clientele.

At nine o'clock the next morning, Savinat came back. Rolland and Florine were having breakfast together at a table in the café.

141

"This is the end for Father Monnard, old boy," he announced, after a brief greeting. "His mother and the curate found him in a dead faint on the stairs last evening, all dressed to go out, half-an-hour after I had been there with your message. He hasn't come to himself, really, since."

Rolland had sprung up from his chair. One thought was imposing its tyranny upon him, shooting its lightning flashes through his brain: He was coming to look for me. . . .

"His mother is asking for you," Savinat concluded. "I haven't any advice to give. . . ."

"Go," Florine commanded, in a voice which accepted defeat.

On the stairway he passed the curate of Saint Sylvère, still in his surplice. He had just given the last rites to the dying man. Rolland drew back against the wall, and the priest murmured as he went by, "You are arriving just in time. He spoke again, a moment ago. He is asking for you." Then he added something which Rolland did not understand: "If it had not been for this attack of delirium, he might perhaps have been able to keep going for another week."

Madame Monnard appeared at the bedroom door as soon as she heard the footsteps on the stairs.

"He expects you," she said, in a very low voice. "I took it upon myself to send for you."

Her face showed only anguish; Rolland could read no censure in it. It seemed to him that he was walking in a dream, where the people you meet speak to you only in words that have no meaning. Madame Monnard left the room as he entered, but before going out she leaned over the bed to say, "Pierre has come."

The dying man's eyes remained closed, at first; but after a minute he muttered, "My glasses. . . ."

Rolland picked them up from the night-table and, after an instant's hesitation, himself put them in place. The near-sighted eyes, clear now, were registering nothing, any longer, except a dreadful fatigue.

"My poor dear Pierre—"

The voice was so close to complete extinction that Rolland had to lean very far over, and it was as if some relentless force were pressing on the back of his neck. He heard, so, the faint words:

"My fault. . . ." Then the dying man seemed to be gathering all his strength together to declare, "We must wait. . . ."

Rolland leaned down farther still. There was something he wanted to be sure about, no matter what torment it might bring. He had to know; otherwise something priceless would be lost.

"When you fell, were you coming to look for me?" he asked, in the too-clear voice which he had never learned to deaden.

The eyes closed. Was it on a final secret, or on the mind's emptiness?

Rolland rose. It was the kind of blank disappointment a man feels aboardship when a fish gets off the hook and the line goes slack. The man on the bed seemed to be plunged into depths, now, from which no word would ever come again.

Madame Monnard was returning. "Could he speak to you?" she asked. "He was so afraid he would not be able to."

Rolland nodded. What was the use of undeceiving her, of telling her that all he had got were a few disconnected words? They both sat down beside the bed. Rolland was waiting for Madame Monnard to speak. It was not possible that she should accept him so, in this place, after his brutal desertion. But Rolland came gradually to understand that the silence would not be broken again, and he gave himself up to it. He was finding within himself, anew, the great empty quiet of the open sea, when he would be following a course in the rocking cradle of the ship, his eyes on an unmoving horizon. The creaking of an outside shutter, swaying in the breeze, seemed to him the grating of a block.

"The spirit of God . . . on the waters. . . ."

The dying man had leaned his head across the pillow to pronounce these words in a voice which, to both the listeners, seemed strangely strong. Madame Monnard got up.

"Do you want something to drink?" she asked, her own voice broken.

There was a glass there, with champagne; she took some of it up in a teaspoon; Rolland slipped his arm behind the pillows and gently lifted the panting chest. But the wine fell away from the mouth that had closed again, spilling over the chin and then down on the throat.

He died at two in the morning. He really escaped them, so gently that they did not note the stoppage of the breath which had become imperceptible, and which, by force of their listening, their ears still projected upon the blanched lips for several moments after he had gone.

More than twenty priests came to the burial, from as far away as Cancale and Dol. At the funeral luncheon, Rolland was amazed by the naturalness with which these colleagues spoke of the dead man, exactly as *they* would do, the men of the ocean-going ships, when they exchanged memories, in the crew's quarters, of a comrade who had just been buried at sea. They quoted words of Father Monnard's, his little jokes and teasings, and then slight incidents of his illness, so that one would think none of them had even glimpsed all the broad reach that he, a common seaman, had divined in that heart and soul. And he was thinking, too, of the mate, who at that moment must be walking up and down on a ship's deck, his head bent over, his hands behind his back. "You will love him. . . ." He had seen rightly, as always. But he, Rolland, how much better would he be for that?

The priests were now talking of the monthly conferences, the deanship meetings to which the rector of Trézel loved to go, and which he had enlivened by his bright spirit.

"One can really say that it was in trying to get there that he died," averred the curate of Saint-Sylvère. And for those who still did not know it, he explained that when he had picked him up on the stairs the priest had muttered, "To Saint Servan."

For it was at Saint Servan that the conference was being held that day. He had remembered it in his delirium. . . .

Rolland, who was lifting his glass of cider, set it down again, as if it had turned suddenly to lead.

The next morning, at Saint-Sylvère, a few minutes before going into the classroom, he stopped Savinat.

"You understand," the latter explained to him, "I wasn't going to tell his mother where you were and what you were up to! . . . I told her a tale about an old pal you'd just run into. You had dinner together, I said, and rather than make them wait up late for you at the rectory you had decided to spend the night with his family. A lot of good that did! I went to get my bike again, in the yard, and the back tire had gone flat! While I was pumping it up, the door opened. 'My son would like to have a word with you,' she said. Well, old boy, there was nothing I could do. His mother had come down after me. . . . 'Look me in the eye,' he said to me. 'I am not to be lied to, because I am about to die. He didn't go to class this morning, did he? You have just seen him. He is with a woman.' It was as if he had followed you! All I could do was give him the address. He thanked me. And he said to me, 'I had not time to open the door for him. When he thought people were trying to shut him in, he jumped out of the window.' He was delirious already, you see. Anyhow, as I was leaving, his mother asked me my name. The next morning a kid brought me word, from her, that I was to get you right away. It was the kid who told me what had happened: that they had found him on the stairs."

He was silent for a moment. Then, as Rolland made no answer, Savinat added, in a firm voice, "And that did not surprise me."

The windows of the schoolroom had a ruddy glow: Huet, the class patriarch, had just lighted the lamps. Already steps and voices

144

were drawing near in the still-black darkness. Savinat spoke again: "Aren't you going in?"

This time, he was not expecting any reply. He contented himself with remarking, in a lighter tone, "You can boast of having got old Rémy in a stew!"

Rolland shrugged his shoulders, and went away. There was nothing he could do about that. Everyone had his own burden to bear: his was enough for him.

In sum, he had repeated the same fine maneuver with the two Monnards. He had taken first one and then the other for a low-down cheat, and he had called down curses upon them and run away. The Monnard of the sea, with his strong hand, had locked him in the sail locker. After that, at least they had been able to have an explanation. But the other. . . . He had tried his best, poor man, to bring him back. He had only been able to carry to his death one last suffering, one further torment, his final gift. . . . "They let themselves be broken, my dear Pierre, and it is irreparable. . . ." Ah, it was!

He entered the Hydrographic Institute at Saint Malo eight days later. During the first week, an examination skimmed off the cream of the candidates for the ocean-going service and threw the rest into the coastwise trade. Rolland was inscribed without difficulty in the ocean-going course.

So that he might have nothing to reproach himself with, he had made part of a group, on the eve of his entrance into the Institute, that had gone to shake hands with Papa Rémy. The old schoolmaster had not even looked at him as he said, "I do not know you, sir."

Rolland had merely shrugged his shoulders, as he had done a week earlier at the door of the classroom: what was done was done. He realized that clearly. Others would have had to realize it. . . .

One morning, as he came out of school, he found Florine waiting for him. And it was with the same air of powerlessness—of being really unable to do anything for her, either—that he approached her. Yes, it was all over. . . . Already? Yes. . . . No, she herself had had nothing to do with it. . . . A business of priests? Yes and no.

She looked straight into his eyes.

"I know that you will come back," she said.

"In that case, you don't have to worry."

He left her. His classmates had already scattered through the narrow Saint Malo streets. As for him, he went down above the harbor.

At least, there was a harbor there!

Book Two   THE MATE

BOOK TWO

XIV

"*ANTONINE! Ho, Antonine!*"

It was strange that one should be calling a woman, with this voice, at this hour, in this place.

The voice was one of those which carry to a distance and are made for bawling out orders, and it was an order which it was flinging out impatiently, now, into the cold dawn mist.

To the right of the man, who stood motionless with head thrown back, waiting for an answer to his shout, the gentle lines of dunes were like low, unmoving clouds. At his left the halos of beacon lights, set in strict alignment, were being extinguished one after the other, while here and there in the fog other lights were being lighted, with softly blurred edges and a reddish glow. At his feet, clearly seen for only a few yards, ran a line of sharp-cut masonry, and on the other side of that waves were lapping, glimpsed in patches as of grayish phosphorescence in what was still a black hole.

The man had piercing eyes; through the pallid density they were already making out four slender columns, like thin lines of smoke rising straight in the air, and it was toward these that he shouted again:

"*Antonine! Ho, Antonine!*"

Then he growled, "Damn foot-sloggers' lighter! They're going to keep me here pickling, are they? They're asleep!"

He spat out the word scornfully. Then he realized that his voice would reach the sleeping ship only after she woke up. Willy-nilly, he would have to wait for her awakening. The cold gripped him, that penetrating cold of early morning. Pierre Rolland buried his hands in the pockets of his waterproof coat, glumly pulled his spongy cap down on his head, and began to walk up and down the dock, his steps quickly falling into a measured cadence because they were finding the rhythm of interminable watches once more.

The forced promenade was not making him feel any more attracted to this apathetic ship, on which he was only sailing under compulsion. He had been almost promised a command. Instead of that, he had had a telegram from his shipping firm: GO IMMEDIATELY TO PORT TALBOT, TO EMBARK ON THE FOUR-MASTER ANTONINE, IN THE CAPACITY OF SECOND CAPTAIN.

Second captain: first mate. . . . That meant he was going to start in again at the business of traveling the fore-and-aft gangway. Once more, he would let no blow from the sea pass by without getting a piece of it. Tomorrow, as yesterday, he would command only at the foot of the mast, elbow-to-elbow with the men, and in the work which, often, he would not have ordered himself.

For he had not been pampered under his last captains!

His recollections were far from lying stagnant in the depths of his memory. They were moving there in profound currents, hot or cold, and they rose to the surface of the present only as the surface was in accord with them, with their warmth or their chill. On this September morning, in the acrid sootiness of the fog and the bitterness of the recent disappointment, only hateful images took form. Nothing came back to him now of the two years spent under the command of Monnard, at last made captain, first as junior officer and then as first mate: two years of easy obedience to a chief whom he admired and loved, one look from whom would put a stop to his fits of anger, as one penetrating word would drain the dark moods from his heart. In this autumn mist the past became definite only from the starting-point of a grave dug in the nitrate desert of Iquique where, on an afternoon of searing heat, Rolland had laid the former mate of the *Galatée*. Monsieur Monnard's death had been stupid and senseless, as it should never be for men like him. A prick from a rusty nail, a thing one dismisses as of no consequence; then tetanus, and six days of horrible suffering, during which one did not know whether it was will power or muscular contraction that locked the dying man's teeth together. . . . Then, finally, this blinding hole in the ground, in front of which Rolland had clenched his fists in rebellion, and in which he felt, at twenty-five, that he was burying his youth. . . .

He had returned to Chile the next year and then gone on to Frisco, on the *Astrée*, under Captain Bouteloup. Old Bouteloup was a good fellow, a damn good fellow, who didn't want to tire out his crew or to make trouble for anyone. The unfortunate thing was that the wind and the sea were not always in agreement with him. He had given Rolland his first black look when the latter had reported a relaxation of duty on the part of the second mate, to the extent of leaving the poop during his watch in order to go to the galley for a morning cup of coffee. Papa Bouteloup had reacted only by a vague grunt. Then the thing had happened that was bound to happen.

You go to bed one night at midnight, off the coast of Argentina, after turning the watch over to the second mate, with the barometer up, the night clear and star-lit, a nice breeze from north-northwest, a speed of nine to ten knots; and you are wakened at five in the morning by lightning and thunder and a howling wind. Just then, you are thrown out of your bunk, to find yourself on the sofa on the other side of the cabin, a flying-trapeze feat whose success is to be attributed to the ship's rude lunge to larboard. And you say to yourself, "If only he has taken precautions and hauled in his upper sails!"

Like an echo, you hear the junior officer, distracted, screaming, "Lower the royals!"

And you think, Well, this is a pretty mess!

For you had realized at once that the pampero had struck you its classic blow, its great leap northwest-southwest, swift as a back-stroke at billiards. If by ill chance the officer on watch has not reduced his canvas in time to keep the vessel safe, the ship takes on enormous speed, heels over on its side and, griping more and more—in spite of the man at the helm, who is pulling as hard as he can and feels his wheel turning backwards, by its own force, in his grasp—swings head to the wind and is taken aback everywhere. All the sails, caught inside out, beat their yards furiously against the masts. Nine times out of ten, there is a de-masting!

All that races through your head in a few seconds, at the moment when the vessel heels over again, this time to starboard, sending you back into your bunk, headfirst. You rush out into the passageway in your nightshirt. The ship is listing so badly that you don't walk on deck any more but on the starboard bulkhead, and when you have got the door in the poop-rail open, it's not a pretty sight that meets your eye!

It is as dark as the pit, but a flash of lightning shows you the *Astrée* on her side, the starboard rail under water, half the hatches washed by the sea. The sturdy mainmast has kept all its canvas in place, and the gale, taking the sails wrong side around, is slamming them against the rigging. Just go ahead and work ship, gybed like that, if you're tempted to try it!

And in this crackling of thunder, these yelpings of the wind, this drumbeat of the rain, you neither see nor hear any human being at all. So then you go toward the bow, clinging to the gunne'l of the port rail which makes a screen, after a fashion, between you and the breakers. In your passage, you loose the halyards of the royal and to'gants'ls, when and as you come upon them, and above your head you hear someone shouting to you, "The forem'st is down!"

It is the Old Man, also in his shirttails, who is staggering along the flying bridge and pointing you to the bow. When you get there you find the mast broken off at the level of the tops'ls, and the yards overboard alongside and bumping the hull all together, with enough force to bilge the whole thing.

Fortunately, if the pampero is the speed champion among hurricanes, it lacks staying power. And when the wind has slackened, when the sea subsides, you have nothing more to do but saw down those tangled hawsers and cut into that underbrush of rigging that is holding the torn-out yards glued to the quarter and bent on staving you in. When this had been attended to, you could only limp along on three legs to Rio de Janeiro, with a bent bowsprit and two masts damaged; for there was no question of mastering Cape Horn, crippled like this! So there was what it cost not to have given a dressing-down in time, and on the instant, to a negligent officer!

You were the person responsible for getting everything into condition again at Rio, for Papa Bouteloup had fallen ill after this hard blow and had been advised to go to Nictheroy, in the hills. Then, just as a really extraordinary job of work had been finished under your direction, accomplished in record time by the crew and almost entirely with the ship's own equipment, just as you had given orders to the cook for a first-class luncheon to celebrate the return of the Old Man—who could not fail to clasp you to his heart for such an achievement—just then, the bos'n comes to inform you that the temperature in the hold has gone up more than twenty degrees. There is every reason to believe that fire has broken out in the cargo: that spontaneous combustion of damp coal, which nothing and nobody has ever been able to prevent. . . .

So that was how it was. When the skipper and his guests came alongside, and Bouteloup, at his most expansive and calling his colleagues to witness, cried out, "My word, boy, that was damn good work! I would never have believed that you would have got ready to sail so quickly, and without any snags. I congratulate you!"—well, just then, you had to reply, dolefully, "You are very kind, Captain; but look now, there is a fire in the hold. I am afraid we shall have to unload the cargo."

A nice start for the luncheon apéritif!

And in fact, after they had shoveled tons of hot coal around so as to get the air into it, you reported that the fire had gained such headway that a complete unloading was necessary.

After that, when you got back to Dunkerque, it did not take long to learn what the ship-owners accepted without question: that the breaking of the *Astrée's* mast and the burning of its coal were to be laid at the door of the first mate, a pretentious young man who had taken advantage of Papa Bouteloup's kindly nature to set himself up as master on the ship, and to sail head on, all sails set, into an all-out pampero; who thought, moreover, that he would lose caste if he went down into his holds to feel the pulse of his coal cargo. A lad who needed to be broken in!

The next one was Thomas Arlozzi.

Oh, that man!

Rolland slowed down in his walk, and turned around. Behind him the houses of Port Talbot were beginning to show white. The lighter windows had at last taken on their rectangular shape, the mist was thinning. The gray ridges of the dunes were emerging more clearly now, but the fog continued to be heavy over the harbor, and the *Antonine,* which Rolland was looking at, still appeared to him with blurred outlines, as if seen by myopic eyes. Above the long dark splotch of the hull, the masts rose in wavy lines that did not yet show any connection with one another. Rolland abandoned this vague and diffused ship to fix his gaze upon another, which the memory of Arlozzi itself rendered quite distinct: the four-master *Espérance.*

He had crossed its gangplank, as first mate, ten months before, and had found on the deck an excited and gesticulating little man who was barking at the heels of the big slow longshoremen. Arlozzi had planted himself in front of Rolland, legs spread apart and head raised for a stare which was meant to be imperious and was only insolent.

"Monsieur Rolland, I have one principle: everyone to his own place. Everything will go well, therefore, if you understand the respective positions of a captain and of his first mate."

Rolland had had no difficulty in guessing the reference that had given rise to this profession of faith. He had replied merely, "This will be my third voyage as mate. So I must have learned my position by this time, or I never shall learn it."

The captain's expression had darkened, and he had added, still more curtly:

"I must warn you also that I require the maximum from the officers, as from the men."

In general, when this is said it is not done! After three minutes' conversation Rolland would have sworn that he had neither the conscience nor the self-abnegation nor the courage which made it possible for a Monnard to ask everything and obtain everything, without even raising his voice. This address of welcome merely

153

proved what Rolland in any case suspected: that he was a marked man, and that Captain Arlozzi, more or less officially, had been given the mission of bringing him to heel. Very well!

The new first mate realized in advance that his strategy of defense would demand every instant's attention: it was a matter of never letting himself be surprised by this Corsican in any piece of negligence or breach of regulations. He had adopted, without trying to, the glacial air and the silences of Monnard on the *Galatée,* and he was genuinely amused to see the captain hanging around him, seeking tirelessly for the mistake, misconduct, or forgetfulness which would permit his being humiliated before the men. Whenever Arlozzi thought he had found an opening he would dash precipitately into it, only to be brought up short by an unanswerable argument which Rolland would be holding in reserve.

Goaded by his tenacious and inventive hatred, the man had had to go on wagging his accursed tongue after the ship had docked— at which time Rolland had left him with a mere touching of his cap, not shaking his hand. When he made his official call, immediately after landing, the first mate of the *Espérance* had been welcomed with smiles by the ship-owners. "The first available ship will be for you," they had said. To be sure, they had added, "Provided it is a small one." But that was to be taken for granted. . . . Now, instead of a small ship to command, he had received this curt order, by telegraph, to embark as first mate on the *Antonine.* Arlozzi had passed by. . . .

He had also, without doubt, warned his fellow-captain, who would be waiting for the new second-in-command on that sleeping ship. Rolland was going to find a chief with a mind warped in advance against this undesirable that had been imposed upon him, the impudent insurgent who recognized no authority, neither the wholly paternal authority of Captain Bouteloup nor that of "Tomaso," hard as it was. He had been able to sail a ship correctly only under the orders of Monnard, to whom his commission as an officer was due. . . .

It would soon be time, all the same, to make the acquaintance of this new skipper. Captain Thirard: the name told him nothing. He had disdained any quest for information. . . . Now the day had emerged at last from the night's darkness; but it had come out dirty, as when one gets up from a fall in a mud-puddle. Everything was gray and flat: the dunes, the town itself, stamped as with a pressing machine against the chalky cliff. What was left of the fog was concentrated over the harbor, where spirals of yellow vapor were drifting about in a raw wind. Blowing across the *Antonine,* these eddies, so like smoke, seemed to bring the ship vaguely to life, setting dull shadows to play upon her.

"*Antonine,* ahoy!"

This time heads, first one and then another, appeared above the ship's rail. Seeing them outlined so, Rolland realized that with daylight the vessel had come in surprisingly close, advancing perhaps forty or fifty yards. The two dark silhouettes were still in profile at the level of the gunnel, motionless as the figures one aimed at during shooting exercises in one's military service. He called out to them:

"This is the new mate, come to take up his post. . . ."

He felt that his voice carried to them, though it was clipped short of all resonance in this humid air.

"Are there no officers aboard, that you are leaving me shouting here for more than an hour?" he demanded. "See that someone comes to get me, and my trunk—and be quick about it, eh?"

It was just as if he had shot at the two silhouettes and hit them both: they went out at one stroke! Finally, at the end of what seemed to him an interminable time, a sailor climbed down the gangway ladder, got into the dinghy, and, hips swaying over the stern oar, came muddling along toward him. He drew up alongside and touched his beret with a finger which Rolland refused to see. Standing upright like a dark block in his streaming rubber coat he made a movement of his chin toward his narrow trunk, which the man took aboard, and stepped down and seated himself in the boat without speaking a word.

The deck was being washed as he came aboard: a slow and languorous washing, with no force behind it. The men dropped their work to watch him pass them and go into the officer's little cabin.

He found the two ship's officers there, having their breakfast. They were dipping slices of bread in their bowls of black coffee; and it was these broad thick chunks of bread that first caught his eye. They were assuredly the most substantial things he had seen since he had first looked at the *Antonine,* whether aboard or from the quay.

When he had let his gaze rest for some time on the bowls of coffee, he took stock of the men. Berteux, the second mate, seemed to be about twenty-five years old. He was screwing up, in this greeting, a gaunt and unpromising countenance, with a bitter mouth, and he averted yellow-streaked eyes under the scrutiny of his new chief; Rolland noticed the restless blinking of his eyelids. Poullain, the third mate, must have been two or three years older than the other. Tall, and broad in proportion, he wrinkled his forehead under a stubble of heavy hair, and opened eyes that were abashed like those

of a child caught with his hand in the jam-pot. Not hard to cata-
logue, that one: probably a good fellow and easy to get on with, but,
considering his age and his grade, certain to be thoughtless and more
given to larks than to studies.

When Rolland introduced himself they got up, but clumsily; Poullain hefting one buttock and then the other; Berteux, on the other
hand, too quickly, with a start.

"I was not expecting to find you here," Rolland said dryly. "This
is the first time that I have seen a ship's first officer so casually
received."

The sharpness of the rebuke stiffened them, but only with surprise: apparently this was not the current tone on the *Antonine*. At
last Poullain made their apologies:

"We did not think that the dinghy would bring you out so quickly,
sir, and we were finishing breakfast."

"No, you were beginning it—although you should have been on
the deck, waiting for me. I myself have had to wait more than an
hour on the quay, until someone here woke up to hear me calling.
That is the mark of an inadmissible carelessness."

Berteux and Poullain exchanged glances which obviously meant,
"This is the last thing we expected!" But after a nervous grimace that
puckered up his angular visage, Berteux took the bull by the horns.

"That is true, sir," he said. "Things are not going as they should,
here. But I can assure you it is not our fault."

He had thrown a vehemence into the last words that made his
chin quiver and left his eyes dilated and his forehead in wrinkles.
Poullain gave a slow nod of agreement.

"And whose fault would it be?"

Berteux did not hesitate. His thin face thrown back, he almost
screamed, "The captain's and the crew's!"

"Very well then, you are covering yourselves above and below,"
Rolland replied. "Why the captain?"

It was Poullain who answered: "He is sick."

Berteux went on with more detail, and now in a duller voice: "He
says himself it is chronic laryngitis, quinsy. But it is certainly something else: he has changed too much. In any case, it has almost
entirely taken away his voice; you can hardly understand him. There
can be no question of his commanding."

All right, so they chose me! thought Rolland. What he said was,
"But there was a first mate, the one I am replacing."

"He is in the hospital, with pleurisy," Poullain explained.

They were both looking at him now, with eyes of an innocence
that is at last recognized. "You see how it is," they seemed to say.

156

"What was there to be done against such a run of bad luck?" Rolland stared at them, one after the other.

"But you are here yourselves, and apparently in good health," he said. "Even if the captain does not appear on the poop, he can give you orders in his cabin, and you have only to have them carried out."

There was rancor in Berteux's answer. "He does not wish to have any association with us, as it were, apart from the irreducible minimum of service."

"Is that their own fault, or is it his?" Rolland was asking himself. "Is it a case of incompetent subordinates, or a crabbed invalid who fumes in his cabin and takes out his ill-temper on his officers between two garglings?"

"We shall see," he said, aloud. Then he asked, "Have you been here long?"

"A couple of weeks," Poullain answered. "We've come out of dry dock, after a grounding."

"Oh, you ran aground?"

Berteux hastened to explain. "It was the tug's fault. She ran us on the rocks in a fog. It is since then that the crew has become unmanageable. The first mate gone, the captain never seen—they just let go, they don't obey any more."

"Even so, that would not have come about all at once, by itself," Rolland objected. "You had to take action about something? There were some men who, driven into a corner, expressly refused to obey you?"

"Yes, there were two," Poullain declared. "The most worked-up, the bos'n, Kréven, and a Negro named Bako."

"Oh, that one!" cried Berteux, while Poullain shook a discouraged head.

Bako. . . . Rolland had known a man from Martinique with that name, on the *Astrée*. He had come aboard at Frisco with a replacement group when old Bouteloup had succeeded in getting some men shanghaied, which was a good thing! This Bako, Rolland recalled, had come up the gangplank with a young goat in his arms, a kid that was more of a pet even than a dog. The West Indian had taught it to chew tobacco! He had made a little net, the size of a nut, that was fastened to a string; he would put a plug into it, and the kid, liking the tobacco, would try to swallow it; but Bako kept good hold of the string, and the little goat had had to get used to merely chewing. After a few lessons, pupil and master were chewing their plugs together. The kid even succeeded in spitting out the juice, to a distance which filled the crew with wonder and the teacher with pride. "The only thing left for him to do is pick up his quid in his cap," the men would joke.

157

On Sundays, the officers would amuse themselves by getting this Bako to sing songs of the Islands: *"Doudou Moué,"* or *"Assez Causé, Assez Palé";* and the men would make him climb the back-stays like a monkey, without ever making use of the ratlines. He was as lacking in wickedness or malice as he was in civil status: it was not possible that this big savage child should have given both these officers those bitter and disheartened faces! Rolland determined to get to the bottom of all this at once, and, with Berteux at his heels, he set off for the crew's quarters.

"He is stubbornly refusing to work," the second mate explained, on the way. "For six days now he has stayed in bed."

It was rather dark in the fo'c'sle. Nevertheless, Rolland made out the man he was looking for, stretched out in his bunk. He had his face turned to the wall, and he did not stir when the officers entered. Rolland caught hold of his shoulder, turned him over on his back, and scanned the dark countenance.

"Look here, you," he said. "You wouldn't by any chance be the fellow named Bako that I knew on the *Astrée?*"

"Yes, Missié Rolland."

"You know that I am the first mate here now, on the *Antonine?*"

"Yes, Missié Rolland."

"And the first thing they tell me when I come aboard is that you are now a rebel, a good-for-nothing, and a lazy scamp into the bargain, since you haven't been willing to get out of bed for the last five or six days."

Bako sat up angrily, on his bunk, to swear, with cannibalistic dumb-show, that this was not true, that he was very sick because he had fallen from the orlop deck into the forward hold, and that Missié Berteux had refused to get him the doctor.

"If me strong, jump like goat," he declared.

The second mate was about to make a retort to this, but Rolland stopped him.

"Good. That makes things a little different. But I am sure that Monsieur Berteux is right, and that you haven't broken any bones. Now then, listen: me, good fellow; me, get the doctor. But if you not sick, me stick my fist in your face and my boot in your buttocks; after that, you sick. You get me?"

"Yes, Missié Rolland."

They went out. For the first time since he had set foot on the *Antonine,* Rolland was smiling.

"It's as easy as that," he said. "Your anarchist will be at work tomorrow morning."

He was mistaken in this: it was no more than half an hour later that Bako was to be seen frantically shining up the copper of the deck light. But Rolland did not immediately learn the extent of his victory, for he had gone to see the captain.

He had hesitated for a moment at the cabin's threshold, stopped by the odor: that odor of a sick man in a stuffy little room, who lets himself be steeped in the brine of his perspiration, the foulness of his breath, rather than open a porthole. To receive his new mate, Captain Thirard had just pulled on a pair of trousers from which his nightshirt was sticking out in bulges and had thrown an overcoat over his back without even putting his arms into the sleeves. A red muffler was wound around his throat, so heavy and so tight that it held his head stiffly upright. His mouth was buried beneath a bushy mustache of a washed-out chestnut color, the prominence of which was arresting in the shrunken face: One might have thought the mustache was forgotten by the disease which had cleared away the rest. . . . The feverish eyes were fixed on Rolland, as he came into the room, with an anxiety which at once struck the new mate. Then the captain rose from behind the little table where he was writing and held out a hand which should have been broad and solid, but in which one felt all the dryness of the bones underneath the damp skin.

He spoke: it must have been words of welcome, but Rolland did not understand them. The voice was no more than a raucous murmur, endeavoring to draw out the sounds and missing them all. One felt it rubbing along rugged partition walls, growing hoarse there, becoming distorted in a twisting passageway. There was the dreadful distress, in listening to it, of a drowning man's struggles, when one cannot go to his aid.

From Rolland's attitude, the captain had at once realized that he was not making himself understood. As with all sufferers from ailments of the throat, he was irritated by this. He sat down, shrugging his shoulders, and pointed out a chair in a corner of the cabin to his new second-in-command. Rolland picked it up, carried it to the table, and sat down in front of the captain, face to face with him, their knees touching. Thirard looked at him, hesitated several seconds before the gesture which so calmly confirmed the fact of his infirmity, then accepted it with a nod of his head.

From then on, they spoke only in the voice of the confessional; and in this way Rolland learned of all the affronts of fortune that had made them miss their sailing date. The *Antonine* had left Dunkerque in tow. The fog had caught her off the Isle of Wight, and had never lifted. Misled by the blinding mist, the tugboat captain had thought he was doubling Longship, and had come around too soon to starboard. All of a sudden, he had run the *Antonine* right on Land's End, the ship's boom in the rocks. As the weather was moderate and the vessel could still float, the captain had succeeded in getting her off again, and then in shaping the course, in tow, to Port Talbot, where the repairs had been made.

"I have received final instructions as to our destination: to Thio, New Caledonia, in ballast. We should have shoved off two weeks ago. So now there is only one hurry on my mind: to beat it out of here!"

All through his recital he had been gasping as if he were running as he talked; but he cried out the last words, almost in a loud voice. An anguished fit of coughing interrupted him. He turned away.

He wants to sail, Rolland thought, though the only thing for him to do is to leave the ship and go to a hospital.

But he knew how stubbornly a captain clings to his command. If he comes down from his poop, ten men will rush up to it to replace him—and to go back to it again, later on. . . .

"I am counting on you, Monsieur Rolland, to see that everything is ready," the low murmur began again, "and, once we are on the way, to see that everything goes well. I must tell you that up to now I have been rather badly seconded. In that business of running aground, Berteux lost his head; and, too, he is often blundering and tactless. Poullain is a good officer, but only when he is under good command. On the other hand, the bos'n, Kréven, has been splendid. You will be able to rely on him."

He rose, by way of dismissal, and Rolland went out.

It seemed to him that he had just been calling upon a hostage. But imprisoned by whom, by what? Throughout the interview there had been no allusion to the captain's illness, to the disturbance it was causing in the ship's routine functioning. By habit, Rolland appreciated silence; but what was this silence hiding?

He did not see the captain again during the three days which elapsed before the sailing: three dismal days, in contact with a sullen crew which he was keeping an eye on but which he seemed only just to see. That was Monnard's method: to commit himself only when it would be worth the trouble, but then to go all the way!

On the other hand, Berteux and Poullain felt themselves bound to exercise zeal. They never left the deck now, and they stuck right to the men's backs. Poullain, for his part, went about it with some discretion: his reprimands were rare, and always well-founded. But Berteux, strong in the tacit authority of the new mate, exercised no restraint, flung out orders in bunches, and seemed, with nervous jerks of his head, to be poking about in every corner of the ship for things to arouse his indignation. A man couldn't even give a hand to a comrade without being bawled out!

Rolland would listen to him reeling off, for hours, all the commonplaces of the maritime vocabulary of reproof. "You haul off like fleas in tar," "That's good to make eddies, but not to leave much of a wake. . . ." It all sounded false, gave the impression of something learned and repeated, so as to "act the sailor." The men would listen without seeming to hear, but with faces that were contemptuous and full of hatred. Rolland merely thought, He'll bring himself into line, like the others, when the time comes. He'll have to.

It had not escaped his notice that there was another man aboard who kept silence, as he did, who seemed absent, like himself, even to the point of seeming not yet to have become aware of the new first mate. Athletic, with a stern lean corsair's face, the bos'n Kréven used sometimes to walk back and forth on the deck, his hands behind his back, his eyes on the deck planking, as if he wished to make it plain that he was there because he was doing his duty, but nothing more. Yet Rolland noticed on one or two occasions, when Berteux and his bawlings were running rampant from one end of the ship to the other, that Kréven had paused before a group of men at work and looked at them, without saying a word; every time, that had been enough: those who came under that gaze speeded up their activity.

On the morning before sailing day Rolland came unexpectedly upon the bos'n taking a sponge bath on the deck, his bare torso bent over a pail. As the officer went by, the man straightened up to dry himself. His body and arms were covered with tattooing: on his chest, a guillotine with the inscription, *The sun saw my birth, the scaffold will see my vanishing;* on his back, in bold-faced capitals, THE PAST HAS BETRAYED ME, THE PRESENT TORMENTS ME, THE FUTURE TERRIFIES ME. The right arm explained the origin of this literature: it indicated a registration in the African battalions. The bos'n of the *Antonine* was an alumnus of a disciplinary regiment. Rolland knew that aboardship that could mean either the best or the worst.

In the officers' quarters the evening before, Berteux had spoken again of Kréven. Rolland had felt that the bos'n was something of an obsession to him. Was this because the second mate felt himself already judged, and cruelly, by the former soldier-under-punishment? However that might be, Berteux had reported that four days after the ship docked, Kréven had presented himself to the captain, in his best shore clothes, his hair well brushed and his cap at the conventional angle, and had demanded an advance on his pay.

"You have been ashore four days and you haven't a sou left?" the captain had said to him.

"A bitch got away with my wallet the day after we docked," the man had explained, briefly, "but I've got her bearings. . . ."

He had spoken in a tone that moved the captain to warn him: "No settling of accounts before we sail!"

Kréven had shaken his head.

"Nothing like that, Cap'n! That wouldn't be time enough! She's got to stew awhile. . . . All I've done is let her know that I was leaving and that I would be back. . . ."

Berteux had shaken his head, as if to say, "What atrocious behavior!"

Rolland had not uttered a word. He was rather of Kréven's opinion: revenge is the last thing that should be hurried. Generally, the men who are capable of postponing it, for years if need be, in order to make it perfect, are not the people to shirk or skimp on the other things. So this was rather on the good side. It remained to be seen.

XV

THE SAILING was set for the next day, and the weather was getting dirty. Winds from the southwest were sending whitecaps all the way into the inner harbor, and the rain came lashing down in sudden squalls. If the wind grew just a little stronger, Rolland was thinking, the tug, after a little turn in the English Channel, would not fail to take them back to where they started from and let them wait there for better days. Boredom would then complete the dissolution of this already rusted-out crew. Rolland would have preferred a hundred times over to pick up the men as they came off the little freighter which would bring them from France, or else to collect them as they stepped off the English train. This had happened to him before.

But one day, on an earlier voyage, as the ship left North Shields, the boys who had gone aloft above the to'gants'ls had vomited thick red wine all over the place; and at the same time one of them, too sick to work, had thrown up green bile in the crew's quarters. This was surprising. But the bos'n had explained it:

"It's nothing to be astonished at: that fathead, he drank the whole bottle of disinfectant he found in the train toilet. He might kill himself, the boob!"

The fellow had gone up the rigging with the others next morning, however, well purged of his creosote.

There had not even been the solace of these fantastic intoxications for the men of the *Antonine*. They had neither wine to drown their

162

viscera nor danger to tauten them; they were as if becalmed too close to land. They scarcely knew where they were going, and they did not much care. To Thio on orders, a hole in New Caledonia where they were to load up with nickel. So far as their drudgery and suffering were concerned, it was not much different from Chile and its nitrate. The Cape of Good Hope is not so cold as Cape Horn, but it is often just as difficult. And then, in the Coral Sea they would have to tack about, till they were fair worn out with tacking, between the coconut-palm islands.

As for the land that would be opening out before them at the end of the voyage—they would be able to salute it from a distance. Unless the ship were dashed to pieces on it, they would not go ashore. The places where they did set foot, moreover, scarcely differed from one another in anything but the name of the liquor they drank in each, which soon blurred them all in the same mist. A few minutes of curiosity as they jumped on the dock, as they hauled off into the first street. . . . But that was quickly extinguished. It is something that demands a regular training, to keep looking for hours and hours, without blinking, at everything you come across: you have to have an education, to be surprised at things. . . .

As Rolland passed the sailors on the deck, this streaming morning, he was asking himself if he had really succeeded, since leaving the Hydrographic Institute, in separating himself from them. What enrichment had he gleaned from his five years as an officer? The taste for command, certainly, and the habit of it. But if one set aside this profession of leader which he had learned, how did he differ at the present moment from what he had been as topman on the *Galatée*? Walking the deck of the *Antonine,* in the rain, he was counting up his memories, his joys; and he was surprised to find himself so poor in them. He was jumping from Europe to the Americas to gather them up, and what was he discovering? Nothing but prostitutes, as before. Not altogether the same, in appearance: better housed, smarter, with a better line of talk; the top of the basket among sailors' trollops; but when one bit into them they had the same taste as their predecessors. As soon as he had discovered that, he had kept them pitilessly subjugated to their task, without allowing himself to be imposed upon, and he used brutally to knock over the fragile stage setting in which some of them tried to hold him.

Captain Thirard, bundled in his red muffler, loomed up on the poop at the precise instant when the tow-line was tautening, in the first slight surge of getting under way.

In those days of the sailing-ships every captain would thus be standing erect at his post, at this moment which might well be called solemn, as if to lead the parade. They all felt that the chief must vouch for himself before the spectators who were standing on the wharfs or the breakwater. Thirard was not failing in this duty, any more than anyone else; and this obviously meant that in spite of his swollen throat he did not intend to surrender any of his functions. On the whole, Rolland was satisfied with that. He would not have liked a poop where the captain wished to command, without being able to, and where the mate commanded without the right to do so.

Seeing his commanding officer for the first time in broad daylight, he was struck by the emaciation of his face. He was isolated from everything, it seemed—the sea, the ship, the men—as in a kind of prayer. The unmoving gaze fixed on the horizon was stamped with a painful assuagement. They were leaving, and, for the moment, this was the only thing that counted for Captain Thirard.

Then Rolland caught sight of his bony hand which, as they went through the locks, was indicating the movements of the wheel for the helmsman. At this instant, the men up forward in the bow began to sing, a raucous and bawling song, absolutely incongruous under this pallid sky, on this gray choppy water. Rolland had no hesitation as to what this music meant; he joined the captain and suggested, "When we have loosed the tug-line, or even before, I will go and do some digging about in the crew's quarters. They have certainly brought several bottles aboard."

The captain beckoned him to come up close to his lips.

"The owner's name on each bottle," he specified. "If any of them protest, throw their bottles overboard."

The order was fair and comprehensive. Rolland made a note of it.

"See to it that everything is ready to cast off the tow-line, quickly."

The captain whispered the words and vanished, driven from the poop by that dreadful sound of a choked-up air duct which the humid atmosphere was causing in his throat with every breath. For Rolland realized at once that if he was not taking advantage of the brief leisure of the towing, as other captains did, to speak a little of something beside the ship's duties, it was not at all from severity or brusqueness but because every word was an effort, and he had to confine himself to essentials.

It was obviously his intention to get rid of the tug very quickly. All captains are sparing of towing, and Thirard could not have had a happy recollection of the tug that had run him aground. But Rolland suspected that he wanted to be speedily dependent upon himself alone, without running the risk of being led by the nose into a port if the weather turned bad. As a matter of fact, the tugmasters

164

are pleased enough to get people out of harm's way when things begin to look dirty; they are paid accordingly. The chances were now that the *Antonine*, once she was free of the tug, would not head back toward Port Talbot, whatever the state of the sea might be.

The first mate was feeling the increasing unpleasantness of the weather. "Rain is rain; wind is wind; but rain and wind, that's nasty weather," sailors say. So far, there was only rain; but it was already so stinging that one could be sure that the wind was not far away. The captain had instructed Rolland to see that everything was ready for the canvas to be run up in short order. The mate went down to the deck, therefore, and was surprised to find the halyards already cleared to be brought to the capstan, and the pressure up in the little steam boiler for hauling. Someone had got ahead of him. Berteux whose watch it was? He was astonished at that.

He went on toward the bow and found Kréven busy making a boat more secure. He called him.

"Get the men together, and bring them to the quarters."

He went to the fo'c'sle ahead of them. A few moments later, the first sailors came in, their eyes suspicious, lined up along the tiers of bunks, and stood watching him.

"You have brought brandy aboard, in spite of the rule against it," he said. "Will whoever has it bring it out?"

Not one of them budged. Rolland waited the proper length of time, then ordered: "Open your chests!"

They obeyed with an unhoped-for docility. As dexterously as a customs inspector, without disturbing anything, he felt through and around the layers of clothing and underwear; but nowhere did he encounter the rounded resistance of a bottle. When he got up, after exploring the last chest, they were all looking at him with mockery in their eyes. The ones in the back row were even lowering their heads so as to hide their laughter behind the backs of their comrades. Rolland did not appear to notice this, and now turned up the straw ticks, one by one, first at the foot and then at the head of the bunks. There was still nothing, though that was a classic hiding-place. In the first row, unmoving and indecipherable, Kréven was following him with his eyes; and the mate was at once sure that the bos'n knew where the brandy was hidden. There was no question of asking him for information. He had to find this liquor himself; but he had already spent too much time looking for it in the crew's presence.

"Bos'n, take the men back to work," he said.

He himself strolled off to the farther end of the quarters, his hands in his pockets, waiting until they had gone. And suddenly the raillery died out of their eyes. So he wasn't giving up after this mortification? Some of them turned around, before they went out of the door, to throw an alarmed glance at him: heaven send he doesn't find it!

He did find it, after an examination that lasted two minutes. A plank of the lowest bunk had been taken up, and in the sort of box formed by the bottom of the bunk and the deck planking, full-sized bottles wrapped in rags turned over under his fingers as soon as he stuck his arm inside: eight bottles of brandy, three of liqueurs. He drew them out one by one, laid them in a row on one of the straw mattresses, and called Kréven back.

"Have all this taken to the lazaretto," he said. "If they had handed it over themselves, I should have had the owner's name put on each bottle. They didn't do that; and I am going to put all the bottles in safekeeping until there is a new order."

Kréven, without a word, turned around to call two sailors.

The four double strokes of the helmsman's bell announced the hour of noon. Rolland saw the men approach the galley to get their rations, very much excited but falling silent when he looked at them. Then he hurried through his own luncheon in the wardroom, sitting opposite Berteux, who was worrying about the weather.

"We'll get a sou'sou'wester' before evening," he said. "And in the Bristol Channel that has meant a bad time for more than one ship."

Rolland's silence bespoke awareness of this.

When he came out again on the poop, he caught a glimpse, through the close latticework of the rain, of two steamships coming in, grinding hard at the waves. Then the silhouette of a tall gray bit of land appeared off the port bow, was blotted out, showed again above the water: Lundy Island, a big dirty-looking pile of rock thrown down right in the middle of the Bristol Channel, as if on purpose to hold up half the ships that came through. The tug had hardly passed it when the captain came outside.

As on the first time he had seen him, Rolland remained nonplussed, for a few seconds, by this mute, almost spectral, apparition: the tall emaciated body, at the end of which the face, muffled up as if in a sack, made a long splash of pallor. Captain Thirard threw the mate a glance that commanded attention, and then, with his two fists brought together and abruptly separated, he made a gesture of breaking loose: the command to cast off the tow-line and run up the sails.

Rolland called out the ritual orders. The jibs, first, were unfurled, smacking; and as soon as the tugmaster caught sight of them he came to starboard to let them fill.

166

"Haul the lower tops'ls taut. Hoist the upper tops'ls."

It was no longer—as it had been on the *Galatée*—the strenuous effort of the men's backs that clothed the *Antonine* in its canvas. The heavy sails would go up by themselves, in a few seconds, thanks to the steam-powered windlass; and, suddenly distended, they would strike the masts with a rude thrust of the yoke, like a powerful Percheron pulling at its burden.

Which ones should be unfurled, in this weather that was still moderate, but more and more threatening? Rolland threw a glance at the captain and thought he understood, from his immobility, that he would tell his new first mate nothing, either by word or gesture. His body stiff, his two hands clinging to the compass binnacle, the man must be holding himself erect only by an intense effort of will, and he was guarding like a miser what he had left of strength. Turning toward him when the upper tops'ls were up, however, the mate encountered a fiery look bent upon the to'gants'ls. He translated, and turned back to the deck.

"Let out the fore topgallant."

The tug was already lying off to starboard, like something useless and soon to be left behind. The sails were going up everywhere. The vessel, already heavily slanted, was tossing in the swell, opening out broad fan-shapes of water at her bow. Once again, Rolland turned toward the captain. He saw him lift his head again and, with his eyes, indicate the upper to'gants'ls that were still furled.

He was going it strong, this sick man! All sails set, except the royals, in this weather! But on the poop the burning eyes were fastened upon his, and then lifted, peremptorily, toward the upper sails that were to be set. And Rolland called out, "Unfurl the upper to'gants'ls, everywhere!"

On the deck, the men hesitated for a second. Berteux, nervous, was twisting his head around, looking for someone to whom he could say, "He's crazy!" Poullain had his mouth open, as if the order he was trying to swallow would not go down. Rolland took one step and called out to the men:

"You heard me? You'll be sorry if I have to repeat it!"

They went up the rigging. When the to'gants'ls were all in place the *Antonine* listed still farther. She was attacking the waves on the bias, scissors fashion. But this scissors, with all sails set, could slip and lurch dangerously. The helmsman needed all the strength in his arms to hold back the headstrong vessel, and keep her from going head on into the heavy wind.

When the watch came down from the yards, a man gave Rolland a look and hummed, in English:

167

"When the rain's before the wind,
Then your tops you must mind."

Rolland recognized the proverb: "If the rain precedes the wind, watch out for the halyards!" The advice was appropriate to the occasion, but the man had sung it softly, as if to himself, so there was nothing to be said. He must have learned it on an American sailing-ship, after getting himself shanghaied. A "black-ball," probably; but it was not at all displeasing to Rolland to come across one or two of those on a ship's deck. He spoke to the man.

"What is your name?"

"Caroff, sir."

Rolland nodded to show that this registered. Then he gave his attention again to the *Antonine*.

She was running along impetuously, with a tilt like a yacht in a race. Such speed was, and could only be, a fragile achievement of balance. It would perhaps last for a certain length of time on condition that the wind remained as it was now: very strong, but steady. If a sudden gust should come along, they would roll gunnel under. There must also be a man at the wheel who was able to steer, as he must, without the deviation of a hair's breadth. Rolland cast a glance at the helmsman. Beside him, so close they could touch him, he saw two long pale hands moving, seeming to turn an invisible wheel, and the man at the helm was following these indications, every muscle tense. Captain Thirard was standing guard over the course.

Like all those captains who were "speeders," he was gambling on the steadiness of the wind and intended to take advantage of it to the last minute, so as to make good progress and get into the open sea as soon as possible. These workings of ship could only be judged by the result. Could he manage to anticipate and prepare for a sudden shift to the northwest, if that should occur? There was the point, actually a point in space and time, which he must seize hold of. It was not the risk that was troubling Rolland, but the man who was taking it, and of whom he as yet knew nothing.

A gesture from the captain summoned him. When he was by his side, Thirard raised two fingers and pointed to the wheel: it would need two men to hold it. Rolland signaled to an extra man.

At five in the afternoon, when the rain was slackening and the wind seemed to be abating slightly, Captain Thirard made another gesture, a gesture like X-ing out a word: Lower and furl some of the canvas. Rolland immediately gave the order: "Haul down the flying jib and the stays'ls. Upper to'gants'ls on the downhaul."

The men toiled laboriously to take in and furl the sails that were

168

heavy with rain. They were grumbling at the order that had come too late, when the wind was rudely disputing their control of the canvas. Rolland thought that the captain was yielding to the approach of darkness. If he had committed himself as the Old Man had done, he would have stuck it out longer, for nothing in the look of the weather seemed to warrant these sudden precautions. But the men had scarcely come down from the yards when the same sharp gesture of the thin hand sent them back again, to furl the lower to'gants'ls. Then Captain Thirard had them fit the robins, again, on the mainsail abaft. Only then did he beckon to Rolland, and whisper in his ear, "Go get your dinner."

The countenance which Rolland had just caught a glimpse of, lighted from below by the glimmer of the binnacle lamp, was so ravaged that he murmured, his own voice very low, "But you, Captain—"

Without replying, the captain seized his arm and pushed him toward the companionway, a gesture which Rolland would never have endured from anyone else, but which he gave in to now because it was the only language possible to his chief.

In the cabin, an abrupt pitch of the ship toward the port side upset his scalding soup on his knees. But before he had reached the poop the *Antonine* had righted herself. The man up there, who had foreseen the southwest blast that was now hitting them, had borne away in time.

Six days, six nights, of tacking back and forth, in bad weather, in that accursed Bristol Channel, without succeeding in passing the Scilly Islands on one side, Cape Clear on the other! Workings and workings: and I clew you, and I furl you, and I hoist you again! Tacking about, ten times a day, and doing it with a fresh wind astern, which was longer and harder. Boots galloping from one end of the deck to the other, and yells, "Look out for your legs!" It was the first and second mate calling that out to you, when they let go the braces, line as thick as a man's fist, that would unwind and spin out, lashing at you like the thong of a whip. If you let yourself be caught by it, you were in danger of being swung over the side, at least, or coming off with a broken leg. And you would hardly have skipped over that when the officers would be in your hair again:

"Heave, heave; hand over hand; heave, heave! Go to it, go to it; haul in the slack! Keep at it, keep at it! Don't slow down! Heave, heave!"

They flogged you with cries, like whipping horses, to drag out all the speed your guts could give. You unwind until you don't recognize your hands any more, or you heave until your skin is like to split. And when it is finished, that tack, when the ship has altered course and is gathering headway, that new first mate looks at his watch:

"Twenty-five minutes! Movements of a tortoise! I call that tacking in the style of the Grand Banks!"

The style of the Grand Banks! It was all very well for him, wasn't it, to treat them like codfish shovelers and give himself the airs of a frigatoon! As if it were possible for thirty poor beggars to go any faster in turning a hand-cart two hundred and seventy feet long!

Two or three times during each night watch, the two watch crews would be called back to work. As they went out of their well-closed quarters, where the swaying glimmer of the lamp touched men and things, leaving out nothing, the men would hold back for a moment before the darkness, and the spindrift that sprang at their faces. Then Kréven would push them toward the shower-bath that awaited them on the fore-and-aft gangway; and much worse than a shower-bath! Water to their knees, to start with, water that was moving, sliding back and forth from one side to the other, and that at once tried to sweep them off their feet and over the gunnel rail. They would catch at a clew line. Without seeing it, they would know it was what they were after, and they would begin to pull as if they were under a waterfall, so many heavy seas would be streaming down their backs.

"Attention!" the mate, who was watching out for the swell, called to them.

Before looking out for themselves, they had to think of the rigging lines, that had already been gathered in and must not be lost; everything was made fast. Then they caught hold of whatever was at hand: a stay of the shrouds, a bulwark timberhead; they hugged a windlass; they crooked their legs around the foot of a pin rail. There was no really good place! First you would feel as if you were lifted up very high; then the ship would drop over to the port side, just under the swell that struck it, at the foot of the wall of water that broke and crashed against the deck. You would be crushed under its savage and icy assault. Then there would be the mass of water dashing up from the stern, with the rip and roar of thunderbolts when it broke against the bulwarks of the deck-houses. The roller would go over you, send you sprawling with your ribs bent, scrape your face on the deck planking, its attack ending only when the wave finally collapsed and gushed up in fountains of spray against the fo'c'sle rail.

That was the first chance you would have, after easing yourself up a little, to swallow a mouthful of air, outside that seething water with which your chest, like a bucket, was filled. So you would recover a little strength, to knot your arms and legs more firmly around some fixed point.

For the old tub now rolled the other way again, the *Antonine* dropped off to starboard. All the water surged back, rushed over the rail, sometimes a full yard above it. This was no longer the steam-roller crushing you, but a dizzy pouring out from an open chute along the whole length of a man's body: over his back, under his belly, a suction at every finger to pry it loose. This, again, only ceased when the ship heeled over heavily to the port side. It was the turn of the others, over there, to be drenched now.

Lungs half emptied, they got up again, coughing, spitting, blowing their smarting noses between two fingers.

"Come on! Bouse the weather clews!"

Groping their way through the water, they found their tangled clew lines straightened them out, began to heave again.

"Aloft! Furl!"

They vanished one by one into the shrouds, even to the last one's boots. Rolland, at the foot of the mast, waited without seeing anything but with his head raised, for the time it would take for them to scatter over the yards and to begin getting hold of the wet canvas. Then he called out into the black downpour raining into his eyes, "Try not to grow moss, up there!"

From the pitch-dark sky a furious voice descended upon him. "Go to hell!"

He smiled. He had only been trying to wake them up. They were awake!

Almost at once, he had to repress a start; on his arm was the lean and feverish grasp which he had not forgotten since the day it had driven him from the poop to get his dinner, and in his ear was the murmur of a command:

"A drop of brandy for the men. . . ."

The words had scarcely been whispered when the tall shadow was lost in the darkness of the deck.

So the captain had come there tonight, into the icy water that washed the fore-and-aft gangway. He had not left the poop, so to speak, since the bad weather set in. Every time Rolland had taken the watch he had found him there, standing beside the helmsman, or transmitting his orders by signs. A closed fist meant, "Bouse the clew lines." When he struck his side, he was saying, "Bouse the buntlines."

In measure with the passing of the days, the men were becoming more outspokenly indignant at his sending them back and forth like this across the Channel, the ship's nose sometimes all but touching the red roofs of the English cottages at the moment of changing the course. He was wearing them out by trying to force the passage, attempting to clear the channel on a contrary wind, losing in one tack what he had just gained in two.

"Let him go stew in his cabin, and let us heave to, good God!"

Caroff, who boasted of having a sharp eye, would sometimes fix an appraising look upon him when he was leaning on the side-rail of the poop, his back bent, his arms flexed.

"Don't worry," the sailor would say. "He's no great shakes any more. Pretty soon they'll truss him up, and the sooner the better!"

In their hearts they were troubled above all, and made uncomfortable, by being commanded by a sick man. Ashore, they used to like to boast about their captains: "A bang-up guy! A fellow that's not afraid of anything!" For they themselves would bask in the glory of their skippers: even, and especially, if the captain was hard and heartless; to them he would be "the worst damn son-of-a-bitch," and they would boast of that, too. It was just as much an honor to have stuck it out with a man who was feared and dreaded as it was to have weathered a cyclone! But a man who was helpless, who could not speak, who was always choking, a captain of gargles and soothing potions—that was something to make fools of them!

In the long run, however, he had won from them the beginning of an irritated respect, just because they had never seen him separated from the poop in all this rotten weather. He wasn't trying to steal his pennies, he was sticking to his trade, which, naturally, was to possess you down to the marrow of your bones. But, exasperated by the fatigue of the incessant workings and their repeated failures—since all they were doing was going back and forth in the same furrow—they had concluded:

"He is making us foam at the mouth to revenge himself for foaming at the mouth himself."

Rolland was not very far from the same thought. He believed the captain to be moved by that oversensitive vanity of the sick, who cling to their old place for fear of being no longer reckoned among the living. His assumption was, "He must want to show them that he is still able to get the best of them."

During these days of bad weather he was concentrating also on the thoughtful observation of those who would remain in the race with him until the end: the officers and the men. This was too good an opportunity to be missed, this chance of seeing them bared to the soul by the terribly hard time they were having. In studying them, he forgot his own harassment.

About Berteux, he had not had to change his opinion: a barking dog, who always demanded more than was due him so that he might get just about what was absolutely necessary. The more open to argument an order might seem, the more harshly—naturally—he would require its execution. On two occasions Rolland had had to back him up when he had routed the men out of the sorry corners where they were getting their breath, to send them back, then and there, on work which could have waited. He could not help hearing Kréven say, on one of these occasions, as he went off at the head of his rebellious watch: "They don't know their trade, they have to learn it. You are paying for their apprenticeship. So much the worse if you break under it."

Since then, the bos'n had enveloped the second-in-command in the same reprobation which he manifested toward the junior officer. He had adopted, in regard to the mate, the attitude of icy contempt, the mechanical obedience, which Rolland recognized from having practiced it so long with Arlozzi. To him, he thought, I am failing in my duty of consideration for the overworked men. In taking Berteux's order on my shoulders, I become responsible for something odious and senseless. I must find out whether this Kréven is capable of seeing farther than that. It will be well worth the trouble."

If Berteux had shown himself, in the general drenching, as just what Rolland had first judged him to be, Poullain, the third mate, had happily surprised him in the course of this test of strength: a man to carry out orders, but indefatigable in that, and a man whose high spirits, no matter how much cold water was thrown on them, had persisted beyond any expected norm. Rolland had seen him get a wry smile out of the men, at the moment of their worst efforts, by a bit of banter that had the right punch and was yelled at them in the right tone. Every man has his own manner; and Poullain's, far as it was from his own, had pleased him. Then, too, he was never sparing of his Herculean strength; he was the first to haul on a halyard, to bouse a buntline, and in such a way that the men had to work their hardest to keep up with him. Rolland had registered his appreciation of all this only in a change of tone by which his subordinate had seemed, the first time, to be much impressed; it had stamped his face with a contentment which all the hard hours since had not been able to efface.

After the officers, the men. . . .

Rolland was obliged to admit that the man who selected them must have sorted them out one by one, carefully, not accepting the lot wholesale as handed out by the trader in men ("The best seamen on the place, I can tell you, Captain. . . ."). Yes, Thirard must have wrapped himself up in his red muffler and gone into the depths of some café to scrutinize their faces and their certificates. For each of them he would have brought out his hoarse queries: "Do you know how to sew sails? Are you a good helmsman?" And that would be not so much to listen to the answers, which would be, as expected, always in the affirmative, as to note the tone—correct or not, forced or hesitant—and to spy out the features, the look in the eyes.

The result seemed to be a crew of grumblers, muttering, snarling, working in a constant hum of scolding, like honey bees: a crew which a Berteux must at once rub up the wrong way. But the more tired they got, the more they would roar and grumble. That was a sign, and a good one! When the steam seeps out at the joints, the pressure is holding. Rolland did not worry about them until the sixth day, when, really exhausted, they fell silent.

Kréven, and Kréven's fists and Kréven's boots, had then to come into the picture, though without the first mate's seeming to notice it. There had been discrimination and discernment in the business, though. The bos'n had kicked back to work, rather harshly, two or three surly fellows whose slack arms Rolland had noticed as they came up at the tail-end of the line.

At last, on the seventh day, about one o'clock in the morning, the wind, very fresh, shifted clear around to the northwest. It was high time; the men were worn out. Rolland himself felt as if he had turned to lead and cotton batting. Now he had the upper to'gants'ls run up again. The ship, nose to the south and on the starboard tack, charged straight ahead in the darkness.

Feeling her vibrate under his feet, and run freely, Rolland, whose eyes were close in a nervous relaxation as complete as an ebb-tide, had the impression that he himself had just stepped aside, and that the *Antonine,* come to life again, was going ahead on her own. She had discovered once more the joy of speed and the taste for the open sea. He gave himself a shake, and said to Poullain, "It's going to be living again, after all!"

The junior officer, not understanding, still agreed.

"It certainly hasn't been any sort of a life this past week," he said.

XVI

TOWARD the end of the morning they passed the Sorlingues, a group of one hundred and forty-five islets, English, spread out in advance-guard formation to the southwest of Land's End. They were getting "dechanneled" now, and they were not sorry; for the English Channel, whether going or coming, is rarely pleasant.

After the storms of the last few days, the sea was suddenly full of inhabitants. Around the *Antonine* there was an incessant square dance, so to speak, of steamboats and of sailing-ships of every known rig; and the men, who knew that the solitude of the open sea was lying in wait for them, were never tired of watching the scene.

Poullain kept busy at the bow. Rolland stayed on the poop, where the captain had not appeared again since the wind had come to terms with them. With the new speed of the ship the mate, unwearying, was tasting that complete relaxation, that abandonment of body and mind, which was brought to him by the vessel's easy gliding motion and the level murmur of the breeze upon his ears. It was a voluptuousness of the sea, which he had always sensed slowly and deliberately, this understanding between the ship and the winds and the waters. Yet at the same time, his whole mind was watching over the *Antonine's* progress, studying the ship's qualities in free-running action. She had a broad roll, but "big roll, good gait"; and the stem was boring into the water with a round and ample movement that was eating up the miles.

The bell on the fo'c'sle sounded three strokes, and the man in the bow called out, "Ship right ahead!"

She was a steamship, on the same course as themselves. They could soon make out her red funnel with a black band around the top.

"A Transat* cargo-and-passenger ship," Rolland announced.

The men on the deck had also recognized her. Rolland, meanwhile, was seeing the stern of the steamer growing gradually taller and broader. It became evident that the *Antonine* was gaining on her. And he was swept by something like a wave of desire.

"We've got to get the best of her!" he cried.

The helmsman, a man named Perrot, from Douarnenez, a good fellow, placid, round all over, with shiny cheeks, looked at him in astonishment: he was surprised that this officer should want to race, as the lively and jovial officers did who never let an occasion slip for a bit of fun, or as the mean ones did, who liked to humiliate a colleague. He had not yet placed the new first mate in either of those categories.

But already Rolland was ordering: "Hoist home the to'gants'ls, the royals!"

The upper sails, somewhat slackened in the ship's sailing pace, were at once hoisted chuck up again and were ready to pull their hardest.

"Ease off the sheets a little on the mains'ls and the fores'ls."

---

* "Transat" is the popular shortening of *Compagnie Générale Transatlantique,* the French Line. Tr.

The men let the lines run out, and the major sails turned almost imperceptibly to take in more breeze. Then, having carried out these movements with a sporting rapidity, the entire crew betook itself to the windward rail, to enjoy the race. Even the cook had deserted his ovens; his broad white back made a rounded splotch among the dark backs of the attentive sailors.

Rolland was experiencing that powerful simplification of the short-distance race—the sprint—in which the entire being seems reduced to a single line: the line that is growing shorter between oneself and the man ahead. At such a moment the first thing to disappear is the sense of speed; for eye and mind are no longer measuring anything except the difference between two swiftnesses— that is, a slowness. No matter how fast the *Antonine* coursed along, listing far on its side and vibrating with the swelling of her sails, Rolland felt only the endlessness of the time it took to swallow up the distance between the stern of the steamship and his own ship's bow.

The liner had just run up the French colors, and she really seemed to be forcing its steam. The men on the sailing-ship's deck had already noticed that.

"Our brother's speeding as fast as he can!" they cried.

For a brief period the distance between the two ships remained the same. Then the breeze freshened further and the *Antonine* began to gain, hand's breadth by hand's breadth, in the men's impassioned immobility. At last the darting stem of the big four-master came in line with the steamer's taffrail.

She passed it slowly, slowly, then gained more and more, and the sailing-ship's poop came up abreast of the steamship's bridge. Rolland saw the commander standing there, a good sportsman, who was the first to salute him, his hand to his gold-braided cap. He obviously took Rolland for the captain of the *Antonine*. At the same moment, the flags of the two vessels were each dipped three times.

"Hip, hip, hurrah!"

The conquerors, on the deck of the *Antonine,* saluted also, repeating the shout three times. Then, the exchange of courtesies being concluded, the joking broke out. They were taking advantage, while they could, of being still within shouting range.

"Do you want a tow-line?" called Neveu, a lad from Paris, making a derisive feint of sending a coil of line over the bulwark.

"Don't push your tub too hard," shouted someone else. "Coal is expensive!"

The good old jibs were flying over the rail toward the steamship when the sailors from the southern ocean caught sight of some women on the deck of the vanquished ship, looking at them and smiling; and they all fell silent, at once.

Suddenly a strong voice rose from the *Antonine,* a voice which the liquor of a hundred ports had not been able to make husky, nor all the northern mists to blur. Caroff, the "black-ball," who had sailed under every flag on every sea, had sprung up on the rail, and holding to one of the shrouds with one hand, he was addressing to the steamship's passengers his rendering of the famous sea chantey of the great American sailing-ships:

> *"Sailing, sailing, over the bounding main,*
> *Full many a stormy wind shall blow,*
> *Ere Jack comes home again. . . ."*

"Sailing, sailing," repeated the *Antonine's* crew, in chorus, enraptured by the sight of the handkerchiefs now waving wildly toward them all up and down the defeated liner.

It was at this moment, the pride of which Rolland was savoring as he stood in the commander's place, that a hairy black monster bounded up the companionway to the poop. Sultan, the captain's dog, circled the poop in three leaps, and disdaining to bark at the steamship dragging behind, turned on the mate, teeth bared. Thirard used to let him loose, like this, two or three times a day, and the animal would bolt out into the open air and gallop at top speed from one end of the ship to the other, all his instinct for space unleashed. But very soon he would subside anew under the poop, to go and scratch whining at the sick man's door and be shut up once more with him. In these frenzied excursions he would not recognize anyone, or allow himself to be held up by the men who were vaguely moved by his self-abnegation. He seemed to want to get his fill of the pure air as quickly as possible, and to relax his muscles to the utmost, so as to cut short the moments which he must steal from his companion.

This morning, however, instead of those full-speed dashes between stern and bow, the dog planted himself, open-jawed, one step away from Rolland, and stayed there for several moments; then he sprang forward and fastened his teeth in the mate's boot. Rolland had to steady himself against the binnacle to keep from staggering; then, with a thrust of his heel full in the animal's ribs, he made him let go, and flung him against the base of the wheel. The dog got up without so much as a yelp, but he looked the mate full in the face for an instant before he turned around to make his way heavily toward the companionway.

"But whatever has come over him?"

Rolland had asked the question aloud, without really meaning it. Like all men of the sea, he understood animals; and this one had just been treating him like a thief. In his own village he had seen farm dogs springing at the legs of tramps, just like this, when they pushed at the gate. . . .

The helmsman answered, merely: "It's because he is kept shut up. He'll end by going mad, maybe!"

The dog had gone down the companionway, meanwhile, and was coming out on the deck when Rolland heard someone calling, "Sultan!"

Kréven, at the foot of the poop-deck rail and under the very eyes of the mate, was walking toward the animal, who was waiting for him uncertainly and looking from time to time toward the open door. The bos'n grasped him by the collar and, crouching down beside him, stroked his head for a long time, while with the other hand he massaged the side that had been bruised by Rolland's boot.

"You're a good dog," he said. "You're doing your job. . . ."

As he got up, after letting Sultan go, he underscored his defiance by a brief glance at the officer.

The next morning, as he went off watch—a watch which had been liberally pelted with cold rain—and while the members of the port crew, drenched, were making their way toward their quarters, Rolland called Kréven, who was going to the deck-house.

"Look here, bos'n, I should like to have a word with you. Will you come with me to my cabin?"

"Very well, sir."

"Now," Rolland said, when they had entered the narrow stateroom, "we are on the right course, and I hope we are soon going to catch up with good weather. . . ."

As he spoke, he had lighted a little alcohol lamp and set a pan of milk to heat, with rum added. It was the drink he liked best when he was wet through and through, as he was this morning.

"For several days," he continued, "we have been slaving together, under rather bad conditions. We have rolled along the fore-and-aft gangway together, and we have struggled together to haul ourselves out, as best we could, of that damn hole they call the Bristol Channel. I think, then, I can say that we know each other."

The milk was commencing to boil. He poured it out and handed a glass to Kréven.

"What I have seen of you during these days persuades me to put a question to you," he went on. "But it is as man to man, forgetting for the moment that I am your superior. I know that you are very much attached to Captain Thirard. Do you believe me capable of profiting by circumstances to take his place, instead of helping him to keep it?"

Kréven took time to empty his glass, so that he might set it down and answer correctly, looking Rolland straight in the face.

"I did believe that, sir, but I do not believe it any longer," he said.

"Good. Then from now on I count on you, as you can count on me."

"Very well, sir," Kréven replied.

Then he saluted with a little movement of his head, and went out.

And in fact it was very well.

They were getting down toward the zone of good weather, but they still ran athwart some bad days now and then. Off the Gulf of Gascony they met more squalls. Then the wind veered forward, and steady rain settled in. It was as they were passing Cape Finisterre that the wind and the sea became pleasant again. And, at once, the married men had to submit to the joking that was a convention of every voyage when the sky cleared. Already, when they had declared their status in the crew's quarters on sailing, their bachelor pals had cried out:

"You married? That's all to the good. We'll have a fine wind. A ship can't have too many cuckolds."

And now Caroff was going for Brisville, a big fellow from Normandy who was as placid as a pasture field.

"To give us winds like these, it's sure and certain that at this very moment your Jeanine is having her feet kept warm by the customs man at the dock. . . ."

But Brisville had his retort ready: "A customs man? Oh, but I'm not afraid of them. They soldier on the job too much."

These good-weather phrases, picked up in passing, were just about all that Rolland now had to give him knowledge of the crew. Kréven, from the moment of leaving "his" mate's cabin, had taken on the job of intermediary between him and the men.

"You can set your mind at rest, sir," he had promised, when the next watch came on duty. "I will see that everything goes on like in a family."

And in fact, if an "incident" did occur it never got past the rail that separated the deck from the poop. The bos'n would settle the affair. Sometimes it would even settle itself.

One Sunday, when the ship was whipping along at eleven knots off Gibraltar, the men were busy hanging out their underclothes on the girtline, or were smoking their pipes and talking lazily, sitting on the raft. Rolland was walking up and down the "main street," and as he passed them he could hear scraps of conversation so simple that it seemed to him that the men must be resting even their minds.

"Holy Moses, but Charles is strong! He carried a cask of red lead up from the storeroom, all by himself!"

"Marius is strong, too—and he's a smart bastard."

"Yes, but he's a stinker."

"And how! Just go talk to Domino about him!"

"Charles—now he's a grand guy."

The bell struck for mealtime, and cut short this litany.

Rolland suspected that there were on the *Antonine*, as on all ships, one or more of those much-dreaded characters who tyrannize over the other men, making themselves bosses over the fo'c'sle that groans under the weight of their insulting domination. They are not always the heftiest fellows. Their prestige comes most often from fear of the injuries they are capable of inflicting when they have a chance. An officer does not find out at once who they are, and nobody gives them away.

Now, Rolland had learned the name of this petty despot on the *Antonine:* Marius Fourcade, a member of the port watch, a "moko" * from Toulon, twenty-seven years old, with biceps but with a face full of hatred, whose muscular and cruelly modeled spareness accounted for much of the fear that he inspired. These Bretons, Normans, Flemings, with their full, open faces, were instinctively distrustful of narrow and sharp-featured visages. A mediocre seaman, Fourcade was nevertheless capable of half-killing himself out of mere swank; but he usually left the hard work to the others, the serfs.

It was in connection with the footrope of the main tops'l astern, that he had had the run-in with Domino, whose name was Pierre Lomineau, a peaceable-natured lad from the Vendée, topman on the same mast. Domino was sure that the stirrups of the footrope were too long. Marius was asserting the contrary. To bring the discussion to an end, the "moko" had made himself plain:

"You shut your mouth or I'll kick you off it."

Uttered at seventy-five feet above deck, to a man keeping his balance on a steel line, this was no empty menace! Domino said nothing more.

Émile, the novice, also kept quiet whenever Marius, seeing him in the quarters with his nose in a book, would call out, with a scorn that twisted his mouth awry, "This gentleman is joining the ink-lickers, so he'll learn how to steal rations and starve the good guys to death. Maybe we'd better squash it while we can."

* A slang term for a man of the Marseille neighborhood who is a bully but who at the same time is possessed of more cleverness and glibness of speech than our word "bully" generally connotes. Tr.

180

Everybody knew that Émile, the "beaver," a well-brought-up boy, shy and obliging, who buried himself in his books during his off-watch periods, was going straight into the hydrographic school when this voyage was over. Rolland also knew this, but he had not yet thought it fitting to talk about it with the future candidate for officer's training. Like Monnard before him, he judged that he must first have seen the boy at work, under circumstances in which he could take his exact measure. Marius, however, had not waited so long. He was beside himself when he saw a young "chief" being thus born and developed under his very eyes. Coming upon the lad bent over his book, he would often raise his clenched fist; but he refrained from hitting him, because Émile came from the same neighborhood as Big Charles, also on the port watch, the man who had, all by himself, carried a cask of red lead, hugged to his stomach, up from the hold.

The extraordinary dénouement occurred this very Sunday noon. The ration of salt pork was steaming on the table, and each of the sailors had sliced off his share. Only Marius, lagging in some corner of the ship, had not yet come in; and this obliged the novice to wait in contemplation of the piece of pork, without touching it. For the rule is categorical: a novice, a "beaver," has no right to go into the common dish until all the seamen have been served.

Émile was hungry, with the hunger of an eighteen-year-old, the hunger all boys feel at sea, where they devour their food like cannibals. Unable to stick it out any longer, he sliced off his hunk of meat. And just at that moment Marius entered the room.

His eye fell at once upon the novice, who had stopped dead, thunderstruck, his sizzling iron platter in his hand. He swooped down on the novice, roughly grabbed the plate from him, went out of the door again, and flung container and contents overboard.

"That will teach you manners, you future ration-robber!" he said.

The boy, who had always put up with everything without saying a word, yelped, the yelp of a famished dog whose bone is snatched away from him, and sprang at the sailor's throat.

Fourcade staggered under the unexpected shock. His feet struck the legs of the bench, and he tumbled to the floor, Émile still on him, riveted to him. Made ten times stronger by his rage, the ravenous youngster went on pounding him furiously, while the men surrounding the combatants, freed now from their own terror, shouted, "Go to it, Émile! Bash his face in, the dirty skunk! And let him tell us what's what afterward!"

The affair could not possibly end, as in a story, with the triumph of right over might. The "vanquished" was pulling himself together; a couple of ugly blows with his fist gave warning to the "conqueror," who hastened to get his bearings in flight, and ran straight into Rolland. In one breath, he told him what had happened.

"All right. Stay here. To begin with, you will change your mast."

For the novice was a topman on the jigger m'st, as was Marius.

In the fo'c'sle, meanwhile, the "moko" had got up; and as his immediate requirement was for someone to fall back on, he searched the circle of faces around him. But he saw only the faces of antagonists. He tried to brazen it out.

"I'll get hold of him again," he snarled. "In the meantime, if there are any of you who are backing him up, just say so."

"Shut your mouth," Domino flung back scornfully. "When a fellow is knocked down by a novice, he gets up and shuts up, see?"

Hard faces were watching him. There was not one of them who was not prepared to make him pay, and immediately, for the shame of their former capitulations. He sensed this, and with a shrug of his shoulders he went off to take cover at the other end of the quarters. That afternoon, Kréven beckoned to him.

"Orders from the mate," he said. "If any accident happens to the novice, you will be held responsible."

This was the value of good weather: the men could let themselves go and work out their difficulties by themselves. . . .

As for Bako, the pseudo-mutineer, he was always overflowing with zeal, especially since Rolland had entrusted him with the "barnyard" in addition to his work in the storeroom: the three pigs on which he turned the hose every morning, which he curried with a brushwood besom, and with which he conversed interminably.

To be sure, there was Berteux, always a discordant note and detested by his starboard watch. He was the little dark cloud on the horizon. Rolland had once said to him, "You talk too much, Berteux."

Since then, the sound of his voice was heard no more in the cabin. And on the poop he opened his mouth only when he had to. That, at least, was something gained; but it was accompanied by the bitterness of a man with a mania for authority, whom the reproof had wounded to the quick. Rolland was sure in advance that he would henceforth make a point of confining himself to his set duties, refraining from all initiative and keeping strictly to the letter in giving orders. In good weather that was of no importance; when the weather was bad, it could be arranged for Kréven to prop him up, if need be.

For it was becoming clearer every day to Rolland that Kréven was the real "master of the crew." * When a work-ship order was being

---

* "Crew master"—*maître d'équipage*—is the French bos'n's formal title. The men call him the *bosco*. Tr.

carried out at the change of the watch, the absence of the bos'n was immediately felt in the slackness of the men, who would haul on the line with reluctance and grunt like a whole pigpen. As a matter of fact, Kréven was not always at his post when a watch went on duty. He did not wake up until he was called, and those who were charged with this task did not much care about dragging him from his leaden sleep. For he was not at all gracious when he was wakened, and a punch in the jaw was more swiftly forthcoming than a thank you. When Rolland did not see him, on taking the watch, he never failed to send the cabin boy or the novice to call him. But they were forbidden to say anything to anyone else, and were ordered not to leave off their "Bos'n, Bos'n!" until they had seen Kréven standing up. From then on there was nothing to do but wait.

A few moments later, invariably, the gruntings on the deck would come to an abrupt stop. There would be an end, that is, to those complaints and accusations which are so universally tolerated that the men, joking, would claim to be giving up 5 per cent of their pay for the right to go on with them. . . . Then a muffled blow would be heard, and Kréven's voice: "There, you bunch of idiots, that will teach you to soldier on the job! Come on now, heave her up! And don't bawl! We've heard enough out of you!"

That was all it needed. On the instant, the watch would find its punch again.

When Rolland was on watch himself, in wind or rain, he literally had Kréven constantly at his feet, sitting on the grating of the wheel, on the leeward side, ready to jump to the required tasks when the order came. The mate congratulated himself on this devotion without being too much surprised by it. One has to be a landlubber not to know that intelligent rebels make the best chiefs at sea.

More to give evidence of his esteem than because he considered the thing possible and desirable, Rolland had asked him, "Have you never thought of becoming an officer?"

Kréven had shaken his head, with that smile which did no more than curl one corner of his lips.

"No," he had answered. "When I was young, I didn't much care for hanging around teachers and priests. And they are the only ones who can get you into the schools. You know that, sir."

Yes, Rolland knew that. The face of Father Monnard and old Rémy rose again before him. In other little holes along the coast there would be tall lads with numbed hands and hobnailed boots who, after years at sea, were going to the rectory, or to the schoolhouse after class, to try to get hold of a little spelling and mathematics. A Parisian would have regarded this as an edifying story, an example to be held up to youth. But whose fault was it if only elderly schoolmasters and parish priests were worrying themselves about the development of officers for the merchant marine? Rolland had known some damn pigheaded fellows, in the bunch of "candidates," who had been made docile by ambition. But to tame a Kréven! He had disdained the breaking-in which Rolland himself had accepted. And the mate could not help feeling a vague embarrassment before the bos'n, for having consented to domestication: a further proof that the common seaman was not altogether dead in him. . . .

"And then, I've gone through some pretty queer doors," Kréven had added. "I've been at some pretty queer trades, to get enough to eat. So, when I was able to, I swore to myself that I would only do what I liked doing, with people I liked working with. I want to choose. And that doesn't go with gold stripes either—not to mention that they'd get in my way, rather, ashore."

He had laughed again, at some of his memories.

"People you like?" Rolland had echoed. "The captain?"

"Yes, sir," Kréven had replied gravely. "This is my third voyage with him. It will be the last. He will not finish it. But he is the kind of man, and the kind of sailor, that I love."

"He will not finish it?" Rolland had echoed, again. "Come, now!"

Kréven made a gesture which meant, "You will see. . . ."

Rolland watched for the captain to come up, that day. Like any ordinary commander, Thirard used to make his appearance on the poop about seven in the morning, shake hands with the officer of the watch, with a movement of his lips in greeting, look at the log-book, check the course, and then go down to the deck and, like other captains, inspect the canvas. But Rolland had more than once had the impression that all this was as empty as the hull of an abandoned ship, that all these professional gestures were without real content. He felt an absent-mindedness, a lethargy, on the part of the vessel's master: this was a disconnected mechanism, one might say, turning in a void. At first he had thought, "Would he be drinking?" There were captains—and too many—who were tipplers. But, no, there was no sign of that: merely an accepted lassitude, an indifference which was laboriously pushed aside only to give the essential orders, especially in regard to the course.

On other days, it would be obvious that the captain was suffering. He would come to the poop with his face drawn, his eyes leaden from loss of sleep, his lip curled back in a grimace of pain. One might have thought he had had a prolonged beating. But these were the days when he stayed out the longest, when he walked the deck endlessly, up and down, his dog at his heels. And the men would mutter, "It's got him bad again. Walking must make it quieter."

For he was clearly seeking to wear down a throbbing pain, and the ship was nothing more to him than a space in which to stretch his legs. And yet, at the slightest respite that his throat would grant him, he would pause, look about him with eyes that had become piercing again, and make a beckoning gesture. Nine times out of ten, Kréven would have reached his side before the officer of the watch, to have the neglected piece of work attended to, that his hand was pointing out.

There were some days, finally, when he did not appear at all. His cabin would be closed to everyone except Kréven and the cabin boy. Rolland would then receive a note which gave the course and prescribed the work for the day. When Kréven came out of the cabin his face would be as indecipherable, and his general appearance as indifferent, as if he were coming out of the sail locker.

Rolland had no cause to take offense at these visits. Kréven had forestalled that.

"He trained me, himself, to take care of him, when he first got sick," he explained. "He feels easier with me, for nursing." And he added anxiously: "It isn't pretty: it's festering, and his neck is beginning to swell."

Tubercular laryngitis? Rolland had thought. Syphilis?

Now came a morning when Kréven knocked on Rolland's door after he left the captain.

"He has had a terrible night," he said. "He is still suffering the tortures of the damned. He is asking for you, sir."

It was the first time he had done that. Earlier, Thirard had made himself plain: "If I need you I will have you called. Unless there is an emergency, have the cabin boy let me know ahead if you wish to see me."

Emergency, that is a simple matter to determine. There is an emergency when the officer of the watch, at night, takes it upon himself to wake the skipper. Well, Rolland was not much of a man for waking captains, and with these easterly winds the watches were gliding by without incident.

When he entered the captain's cabin, now, his gaze went straight to the man in the bunk, who raised himself on one elbow to welcome him. Everything about him was new and dreadful: the shaggy thatch of gray hair with stray locks plastered together by sweat on his forehead; the bloodshot eyes; the face the color of yellow wax. Yes, it would have been a head of wax, such as Rolland had seen in exhibitions at country fairs, if it had not been for the terrible life of that distended throat, denuded now of the red muffler and seeming to hold the marks of a strangler's fingers hollowed out in the swelling.

185

Thirard jerked out three words of explanation: "An attack—long. . . ."

Before Rolland had found anything to say in answer, the captain had fallen back on his pillow, his eyes on the ceiling. The mate thought it was a fainting-fit, but the sick man murmured, "You are —keeping—a good course."

Rolland raised his own eyes then: a compass was nailed above the head of the bed, wrong side around. Flat on his back, Captain Thirard was checking his ship's headway.

"The weather?" he asked.

"Very fine, Captain. Winds from the north-northeast. We are making our eleven knots. The barometer is at seven-seventy-seven."

"Will it last?"

"I think so, Captain."

The hand, all sticky with perspiration, seized the hand of the mate and pressed it with spasmodic movements of irritation, while the voice hissed, "You should not say I think so. You should be sure."

The head turned on the hard pillow, the exhausted eyes sought the other's gaze.

"You understand, Monsieur Rolland, I should like to be able to rest—without worrying!"

"You can do that, Captain," Rolland declared.

It was still only a polite phrase, and, as such, Captain Thirard refused it as he had refused the other. He had kept the mate's hand in his, and he shook it in cadence with his next words:

"Can you take over—from me—absolutely—for twenty-four hours —whatever happens? Take all—responsibilities?"

Roland did not hesitate.

"Yes."

The sick man attempted a contraction of his mouth, which showed his yellow teeth and was meant to be a smile of gratitude. Then he raised his arm as a sign of dismissal. Rolland still waited: not everything had been said.

Impatience vibrated through the voice that was still more chopped and broken, as if the sick man were afraid of losing one minute of the hours just granted him.

"Then the responsibility is yours, sir; and thank you."

It was the formula that turned over the command. Rolland bowed his head, wished the captain better health, and went out.

XVII

THE *Antonine,* hove to since the evening before, under her fore stays'l, her lower tops'ls, and her mizzen stays'l, was riding out one of those storms from the east which one gets a taste of once in a great while in the extreme western reaches of the Pacific Ocean. She was lying to gently, not laboring. Nevertheless, these were days lost, days to be struck out of one's existence. If they had just been the only ones! But since the ship had come out of the southeast trade winds and entered the zone of variable breezes, Rolland no longer understood what was happening; or, rather, he understood too well. . . .

The first part of the voyage had gone as well as anyone could ever expect. They crossed the Equator on the 4th of October; then, very quickly, caught up with the southeast trade winds and the southern spring. The weather had continued to be fine, on the whole, with only the interruption of a few squalls. On the 8th of November they rounded the Cape of Good Hope, full wind astern, with waves that were long but rough, and they had had several days of being tossed about there. During these weeks it had quickly become apparent to Rolland that the captain was growing cautious. Too much so, for his taste! And Poullain himself, who was far from being a break-neck, was noting that Thirard was actually putting up very little canvas, and that he was hauling it down long before the wind rose.

They had attributed this to his condition. Illness makes the most audacious men timid, they reasoned—for this man had a reputation for hard and dauntless sailing, and Rolland had been able to see that for himself in the Bristol Channel.

Then, when they had left the Cape behind them, they ran into heavy weather. Every evening the low sky would be hacked and torn by storms. Sudden squalls would smooth down the hollowed sea before scattering it aloft again in lashing spindrift. There would be rain, then more squalls, gusts of wind that jumped from northwest to southwest. It was hard weather, certainly, but it was the right weather to make progress on the course.

And they were taking practically no advantage of it. . . . Regularly, every evening, the Old Man would give the order to furl canvas. With the daylight watch, Rolland would go back to the

187

command of "Set all sails!" But the lost miles could not be recovered.

Things were worse still when the door of the small deck-house had been stove in one night by one of those breakers that the sailors call "polishers" because they polish off the deck. After that, the captain had the sails trussed up more than ever. One might have said that he believed the ship to be sick like himself, incapable of weathering a storm, and the men anemic and prostrate.

One evening, the weather took on an extremely peculiar appearance. The sea became less heavy, the air more limpid around the ship. But thick banks of fog, unmoving, with clear-cut outlines, were resting upon the water a few miles away. From their look of tall gray cliffs it might have been supposed that this was land; and the *Antonine* seemed to be sailing in the middle of some bay, closed in on all sides.

Rolland had never had the sense of being so narrowly shut in, in an irrational situation. The captain had not appeared on the poop for two days. The mate knew, through Kréven, that he was struggling again with the horrors of suffocation, and that the swallowing of every meal was torture.

For he wanted his body to be nourished, in spite of the torments that were the price of every effort. He wanted to keep up. . . . But Rolland was wondering more and more whether this stubborn persistency in maintaining his hold on his official duties were not directed against himself. . . .

For any captain, any captain whatever, who was ill, would temporarily have turned over the command of the ship to him, as he had believed Thirard was about to do. That was what happened on all vessels where the master of the ship had confidence in the "second captain." After all, that was his official title, which was abbreviated to "second." * And "second captain" really meant substitute, replacement for a commander who was unable to perform his functions, and not just "that which comes after the first."

But, day and night—and especially at night, since he did not sleep—the captain of the *Antonine,* in the depths of his cabin, between his compass fixed to the ceiling and his barometer stuck at the side of his bunk, was watching the ship's progress, hour by hour. One was obliged to recognize a truly extraordinary instinct in him, which enabled him to discern the state of the weather from the motion of the ship, the sound of the wind, the crash of the waves.

And, then, he would come up to the poop at any hour. The officer of the watch would see the door of the chart-house being pushed ajar.

* The first mate is familiarly called the "second," that is, second captain, or second-in-command. Tr.

It would open slowly, as if there were someone spying from behind it; but that was only because this was the final bout in an exhausting effort, and the captain was trying to get his breath before he appeared outside. Then he would be seen framed in the narrow doorway; and whenever this happened Rolland could not help thinking of a picture in his catechism book, "The Last Judgment," where the dead were slowly pushing aside, like this, the marble slabs that sealed their tombs.

If it was at night and in heavy weather that he would thus pull himself up to the vessel's surface, he would not be seen at all, for he would be in darkness, as the others were. Then he would rap with a key on the steel door, by way of summons, and when the officer of the watch came, he would murmur an order, which was always to clew up and take in canvas.

Where could it come from, Rolland was once more asking himself this evening—that exaggerated caution on the part of a man whose entire past gave it the lie? With others, the timid ones, it would be the fear of being taken unawares by a sudden gust of wind with too much canvas set, and of rolling gunnel under—"capsizing," as the landlubbers say. Sometimes that happens so quickly! Among those who are too much "good fellows," there is solicitude over exposing the men to the danger that is always present when they must struggle for a long time in the yards over the mastery of a sail in a tempest. Here, Rolland would have sworn this evening, it was something else. The mate no longer believed that this was the stubborn willfulness of a sick man, to whom nothing was left but the resource of opposition, to manifest his authority. ("You want to put on canvas? I tell you to take it in, because I am the master.") It was, rather, the determination to supervise the vessel in actual fact, and, for that purpose, to avoid risks, shamelessly. At these slow speeds, he was still holding the *Antonine* in those hands so thin one would have said they were breaking, so unstable one would have thought they might crumble away.

If the four-master had been carried along at a lively pace in the heavy winds, on the contrary, her commander would have had to have the endurance that is required by long watches, the powerful voice that called out sudden orders and forced their speedy execution: all things which he, unhappily, no longer possessed.

As for delegating his authority to a "second" who was a man just made for hard seas, he would refuse to do that as long as the breath of life remained.

This was what Rolland always came back to, the note of resentment on which his reflections always ended.

When he went below to the cabin for dinner, the table had not been set and there was no sign of the cabin boy. Berteux was already waiting, and the lines of impatience on his forehead stretched up to the roots of his hair.

"Of course he is still with the captain," he remarked, in his most acidulous voice. And, as Rolland said nothing, he added, "One may say we are being given the go-by."

It was a fact that the cabin boy had been neglecting the cabin for some time back. When he was spoken to about it, he would bristle up and reply, "I was with the captain. The captain told me to stay. The captain says I am to go back to him at one o'clock. . . ."

Rolland did not insist. He realized how heinous a thing it would be to deprive the sick man of the small services the youngster could render. The cabin boy took care of his room, brought his meals to him, served them; most of all, he had to be uninterruptedly available to act as liaison agent between the captain and the poop. In theory, he was stationed in the pantry, where the Old Man would summon him by pounding on the partition-wall. But Rolland had noticed that he used to spend hours, also, in the captain's cabin, and that surprised him on two counts: he was surprised that the captain should take pleasure in the boy's company, but he was even more surprised, perhaps, that the boy himself should take his duties as nurse so much to heart. It could not be very cheerful for a youngster —this room that stank of stuffiness and medicine, this tête-à-tête with the wretched man who lay prostrate in his bunk or was bent double in the effort to get a little breath! The natural thing, it seemed, would have been for the boy to escape from that, run out to the deck, to the fresh air and the work in the rigging which he adored, because he was as clever as a monkey, and because that won him the attention of the men.

The cabin boy, however, was the person on a ship to whom Rolland had given the least thought, always. He had never suspected that it might come to be monstrous to isolate a thirteen-year-old boy among thirty rough men. When he was a sailor, he had seldom struck the cabin boys. If his boot flew out toward their narrow buttocks, there was always some reason for it. As an officer, he had demanded satisfactory work from the boys as from all the others, and he had always shown justice toward them as toward the rest. But the lads had never got from him any of those good-natured insults, that teasing, of which Poullain, for example, was so prodigal, and which would give them for a whole afternoon the bright face of a happy child who feels himself at home.

At last the boy came into the messroom, and Rolland could not help noticing his absent-minded and serious look.

"So," said Berteux, "you've decided that we are under your orders now?"

The youngster did not answer. He set the thick plates down on the table, mechanically.

"And are you sleeping there in the captain's cabin now?" Berteux persisted.

"It's him that wants me to stay," said the boy, with an air grown suddenly hard and inscrutable.

"But it's just what you like, isn't it? When you're with him, you aren't doing a lick of work."

The cabin boy, who was wiping a glass, stopped dead and looked the officer over. "But it isn't because I'm not doing any work that I like it," he said.

"That will do," Rolland broke in. "Run along to the galley."

"It's two days now that we haven't seen the captain," Berteux remarked when they were alone again. "That is a sign he's no better. And what is it he's got? When we left France, they told us it was chronic laryngitis. But with laryngitis you don't go all to pieces the way he's done. And these attacks of strangling, this not being able to swallow! What I think is that it's tuberculosis."

Rolland made an evasive gesture. The cabin boy was coming back with their dinner.

"How is the captain getting on?" Berteux queried, and added, "If you don't know, who would?"

"Badly," replied the boy curtly.

Rolland looked at him, and asked, in his impersonal voice, "What do you mean, badly?"

To him, the lad consented to give an answer. "He couldn't breathe, all day. Before I came here I helped him get to bed."

"He hasn't asked for anyone?" Rolland went on.

"No."

The boy went back to the galley to get the second course, and Berteux continued: "He doesn't ask for anyone, and he bolts his door! All the same, it is unfortunate that he prefers to be taken care of by a cabin boy and a bos'n, instead of by his officers. The little we learned at the Institute might be of some service, after all!"

Rolland went on eating, without making any reply: since the second mate did not realize that the sick man's first wish was to hide his disability, at any price, there was no use in explaining it to him.

Berteux's voice sank to a confidential murmur. "Did you know he was giving himself injections of morphine at those times?"

Rolland raised his eyes. "How do you know?"

The junior officer gave him a knowing little smile. Then he dug into his pocket and laid an empty ampoule on the oilcloth table-cover.

"I found this yesterday, quite by chance, as I was going through the corridor. I saw something shining. The cabin boy must have got it stuck under the baseboard when he was sweeping."

"Yes, I knew it," Rolland lied. "When that happens to him he lets me know in advance."

"In that case, it's in order," Berteux admitted.

When the midday meal was finished, Rolland stopped the cabin boy as he was clearing the table.

"Go tell the captain that I need to speak with him," he said.

The boy returned in five minutes.

"You can come," he announced.

"*Sir*," Rolland appended, with a hard look at him. "Go on, repeat, 'You can come, sir.' Do you think you are exempt from having manners because you have become a *valet-de-chambre?*"

He was far from suspecting that the lad was not at all unmannerly, but, instead, hostile. The cabin boy had guessed that the mate was going to attack the captain. And the captain used to say to him—to him, Yves Joubier: "You are a good little fellow. Stay with me."

No sooner had he entered the room than Rolland came near to leaving it again, on some pretext or other, without letting fall a word of what he had come to say. The captain had evidently got out of bed to receive him, for the bunk was open and the sheets mussed, but he was bent over in his armchair and did not straighten himself up at all. In the half-light of the cabin he had now the color of washed-out straw. The eyes were more sunken, the drawn face was further molten down. The skin itself seemed to have been made thinner, until it was no more than a fragile film that the bones threatened to break through. There seemed no longer to be any blood or muscles underneath it: a mummy, in short.

"What is it that is carrying him off at this speed?" Rolland was wondering. "Tuberculosis is slow . . . In any case, he is done for, and it stands to reason that he will have to be defended, if necessary, against himself." This reflection decided him.

"Captain, I had to talk with you," he began. "It is necessary for me to know whether you have confidence in me. You ought to take care of yourself, and rest. You cannot do that, thoroughly, if you are preoccupied with the care of the ship. Will you leave that care to me, until you are able to take up your duties again?"

The short, direct sentences were shot like arrows upon the man sunk into the chair. He listened to what was practically a summons to abdication without any show of feeling, apparently absorbed in the effort to breathe.

"We can reach our destination in twenty days," Rolland continued, "if we go farther south to get the carrying winds. Do you authorize me to change the course?"

There was a long silence. Then Captain Thirard raised his right arm, held it out for an instant, and let it fall. "You do it," the gesture said, "since I can do nothing more."

But Rolland refused to accept this too-vague investiture.

"Excuse me, Captain, but I am asking you to tell me—yes or no."

"Yes," the strangled voice whispered. "You go ahead!"

When he had gone out and closed the door, Rolland shrugged his shoulders. "He isn't happy about it," he said to himself, "but he had to be made to listen to reason. That is to his interest as well as to other people's."

As soon as he got back to the poop, he shifted the course to starboard and ran up more canvas at once.

Two days later the mileage figure began to go up, in the logbook: two hundred and thirty-four, two hundred and fifty, two hundred and eighty. . . . Rolland had indeed gone farther into the south, where he met winds from the west that were stronger and steadier. Sometimes they would run into snowstorms, and the man at the bow was on the watch for icebergs night and day. But the meridians, which were already drawing closer together before converging at the Pole, were crossed in quick succession: the ninety-fifth, which is almost the dividing-line between Burma and Siam; the one hundredth, which slants across Sumatra; the one hundred and fifth, which is Indochinese. Every day, so, in these southern reaches, they would be passing vast countries that are spread out above the Equator.

The ship's speed produced her tonic effect, as always, and the powerful wind kept the men on their toes. Now that he had his hands free, the mate was bringing the ship along swiftly and well. There was no going moldy at the foot of the mast, you bet, when he called you to work the sheets, for when he got into it himself it was worth your while to step lively! For the first time in weeks, they felt that they really were commanded, and accepted the new regime.

"Seeing that the Old Man isn't up to it any more—" they would say.

The captain no longer counted for much on the ship. Some of them—the oldest—would occasionally think of him with a little pity: "What sickness can do to a man, after all!" But that would be the end of their compassion. They were incapable of being moved to tenderness; and only tenderness expands the heart.

As for Rolland, he had the log-book taken to the captain every day, as was his duty, just as soon as he had set down the regulation notes in it. The sick man would put his O.K. to the record, with a hand which he had to struggle to keep from trembling.

After a period of cloudy weather with heavy and fairly steady breezes, the *Antonine* again fell upon unsettled winds interspersed with calms. One sensed that the play of the breezes was turned aside by the proximity of an enormous land mass: Australia loomed up like a screen, two hundred miles to the northeast. At the end of three days, the winds resumed their force. They doubled Tasmania under a gusty sky, making a broad sweep around the South Cape, the second of the earth's three great promontories off which they were to pass in the course of this voyage. They were keeping Cape Horn for the return trip.

One evening the captain came to the surface again and appeared on the poop. There was a good breeze blowing, but the *Antonine* was carrying full sail. Thirard did not so much as glance at the royals stretched taut like balloons, at the stays'ls whose long puffed-out triangles seemed to distend the ship lengthwise in addition to all that was already swelling her out across. He pushed the door of the chart-house ajar, as usual, and Rolland, who was not expecting him this evening any more than on other days, gave a start of surprise which he immediately checked, and stepped over to greet him. When he asked how he was, the captain replied merely by a vague gesture; then he said, in almost normal tones—for during this period of retirement he seemed to have recovered some strength and some voice—"Tomorrow is Christmas. Have you thought about it?"

"Yes, Captain. I have put the men on Sunday duty."

"Have them given their double drink ration this evening. And tomorrow at noon get them together in the saloon, first one watch, then the other."

Having delivered these orders, the captain left the poop as if nothing, on this vessel in full course, were of any further interest to him. Rolland felt the pride of this relinquishment, which bore public witness to his authority, more than the strangeness of what had just been said. Yet it was strange. Get the men together? But he would not make a speech to them!

. . . The captain did not make a speech, and this unusual assembly was marked by an extraordinary silence. When the helmsman had struck the noon bells, the men of the starboard watch took their places in the saloon, which they were now entering for the first time and which filled them with reverence: its maple and rosewood wainscoting, its mahogany furniture, its armchairs screwed to the floor. The rug, especially, intimidated them more than the fore-and-aft gangway on a stormy day: the important thing was to keep from setting their boots on it. Everyone held his mug in his hands. Kréven had instructed them to come supplied.

The captain appeared, followed by Rolland. He was carrying a full-sized bottle of rum: good rum, captain's rum, with a Negro on the label. He filled each mug half-full, then he raised the bottle:

"A good Christmas to you, my friends, and to your families. . . ."

They were so stunned by this that not one of them dared take a drink. Besides, wouldn't that have been almost indecent in front of this poor man who was not drinking, who could not drink, who probably never would drink again? It was the cook who saved the situation, by finding the right thing to say; cooks have practice in that, as part of their profession.

"To your better health, Cap'n; to your recovery," he said.

The captain thanked him, with little jerks of his head. Released, they raised their mugs and drank.

Then the Old Man went down the row with a box of cigars: fat ones, with gold bands! They took them, cautiously. Most of them chewed tobacco.

As they went out, they were pondering over this astounding ceremony. They felt, confusedly, that in this unprecedented gesture there was something which reached out very far.

The temperature was becoming milder day by day. On the twenty-seventh, they met with a northwest blow as they were passing Bass Strait, where a draft of air runs between Australia and Tasmania. Then the weather became fine again, and they made good progress. The nights were mild once more, all studded over with the Tropics' stars.

On the fifth of January, in the morning, they caught sight of what looked like a bluish-toned fog-bank on the port side. Poullain, who was on watch, pointed it out to Rolland.

"There we are," he said.

XVIII

LEANING against the "turtle," the booby-hatch that pro-tected the steering-gear behind the wheel, Rolland looked at the great island as it drew closer. It was still no more than a chaos of steep isolated hills, a disorderly cavalcade of savage mountain ranges, sometimes splashed, around their base, with the dark mottlings of forests. Poullain, who was making his fourth voyage to New Caledonia, pointed to a cylindrical summit like a gigantic drum.

"The Round Table," he said. "You can see it from both coasts."

The men had their eyes fixed lower down. They were showing one another the red-toned gashes in the mountain, the long scratches on its sides.

"It's all nickel," they were saying. "How long would it take you to shovel out all that!"

Captain Thirard came up to the poop at the moment when everybody's gaze, forsaking the land, was falling back on a moving line of spray which ran parallel to the coast, and which, at intervals, was tossing up tall jets of snow-white water: the Great Barrier. Nobody could say that it did not come lawfully by its name: a belt of reefs about fifteen hundred miles long and sometimes twelve hundred yards wide, strung out within fifteen miles of land. It circled the island as a broken thick-set wall, but cut down to the surface of the water so that it resembled abandoned foundations. It followed the contour of the coast so faithfully that it might have been thought to mark an initial design: as if the first visualization had been too large, and New Caledonia had been pulled back from that original plan.

This time, it was necessary to go through a breach in that wall which seemed built by giants; but these breaches were few and narrow. Taking them through was, without doubt, the business of the pilot, whose cutter could already be glimpsed through the binoculars as she put on sail to run out to meet them. But the *Antonine* must first be pointed toward the center-line of that invisible gap; and Rolland was by no means sorry that the captain should have had a chair brought up for him and set at the helmsman's side. Yet it was a pitiful thing to see him there, his body bent double, but his head thrown back and his eyes raised to find his alignments. He knew, as everyone knew, that New Caledonia was not called the Sailing-Ships' Grave for nothing, and that the Barrier was marked, as with buoys, with the skeletons of ships.

They hove to half and hour later to take on the pilot, a young fellow in a straw hat and khaki jacket who, as he chatted about the rain and the good weather, would be able to get you into the channel just as he would step over his own door-sill when he went home at night. That channel was so narrow, however, that the men leaning over the side saw monstrous heads of white chicory, that were clumps of coral, waying under the seething eddies. Then all at once there was calm water, so blue and so limpid that the boys looked at it for an instant in sheer pleasure, like tourists.

Their gaze returned swiftly, however, to the nearby land. They were scrutinizing it without any feeling of personal friendliness, as one does women, or places, that one cannot approach. They would not set foot on it. For days, perhaps weeks, they would load nickel ore in the roadstead—that nickel of which all they knew was that it was what gave shining handle-bars to bicycles. Then they would return through the Pacific Ocean and around Cape Horn, after which they would trudge along up the Atlantic, just as if they were coming back from Iquique or Frisco. . . . And not one of them would have protested that this journey around the world might have won them a few days of relaxation ashore, somewhere in mid-course. It was like that, it was the rule, and they noted it without resentment.

"You'll have the right to make a tour of it through the telescope."

"You'll always be able to touch the wood of the wharf when you go out in the boats. But as for going ashore, nix on that unless you're assigned to get provisions or take on water."

"When you drank your last glass of gin or whisky at Port Talbot, you could have told yourself that you wouldn't have as much earth under your feet as that glass would hold until you got back to Dunkerque or Hamburg or wherever."

Gourvais, an old hand, nevertheless remarked regretfully, "At Frisco, or in Australia, we tie up at the dock. It's pleasanter."

"Well, here you have to save your money whether or no," someone put in. "No drinks and no women."

Caroff summed up: "What's wanted, anyhow? A sailor to be glad to go to sea? Well, then, since you're in a worse temper here than you are on the water, you'll be as satisfied as all-get-out to go back to sleep on the ocean, like the gulls. That's all right! Run over there and ask your pals if they aren't just waiting for the moment to spr-r-ead their sa-a-ils!"

He was pointing to a three-master in the roadstead, still with her canvas furled but visibly heavy in the water, the loading of which was being completed; there were two black scows clinging to her flank, like horseflies.

"It has a kind of dowdy look, your Thio," Big Domino put in.

There were a few small houses with zinc roofs, Thio-Mission, at the foot of an overhanging cliff; a little wooden wharf, above which the parallel cables of the funicular for the ore stood out dark and astonishingly distinct against the white sky; and, against this wharf, tall metal scaffoldings, iron frameworks for carrying cranes, which the boys on the *Antonine* were regarding with a jaundiced eye.

"With that damn mechanical stuff, they'll have loaded us up in three days, the bastards," they said.

197

That "damn mechanical stuff" did part of their work for them and saved them trouble, but they loathed its rapid action. In spite of everything, land is land. . . . It rests the eyes, it is a neighborhood. . . . And even if you don't go to it, it comes to you, with its fresh provisions—its fruits, oranges, coconuts—and the customs officer. This latter would be living aboardship, as long as the loading continued, and through him a man could take stock of the curiosities of the country. Then, too, the boatmen, when they went to get water, would manage to lay in some clandestine supplies of liquor, which was very cheap. . . .

They came to anchor, in twenty fathoms of water, at the beginning of the afternoon. At once, the men took up their shovels and began to fill big baskets with ballast to be unloaded from the hold: the gravel that had occupied a third of the space now to be given over to the cargo of nickel ore.

"You don't see our kind of diggers often, do you?" Neveu demanded. "We fellows, we've got the land right where we live. That way, we don't have to go alongside."

Joking or not, he would come harking back to it. He was itching to take a turn in the countryside, and the chances were that he would succeed in doing so.

Rolland would be going ashore, according to orders. This time, they would come from a recluse. Captain Thirard had already made it plain that no more than the men would he set foot on the island. His reasons were obvious enough: the weakness that made a stairway a calvary to climb; and, with it, shame at showing himself as he now was to his fellow-captains, the middlemen, the agents in the offices, the mine directors. For him there would be no more of that pleasant life of the island for which the skippers all lived, more or less, once their ships were anchored in the roadstead. Thanks to Poullain, Rolland knew some of the island detail.

"It's at Thio-Ville that everything goes on," the third mate said. "You get there in twenty minutes, on a little train that leaves at eight o'clock every morning and takes the school boys and girls— especially the girls. Those damn kids, in this climate they're women by the time they're twelve, and they know how to lead the men on—you've got to see it! The last time I was here the mayor, old Papatzi, had had to add a car 'for ladies only' to his ramshackle train. But that didn't make any difference!"

"And those houses right down there, what are they?" Rolland asked.

"That's the Mission village. That's where all the people live who work in loading the ships. The Canaques live there as a tribe." Poullain began to laugh. "You must be sure not to miss getting acquainted with their king, Philippo. He wears formal dress, if you please, with the shirt on top of the overcoat; it's only the shoes that he's never been able to get into, but he carries them slung over his shoulder by way of insignia."

"Why the name, 'Mission'?" Rolland asked. "Are there missionaries?"

"Only one, but he is somebody! A Marist, Father Paul. It won't be long before we see him coming aboard."

As soon as a ship came to anchor in the roadstead, Poullain went on to explain, the priest would hurry to greet her, unless he was on a trip back in the hills. His great delight was to eat a piece of salt pork in the cabin. In return, he would place all the fruit in his gardens at the disposal of the visiting captains, and they would come back from calling upon him with their boats full of cocoanuts and oranges. He grew a damn good coffee, too! When you had a sip of it you were getting something very different from old Jules's belly-wash!

Poullain went on talking, leaning his elbows on the rail; and it was as if the high wall of cliffs had been split open before Rolland's eyes, so as to let him see into the heart of the welcoming land: fabulously rich, yet still swarming with what was left of a vermin horde of convicts and released prisoners, like parasites on a sturdy beast.

"It wasn't so very long ago," Poullain had said, "that you would never hold out your hand to anyone before he had assured you, 'I am a free man.' "

He was about to embark on the inexhaustible chapter of the penal colony. Rolland interrupted him to go down to see the captain.

When he entered the cabin, Thirard, who was stretched out on his bunk, got up. He had the anxious, frowning air he had had at Port Talbot. When he recognized the mate, he lay down again.

"You are alone?" he demanded.

"Of course."

"They won't be long in coming alongside, to make my life a burden," he said wearily.

Rolland guessed his fears well enough to suggest, at once, "If you wish, Captain, I will give orders that you are not to be disturbed; I can explain that you are not well and cannot receive anyone."

"So that they will think I have gone to pieces entirely? No, listen . . . you will have word sent to me, and you will hold them for ten minutes."

Ten minutes: time to give himself a shot of dope,* slip into his trousers, put on a jacket instead of the bathrobe that clung to his

* The phrase is *de se doper avec une piqûre* in the French original. Tr.

199

bones; ten minutes to bring himself to stand upright, to look like a man. . . .

Having set up this fragile defense, the captain gave his instructions. Rolland was to betake himself to Thio-Ville next morning, for general orders. Thus they would find out whether they were to take on their cargo in this roadstead or at Kouaoua or Kanala; that was up to the management of the Nickel Company. Rolland was also to take the report, lying there ready on the table, with all the papers, and deliver them to the consignee, who would take all necessary steps. The mate was to say that he wished to offer the captain's apologies for not coming in person; he was remaining on his ship. *He was remaining on his ship*—might that be rightly understood!

Raised on his elbows, he had almost cried out the words, in a kind of strangled bark. His head stretched out on his neck, his eyes starting from their sockets, his face drawn long above the lean snout, he looked like some scrawny old dog that is waiting for a kick and trying its best to growl. The former torment had bitten into him at the moment when the anchor bit into the floor of the sea. The land was menacing him anew, with its executives and its doctors, who would be passing the word to each other that he was to be taken ashore, stuffed into a hospital. . . . The hospital— No, no, no, not for him! He had just been making that plain to his second-in-command, who would have to make it plain to whomever it concerned. Rolland bowed his head in acquiescence: he would tell them. . . .

This seemed to quiet the sick man, and he added, "There are only two men whom I should like to see: Berlot, the skipper of the Tamanou, an old comrade; and Father Paul, the missionary. Especially Father Paul. . . ."

Rolland promised to call at the Mission.

The night was falling with the swiftness of a dropped curtain when he left the cabin. There was a feeling as if the sun were burying itself behind the mountains as in a deep sea, and there were only a few mauve reflections, now, cropping out on the surface. The cliffs had turned to violet. And in this sudden twilight Rolland had not taken two steps on the deck before he was giving himself a series of slaps, on cheeks, hands, nape of the neck. Poullain, approaching with his long stride, began to laugh.

"I've forgotten to add that to the program," he said. "The roadsteads of New Caledonia, that means mosquitoes: mosquitoes and the southeast trade winds."

. . . When Rolland came on deck next morning, at swabbing time, the land seemed to be sound asleep. For some minutes still, the daylight would be leaving a light mist, like a thin wash, spread over the sea. Poullain was standing waiting at the top of the ladder that hung from the *Antonine's* taffrail. The big long-boat, made fast aft, had already been brought into position and was almost completely filled with two enormous leather bottles. Rolland had decided to go ashore with the first water party, so as to have time to explore the Mission before taking the little train for Thio-Ville. When he had given his instructions to the second mate, who was remaining on the ship, they put off: Poullain, who took the helm, the first mate, and a sailor, Gallais, who at once hoisted the jib, the fores'l, and the lugs'l.

"Push along, Gallais, and haul your jib taut," Poullain ordered. "We'll make a good tack with the last bit of land breeze."

"It isn't going to last long," said the sailor. "That damn screech from the southeast will be coming up with the sun . . ."

". . . And we'll be drenched all day," Poullain finished the sentence.

The third mate and Gallais, with the big long-boat, were to assure the supply of fresh water for the ship's boiler, the "little horse" which would be constantly under pressure during the loading. And it would guzzle down water, the old brute, with that blasted winch for hauling in the ore, which, once it was set going, never stopped from six in the morning till six at night. So there would be no time to lose, in this shuttling back and forth between the ship and the wharf, filling the two big leather bottles that weighed the long-boat down to the gunnels, emptying them, and filling them again.

There as everywhere, when you had a good wind going, you had a wind against you coming back. With the long-boat weighted down like this the spindrift would whip you in the face, too, and every trip, would soak the couple of duds you had on your back. Only—what Poullain wasn't saying—there were compensations, for a sociable young man. Along the wharf where another sailing-ship's long-boat was also filling up, he'd find a comrade to talk to, and he'd have a bit of fun with him in a little music-hall while the sailors were looking after the filling of the water-bottles. Poullain knew his way about in the women's quarters, also: white or black, it was all right with him. The leather bottles wouldn't be half-full before he would have arranged a rendezvous.

Now the long-boat came alongside the wharf. The junior officer went at once to the office of the Port, to make his declaration and get his water permit. Rolland made his way to the Catholic Mission.

He followed the bank of the river, which, beneath an arbor of screw-pines, led to Thio. It was one of those short Caledonian streams, cut up by rapids, navigable only for small boats, and that for only a few miles. A bar tossed up its white foam where the stream met the sea, and Poullain had avowed to the first mate that he used to be capsized there regularly with his dinghy, on his previous voyages, whenever he went to Thio-Ville and was not able to take the school train.

"One dries off between warm arms," he declared.

Upstream, the Thio River became suddenly calm. Like the sea, it had an extraordinary limpidness: water from the rock! Broad panoplies of leaves, sharp silver needles, hung down from the pine trees that bordered it.

The Mission was scattered about in square huts, with zinc roofs, on the right bank of the river. The chapel boasted of a bell turret, a wooden cubicle whose louver boards reached just to the height of Venetian blinds. But Father Paul had impaled a cock on the metal cross, a French chanticleer whose golden feathers glittered in the morning light.

A hubbub of voices, like a dispute among parakeets, drew Rolland toward a long wooden barrack hut. His arrival brought a swift end to the racket. Some thirty Negro girls, barefooted but stowed into cotton dresses like sacks, were staring at him with their white-rimmed eyes round as marbles under the ball of their crinkled hair. He turned away from them and caught sight of an elderly nun, who had just stepped out on the threshold and was watching his approach, a stern and heavy face become expressionless beneath her wimple. The church's quartermaster, she was: especially made, one felt, for forcibly impressing the rudiments of religious instruction upon the toughest pates and exacting obedience to the Ten Commandments as daily duties. Rolland gave her his name and asked to see Father Paul.

He was told that the Father had left for the hill country to visit his flock, the evening before, and would not be back for a week. Then he explained that Captain Thirard of the *Antonine* wished to see him, and that he was ill and could not come to the Mission.

"He must be ill, truly, not to come," she said. "It is a habit he never fails in."

The nun's air, as she spoke, was distrustful, and she was watching Rolland from eyes that were raised in a slightly lowered face.

"He has been ill since we left France," he added, more curtly. "That is a very long time, and I am afraid the trouble may be serious."

She nodded.

"That is what I was thinking," she said. "Otherwise, he would be here already."

She demanded details. Rolland was surprised to find himself speaking freely and at length, acknowledging his worries, in the midst of these Negro girls who were devouring him with their eyes.

He felt that she was listening to what was not put into words, that with her woman's intuition she divined on the spot things it had taken him months to understand.

"The Father will go to him as soon as he gets back," she promised. "But he must also see a doctor."

Rolland shook his head, without speaking: that would not be so easy. . . .

"He won't be asked for his opinion," the sister said. "When the doctor is brought aboard, he will have to receive him."

Then, immediately, she thought of what might give him pleasure. Rolland was to be sure to stop by at the Mission on his way back from Thio; he was to take the captain a basket of oranges: sick people never got tired of them.

"And apples!" she cried out suddenly. "We have apples—think of that! He will eat them stewed."

"Yes," agreed Rolland, "apples."

It was obvious that apples came from far away—as far as France! The thought of this windfall brought a sudden animation to the good sister's countenance, and spread a broad smile across it: one of those smiles that take one aback when they appear on an austere visage, because they leave no austerity there.

She pointed the way to the station, hardly two hundred yards along the river. Then, as the group of little Negresses had grown to be a dense swarm around them, she opened a path for him with an authoritative fist, pushing shoulders aside, shoving back breasts that were already firm.

The station was obviously a mere hut, with a square hole cut in the wall for passing out tickets. The railway, where the engine was puffing on the narrow-gauge track, was like one of those country-fair railways that go round in a circle and plunge into a canvas tunnel. The cars were open: platforms under sheet-iron roofs, with wooden benches running lengthwise and now filled with chattering schoolgirls. Some of the girls were white, for there were some European households at the Mission, but most of them were half-breeds, and about twelve years old.

It was true that they were fully developed, these youngsters; the sun took care of that. But to go on from there, as Poullain had done, and regard them as women. . . . They had the thick flat noses of their Canaque mothers, the saber-cut mouths, the too-long, almost simian arms.

So now he remained standing on the narrow platform, turning his back on the bunch of schoolgirls whose prattle became a more frantic hubbub as the train started. They were going to learn to read and write. . . . At their age their mothers, savages, had been weaving rush mats and braiding hair cords, molding pottery from clay, flanking the fire in outhouse shelters to bake it, after drying it underneath them. For the rest, they would have debauched themselves, until they were married, with anyone who wanted them; and the priest, the sisters, the Thio schoolmistresses, all together would have been hard put to it to make their daughters admit that this was not to be recommended. The discipline would succeed, practically, so long as the youngsters were under ten years old, but after that it was time to hide with the boys in the forest.

Like many seafaring men, Rolland admired the missionaries all the more insomuch as he was convinced that they were giving themselves useless trouble. Everything they succeeded in implanting in those primitive brains remained as foreign to them as their tricks do to trained dogs. Gestures, words. . . . Like the others, he had a whole collection of real-life stories to bear out this conviction: stories which not one sailor would ever have told before a missionary, for fear of hurting his feelings.

This line of thought led him back to the good sister and her apples. It was a dreadful thing, all the same, that this apple-sauce should be such an event: that a ship's captain, after sailing halfway around the globe, would have nothing to hope for but a dish of stewed fruit!

The broken-winded engine snorted over a bridge, wound its way among great trees for a few minutes longer, and then stopped at Thio-Ville. The schoolgirls, chirping shrilly, got out. The oldest of them had taken each other's arms and were turning around, laughing, toward Rolland. It was, he thought, the precise duplicate of the exodus from the dressmaking establishment in Saint-Sylvère: the same giggles, the same nudgings. . . . Emphatically, they were all the same, under skins that might be fair or chocolate-colored, and at all the ends of the earth.

Thio-Ville was no more than a large village. Little square houses buried in luxuriant gardens, bordering a narrow road itself encroached upon by trees. Rolland soon discovered the headquarters of the Nickel Company, a spacious double house, built of wood, that looked Scandinavian. He was ushered into the office of one of the assistant managers, a room lined with green file-cases, like a lawyer's office; and there he was received by a stout unceremonious man, his collar unbuttoned, already perspiring, who displeased him by holding out a moist hand across his desk, without getting up. When Rolland said that he had come, in pursuance of instructions, from his "ailing" captain—he had searched a long time for that adjective—the other raised his eyebrows. He made no comment, however, and informed the mate briefly that a telegram from the shipping firm instructed the *Antonine* to put off again from Thio and take on its cargo of ore in the roadstead of Kanala, forty miles to the northwest. The only trouble was that the Company's tug was out on duty, and would not be here to tow the ship for another two days. Nor could they count on the *Tamanou,* a coasting-boat, Berlot the owner, which occasionally substituted for the tug; it was at Nouméa for an overhauling.

"By the way, where could one find this Berlot?" Rolland asked. "I have a message for him."

He did not consider it relevant to say what the message was.

The stout man gave a little start and a giggle, that closed his right eye.

"That depends," he said. "If it is an official message for the skipper of the *Tamanou,* you can leave it in one of the ports where he puts in. If it is for Berlot personally, take it to his mistress, a woman by the name of Pillou, who lives close to Kanala, as a matter of fact. He goes back there from every corner of the coast, between two sailings. . . . You know him, this Berlot?"

"Not at all."

"He's a character! Nobody ever gets bored with him, or sore, except when his wench throws him out. Then he gets drunk and becomes obnoxious."

The assistant manager had picked up a little ink-stained ruler from his desk and was turning it over between his thick fingers.

"So your captain isn't well?" he said.

"Not very."

"He couldn't come himself? He sent you?"

"Of course."

"That is not the custom. All the captains come themselves, to present their papers and receive their orders. That is elementary, and Thirard has always done it up to now. What is the matter with him, then, that he cannot move from where he is?"

"He has a very bad throat ailment. And he has lost his voice."

The assistant manager opened his eyes wide.

"And that is what keeps him from coming as far as this?"

Rolland felt that things were going badly, and that he would be making nothing better by his answer: "It has exhausted him very much, and then with the cold here, this morning—"

Clearly, the other man was wondering whether he was being made a fool of; Rolland realized that from the glance he threw at him. The assistant manager had taken up the report which the mate had delivered to him, and was commencing to read it. Without interrupting his perusal, he inquired, "It has been a good voyage, coming out?"

"Quite normal," said Rolland.

"No incidents?"

"No. A few trifles, as always."

The other man did not utter another word until he had finished his reading. Then he leaned back in his chair and looked Rolland straight in the face.

"But listen here," he said. "This trouble in the throat, it doesn't look like one of those little things that can be cured with a couple of cough-drops! One only has to read this report. . . . The captain speaks of you, here, with high praise, but precisely; he points out that he has had to leave everything to you, on two occasions, during the voyage. He speaks of attacks. Attacks of what? He seems to be saying, also, that he has found it impossible to exercise his normal functions of command, since sailing, because of this 'loss of voice.' A loss of voice that lasts three months, and that prevents a captain's coming to get his sailing orders!"

He had got his teeth in it! Deep in his heart Rolland was cursing the sincerity of that honest and unhappy man, who did not hesitate to avow his own weaknesses, rather than play down his first mate's deserts. If he had only let him read it before handing it in, this damn report!

The official was turning over its pages, with an air of distrust. He laid them aside, and concluded: "A disturbance in the throat, that lasts so long, and that reduces a robust man like Thirard to such a feeble state that he is glued to his ship, and even to his cabin during the voyage—that is something to keep an eye on. Don't you find it so? Well, we shall see. . . . The loading at Kanala will take a certain amount of time. That should enable him to get on his feet again, and make sure of the return voyage."

"I hope so," said Rolland.

But he was not deceived by this effect of candor. And his uneasiness could not have escaped the assistant manager, who, as he accompanied him to the door, threw him another sharp glance. "What's the man's game?" the official was obviously wondering.

Rolland was asking himself much the same thing, as he crossed the dry earth of the "garden." It would have been so simple, and at the same time so true, to say, "He is done for. He doesn't get out of bed any more, except for a few hours, and that by a miracle of strenuous energy. One of these days—perhaps tomorrow—he will stop getting up at all. And I shall have to drag a dying man through weeks and weeks of ocean until he goes to his grave in the water; for I shall not get him back to France. First for his own sake, and then for everyone else's, he must be persuaded, if necessary he must be obliged, to leave the ship."

206

If he had not said this, it was because, in the first place, that greasy fellow had at once aroused his disgust. To go fifty-fifty with him in a scheme, even an entirely permissible one, was simply not to be thought of. And then, too, and more than anything else, there was the other, the poor soul who was clinging like a shipwrecked man to the planks of his boat. To strike at his hands, to force him to let go because he was increasing the weight of the lifeboat! They would do that without any aid from him!

All this, however, had put him in a bad mood. He walked all around Thio—it did not take long—without shaking off his preoccupation. He saw nothing in the overgrown village, moreover, that would have had any power to distract him. A few chickens in the unpaved streets, a pig crossing his path, and, seen through the open windows, some women at their morning housework: black women and white women, and those neither beautiful nor ugly.

He went to Mother Girard's: a little café with wooden tables, very clean. Shortly, two overseers from the Nickel Company came in: one thin, one fat. From the door-step, the fat one winked at the girl behind the bar. She responded with a smile of familiarity.

"What will it be?"

"The usual."

Oh, my God, the usual! That sure was worth the voyage! To have treated yourself to a journey halfway around the world; to have put France just under the soles of your shoes, so to speak, on the other side of the globe; all that, so as to sit down in a village bar in front of a pernod!

Elbows on the table, he raised his head. Just opposite, a man was observing him: a clear, hard gaze under brown eyebrows, a thick head of chestnut hair that set off the line of the willful forehead, a flange of beard that was not enough to blur the sharpness of the chin. . . . The mustache curved its brown shavings over the short upper lip. The shoulders were square without being broad. . . .

Rolland was looking at himself without real recognition.

In his cabin he had one of those mirrors that cost four sous, and in it he saw nothing but his hair, at the moment when he was combing it. Here, there was this large glass, set at a forward angle, which gave back this surprising visage. No, it was not a seductive appearance he had, with that long face, that sharp nose like the bow of a ship, that short dark pirate's beard. Where had he got hold of a face like that, in place of the flat features of the Bretons? Was it because old man Rolland had come from Cancale, and the Cancale people are cross-bred with Spaniards? Be that as it may, whenever he took that head of his anywhere, people seemed to be taken aback, put on the defensive. He remembered the eyes of sailors, suddenly stony, when he came unexpectedly into the fo'c'sle; and the one who had muttered, the day he went aboard the *Astrée*, "Here's a fellow you'd better not get too free with." That was how it was. He froze the men, and stiffened even his fellow-officers, at the first encounter. This morning, he was far from thinking that they were wrong. . . .

And women?

Those to whom he addressed himself had no choice. But the others? That was what he was asking himself about now, as he scrutinized his face, with no friendly eye, in the mirror. The others? . . . He might perhaps attract, and please, those who liked difficulty, the Kréven type. But were there any?

XIX

THE NEXT DAY, which was Sunday, an old Canaque— he had a jacket and trousers, that one—brought a letter to the captain: Monsieur Bouttier, the manager of the Borné mines, one of the richest veins of nickel in New Caledonia, invited him to luncheon, along with one of his officers. The two men had become acquainted three years before on a steamship that was taking them to the large island, one after holidays in France, the other to take command of a three-master, at Nouméa, that was without a captain.

"You go, Monsieur Rolland, with Poullain. You will make my apologies to Bouttier and his wife," Captain Thirard said.

He presented the proposal with that detachment of the sick from their former pleasures which always surprises the healthy, whose world has not been transformed.

For the trip up to the mine, Rolland and Poullain had to be-straddle the little Caledonian horses that were waiting for them at the Mission. It was a climb to be long remembered: goat tracks that cut into the mountain—and with such narrow gashes!—and rocky corniche roads where one could not have stretched out a towel without having to fold it above the void. One leg would be hanging over the abyss; and when a stone slid under his horse's hoof Rolland shrank back in spite of himself, as he had never done on a threshing yard. After two hours of this ascent, they at last arrived at the mine. Rolland would have called it the quarry, for it was no more than an amphitheater open to the sky, with cyclopean tiers of chocolate-colored ore streaked with greenish veins. The manager's house was still farther up, where there began to be trees: a timber-built house painted light blue, with a shallow stoop under a wooden canopy.

Even before they had alighted from their horses, a man had come down the steps to greet them: a man in his forties, who at once paused in surprise when he did not see the captain among the arrivals. The news Rolland gave him seemed to fill him with consternation. What! Thirard, come to such a pass! It was not possible! He had been bursting with health the last time he was here!

When she met them in the vestibule, Madame Bouttier joined in her husband's dismay. She must have been about ten years younger than he: a fresh-skinned brunette, but already well-upholstered by the indulgence of solitary women in good food. She had very beautiful eyes, easily moved to tenderness, and they were filled with sincere sorrow when Rolland repeated the report of the *Antonine's* anxieties. Like the good sister at the Mission, she spoke at once of a doctor, and then of hospitalization at Nouméa. Rolland had to explain why this was not desirable, and he was grateful to her for her immediate understanding. Monsieur Bouttier promised to do his utmost to visit the captain on his ship, even at Kanala. They seemed really stricken by the misfortune of a friend. Rolland reproached himself for feeling vaguely surprised by this. But already Madame Bouttier, coming back to her duties as mistress of the house, was telling him how delighted they were to welcome him.

As he seated himself on her right, at the table, the first mate of the *Antonine* cast a glance of alarm at the array of glasses and knives-and-forks with which he was going to be obliged to disport himself. This was actually the first time he had come in contact with the luxury of the well-to-do middle class and their little-known code of proprieties. He had changed caste at sea, by passing from the fo'c'sle to the chart-house, without ever having been in a position on shore, between arrival and departure, to adapt himself to the exigencies of his new rank. So he had not ceased to be afraid of the common seaman whom he felt still living within him, and this fear made him stiff and self-conscious as nothing else could. Madame Bouttier's gracious manner and genuine cordiality at last brought him to feel at ease. Yet she would sometimes ask embarrassing questions.

Poullain had just been recounting the history of one of his former captains, a Basque who kept a statuette of Saint Anthony of Padua in his cabin. When the vessel ran into a dead calm, he would go before the statue, lift a finger to his cap, and say, "Great Saint Anthony, you who make it your business to recover lost articles, there'll be forty sous in it for you if you put us in the way of finding the wind again." But if the calm persisted, the saint would be subjected to an odd sort of litany. The captain would make him fast with an end of line, well rigged around the neck, and fling him, raging, into the water. "Go look for the wind, you false saint, you thief of paradise," he would yell. "You aren't dealing here with bigots who can't teach you what's what!"

"And I must say," Poullain concluded, "that I have often seen the wind come up almost immediately."

Madame Bouttier turned to Rolland.

"And you—do you believe that Saint Anthony finds the wind again?" she asked.

The question went deep, and far! In common with ninety-nine seafaring men out of a hundred, Rolland, if he had a knife at his throat, would not have been able to answer yes—for fear of being taken for an easy mark—or no, for fear of giving offense to Mystery, all the Inexplicable that broods over the sea and sometimes lies heavy upon it. Then, too, Madame Bouttier asked the question without smiling, almost earnestly; he had the impression that she was demanding some kind of testimonial from him. Does one know what may be in the minds of women isolated as she was? There are some who are much stirred up over religion, and to whom, one must not answer just anything, where it is concerned. Finally, and especially, this was a matter of the wind: that capricious despot that veers forward or aft, that chops around or goes straight ahead, that strokes or smashes. Seamen believe that it is alive, insomuch as they whistle to call it—not like a dog, to be sure, but to induce it to whistle with them. Rolland could not have sworn that he had not done that in his time, like the others. And an old captain had once told him the story of mad sailors on his ship, who, driven to frenzy by weeks of calm, short rations, and stinking water, had chased the cabin boy up into the royal yards, wanting to unleash the wind by throwing him into the sea; as had happened to that Iphigenia who had since given her name to some fine ships! All that, again, was a far cry from Saint Anthony! So he answered, "With the wind, Madame, everything is possible."

And Poullain added, "I'm telling you, too, Madame, that every time Saint Anthony brought back the wind the captain would hand out an apéritif. It would not have been the thing to act as if one didn't believe in him!"

This time, Madame Bouttier started to laugh. She laughed with her head thrown back and her throat quivering, like a bird taking a drink.

The Canaque butler, barefooted but buttoned up to his chin in a white coat, came in with a creamy mocha cake. On the icing a ship was outlined in sugar with the name, *Antonine*. Poullain cried out in delight. Rolland was satisfied to turn toward Madame Bouttier and thank her with a smile.

He was comfortable now. The wines had made him feel in his place again, on a level with his hosts. They went into the drawing room for coffee. It was paneled in rosewood, and had wide doors opening on a garden. But the furniture was in "modern-style," * with its lines in segments of circles, and curves in its slender legs; there were vases in convolvulus form, and other vases, on grasshopper feet, were overflowing with unfamiliar flowers. Poullain went into ecstasies over a bronze bust, "Pansy": a woman with her breast armored in pansy petals was sporting another full-blown pansy as a crown for her knot of hair; two other pansies set off her ears. The junior officer knew how to shower agreeable praise on something he deemed beautiful, an art that Rolland lacked. He expressed his approval only with a movement of his head, as if he were saluting. But Madame Bouttier did not seem to hold that against him, and it was obviously for him that she was taking the most pains. Several times he caught her gaze resting upon him with that smiling curiosity which betokens a feeling of sympathy. He would have liked to be able to thank her for it, to tell her, in confidence, that this cordiality was very important to him—these smiles that were addressed to what he did not say, to what he was, to what she divined in him. For social affability found him defenseless, warmed through and through, ready to take the consideration of a good hostess for an expression of personal liking. . . .

They fell to talking of France. The Bouttiers recalled it with the nostalgic enthusiasm of colonists, and set the highest value on things which would have left the two officers cold if they had read about them in a newspaper in a French port. Some bits of news passed entirely over their heads.

Then Monsieur Bouttier began to speak of the ships that had anchored in the roadstead of Thio in the past year. There was the *Ville de Bayeux,* for one, that had run aground off the channel and had been stranded on a reef for thirty-two hours before she could be towed off. Faced with the price demanded for repairs, the owners had preferred to sell her on the spot. An assistant manager of the *Compagnie des Longs-Courriers Normands* had come to Thio to settle up the business.

"But you know him!" Madame Bouttier suddenly broke in. "Didn't you once sail on the *Galatée?*"

"Yes," Rolland answered, suddenly shy again on hearing the name

* English term in French original; turn-of-the-century period. Tr.

211

of that ship, the last his pride would have wished to hear spoken in this drawing room.

"Then you knew Monsieur Barquet."

The "Monsieur" led the former topman astray.

"I knew his son, yes," he said.

"But that's the one! He was the apprentice, wasn't he?"

Rolland steeled himself a little before answering, but now he could take it.

"Yes, when I was a seaman," he said.

Madame Bouttier seemed altogether delighted at this.

"Then it was you who saved his life off Cape Horn!" she cried.

It was not off Cape Horn, which the *Galatée* had passed some distance back when the accident occurred; and Rolland had not saved the apprentice's life; at least, so he said.

"That is not what he told us!"

"You saw him?" he asked her.

"Yes, he came up here," she said.

And her husband added, "If you had got here six weeks earlier, you would have had lunch together. And do I know him! I come from Fécamp, and his father and I were in high school together. He died two years ago, when Jean was in Japan as junior officer on the *Du Guesclin*."

"He kept on at sea?"

"Yes, he was at sea three years, I believe. Then when his father died he took over his shipping interests, and he is associated with the *Longs-Courriers Normands*. That is how he happened to come here, to close up the business of the *Ville de Bayeux*."

Monsieur Bouttier was saying all this as if it were the simplest, the most commonplace, thing in the world: Barquet—"Débarqué"— who used to shake in the wind like a scarecrow; Barquet with his open mouth, his ways like a nun, his jitters, his crass ignorance that didn't know one end of a ship from the other; Barquet junior officer, shipping-man, assistant manager! It would have to have been in France, on the other side of the world, the antipodes where everything went along upside down, like flies on the ceiling! All one could think of as senseless or unjust became natural like this when it was a matter of people with money!

For he was no more willing than he had ever been to go beyond that. The-son-of-his-Papa whom Captain Le Gac to start with had shut up in his cabin, for fear something or someone might hurt him, had found others to pass him on from hand to hand as far as an assistant manager's armchair. Barquet had bought his way on land, as he had bought his way on the *Galatée;* that was the explanation of his pretty career.

As if she had somehow divined the essence of all this, Madame Bouttier added two sentences that brought Jean Barquet's "mission" down to more acceptable proportions! "He came especially to see his sister, at Nouméa. She married a captain in the colonial artillery eighteen months ago, and followed him here."

She was throwing Rolland back once more to the *Galatée*. He saw, again, the photograph he had dirtied, Barquet's dash to snatch it from him, Monnard's scornful face when he was burning the obscene pitch marks with which he had spotted it over. It was one of the most humiliating memories of his life; and here it was being offered to him with the chartreuse! What did they still have to drag out of his inmost self?

From then on, he was only making a formal call. He listened without paying attention, for the proper length of time, while the manager talked to him about nickel, about the difficulties of mining it and working with Canaque labor, about the vexatious meddlings of the board of directors; then he pulled out his watch, gave it a glance, and rose.

"You must excuse us," he said. "It is about time for us to get back."

"Already! You are not in such a hurry as all that!"

Madame Bouttier was looking at him reproachfully, and he thought that it was not mere politeness. "But what have I said, what have I done?" she seemed to be asking. He turned away from her as if she had betrayed him, and it was to her husband that he replied. "Yes, it is time for us to go: high time already. . . ."

"Aren't they the grand people!" Poullain exclaimed, as they were starting away. "They gave us a splendid party, didn't they?"

"Because they are bored with themselves," Rolland retorted, beginning to attack the descent.

They did not exchange another word until they reached the ship, where Berteux informed them that the tug *Tayo* would be on hand the next day.

The *Antonine* left the roadstead of Thio next morning, in tow for Kanala. On the port side there were forty miles of tall wooded cliffs following one another in procession. The reefs, gray or dark-red, would sometimes curve their masses like curly fleece at the level of the water, and sometimes lift solid blocks and peaks as sharp as needles above the calm transparent sea.

On the *Antonine,* released now from her labors, it was the little steam boiler which was for once becoming the center of interest. Every last grain of tartar had been chipped off it by the pointed hammers of the watch; it was as clean as a whistle. Papa Burrey, the mechanic, had given it a thorough overhauling, oiled all its joints, ground its valves, and at last declared it to be all in order for a swift loading. As the ship started, the cabin boy had brought Rolland a note from the captain: he would like the boiler to be filled as soon as possible, so that it could be fired by four o'clock the next morning, in case the barges should have been made ready at Kanala. No captain likes to lose any time, but, ashore, that was certainly an early hour!

Papa Burrey, therefore, had installed a big hand-lever on his "little horse," the steam feed pump, and the men would take turns working it to fill the boiler. They went at it with a good heart, because it was a novel task, and because it entertained them to strike the pistons in a cadence which the sturdiest would succeed for a few seconds in matching to the rhythm of the steam. It was a game they were playing, youngsters that they were, when they hung onto the lever of a pump and worked it fast enough to get a good spurt, full and steady. Poullain acted as umpire, praising the quick boys and crying down the dawdlers. And then, at the height of the fun, the key piece of cast-iron where the hand-lever rested—too long maltreated by the joltings of all these confounded pumpers—broke square in two. . . .

Poullain, utterly crestfallen, came to report to Rolland.

"Bad luck, old boy! Go report it to the captain," the mate said.

Thirard was sitting in his cabin, with his head in his hands, but at the news of the accident he stood up and turned paler than ever, if possible, as he advanced on the third mate, who had remained standing close to the door.

"Damn good-for-nothings, idiots!" he panted. "Now we'll have to have another piece cast. And that can't be done at Kanala."

He took several steps, to quiet down this anger which was terrifying, because it was using up, to no purpose, the strength which was already so dreadfully reduced. Then he came back toward Poullain, without choosing to notice his air of distress.

"Well, get us out of this mess! Go down to Thio with the little boat and bring back a new piece. And be as quick as you can about it!"

He succeeded in speaking aloud, in a voice that was horribly hoarse and broken, as he repeated, "I said, as quick as you can!"

Poullain almost ran out of the room.

"It'll be twenty miles from here to Thio, since we're almost half-way," he explained to Rolland, sponging his forehead as he spoke. "Then forty miles from there to Kanala. Shall I take the long-boat and four men, sir?"

"Why not the dinghy?"

"Because I've got sixty miles to go, and I count on having the breeze."

"Very well, take the long-boat. I needn't tell you to speed her up. . . ."

They signaled to the *Tayo* to slow down, brought up the long-boat, and Poullain set off with four sailors. The boat started out with a good carrying wind but soon struck a calm, and the men had to take hold of the oars in order to avoid the reefs. Nevertheless, Poullain hauled off the twenty miles in six hours, which could be considered a record, and at five in the afternoon he entered the Nickel Company's workship with the broken piece under his arm.

"We'll make a new one for you in steel. That won't snap off," the superintendent said. "You will have it tomorrow evening."

Poullain glowed: two evenings to spend in Thio—for one could not think of sailing along the coast, among the reefs, in the dark! That would be well worth a journey of sixty miles!

After he had moored his long-boat broadside on, and arranged for food and lodging for his four men, he rushed straight away to look up his acquaintances. Where Rolland had strolled about for a whole morning without making any discoveries, he went into three houses where women came running to the summons of his ringing voice. He did not leave the last of the three until rather late the next morning, and when he went back to Thio-Mission he caught sight of the *Tayo,* returning from Kanala, where she had cast off the *Antonine*. Poullain went aboard to see the tugboat captain, and told him his adventure.

"Well then, Commander, it would be very kind of you to explain to me where Kanala keeps itself, and you would be doing me a service if you gave me a map."

"A map," the captain echoed. "I have only one. But I will make a tracing for you, and that will do. You aren't likely to make a mistake. It is the first bay after the Pennel farm, a big white building with cocoanut palms around it. You can't help noticing it: it's the only place of its kind on the coast. Only, you must leave early tomorrow morning," he added, "so as to haul out on the land breeze. Until then, Monsieur Poullain, please make yourself at home on the *Tayo*."

They went off together for an apéritif, and directed their steps to Mother Girard's. There they met up with the mayor of Thio, the chief warehouse-man and the workshop superintendent from the Nickel Company, and two or three others, who were at once of a mind to clink glasses with an officer from a sailing-ship, especially when he was such a damn good card as this one!

215

"Why don't you have your men tie up your long-boat to the stern of the *Tayo?*" the tugboat captain suggested, as they left the café. "They will sleep aboard; you, too. That way, you will be sure of having them there at four o'clock tomorrow morning."

Poullain thanked him, and went off to gather his men together again and bring up the long-boat. Then he set out to make his farewell calls, get his new piece of apparatus, and have a last drink with the workshop superintendent. It was late when he got back to the tug, and the captain met him with a rather curious air.

"You are going to take on a passenger en route," he announced. "I spoke to you of the Pennel farm: Madame Pennel is about to have a baby, and the doctor here has been sent for, for her confinement. You will pick him up there as you go by."

"But where am I to take him?" demanded Poullain, in amazement.

"To the *Antonine,* nowhere else! He is to see your captain, by order of the Company. They mean to find out, whether or no, how things stand. You know, I have a feeling that he was wrong not to call on them in person."

"If he had been able to!" Poullain exclaimed.

"Oh, is it as bad as that? As a matter of fact, I suspected that this was coming. This afternoon, when I called at the office, they asked me bluntly how I had found him. I was obliged to tell them that I hadn't seen him. It was the mate who had made all the arrangements, with the captain's apologies: he had had a fit of choking, he said. Well then, naturally, they asked themselves, 'Is he hiding, or is someone hiding him?' In either case—"

"I understand that," said Poullain, very much annoyed. "But to come down on him like this, without even giving him any warning! He is not hiding. He is not being kept hidden—that still less! He does not wish to leave the ship, and there you have it! Except for these attacks, he's holding on all right. But since we reached here he's had one, and it's got him down. At those times he's not a pretty sight. Any old medical officer would put him in hospital as a matter of course. What's he like, this one of yours?"

"A former Navy doctor who has settled here, a Dr. Lefort. Oh, a good fellow!"

Poullain shook his head. "Yes, but a top sergeant! That's not going to work out, not any!"

The tug's captain changed the subject as he refilled the apéritif glasses.

"Wait and see. . . . It isn't going to keep you from having dinner, is it?"

Poullain sneezed. "As you say, Captain, we must wait. . . . What can we do for him this evening? Drink his health. . . . Then let's go to it!"

They did not turn in that night. The supper for four people (the captain had invited his mate and his mechanic), stretched out by Poullain's story-telling, lasted until morning. As it struck four, the officer got into his boat, with the new piece of apparatus and provisions for forty-eight hours, the latter a gift of the tugboat captain, who had been delighted with this jovial companion.

"Well, we shan't see each other again," he said regretfully, as he shook hands. "It's Berlot who is going to pull you out of that hole you're in now."

"You don't know me!" cried Poullain, already on his way down the ladder. "Nobody can ever get rid of me; I always come back! Something else will bust in the boiler!" But as he was an honest fellow, and fearful of calling down an untoward fate, even as a joke, he added, as his sailors were pushing off: "I'm not asking for it, get that!"

The men on the *Tayo* saw him run up full sail to take advantage of the land breeze. Standing at the wheel, he made sweeping gestures with his left arm; then he sat down. The weather was clear, and at this end-of-the-night it was mild—too mild! A chill would have waked a man up, whereas in the cradling movement of the long-boat, the monotonous slapping of the waves against its sides, Poullain felt his head getting heavy, his eyelids turning to lead. One of the older sailors, Cario, came up, without saying anything, to smoke his pipe near the tiller. . . .

"Bear away, Monsieur Poullain!" he called out suddenly. "There's a big rock right ahead."

Poullain gave a start.

"So there is! My God, I was asleep! And we are running right on Bouétamiré, the sugar-loaf where the Canaque chiefs used to be buried. . . ."

A push at the helm, the sheets eased off, and they passed it, dangerously close.

Poullain was not sleepy any more; besides, it was almost full daylight now. With a first-rate tot of grog, they all felt fit again. Cario was no longer watching the tiller, but the sail: the land breeze died down at dawn.

"The bitch, she's giving us the go-by," one of the men grumbled. "We'll have to haul a dead weight."

Half an hour later, in fact, they were in a "white calm," with a thin thread of current bearing toward the shore, and they got the inevitable order:

"Man the oars!"

The four fellows went at it with a good heart, to warm themselves up; for the air had grown chilly as the sun rose. At the same time, the water became deeper. This was no longer a gray surface, as it had been a little while ago, but a profound domain blossoming with extraordinary corals.

"Have a look, Monsieur Poullain—wouldn't you say they were heads of endive, those white ones there?"

Then there were garfish, pretty fringed fish that came to escort the long-boat, keeping their heads at the surface of the water and swimming with a flexible movement that made them look like blue seaweed.

"Stand by!" called out Gallais, a Breton from Saint Briac.

He had pulled in his oar and let down a line.

"I've got him!"

And he brought up a splendid garfish.

Poullain was beginning to be afraid that his rowers, tempted by such fishing, would lose their energy! But fortunately a breeze came in from the sea, and they went back to the sail. At one in the afternoon, Poullain caught sight of the white house. It stood at the top of a wide path that descended in a gentle slope to the sea.

"If that damn kid could only stay in his nice warm nook until tomorrow!" Poullain growled.

The men looked at him in astonishment. What he was thinking was that if the doctor was still held up by the confinement, he himself would be free of the job of taking him to the ship.

But when they were still more than half a mile from shore, a canoe dashed out from behind a rock; it was paddled by a Canaque, and in the stern sat a man in a white suit, with a linen helmet. Five minutes later, the doctor was stepping aboard the long-boat: a man of about forty-five, with gray hair, a stiff little beard like a shaving-brush, and long narrow eyes that gave him a vaguely Chinese appearance. He did not conceal his vexation at being prevented from returning to Thio that evening. The baby had been born at eight o'clock in the morning; that meant he had been waiting five hours for their long-boat.

"What has he got, your captain?" he demanded.

"Something the matter with his throat," Poullain answered cautiously.

"And that keeps him from coming to Thio for consultation?"

"It has made him very weak. . . ."

"Ah," said Dr. Lefort.

Poullain realized that he was going over in his mind the throat ailments that might make the captain of a sailing-vessel so weak he could not leave his ship. The process seemed to calm him. He appeared to be less certain, now, that he had been disturbed for nothing.

Poullain dug into his pocket. One of his acquaintances had made him a present of three cigars, semi-Havana, wrapped in tissue paper. He offered one to the doctor, who accepted it. When he had lighted it, the passenger relieved his mind of his major preoccupation:

"I shall be obliged to spend the night at Kanala. I do not know if you are acquainted with the place. It consists of six houses and a bar."

Poullain assumed an air of stupefaction.

"But that is nonsense! You will dine and sleep aboardship."

"Very well, I accept," responded Lefort, as if he were saying, "That's to be taken for granted."

"There is only one thing that is troublesome," Poullain pointed out, his eyes on the smoke of his cagar. "It is that the captain is not expecting your visit."

He spoke in a low tone, confidentially; there was no need for the men to hear. The doctor's reply, on the other hand, was flung back too loudly:

"So what? After all, he isn't a baby, afraid of a spoon in his mouth!"

Poullain explained, laboriously, that Captain Thirard, oversensitive like all sick people, might construe this visit as a measure taken in distrust.

"And suppose it were?" retorted the doctor, whose military outspokenness was gaining the upper hand, and whose forehead was wrinkling dangerously.

"In that case," Poullain replied categorically, "he would slam his cabin door in your face, and nothing would be any the better! They won't make him consult a doctor by force, will they? Any more than they will call the police to haul him off his ship, if he insists on staying on her."

The physician, slightly perturbed, shrugged his shoulders.

"Have you another sick man aboard, who might justify my visit? No? Well, then—"

"But you might have come for health inspection," Poullain suggested. "They were saying at Thio that there was a case of yellow fever on the *Suzanne,* the boat that was in the roads when we arrived."

His passenger rejected this bit of news with a surly toss of his head.

"That's all rot! Because they were coming from Saigon, they saw yellow fever everywhere. The fellow had acute jaundice, with temperature. Not enough pernod!"

Cario, who had heard this, turned away laughing. But Poullain persisted. It was a fact that there had been fear of yellow fever. Going on from that, he added in a lower tone, what was there to prevent the doctor's saying that the Health Office had ordered an inspection of every incoming ship, as a matter of form?

"It would be such a little lie," he said, insinuatingly.

"If you are set on it—" said the doctor. Then he pointed to a broad silver-gray cliff. "Kanala Bay is just behind. . . ."

The entrance was wide, between tall cliffs covered with forest. A chain of high hills rimmed the water, in a design like a broad boot, and these were cut into by the deep gashes of gullies. It was low tide, and coral banks stood out above the water. The *Antonine* lay at anchor in the middle of the bay, unneighbored, a spot of black on the dazzling sea.

They came alongside.

Rolland was waiting for them at the ladder, amazed to see this surplus passenger. Poullain introduced the doctor and explained the reason for his coming, the pretext that would have to be given to the captain. The physician was listening, with no very good grace.

"You, too," he demanded of the mate, "do you think this tale of yellow fever is absolutely necessary?"

"What I am asking myself particularly," Rolland answered, "is whether there is any chance of his believing it."

"Then what?"

"One can always try," suggested Poullain.

And as their silence seemed to give consent, he went off in a hurry to announce the visit to the captain. He came back five minutes later, glowing.

"It's worked splendidly! He is waiting for you, doctor."

They themselves were a long time waiting for the doctor to leave the sickroom. When he came out on deck again, and made his way toward the two men standing near the poop-deck companionway, one look at him gave them warning.

"Well, doctor?"

Lefort threw a glance at the sailors lounging on the fore-and-aft gangway: "Not here . . ."

They went to the mate's cabin.

"Well," he said, "this is the worst cancer of the larynx that I ever seen. He must be a man of extraordinary energy to have stood it, and to go on standing it! When they reach the stage he is at now, they are no more than rags and tatters of men, that you can do what you like with; it isn't that way with him!"

It was Poullain who asked, "Is there nothing to be done?"

"Absolutely nothing. It is too late for surgical treatment. If the larynx were removed it would not change anything—and he could not stand the operation. The only thing is to go on with what he is doing: spraying with cocaine, morphine when the pain is unendurable."

"Does he know what it is?" Poullain asked again.

"If you could tell me! . . . He talked to me about edema, but I am convinced that he didn't believe in it any more than I do."

"How long can he go on?" Rolland put in.

"At this rate, a month; six weeks at most. But a hemorrhage might just as easily carry him off tomorrow. It is one of the most rapid of all cancers in running its course."

"You are not going to make him go ashore?" Rolland asked, in a more muffled voice.

The physician did not reply immediately. At last he said, "Since I left him, I have been putting that question to myself. I naturally advised it. I even suggested that he go back to France by steamship. He would not hear of it! He said that he had been able to perform his duties so far—"

Rolland and Poullain spoke with one voice: "That is true."

"—and that he was still able to do it. Being the man he is, he will stick it out to the end. If there were one chance in a thousand of any improvement, I should not hesitate: I would make him leave the ship, even if it had to be done by force. But there is no such chance. The only question is whether he is to die in a hospital or on his ship. It goes without saying that he would have a more tranquil end in a hospital, but the blow to his morale would be terrible, and I must take that into account."

He paused, and looked at the two officers slowly, one after the other.

"There is another question to consider: whether the ship may have to suffer, from his presence on board. That, gentlemen, is a question for you to answer."

"She never has suffered, up to now: on the contrary," Rolland said.

Poullain nodded in confirmation.

"No, but that may come," said the doctor. "Think it over. You will be here for some time. That makes it possible to postpone a decision."

"That is so," Poullain agreed, with relief. "Let us wait." He had already said that, on the tug. Now he added: "The captain of the *Tayo* made me a present of a bottle of vermouth. I think it's coming to us to have a taste of it!"

XX

AS SOON AS the boat came alongside, Rolland turned his back on the shore and looked at the water playing over the red pebbles at his feet. There was something returning to him out of his earliest childhood: the pleasure he still felt in seeing the sea reach its final boundary, thinned down to a mere moving film of frothy water; in listening to its sound like the crinkling of fine silk; in following its overlappings as it slid across the sands. It was an infrequent pleasure, for usually one landed only at quays, at wharfs. Yet never did a shore appear more familiar than at this rim between land and sea, where all lands were like one another as they welcomed the tide.

When he turned back to the shore again, the harmony of this new land filled him with a sense of well-being, a contentment that was strong and that he felt would be enduring. He did not know how to analyze the sources of this serenity; everything had part in it: the foliage that gleamed like silver, the vibrant clarity of the sky, the muted sound of the surf behind him, even the new savor of the air he was breathing deep into his lungs. He was taking it all in at one time, through eyes, ears, mouth, unwilling to let go of anything in order to mark the details of his enjoyment; that would have been both a labor and an impoverishment.

Yet he was satisfied, and in a way proud, to be able to take such an interest in a completely unknown landscape, to be profoundly aware of how novel it was. It was really the first time such a thing had happened to him. Up to now he had, like his sailors, followed, at every landing, the slope that led very quickly from the mysterious to the banal. A few minutes of curiosity, and their experience of the world would soon resolve the strangest and most alien countries into something they had already seen. With his first steps on this island, Rolland felt that he was becoming capable of wonder; it was a sign that he was changing his caste.

Kréven, who was making his third "nickel voyage," spoke of the country as they made the boat fast.

"No snakes, no wild animals, a good climate; everything grows here, as it does in France. And the Canaques, they're grand guys!"

"It's too bad," Rolland remarked, "that it should have been dirtied up with a penal colony."

This was the reflection that all the captains used to come back to, and that he was making his own. In the face of the lovely results of penal colonization, the government had not ordered any further "transportations" to New Caledonia since 1897, but there were still more than three thousand convicts undergoing punishment there. Kréven threw a sidelong glance at the mate.

"Yet those are men——" he said.

Rolland's expression forced him to explain:

"A fellow gets in today on the *Antonine*, and he says to himself that he might, if you're damn particular, be coming in on the *Loire*.* It's often just a question of chance."

"Where I come from," Rolland recalled, "they work themselves to death to clear the weeds and stones and stumps out of a bit of moor; and here it seems that a convict, at the end of his term, can receive two or three thousand square acres of land, all ready for planting, a cabin, tools, money, supplies for five years, not to speak of a woman, a hussy who'll pick up something on her own as a streetwalker. That amounts to telling you that honesty doesn't pay!"

Kréven abstained from any answer, except by the shadow of a smile. He obviously approved of the general exploitation of official guilelessness. When the boat was staunchly moored, he turned around and, pointing to a narrow gap among the pale tree trunks, said, "That path must go there, too."

They were looking for Pillou's farm. Since the *Antonine's* arrival at Kanala, the captain had been asking again for his "fellow-townsman" Berlot, the owner and skipper of the *Tamanou*. Rolland had decided, therefore, to make an advance into the country as far as the home of this Pillou woman with whom Berlot was infatuated, if the assistant manager at Thio was to be believed. There he would perhaps get news of him. At Kanala, they had advised him to "go up the gully." So he and Kréven had taken their little boat, determined to go as far as possible in it; but they had met with nothing but disappointment. First, because their throats were burning in the blazing sun, they had sampled the water in the stream.

"Fine! It's fresh!" they said.

Then they put down their bucket and brought it up full to the brim.

"My God! It's salt!"

There was only a thin layer of fresh water on the surface of the briny current.

* The convict ship.

Then the mosquitoes—one's hands would be first black with them, and then red after they had been killed. . . . This had disgusted them with navigation. They had tacked about and returned to draw up the boat onto the narrow beach, from which they would be able to cut across to the farm by way of the cliff. While Rolland was finding some minutes of diversion in looking at the edge of the water, Kréven, keeping to the specific and the practical, had at once searched for a possible route, and thought he had found one in this promise of a path. They took a chance on it.

The first curious species of native trees, with pale foliage like false birches, and white bark that crumbled into flour under Rolland's fingers, merely fringed the seashore. Higher up, there were candleberry trees, ironwood, tamarinds, and others unknown to him, whose light trunks shot up through the thick underbrush. Tropical creepers hung from the branches like bunches of tangled rope: a wild rigging, all muddled by a storm. . . .

They made their way through a narrow tunnel hollowed out under the sturdy foliage. The quality of the light was the same as Rolland had perceived a little while ago at the bottom of the blue-toned water: limpid but cold, and without reflections. It reached them only as it was poured from leaf to leaf and decanted of all vibration through those multiplied screens.

The silence was surprising, too. The soil, as soft underfoot as a velvet-pile carpet, absorbed the sound of their steps. Even more surely than the sun, the breeze was blocked by the dense foliage of the trees and the close lattices of the creepers. Not a leaf was rustling. There would have had to be a cyclone to make music here! And even it could have swept around and around this cage of vegetation without finding its way through the bars. . . . There were no bird songs to be heard.

Rolland was walking ahead of Kréven, taking long strides and seeing no more of the hill-slope than he used to see of the land beyond the edges of the road that was blotted out by the darkness when he rode his bicycle at night. He had speeded up his pace, because this mute dimness oppressed him. Then, suddenly, he stopped short: there was the patter of a sinewy gallop on the soft earth, a gallop of small hoofs, but so swift that Rolland expected to see one of those deer emerging, which Poullain had listed among the local game.

It was only a goat; and astonishingly French in aspect, with its yellow-gray coat, its Chinese beard, and that sharp-cut backbone which offends the eye. It planted itself in the middle of the path, with the insistence of animals that have only their sight to tell them the intentions of the human beings they meet; then it turned at right angles and was off again, at the same high speed. Its appearance had done away with all Rolland's sense of strangeness in this place. The she-goat seemed so much at home, under these alien trees, that it robbed them of all mystery.

The forest came to an end with the hill-slope. The canopied path came out in the open at the top of a hummock. The crude blue of the sky and the blaze of the sun together, struck them in the face.

They paused to get their bearings. There was still the high palisade of tree trunks to left and right, but in front of them the underbrush slipped down to the depths of the valley, where the shrunken gully cut through a close thicket of trees. That was where the house must be.

They were about to start down when they caught sight of the herd of goats, lined up right beside the edge of the forest, where the tufts of grass, protected by the shade, would be less dried up. Almost at the same time, they discovered the woman.

She was sitting on the ground, leaning against a screw-pine, and as they looked at her with the full glare of the sun in their eyes she seemed black.

A Canaque, Rolland thought.

It was only when they had come quite close to her that they saw she was a white woman.

She had not stirred at their approach. Like her goat, a few minutes before, she was examining them. But it was soon Rolland alone on whom she bent her steady gaze. She neglected Kréven, in whom she had divined the subordinate.

Standing two steps away from her, Rolland made no haste to speak. He, too, was observing, and with a fixed gaze. She was very dark, with black eyes that glittered as if they had metal filings in them. The narrow face seemed to be retaining the bitterness of what it had been when it served to give pleasure, of what it might still be in some other place than in this barbarous and remote corner where one's hair became a mane, and sunburn bit into one's soft-toned skin. The body was at the same time slack—too long the play of outside forces, one might say—and muscular: capable still of reaction and combat. The pressure of her breasts against her dress showed that she had given up the European corset, and the cotton fabric followed the lines of her long thighs. Without taking his eyes off her, Rolland was searching for a sentence with which to accost her. At last he pointed to the goats, and asked, "They don't make it too hard for you, looking after them?"

"No."

The mistrustful curtness of the tone made him realize that he had gained nothing, and that his approach to the subject was missing fire. It would have been better to have said at once, as he did now,

225

"We are looking for Monsieur Berlot, the owner of the *Tamanou*. It seems that he can be found at the house of a man named Pillou. Is it this way?"

Before answering, she asked him, "Are you from the ship that came into the roads yesterday?"

"Yes."

"Is it for information that you are seeking Berlot?"

From this "Berlot," as from the still unappeased defiance with which she regarded him, Rolland realized that he was not dealing with a mere goatherd. He explained that the captain of the *Antonine* wished to see Berlot, one of his old seafaring comrades, and that, being ill, he was not able to come ashore. Her reply did not greatly surprise him:

"He was staying with us, but he is not here now. He sailed day before yesterday. I can give him a message," she added, "when he comes back."

She got up.

"You will come as far as the house," she said.

It was the phrase Rolland had heard so many times in Brittany when he used to speak to a farmer or his wife, for any reason at all, in the fields: that beautiful phrase of rustic courtesy. They would not hesitate to leave their work to escort the passer-by to the farmhouse, which was usually a long distance away, even though he had already said everything he had to say. But this woman did not offer her invitation as it was offered in a buckwheat field: she seemed still to be wondering about the two men, and to be wanting to find out more about them. Rolland, on his part, was scrutinizing her with still more attentive eyes, now that he knew that this was Berlot's mistress. Their two curiosities were already a link between them, and he was conscious of it.

She swept a long bamboo rod across the ground, and went off with it to the edge of the forest to drive home her goats. Those that loitered for a last mouthful received a swift and accurate stroke on their hocks, and they would bound forward as if propelled from a catapult. Then, when they were herded together, she drove them over the slope of the hill, which was overgrown with the dry leaves of the hated weed that the people call "blue grass," a vervain which invades these fields even more than the couch-grass does those of France. Then the woman went down the hill with a step as sure as her goats', and Rolland watched the free swing of her body as she walked.

Ten minutes of walking brought them to a small grove of guava trees at the bottom of the valley. She shut up her goats in a yard with a wooden fence, and went ahead of her visitors toward the cottage. From the moment she rose to call her herd, she had not seemed to be aware of the fact that two men were following her.

It was a wide-spread house, with square windows that rose to the border of the thatched roof. A wooden bench was backed up against the outside wall near the entrance door, under a sort of lean-to roof. The woman went in first.

It was dark inside, as it is in all dwellings in countries of burning sun, arranged to apply a poultice of shade to eyes too long scorched by the light outdoors. There was a table, a few chests of drawers, a low bed, all made of precious woods—those which in France are sold for thin veneers, and which here were solid and hardly quartered off at all. She set a bottle on the table, to say nothing of glasses, and poured out the drinks with the indifference of a barmaid in rush hours. When she bent toward Rolland, to refill his glass, he stared at her without meeting her eyes.

He was seeking assiduously for a way to start a conversation, and he found himself running up against perils in the simplest question, everywhere. It was hazardous, for instance, to remark, "Well, it's a pleasant country, isn't it?" . . . or, "You don't get too bored here?" If this was a liberated prisoner he was talking with—and her defensive attitude was making him fear that such was the case—he would be driving her to bay for the only reply, "Pleasant or not, whether I am entertained or whether I am bored, I have no choice." Still less would it be in order for him to inquire, "Was it a long time ago that you left France?"

He contented himself with saying, as he pointed to the sky of lapis lazuli outside the window, "Do you often have weather like this?"

"Yes, it's the usual thing here," she answered.

"We are fortunate, in any case," he said, "that the first person we encounter here should be a beautiful woman."

"Go easy," she advised.

He insisted that she was a beautiful woman, and he knew what he was talking about. To mention no more than what he was seeing, it was certain that those eyes of hers were in a class by themselves. He took another drink, and added, "If you need me, some day when there's a big wind, don't hesitate."

"Need you—for what?"

"To moor you fast to your bed. You wouldn't be in any danger of being carried away!"

She answered him seriously: "You know, that happens."

"Never when I'm around! Because I'd reef your sails. And if the wind blew too hard, I wouldn't even hesitate to strip your canvas."

She shrugged her shoulders. "When there is a big wind here, we

227

call it a cyclone," she said. "On those days you'll do as others do: stay indoors."

"If it were with you, I shouldn't find the time long," he said.

And there he was; that was all; he had run out of things to say. It was impossible even to get hold of the most threadbare commonplaces of port gallantry. Oh, if Poullain had been in his place! If, even, she had not let him down as she was doing! He fell back on the country, the farming, the Canaques. She replied in monosyllables, sometimes leaning over to refill the glasses with red wine, then returning to her waiting pose, elbows on the table, chin in her hands.

Rolland, who was sitting directly opposite her, felt himself more and more drawn by that strange cold visage. The dark eyes that were watching him never blinked, nor were they trying to appeal to emotion, to sweep him off his feet. But their stress was sufficient indication of what he was meant to understand: that she was a tart, and would ply her trade when occasion offered.

But she was a tart with thin lips and a thin body, of a type which Rolland knew well: hard and self-contained hussies who would go through the paces of physical love successfully, by a prompt and exacting mechanical action, but who yielded nothing of themselves, neither a word nor a spontaneous gesture; women who brought a stern conciseness to the encounter, turning it into a brief and terse struggle. He had always been more attracted by these muscular exhaust-boxes than by the woman whose words and bodily responses were a flowing tide. He was not disgusted with them when they had served their purpose, as he was with the others. They remained firm, tense; and, insomuch as they had given nothing of themselves, they kept their enigmatic charm. He had entirely forgotten his first suspicions: he was not going to begin to see the convict prison everywhere, like a journalist! He was wondering now how to suggest an assignation: "Where? When? How-much?" He had read that somewhere; and the insolence of those three words had pleased him: convenient, quick, but not always easy to introduce!

Then, too, he felt uncomfortable about Kréven: not in any way from modesty, but because to him this would mean, "I am going to have a good time while you are working." Since the beginning of their conversation, however, the bos'n had shown as complete an indifference as if they had accosted a customs agent to ask their way. Now, sprawling over the table, he seemed to be entirely engrossed in his glass of wine, which he held encircled in his two hands and was looking at, unmoving.

Just then the door opened. A panel of harsh light fell on the end wall, and, with it, a man entered the room. He was disconcerting, as a scrawny pig is; for one felt that he was intended to be fat, with the flabby, empty creases in his weasel face. He threw a sharp glance at the strangers, from the door-sill, and then immediately smiled at them.

"My husband. . . ."

The woman spoke almost with defiance, as if she meant to add, "I have one; why not?"

At once, Rolland was all on guard again. The man stank of the released prisoner. This could not be a free colonist, with that servile gaze, the mawkishness of that thick underlip, that bent-over look. And she, he was now asking, where would she have come from, if not from the "convent"? Poullain had been to see that "convent" on his first voyage to the island: a place at Bourail where some ten or twelve nuns kept a fish-pond of women, sent out by the reformatories to marry the bachelor or widowed convicts when they had served their prison terms. Poullain had been showered with smiles and sheep's eyes, during his visit, to a crushing extent, and he had delighted in the suave, "Pardon, Mother," which the "candidates" pronounced with a soft slurring of the "r," to add to the seduction of their voices. In front of the institution building there was a courtyard planted with stunted trees, and in the middle of this was a green latticed summer-house. It was here, once the selection had been made in the parlor, that the engaged couples would meet, watched through the gratings by a nun and a guard. When the interview became too affectionate the nun would cough, and the guard would step into the summer-house. . . . Seeing her husband, Rolland was ready to take his oath that this woman had come out of the house of correction by that door; and that was not making him feel kindly.

He did not have to refuse an offered hand, nor to hold out his own in greeting. The man who was coming in was all bowing and scraping. He seated himself at the end of the table.

"Well," he said, his eyes half-closed. "You've strayed as far as our neck of the woods, have you?"

"They wanted to see Berlot," the woman said curtly.

"Ah, Monsieur Berlot. . . . You are out of luck; you have missed him by two days. He sailed from Muéo day before yesterday."

"This is where he stays, between his voyages, isn't it?"

"No," Pillou answered, with a humble smile. "We are not fitted up, after all, to give Monsieur Berlot lodgings! But he likes to come here to rest, in the quiet, between two coasting trips."

"When you see him again, if we are still in the roadstead, tell him that Captain Thirard would be very glad to see him. But he would have to come aboard the ship, because the captain is ill and cannot go ashore. I can depend on you to let him know?"

"Absolutely, sir, absolutely. But look, Denise, the glasses are empty. Go get another bottle."

She did not budge. It was Rolland she was watching: his hand that had just pushed his glass brusquely aside, his face become suddenly hard. He had dropped into the house of an ex-convict, he was sure of that. It must be a common occurrence in the countryside. One might find oneself, sometimes, sitting before a glass of wine offered by a murderer, and there must be certain cases where acceptance would be the right thing; but not from this man!

"No, we are going," he said.

He stood up. Kréven rose after him. The man, stopped short, was looking at them. He had immediately recovered his oily smile under the affront; and Rolland was asking himself, as he reached the door, what it was that was out-of-the-ordinary about him. He thought he had found it: Pillou had not made one gesture since he entered the room; he kept his arms close to his sides: the habit of standing always at attention, probably too recent still.

"That's all right, then," the man promised, as he followed them to the door. "As soon as we see Monsieur Berlot, we will tell him."

The woman had remained seated and was deliberately returning insult for insult—which made Rolland give her a glance of observation before he went out. Head and shoulders held straight and unmoving, she had her eyes fixed on the floor; she, too, seemed to be recovering the attitudes of prison.

And behind them the mawkish sticky voice was even more saccharine as it urged, "You must come again, gentlemen. I am not often at home myself, but my wife is always here. Or, at least, she is never far away."

Rolland did not turn to cast a glance at the merchandise thus offered. But he touched the brim of his hat as he went away. It was the first time that he had felt called upon to be impolite, in leaving a house where he had been welcomed; and that troubled him.

"There's a married woman who can't be hearing herself called 'Madame' very often," he remarked to Kréven as they started up the hill.

The bos'n's only reply was a swaying movement of his head. Rolland, who had wanted to please him by taking him ashore with him—though this was not usually done—felt a little annoyed that he should have turned out to be such a glum companion.

As soon as they reached the ship, he went to the captain and reported on his mission. Thirard listened with his eyes closed, and that tight fold of nausea around his mouth which was brought there now by the word of any delay, hitch, or anything that upset the routine on the ship. To Rolland, this was a sign that he was stricken to his innermost depths, all his substance corroded: this morbid impatience, this inability to wait, to endure, although endurance is the essential virtue of sea chiefs. Now the sick man shrugged his shoulders and murmured, "It is high time for Berlot, too, to get back to France!"

Rolland looked at him, almost in terror: was he really thinking that he himself would be able to get back to France? Now that the mate *knew,* he went into the captain's room as into the cell of someone condemned to death, wondering if he believed in his recommendation to mercy. . . . Thirard, however, with the same look of exasperation, began to drum his bony fingers on the table-shelf and grumbled, "Berlot gone away, the loading delayed two days, nothing is going right!"

Rolland reassured him, as one would speak to an unreasonable child: "But see, Captain, they will send him to you as soon as he gets in. And now that the apparatus is in place again, things will be booming by tomorrow!"

But in the night they were wakened by a sledge-hammer blow against the ship. There was a terrible bucking, a double explosive snapping: the breaking of the two chains. Then at once they were caught in a crazy gyration, like a whirligig at a fair. Rolland hurried out on deck into a volley of hurricane wind and hail. He felt the vessel slipping swiftly away under him, on a straight course. The *Antonine* seemed to be gliding on those smooth and swift waters that churned into foam before a barrier over which they were about to plunge. Then there was the jamming of a brake, far below: the whole keel that struck at the same time, and a man calling out in the darkness, "We're aground!"

As if the sudden tornado had had no other object than to ground them, it died down like a shot. They were flung back into silence and immobility, in a state of stupor since they no longer moved an inch, once the attack was over, and no longer heard a sound. The ship's lanterns were brought up, and Rolland gave the order to investigate the holds.

"Coral is elastic," he heard Kréven's cold voice say. "All it will do is clean up the ship's bottom."

This was true. Berteux came back to report that the holds were free of water. The ship was uninjured. She had hollowed out a bed in the soft coral and was resting there.

Rolland went below to the captain's cabin.

"We have run aground," he reported, "but the holds are dry."

Thirard made a gesture of assent. "Yes, you will get off tomorrow morning, with the tide."

Was it an order he was given, or a reassurance? Like a blind man, he had followed the accident by sense of touch, and he did not seem to attach any importance to it.

The next morning, Rolland had the big waist-anchor let down from the long-boat. In this way he established a fixed point from which he would try to haul off. The thick cable was rigged to the windlass, and they began to heave at it a little before the slack of high tide. The steel wire rose from the water like a rigid bar. The winch slowed down under resistance but was enveloped in a hissing cloud; and Rolland knew that the steam would not give way. Either the ship would obey or the anchor would drag. It was the ship that answered the call. They won out swiftly, and soon the *Antonine* began to roll a little. Faces cleared. Bako, the Martinique Negro, made the sign of the cross three times in quick succession. Caroff expressed his opinion:

"It was more of a stunt, all the same, when the tug ran us on the rocks. This here is a lark. I don't mean to say, though, that coral isn't good to make necklaces for your girl friends."

It was Rolland's thought that the captain, also, with the instinct of the very ill who only mobilize themselves for catastrophes, had refused to take the accident too seriously.

He did not recover his broken chains, still lying at the bottom of the sea, until two days later, when the bay was dragged with a "creeper," a strong grappling iron pulled by the long-boat. It felt around, merely, all day; but in the evening it gripped into something. The Canaque divers went down; sure enough, it was the chains.

These divers had been brought in by Poullain after a day of searching and palavering. He had gone out to corral them in the villages, on the banks of the gullies where their canoes were wafted along under rattan sails. He had been sent from one hut to another, as in France one is sent from office to office. Finally he had arrived under a high thatched roof like a candle-snuffer: the hut of the tribal chief, dark and stinking. An old man had risen from a cot, an old man with gray skin like dried fish. It had taken an hour of explanations and arguments to settle the business, and hours more to find the men.

When Poullain had taken his leave at last, the Canaque had said to him, "You are going to France? If you see President Loubet, give him my greetings."

When the woolly heads bleached with lime reappeared on the surface of the calm sea like tufts of white sea-weed, and when the divers announced that they had found the chains, a piece of line was passed to them which they made off to shackle at the bottom, and then everything was hoisted aboard, chains and men.

"Now we're quits," said Cario. "This place has only one tornado a year."

The loading of the ore began at last. It was brought down from the mountain by a funicular, and put on barges which three Canaques rowed out to the ship. Rattan baskets reinforced with bands of steel wire were sent down to them, they filled these with the ore, and the little steam engine did the hoisting. But it was only a few hours before the boiler ran out of fresh water; and Poullain, who was in charge of keeping it fed, had explored the bay without finding an available water supply; they were using salt water already! So Rolland decided to go and look for water himself.

He pried in vain into all the creeks, delved into the mosquito-infested gullies until his dinghy had its nose in water-falls. At last he came upon a little workshop, where a European and a Canaque were repairing a boat. This time the Frenchman had an honest and placid artisan's face.

"A spring?" he echoed Rolland's question. "I fixed up something for a boat once. Come on, we'll see if we can't get it in shape again."

Rolland followed him into the forest.

As they went along, his guide told him the names of the trees: the sago palms with their slender trunks, the heavy-timbered tamarinds, the black beeches that were the most beautiful trees on the island, the ebonies, especially the *boraos* with their veins of yellow and purple, that had the suppleness of ash trees and made perfect ribs for boats. As for Rolland, he was counting his steps and worrying over going so far back from the sea.

"Here it is!" And the man motioned toward a pool, roughly walled around, and full of clear water. Then he pointed out what looked like a mound of earth covered with lianas. "The pipes are there. There ought to be some in the lot that can still be used," he said.

The next day Papa Burrey and Caroff succeeded in running a conduit as far as a little cape where the long-boat could come alongside. Caroff was able to make some first-rate connecting pipes out of clay, baked in wood fires. Old Burrey, the mechanic, had built some level courses out of small stones, and contrived an easy slope that carried the water at a slow flow to the beach. There, with twenty-five yards of rubber hose, it was possible to fill the big containers, in the long-boat, which would feed the boiler. It was a matter of getting more than 30,000 quarts aboard, both for the stay here and for the voyage.

When Rolland reported to the captain—"There you are, Captain,

233

we'll have water!"—Thirard barked at him, with a fury that was truly beyond understanding:

"My God, you've taken your time about it!"

They were clearing for action at six in the morning. The actual work began at seven, when the noise of the steam-driven windlass, magnified by echoes, would fill the bay and break the morning silence to bits. This kept up until six in the evening, with an hour out for the men to have their midday meal. "We're working harder than the convicts," they declared, on the second morning.

This fact emerged from a strict counting-up of working hours: eight-and-a-half hours for the prisoners, with nine hours of good uninterrupted sleep; ten hours for the sailors, with watch duty at night—two hours of watch for each man. That made three-and-a-half hours to the credit of the convicts, as bonus. It was Caroff who had made the calculation, with the same attention that he had given to the pipe-lines.

And it was indeed convict labor, in this iron hull which the tropical sun heated to scorching point. Shovel in hand, in the hold, they would stow away the ore which the men at the windlass were upsetting in full basket-loads on their heads. The barges must be emptied by evening. Between two shovelfuls they would spit out monotonous oaths, along with the yellow nickel dust: maledictions that repeated the same theme: "They're driving us harder than the fellows in jail."

To be worse drudges than the convicts—it was incontestable, and it was at the same time flattering. . . . If, as sometimes happened in an island roadstead, one of those shaven men, in a shirt with his prison number stamped on it, were to come out on one of the barges and talk with the sailors during a breathing-spell, Caroff, his "schedule" in his hand, would have been quick to attest their own superiority: "You fellows aren't in it, see!"

That was a satisfaction, to be demonstrating that one was capable of sweating even more than those whose business it was to sweat!

At the end of a week, the captain once more asked for Berlot; "a week" was what they had told him. Rolland had been far from seeking an occasion to go back to the Pillou farm. When he thought of the goat-tender, it was to growl: "The only possible woman in all this hinterland, and it's ninety-nine to a hundred that she is the wife of an ex-convict and a released prisoner herself!" That was enough to give him a distaste for her, as for something unhealthy. Yet sometimes a doubt would assail him: it had only been an impression after all, and if he were deceiving himself it would be too stupid. . . . He would have to make inquiries, at Thio. . . .

When Thirard begged him to ask once more about the *Tamanou's* arrival, he set off, determined to clear up the situation.

"Look out for the goat!"

A powerful gray-bearded animal, bigger than a calf, shaggier than a liana, with a tawny coat sweeping the ground, burst out from among the trees. Instead of the convex horns of European he-goats, this one's sprang out almost in a straight line from its stubborn butting forehead, and were curved back, just at the end, in sharp hooks. It sent a heavy stench ahead of it. At the moment when it was lowering its head to charge, the woman rushed up, caught one of its horns in her two fists, and pulled to one side. There was a brief struggle, but the sinewy wrists would not let go. The woman would leap back to avoid the creature's thrust, her bosom turning and following the movements of the rough head; and she jerked her own head backward in the same way to toss back the hair that was falling over her eyes. At last the goat gave in, slid along a step, and allowed itself to be pulled toward the fenced yard. When it had rejoined the nanny-goats there, Rolland leaned his elbows on the fence and looked at it. The huge beast, obviously a beast of the forest, stood planted on its heavy feet, and was surveying him.

"Where did you fish up a billy-goat like that?" he asked.

"He is handsome, isn't he? He comes from a crossing with the big wild antelopes. There are still a few of them left on the island, but the hunting is destroying everything."

"You didn't have him the last time."

"No, we had lent him to a neighbor."

She had come back to stand near him, smoothing out her disheveled dark hair with both hands. Still all excited by combat, she seemed at last to be alive, with red cheeks and shining eyes, and with more of a willingness to talk.

"How many nanny-goats have you?"

"Thirty-five."

"That needs some tending."

"Yes, especially when they are going to have their kids."

Actually, he was standing there scrutinizing the flock as if he had encountered some cowherd at a fence between the fields of his own countryside, and had paused, in rustic courtesy, for five minutes of conversation. If he seemed, so, to be taking an interest in the goats, it was because now, when he was so close to her, the thought was going through his head like a shooting pain: Why is she here? Is it because she wants to be, or because she is forced to it? The idea of possible crime remained inseparable from the woman, now that he had met up with her again, and set her apart even from desire. As for her, she was gazing at her herd of goats as if nothing else existed in the world.

"Are you going to have many kids?" Rolland continued, because he really had to say something.

"Oh, they are almost all having them. César is a husband who takes his wives seriously."

This time she did turn around, and her eyes fixed themselves on the man's in a brief smile. For a moment Rolland thought of nothing but the prostitutes in the ports who, after the exchange of two sentences, would cut in, "Well, are you coming?"

She was making the same proposition: "Won't you come to the house? It's more comfortable indoors than out."

As he followed her, he felt again that curious alarm which was like some vague fear of infection. When they reached the house, she waved away a Canaque woman, with pendulous breasts under a short cotton dress, and, as on the first occasion, went to get a bottle, which had kept a cool moisture on its dark glass. She opened it and filled their glasses. Then Rolland asked if Monsieur Berlot would soon have finished his coast trip. There were still three or four days, she said, to wait.

Silence fell between them. As on the first visit, she had again seated herself opposite him, and he was looking at her with only one thought in his mind: How was he to find out? She herself, passive, accustomed to man's hesitations, was leaving him plenty of time; and she began to ask him commonplace questions: How many officers were there on the *Antonine?* Was this his first voyage to New Caledonia? One would have thought there was an assistant school-mistress standing behind her, or a woman supervisor. Then when she came close to him again, to refill his glass, he seized her by the wrists, to make an end of it.

He never knew how he had been able to keep back the question that was hovering on his lips: Which are you, a free woman or a convict? Nor did he know which of the two had pushed the other toward the low bed. There had been several seconds of vertigo, which he was never able to recall. In any case, no woman had ever given him so strong an impression of being absent from the body of which she was lending him the use. He would have nothing to keep of her but the pungent fragrance of her skin, a plant fragrance, box or ivy. . . .

Yet he had scarcely set his feet again on the dry earth of the floor when even this faded away, leaving nothing but uneasiness. "If she is an ex-convict, then I am a fine scoundrel!" What he was thinking was that one excuses a crime in consenting to remain in ignorance of it. Yet he had too much pride to try to gain serenity for himself, after the event, by questioning her.

"You haven't even finished your glass," she said.

She was proposing to take matters up where they had left off, before their short and savorless parenthesis. But he was already on his way to the door.

"Then I can count on it," he flung out as he left, "that when Berlot gets back—"

He did not even notice that she made no reply.

The loading was moving along smoothly, kept to a good pace by Papa Burrey's steam-engine, that snorted away all day long. The men used to curse it. It was sparing them the hardest toil, certainly; but, tireless itself, it ignored their extreme fatigue and imposed its own inhuman rhythm upon them. Rolland did not blame them for protesting: on the contrary. He felt as they did.

For they were the last to keep a loathing and distrust of the machine, the first to have a presentiment of its menaces. One by one, the "turnspits" were already ousting the sailing-vessels. More than one sailor, through curiosity or self-interest, had made a voyage on a steamship, with a remorseful sense of betrayal. They had returned outraged, as if they had been castrated. That was no job for a seaman! Cut off from the ship, from the sea, from everything! . . . Chambermaids, that was what they had made of them! Washing, polishing, scraping, scouring: "If you know how to chip rust and slap on the red lead, that's enough—you're a sailor!" Everything that was of value to them—their courage, their skill, their experience with wind and water, with the ship and its course, their instinct for the weather—all that was just exactly zero! "On those boats you aren't a man any more—you get what I mean?"

With a dim awareness of the scope of the drama, they were playing the prologue. With the turn of the century, the machine was being lined up alongside of the workman. Oh, only to assist him, he was assured—like Papa Burrey's steam boiler. . . . After all, a basket that set the load down at your feet was something different from hauling up the ore by the armful, at the end of a tackling gear.

Then, too, there had been the Exposition! In their villages, in port boardinghouses, they had all seen it, thanks to the "souvenirs" in the shape of little bone penholders that held panoramic views. One glued one's eye to a sort of glass blister, and could wonder at the Eiffel Tower, the Ferris Wheel, the Moving Sidewalk, the Hall of Machines. It interested them, as it did everyone else. Not one of those sailors would have had any notion that "progress" was depriving them of their means of livelihood.

There remained the captain. He, certainly, was a case apart, for officers and men. Since the terrible word had been pronounced by the doctor it seemed to both Rolland and Poullain that this word was escaping from them, from their look, from their slightest phrase, at every contact with Thirard. When one is hiding something like this, one always has the sense that the other is looking for it, that he has discovered it. Thirard would scrutinize them now with a distrustfulness he had never before shown, not even at the time of the sailing. And, what was even more irrational—since there was really nothing to be done aboardship, and other captains would have gone off on excursions that lasted all day—he was using up the last of his strength in being on hand from morning to night, in roaming around the ship, in looking for the fleas on every dog! He was as bad as a top sergeant!

The worst feature of the situation was that the crew, the petty officers, the officers, were accepting everything with that saddened inexhaustible patience which one has for the caprices of the incurably ill. When they saw him walking back and forth on the ship, with his long bird's skeleton, his crucified face, they would say, over and over again to one another, "It's all up with him!" And it followed, of necessity, that he was always right. . . . But they would say, also, "All the same, it would be better if he went to the hospital."

First of all, they meant better for him, because he would die quietly. And then for themselves, because if he should take a notion, when they were at sea again, to take over the active command when he was not able to, simply to show that he still counted for something, that would be a very queer kettle of fish. . . .

Obviously, the sick man sensed all this; and Rolland, who made it his first duty not to leave him, to be always at his beck and call, followed his mounting irritation as if with his actual eyes. Finally, one day, apropos of the most unimportant of odd jobs, Thirard turned on the mate and cried out in his dreadful undertone, "Who is it that's commanding here? They haven't taken me off the ship yet, have they?"

The look of hatred with which he underscored this apostrophe brought Rolland a sudden enlightenment. The captain believed that there was a conspiracy afoot to get him ashore; that Rolland wanted to take his place; that he had brought the doctor aboard in order to clear him out. . . . And that was why the wretched man was exhausting himself by those tours of the deck!

That evening, when the night's sudden coolness had set the captain back to his cabin, Rolland presented himself before him. Thirard had just gone to bed. He merely turned his head toward his caller.

238

"Captain," Rolland began, "Monsieur Triger, of the Nickel Company, has just sent word by one of the foremen that he is leaving tomorrow for Nouméa in his automobile, and that he has an extra place in the car."

"Very well, go along." The captain flung out the permission with a shrug of his shoulders which was like a shudder. Then he turned over on his side to look into Rolland's face. "What is it you want to do at Nouméa?" he demanded, in his shattered voice. "To complain of me to the Company?"

Rolland pulled up a chair and sat down at the head of the bunk.

"It was not for me, Captain, the place in the car. It was for you."

The fleshless head began to wag back and forth. "Ah, I understand. . . ." The burning eyes did not quit Rolland's; and he, on his part, did not lower his own. "Go on," the captain panted. "Spit it out!"

"That is what I came for, Captain. When the doctor from Thio was here, he repeated to me what he must have said to you: that he advised your going to the hospital, and waiting there for a steamship to take you back to France."

The skin-and-bones hand shot out so close to Rolland's eyes that he blinked.

"To you the doctor said 'the hospital,' not the steamship."

Rolland, startled, had to wait several seconds before going on: "I replied that this was for you to decide, Captain, and for you alone. I also told him that insomuch as you had been firm in the performance of your tasks as commander up to now, you would surely be anxious to remain aboard your ship. That is what I said, not one word more. But I had to let you know of Monsieur Triger's offer, in case you might have changed your mind."

Captain Thirard turned his head away. He was looking at the ceiling now, at the upside-down compass, and he did not move.

"It would be to your interest to have me go," he said.

"Frankly, I think it would, Captain. If I take the vessel back to France, that will probably amount to a ship's command for me. But I have come precisely to ask you whether, from my attitude up to now, you believe that I am disposed to put my interest before yours."

Thirard sat up abruptly on his narrow mattress.

"Ever since Port Talbot, I have seen you at work," he said, in his jerky voice. "You have never tried to take advantage of the situation. . . . Yes, I had been warned against you. They had said to me, 'Look out for him; all he will try to do is to get free of control.' Then, this visit from the doctor, the idiotic pretext he gave me for it, his insistence that I go to the hospital . . . I did believe that you had

had enough of me, of towing the wreck that I have become. Oh, it would be natural for me to think that! Because you are no longer the same, since the doctor was here. . . ."

Again that terrible word rang in Rolland's ears, the word that had been spoken on the poop and of which the captain was ignorant, that word which tightened his own throat whenever he came near the condemned man. To hide it within himself, to screen his pity, he had stiffened himself to a point where the other believed him hostile.

"On my side, Captain, I saw very well that you no longer had confidence in me," he succeeded in saying. "I could not be the same. And then I kept asking myself what really was to your interest: to go ashore or to stay on the ship?"

Thirard began to laugh, a laugh that wrinkled the yellow skin under the short gray beard. Then he spoke aloud, in one of those curious respites which would allow the voice to escape almost naturally:

"But that is easy to decide! If I had the slightest chance of being cured in the hospital, that would be something to argue about; but I should enter it only to die there. You know that as well as I do, Rolland."

It was the first time that he had not said "Monsieur," and the mate was even more struck by that than he was by the calmness with which he acknowledged himself to be lost. The captain fell back on his bunk again, but he was lying now on his right side, so that his face might be close to Rolland's.

"I can tell you everything now," he said. "You have, after all, the right to an understanding! Here it is, then. . . . I am poor. I had my savings, like everybody else. I had put them in a little bank in Fécamp. Two years ago, the banker was arrested; he had made away with everything. So, when I am gone, my wife will have nothing to get along on but my pension, augmented by the money from this voyage. My 'interest'—that is to say, hers—is, therefore, that I make the return passage; even if I do not finish it, it will be counted for my widow. . . . This passage—there is no question of my undertaking it against opposition from you, or without your support and your devotion. . . . Now I have told you everything," he ended abruptly. "What do you advise me to do?"

"Taking everything into consideration, Captain," Rolland replied, "I think that you ought to remain on board and keep your command. So far as I am concerned, I assure you that you can depend on me."

Thirard bent his head very low in acknowledgment.

"On my part, you can be sure of my complete confidence," he said.

It pleased Rolland that he should have replied to him as to an equal. Meanwhile the captain's eyes were searching the cabin, until they found, on the table, a little Chinese cabinet with the lacquer flaking off. He asked for it, and when Rolland brought it to him he took out a small jewel-case from under a packet of letters. It was a vermeil scarf-pin. He held it out.

"Will you accept this as a souvenir?" he asked. "It will be the souvenir of a man who esteems you greatly."

As Rolland was thanking him, the voice became choking once more; but it seemed to the mate that it was not only illness that was breaking it into these gasps.

"There is something else—I must ask you—something else—more difficult."

His face had grown red, and it was pitiful to see the sudden flow of blood into those livid cheeks.

"Yes," he stammered. "It is about—about the morphine. I can swear to you that I only take it when, truly, I cannot hold out any longer; it is that or the revolver. But now I have to have stronger doses to ease the pain, and I am afraid of running out of it. So, then, at Nouméa . . . through Triger? . . ."

"You can depend on me, Captain," Rolland repeated. "I will attend to it."

For the first time the sick man's eyes were misty, with tears which the flicker of his eyelids was trying to brush away.

"Ah, my dear Rolland, to have been a man, the man that, after all, I have been, and now to be obliged to ask you that! . . ."

At dinnertime, as the officers were unfolding their napkins in the cabin, the cabin boy came in, with an air of importance, holding at arm's length a bottle of champagne.

"It is from the captain," he announced.

Berteux and Poullain looked at each other.

"Did he tell you why?" Berteux asked.

The boy shook his head.

"No. He said, 'You are to take this to the officers, from me.'"

For a long time Rolland, because he was conscious of all the falseness of the situation, had imposed a complete reticence upon the cabin in regard to the man who never made any appearance there. The question of his health was alone touched upon, and that with caution. So Poullain dismissed the subject, but with all his characteristic openheartedness:

"Poor man! If it could only mean that something good had happened to him!"

The next day, Rolland delivered to Monsieur Triger two letters for the Company's executive office at Nouméa. In one, the captain asserted his determination to remain on his ship, and released the Company from all responsibility in regard to him; they had proposed hospitalization and repatriation; he was refusing, as he had a right to do, since he was still effectively performing his tasks as commander; in case that should become impossible, the command would pass, *ipso facto,* to the second captain, in whom he had complete confidence.

In the other letter, the "second captain" declared point-blank that he would refuse the command of the *Antonine* if the directors offered it to him after insisting on Captain Thirard's evacuation. He had no intention of replacing him except in case of absolute necessity.

When Monsieur Triger returned from Nouméa a few days later, he brought no reply.

"There could not be any," he explained to Rolland, "since everything remains in order, and you are forcing their hand. However, you can pride yourself on having astonished them! You had only to say *Amen,* and you would have taken over the command. A little sooner, a little later, that would make no difference, and it would have saved you a lot of queer jobs."

"Do you really think it would have made no difference?" Rolland asked.

Monsieur Triger did not try to argue further. He spread out his arms, in the gesture he must have seen made by the executives in Nouméa.

"After all, as they said, it is your business," he concluded. "And speaking of that, I have your ampoules. I said that it was for Dr. Lefort in Thio and that I had forgotten the prescription. I am not worried about that: Lefort will send me his prescription, and antedate it."

"You are both very generous," Rolland declared.

Monsieur Triger wrinkled his eyelids.

"And you," he said. "In this business, aren't you being just a little generous yourself?"

XXI

TWO DAYS LATER, which was Sunday, the captain sent for Rolland.

"You can take a day off," Thirard said. "Tell Monsieur Berteux and Monsieur Poullain they are free for the day, too, I will attend to the ship's duty, with Kréven."

He seemed to be having a period of abatement: calmer, less depressed, released for a time from those terrifying spasms of asphyxiation which had made him like a fish gasping on dry land. When he said goodbye to the officers he even added—and this gave them a shock—"Have a good time, boys!"

Poullain and Berteux determined to go up to Kanala—ten houses, a butcher shop, a bakery, a co-operative store, and a bar—and explore that metropolis. The third mate, relying on the tips of a colleague on an earlier voyage, insisted that one could have a good time there. But where would Poullain not have found a "good time"?

So the *Antonine's* junior officers went off together.

The friendly companionship between these two never ceased to surprise Rolland. One might have thought that Poullain's indomitable good humor needed Berteux's petulance and constant grudges as a stimulant. The scrawny bilious-natured fellow stuck to the other's rotundity like a horsefly to a mare's plump flanks, and Poullain snorted all the better for it.

As for Rolland himself, he wandered on the reefs all morning, looking for oysters. It was an almost-forgotten pleasure, from the days when he used to go poaching at low tide on the sands at Erquy. Then in the afternoon he had himself taken ashore, and went back to the road to the Pillou farm.

He had sworn that he would never again set foot on the place. Since he had not been capable, the last time, of finding out with whom he had to deal, he was calling a halt to the business. There was no question of going back to the beginning, after the surprise stroke of that last zigzag! To think that he had perhaps been pawed over by the hands of a murderess! That made him sick with shame.

As he emerged from the tunnel of creepers, at the top of the ridge, he saw coming toward him a woman whom he did not recognize until she was close by. It was she, but in such unforeseen guise! Dressed in her Sunday best: a pink cotton print frock, with flounces; a sailor hat poised on her coils of black hair; a parasol, and high buttoned shoes. . . . The aggressive costume fairly shrieked in this solitude, and she wore it like a challenge. He was first astounded, then tempted to laugh, and at last vaguely touched.

"You were coming to the house?" she asked.

"Yes—and you were leaving it."

"I have to go to dinner with some neighbors. Their carriage can't get down this far. I was on my way to wait for them on the road."

"Then I may escort you a little distance?"

He made the offer with real zest. It had occurred to him that it would be pleasant to walk along beside this good-looking woman, chatting, as with a woman acquaintance on a Sunday in the country; insomuch as that was now possible, and they would not meet anyone. A country stroll! He had sought for one vainly—he did not remember when he had had that pleasure—there was never any time. . . . And now he had a crazy desire for it: much more desire than he had for her.

She looked at him for a moment, from eyes half-closed in the bright sunshine, without replying; then she shrugged one shoulder.

"You didn't come for that. . . . I don't have to go for a quarter of an hour or so. Come down to the house."

"As you wish," he responded.

She dashed ahead of him in a precipitate retracing of her steps. Her haste to get on with the unexpected job was so obvious that he stopped short.

"Never mind: it isn't worth the trouble," he said.

She turned around, suddenly aroused to interest, like all prostitutes, by the anger they have unleashed in a man.

"Oh, don't act like an idiot!"

She caught his wrist, and let go of it only to take her key out of her pocket. As soon as they entered the house she reached her arms up to remove her hat-pins, a woman's gesture, the gesture of a real woman, which he had almost never seen: the port girls go bareheaded. But she at once unfastened her bodice also, and this promptness was such as to make him lay his ten-franc piece on the table, between the parasol and the sailor hat.

"I should have liked to give you a present," he said, "but there is no question of buying anything here. You will buy it for yourself. . . ."

"Pick that up," she said.

"Why?"

"I tell you, pick it up."

He raised his shoulders, and put the gold piece back in his pocket.

She was plainly concentrating, this time, on not showing any unresponsiveness. The insulting lethargy of the first encounter had given place to a banal wish to please, which nevertheless relieved the man of any pretext for deceit. It was he who first wished to leave the low couch. She held him back.

"You have time."

Her plan for an excursion seemed entirely to have gone from her mind. Her arms were lifted and arched in the movement of a little while ago, when she had taken off her hat, and her fingers were under the twisted rope, tight-bound and glossy, of her hair. Propped up on his elbow, he was questioning this prone body with a curiosity that had in it nothing sensual. Who and what was she, actually? The query tormented him no less for having changed its direction. Some women, in the silent reaction that follows the act of love, answer it well enough. The relaxation of the flesh, its exhaustion, is evident in this repose which is like no other; but at the same time the subconscious being emerges, that innermost being which has just been thrust up to the surface and has not had time to bury itself again. But this long and slender body kept its secret: the high dark-toned bosom remained firm; the hips continued the spring of the sinewy thighs and the straight extended legs. It was the body of a swimmer. And he was recalling the water of the lagoon, that transparent water which he would hardly have disturbed as he glided through it.

It was actually because Rolland's thought made the woman one with this island, and with its extraordinary waters, that he asked, as from the depths of a dream, "Have you been here long?"

He did not see the sidelong glance she cast at him, brief and sharp, like someone who has just been hit with a stone and looks to see where it came from and whether it was even meant for him. He had heard echoing through the room, as if asked by another voice, the question which he had so long held back, and which was escaping him at the moment when it no longer had any object. He was already seeking for a way to recall it when she retorted, through tight lips, "Does that interest you?"

Both with bad faith and bad humor—because the tone had displeased him and he was reproaching himself for his blunder, he charged in: "Oh, not at all! Whether you were born here or came from somewhere else, and when, and why, and how, I don't give a damn—get that! If I did, I wouldn't be here."

"Just imagine to yourself," she said, in that unassailable voice which challenges a slap in the face, "that I have killed my grandfather, my grandmother, my father, my mother, my brother, and my little sister. Is that enough for you? You should have asked me sooner, if it excites you so."

This outburst of spleen reassured him completely, and he broke into hearty laughter.

"You couldn't add three or four little cousins to the mincemeat?" he said.

But she was not laying down her arms; on the contrary.

"If you want to know," she continued, in the same severe voice, "I am the daughter of ex-convicts. Here, that is enough to put you a little lower than a Canaque. If you share this opinion, you know where to find the door."

"A hell of a lot I care!" he said.

It was true that he did not care. After being afraid of running on a rock, he discovered himself on a mud-bank, from which he would get free when he chose. . . .

At this moment, they heard the sound of steps on the hard earth outside. A hand tried to lift the latch, but noiselessly, with a robber's smoothness, and then there was a knock—a few discreet little raps—on the door. Rolland jumped up. Swift fingers caught his arm and kept him from moving. Then, turning her head toward the door, she called out, "Go around in front and tell them to wait."

The footsteps were heard again, and died away.

"Was that your husband?" he asked, in an undertone.

"Who do you suppose it would be?"

"And—he is going away?"

"You weren't reckoning that he'd bash in the door, were you? He isn't that kind of man." Then she added, in a different tone, "You were speaking of the countryside, a little while ago. Supposing you found it to your liking, and wanted to stay on; could you give up your ship, and settle here?"

"Me?"

Utterly dumbfounded, he thought at first that she was planning—God knew why!—to get him to leave the boat, and the sea. But from the irritated toss of her head he realized that he personally had nothing to do with her question.

"I said 'you' as I would say anybody. . . . An—officer, on a ship that called here: if he wanted to, could he stay?"

He thought of Berteux and Poullain who, at this moment, were wandering along the single parched street of Kanala. They, too, were outside the picture. Then who? . . .

She realized that the question was too surprising, and she hurried to explain.

"I am asking you that because I have been thinking of Berlot. He did that. He left his ship and stayed here. How was he able to work it?"

"I have an idea that he didn't ask anyone's permission, so that it wouldn't have to be refused him."

"I don't know anything about it myself; it was a long time ago, and he doesn't talk about it. But I have never heard tell that he had any difficulties. If you wanted to stay here, for instance, how would you go about it, to avoid trouble?"

Oh, what a tart she was! Only tarts—or old married women—could pass so serenely from love to an idiotic conversation, and insist on sticking to it! On the instant, Rolland lost all interest in the body that was lying by his side, the body over which he had been leaning but a moment before, because it was not like a body sold on a bargain counter. With that body, she ought to have been someone, among women. But she had thrown it into the street. A lost woman. . . . The "bourgeois" term sprang to his mind, with a new meaning: lost to all that she might have been, with what must still be called her beauty, and the willful strength he divined in her. . . . In the ships' crews, the failures—there were some—had always found him ruthless. She, too, was ceasing to exist. . . .

He got up; and it was the absurd problem she was putting to him which suddenly fastened upon his mind. What would he do, himself, if in some extraordinary fashion he should be seized with the desire to stay in a country where his ship called? Not this one, pleasant as it was, but a "green isle" such as seafaring men still dreamed of, an island that they never found in any sea and that trailed the ancient breath of paradise. . . . He reflected before he answered, and when he did, it was much more for himself than for her.

"From the cabin boy to the first mate, everyone goes through the Marine Office before the ship sails. The commissioner enters you on the roster of the ship's company, and the embarkation is noted on your registration card. You are signed up, then, for the entire voyage, and if you leave the ship en route it is a desertion."

"But if the captain agreed to it?" she objected.

He was forced to admit that such a thing was possible. In that case, there would be a mutation registered by the Marine officer. But the captain would never agree unless there were an acceptable replacement ready to hand.

He was dressed now. She had not stirred from the bed. He turned back toward her.

"Have you a lover whom you want to get away from his ship?" he asked.

"I have already told you that I was thinking of Berlot," she retorted. "He left his boat, here, a long time ago. He went off into the bush and stayed there while the vessel was in the roads. He has never had any trouble about it; but if he wanted to go back to France, wouldn't they be looking for him? . . . By the way, Berlot is back."

The next day, in fact, the dinghy came alongside, with Berlot aboard. Poullain, who had the watch, had heard a sharp whistle from the beach and had perceived the outline of a stocky figure, making semaphore signals, over and over, on the shingle. Through the binoculars, this had been seen to be a broad and ruddy man, with a face rimmed by a gray beard. The lieutenant had sent the boat to get him.

Berlot made a conquest of Poullain the instant he stepped on the

247

deck. He was one of those men who are at home everywhere, whose hearty friendliness demands an answering smile, and who are bursting with vitality and good cheer. He made his way toward the stern without waiting to be escorted, roaring as he went, "Where is he hiding himself, that false comrade, that miserable tool of the Custom House, who didn't wait for me to tow him in?"

Rolland was observing him with a keen curiosity. Was this the man who, as soon as he landed, went running to the Pillou farm? Actually, he was thinking, it is of no importance, either for him or for me! He must have a woman like that in all the island coves where he tied up. He was that robust and lecherous man in his fifties who takes a vacation from alcohol and women only when he is at sea, and and who goes on like that, with not a wrinkle added by the years, until he has a stroke of apoplexy: a current pattern in the coastwise trade. . . .

The mate presented himself, was seized in a pincer's grip by the vigorous fist, and, while Berlot persisted in shouting out his demands for the captain, his fellow-townsman and old schoolmate, Rolland warned him, as he thought he must: "You are going to find him changed, since the last voyage."

"Yes, I know."

This time, he spoke in a low voice, in a quite different tone, which meant, "Don't take me for an imbecile. I know what I'm doing." So Rolland let him go down into the officers' quarters.

When he came out, half-an-hour later, he had the same preoccupied air as the doctor from Thio. Rolland was pacing up and down the deck, where the windlass was still spouting out its shattering noise. Berlot joined him on the fore-and-aft gangway and went with him to the edge of the poop-rail, off to one side.

"If I had expected to find him in that state!" he said. "It's no good to be warned—they told me, at Thio—it knocks you out just the same! You yourself, you've only known him sick. . . . And, by the way, what didn't he say in praise of you! You have been generous, but you have reason to be. He deserves it. He is a sailor and a man."

Kréven's very words. . . .

For almost another half-hour, the skipper of the *Tamanou* talked of Thirard, as one talks of a man who is dead. And as these recitals went on, Rolland saw muscles and flesh superposed on the living skeleton he knew, and the firm features of a daring sea commander who was yet as methodical and dependable as a compass.

"His decks, white as snow! His brasses, shining like the sun! Inspection three and four times a week, in the men's quarters, the galley, the storerooms . . . that, everybody can do. But with him

248

the seamen were proud of the fine way their ship was kept up, and the two watch-crews would be bursting with jealousy to see which would make its side the best-looking! And listen, the most gorgeous thing of all, that happened when he was captain of the *Ganymede:* he'd passed Staten Island and left Saint John's Cape to the northeast, and a hurricane struck him from the southwest, with the barometer down to seven-twenty—"

Berlot went on with a long story of sails torn from their masts, lifeboats stove in, the vessel with a disabled rudder, a man fallen from the rigging, and the albatross digging into his skull under his comrades' eyes: all that tragic breaking up and crumbling away of a great sailing-ship that is prey to the fury of Cape Horn. . . . "And you can judge of the state of the fellows' morale!" he continued. "But what did Thirard do? He drew up a formal report, according to regulations, of how coffee and sugar and two casks of wine had been damaged by the sea's coming into the steward's cabin, and he made two sailors step up and sign it, his official record, as witnesses. And I can't tell you how this formality, executed at length in the midst of their torments, as calmly as if they were in port—I can't tell you how it set the crew on their feet again, in one stroke!"

With that, Berlot pulled a fat turnip watch from his pocket.

"It's getting toward the lunch hour. He told me he wanted to be there. That's going to be the moment to have a good time."

And he had a good time with such furious determination that he came off victorious in the end. . . .

At the start, it was excruciating. Thirard had come into the cabin where his officers had never seen him and had sat down before an empty plate, which remained empty. At once Berlot, the corner of his napkin tucked in under his thick neck, his two fists on the oilcloth, had thrown himself back in his chair and assailed the captain with loud-voiced witticisms. Thirard listened to them with a distracted air, as if Berlot had been speaking across him to someone else; the officers were in agony. Was it conceivable, such utterly bad manners, such boorish snortings and guffawings in the presence of an almost dying man! If the unhappy invalid had not been on the opposite side of the table, they were thinking, Berlot would have been assaulting him with hearty thumps on the back—"that damn good old boy, Thirard!"

He had obviously made up his mind to treat him, as in the old days, like a pal whom one gets hold of again over a good luncheon. But the artifice was so gross, so unseemly, that Rolland, exasperated, was about to call a halt on it when he ventured to cast a glance at the captain. And what he saw was extraordinary! Thirard was expanding under these buffetings! In finding his old friend just as he had been on the preceding visits, when the officers' cabin used to rock with his laughter, he was escaping from the present. . . . A force of nature, Berlot! This was a facetious old elephant, with a free and lively eye, who trampled on everything—decency, anxiety, even suffering—without any wish to perceive what he was crushing, but who cleared his way, and swiftly! Already, in his wake, a draft of pure air blew into the cabin. He was ending by imposing his savage buffoonery, through sheer force. And Rolland was soon obliged to notice the adroitness of the "You remember?" which he was now introducing more and more often: these memories of childhood, of youth, which Thirard would verify with little nods; these tales of girls pursued at country fairs, whose flights Berlot was miming and whose shrieks he imitated—"A damn good woman-chaser, your captain!" And the other, with his pitiful smile, seemed to be saying, "Yes, I was that."

Then Berlot told them tales of the Canaques, showed them the dance of the *pilou-pilou,* and explained, with a demonstration, how the natives celebrated their ritual cleansing on the beaches blazing white in the sun: they would fill their ancient ceremonial jugs with sea water and drink it down in great gulps; then they would leap into the air in rivalry as to who would be first with the purification. After that he reeled off stories about women, white or black; but Rolland noticed that he made no allusion to the cabin in the gully.

Finally, he gave them the latest news of the Russo-Japanese war and sang them a satiric popular ditty about it.

When they got up from the table, they were dizzy, as when one steps off a merry-go-round at a fair; and they felt ashamed, too, of having laughed so much. The captain kept hold of his guest's broad hand.

"We shall see you again?"

"You'd better believe it! In the first place, you can't leave without me. I'm the one who's to take you out of here."

Then Berlot seized Rolland by the arm.

"Come and let me show you where you can fish for rock lobster with torches," he said. "To be sure, they are little ones; but when they come into the light—"

They went out together. As soon as they reached the deck, Berlot wiped his forehead.

"Good God, I shall never forget this luncheon, with his poor face opposite me!"

"You have done him good, nevertheless," Rolland said.

The other man shrugged his shoulders.

"One never knows . . . at the moment, yes, maybe; but afterwards . . . ."

The next day, Berteux took Rolland aside.

"I must report to you, sir, that Kréven is leaving the ship every night."

"Since when?"

"For the past week, at least."

"And it is only today that you tell me about it?"

"I was waiting to be sure. I had ascertained several times that he was not in the little deck-house, and last night I saw him go off and come back."

"How?"

"He swam. He must have clothing hidden onshore."

"What time did he leave?"

"About eleven o'clock."

"And he returned—?"

"At five in the morning."

"When he came aboard again, did you ask him where he was coming from?"

"Ah, no. I preferred to inform you."

His tone, and the expression of his face, added: "Ask him about it myself, so that you might accuse me again of kicking up incidents with every step I take? No; he's your precious pet, you straighten this out yourself!" And a little gleam in his yellow eye concluded, "You certainly know where to place your confidence!"

Rolland understood all this, unspoken but perfectly plain.

"You did right. Send him to me," he said.

Five minutes later, Kréven came into the first mate's cabin.

With their first mutual glance each one measured, in the other's face and attitude, all the backward road they had lately traveled. Rolland had become again the inscrutable and inflexible chief that he had been at the beginning of the voyage. Kréven had retreated even farther into his past. The mate realized that the bos'n no longer belonged to the ship. He had actually left her, was hunting down his pleasure on land, and was ready to hate and disown the vessel from which he was escaping, as all deserters do, by revulsion, as soon as they have crossed the gangplank. Rolland had been face to face, in the past, with men who had swallowed the mysterious "knock-out drops" of the shanghaiers; this was just like it. He also remembered how he himself had been nabbed by the bos'n's sturdy wrists, under Monnard's orders, at the moment when he, too, was quitting his ship. But with him it had been only the unleashing of sudden fury and instinct; Monnard had not seen in his eyes the resolution he now saw in Kréven's. And then Rolland, a sailor on the *Galatée*, had had only a sailor's past, without anything in common with the unknown

251

past to which Kréven had just been returning, and in which he was entrenching himself.

"I am told that you have been going ashore every night for the past week," the mate said. "Is that correct?"

"For the past ten days; yes, sir."

"You know better than anyone else that you must not leave the ship without permission." It was not a question, and he did not wait for an answer. "You went to Kanala?"

"No, sir: to Pillou's farm."

Only Rolland's more pronounced immobility gave any indication of the unexpected stroke. Yet he had been a hundred miles from imagining that Kréven was going to meet her! He was seeing him again as he sat at the farmhouse table: indifferent, barely polite. He had not even looked at the woman; or, rather, one glance had been enough for them to recognize each other, and since then they had been together every night.

It was not of her that he was thinking. Her turn would come! But, for him, a woman never counted, so long as there was a man concerned. And this man was, so to speak, excessively present: all the breadth of his shoulders thrown into relief by the narrowness of the cabin, his hard face on the defensive—more so than the case deserved, in fact. For if there was a disciplinary slip it had been unobtrusive; after all, it was only one watch.

But it was precisely the mediocrity of the business that had revolted Rolland, when Berteux had reported it to him: that Kréven should have lowered himself to a novice's escapade. Yet there was obviously more to it than that: the man was not one who would take the bit in his teeth, like this, for a mere lark; and it was really because Rolland felt that the main point was escaping him that he went on:

"You knew that, on your part especially, that was not to be allowed."

Kréven's bearing became stiffer still.

"You have never had any fault to find with me, sir, so long as there was work to be done. I have always done my full duty. But here, on nights when I was not on watch, I was doing no harm to anybody."

"But the men!" Rolland retorted sharply. "They knew, or they will know. What becomes of your authority over them? And the example you give?"

"I have thought of that, sir. If it were necessary, I should have made them understand very quickly that it was no business of theirs."

It was the pronouncement of a petty despot, sure of his power and always ready to bring his tribe to heel.

"Yes," Rolland responded. " 'Do what I say, not what I do.' I expected something different from you." He threw a glance at the impassive man who was listening, in so correct an attitude, and concluded, "The captain will decide how to deal with all this."

Kréven made a gesture of agreement, and turned to go out.

"And also," Rolland added, "it is not necessary to tell you that these moonlight rambles are at an end."

"Oh, there would be no more reason for them now, sir!" Kréven said.

A very odd response! Rolland's curiosity, stirred by it, drifted to the woman, again hard to thrust out of the picture. It was she who possessed the explanation of this escapade, she who had wrought the astonishing change in this man. And she had needed so little time to do it!

"Why, no more reason? There has never been a valid one," he said.

"Because the skipper, Berlot, has come back, and now it is his business," Kréven replied.

So the bos'n had been only a stopgap. With the return of the rightful master he was effacing himself, handing over the place he had kept warm. . . . That was so little like the man Rolland had believed he knew that what he felt now was a deadly anger with himself for having given him his confidence, and he made a gesture with his chin to show him the door. At the same time, he was driving out the woman whom the bos'n was handing back to her old man with such placid cynicism. At bottom, that was all she was worth!

. . . By the next morning, the mate was regarding the bos'n's misdemeanor with more indulgence. He would keep him at a distance, certainly. But he was not going to upset the captain with this tale. Since Berlot's visit, Thirard had been enjoying a kind of truce, and it would have been criminal to mar this respite. Just the evening before, Rolland had persuaded him to take a little jaunt to the land, and the dinghy had set him down in the shade of some big trees; he had taken writing materials with him, some paper and a small bottle of ink.

For the rest, the two hundred-ton barges would make themselves fast every morning to the flanks of the *Antonine,* and would go away empty at night. The days were marked only by the trivial happenings on shipboard: the pig that burned its mouth out when it got into a basket of peppers, the lazybones who reported sick and whom Rolland cured in a trice with ipecac and sodium sulphate that he made the man swallow in his presence. Then at last the *Tamanou* appeared, one morning, at the entrance to the bay. The loading was being completed, and the little steamer would tow the *Antonine*, next day, out beyond the barrier of coral reefs. She had scarcely come to anchor when Rolland saw her rowboat approaching, pulled over the dazzling water by two long-armed Canaques. In the stern, he at once recognized Skipper Berlot, in the distance a ruddy blob of a face under a white helmet.

The boat came alongside. Rolland was at first surprised by the series of furious oaths poured forth by the ship's master when one of the Canaques, not moving quickly enough, made him miss the ladder. This was not the same voice, that full-bodied voice that had set the cabin windows to vibrating; these were malevolent vociferations, out of all proportion to the incident. Then he thought he understood, when Berlot hoisted up on the deck a face that was unrecognizable, creased all over with lines of rage, and when he cast all about him the circular glance of a man who is searching for someone to fight with.

"Thirard is in his cabin?" he asked.

"I think so. I will have him told—"

"No need for that!"

Berlot had already dived beneath the poop.

That's that! thought Rolland. "He has learned of Kréven's excursions, and he wants to give him the works. I was a fool not to warn the captain." The whole affair, however, was sinking to the level of the grotesque. The old fellow there was on his way to complain to the properly constituted authority of having been cuckolded by his mistress! If he was going in for auditing his accounts, there was no reason why he might not presently be coming to settle the score with him, Rolland! That would be piquant!

"Kréven!"

Berlot, his head thrown back, was roaring as if he were in his own house. The bos'n, standing near the rail, was watching the loading of the last baskets of nickel. He turned around and made his way without hurry toward the stern, where he joined Berlot and disappeared.

They remained shut up for more than an hour. At last the coasting skipper and the bos'n came out again, together. Kréven's face wore a look of abstraction. Berlot had stopped at the foot of the poop companionway and was talking to him, with a dejected air. When they parted, Rolland heard the *Tamanou's* master say, "Tomorrow, then, at ten o'clock."

The mate was more astounded by this appointment than by all the rest put together. The *Antonine* was sailing next morning at seven. The *Tamanou* had to take the ship out of the bay, lead her through the opening in the reefs, and cast her off, out to sea. That would be a matter of an hour. Free of the tug, and with the southeast trade winds, they would be far away by ten o'clock! Yet Berlot, having tossed out this order, was going back toward the ladder without caring to see anybody or anything. As for Kréven, he was returning to his place as if nothing had happened.

Five minutes later, the cabin boy came to look for Rolland.

"The captain asks to see you, sir."

The moment he entered the room, Rolland realized that he was stumbling into the very midst of an attack. The sick man was seated, leaning forward as always, and the mate saw that both his abdomen and his cheeks were drawn in, his entire torso compressed, in a violent endeavor to get his breath. Thirard was so plainly putting all his strength into this that there could not be enough left to him for speaking. Yet he brought out two words, in a sputter: "Kréven— leaving."

Rolland knew that he must neither question nor interrupt. Words were too dear to be asked for in more than the exact sum due. But he did not try to hide his stupefaction at the announcement of this new perplexity.

"Sailing—with Berlot," Thirard hiccuped.

With Berlot! Not only was a bos'n like Kréven being let go, but he was being sent, on a buttocks-awash* in New Caledonia, to be second-in-command to a skipper whom he was cuckolding, in order, evidently, that he might continue to do so! And that, beyond any doubt, at the request of the cuckold and with the blessing of the captain. . . . Oh, this was a ship of madmen! Or rather, alas, she was a ship commanded by a poor, poor soul.

"Very well."

What else was there to say, except, "You have done this on your own. You are presenting me with the *fait accompli*. I leave to you the honor of the fine work."

With this in his mind, unspoken, he was overwhelmed by the captain's long gaze of reproach. "Already adversaries, in spite of all you had promised me?" it seemed to say. The sick man shook his head, in a poignant distress: did Rolland not realize, then, that a dying man, such as he was, must be reduced to a few words to explain everything? He speeded up the spasms that were his respiration, as if he were trying to give himself a good start, and he spit out the next phrases:

"For a bitch—that Pillou—kick Berlot out—if he doesn't bring— the other. . . . Berlot's a rag!"

* Literal translation of sailors' term of contempt for a very small boat. Tr.

Having said everything, he dropped back to the bottom of the pit. Rolland jolted him out of it, without mercy.

"But, Captain, did you sign the transfer?"

"Forced to. . . . That or desertion."

"And have you found someone to take his place?"

"Berlot is attending to that."

"Have I your authorization to speak to him, Captain?"

A nod of the head, a shrug of the shoulders, both equally feeble. . . .

Rolland went out. When he reached the deck, he saw a basket of ore coming up, and in the depths of the hold there broke out a wild hurly-burly of voices. It was the last basket, and the boys were saluting it.

"When you have finished, bos'n, come to see me in the chart-house," he said.

He lighted a cigarette while he was waiting, but he let it go out after a few puffs. Oh, what a disaster it was, to have nothing but the empty shell of a skipper in the captain's cabin beneath the poop! A strumpet wants a man, the best man on the ship: all right, here he is! We're sending him to you, well wrapped up in the regulation papers, for fear he might get hurt. . . . Sitting here, he was seeing what had happened: Berlot clattering back to the cabin in the gully, all gay and lively, after the luncheon on the *Antonine,* and then: "Don't touch me! And never again, if he goes! Take him on your boat!" That was it, the means she had been seeking, stretched out beside him that day. And the old man had moved heaven and earth, threatened to chuck everything—his coastal service, his towing—if he wasn't helped out of his predicament. He had done it raging in his guts, but well broken in; for this was certainly not the first time he had had to share her in order to keep a morsel for himself. But the other man—what was he accepting? And the captain, who had at once said Amen? Oh, a Monnard would have toppled the fellow to the bottom of the hold, with the hatch fastened down over him and the rod across it, and it wouldn't have been unbolted until the ship was out to sea! That is what he, Rolland, would have done, and how! If his hands had not been tied. . . .

"You wished to speak to me, sir?"

Kréven stood framed between the stanchions of the open door.

"Then it seems that you are leaving us?" Rolland said.

"Yes, sir."

"It is a promotion, I understand? You step up to be second-in-command, in short, on the *Tamanou.* I wished to pay you my compliments."

He was seated as he spoke, not looking at Kréven, tapping the end of his pencil on a chart sheet. Suddenly he got up, so roughly that the chair was overturned behind him. He brought his fist down on the bos'n shoulder, a gesture of arrest.

"And then, I wanted especially to tell you to your face, man to man, that I have been mistaken about you, Kréven, and that you are a pitiful creature in the first place, and a dirty swine."

The other man had gone white. Its mask torn off, the face was coming to life again with a maddened violence. Beneath the wrinkled skin of the forehead the eyes were wide open and haggard, while the mouth, open too, was being slowly pulled out of shape; the nostrils were compressed; and for a moment this distorted countenance made the mate think of that other visage, below. There was the same twitching, to capture the fugitive air. And it was also in almost the same hoarse voice that Kréven demanded, "I suppose you have made me come here, too, to tell me why I am that?"

The question was meant to be scornful and defiant, but the voice could no longer rise to the heights of sarcasm. It stuck to his lips; the words were badly enunciated, as if he had had a blow on his head.

"If I tell you," Rolland retorted, "it is because you are no longer capable of finding it out for yourself. You are a pitiful creature, whom a common prostitute can make give up his job."

"You haven't always been so squeamish," the man snarled.

"I left her where I took her, and I took her for what she is," Rolland responded. "Besides, when she was with me, she was already working for you. She wanted information, to make good on your scheme; she was paying for it. And to think that it was you who had put her up to that stunt!"

Kréven was deathly pale. "It's lucky for you that I respect you," he uttered. And Rolland burst out laughing.

"Your respect? Oh, no, old fellow, you're behind the times! You'll have to learn to talk all over again. What can respect have to do with you now?" He scanned the face before him and concluded, with a fierce contempt, "My word, I might think I was listening to Pillou!"

At the man's forward spring, at the stiffening, as in tetanus, of his body, Rolland said to himself, "This time he will strike!" And in the shame he felt for the man who was being trampled upon, he hoped for that assault.

But Kréven had succeeded in stopping himself. But he was panting, and his forehead was drenched in a perspiration that did not run down his face, but stood out on his skin in fine little drops like a drizzle of rain. At last, because his self-mastery gave him the right to, he asked, in a voice once more firm, "May I speak, now?" And without giving Rolland time to reply, he added, in the same clear tone, "Yes, you have still to tell me that I am a dirty swine for having got myself in right with the old man, taking a job on his boat: a dirty swine, or, if you like it better, a pimp."

"I like it better," Rolland said.

Kréven's curt gesture discarded this. Arrows that pricked the skin had no place from now on. He had reached the heart of things, delved into himself so deeply that he could not be struck at any more.

"To let go of everything at the first nod from a 'common prostitute,' as you say—I did that once, in the Legion. I was taken in, and I paid for it. Here, ten years later, I had made up my mind to do it again; we were going to sail for the Tuamotus, she and I; and then things worked out differently. . . . If I had decided to desert, it was because it was worth it. Women—as you say, one takes them, one leaves them; and, without boasting, I have certainly left a bigger lot of them than you. But this one—I am keeping her, because with her, it is different. . . ."

"The soul-mate, in short," Rolland cut in, with a smile which the other visibly held back from wiping out with his fist. "But what interests me is your job with Berlot."

"He came to me, to beg me to sail with him. I did not have to ask anything of him."

The same smile played over Rolland's features, and again the dreaded fists were clenched.

"Naturally! Somebody else was taking care of it, and she will pay the embarkation fee."

Kréven gathered himself together, his face close to the mate's as he cried, "It's my business, whether the old man blows his brains out or not—as he has sworn to her he will, if she drives him out. I am not a bourgeois! My woman will be *my* woman, and if I have decided that she is to 'pay,' as you say, she will pay, whether she enjoys it or not, because that will be the correct thing, and because I will have said so. And when that day comes, she will pay again, on that, for the captain; she will pay for you!"

Rolland could not restrain a start.

"You are losing your mind!" he said.

"For the captain," Kréven repeated, with emphasis, "and for you!" He dropped his eyes, as if his gaze were pointing to the deck planking, and he dropped his voice at the same time. "I've told you, this is the third voyage I have made with him. On the first, at Iquique, we were caught like rats in the middle of a revolution. I picked up this, but I got him out of it."

He had swiftly opened his shirt, to show a scar, above his right

258

breast, where the withered flesh was twisted so that it looked like a pink marshmallow.

"On the second voyage, right here at Nouméa, it was he who pulled me out of an ugly mess that might have kept me in this country then. And on the third, when he is almost dying— It was when I said, 'I can't give him a raw deal by deserting; he has more than his share of raw deals as it is,'—it was then that she said, 'Then we'll have to find a way. . . .'" He stuck one hand in his pocket, and shrugged his shoulders. "The way—it is what it is! But when the tug-boat skipper, there in the cabin, explained his scheme for the *Tamanou* to me, it was a very queer business! Berlot, begging me to sign up on his ship, slobbering with rage all the time, wanting to strangle me; and me spewing him out, him and his tricks! For I had come back to my first idea of beating it into the back country, as I'd done in Morocco, making a get-away up into the hills to start in with the Canaques, among the tribes where they still chew up a man once in a while, so as to be left in peace. They'd smash my skull in less with their hatchets than that old man would, who was giving me hell while he was down on his knees to me! I told him that. Then the captain shook his head no, and then he said to me, 'Since your mind is made up, go with Berlot. That is best, for the crew and for me.'"

Kréven wiped his forehead with the back of his hand. Then he looked into Rolland's eyes.

"You know what it is when he has an attack and tries to talk. It's as if the words were thorns that had got into his throat, and he was pulling them out one by one and throwing them at you, all bloody. You can't argue. He wanted to save face, as people say, for the men, for the ship-owners, for himself, and perhaps a little for me, too. So, then, I said yes. I said it for him, and also for you; because for you, too, after the place you have made for me here, Kréven the deserter wouldn't be a very shining spectacle!"

"Do you think that this is more so?" Rolland asked.

Basically, he knew nothing about it any more! Everybody was falling over everybody else to get into the picture. Before Kréven spoke, the affair had been only a triangle of complaisance. Now, the captain, the crew, the ship's owners, he himself, were all involved. And there were still others, who were not called into question, but who would agree: the Marine officer, for one; and the Nickel Company, that must be thoroughly delighted to sign up for its *Tamanou* a bos'n who was a picked man and could be depended upon to stand in for old Berlot—who might well have an attack, one of these days, that would send him to take his longitude on his deck. There was a woman at the bottom of it? So what? That would be getting to be

259

almost the way it was in high society, where women directed the dance from a distance, and pulled the strings. . . .

Without speaking another word, he stepped in front of Kréven, out of the door, and down the poop companionway. In the fore-and-aft gangway he just escaped bumping into a bucket of sea water, in which the men had been washing their hands as they came up from the hold. It was filled with a reddish soupy liquid, and Rolland stopped and looked at it. The water was muddy, he was telling himself, because everybody had just been stirring it up, but in an hour it would be clear again. Perhaps, with time, this other mess that had been poured out before him would come to seem cleaner. . . .

Kréven, who was following him, thought that he was making note of a piece of negligence. He turned around, snapped his fingers to summon a sailor, and pointed to the bucket, which the man carried away and emptied over the rail.

It was the last order he gave on the *Antonine*.

XXII

THE *Antonine* left its anchorage the next morning, the 10th of January, in tow to the *Tamanou*.

The new bos'n whom Berlot had found had arrived the evening before. His name was Ernault, and he had been "boss man"—that is, crew-master, bos'n—of a vessel lost four years before on the coral reefs. Instead of having himself repatriated, he had chosen to have a try in the colony. He had not succeeded there, because he was out of his element, and now he was going to sea again, jaundiced by his failure on land. Rolland had summed him up at a glance: a slow man, and slack. What a change from the other!

He had warned him: "You will take the place of a bos'n who had a great deal of authority over the men. I hope that it will be the same with you."

The long visage had lengthened still further at the announcement of this difficult succession.

Berlot had come aboard the *Antonine* a few minutes before sailing, with the fidgety and arrogant air of those who have been guilty of a dirty trick and insist on brazening it out. He had gone in, so, to the captain's cabin; but when he came out, ten minutes later, he was not swaggering any more. What he had seen and heard there had detached him, for the moment, from his own troubles. He had joined Rolland, and spoken to him in a low voice:

"He knows it is all up with him; he has just told me so."

The mate had merely nodded in agreement.

"You have done the right thing, taking him back on the ship," Berlot had added. "He is satisfied." And then, turning on his heel, and without even holding out his hand, he had said, "To go to pieces with that or with something else—"

It took several days to sail southeast through the broad channel between New Caledonia and the Loyalty Islands: and there were days when they were obliged to tack about, nose in the wind. After that, there would be the Pacific Ocean, free of all this swarm of coconut-palm islands. They were starting on a return voyage. To what? Rolland was thinking. . . . To France? Not even that. To a port; that is, a portal: a door which opened upon the country, but through which he, the sailor, would not pass. There was no time. And, besides, what would be the use? There was no one waiting for him. He had had no home to go back to since, on returning from the next-to-the-last voyage, he had found at the Marine Office the word of the death of Marie Ernestine Adéle Rolland, born Jagot, deceased at Erquy at the age of sixty-nine years.

He had kept his word and had put a stop to the washings as soon as he became an officer. She had no longer gone down to the brook with her wheelbarrow, an old piece of sacking thrown over her back in bad weather. He had asked himself, since, whether he had done right. She had had to break the ice every winter to wash her clothes —and she had been stricken with bronchitis in the first December that she was able to spend beside the fire! Without her, the return to France was no more than a change of direction.

He looked out at New Caledonia as they left it, watching the land grow smaller in their wake. Indisputably, it was a beautiful land, far different from the sterile saltpeter desert of Iquique and the Chilean coast. But what was he taking away from it? Not even the memory of abundant binges, like Poullain. An encounter that had been as banal as the work of bringing a ship to the dock, but that at least left no emotional regrets. No, there were no regrets of that kind, but there was a question, the question brought up by this Pillou-Kréven matter: always the same question, but this time put to him with added force.

For Kréven he still felt a cold scorn. He had respected him. More than that, there had been a friendship between them. Well, Kréven was a deserter. Good God, then she didn't exist—a ship that would sail on without stop-overs, without women; and without a man, a real man, letting you down for a tart who's given you the run-around; without your going ashore to find out that a Barquet has become the master of captains and of ships!

He caught sight of Ernault, his bearings completely lost, wandering along with his eyes glued to the sides of the deck as if he were looking for a pin. He pictured Kréven going to sea again one day, as this man was going to sea again, beaten, broken to heel. No, never! He knew very well that this was not that lad's style. He would blow up everything, and himself along with it, rather than own himself a failure.

Meanwhile, his absence was already making itself felt. The mate had just given the order for the deck to be cleared up as soon as the anchors and chains had been brought in. But the work was being done half asleep, while that big boob strolled up and down without noticing anyone, like a watchman in a public square. The men were turning lines and halyards around the toggles, like good old women in their eighties winding up wool. Neveu was bawling for his thread to stitch and sew the bolt-ropes, and Ernault did not even seem to hear him. Papa Jules, the cook, was making a great hullaballoo throwing out the novice, who had been trying to heat his chunk of pitch and soot on the stove, to wax the thread.

"Never while I'm in charge of the galley!"

"It's the bos'n. . . ."

"I spit on him! If he wants to get my poker in his belly, all he has to do is come in here!"

This was only a "manner of speaking." But the point was, he would never have said that where Kréven was concerned!

Rolland was thinking that Caroff would have taken his place in the little deck-house better than this sorry recruit. Caroff was a grumbler, but without bad faith. As he had sailed far and wide, he knew that the first attribute of food rations is that they shall last until the end of the voyage; from this it follows that one must reckon with all hazards, and economy is the law of the lazaretto. A sailor who has grasped that has grasped everything. Caroff also knew all the fine points of the seaman's trade. Unfortunately, his attitude of indifference might quickly have robbed him of all authority, and above all, he had never concealed his repugnance for command. The mate, who had speedily detected the jeering look with which he was following the comings and goings of the new bos'n, realized that some fun was already promised for this quarter: too much. So the next morning at six o'clock, although that was the end of his watch, Rolland stayed on deck.

"The washing."

Ernault was calling to the watch without conviction, in the voice of a grocer saying, "Who's next?" Nevertheless, it seemed to produce its effect. Marius and Domino picked up the buckets, and the others got the brooms. They began with the pens for the pigs and the chickens, below the quarter-deck. Four young pigs had been brought aboard at Kanala, and they were already civilized. There is no animal that is cleaner than a pig; and these came up of their own accord to be showered with water from the buckets, and then to be scrubbed down by Bako with heavy strokes of his briar brush. After that, it was the turn of the deck, now getting white under the swabbing by worn besoms and the rinsing with buckets of sea water. Ernault had gone back to his promenade. A bucketful of water struck full across his boots. He pivoted on his heels, and looked at the man who had thrown it. It was Marius, who was making his way calmly toward the rail, swinging his empty bucket. But as the new bos'n turned around, his gaze met Rolland's eyes. They were saying, quite plainly, "Now what?"

Ernault's reaction surprised even the mate. The bos'n snatched a broom from the hands of the man nearest him, and as Marius came back with his bucket full of water, he stopped him, took the bucket from him, and handed the *moko* the broom.

"Take that," he said. "You are much too clumsy!"

The man stood there flabbergasted, looking like an idiot. The others were laughing out loud. That was well played, Rolland thought. After all, those big ordinary overgrown fellows had their own ways, which were not always bad!

The day was spent in making wide tacks, in the bright sunshine: a lot of distance covered for little distance gained; a course like an accordion, which brought you at night just a little south of the point you left in the morning. Rolland did not like these zig-zags, which emphasize the slowness of the sailing-ship obliged to deal cunningly with a wind that the steamship ignores. In the cabin that evening he avowed his eagerness to get back, in the Pacific at last free of islands, to that pace of "full and by" which the *Antonine,* with her fine lines, maintained so well.

"Oh, yes!" cried Poullain. "When we just get clean water under our tucks!"

The cabin boy was coming out of the galley with the captain's dinner on a tray, a dinner to which Papa Jules gave concentrated attention. For weeks past there had been nothing solid, nothing but a thick soup and a clear bouillon, to which since the call at Thio the good sister's gift had made it possible to add some apple-sauce.

"What you give a baby," remarked old Jules, whose wife had reared four.

But he put the minute care of a kind and good man into the crushing of every smallest lump, though he was on the heavy-handed side in his cooking for the crew.

The cabin boy would set the tray on the table and vanish; and Thirard would then come to grips, alone, with the torture that was his meal. It took him more than an hour to swallow a few cold teaspoonfuls, and it was the most terrible hour of his miserable day. During the voyage out, when the cancer had begun to bite into him savagely whenever it was irritated by the least morsel of food, the captain had said to himself, "I must eat, or I shan't be able to hold on." At Thio it had been, "I must eat, or they will take me ashore." Now he had no courage left.

And this evening he looked at the tray the cabin boy had just set down, as if he were being brought to bay before a superhuman task which he was giving up trying to undertake. What was the use? The return voyage was credited to him, now that it was begun. Was it not enough now to have to go on breathing? To dread every breath as seasick landlubbers dreaded every wave? He opened the porthole and emptied the three plates, one after the other, into the sea. It was his first capitulation.

When Rolland entered—he came every evening now—he found him sitting quietly. Only that billowing movement of the head and shoulders persisted, stretching him out with every effort at respiration, lifting him up, to fall back empty.

He had been following the different changes in the ship's direction on the compass he had nailed to the ceiling. He knew that the weather was good, with a nice breeze. He gave some directions about the course, and then he looked thoughtfully at the mate.

"I feel remorseful, now, for not having rid you of a burden," he said. "I was thinking of no one but myself, all through."

Thinking of himself, in refusing hospital care to stay in this scorching hot cabin, on a ship that would not always be running along with this supple ease! Yet Rolland could not fail to understand what the words meant: "I wanted to keep a command which I would soon not be able to vouch for." And it was to this that he replied, "You are by no means a burden, Captain. So far as I am concerned, there is more peace of mind in having you aboard."

Thirard thanked him with the shadow of a smile. That was true: his seaman's sense, his experience, could still be useful, since his brain was unimpaired.

"Yes, but later—" he murmured.

Later, when the attacks of suffocation, which were still intermittent, became one long crisis, when he would be gripped by that dreadful rattle day and night, writhing in agony in this cabin—

"Later, you may be better," Rolland said. And then, as the sad eyes reproached him for the futile untruth, he continued, "Even if, later, you are no longer able to do anything about the ship, everything that you are doing now is a help."

Thirard made another gesture of acceptance.

"In any case," he promised, "when I am no longer good for anything, you needn't worry: I shan't bother you in dying." He saw Rolland's look of alarm, and added, "No, I shall not kill myself. Still, when one jumps out of a window to avoid being burned alive—it would be only that. But I shall not do it. Because of my wife. For her, it would still be suicide."

For a moment, Rolland's thought went out to that far-away woman. It was to increase her widow's pension that the captain was here, it was for her that he was consenting to be slowly devoured alive, rather than cause her the grief and anxiety of a proscribed death. Thirard was close to fifty years old: he must have been married for at least twenty years. She must be, like so many captains' wives he knew, serene, thrifty, patient, resigned to interminable waitings. Since there was no longer a question of passion between them—if there ever had been—what threads could then be woven between two human beings, how could such a fusion be brought about with the companion of one's life? It is the almost scandalized question that is asked by the young, in the presence of an old union.

Thirard leaned back, then straightened himself again to ask, with singular concern, "Do you believe in God, you yourself, Rolland?"

The question caught the other man up short. Rolland indeed believed that he believed in God; but since he had never been asked about it, as a challenge to be met then and there, he really did not dare to declare himself.

The ghost of a voice continued: "You—you can wait. For me, it is Yes or No. If it is Yes, then why this?" He pointed to his throat. "If it is No, that is worse, in a sense. . . . If it were Yes," he added, "it would be because of my wife."

It seemed right to Rolland that one should reach a decision in this way on the existence of God. He felt confusedly that one could be subject to the contagion of faith, even from far away, and that a life was sometimes a proof.

The captain made a gesture toward the empty dishes on one corner of the table. "Will you ask them in the galley to send me some more bouillon and stewed apple?" he asked.

"Your appetite is coming back, Captain. That is a good sign," Rolland answered.

He was feeling really happy, as he went out, about this appetite.

He could not suspect that he had recalled his chief to the duty of living a little longer.

When he reached the deck, he was stopped short by an extraordinary spectacle. The *Antonine* was literally covered with sea birds. They had lined up on the yards and the boom; they were perched on the hatches, the deck-houses, the windlass; the boats had a fringe of birds around their rims. The men, who had started to chase them away, were recognizing some of them: sea-mews, gulls, skuas.

"That black one—I'd say he was a cormorant."

"Those gray ones—you wouldn't think they were plovers, would you?"

Others were quite unknown. But they all refused to leave the ship. Sultan, the captain's dog, almost beside himself, would leap up into their solid lines, and they would dodge him with a flap of their wings and then settle down again. The men would pursue them as far as the lower yards; and sometimes they would mow down rows of them on the edges of the hatches, where they were pressed close together. The birds would fly up, screech, fall back, but they would not fly away. Papa Jules, who had come out and was standing at the doorway of his galley, was condemning the futile slaughter; in order to stop it, he was protesting that he would not cook these inedible fowl, with their oily flesh and fishy taste. The men told him to go back to his saucepans; this was not a matter of food, but of entertainment. Not one of them, not even Rolland, felt any wonder either at this unusual visitation or at the passivity of these creatures that preferred being crushed to death on those wooden planks to flying off into the free and tranquil air. No one asked himself what was the unnamable terror to which their fear of man had given way. The only one, perhaps, who might have been able to guess that this phenomenon portended danger was lying in his bunk, as prostrate as the dead and dying birds.

He came up to the poop, however, toward three in the morning. The birds had fled at nightfall. Poullain had crushed the last two, that had swooped against the wheel, and he was now walking up and down, smoking. Berteux, the head of the watch, had gone to make a tour of the bow. The breeze had calmed down somewhat, and the *Antonine,* with all sails set, was scudding east-southeast. Poullain had just had the braces tautened when the captain appeared, bareheaded and with his old coat thrown over his shoulders. As soon as he came in sight the junior officer went to meet him, as usual.

"The barometer is going down very fast, Monsieur Poullain."

This shattered voice always affected the third mate deeply. Now, again, he was more impressed by it than by the fall in the barometer.

He had noticed nothing during the night to make him anticipate that. There was the same sky, a-swarm with living stars—alive as they are in the Tropics, with not one ever keeping still, all of them making eyes at you all through your watch. There were some untoward shifts in the trade wind, perhaps, and a moisture in the air that drenched you in perspiration when you were doing nothing at all. But there was no indication, in any of this, that would send you sticking your nose into the drum of the self-registering barometer. And yet the captain, all bent over, was already going back into the chart-house and beckoning the officer to follow him. It was a fact: the barometer was falling, and fast.

Poullain thought of the birds. Was their invasion not an advance announcement of the barometer's plunge? He spoke of it, and thought he heard the captain mutter, "A bad sign. . . ." But already the emaciated body, panting and at the end of its strength, was propped against the partition wall. Poullain, big and tall and overcome with pity, leaned over.

"You must go back to your bunk, Captain. If the wind blows up, I will send you word."

The captain thanked him with a movement of his head, and made his halting way down the steps.

It was of him, and his suffering, that Poullain thought first, when he was alone again and returned to his interrupted walk. How many times would he be able to drag himself up here, like this, before the end? And the end, people said, was terrible. . . . Asphyxiation, but slowly measured out for days; death by being buried alive in the open air. And the others, who could do nothing but look on . . .

Berteux, returning from his round, came up the companionway to the poop. Poullain told him about the captain's visit, and they both went into the chart-house. Yes, decidedly, this was bad! A drop of three divisions since they had gone on watch. Poullain tapped on the glass, an encouragement which would sometimes succeed in sending it up one-tenth or so when it was favorably inclined. The hand remained inert, as if it had become very heavy with a weight that was slowly drawing it toward the figures of catastrophe.

Yet neither of the two officers had ever known a more complete contradiction between the instrument and the weather. A breeze, a calm sea, a clear sky. . . . But look, the sky was not so clear as it had been a little while ago. The stars over the northeast horizon were a little blurred now. And there was a sultry warmth descending upon them from that sky, instead of the chill that usually marked the approach of dawn.

The breeze, however, remained steady. They were still hugging the wind, to get out of this accursed channel as quickly as possible.

267

However, it was a fact that they had been tacking ever since they left Thio, and not making much headway. The trade winds, which were ordinarily steady at east-southeast, were now in the south. So then, to make for the south with almost southerly winds—that was a damn hard problem for a big square-rigged ship, especially when they lacked the range for a long tack.

They would have to veer, however, when the watch changed, and Berteux had made ready for the operations.

Rolland was turning to now with his watch. The look of the weather struck him at once, and he jumped to the barometer: 735 mm.

"Good God, Berteux, why haven't you let me know of this?"

"The captain knew about it."

Berteux, for some time past, had been playing the captain against the mate, and this was so stupid that Rolland paid no attention to it.

"The weather's turning into dirty linen," Poullain remarked, as he joined them.

This was not to be denied. But there are too many murky dawns to permit taking them as the basis of prophecy. It was a chalky sun, nevertheless, that was rising above the horizon on the port bow, and there were copper-colored streaks scratched all across the sky in front of the ship, like long strings of tawny cotton drawn out by a carding machine.

"Cat's-tails," said the helmsman, who was listening without seeming to.

Now every seaman knows that when one sees the tail, the claws are not far away. But it was not the helmsman who gave a name to the danger.

They had changed the tack, and were running into the southwest now. Ernault, the bos'n, had just called the men for washing duty, and they were already lugging the buckets they had filled at the pump. The water seemed thickened and sluggish, so much so that when it was thrown out on the deck they were surprised to see it flowing in swift transparent streams as it did every morning. The sailors worked languidly, casting frequent glances at that disquieting sky, and then at the poop. The wind was not growing any stronger, but it remained oppressive, although the breeze is usually so buoyant in these localities. Then, too, the mate was going too often to look at the barometer, and he would come out of the chart-house with the wrinkles across his forehead that they saw there on bad days. The pigs, the chickens, even Sultan the dog, had the same disturbed look. When the men flushed out their quarters they had seen them

268

huddled together in their pens. All this was a further announcement that they were in for something ugly.

The washing had brought them to the foot of the poop-rail. There they were in a good position to keep their eyes on the first mate and Monsieur Poullain, who were walking up and down on the windward side without saying anything to each other.

It was then that Ernault raised his head toward the officers and muttered, in his toneless voice, "There'll be a cyclone tomorrow or next day, and it isn't going to be a surprise to me! The last one that went over the island destroyed everything I had—just tore it all up and swept it away."

The damn nitwit! A hell of a lot they cared that his cabin had been blown to bits and his sugar cane into matchsticks! Or, rather, why hadn't he taken root with his cabbages, instead of coming here to say what should never be said on a ship! But he had gone back to his swabbing already and seemed altogether astounded to see the brooms still held aloft and the men stock still in the middle of the deck, their full buckets at arms' length, as if they had been called to platoon drill.

"Well?" he said.

They looked at him with loathing: it would be well washed, that deck of his, and without anybody's breaking his neck over it, either!

Eight bells sounded: four double strokes. Berteux stepped up on the poop. At the same moment, the captain appeared framed in the doorway of the chart-house. He beckoned to Rolland.

"Will you look at the log, sir, and come with me?" he said.

He went back into the iron cubicle. Rolland came out ten minutes later, less surprised by what Thirard had said than by having heard him speak for some time, and almost with ease. He called Berteux.

"Monsieur Berteux, tell the bos'n, the carpenter, the mechanic, the cook, and the two men of each watch who have been longest with the ship, to be ready to come down to the saloon. You will come, also. Poullain will take your place on the poop."

Only a few seconds later, the cabin boy presented himself.

"Monsieur Rolland, the captain asks that you will have the leading men of the crew come to the saloon."

The little fellow spoke his piece very well, without showing any fear, but with the grave face proper to the situation.

Now, lined up in the saloon, bareheaded, in their boots and oilskins, they no longer seemed at all embarrassed, as they had been at Christmas, by their arms and their legs. For their ship and for themselves there was now a question of life or death. They must accept or reject the Old Man's decision. Rolland, after a glance at

269

their unmoving faces, felt that they were fully his equals: it was a reinforcement which the men were bringing to the officers.

The captain spoke in the voice that seemed to come rumbling from the depths of the earth: "My friends, the aspect of the weather, the sudden downward plunge of the barometer, the birds you saw yesterday—all this indicates the approach of a cyclone which will probably strike us before tomorrow. We are at this moment seventy miles east-southeast of Thio. Monsieur Berteux, will you spread out the map so that everyone can see the exact point?"

Berteux unrolled the map and put a pencil mark on a spot between the coast of New Caledonia and, to the north, Maré, the most southern island of the Loyalty group. They all bent over it. Then Thirard continued, measuring out his breath:

"We are thus not clear of the dangers of the coast, and we should certainly be lost with all hands on one of the islands by which we are surrounded if the cyclone should catch us in a position close to that which you see marked on the map. This is what will happen to us, almost of necessity, if we continue to tack as we have been doing since leaving Thio, in an effort to gain the open sea. Do you understand me thoroughly, and do you share my opinion?"

They had just placed themselves, on the map, between those two arms of the trap, those islands that paralleled one another so astonishingly; and under their eyes there was still the space all speckled over with hundreds of black dots which they had looked at and thought about: so many reefs. They responded with one voice, as in church, "Yes, Cap'n."

"Then," Thirard went on to explain, "I believe that our best chance of getting out of it is to bear away on Thio, to go back into the roadstead and ride it out at anchor. I am not allowing myself any illusions. If our chains break we shall capsize. But it will be in a much less rough sea. We shall have—the ship and ourselves—a chance to escape from it. Do you agree with me?"

"Yes, Cap'n."

"Good. Then, rely on me. I do not need a pilot to go through the strait. I trust that the good God will grant me the strength to keep on my feet, and eyes to make out the sea marks. . . . Monsieur Rolland, bear away, set the exact course."

No sooner were they out of the room than they expressed their astonishment:

"Not to be able to talk, and to make himself understood like that!"

As they ran to their posts for the working, they were saying, "We are going back to Thio." And they did not doubt that they would arrive in time."

"With this breeze, we'll be there before the shake-up," they said.

When the *Antonine*, her sails distended close to the bursting-point, was charging toward the northwest, Rolland noticed that the aspect of the sky had changed. The reddish-toned cirrus masses had disappeared behind swollen banks of white cloud already tinged with black. The wind was blowing up stronger, too, and long close surges of sea were sweeping down from the north. The *Antonine*, overloaded with canvas, was cutting a rude furrow through them. Rolland consulted the log, and then the barometer: speed, thirteen knots; barometer, 730 mm., which meant that it was now dropping more than two millimeters an hour. This showed a steady lessening of the distance between the ship and the cyclone. The log and the barometer; the log against the barometer! Everything was at stake between those two: the ship's speed and the hurricane's. They must keep the canvas up, then, even if the wind became still worse; they must not take in sail until the very moment when everything was about to be carried away.

The mate came back to lean over the hand-rail, and heard a man calling out, below. "She's never speeded like this! If we're caught, it won't be the ship's fault!"

Rolland was pleased by this tribute to the vessel. When the sailor's glance met his own, he made a little sign to him. It was almost noon. At this rate, and assuming that they could go as straight ahead as a steamship, they ought to be off Thio about four o'clock.

The officers hurried through their lunch in ten minutes and went back to the poop. The men had not taken long, either, to gulp down their meal, and in spite of the drenching spray they were flowing back along the deck, eager to see it all, to lose nothing of this vibrant swiftness that was carrying them toward a haven. But in those ten minutes the sky had been again transformed. A thick black band now stretched across it, from northeast to southwest. They were running head on toward this wall. Huge thunderheads were emerging from it, and their red glow was spreading over the sea, the ship, and the men, like fixed reflections from a blacksmith's forge.

"The lamps are being lighted," said Caroff. "Look out for the dance that's ahead!"

It was at this moment that the cabin boy, wild-eyed, leaped up on the poop.

"The cap'n! He's dying!" he cried.

Poullain and Rolland looked at each other. Truly, he was choosing his moment! This was the last straw!

"Don't take in sail until the final second," Rolland ordered, before he followed the boy.

Poullain's gesture accepted this as a matter of course.

As he pushed open the door, Rolland was expecting to find the captain prostrate, with no life left. It was worse. He was standing up. One might have said that the cyclone, still hanging over the ship outside, was already here, in the heart of the vessel, that it was shaking, striking, flinging back and forth the inhuman being that was shut up in this cabin. A horrible minotaur's mask, a yawning mouth from which a black tongue protruded with a savage rattle, nostrils dilated like a wild beast's snout, eyes thrust out beyond the bloodstained lids. . . . He had thrown off his jacket, torn out the buttonholes of his shirt. The red muffler was lying on the floor, and Rolland cast a horrified glance at his neck, a neck the color of wine dregs, encircled by a necklace of ulcerated lumps. Thirard had not seen the mate come in. He was hanging onto a heavy shelf, his fingers biting into it like talons, and, arched against this base, he was distending and twisting his body with the violence of a madman, one of those madmen of olden days who used to be smothered under mattresses. He was pulling at the air, to force it through the narrow pass of his blocked throat, as Rolland had never seen a man pull on a line at the worst moments, when life depended on the effort of that pull.

Then he let go of the wooden ledge, turned back upon himself, and seized his throat as if to tear out the thing that was strangling him. For this was strangulation, a veritable murder by an invisible assassin; and one had to stand there with dangling arms and let him struggle, with nothing one could do, nothing one could say. A woman would have put her hand on his forehead, pressed his arm, wiped away his perspiration: completely useless gestures, yet something that would have brought him close. For a man, a "second captain," that was out of the question.

And the others, up above there, sitting tight while they waited for the hurricane, that insane wind which, from one moment to the next, would bring them as close to death as was this wretched man. . . . And not one tiny breath of this wind, which was about to swoop down upon them after overturning houses, sinking ships, snapping off trees and masts as one breaks sticks across one's knees, would make its way into this throat. The cyclone would stop at the edge of those blackened lips.

Rolland just checked a step of recoil. The monstrous creature was advancing upon him, beating his hands upon his shoulders, lowering his head, his forehead, to scrape them against the rough cloth of the mate's coat. Rolland felt the sharp fingers dig into his flesh. The half-bald head was directly under his eyes, the skin yellow, with swollen veins. And he thought, Go on, go on, if that can ease you! . . . In spite of the pressure upon him, he forced himself not to stir.

Then, after a spasm that set him to trembling with all the trembling of the agonized man, the hands loosed their hold. He felt a profound relaxation throughout the body that was buttressed against him, and a fetid breath struck him full in the face. The air had got in! Rolland reached out his arms, supported that now-sinking body under the armpits, and carried the captain to his chair. Then, watching him, he sponged his own forehead, for he, too, was streaming with sweat.

I do not know what is waiting for us up there, he thought, but it cannot be worse than this that is here.

The sick man seemed to have forgotten him again. Slumped down in his armchair, his chin on his chest, he was breathing in short, avid gasps. The pitching of the *Antonine,* rudely buffeted now by the swell, sometimes almost doubled him up. Rolland waited for a few minutes, then spoke.

"Would you like me to give you a hypodermic, Captain?"

He had learned how to do that in his training course, as well as how to reduce a fracture and to pull a tooth. It was the first time he had made any allusion to the morphine. The captain shook his head in refusal.

Rolland was not satisfied. The doctor had said to him, before leaving the ship. "If he suffers too much, knock him out with morphine." This, if ever, was the time for that! Then, too, if they did not reach Thio and find shelter there, he would have other things to do than coming down here to attend to the invalid. Since the captain would be nothing but a cipher, in what was ahead of them, let him at least not be one misery the more!"

"You would rest better," he insisted.

"Exactly where are we?" the captain asked.

A few moments before he left the poop, Rolland had taken a meridian altitude on a corner of sunshine stifled—it, too!—by clouds. He indicated the position.

"When we are in sight of Thio—come and get me."

The order escaped from him like the last puff of steam from an engine whose pressure is exhausted. He made two slight gestures with his head, which could only mean, "Thank you. Now go away." And Rolland went out.

He found nothing changed on the ship or on the sea, when a quick look around had put him in possession of first the one and then the other. There was still the same assault of the swells, the same foaming of powerful wave crests, across which the *Antonine* was dashing wildly, like a dog determined to drive back the panic flight of a flock of sheep. But the sky's structure was now that of

273

a giant oven built of dark blocks, and from its vault, broken at the zenith, fell a sulphurous glow like that diffused by the last embers of a dying fire. The barometer was hastening on its downward course. The distance between the *Antonine* and the cyclone was diminishing at a swifter pace. Where would the encounter take place? Would they have time to reach the Thio roadstead?

The sea was getting heavier. Its first breakers were cracking like whip-lashes into the fore-and-aft gangway. The wind, too, was working itself up and howling. This was no longer the even and measured trade wind, which has its tour of the world to make and watches its breath like a long-distance runner. One might have said that it sensed its colleague's dash from the north and was itself charging to meet it. Thus, in a herd of animals, a stampede is contagious and carries even the most sluggish along with it. . . . The ship was growing tired. She had begun to resound like a base drum under the blows of wind and sea. The masts were quivering; the sails, stretched and rigid as cauldrons, were pulling as if to up-root them; the rigging was vibrating like sharp-drawn strings. But the log was still saying thirteen knots, and this was not the moment to take in sail!

At three o'clock, they caught sight of land to the west, like a darker and more stable mist. At four o'clock, under the asphalt mass of the sky, on a sea sharp-pointed like a harrow, Rolland had the canvas reduced off the harbor channels of Thio.

The battle was not won, for all that! Ahead of them, the reef barrier was flinging a defense wall of explosions into the darkened air. There seemed no longer to be any opening in that barrier. Behind those geyser spoutings the mountains, cut by the avalanche of the low clouds, seemed flattened as by a steam-roller. There were no more differing planes, there was no more relief: the coast was pasted flat against the dark verdure of the hills.

Then Rolland remembered, with a hope that he dared not avow, the order breathed out down there a little while ago: "When you are off Thio, come and get me." The mate knew, as everyone on the ship knew, that two years ago Captain Thirard had succeeded in this same operation, in less unmanageable weather, to be sure, but also with little visibility. It was the same man, or what was left of him, who must now again force a passage through the coral reefs; for the pilot, needless to say, would not be waiting for them at the entrance!

Berteux was already working to change the ship's head and approach the land, when Rolland went down to the captain's cabin. He was wondering, with an apprehension not wholly concentrated

on the sick man, what he would find there. An hour before, he had
sent the cabin boy for news:

"Go ask the captain if he needs anything."

The lad had come back at once.

"He is sitting there with his eyes closed. He didn't answer. He
must be asleep."

The prostration that follows the attack. . . . Would he have
strength to rouse himself from it, to drag himself as far as the
poop, to murmur an order?

But he found him out in the narrow corridor. He was moving
along, stumbling, scraping his shoulder against the partition wall.
Rolland caught hold of his arm and supported him as far as the
short stairway. As in the morning, he had an armchair brought up to
the poop, and the captain was seated in it. Then Rolland turned
toward him, awaiting orders, but not hoping for them too much.

For the mate's gesture was only that of a young tribal chief in the
presence of a threat never before encountered, when he has the old
man brought out of the cave—the impotent old man to whom
nothing is left but his eyes and his memory—to place him face to
face with the peril he has once conquered. In those hours of con-
tinuous grazing of the ship's breaking-point, Rolland had succeeded
in bringing the *Antonine*, in record time, to the gateway of safety.
To do that, he had kept up an insane spread of canvas, which the
most reckless speeders would have hesitated to maintain. He had
won. But to go through this gate, he must abdicate. Let it be done
quickly, and no more talk about it!

His head drooping over his shoulder, his eyes half-closed, Captain
Thirard was obviously seeking to rediscover, on this confused shore,
the sea-marks that would give him the necessary alignments. But
how, with those wavering eyes, was he to find a house gable in this
daub of pitch, a conspicuous tree in this green-and-gray wash that
was now the forest? Rolland was sure that he would not succeed. He
was already dashing into the chart-house—as if he were stepping
over him—to get the map, and the "Nautical Instructions," when
he saw the pale lips move. The captain was whispering orders which
Berdeux was passing on to the helmsman.

The *Antonine*, on the port tack, was just about to enter the
harbor passage when a violent shift of the wind struck it, almost
head on. The trade wind, already driven out of its course by the
cyclone, was buckling completely, was falling off to the west, and
seemed to be thrown back by the screen of the mountains. The sails,
no longer filling, quivered. At a swift and sweeping gesture from
the captain, the helmsman had only time to put the wheel all the

way to starboard, to avoid the ship's being caught aback. The big four-master fell off rapidly, just missed the reefs, and at once picked up speed. It was all over for Thio. The wind had been taken out of their sails. Literally, the land was spewing them out again.

XXIII

THEY HAD ALTERED the course, thereupon, in order to fill the sails again, and were fleeing with their head to the north-east. The men's faces showed the fury of people who have just had a door slammed in their faces; they were choked by a white-hot rage, as the Old Man was choked up there on the poop, as they watched the land being blotted out by the eddies of rain.

"Ten minutes more and we'd have made it, and then never mind about rain!"

Their nerves were already in tatters from their long suspense, and this shower was as if someone had stuck a fist full in their faces. Accustomed as they were, at sea, to having things not go as they wanted them, broken in to the winds' whims and evasions, they were nevertheless choked with wrath over the perfection of this blow. How were they not to feel a diabolic will to refuse them asylum, instead of that incoherence of the winds which precedes the air's great convulsions?

"When you tell it, nobody will believe you!" Cario—who was nevertheless one of the calmest of them ordinarily—was summing it up, his head raised toward the dark sky, his lips curled and uttering most frightful blasphemies. "All right, then, just send it along, your god-damn cyclone! All right, let it smash us; but get it over!"

They had to have a reason for all bad luck. "Who is it hasn't paid his jane?" they'd say when the wind was against them. Now it was Marius, hauling sullenly on his line, who growled, "Look, you don't have to hunt for it! With the Old Man rotting from the head down, like a week-old fish! The land was scared of him, as soon as he showed it his face!"

Struck by this, they turned toward the stern. The captain had left the poop.

Marius, beside himself, shouted into the wind: "Let him hide, and let him die! And we'll toss him to Davy Jones's locker. He's bringing death to the ship, I'm telling you!"

When the vessel had stumbled into the squall, the captain had flung out his arm in a disheartened gesture, and his head had fallen back into the red muffler. Rolland, dashing off to the working, had ignored him. When the *Antonine* had again set its head toward the open sea, Thirard had tried to get up, but the ship was rolling terribly, and the sick man had twice been thrown roughly back into his seat. It was then that Poullain had signaled to Charles, who was coiling a line on the poop.

"Help the captain down to his cabin," he said.

The big seaman had almost carried him away, held against his stomach, like his famous drums of red lead. But before he let himself be picked up, Thirard had called Rolland, to whisper to him, "Not before tomorrow . . ."

The mate himself was convinced that the game would be played this very night.

The wind was getting stronger. The waves were rolling over the stern: huge rollers that were filling the well-deck. It was again necessary to haul in canvas.

The men went up awkwardly. In spite of the turmoil above and below, Rolland heard Gallais yelling, when Corio stepped on his hand. Then there was the jingling of the rings on the stays, when the lower stays'ls were hauled down; a jingling like curtains sliding over their rods. In just such a way would the "bourgeois" families draw the curtains together in the evening, so as to be more snug and secluded in their homes. . . .

Rolland raised his hand to form a megaphone, and called out: "Come on, stir your stumps a little, my God!"

For they were taking their time! Granted, they were going to strip the ship, piece by piece, as has to be done in heavy weather. But after that? Furled or not, the sails might make a get-away and take the masts with them. What did the mate know, after all, about a cyclone?

Oh, that word! If Rolland had had his hands at the throat of the man who had pronounced it, how he would have made him swallow it, even if he choked, like the luckless man down there! A word is more noxious than a thing. . . .

His head was still lifted toward the upper tops'ls, which the men had almost finished furling; and above them he saw the sky. It had taken on the look of a moving ice-field, broken pieces that were not coming together again, dark blocks following one another, with gray intervals in between; and it was shedding the light of a prison cell, which one felt to be filtered down from far above, through that hard disjointed mass.

When the men were on deck again, Rolland called them around him, with a gesture.

"You know already that the cyclone is going to hit us," he said. "There is just one thing that can bring us through it." His eyes met one after another of the tense looks fixed upon him, and he spoke with emphasis. "To obey."

They scattered, their heads lowered, carrying the word with them, planted within their skulls.

At seven o'clock they passed the Gazelle reefs, which lie forty miles to the northwest of the coast of New Caledonia: a few dark heads swimming in the spray. By eight o'clock, complete darkness had fallen, three hours earlier than the evening before. It had become suddenly so thick that they had the feeling of running along in a trench so deep that no gleam of light ever got down into it. The only things that remain distinct were the mate's face, streaked with hard lines of shadow by the binnacle lantern, and the blinking of the ship's signal lights. In flight, under the lower tops'l and the fores'l, the vessel was now rolling gunnel under and shaking off the water that swept over it, with a great splashing noise. Both watches had assembled on the poop.

"My God, how dark it is! How can it be as dark as this?"

To find a line to be tautened, they had to feel their way like blind men, and, when their fingers encountered a body, to follow it as far as the arm, and then run down that to the other man's hand, holding the end of line. Yet their courage was returning as the hours passed. They had often ridden out weather like this. To be knocked flat by the heavy seas that washed over the deck, and mercilessly buffeted by the swells; to cling with arms and legs to any firm projection; to tear their fingers open in furling the sails; to swallow mouthfuls of salt water and only spit out a quarter of it—that was the bad side of their trade, but it was still their trade all the same. It seemed to them that to carry on as they were used to doing would hold the weather within known limits; that to go on like this, crushed by toil and weariness, must conjure away the evil fate; and that the obscure power in whose hands they were would be satisfied, as usual, with beating them, felling them, draining all the strength and the warmth out of their bodies, without going so far as to sink the ship.

Then, too, and especially, a cyclone, to them, was something that must strike like a whip-lash, as the tornado had done at Kanala, sweep away everything—rudder, yards, the whole kit and caboodle—in that single stroke.

"Believe it or not, this is lasting too long," one of them said. "If it had been going to blow everything to bits, it would have done it."

"As Monsieur Poullain was saying," added another, "maybe we are only going to catch the tail-end."

They were bellowing right into each other's ears, in the pitch-black darkness, sometimes swept off their feet by the ship's rolling, and wiping the trickling spray from their mouths and their cheeks with the backs of their hands. They knew that they were still masters of the ship.

Around midnight, although the wind was raging, they found themselves all of a sudden, as in a harbor, on a smooth sea. There was an abrupt stoppage of the rolling that had been heeling the bulwarks into the water and grazing the lower yards with the swell, the pitching that had been turning their stomachs upside down. The ship was running on as even a horizontal as if she were on rails: the swift gliding of an express train, engulfed in the roaring tunnel of the night.

For the wind was not letting up. It was still driving them at a terrifying speed, which they were better able to measure on this level surface. It felt to them as if they were being carried ahead by the smooth and dizzying rush of a current in the uncontrollable moments before it plunges beneath the earth, or they were darting along the glossy rim of a whirlpool. This calm of the sea under the increasing fury of the sky struck them with stupefaction; and they would jump to any assumption rather than suspect their terrible success: they were sailing so close to the invisible reefs as to find this sheltered and dormant water right against the rock.

"Astrolabe."

Rolland, on the poop, had grasped the situation. Yet he gave a start when the disembodied voice breathed the word in his ear. He had not heard the captain come up, nor the door of the chart-house open. "Astrolabe"—that was the name of the mass of rock and coral which forms a block at the northeast of the New Caledonia-Loyalty channel. So far, they were passing them; but so terribly close that they might even yet fall into the trap. For there was more of it to come. The bank of reefs stretched north for miles; and the ship's course belonged to the wind, solely to the wind, which was sweeping the *Antonine* before it, headlong.

The two officers waited, side by side, without speaking. Every next second might be the one that crushed them. Then Rolland felt a touch on his arm, and a whisper so close to his ear that the breath and the words reached him at the same time:

"Have boards, thick planks, taken into the sail locker, with carpenter's tools."

Boards, tools, in the sail locker . . . Yes, if five minutes from now they were not dashed to pieces on a rock, they might need to shore

279

up a stove-in door, when all the crew would have taken refuge in the big locker where they sewed the sails. For the quarters, the deck-houses, would become as inaccessible as the reefs that were slipping away off port bow.

He moved away from the compass and flung the order into the black pit of the deck, and he did not turn back toward the stern until he had heard the heavy planks being dragged to the foot of the poop. Then he no longer saw the captain. But the two men at the wheel seemed to be looking at something at their feet. Leaning down, Rolland saw that it was Thirard, who had let himself slip to the floor. Sitting there, bent double, he was leaning his rounded back against the compass binnacle.

"Are you feeling worse, Captain?"

As he did not receive any reply, Rolland reached out his hand and felt the spasmodic jerking of the emaciated shoulder as he touched it. He called two of the men, then, to carry him away—something that had become habitual, as in the home of a paralytic. As they picked up the prostrate body, however, one of the sailors shook his head: what was the Old Man doing there, to make them more trouble? He wanted to command, and he couldn't. . . .

The calm beneath the ship did not last. Their flight at thirteen knots before the hurricane had soon left the Astrolabe in the southwest. When Rolland felt the trough of the waves under his boots once more, and the ship starting her wild dance again, he drew a deep breath: hard as the sea might be, it was not so hard as the rocks!

It was at this moment that through all the rumbling and howling and thundering about him he made out a frantic hubbub toward the bow: the beating of frenzied wings against the sky-lights of the chicken-pens, the desperate thrusts against the planks of the pigsty. The chickens and pigs were trying to get away. Bako attempted to dash toward them, but Caroff, standing beside him, caught him and held him back.

"Stay where you are, Blackface! You'll be carried away if you go."

The Negro, who adored his animals, was in tears.

"But they can't get out!" he cried, in his Martinique patois. "They've no way of saving themselves!"

"Have you any way of saving *your* self?" Caroff demanded roughly.

At one in the morning, when the ship was swept with water from end to end, Rolland sent the men to the sail locker, under the poop, with the cook, the mechanic, and the carpenter, who had had to be evacuated from the petty officers' deck-house. He himself remained at the compass, lashed fast, like the helmsmen, by a line fastened to the hand-rail of the chart-house.

At three o'clock, the fores'l went. They felt it only as a thunder-bolt in the darkness, or the impact of the ship against a buffer-stop. With dawn, the look of the weather was horrible. There was no longer either sea or sky, but a vast spouting back and forth between the two that confused the one with the other, a jig danced by drunken mountains leaping from all directions and whipping out thongs of stinging water the while. All the separate noises, too, were absorbed in the uproar of the waves as they struck against the stern and buried the ship under avalanches as they fell. Rolland had savagely shaken Cario, one of the helmsmen, seizing him by the collar as he surprised him in the act of turning around.

"The compass! Good God, look at your compass, nothing but your compass! You have no business looking at the stern. That's my affair, not yours!"

He was afraid that the fear of what was coming upon them might make them give a lurch that would be fatal.

The storm had reached the point where it became master of the human countenance. Its paroxysm would unclench a man's lips, distend his cheeks, possess itself of the eyelids, which were no longer obedient and would blink in spite of him. When one's eyelids flutter like that—like the ringing of an electric bell—it is a sign, and all seafaring men know it, that the wind is not far from carrying away all the rest of the man.

Rolland and the two men at the helm, Cario and Brisville, re-mained exposed to every blast. They alone were defending, however little that might be, and with the strength of their loins only, the "turtle"—the box that held the wheel. They were battered and lashed on the back, the nape of the neck, the head. They would be stunned by blows as they were stung by whips, they would be emptied of all thought, almost of all consciousness. The helmsmen became at last, like their tiller, no more than an insensate and streaming block in which subsisted merely the instinct to keep turning, even if submerged: "Hold the course. . . . Ten to star-board . . . right . . . Twenty to port. . . ."

Suddenly, somewhere near ten o'clock, they felt themselves flung forward as if by an explosion. Lifted up by a monstrous blast of wind and water, they went all the way to the end of the line that was tied around their waists, and that now stretched them out on the deck. An unheard-of uproar reached them in the depths of their own prostration: the sails that were bursting as an inflated paper bag pops when one hits it—even the sails that were furled and tightly bound in; and behind them, above them, the crashing as of felled trees. A mast? The yards?

At the moment that their bodies shot upward, they felt the same

281

movement in the ship, as if the wind had snatched her out of the sea. Raising himself on his knees—his forehead cut open—Rolland for the space of one second saw the *Antonine* wholly reared up on the summit of a monstrous wave, and as if brandished there. Then she fell back like a stone to the bottom of a seething crater.

One might have said that she had laid itself open to the cyclone down to the depths of its being, that she was distended to the breaking point, like her sails. A harsh vibration quivered through her and reached the three men, who, driven back now by the irresistible gush of air and clawing at the deck planks with their fingernails, were trying to crawl as far as the chart-house. Brisville, flat on his stomach, wiping his bleeding mouth, yelled in a curious high voice, the voice of a Norman villager in the hubbub of the country fairs, "This time it's him for sure, the Beast!"

The gust picked them up again, threw them down, flung them back and forth, on their backs, on their bellies. Cario, thrust against the charthouse, succeeded in getting to his feet and gripping the hand-rail. He hauled up Brisville, and the two of them brought in Rolland, who was turning over at the end of his line, as a fish does when it wants to twist and shorten it. When, bruising themselves against the door jambs, they succeeded in slipping into the chart-house, where they no longer felt on their mercilessly beaten bodies the drubbings that had rained upon them outside, Rolland gasped: "The royals—are still up. The wind is low."

A hell of a lot they cared, the other two! Low or high, they were under it. Something, somewhere on the poop, was bumping against the deck, almost at regular intervals. Brisville listened.

"The bell is tolling for us," he said.

Rolland turned around, fiercely. "Get away!" he shouted at them. "Get out of here! *Quick!*"

The companionway was jerking and buckling as he drove them to it.

XXIV

THE SAIL LOCKER measured about fifty by sixteen and a half feet. That much space was necessary in order that the sails might be properly stretched out as they were cut and sewed. It occupied all the starboard section in front of the poop, and opened on the main deck. On the port side was the steward's cabin; at the stern, the saloon, with the cabin and the officers' cabins grouped around it. Thus the ship gathered together at the back her most precious lives, her provisions, and her chairs of state. The poop itself would henceforth be the last asylum to be demolished: an asylum only, since neither orders nor workings could issue from it any longer.

The men, standing upright in the long room, had been knocked down like ninepins when the cyclone struck the *Antonine:* a confusion of boots, arms, heads, bodies, such as no charging waves have ever brought together on a deck! And as they disentangled themselves and tried to get up they had at once realized, from her sweeping undulations, that the ship was nothing any more but a cork that the sea was tossing from side to side.

"It's all up!" they had said.

Rolland himself had not come down to the sail locker. He had stayed in the chart-house, a cube of iron rooted in the flooded poop and still emerging from it like the conning tower of a submarine. Hanging on to a ledge with both hands, he was trying to look out, his face sometimes crushed against the glass of a porthole, sometimes thrown back by the mad combined pitch-and-roll of the ship.

It was truly, in any case, seeing for seeing's sake! Nothing could have been more futile, since it was no longer possible to take any steps at all. Yet he was bringing an eagerness to it such as he had never put into his scrutiny of the weather when he was in a position to work ship. This tumult as of the end of the world; these maddened leaps of the *Antonine,* of which he would never have believed any vessel capable; these shattering crashes over his head, against his eyes—all this intoxicated him like the *pilou-pilou,* the savage dance of the Canaques from which they emerged with the wish to kill. The blood was dripping into his eyes from the cut in his forehead; wiping it off with the back of his hand, he smeared it all over his face.

He had first looked through the after portholes and had made out, under the torrents of water, something like a huge bush made of wood and steel, which the waves were lifting up as on a pitchfork: that had been the jigger topm'st, the gaff, and the boom, with their rigging.

Toward the bow, he was able to discover nothing, neither deckhouses nor fo'c'sle; all was covered by the sea. But in brief flashes of light between two water-spouts he caught a glimpse of the masts, and the davits shorn clean of their boats. They were all gone, the boats, except the long-boat, astern to starboard. The yards, without arms or lifts, were making rolling gestures that were like a semaphore manipulated by a madman. If only they didn't fall on the deck!

He noticed also, at the jigger, a triangular strip of canvas, the size of a handerchief, raveled out, as if systematically, at the end, like a bit of lint: that was all that was left of the tops'l! The rigging, for its part, was little by little coming to pieces. All those lines, fixed and taut, that had snapped their moorings were whipping furiously against those that were still holding. Twenty dark whipcords, one might say, eddying about the masts and desperately set upon slashing everything. He even saw—and this staggered him more than all the rest—the port sheet of the main lower tops'l, which was hanging at the end of its yard, coiling around one of the lifeboat davits, pulling it loose, and whirling it around above the deck: one of those ferocious games of inanimate objects, so adroit that one cannot keep from thinking that they have been planned.

Shouts called him below. In the sail locker they had just been hearing other crashes, and these came from inside. There was a banging and thumping in the big storeroom, the one below the lazaretto for daily rations, which they all knew, with its compartments for demijohns of rum, wine, and oil, and its bins of beans and split peas. None of them had set foot in the big storeroom since they left Port Talbot; but, no matter, they didn't have to go see it to know what it contained! Casks of wine and kegs of salt pork were stowed there on stands fixed at the height of a man's middle; to make sure of support, props of heavy planking had been fastened to the ceiling, over the rows of casks, before the ship left France. It was these which had just given way.

Taking several men with him, Rolland slid through the storeroom's trap-door. From the ladder, he caught a glimpse of two wine casks rolling up and down the long room: stopping, dashing forward, jolting to one side. They had already battered in the boxes of tinned food, and broken the lower shelves. Pausing on the last step, the mate called for a lantern, since is was almost impossible to see in there. The big storeroom was only lighted through the trap-door which opened into the everyday lazaretto, and there wasn't much light getting in there through the dripping portholes. When the lantern had been passed from hand to hand, Rolland jumped down, first. But behind him, the men hesitated. These Bretons and Normans knew what a wine cask was, even a 50-gallon keg of cider; they had let them down often enough into the wine-cellars, or rolled them into the still-room. But to see one of them dashing free like this, whirling about, plunging with the rolling of the ship—that was no go!

Rolland had already caught up a bag of rice, which he was holding tight against his body as he half-walked, half-slid toward one of the casks which the ship's roll was now pressing close to the steel bulkhead. At the precise moment when it was swerving off again, he threw the bag under it. Already four men were bearing down upon it, wedging it with small beams, holding it fast with bars and loops of rope under its staves. They were about to lash it down when Rolland yelled, "Look out!"

In a violent pitch of the ship to leeward, the other wine cask came rushing down on them at full speed, and straight ahead. They had only time to stagger out of its way when it came knocking against the edge of the cask they had shackled, as if to free it. Then, once more at the mercy of the ship's roll, it left it and went careering across the storeroom again at lightning speed. They thought it was going to crash against the wall and break open—for it is easily broken, a wine cask!—and they hoped for this and at the same time dreaded it, because of losing all that wine. But the ship keeled over on her other side before the cask struck, and it retraced its course.

"Caroff!"

Rolland signaled to him, with a rounded gesture which the seaman understood. Together, taking advantage of the cask's slowing down on the deck which was horizontal again for a moment, the two of them wheeled it around by a quarter-turn, then jumped back. It was the pitching that caught it now and shifted it back and forth on the ship's axis. But that freed the men from one menace while they were struggling with the other, finishing the work of getting the first cask tied up. Rolland and Caroff, who were keeping their eyes on the cask that had escaped, saw it first run down the slope toward the bow, then veer right around and go off toward the stern, where, without breaking, it landed full against the base of a great iron tank. This was a biscuit chest which had been transformed into an extra reservoir, because there was never enough fresh water on the ship. It was full now, and it weighed four tons.

Rolland caught hold of another bag of rice, and tried to repeat his stroke. This time he did not succeed so well: the space of a yard remained between the tank and the improvised wedge, and the wine cask was knocking about heavily there.

"Perrot."

The man who was summoned slid down the slope and reached Rolland's side. With his back against the water tank he tried, with the heel of his boot, to wedge the cask with the rice bag; it was already disturbingly flattened out, and Rolland was looking around for something to add to it.

It was just at this moment that the *Antonine* reared up almost vertically in the trough of a wave. The men were all thrown back, on their knees, on their stomachs, to the other end of the storeroom: all except Perrot, who was caught between the wedged wine cask and the water tank. He was the only one who did not cry out; for, flung stomach down upon the big cask by the monstrous blow from the stern, he had not seen the great block of iron, behind him, pulling out the timbers that held it in place, and pitching forward. . . .

When the ship, seesawing back with the same force, flung Rolland and his men back toward the water tank, a dreadful torso was protruding from under it. But behind the point where it appeared, there was hardly any elevation of the iron tank, so completely was the man crushed beneath it, his legs and thighs a pulp. They looked at him with more terror than pity, the gaze of wild animals in the presence of one of their number caught in the jaws of a trap. He was a quiet fellow on the port watch, this Perrot, who had never done anything to get himself talked about. The wine cask, meanwhile, under the impact of those one thousand gallons, had burst open like a red currant, and the men were splashing in wine and blood.

There was nothing they could do against that iron mass, which no crowbar could have lifted: nothing but listen to the wretched man screaming, out of that black hole that no longer resembled a mouth, "Kill me! Why don't you kill me?"

Already two of the men, unable to stand any more, had slipped out, up the ladder; and the rest were about to follow.

"Burrey, your sledge-hammers!" Rolland ordered, in a toneless voice. "We'll try to break it."

The mechanic stared at him, dumbfounded; break it, a thing like that! It would take a good hour! Rolland caught him by the shoulders as if he were the cabin boy, wheeled him around, and shoved him toward the ladder. A new brutal lurch of the ship flung the mate himself to the floor, and he dragged himself on his hands and knees until he was again close to that agonized face.

"My poor old boy, we're going to get you out," he said.

The tortured creature glared at him with hatred, and his head swayed furiously from left to right, his cheeks striking against the deck planking.

"No!" he cried. "Kill me! Kill me right away! If you don't, you have no more heart than a dog! Why don't you shoot me?" And he began to repeat, in a lower tone, like a litany, "Shoot me, shoot me . . ."

Meanwhile, the others were dancing. Except for Rolland, who was still on his knees and had a better purchase of the floor, they were all dancing, with short steps, arms held out: wheeling, changing places, doing all they could to keep their stance on this seesaw. Some-

286

times it was only by an abrupt swerve that they avoided stepping on the trapped man.

Papa Burrey came back, looking haggard, and holding three large sledge-hammers in his hands. Perrot caught sight of the heavy steel and began to implore him, "Smash in my head, Burrey! You have the thing to do it. Smash in my head!"

The mechanic, his jaws quivering, remained standing where he was, his great wheelwright's hammers held out at arm's length. Rolland took two from him and reached behind his back with the other, not looking around. It was Caroff who seized it, and who attacked the iron tank at the same time as he did. Burrey at last understood what they were doing, and set to work beside them.

They pounded away for minutes that seemed endless. The tank was dented in, but did not break. Papa Burrey, skillful as he was, missed a good mark in one stroke out of three. Finally, at the spot he was hammering on, he made a small glistening hole, which his fierce blows enlarged quickly. Now the water came pouring out into the storeroom, up to the lips of the wretched victim, who had ceased to speak. But they had to wait ten minutes before the tank was empty enough for them to lift it with their handspikes and get the dying man free.

They hoisted him by the arms up to the trap-door, while his head, unsupported, kept hitting against the rungs of the ladder, and they laid him down in the lazaretto, between two cases of beans. It was then that the captain appeared at the door.

"Carry him into my cabin," he said.

They did not carry him; they dragged him. Not one of them would have dared lift him by his crushed legs, that dangled all slack behind him, as if he had had sand, instead of human limbs, in his trousers and his boots.

When they had settled him in the captain's bunk, they saw Thirard calmly open a drawer and, wedged against a table and keeping astonishingly steady in spite of the ship's pitching, break the end of an ampoule and fill a glass syringe: movements so habitual, so practiced, that it would have taken more than a cyclone to make them go away. . . . He raised the injured man's loose-hanging arm, brought it up over his chest, and with a sure stroke drove in the needle: the first injection of morphine, meritorious alms, and priceless.

Toward the end of the afternoon they once more heard muffled and repeated blows, as if the ship had grounded. Through the streaming portholes they saw that this was the boom on the port bow, a spare topm'st which had pulled out its lashings and was going about on its own, like the wine casks. But it was on the main deck that it was performing its labors. It was rushing back and forth in mad haste, not so much as a battering-ram staving in something as a bludgeon knocking something down. One after the other, it was tearing away the bulwark timber-heads; one by one it was breaking the chain plates of the shrouds, those irons which make them fast to the body of the ship. The men saw them, those steel shrouds that they had so often climbed, popping off in the squall like kite tails. The jigger mast, which they were no longer holding up, was bent down.

The boom was active through its sheer mass, also, as it was alternately lifted up and struck down by the flux and reflux of the waves. Its enormous weight would fall back upon the cement paving of the fore-and-aft gangway, crush it to powder, and hollow out funnels through which the water rushed streaming down upon the nickel in the hold. Up to this point the derelict craft, still water-tight, had kept the flexibility of a living ship: she plunged down, wheeled about, but, with every blow, would rebound again to the surface. They felt her growing heavy. There was no proper play to her rolling now, because she was heeled over on her right side when the waves struck; and she was being struck the harder because she was now half-inert, because she had lost, so to speak, her instinct for floating. Before, the sea had swept over her. Now, she was settling into the sea.

And hundreds of things which up to this moment had held sturdily were finally, at the end of their resistance, letting go. Bolts and rivets, tormented for hours, gave in one after the other. And through the holes where they were torn out, the water was rushing in everywhere. At six in the evening, when the haze of gray water—which was after all the daylight—turned black, they were wading up to their knees in the sail locker.

That night belonged to the captain.

He alone among them all was privileged in having received his mortal sentence weeks before; and so he was the only one not to be taken unaware by the threat of death that was now pounding on the steel doors, entering gallon by gallon into the hold. What he had to defend himself against was merely the forbidden hope that in going down with his ship he might escape days and days of agony. His duty—undoubtedly the last—was to force himself to confidence, and to force it upon the others.

He was going to do it, but he would do it alone. By noon Rolland had, with violent words, imposed silence upon Berteux. Yet the second mate was only saying what they were all thinking, men and

288

officers, with Rolland at their head: they were lost; the ship was about to sink, like a box full of holes. Berteux stopped talking, but he was choking with resentment. It was not that he was a coward, or that what he wanted to cry out aloud was fear. On the contrary, what he was bursting with was the fact of having been right: from the beginning of the bad weather he had foretold the worst, and now he could not say, I told you so! He was drowning from within, in his own bile: a prophet forbidden to lay claim to the dire prophecy which he sees fulfilled! As for Rolland, he was being eaten away by the necessity for waiting, unable to do anything or to see anything, tensed for every plunge of the already water-logged hulk.

Captain Thirard, on the other hand, knew how to endure. But he must now teach it to the others. At eight in the evening he came into the sail locker, a lantern in his hand.

The water was washing about wildly, beating against the bulk-heads and the door, sapping at the men's legs. Yet it was, and would continue to be, necessary to remain standing. You'd keep on your feet, in the water up to your thighs, even when your legs were knocking against your belly! The water was running in through all the holes in the poop, and it was impossible to get out, because now that the door opened on the sea, you could not call it the deck any more!

The captain's lantern sent its beams back and forth on this buffeting spread of water. Thirard raised it level with his eyes to find the men, who were wedged into the corners of the sail locker. At the same time, he was throwing the light on his own head: that head of a walking corpse, the empty skin of his cheeks—but also his eyes. They were everyday captain's eyes, the eyes of those days when the log-book would say, *Fine weather, ordinary work of sailmaking and seamanship.* He fixed those eyes on each and every one of them, recognized them one by one; and his gaze brought them back to themselves, gave them a hold once more on something which was no longer their own fear. Those eyes existed for another man, and that seemed to them to increase their chances of existing. . . .

He did not speak at once; he was listening to them. There were voices in frenzy, screaming. "I've had enough of it, good God, I've had enough! It's time for the end. Let it break up once for all, and leave us alone!"

There were calmer voices, too, that asked: "Well, it is the end, isn't it, Cap'n?"

And there was Caroff: "I think we're stitched into the devil's skin, and he in ours!"

"The devil's skin . . ." "It's blowing the skin of the devil," the men used to say of unnatural weather, of hurricanes that smash everything, that fair tear out a man's eyes. For all of them, up to now, that had been nothing but words. But to listen for so many hours to hell screaming outside, around them; to feel themselves gripped by a giant hand that was tossing their ship about like a pebble; to be enveloped in the noisy flapping of enormous wings: in all this some of them were rediscovering the terror of a monstrous presence, welling up from the obscure depths of their childhood, and perhaps forgotten too long.

It was then that Captain Thirard spoke to them.

He spoke very simply of specific things, which immediately impressed them even before they understood them fully, because they were *hearing* them! That was more unimaginable than all the rest: that smothered voice, those murmured words—they were hearing them so clearly that this whispering seemed to them to balance all the howling and hooting, all the crashing, of the cyclone.

Leaning against the heavy door that opened on the deck, as if to close it better, seeming to be unaware of the water that was slapping his thighs and his stomach as it was theirs, he assured them that the weather would have calmed down, and for good, before noon the next day; he gave them his word for this. That might seem to them as far away as the end of next year, but they must hold out until then, because the ship itself would hold out. He was sure of that!

When he went out, Marius, out of his mind with fear and hatred, yelped, "A hell of a lot he cares—he knows he's pegging out anyway. A little sooner or a little later—"

Domino roared at him: "There was nothing forcing him to come. He only came to talk to us. And in the state he's in!"

As if he had heard the *moko* blaspheming, the captain had something special to say to them, on his second visit to the sail locker.

"You will all come out of it, I can give you my oath on that," he promised. "When one is getting close to death, one knows where it is going. I know it is not coming upon you."

Having said that, he went away again, swinging his lantern like a railroad station-master. He left them convinced, and taken out of themselves. Caroff nodded his head, with a little whistle of admiration. Marius was about to open up again, all the same, when Big Charles, who was keeping his eye on him, took two floundering steps and came up beside him, fist in the air.

"Are you going to keep your dirty sewer of a mouth shut?" he cried.

Bako, who up to this point had been talking to himself, without ever stopping and without disturbing anyone, alternating his own funeral orison with that of his hens and pigs, fell silent at the same time.

At midnight the captain came back again, this time to declare to them, on his honor, that they had avoided the center of the cyclone, a sort of trough of calm, after which they would have been assaulted by blasts still more terrible than those which were beating upon them now. If it had been anyone else, they would have loaded him with abuse over this "center," and his way of calmly telling them that there was something worse than what they were sampling and that they ought to be content with their lot! Yet not one piped up with a word. He had already told them so many extraordinary things that they swallowed this one, too.

He did not return until three in the morning, and then he had a bottle of cognac under his arm. He found them sick with fatigue, ready to give up, in this seesawing pool in which they had been splashing for so long. And they had been standing up for fifty hours, since they had tacked about off Thio! They were all drenched, even to their hair. Twenty times an hour they had been swept off their feet by some furious jolt of the derelict ship, and had slipped and plunged and picked themselves up again.

Thirard was looking at them with an informed and attentive sympathy. He knew those moments when, having suffered too much and too long, a man curses that something in himself which insists on living. They were beginning to look like him: the same desperate eyes of animals being beaten to death, the same white lips, the same grievous stupor. But they had taken only a few steps on that road: they would not be long in returning from it.

"Have a little drink," he said. "It will warm you up."

They flung themselves upon the bottle without a word, greedy as babies who see the nursing bottle approaching, their eyes popping from their heads, their arms stretched out, their feet tapping with impatience. The cognac passed rapidly from hand to hand. Yet they had not parted company with their sense of justice, and as each of them, with one swift glance, gauged what was the due amount for him to drink, they rediscovered that feeling for cubic content with which they used to watch Poullain and his measurements, when the rum rations were handed out. Old Burrey, who was the last to drink, left the correct level at the bottom of the bottle, and after wiping off the neck with the underside of his sleeve he held it out to the captain.

"And you, Cap'n?" he said.

With the smile of a good fellow, the captain refused. Burrey's face reddened. What had he been thinking of? With that throat! The mechanic drank down what was left.

With the dawn, and after a brief period of relative calm, the storm seemed to redouble its force.

At five o'clock, Rolland—who had gone back to the chart-house with the first gleam of light—saw the long-boat break away at the stern. Torn from her lashings, she had lifted herself straight up on the stern-post, as if to show herself in her entirety, with her seats and her lockers, for the last time; then she had fallen away, keel in the air, into the spray, and had disappeared under a wave.

The tasks performed by the mate during the night had been only those of a flood victim: to haul things up as far as possible and fasten them there. He had helped to raise Perrot, the man who had been crushed, when the water had threatened to reach him in his bunk; he had gone to get dripping mattresses out of the officers' cabins, and with the help of the cabin boy, had slid them under the gasping man. At this instant he had looked at Thirard and pointed to the head of the berth.

"What about yourself, Captain?" he had said.

The captain had made a gesture toward his throat.

"For the first time in four months, I don't feel it," he answered simply. "Why? How do you explain that?"

There were replies ready to hand: One nail drives out another. Danger is an anaesthetic—it demands all a man's nervous force, and leaves nothing over for pain. There were the stories of those soldiers in battle who were not aware that they were wounded. . . . But Rolland had said nothing of any of that, because he had seen in the captain's eyes the flame that burns in the eyes of those who are visited by miracle. He had contented himself with nodding his head; at all events, it was a piece of good fortune.

For the rest of the night the mate had worried, especially, about the security of their shelter. He had had the carpenter buttress up the door of the officers' corridor—which was beginning to work loose —with heavy timbers, and in all parts of the ship had everything made fast that was trying to break away. He had not gone at all to the sail locker. There was nothing he could do for the men except talk to them. And that was hardly possible, since he himself was convinced that the situation was hopeless. It was all to the good, certainly, if the captain succeeded in making them believe there was still a chance of their coming out of it; but he, Rolland, had no miracle to promise.

It was only at six o'clock, after completing a general tour— saloon, cabin, sleeping quarters, lazaretto—that he decided to make his way into the crew's den. And he felt as if he were going into a ditch where rutting walruses were fighting, all streaming with water and loud with shrieks. They cried out, as soon as they caught sight of him, that they were done for, that the sea was three-fourths over them already, but that the big boasters were going to have their eyes washed out, just like their pals. . . .

Without replying, any more than if he had been alone, he pushed two of them aside and began to try out the door's stanchions. After an instant of silence—because they were wondering what he had come for—they started laughing. Oh, he was worrying about the door, was he? Well, he needn't bother! They were going to push it wide open, that door of his! And there'd be an end of everything in five minutes: no more ship, no more good fellows, no more whorehouse of officers, all of them in Davy Jones's locker, all alike!

He heard one of them, it must have been Gallais, protesting: "Shut your mouths about that door! So long as we're still alive—"

But the most frenzied of them were advancing on him already, stumbling in the flood. They were crying out to him, with appalling insults, that he was on the side of the masters, those who had nothing better to do than drown them inch by inch, after shutting them up here like rats. Well, they'd decided: they were going to die in the open air. . . .

Rolland did not turn around until the instant when they all fell silent together: supported, this time, by Poullain, the captain was coming into the room.

"Well, here we are," he said, in his choked voice. "The barometer is rising again; we're beginning to get out of it."

It was, once more, so extravagant, so contrary to everything they were seeing, everything they knew or expected, that they just stood there stupefied, their arms dangling down into the water. It was to Rolland that the captain explained that around four o'clock the instrument had begun to oscillate, going up and down every quarter-hour. It was the time when they had been closest to the center of the cyclone. But when that point was passed, and for the last hour, the barometer had gone up steadily.

Big Charles cried out, "It was just an hour ago that Cario and Gallais and I made a vow to go barefooted with a candle to Notre Dame de l'Épine if we got out of this!"

The captain nodded his approval. Then he added, "It will be calm before noon. That is what I told you."

Domino called out, for them all: "It's true, Cap'n: everything has happened just as you said!"

XXV

THEY SPENT three hours listening to the squalls die down: three bad hours. The immediate danger that was gripping them close, but holding them upright, was being relaxed, like the unlacing of a tight corset, and they were slumping everywhere. By crawling up to the poop, they were at last able to get through to the poop-rail. There, the full extent of the disaster was revealed to them at one blow, like the blow of Kréven's fist when he used to knock them off their straw ticks.

"My God, but we're going down!"

Up to then, the settling of the ship had been something they only felt; now they were seeing it. The water was coming in through the scuppers, as into the open mouth of a drowned man. It was over these scuppers, which were working in reverse, like an overflowing drain, that they now stood hypnotized, without even one look at the debris of rigging and yards strewn out all over the ship and threatening to break the hull with every heavy roll.

"Rafts! We must make some rafts!"

Wild-eyed, they were running around on the poop, looking for everything that could float. Some were already hurrying to jump down on the deck, still swept by the last great breakers. There were spars there, drifting about, and planks that they needed right away.

"You're going to get yourselves washed overboard!" Rolland called to them.

But in him, too, everything was on the point of agreeing with their panic, or, at the very least, of trusting in their instinct, the instinct of the rats that abandon a doomed ship. A few timbers girdled by kegs—from one second to the next, perhaps, that would be all that was left to them. . . .

The mate gave the order to Poullain and Burrey, who had got a hold near him: "Bring the captain back."

He had seen him again, before they got out into the open air, all hunched up in his cabin, struck down again by the returning thunderbolt of his disease. And he had thought, It would have to be like that! He would only have felt like himself again during the worst hours of last night. He must be sorry to see it go, his cyclone!

When Thirard came on deck, carried by the third mate and the mechanic, with his long arms inert around their necks, and when Rolland observed his open mouth and his dimmed-out eyes that looked over the ravaged ship with a dying man's indifference, the mate reviled himself. This was both for having had him ruthlessly dragged up here to his side, and also for having seemed to expect help from him. . . . Then, amazingly, the captain was speaking, his head drooping, his voice low.

The things which he was murmuring, and which first Rolland, Poullain, and Burrey, and then Berteux and Ernault with them, listened to in a circle around him, leaning over almost against his mouth, were things he was drawing out of the very depths of himself, like the things he had said to the men the night before. It was not the miserable condition of the ship that was dictating them to him, but, once more, the mysterious intuition which last night had seemed set in the heart of the cyclone to estimate its force, and which now seemed to diffuse itself throughout the *Antonine,* to withstand her slow absorption by the sea.

"Monsieur Rolland, with your watch crew, do your utmost to free the pumps; we must find out if they can still function. Monsieur Berteux, with your starboard watch and the carpenter, stop up the holes where the rivets have been pulled out, the steps of the masts that have been stripped, all the openings where the water can get into the hold. Bos'n, and you, Burrey, see how to get rid of the pieces of masts and yards that are banging up and down the ship; they ought to be got out of the way at once. You, Monsieur Poullain, make observations and fix a position. My sextant is intact, and I have rewound the chronometers."

He raised his fleshless hand. The men were coming up, in their turn. It was toward them that he was now trying to stretch out his arm, and it was to them that he was looking now.

"Keep calm," he said to them. "Obey the officers. I am responsible for the rest."

"They're spitting! God Almighty, they're spitting!"

Caroff, gone quite mad at the sight of the thick yellow fluid being spewed out by the pumps, was leaping up and down in a sort of wild *pilou-pilou,* a galvanic motion he was not trying to control. By a miracle, both the shafts of the pumps and their fly-wheels had remained unbroken. Then Rolland had gone down to the pump-well, with the water up to his armpits, and plunged in to feel out the pistons, the rods: nothing was out of gear. The cranks had been found again in the storeroom. The huge fly-wheels, driven by arms whose success increased their strength tenfold, were turning like a house afire, and the pumps were spitting from all their pipes.

"If the hull is tight, we're all clear, boys!"

If the hull is tight . . . Rolland was scarcely hoping for it. The work of those accursed spars that had been thrashing up and down the ship for three days; joints that had sprung apart under the frightful joltings of the night before; steel plates opened by the *Antonine's* headlong divings into the trough of the waves: there were too many possible, probable, leaks.

The men's cries of joy on discovering that the pumps were intact had not been enough to deafen him to the echo of the other cry, the cry that had burst from the men when their eyes first fell upon their submerged ship. Once before, on the three-master *Dupleix*, under Monnard—hove to south of the Horn at night in a blizzard in which the helmsman could only just make out the main lower tops'l—Rolland had heard that cry of disaster. A mass of wreckage fleeing before the storm had skirted the ship on the port side and torn away the lower yards in a tumultuous crash: it was a collision that missed fatality by no more than a yard. "We're sinking!" a sailor had cried. But they had not sunk. Would it be the same this time?

"Here's how it is, Monsieur Rolland. The wheel-box is gone, the guides of the helm screw are broken, but the rudder seems to be moving normally in its gudgeons; perhaps we can steer with relieving tackles. The saloon sky-light is torn out; the spanker's gaff and boom have broken at the iron joint and gone off with the topmast; there's nothing to be seen any more."

Ernault the bos'n was making his report to the mate. For the new petty officer, the ship's peril had ended as a sort of polish to brighten up his mind. What he said was clear and concise, like an insurance affidavit after shipwreck.

"The two boats above the little deck-house are gone. The little deck-house itself has lost its door, and is in a bad state. The main to'gantm'st is broken at the cap. When it fell, it tore up the bulwarks. The yards and everything are dragging along the side. Burrey and four men are starting to saw into the rigging that is holding them against the hull. The forem'st has snapped at the level of the deck. It is especially through the space in the mast case that the ship has taken in so much water. Fortunately the forem'st sail and yards tore everything away and it went off; I don't see a trace of it anywhere."

Inexhaustible and merciless inventory! Ernault, fussy creature that he was, was leaving out nothing. He was mixing the wholesale with the retail, the major damages like the tearing out of the forem'st with the broken lanterns in the lamp room, and the state of the large deck-house, which was no more than an empty shell, with Burrey's rediscovery of his anvil chisels and caulking-irons in the little boiler's shed.

"In the cook's galley," the recital continued, "nothing is left but the stove. Papa Jules has already lighted it again, and he is making soup in the cabin boy's dishpans, which he recovered from under the poop."

At last Ernault scratched his head.

"There! That is about all. Now I'm going off to help the mechanic clear out the stuff that's banging all over the ship."

Well might he go off to help the mechanic, the old colonial settler! His report left the *Antonine* in the state in which he had found his plantation after the cyclone that had ruined it: a hulk. Some masts shattered, the others tottering; a gigantic pile of debris like a hedgehog sitting on the stern, while Burrey and his men, with bleeding hands, were trying to force it to relinquish its hold; no more rigging; bundles of cordage tangled into balls as big as a man; no more sails, except the royals; no more arms for the yards that were thrust out in all directions and tracing oblique and absurd lines in the air that was at last clear. . . . The port-watch crew was still pumping, but the big fly-wheels were slowing down. The men, exhausted, and dulled by their turning motion, were going to sleep over the crank-handles.

"Monsieur Rolland, you can have them eat whenever you like."

Old Jules, at least, was emerging as a conqueror from his ravaged galley. There was a hot soup, the first in three days; and there was Poullain, who before generously measuring out the wine ration had been able to find a slither of sunshine between two clouds, and came back to report that they had land some twenty miles to the north—Malicolo Island, one of the Hebrides. The news made an even better filling for their insides than the soup which they gulped down in a hurry; and they rushed through the sketchy meal and went back to work, with their mouths still full.

The teams were spelling each other at the pumps, and the *Antonine* was no longer settling into the water; they would even have sworn that its position was somewhat eased. Berteux's men, on their knees on the deck—which the sea was now slapping from the rear in amiable little spanks, as the incoming tide slaps the boats in a fishing port—were stopping up the scuppers, hole by hole. Burrey and several husky fellows were pegging away with hammer and chisel in the litter of the rigging.

The clearing-up was making headway very quickly. The sky, from minute to minute, was becoming once more a respectable sky of the tropics. But the trade wind had not yet settled in. The feeble breeze was varying from south to southwest. Rolland had had Ernault and his men bring up some sails from the locker, and he was able after a fashion to bend jibs and stays'ls and to put lower sails and cro'j'ck tops'ls in place. It did not look any too well, and Caroff commented: "What we've got is a laundry boat, rigged out with the customers' wash."

Yet when the breeze had lazily filled this dilapidated canvas, when they felt the *Antonine* once more behaving like a working ship—though so little!—beneath their feet, they interrupted whatever they were doing to look at one another, each one to see his comrade's happy face and to show him his own. There were some, too, who did not forget to give a wink to Papa Jules, whom the mate had just shaken hands with because the old fellow had gone on his own to bend the preventer braces on the yard arms, which were swinging in all directions at a rate to tear out their fittings.

When land appeared on the northern horizon, a high purplish cliff with clear contours, Rolland fell, rather than sat, down on a corner of the large hatch. The junior officers work in shifts; not the first mate! He was worn out.

The men were the first to perceive this. "Well, he was dropping his bag ashore, was he? * And what would you expect? He was always on hand. How long is it since anyone has seen him going off to sleep? And nobody ever gave him a thought, neither the fellows themselves nor the officers under him. A hell of a business!"

"Sir," said Poullain, "we have still a good four hours before we reach an anchorage. Berteux and I will finish running up what sail we can. Won't you go and get a little rest? You will be called in plenty of time."

Even when he stretched himself out on his bunk, the fatigue that had spread through his body like an infection kept sleep away for a long time. Everything was jostling against everything else in his aching head. Men and things were competing for first place in a tireless dance. The ship, the shore, Berteux's left eye that was always half-shut and drooping on his cheek, the bit of sail that the wind had knotted like the knot of a woman's hair, the Pillou woman's hair, Kréven . . . ah, Kréven. . . . Kréven in bed, in bed with his strumpet. . . . In bed last night, when they, in water up to their bellies, were waiting for the *Antonine* to sink. . . . "Go to bed, Kréven, and forget the man you were, the man you might have continued to be!"

Another man had gone to bed now, no doubt: the captain. How the crew had looked at him, last night in the sail locker! He, Rolland, on the contrary, had been cursed. Why? Because he had

* The sailors' way of saying that he was all in. Tr.

not known anything to say to them. Yet he had searched for words. But what was there to say? "If you have to die, try to die with your chin up. . . ." It was better to have said nothing.

Well, but where did it come from, that radiance in dying men? Father Monnard, Thirard? All right, there was the barometer going up again—the barometer.

They woke him for the burial at sea.

Perrot had died that morning, and, thanks to the morphine, he had died easily. It was a stroke of good luck for him, the men reflected, that the cap'n should have been sick. On what sailing-ship could a fellow in the crew be treated to the luxury of a hypodermic, so he could slip his moorings peacefully, just like a rich boy? And now Gallais and the carpenter had sewed him carefully, with good tight stitches, into his sail-cloth.

"Put his arm along his side, so he can rest easier. . . ."

"He was a good pal; we'll sew him up right. . . ."

They were worried about their work, nevertheless, because of those damn filthy bastards of sharks. The dirty swine had taken the *Antonine* in tow, sure she was going to sink, and they wouldn't miss their aim at the poor boy as he went down! But Papa Burrey swore that they should not have him. It was unbelievable, what he had been able to dig up in the way of ironwork to armor-plate the canvas sack in which the dead man had been sewed.

The entire crew had gathered around the body when Rolland came up on deck. The captain made his appearance at the same time, in a chair carried by two men. He made a motion of his head to summon the cabin boy.

"You still know your prayers, don't you, my lad? Say one of them, for our poor sailor."

He himself accompanied the youngster with his lips, like a priest saying his breviary. When the "Our Father" was finished, he made the sign of the cross. The men eased up the sack. When the poor devil slipped into the water, almost horizontally, there was no sound at all. But the sharks dived just the same. Papa Burrey, leaning far over, his teeth clenched, was growling, "Get hold of him if you can, you sons-of-bitches!"

And in fact the sharks came back to the surface after a minute of vain pursuit.

The *Antonine* was drawing close to the land now, a mountainous and dismal-looking island. There was the indentation of a white sand beach in the coast line, and behind it the forest rose steep and thick-grown. They took soundings: Twenty-five, thirty, fifty fathoms of line, and no bottom!

It was then that they caught sight of a dark silhouette, leaping up

299

and waving its arms on the sun-flecked beach. The man was surprisingly distinct on the dazzling expanse of sand, and it seemed evident to them all that his dancing motions were addressed to the ship. But then he vanished, absorbed by the fringe of the forest.

A few minutes later, a plume of smoke rose from the dark border of the woods. The *Antonine,* meanwhile, was dragging away along by the beach, at less than a mile from shore, and taking soundings every ten minutes.

Suddenly a chorus of yells arose from the edge of the close-grown forest, where European pines were strangely mingled with cocoanut palms and iron-wood; and out from among the trees burst hundreds of Canaques, running and gesticulating on the white coral sand. The smoke of other fires was rising from the brushwood, and still other Canaques were dashing down over the beach.

The *Antonine,* with her sluggish speed, was like a bathing guard's rowboat watching over a popular resort beach. The strand was swarming now with savage leaps and whirlings. A raucous uproar was rising from it, like an argument among crows. Rolland was observing the scene through the telescope.

"They have tomahawks," he announced.

At Thio and Kanala, they used to laugh at those Canaque tomahawks, because of their phallic shape.

"So long as they have no canoes . . ." Poullain murmured in the mate's ear. "It's still more than half cannibal around here."

Burrey, the mechanic, was already assembling his hatchets, hammers, and cramp-irons.

"Sir—"

The cabin-boy was handing Rolland a page torn from a small notebook. On it, written in a wavering hand, he read: *Stand out to sea, quick. Set course for Thio.*

Without a word, Rolland passed the sheet of paper to the third mate.

"Two hundred and fifty miles," Poullain remarked.

Then he made a gesture with his head toward the beach, where the whirling dance seemed to be getting wilder.

"After all, it may be a stroke of luck that we didn't find an anchorage," he said. "Just so the breeze doesn't die down!"

Rolland was already calling the men to work ship. The wind had settled into the southeast, and soon the *Antonine,* with her head to the southwest, was making progress. Yet it was not until sunset that the Canaques, as they grew smaller in the distance, lost all human form. Nothing was left of them, then, but the movement of dots, wheeling about madly in the twilight, like a dance of gnats.

"The dance in front of the refreshment bar," Poullain summed up.

Berteux, who was passing by and heard this, flung out in his dry voice, "What do you know about it? Perhaps, on the contrary, they were well-disposed. These islands are not inhabited only by cannibals and wreckers. There are even some Europeans."

"Nice well-disposed mugs they had!" Poullain retorted.

The men who had heard him began to laugh. They were forgetting that they still had more than two hundred miles to go, in a disabled and dismembered ship.

They had time to learn it!

They sailed for eight days: eight days of agonizing effort to keep what was left of the masts standing upright, brace the yards whose forks had been carried away and whose saddles had been half torn out; eight days of watching the *Antonine* drag along under its rags of sails, afraid that the wind would grow stronger, afraid also that it would drop to a dead calm; eight days of incessant pumping, for the wretched craft was still leaking, God alone knew where!

When Rolland went to give the captain the noon position on the third day, he had found him senseless on his bunk, the sheets soaked with blood: a hemorrhage, what the doctor in Thio was dreading. He had only recovered consciousness two hours later, and that in such a state of weakness that Rolland and Poullain had taken turns watching over him until the next morning, afraid that every moment might bring the end.

The news had gone the rounds of the ship, and the men were crushed by it.

"I'd give a month of my pay to get him to the hospital, where he could go out quietly," one said.

And another: "It's what he made himself do in the cyclone that used up his last strength."

They were cursing the slow pace of the impotent boat, the too-fine weather, the gentle breeze. They were ready to wish for a strong wind, even a gale, if that would give a shove to the backsides of this good-for-nothing snail of a tub!

On the eighth day, they saw a column of smoke across the stern and soon caught sight of the funnel of a steamship that was catching up with them. They struck the code signal at the head of the forward mainm'st: WE NEED ASSISTANCE. The *Saint Paul*, of the Ballande Company, bound for Nouméa, took the *Antonine* in tow.

Twenty-four hours later, they were moored at the dock.

XXVI

THE *Antonine* had to stay three months at Nouméa. The port was without a dry dock, and that slowed down the work, it had been immediately ascertained, moreover, that the largest repairs would have to be completed at Sydney, especially the remasting. Those three months were hard, as hard as the time spent in a loading port. From morning till night the crew was riveted to its task, with a short siesta at the hottest time of the day. On Sunday, the boys would stroll about in the town, between the zinc-roofed wooden houses of the Place des Cocotiers or the avenue de l'Alma, with a hundred sous in their pockets. They would pass the infantrymen of the Colonial Army, and the naval gunners dragging their heavy boots through the streets. They would wander in groups about the bandstand during the concert; and in due time they would go back to the ship.

For they were keeping themselves as inconspicuous as possible. Nouméa was swarming with policemen and blue-capped guards. The island of Nou and its penitentiary lay at the entrance to the harbor, and the *Antonine's* men had it under their eyes as they worked. The impossibility of ever forgetting the convict prison, the constant sight of the convict boats going back and forth alongside of the ship—all this ended by imbuing them with a vague disquiet which kept them from sprees that went too far, and from brawls. Their vessel was too close to the prison for them not to reflect on how easily one could step across from one to the other; no one could help seeing that!

For Rolland, too, the days rolled by as a sort of dismal calm. A cable from the shipping firm had officially entrusted the ship to him, for the repairs and then for the return voyage. It was less this expected responsibility that disturbed him than the feeling of loneliness which he had not been able to get rid of since Captain Thirard left the boat. He was genuinely astonished to realize the place which this almost-dying man had filled aboardship. At a time when he had known only a skipper of diminished physical power and ability, he had been more and more aware of an accretion of strength, of looking on at an actual rising of the tray of the scales under the weight that the other man carried: would Thirard have been the remarkable man of the cyclone, if his body had not been consumed? It seemed that the very wearing-away of his physical envelope had permitted him to escape from himself so that he might enter into the deepest being of the men. . . .

The captain had left the ship, in a carriage sent by the hospital, on the afternoon of the day they reached Nouméa. The master of the vessel had quitted it on a stretcher carried by the carpenter and the mechanic, who jolted it because they did not keep good step. The men of the crew had bared their heads, as at the passing of a funeral. The captain had opened his eyes only as he went down the gangplank, and had made a faint gesture with his left hand, in token of farewell.

Rolland had seen him only once at the hospital. His throat had been opened up—a tracheotomy—so that at last he was able to breathe. Rolland had been hypnotized by the silver tube which projected from his neck, and through which the air now passed in and out. But the sick man was at the last extremity of exhaustion: he could give his visitor no more than a look.

He died four days later. At the hospital, the Sister had given Rolland an envelope: "To be delivered by your own hands to Madame Thirard, 18 rue de l'Arbalète, Fécamp." On the way back from the cemetery Rolland, who had led the procession of mourners, had been joined by Berlot.

"Well, he is at peace, poor old fellow," Berlot said. "It is in cases like this that one can speak of deliverance."

In less than a month, the skipper of the *Tamanou* had himself grown strangely old. His plump *bon vivant's* flesh was yellowed over as with a sort of veneer. His face was turning the color of wine dregs, with a network of small purple veins where one felt that the thickened blood was stagnating. Rolland told him in a few words what had happened between the *Antonine's* departure from Kanala and the captain's death. It was a recital as dry as a log-book. Then he cast a glance at his companion.

"And how are things going with you?"

A little curiosity was awakening in him, as to how Berlot and Kréven were working out their pretty little schemes! Yet all that seemed so far away. . . .

"They're going all right," Berlot said. "I've got the hang of it now: I'm never sober any more. So everything's all right." He was trying to chuckle. "You might have known," he went on in explanation, "that as soon as she'd got the fellow she wanted, she'd kick me out. That was bound to happen."

"Then he isn't on the ship any more?" Rolland asked.

"Of course he is—more than ever! I told you, I'm always drunk.

He's the one that runs the wretched tub. He runs her very well, and everything is in order. I draw the money, without making it. . . . And then, when he is on the ship, he is not with her. She wanted to come too, but he sent her back. 'No women on a ship,' he said. Well, on the trips, when I'm drunk, I give him hell. He listens to me, and when I'm through he takes me back to my cabin. I shut myself up there and start drinking again. What better would you ask for?"

Rolland thought of that other cabin, where the man they had just buried used to shut himself up, he too. . . .

Then Berlot added, in a lower tone that mingled hatred with fear, "He was at the burial, you know. Didn't you see him? It would surprise me if he didn't come to talk with you."

Before leaving Rolland, he made an effort to change the conversation:

"I've seen your ship. You certainly were hard hit!" he said.

Whereupon, he struck him on the shoulder, in a series of hard little raps that continued for several moments, while a wave of anger made his heavy eyes heavier still. "Ah, well, in spite of that, the one who got licked, in the devil's skin, and who will break under it— it isn't you. . . ."

Ten minutes later, Kréven came up to Rolland on the dock, a hundred steps from the *Antonine*.

"I knew that he was to be buried today, so I came," he said.

Not a muscle moved in Rolland's face. He was thinking, He has learned to talk so as to say nothing—he is developing, on land.

The *Antonine* was still hidden behind the bridge of a steamship. When the ship's former bos'n caught sight of her, he could not restrain a start.

"She's had a narrow escape, eh?" Rolland said. Then, turning toward him, and with a dreadful cordiality, he added, "You see, you left at a good moment. Could you possibly have smelled the wind?"

Kréven, his head lowered, let the insult sink in. Then, after a moment, he said, "I only stopped you, sir, to beg you to tell Madame Thirard that I shall take care of the captain's grave as long as I am here."

Rolland's shake of the head registered refusal. "I have no reason to transmit any pledge whatever on your part. Write to her," he said.

He turned and left him.

I got the best of him, he was telling himself. He was less sure of that during the hours that followed, thinking it over again as he walked the deck. A strange voyage, this, in which one encountered characters like Thirard and Kréven, and was served, with the liqueurs, to a Barquet as assistant manager of a navigation company! Each of them, in his own fashion, brought some queer questions to one's mind. . . . It was a voyage from which a man would return less sure of himself than when he set out.

He returned from it in ninety-eight days.

"Almost a record!" declared Monsieur Blévin, the chief of the shipping firm at Le Havre, who had insisted on receiving him at home, in his personal office.

He had made Rolland sit down in a deep armchair. Other men used to perch on the edge, so as to keep sitting up straight, but Rolland had settled himself in the depths of the chair, without any presumptuousness but with a naturalness that was not displeasing. Monsieur Blévin leaned forward.

"I am authorized to tell you," he announced, punctuating his phrases with brief movements of his head, "that following this voyage, accomplished very quickly and with excellent conditions, we have decided to entrust you with a ship's command."

"I had already been led to hope for that, before my last sailing," Rolland said.

Monsieur Blévin acknowledged the stroke with a swift smile.

"This time the order will not be countermanded," he promised. Then he clasped his hands on his desk, and continued: "I was Monnard's closest comrade at the Hydrographic Institute, and he used often to speak to me about you. That permits me to go into things very frankly, in my turn. You have often caused us concern, Rolland, and myself first of all. Your former captains have always had high praise for your ability both in working the ship and in managing the men. On the other hand, they used to complain of your difficult and too independent disposition. That is why, in spite of your recognized worth, you have had to wait so long for a command."

Rolland was listening without so much as the flicker of an eyelash. This was the ringing of Papa Bouteloup's bell—and Arlozzi's. But no more in the Merchant Marine than in the Navy are captains' observations argued about before the official who communicates them. He knew that. The only interesting thing would be the conclusion, the name of the vessel that was to be given him. This name would indicate his market value quite surely, and better than half an hour of discourse. He waited for it, before making any response.

Monsieur Blévin seemed in no hurry to enlighten him. He was leaning back in his own armchair now, and his eyes were fixed on Rolland's as he went on:

"To be quite frank with you, we considered that Captain Thirard, both as chief and as man, was entirely cut out to keep you under his orders. We were not able to guess at that time—"

"That he would no longer have the strength to break me in?" Rolland interrupted. "You are mistaken. He did break me in. He was ten times stronger than the others, with his little breath of life."

Monsieur Blévin nodded in assent, but he did not ask the details of the breaking-in; apparently he was already informed about that. He spoke a few words of eulogy and regret for the dead man, and then came to the conclusion: "Well, then: we are completing the construction, at Nantes, of the *Andromède*, a square-rigged three-master of thirty-four hundred tons; she is being reserved for you. You are satisfied?"

"Yes, Monsieur Blévin."

It was something to be satisfied with! A new ship, and of that tonnage, as his first command, instead of the old tubs on which new captains were most often sent out to get their hand in!

"The only thing is, she will not be ready for two months," Monsieur Blévin added. "It is a further proof of our esteem, that we should keep you immobilized all this time, to wait for it. In parentheses, you can bless your cyclone and the delay it caused you. Without that, you would not have had the *Andromède*. We would have given you the best we had, three months ago, but after all it would not have been an equivalent."

They talked for a few minutes more, then Monsieur Blévin rose and held out his hand: "Goodbye then, Captain."

Rolland felt a shock, all the more since the other man had spoken the word quite simply, without stressing it.

Two hours later, he set out for Fécamp, to call upon Madame Thirard. Since he first stepped upon the dock, the thought of this interview had been weighing on him more heavily than all the tons of water in the hold of the *Antonine*. He arrived at nightfall, slept in a hotel near the station, and presented himself at the home of the captain's widow at ten the next morning.

She lived in a ground-floor apartment near the Bénédictine distillery. An elderly servant took him into the dining room, where the first thing he noticed was an enlarged photograph of the dead man. It must have dated from several years back, and it surprised, indeed almost disappointed, him: the man in the picture, strongly sensual, with his full cheeks and square chin, was too far removed from the one he had known.

His wife, on the contrary, was as he had imagined her: a woman of around fifty, rather heavy, with a face fixed in its sorrow, an overconscientious air; everything she did she must do thoroughly, even pining away. The emotion which overwhelmed her when he was introduced had the effect of giving him some assurance. He was always like that: when anyone near him let go, he himself became so much the stronger.

He started out to tell her about the voyage, to deliver to her all his recollections of the dead man, without depriving her of any detail; he at once saw that course was full of pitfalls. To extol the heroism of his skipper, as he must, in giving her the picture of Thirard's visits to the poop, he would have to let her know the price that was paid for every one. On the other hand, when he would do his best to pass over in silence the agonies of the cabin, the captain would become almost an ordinary captain, in the excellent performance of his duty. He changed his mind and cut the story short, without being able to avoid the question which he had felt hanging over him since the beginning of the conversation:

"He suffered a great deal, didn't he?"

Rolland could only bow his head.

"I know that you were very devoted to him," she said. "I thank you for that. But tell me—you saw him when the ship sailed— could one have guessed anything like this? He had always had a hoarseness; he used to smoke too much. And he had got very thin, the last weeks. But he would say, 'It is age; when you get to be around fifty your constitution changes.' No matter, I ought to have suspected, when I saw him so tired. But then he would say to me, 'That will be gone, after a week at sea.' He wanted to start out on this voyage: the money it would bring, the increase in the pension. . . . As if that counted, now!"

"Perhaps it was better that he did make the voyage," Rolland said. "He was on his feet till the last day, and in keeping busy with the ship and the crew he would forget his suffering. All they could have done ashore was to prolong it. The doctor at Nouméa assured me that even here an operation would not have saved him. At the rate the disease carried him off, it was already too late when he sailed. And from the point of view of morale, things would have been worse for him in a hospital than on the ship."

"Yes, but I should have been there!"

That was obvious! But, as always, Rolland only thought of the woman after the event. Somewhat abashed, he reached into his pocket and took a thick envelope out of his wallet.

"The captain had the Sister deliver this to me, for you. It would have come faster by steamship, but he did not want that. He said to the Sister, 'I want her to have it at the time when the boat gets in.'"

307

She turned the envelope over and over in her hands, and her eyes were blurred with tears. Rolland realized the hurry she was in to be alone, to open it, and he got up.

"I must tell you further, Madame, that his former bos'n, Kréven, has settled on the island. He charged me to give you his promise that he will look after the grave himself."

She choked back her sobs.

"If Kréven takes the responsibility, I can rest easy," she murmured.

When he was on the street again, he reflected, "Yet I gave that swine to understand that I would not say anything about his taking care of the grave. . . . All the same, it is better that I did."

The dining room he had just left seemed somehow to be almost one with the captain's cabin. Here, as there, a human being was haunted by thought and yearning for another: he who for her sake had gone away to die at the other end of the world, all alone; she who was shut in with her grief as he had been shut in with his torture. Rolland had been the only person who could bring them together just like this. And it was easy. They were one again. This was a case, if there ever was one, when one could speak of two halves!

"At any rate," he said aloud, as he stopped on the sidewalk to get out his tobacco pouch, "there's a good job done!"

He hastened his steps as soon as he had lighted his cigarette. Now, to weigh anchor and get out of here, full speed! Fécamp, that was Barquet's town. All sorts of things happen, and at the next corner he might well collide with the Assistant Manager, coming straight across his bow! That would not be a pretty maneuver, from his point of view! In his new situation, it was something to be avoided: they all hung together, the companies. . . .

So he went prudently back to the station to get a ticket for Lamballe, the railroad stop nearest Erquy. The only relatives he had left there were two old aunts, one of whom made shell-work flowers for the summer visitors, while the other kept house for the priest. There was no question of a two-months' mooring under their Breton caps. It would be "How-do-you-do? How-do-you-do?" and a visit to the cemetery; after that, straight to Nantes, to see his ship being finished.

While he was getting into his train, Big Charles, Gallais, and Cario, a hundred leagues away, were also liquidating the situation, in carrying out their vow to Our Lady of the Thorn: barefoot, and each with his candle. As a storm had loosened all the sharp pebbles on the road, they cut themselves with every step; and never had they sworn so many oaths as on this pilgrimage.

Book Three   **THE CAPTAIN**

BOOK THREE

XXVII

"WHEN DO YOU LEAVE, Victor?"

"Not for four days."

"And you, Edouard?"

"I'm asking you! I've been waiting a week already for a replacement part for my donkey engine. Makes me think of Willaroo, where we found the wheat an inch and a half high and had to wait till it grew and was harvested so we could take it aboard!"

"How about you, Rolland? When do you sail?"

"Tomorrow morning."

"That's bad! We'd have got together for something or other . . ."

Rolland raised his hand. "Don't let that stop you," he said.

Captain Cordier wagged his head back and forth from one shoulder to the other. He was a big-framed man, with hair that stood straight up and fleshy lips always ready to part in roars of barbaric laughter.

"Sure, that won't stop us," he said. "But you see, Rolland, that it works out all wrong. Four and three—they're two different things. Four at the table, it's squared off; three, that leaves an end dragging behind. This way, we'll have to put it off till the next time: in Frisco, or Hamburg, or Antwerp. Better in Antwerp, eh, Edouard? At Anna's place, or little Rose's. How many times have you made Rose turn her Blessed Virgin to the wall?"

"Pay no attention to him," said Bouriès, a spare-built, clean-shaven, alert young man. "It's jealousy. He's bursting with it."

"Yes, all she did was darn your socks," Cordier remembered. "You've told us plenty about that. But do you want some advice? Those socks—don't show them to your wife. On my last voyage, I took mine home; but how would I have time for such finished work, such a beautiful checkerboard pattern? When my wife found them, she looked at them with a dirty eye and said to me, 'You didn't do this!' So now, boys, some white stitches, some black stitches, and all in a bunch—that way, there's no trouble."

311

The four captains were seated at a table in a bar, with the outside shutters closed against the Australian summer. They had just stumbled into each other again at Hobart, meeting once more at one end of the world—for the moment it did not matter which. Their table was an island where as yet neither anything nor anybody was coming ashore.

"Who brought you in?" Cordier asked Bouriès.

"Harris, as usual; and, as usual, in French!"

Captain Bouriès made his smooth-shaven face still more rigid, to take off the appearance of the Hobart pilot, while he reproduced the Australian's mispronunciations in a gutteral voice. Cordier slapped his thigh.

"That's him to the life!"

"And if you repeat the order after him, he pulls a long face," added Victor Drobin, the captain of the *Nanterre*. He was a thick-set fellow, half-bald, with a sleepy air and a countryman's voice that stuck his words together, thickening them and slowing them down, as clay sticks to the soles of one's boots."

They spoke of the voyage. A few sentences were enough for the essentials: notes on the routes they had followed, the state of the weather. They all reported heavy winds since they had passed the Cape, but agreed that they needed these to cut ahead on the course.

"I lost a man all the same," Drobin said.

It was a sailor who had fallen from the yards while furling the main upper tops'l.

"We sent him out a buoy, but he wasn't able to reeve it," Drobin added.

As for Rolland, he had just handed an "undesirable" over to the consul. In a few dry sentences he related how he had caught the man distributing copies of the *Libertaire* among the crew, and had succeeded in putting him on the spot for threats and insubordination.

"We shall have to realize in the end," he concluded, resting his fists on the table and leaning toward his noncommittal colleagues, "that the stake is between those fellows and us, the captains. When you get back from a voyage, the administrator at the Marine Office will keep you cooling your heels for hours. But you'll see fellows in blue boiler suits, yellow shoes, and gangsters' neckties go into his office as if it was their own. When they leave, they'll walk right up to one of your men. 'Your captain's a swine, isn't he?' 'Yes.' 'Come on, then, tell us about it.' When I see that, it's about all I can stand, and when I get hold of one of those fellows, he gets what's coming to him."

Bouriès contributed a recollection: "The same thing, or just about, happened to Joly, when he was captain of the *Clotilde*. What he did was arrange to have all his undesirables shanghaied at Portland."

Rolland got up. "You will excuse me. I still have a lot of things to attend to between now and tomorrow."

The others held out their hands, without rising.

"Well, then, till we meet again," said Cordier. "And if you run across old Tancrey, my equipment chief in the shipping office, tell him that I spit in his eye, and that I am not going to bring him back one damn keg of salt pork as surplus."

When Rolland had gone, Cordier sprawled on his elbows over the table.

"I hadn't seen him for seven years," he said. "The last time was at Tacoma. He was still commanding the *Andromède*."

"I ran into him at Geelong eighteen months ago," said Drobin. "He was captain of the *Marie-Laurentine*."

"Yes, it is only this year that he has had the *Argonaute*."

"She's a beautiful ship," Bouriès commented. "I saw her yesterday. The Bordes firm hasn't anything better."

"That may be," Drobin admitted, "but in my opinion she's above all a fast sailor in moderate weather."

"With that chap," said Cordier, " 'moderate weather' is just about any weather that the good God sends."

"Yes," Bouriès agreed, "he is a speeder."

The conversation circled and hovered above the absent man like this before swooping down on him. It was Bouriès who brought it to a point.

"We went out together from Dunkerque," he said. "That was— let me see, this is 1912, so that was three years ago. He had just taken the *Saint Sever*, when Brignon had broken his foot, you remember?"

"And how!" Cordier affirmed. "The way he tore along, that lad Rolland, as if he had Papa Minart at his stern!"

Bouriès chuckled over this recollection, but as Drobin was looking at him with big eyes wide-open in curiosity, Cordier took up the story:

"Haven't you heard about that? It was Blévin, his shipping agent, who told it to me. Blévin had taken it into his head to get him married, when he came back from Nouméa with the *Marie-Laurentine* pretty badly damaged. At least two months of repairs ahead, easily long enough to produce twins! Fine! Blévin headed him toward the daughter of one of his old pals, Papa Minart, who had retired after thirty years of command in the coastwise trade and was living at Val André. Everything started off splendidly. The old man

313

swore by no one but our Rolland, the girl was crazy about him, they were setting the date for the wedding. Just fifteen days before, here he is coming into the company's offices. 'I've learned of Brignon's accident,' he says. 'If it's all right with you, I will go in his place.' The shipping men, who, themselves, had heard something about a marriage in the offing, said to him, 'But do you know that the *Saint Sever* is all ready to sail?' 'Exactly so,' he said. So, pleased as punch, they hand over the command to him, and off he goes! Blévin has never forgiven him."

"At Geelong, I really thought he was going to take the plunge," Drobin put in. "He had become acquainted with a pretty girl, a girl of good family she was, too, and she spoke French. Her parents were big land-owners in New South Wales, and she was visiting an uncle in Geelong for her holidays. He used to spend all his evenings with her. And when he sailed she came to the dock to kiss him goodbye. I said to myself, 'This is it, this time!' And when I saw him again yesterday I asked him, 'What about the little girl in Geelong? This will be the time to telegraph her.' 'The log has been reeled in since then,' he answered."

"That's a lad that will never marry," Cordier declared. "What would he do with a wife? She'd have to hit him over the head to keep him from saying, at the end of two weeks, 'I'm sailing again. See you next year.' He doesn't like to be tied up to the dock, that gentleman!"

"It seems he's made a pretty good anchorage here," remarked Bouriès. "I heard it from Hervy. They've been going around seeing the shows together, and they met all the dancers in *Spring*. It's Rita, a Spanish girl, who's ended by hooking in. Hervy showed her to me: a pair of bows, old chap!"

"He won't stay here an extra quarter of an hour, not for her or any other girl," Cordier averred. "He has speed like a disease inside him. Eighty-six days from Glasgow here, how's that for a shaking-up?"

"Do you remember the time he and the *Margaret* and the three-master *Auvergne* all left Frisco together?" Bouriès went on. "Some go-ers, they were! And big stakes! He beat the two others, one by eleven and one by nine days, and he brought twenty-five thousand pounds to a broker who had bet on him. The fellow sent him a gold watch."

"I am not paid to run races," remarked Drobin. "If you lose sails, masts, and even men to make a high speed record, a lot of good it does you afterwards!"

This was the catechism of the old sea captains, who sailed their ships as if they were trolley-cars, putting on the brakes going down hill and not pushing too hard on the upgrade. Drobin, the only one of the three who was a mediocre man, and who, because of that, paid more attention to small things, observed that Rolland's rigging suffered more damage than any of the other captains' because of his stubborn refusal to take in sail. The other two granted him that, but it was of no importance; what they were after was the exact measure of the man. Three hard knocks he had had gave it to them.

The first was in the reaches around Cape Horn, in the middle of the southern winter. The *Andromède,* encrusted with ice, was hove to, but it was necessary to change the tack, because the winds were shifting. A forem'st topman, who was inspecting his mast, slipped and crashed to the deck. Hardly had he been taken away when a sound of snapping filled the stern of the ship: the spanker boom had broken, a piece of wood twenty-five yards long and thick as a man's body, extended horizontally above the poop.

It had broken, but it did not fall. The rear end remained hanging to the gaff, and the stump, pivoting with the rolling of the ship, was threshing about, pounding at everything within reach. It had broken the spokes of the wheel, from which the helmsman had fled, and the free rudder, in its turn, was now tossing furiously; the ship was about to veer broadside to windward. Rolland had crouched down in the end of the stern, where the thrust of the backward blow would be swiftest and most deadly. He knotted a rope lasso. The monstrous cudgel was coming on rapidly. The captain felt the draft it made, close to his face. But at the precise fraction of a second when the crushing force was grazing him, he leaped to one side and flung out his running noose. Now the boom could bang down on the starboard side, it had the line tight around its end, it was bridled. . . . Men caught the mooring cable with chilled and bleeding fingers, fastened it, and took control of the wheel again.

"If he had had his face smashed in, what good would that have done?" Drobin demanded.

"Since nobody was doing anything—" retorted Cordier.

"In such cases, there is always someone who decides to act," Captain Drobin affirmed. "You only have to give them time for it, since it is that or capsize."

If this was not glamorous, it was accurate. Drobin, without any doubt, would have waited for someone else to meet the situation, because he himself was clumsy and slow. This left the prestige of the quick-moving athlete, however, intact.

The next incident they recalled was that of a fire which broke out aboard the *Saint Sever,* in the open sea off the coast of Chile. The vessel was crammed full of saltpeter, taken on at Iquique, and a fire in a cargo of nitrate is hopeless. After an explosion in the hold had,

315

so to speak, opened up the vessel and had blown off the hatches, Rolland had had the life-boats launched, and the crew had abandoned ship. Even then, the captain had refused to leave.

None of his three colleagues was making any mistake about the reasons for his obstinacy. This was in no way a romantic determination to go down with his ship. A captain they knew had recently fastened himself to the rail of his sinking vessel, rather than abandon it. When they recounted this piece of extravagance, they explained it in two words: "He drank." If Rolland chose to stay on the *Saint Sever,* it was because he knew there was one chance in a thousand of saving the ship, and he would not consent to let that chance go. And the impossible happened: the draft of the explosion put out the fire as one blows out a candle, and the boats that were waiting a little distance away for the captain to jump, or the vessel to break up, were recalled by megaphone. A steamship which happened along had taken the *Saint Sever* in tow to Valparaiso.

"That proves he's lucky," Drobin said.

"And that he keeps his nerve," Bouriès added.

"There is one thing that stumps me," remarked Cordier. "It is that, ruling his fellows the way he rules them, he should never, on the whole, have had any bad run-ins with his crews."

"Perhaps he doesn't boast of them," suggested Drobin, in his dragging voice. "And then, doesn't he hand out plenty of wine and grog? It's not hard, with that, to keep them from grousing."

Cordier and Bouriès exchanged an amused glance. Drobin was famed for a rapacity which earned him the compliments of his shipping firm and the execrations of his men. He cut down on everything: food, wine, rum, soap. It was known that his sailors had wound up by demanding that the keg of salt pork be kept in their own quarters: "So many kilograms, so many days: we'll portion it out ourselves, and the officers' staff won't slice off the lean and leave the fat to us." On Friday he gave each man one sardine. The officer came aft to say that they were putting up a very rough protest, but Drobin could not drag the words out of his throat, to increase the ration. He ended, however, by holding up two fingers: two sardines. Then, at once, he burst out, "And I hope they choke on it!"

Cordier and Bouriès knew all this. It was to be seen on their lips as they smiled. But as they had no desire to end the conversation by inducing an explosion on Drobin's part, they said nothing more about the steward's cabin; and Cordier, who prided himself on going through life with a jug of oil at hand to pour on troubled waters, concluded, as he rose from the table, "Well, everyone does the best he can." And he added: "None of this can alter the fact that as

316

a captain I take off my hat to him. But for me he will never be anything more than a colleague: not a pal."

The other two agreed.

Rolland walked through the wide streets lined with white houses and gardens, and so reached his ship. He had lingered in the ship-chandler's shop, and he did not regret it. Once the purchases had been attended to—and quickly—the shop-keeper, an old Tasmanian with his face wreathed by a white beard, had grown talkative over a glass of whisky, to call up old times in Hobart Town, the old times of the whaling ships and the convicts. In the French captain's mind, thus, images of a different color came to keep company with the flower-decked bungalows, the display counters heaped with fresh vegetables and fruit, the shop-windows with their brooches and belt-buckles bearing the glittering inscription, *Gardens of the South*. Pictures rose before him of shaggy-haired natives, with skin of a bluish tint, pursued by the colonists' dogs and shot in the trees like monkeys; of crowds beside themselves with hunger, besieging the homes of the first captains-general; of women fairly torn to pieces, on the arrival of the "women's boats," by the convicts who were quarreling over them. Rolland knew these savage beginnings of peaceful colonies. He had already listened to the same chant, but in a quarter where its extraordinary overtones were even more bizarre: Pitcairn.

He had made a call of several hours there, during a voyage from San Francisco to Falmouth. And he was recalling it now, as he walked down to the port, as if to shake off the languid mildness of the Tasmanian spring.

Oh, he had found them settled down, and how, the descendants of the mutineers of the *Bounty!* They had loaded him with presents: he had taken back a full boatload of oranges, bananas, and potatoes. When he left, the school children—little girls with tight braids, little boys with long faces—had sung the Centenary Hymn in his honor. He had a hard time hiding a smile as he raised his cap in a final salute: to hear vespers chanted by this spawn of murderers and savages, on this very beach where mutineers and natives had cut each other's throats!

Today, he no longer found this amusing. He knew that it always happens like that, that it had happened like that for himself. He, too, was a fellow who had settled down, the Pitcairn or Hobart species. He was thirty-four years old, and he knew it! What was in his mind now was not—and it never had been—regret for the days of the desert islands or the orgies of the Hobart whalers, nor was it

317

the wish to play a Fletcher Christian role. As he sailed up the Pacific he could still, if his heart was set upon it, land on one of the Hebrides and kill a few cannibals—there were some left! That was not the point. . . .

No, it was simpler, and it was worse, than finding bankers and preachers everywhere, their armchairs planted on the lands that Adventure had cleared. It was in himself that this was happening. He had been a captain for eight years; he had weathered some dirty storms, he had broken in some dirty characters; he had been barely missed, with knife or revolver, two or three times. Those were his adventures, and they would not make a volume! In his trade, all this had about the same significance as a tumble from a bicycle, a fall downstairs, an attack of bronchitis, or similar accidents of bourgeois existence. He was not inclined either to regret these trivialities or to hope for others.

Only, he had enough of his life behind him, now, to know that the rest of it would follow in the same line. He was a captain who was quick, skillful, obeyed, one to whom only the best commands were offered. And that was all. He would continue to be that until he retired on his pension. It was a success, if you like, but it no longer interested him. On the *Galatèe,* at the age of nineteen, when one was bursting with energy and ambition, one had dreamed of becoming just this. And when this is what one has become, a captain who sweeps everything before him in all weathers, who is a terror to his men, who makes money for his shipping company and for himself, but who doesn't give a damn for it, well, then, one becomes aware also that it wasn't worth the trouble to drive oneself so hard toward the attainment of nothing but a routine, a black, boredom.

He himself, for years past, had not been able to get rid of the sense of being stuck in the mud-bed of his trade, of crawling through life like a fouled boat in warm seas, when sea-weeds and mollusks glue themselves to its bottom and drain away its speed. And there were tricks, now, when one had dreamed almost of conquests. . . . Yes, tricks. . . . The mere fact of his being here was one of them. Why had he sailed around the world, instead of going to Frisco by the Horn, the shortest way? Simply because of the law on bonuses, a lucky find of the fellows on desk jobs. The ship-owners got a bonus on the miles covered. The Ministry, logically, advised them to stick to the itinerary that was less long. But then the shippers would give priority to cargo to be discharged at a port of call in Tasmania, or Australia. That justified the "grand tour," and the government, cheated, could do nothing but pay. For you, the captain, of whom nothing is asked but to stretch out the course, there's nothing there to set you afire with pride!

Yet the three men whom he had just left were satisfied, each in his own way. He was the only one, then, who wanted something else, without even knowing what it was he wanted. On the whole, it seemed to him that this profession, which, when he first landed in it, used to appear alive, robust, teeming with blood and muscle, had wasted away, like Thirard on the *Antonine;* that there was nothing left of it but dry bones. He would have to accommodate himself to it, as one keeps a wife who has grown old. Well, then, since this was life—

When he went back aboardship, he found queer faces among his sailors, the air of people who are upset and are concealing it from one other. Gicquel, the second mate, a young man but as steady as an old one, with a cold and reticent face, told him what was the matter: "Sultan chased the cat, Captain, and it jumped overboard and is lost."

It is a most sinister sign when the ship's cat, the creature most attached to every last corner of the vessel, abandons it. All the men knew that. After the thoughts that had just been going around in Rolland's mind, this anxiety seemed ridiculous to him, and there was the shadow of a smile on his face, which surprised Gicquel.

"Try to find another before tomorrow," he advised.

"It won't be the same thing," the second mate remarked.

He meant, obviously, that for the men the replacement of the lost animal would not conjure away the evil spell. So he did not understand when the captain bent a heavy gaze upon him and answered, "Oh yes, it will! Isn't it always the same thing?"

XXVIII

THE SHIP was brought up on her cable and came to a standstill in the current. It was one o'clock in the morning, and the fog was dense.

"There is no use having the sails furled," Rolland said. "Simply counter-brace the canvas abaft."

When this had been done, the officers went below to the cabin to get a bite to eat.

"A hundred-and-one days at sea," Rolland remarked as he sat down. "That is a fine crossing."

They hurried through their snack and went to their cabins; and soon the peal of the fo'c'sle bell as it struck the fog signals, and the steps of the officer of the watch on the poop, were the only sounds to sink into the thick blanket of the air. The fog did not lift until four in the morning. To the eyes of Courtier, the third mate, who was on watch, it first uncovered the contours of the land to the east, and then the hull of the fire-boat on which, through the binoculars, the officer made out the white letters SAN FRANCISCO. Near her thick-set body the pilot's schooner was swaying at anchor. A scattered fleet of large sailing-vessels was spread out over the pallid water, and Courtier recognized four French ships among them.

As soon as it was broad daylight, tug-boats came out from the Golden Gate and shot off at full speed toward the ships.

"With this calm, the tugs* are going to set their prices to suit themselves," said Rolland, as he came out on the poop.

Courtier nodded in agreement; then remarked, "The pilot is starting."

And soon the broad-decked schooner, with her cutwater curved like an amphora and her stern as delicately modeled as that of a yacht, came alongside the *Argonaute,* whose sails were waking to movement in the freshness of the nascent breeze. The pilot, red-haired and athletic, climbed the ladder and flung his black canvas bag on the deck—the gesture which, on any vessel, testified that the man henceforth belonged on the ship. Immediately after the "shake-hands," he insisted that the craft be taken in tow. He averred that it was all but impossible to get through the entrance passage and into the roadstead under sail. Rolland waited till he had finished speaking, then he said, "Have a drink, pilot?" †

"No, sir. Thank you."

"All right."

The captain turned toward Gicquel, who had just come up.

"Call the men to their sailing positions," he ordered.

The pilot looked at the bustle about the deck with a worried air.

"Here comes the tug, sir," he announced.

Rolland did not reply. Instead, he had the to'gants'ls set, and gave the command to weigh anchor. When it was apeak, the jibs were hoisted. The *Argonaute* fell off. As she was beginning to make headway, all her sails well braced for the wind, the tug, which had put on extra speed, came up beside her. From the bridge the captain called out some prices. Rolland shrugged his shoulders.

"Run up the royals, haul the spanker taut," he ordered.

* He uses the English word, in quotation marks. Tr.
† The conversation with the San Francisco harbor people is carried on mostly in English, except for Rolland's one long speech to the pilot later on. Tr.

"What's your price?" cried the tug-boat captain, fidgeting about on his bridge.

The tug was running along in pace with the ship, like an importunate guide, and its captain was pelting Rolland with a succession of ever lower prices. Vanquished at last by the latter's silence, he steered away. At the wheel of the *Argonaute,* Papa Bonjean, who was always entrusted with harbor entrances because he was an incomparable helmsman, jerked his head toward the west.

"Have a look at the sea, Cap'n. There comes the breeze."

The wind was in fact blowing in at the stern, and in a short time the *Argonaute,* with a full wind abaft and all canvas up, swept through the narrow mouth of the Golden Gate. But it was not until nine that evening, after tacking about for a long time, that the ship dropped anchor.

Before supper Rolland turned to the pilot, as he had done before: "Have a French vermouth, pilot?"

"No, sir; only water."

"A serious lad," Courtier commented.

"A furious lad," amended Rolland, who had been enjoying himself. "By coming in under sail we have deprived him of the 'gratuity' * that the towing companies pay him."

At the end of the meal Gicquel went up on deck, and returned quickly.

"The barometer is going down," he announced, "and the wind is rising. I have given orders to the man on watch to let me know if the breeze gets stronger. The second anchor is ready to be let down."

When there is a pilot aboard, the captain keeps him informed and consults him. Rolland therefore translated this news to the red-haired athlete, who answered, "Everybody can go to bed. I'll be on the look-out."

He refused the passenger's cabin that had been prepared for him.

In the chart-house Rolland went sound asleep, as was his habit in port. He was brought painfully back to reality by the howling of the wind as it shook masts and yards.

He had just jumped down from his bunk when his dog growled. It was a German shepherd dog which, like all the dogs he had had as captain, he had named Sultan, in memory of Thirard's pet and companion. The animal was baring its teeth as it looked at the door, the handle of which was being fiddled with by a hesitant hand. At last it opened, and the pilot edged in a portion of his broad frame.

"Plenty of rain and wind, Cap'n," he sputtered.

Then, stumbling against the consonants, he demanded that the second anchor be put down.

* Again, English word in French original. Tr.

321

Rolland had barely reached the bottom of the companionway that went below to the saloon when an uproar made him turn around. Behind him, the giant was bumping down the steps on his back. When he arrived below, he picked himself up laboriously, swayed toward the captain, and blew an alcoholic breath full in his face.

"Plenty wind, sir," he said again.

Rolland was about to catch hold of him, when the heavy jingling of the anchor-chain spinning through the hawse-hole made the drunken man turn around. The second anchor had been let down. Gicquel had been ahead of the order.

The pilot was now zigzagging around in the saloon. A fortunate lurch sent him aground on the sofa, where he passed out. Gicquel came into the room, oilskins streaming.

"I have just lowered the second anchor, Captain," he said.

"Thank you. But look at this swine—he's anchored from the inside! Where did he get it?"

Gicquel gave a sidelong glance at the butler's cabinets that flanked the saloon fireplace; their doors were open.

"A bottle of vermouth and one of brandy—he's filled his bunkers!" Rolland summed up. "What would I like to do to his backsides! A phony that refuses a glass of wine before dinner and gets drunk when he is on watch!"

The storm died down with dawn. The Health Department's launch came alongside at eight in the morning and, after a severe inspection, gave the ship a clean bill. Then the customs men came aboard and sealed the hatches and the storeroom—with a liberal allowance, however, of what might be needed for current consumption. The chief asked for a bottle of cognac. "Only for sauce," he declared.

"Oh, of course," Rolland responded.

After that, there was the coming-and-going of the consignees' boats, bringing instructions and the mail from France. All the officers, and all the men, flung themselves upon their letters and went off alone to read them; all except Rolland, who had nothing but official mail.

At last the pilot reappeared, without his cap, his clothes rumpled, his eyes still wild: Gicquel had just been shaking him out of his stupor.

"Beg you—your pardon, sir," he stammered.

Rolland fixed his stern gaze upon the wavering eyes, and it was only when the man was holding them steady that he spoke:

"You got drunk, by stealing the ship's liquor, when you were responsible for the ship. A circumstance that aggravates the offense is that you yourself had demanded this responsibility, in order to be free of all surveillance. I shall make my report to the chief of the pilot service."

The man was looking at him, open-mouthed, like a groggy boxer. He seemed to be trying to get hold of excuses, pleas; but none came. His eyes, only, were flooded with despair.

"He has a wife and children," Gicquel put in. "He told me that if there was a complaint he would lose his job."

"I have a ship," Rolland retorted, "and he might have lost that."

"Yet he did let you know, Captain, sunk as he was: he asked you to let down the anchor. The very fear of the report, by itself, would make him go straight."

"Do not insist, Monsieur Gicquel. It is just because pilots are devoted and conscientious men that this fellow is not worthy to be one."

The *Argonaute* drew up to the loading wharf in the afternoon. That meant visits: office after office. The deep canyons of the streets were teeming with a busy crowd. There was the clatter of trolley cars; there were still a few buggies harnessed to spirited horses; but more than anything else there were automobiles, high on their wheels, jerking forward. Rolland got into the tonneau of the consignee's car. It was not the first time he had been in an automobile, but it was still a novel diversion for him. The speed, the detours, the sharp turns, the meetings and passings, the grazing of other cars and the avoiding of them—all these maneuvers, achieved before he even guessed they were coming, made him dizzy. When he put his feet on the ground again, it was with the feeling of an acrobat who has yielded to the lure of a foolish stunt and has pulled it off successfully.

He called at the Customs Office—on the consignee, on the supply men, and finally at the Consulate.

He stayed on board the next day. The sails had been dried, and thanks to the hot sun it had been possible to take them off the yards and send them to the sail locker, to be inspected during the following days. The unloading had begun. In the evening Tessier, the senior member of the starboard watch, came in the name of the crew to ask for a little money, "to go drink a glass." Rolland refused.

"You know the rule, Tessier. Sunday morning every man will have a dollar. There's nothing doing until then."

But an hour later Gicquel informed him that he had seen Sergent and Boullard going ashore, one with a ship-in-a-bottle under his arm and the other with his fine model of a four-master.

"To hell with them," Rolland said. "It won't take them long to get rid of what they are paid for their little ships. When the bunker is empty, you'll see them coming back to look for more. But they can dig in their own pockets for dollars after this, I'm telling you."

He told Gicquel he might go in to the town, but the second mate refused: he had letters to write and he needed sleep.

"In that case, I leave you in charge," Rolland said. "I am going to Mother Gibier's to stand my colleagues a round of drinks."

An electric car deposited him in front of "Mother Gibier's" hotel. To the French, she was an old Alsatian, though it was a safe bet that she was German and nothing else. Her nickname came from her custom of asking each of her boarders if he would like to find a "pretty little piece of game" in his room when he came in from the theater. The *"gibier"* was pleasing, the food tasty; and the hotel had become the rendezvous of all the French captains and officers who might be in the port.

Rolland stepped into a large room decorated with ships-in-bottles, relief models of ships under full sail, and albatross heads. Separated from this room by a partition, a French café lined up its tables in front of imitation-leather settees. Here sailing-ship captains and officers were drinking, with women—American, German, Latin-American; not French. The French girls occupied other quarters, in the "red light district."

The drinkers were still maintaining the high pressure kept up in one café after another since lunch. That was plain to be seen, and especially to be heard. Everyone was talking at once, in great vocal outbursts broken into by the girls' shrill laughter and bits of song. Rolland was welcomed with a roaring cordiality, and went to sit down near a clean-shaven and stern-faced captain with a pipe in his mouth. He knew them well, these anchorages where the ship-masters are crowded together flank to flank, like vessels in a tidal basin, with alcohol rippling in their stomachs like the opaque water of a harbor.

"How many days at sea?" they called out to him.

"A hundred and one."

"You've made a record! Wash it down!"

That was what he was here for, and he called the waiter. A corpulent and jovial captain rose, his hands on a woman's shoulders, and commanded, "Just a minute! I have priority in the record of length: a hundred and fifty-eight days at sea. Who can go me better?"

Figures flew back and forth, fragments of sentences were shouted through the smoke:

"A full head wind for twenty-one days . . ."

"More than a month off the Cape, and the sails damaged . . ."

In front of Rolland, an apoplectic-looking captain with a thick gray beard had one arm around the neck of a tall blonde American

324

girl, and with the other hand was keeping time to the song he was teaching her. Leaning back on the settee, she was repeating, with a very bad accent, two lines of which the burden was, "Does your dog bite, Madame?" But the grizzled gallant got up.

"She won't learn it in public. She gets scared. I'll take her away."

And, with his short arm encircling her rounded waist, he took her to one of the private cubicles built around the room, the walls of which, by police regulation, were only the height of a man.

The hullaballoo increased. The captains were arguing; their faces were red, and they would pound on the table with one fist while the other hand was occupied with their companions.

"Listen to them," said the captain with the pipe, "beating mileage records and breaking topmasts. I've got my bunkers full up with their imbecilities for this evening. I'm going. Are you staying on?"

"No," Rolland said.

They went out into the hard light of California Street.

"That sort of thing will end up in the red light district," said the captain from the island of Arz; and he went on to speak of a blind alley where women solicited their visitors from the threshold of their open doors, and two policemen regulated traffic. "They will find Frenchwomen there," continued the Breton. "Frenchwomen who will bawl them out because they don't give their sailors the dollars to come to see them. One captain told me that a cop had called him down for straying into that sewer. 'Captains are not in their place here, sir,' the cop said. And he, our colleague, was having a good laugh as he told it. . . ."

He took several steps by Rolland's side.

"You are going back to your ship? Look out! The approaches to the docks are none too safe. Myself, I am staying with friends who are French. I should have done better to have spent this evening playing checkers with their little girl."

He pressed his fellow-captain's hand, and went away.

Left alone, Rolland walked in the direction of the harbor for a few minutes, then turned at right angles and went back to the center of the city's night life. The instinct of the chase was waking in him again. He had not been attracted by any of the women he had just seen at Mother Gibier's, though some of them were better-looking than one would have had reason to expect. He might have accosted more than one of them if he had found her alone in the street, but there was nothing doing over the counter!

The saloons and music-halls were disgorging their crowds now. Moving abstractedly toward a theater exit from which women in low-necked gowns were emerging, Rolland felt his shoulder being jostled. He could not decide whether the impact had been sought by the woman who was passing him and was turning around to face him, accurately calculated though the collision seemed to be. He looked at her, from her shoes to her hat, with an insolent, evaluating gaze. Under such a gaze a conventional woman would stiffen and with suspicion, pass on; and that would tell him what he wanted to know. This woman, however, gave no sign of being aware of him at all. She was a slender brunette as tall as he, with a thin-lipped mouth and dark eyes that were made darker by her little veil, and she had kept the smile with which she had met the encounter, and which was no more than an amused and reticent crinkle of her lips.

He walked along by her side, and she did not seem to notice him; but she still had her ironic air of a woman who is entertained by adventure. Stepping down from the curb, he took her arm. She let him take it, as if it belonged to someone else. She walked with a rather long step, to which he matched his own without effort, and as they turned into one street and then into another, she did not speak a word in reply to his gallantries, though sometimes she would throw him a sly sidelong glance. He had more and more the feeling that he was addressing himself to a conventional middle-class woman who was on her way home and would stop him in front of her door with, "Here I am. Good night."

She did stop, in fact, before a tall house whose door opened noiselessly when she pressed the electric button. She went in, but as she did so she turned her head slightly, as an invitation for him to follow.

Behind her, he traversed a deserted hall and went up to the third floor. It must have been some sort of hotel, he thought, judging from the length of the empty corridor on which the rooms opened. She used a key, this time, to open a door, and she preceded him into a room with drawn curtains, furnished with a narrow mahogany bed with only one pillow, armchairs, and a round table with gilt inlays on which lay a leather valise. She locked the door, went over to a mirror, untied her little veil, took off her hat and, turning back to Rolland, disclosed hard eyes—the face of one who has lain in ambush.

"You are to pay me a hundred dollars," she commanded, "or I will call for help and the door will be broken in. I shall say that you followed me against my will, that you forced your way into my room, and that you have locked me in here. You know the white-slave law?"

He knew it. He knew that a woman in the street could say to a policeman, "This man is pursuing me. He has made improper advances. Arrest him," and the man would be arrested. If he resisted, the blackjack—a leather casing weighted with lead, which the "cops" carried attached to their belts—would be brought into the picture.

And Rolland knew even better that to be caught in a hotel room with a woman undressed and screaming, and alleging that he had shut her up in order to rape her, might cost him two years in prison. This woman was already undoing her dress; accomplices would be on the look-out, just waiting for her first outcry.

"You will pay?" she demanded, in an icy voice.

"Yes."

He went up to her slowly, opening his jacket as if to reach into his inside pocket and find his wallet. The revere which he pushed aside with his left hand hid his clenched fist. His arm was ready to fly out toward her, and he was calculating just how to strike the point of her sharp chin. She would fall back, stunned. And he would pick up the key that she had laid on the table behind her, and leave. . . .

It was his wallet that he pulled out, to take a handful of bills from it and count them.

That was how it was, now. The captain put down the common sailor within him, at the first move toward action, even when the action was good. And Rolland knew that this time the common sailor was right. After the crushing blow he would have gone away, as he was about to go away, through the silence and the emptiness of the corridors; but he would have had his hundred dollars in his pocket, and in his heart the joy of having taught a strumpet a lesson, instead of the bitter realization of his lack of daring, as well as the shame of having been taken in. The trap, which was new to him, must nevertheless have been an ordinary one, to judge from the precision in which it could be sprung in one direction or the other. He paid, and he went out, without seeing a soul. If he had refused to pay, pseudo-neighbors would have dashed out of rooms in answer to the woman's cries, while she was tearing off her bodice. They would have broken down the door, sprung upon the French-man, and held him until the arrival of the "cop," who was, perhaps, himself in on the scheme. A well-planned brigands' ambush, in the American fashion, and a story not to be told!

In the street, which was already bathed in crude light but traversed now by only a few pedestrians, a thought struck him—when his fury had been somewhat calmed by walking—which was just as clear and just as brutal as the ambuscade he was leaving be-hind: since he had become "Captain Rolland," women had been only waiting for what they could get out of him. He was not so stupid as to be surprised by that, so long as he addressed himself solely to professional prostitutes. Yet when he was a common sailor even those had sometimes refused his money. They would murmur, "I'm sweet on you," as if they were confessing to some ailment. And more than once, when his ship was sailing and he was leaving them,

327

he had been obliged to slap their fingers to make them loosen their hold.

But since he had become a captain they had all aimed at nothing but his pocket: even the two women whom, in each case, he had just missed marrying.

He looked back, now, to his return from his last voyage but one, and once again saw Blévin the shipping manager leaning back in his chair and rubbing his hands.

"Since the *Marie-Laurentine* won't be ready to sail again for two months, what are you going to do in the meantime?"

"I'm just wondering that myself."

"Why don't you take advantage of the long holiday to get married? You won't often find such an opportunity!"

That was true: two months ashore was something very rare in the career of a captain in the foreign trade. They were always waiting for such an occasion, in that fraternity, so they could take a wife.

"My word, I declare I hadn't thought of it," Rolland answered. "And you know better than anyone else, sir, that I have hardly had a chance to. In the time I have had ashore I have always been busy looking after the overhauling of the ship. It has been all I could do to find an hour in the evening to take a turn around and get some new ideas in my head."

"Well, try to think of it," said Blévin. "Haven't you anyone in mind?"

"No one."

"In that case—I hesitate to speak about it to you, but after all, why not? Just a little while ago, at home, I was talking of you with my sister. You know how women are: an idea crosses their mind, and they jump at it. She exclaimed, 'There's the man who would be just right for—' She will tell you the name if you like. What do you risk in talking it over with her?"

"Nothing."

Walking past the unlighted shop windows of San Francisco in the cold gleam of dawn, Rolland was seeing again the girl introduced to him by Blévin's spinster sister in the Blévins' dining room with its waxed and highly polished floor; a Chinese cabinet, inlaid with mother-of-pearl, was all a-glitter, too, with the lacquered shells of sea-turtles; blue Chinese porcelain, on an open case of shelves, quarreled with the Henri II furniture, but no one was troubled by it; a little old spinster with plainly arranged gray hair, but with a high-bridged nose and keen eyes behind her glasses, was scrutinizing him as he came in. Monsieur Blévin had made the introductions.

Rolland had been surprised by Val André. He had liked the girl:

a clear-skinned blonde, a handsome girl, as they said of anyone who was more than five feet six inches tall; arms and a waist that would not yield under one's fingers. He would have let himself be signed up. She would have made a capable wife, as a captain's wife should be. For, as Mademoiselle Blévin had said, it was she who did the housekeeping, and she did it well. Her cooking was to his taste, and she managed everything so skillfully that she would not get up from the table during a whole dinner, practically, any more than if she had had a maid.

Only, one afternoon when they had taken a walk to Dahouet and were sitting close to each other on the cliff there, and when his hand had slid along her body from her waist to her throat, she had taken advantage of the intimate caress to ask him two or three little things. . . . Did captains receive bonuses when they cut down the time of a voyage? That would be only just, with all the money they would have saved the shipping companies. . . . Was it true that the Bordes firm paid more than the other ship-owners? Her father knew Monsieur Antonin Bordes very well. . . .

She asked him all this in a soft and gentle voice without being disturbed when his broad hand abandoned its caress, unaware of the hardening of her "intended's" mouth and eyes. As for him, he had had an idea of sheer genius: he had declared, with the utmost emphasis, that after he was married he would never go to sea again. That was no life! To have a wife one month in the year! When that time came, he would look for something ashore: anything would do, to start with.

He had gone on with this program amiably as he took her home. As she never piped up a word, he had looked at her searchingly and asked, "You are pleased?"

He had taken a kind of fierce delight in the jaundiced smile with which she had succeeded in puckering up her face, and then in her stammering response: "Of course! But if you don't find a situation— And then, it would be such a sacrifice. . . . I wouldn't want you to regret it, at any price."

"Regret it?" he had echoed. "You haven't looked at yourself!"

She had succeeded in tossing off a little laugh.

But the next day old Minart—taking a turn around his table, and as upset as if he were walking the deck of a ship that had run aground—had adjured his future son-in-law not to do anything foolish. Marriage was one thing, a job was another; the two went together, and neither should do any injury to the other. To leave the sea, with his future, at his age! A crime!

"You are right," he had answered. "I will go off to sea again."

And he had gone off, that very evening, to Nantes, to sign up for the *Saint Sever*.

With Margaret, at Geelong, it had been just the opposite. Just a youngster, she was, but a nice youngster with ash-blonde hair, and blue eyes that used to darken when he kissed her; the ways and laughter and speech of a youngster, but all that so fresh, so sincere, that he had been entirely bowled over: to have knocked about as he had, and to be loved by such an innocent child! To make a woman of her! For she had the stuff of a woman: her outbursts, her defenses, her glances at once timid and eager. . . .

He had written her, *I will take you to France.*

And she had answered, *I will keep you here.*

This certainly seemed to be the other extreme from Val André since Margaret turned up her nose at his job and was trying to make him chuck it. At bottom, it was the same thing. Both women were only seeking to annex the man. . . . He had written back to Margaret: *Each would have to sacrifice too much for the other. That could not work out. . . .*

Walking, and thinking, he had reached the docks. So entrenched was he within himself that he passed some disquieting silhouettes almost without seeing them: moving figures that paused at his approach, and turned to follow him with their eyes.

When he got back to the ship, there was a line of light under Gicquel's door. It opened. The second mate was still dressed.

"Captain, Le Bihan and Nédellec have deserted."

"Le Bihan and Nédellec?"

They were two Bretons from Quiberon, given to grumbling but good and courageous sailors, two of the best men on board.

"When did this happen?"

"Between ten and eleven o'clock, Captain."

The second mate went on to report that the bos'n had been making a last tour of the deck when he was called to from the quay; it was two women, well dressed, one of them speaking French; she was, or she called herself, a Canadian. She had asked if she could come aboard. The bos'n had refused, but she had come up closer to the gangway to joke with him. Just then, the bos'n had heard talking at the bow and the dragging of something heavy. He had hurried up in time to see Nédellec sliding down a line into the rowboat in which Le Bihan had already embarked. While the women were buttonholing old Alain, they had had time to let their sea-chests down into the boat.

"The bos'n jumped up on the belaying-pin rack and began to call to them," Gicquel continued, "and Le Bihan yelled, 'Go to hell three times over! Is that enough for you?' As for Nédellec, he said,

'Your prison ship's no place for a man to make his living; a boat with a curse on her, and run like in Colbert's* time!"

Rolland did not ask, "What has Colbert got to do with it?" He had read the phrase in the *Libertaire*. But he did say, "Why 'a boat with a curse on her'?"

Gicquel shrugged his shoulders without answering.

But Rolland understood: the cat's running away at Hobart, this had been fermenting in the minds of the crew for a long time until it had destroyed the confidence of the best men among them, while he had been unwilling to take it into account. It was because they no longer believed in his good luck that Nédellec and Le Bihan had jumped into the shanghaier's boat. This was another defeat, even more searing than the one inflicted upon him by the woman in California Street. But against this he reacted.

"There are two kinds of men I never regret losing," he said, "the idlers and the idiots. And I prefer the first to the second."

"I do regret losing them," Gicquel ventured to reply. "They were two first-rate men." Then he said, "Good night, Captain," and closed the door.

XXIX

IT WAS just a month since the *Argonaute*, after gulping down her five hundred tons of grain a day, had hoisted her last bag with the customary ceremonial and had been towed out through the Golden Gate. Cliff House, the Sutro Baths, and then the foliage of Golden Gate Park, had filed past under Rolland's cold gaze. Once more, he was leaving the land without any sense of regret. He had really had eyes only for the first buoy of the harbor passage, when the tug, after signaling to cast off the tow-line, had responded with three short barks to the formal salute of the sailing-ship as she slowly lowered and raised her flag.

"These damn Yankees don't waste time in politeness," he had said to Gicquel.

By evening, the life aboardship had taken up its immutable cycle again.

That was all that Rolland expected of it: this monastic regularity

* The establishment of the French marine was one of the outstanding achievements of Louis XIV's famous administrator. Tr.

which, never confusing the hours, let them fall like beads in a monotonous chaplet, as the knots succeeded one another in the log line. In the end, that would lull to sleep the feeling of emptiness and solitude which once again had sunk into him among the crowds and the movement of the city. He had his destination: Falmouth for orders. In default of anything else, that made a goal to be attained.

And to be attained speedily and well! His renown as a fast and lucky captain must remain undisputed. Since it was the only thing he had succeeded in acquiring, at least let him keep that!

As the crew is made in the image of its chief, his sailors were strictly obedient, but without relish, to the orders of a captain who was skillful, just, and severe. When they saw him coming from the poop in his little oilskin watch-coat, they would say to each other, "We're going to work ship."

For he made it a point of honor to be with them when they were drenched. He was not one of those captains who kept company with the compass during hard weather and exercised the command by means of a telescope. And that made itself felt when he put his weight into the work.

"If you do your job, he doesn't nag you," the men would say. Yet they would add, sarcastically, "But his amiability would make a policeman jealous."

Among the officers, Gicquel had at once adapted himself to his functions as second-in-command. Rolland had begun by coming up unexpectedly during his night watches, to inspect the canvas. He was suspicious of that fear of surprise which haunts young officers and makes them furl sail a long time ahead, whenever it looks like a change in the weather. In such cases, the captain has a sharp reproof ready; but Rolland never had to administer any here. Gicquel was not taking any risks, but he suited the canvas to the weather. It was up to the captain to go beyond that if he wished to. And in this Rolland agreed with him.

He did not agree with him about Harry.

When Rolland appeared on deck, Harry would always call out to him, in English, "Good morning, good afternoon, good evening, Captain," according to the hour of the day, and without worrying over never receiving any response. A tall youth with a clear skin, fair hair that he did not know what to do with, the torso of an athlete poured into a seaman's jersey: Harry Feldman, twenty-three years old and the son of a millionaire.

He had been imposed upon Rolland, as they were leaving Frisco, by a telegram from the ship-owners. The boy was drinking himself to death, just to kill time; and his parents, after trying everything else, had done just what middle-class parents did in France: as a last resort, they had sent him to sea. Rolland was urged to clean him up with three months aboardship, and then to send him home on a liner.

"I don't like it," he had answered. "Since it is an order, I cannot refuse. But tell his parents that for him as for the others I shall always be merely the captain."

"You need not worry," the shipping agent had assured him. "They do not ask any favors: he is simply to have a bunk, and the same food as the men. But not their work: his mother is afraid of his breaking his head. You will take him over, in short."

When his fellow-captains heard of it, they exclaimed, "It's a sackful of dollars your signing on!"

And indeed he himself knew perfectly well that this could be a great stroke of luck for him. To install the boy in a cabin, admit him to the officers' saloon, treat him with cordiality, make a friend of him who would repay his welcome without even waiting to inherit his father's fortune. . . . But on sailing day Harry had made his appearance in a state of complete and helpless intoxication; two hefty fellows, his "nurses," had literally laid him down on the deck. And Rolland, who freely admitted that two-thirds of his crew came aboard dead drunk, had immediately conceived a fundamental scorn for this child of riches. He had motioned with his head toward the bow of the vessel. "Throw him forward there, in the fo'c's'le. He doesn't deserve to be in the stern."

And as soon as they sailed, let the fellow chip rust!

"I don't want to hear any talk about it," he said.

He had got what he asked for! The boy had taken it like a sport, with never a protest. He would jab at his share of salt pork at meals with the others, roaring out every time in a voice to shake the fo'c's'le, *"Maudit cochon!"* Except for a few obscenities, this was all the French he had learned, and as he made use of it at every meal it became a rite which filled the crew with joy.

The men, moreover, had quickly adopted him. The mere fact that he had been punished was already a plea in his favor. But they had been conquered by the way he took it: his imperturbable gaiety. When he was not laughing—showing all his teeth—he would whistle, as he chipped away at his rust; and the tunes would be just made for keeping time to the blows of his two-peened hammer. A damn good bird!

"A hell of a lot he minds!" they would marvel.

They had learned to say "Hello, boy!" and to return his back-slapping. And he, an immature adolescent, found himself at home with their simplicity. They sensed this, and were bursting with pride over it.

Officially, Rolland had nothing to say against this good-humor on the part of the passenger. Harry was not putting on any airs, and his good mornings sounded sincere. Yet all this forced the captain to the conclusion that he was merely finding within himself resources which he would never have suspected, to weather the storm.

"It is just the change in his way of living that pleases him," Gicquel had said one day.

"Yes," Rolland had retorted, "it rests him so he can go back all the better to his old life."

"I am not so sure. He has been cut off alcohol abruptly. At his age, he can be cured. In any case, nobody is any better at pumping the water from your water-butt!"

"You are young, Monsieur Gicquel," Rolland remarked.

Several evenings in succession, during the fine weather, Gicquel, who spoke English perfectly, had joined the young American for a prolonged stroll up and down the "main street," under the sympathetic eyes of the crew. Rolland had observed these promenades, at first, without saying anything; then one evening when the second mate had just left Harry Feldman to go on watch duty, he had waited for him on the poop.

"I do not much like seeing the officers too familiar with the men, Gicquel," he said.

The subordinate fixed his cold gaze upon him.

"Feldman is not one of 'the men,' Captain; he is a passenger."

"You are playing with words. In any case, I beg you to cease these conversations from now on."

"My apologies, Captain, but that is not enough for me." And as Rolland, veritably dazed, stood waiting, with eyes opened too wide, the second mate explained: "Monsieur Feldman is listed as a passenger. The fact that he is treated as the worst of novices makes no difference. He has accepted the situation in a way which commands respect. Moreover, he is unable to exchange three words with anyone. He is reduced to reading aloud, in the crew's quarters, so as not to lose the habit of speech. This is an aggravation of punishment which he does not deserve. Consequently, Captain, if you deem it necessary that I should end my acquaintance with him, I must ask you for an express order to that effect."

"And this order, you would take note of it when the occasion arose?"

The officer's face went white under the cutting insinuation. Then he recovered himself.

"I shall merely carry it out, Captain. But nothing will keep me from thinking that you are unfair to Feldman, as you have just been to me."

Rolland had contented himself with replying, "You are fortunate, Monsieur Gicquel, that I put up with things from you which I would not stand from anyone else."

Since then, the second mate had received the American, in rest periods, in his own cabin.

The first albatross appeared again. The *Argonaute* was entering the zone of variable winds. The southern spring flung its icy rain and snow against the eyes once more. Then the fog, by putting a stop to all observations, forced Rolland to go far down into the south. Courtier was hoping to see the Diego Ramirez Islands on this detour, but they passed them too far out. Papa Alain, the bos'n consoled him: "Believe me, Monsieur Courtier, you aren't losing anything much. It's nothing but bare rocks. Even when it's clear, you have to be right on top of them to see them at all. And the Cap'n is quite right not to come alongside of them in this cloudy weather." The old fellow spat, and added, "As they say, 'You should beware of the fronts of women and the backs of horses, and give points of land a wide berth.' "

According to the position as reckoned, the meridian of Cape Horn had been left to the west two days later. The winds had shifted to the west-northwest, and the *Argonaute*, fleeing before long swells, her main to'gants'l set, was crossing the degrees of longitude at thirteen knots an hour. On the gray sea mottled with splotches of white spray, on the crests of giant breakers that sent up a smoke-mist of water, the men were pointing, with chuckles, to the ships passing in the other direction, and laboriously trying, under their lower tops'ls, to breast current and wind.

"It sure is our turn to have the wind a-stern," they said.

Then the *Argonaute* started on her course back into the north; and after a few furious wind storms the good weather settled in, almost without any period of transition. The southeast trade winds bore them along to the latitude of Saint Helena, which they left several hundred miles to starboard. Papa Alain had landed there once, but he had a better recollection of the island's water-cress than of the tomb of the Emperor. The officers' table had been set on the poop, as was the custom in good weather.

It was as they were sitting there one evening that they saw two men leap up from the large hatch and fling themselves upon each other without a word: with no bawled-out succession of insults to create the atmosphere of combat and push anger to the explosion-point. Gicquel was the first to identify the fighters.

"It's Bourgoin and the Whale."

Bourgoin was a giant who was misshapen by force of being strong.

335

His neck was rooted in his ears, his arms were like the stumps of yards, he was an elemental being, and he was hungry day and night. For although the steward, in deference to his capacity, gave him large helpings and handed out by the dozen the sea-biscuit that he munched all day long, his fixed idea was the anticipation of mealtime. He was probably the only sailor on earth who, when he was on shore, ate instead of drinking, and that with the same passion with which the others drank.

Guizard, nicknamed "The Whale," was slender and springy. He was one of the two whom the dealer in men had delivered to Rolland to replace the two deserters: a run-of-the-mill port drifter who said he came from Garennes-Colombes. It was impossible to tell from his accent, worn down by years of battering around the world, and there were long odds that the voyage would be over before his true civil status was fixed. He was very proud of having been shanghaied by American whalers, and his nickname came from his habit of repeating on every occasion, from lips curled in disdain, "If you had been on the whale ships!" and, "That isn't in it beside whaling!"

The reason for the quarrel? The worst. One that smolders in the depths of the crew's quarters as coal may smolder in the depths of the hold, to flame out with no apparent reason; one of those profound antipathies of man for man which have their source in the core of a man's being, and which one notes without being able to explain them: a hatred as imperious, and as spontaneous, as love. It begins with the first look that marks the men's fundamental antinomy. After that, as if the thing went on by itself, every word stings.

The fight was following the usual lines of a conflict between a crushing but clumsy force and a sly agility. The Whale would slip away from his opponent's hold and land swift blows on his stomach, but he was falling back step by step and was about to find himself brought to bay against the rail. The men had all got up.

On the poop, Rolland got up too. He had just seen Guizard's hand go into his pocket. He was down the poop companionway in two jumps, and he charged upon the fighters sideways. The impact of his shoulder separated them for a second, time enough to seize the Whale's wrist, twist it, and with a swift kick send the fallen knife slithering across the deck. Then he went to pick it up, and closed it.

"My knife," the man snarled, panting.

"I am keeping it. I will give you another," the captain said.

For a sailor cannot do without a knife. But Rolland knew that a man cannot kill another with a strange knife, when his own is in the captain's possession as convincing evidence.

336

He went back to the two men, gripped their shoulders, and, with a strong thrust, pushed them to one side.

"None of this on my ship," he ordered. "Settle your accounts ashore."

He let them go, but only to seize them again, grasping the front of their jackets and holding them, thus, one on one side and one on the other.

"Here, I am between the two of you. You get that? The first one who touches the other will be striking at me, and that stroke will take him a long way. Now go."

He kept them under his eye for several days, and as they seemed to ignore each other he pigeonholed the whole affair. But one evening Gicquel came to him with a suggestion. "Captain, it would be better if the Whale were to change his watch."

"Why?"

"Because I do not trust him; he is thinking up some dirty trick."

Rolland shrugged his shoulders.

"You are having visions, Monsieur Gicquel. Guizard has been warned. He knows that if he tried anything like that he would find me on his trail. That's enough."

But the mate persisted.

"He has an air that I don't like, Captain. If he were transferred to the other watch they would practically never come in contact. Then—"

"Then, it is I who would have the air of being afraid of him. I have taken the matter into my own hands, and they know they are dealing with me. To change the watch without any reason would be to acknowledge that I am not sure of being obeyed; and that is something I have never done."

Gicquel was still obstinate.

"It could be presented in such a way as to seem altogether natural. All one need do—"

Rolland interrupted him, frowning: "There can be no trickeries when the authority of the captain is at stake. It must suffice. Now go have your to'gants'l run up."

Two days later, at three o'clock in the morning, in black darkness and with a west gale, Bourgoin fell from the yard where he was furling the fore upper tops'l with the rest of the starboard watch, and crashed to the deck. He died that afternoon, without recovering consciousness. Guizard, the Whale, was working near him on the yard.

When the men had come down again, after furling the sail, not one of them uttered a word about the accident. Even their faces were expressionless.

337

"Come with me."

Rolland's outstretched arm stopped the Whale, who, like the others, was on his way for his bad-weather tot of grog after the successful effort in the rigging. To the captain, the matter left no room for doubt: the blackguard had thrown his comrade from the mast. How? Probably without touching him. It was enough to choose his moment, when the other man was working with both hands on the ballooning sail. Then one suddenly lets go of the piece one is mastering; all the force of the canvas falls upon one's neighbor and pushes him back. If, beating the air with his hands, he cannot catch hold of a fold; if the sail is stretched tight and hard like a metal plate, on which one's fingernails slip— This was what Rolland had tried to make the reprobate confess, in the depths of the sail locker to which he had led him. But under blows that were enough to stun him, the other had spat out only his teeth and some threats: witnesses, he would have witnesses! He would make them sign, and they would meet again on land! Rolland had thrown him out with one last kick.

Gicquel had come looking for his skipper at the end of his watch.

"I have to report to you, Captain, that the sailor Guizard, being drunk, must have fallen down the steps of the forward hold, and is slightly injured. I found two bottles of brandy in his sea-chest, and I have ordered the curtailment of eight meals as a punishment for having hidden them aboardship."

The second mate had spoken in his inscrutable tone of voice, and Rolland turned pale.

"I am not accustomed to having the corporal punishment I administer camouflaged by my officers, Monsieur Gicquel," he said.

"In that case, Captain," the other had replied, "you will remove the penalty if you think best."

Rolland had not done so. The voyage continued gloomily, between a silent cabin weighted with the silent reproach of the acting mate, the poop where the officers exchanged only such words as were concerned with their duty, and the deck where the men made a poor show at concealing their disaffection for this ship and their hurry to get the voyage over.

A prison ship, Nédellec had called it when he ran away. Yet the men were no worse treated here than elsewhere. The food on the *Argonaute* was better than on many ships, and tots of grog and double wine rations came far more often. In spite of that, there was an oppressive atmosphere of the military barracks, the prison, which is what men of the sea dread and loathe more than anything else. It was significant that when they spoke of the master of the ship, it was not as "the Old Man," or "the Skipper," or "the Cap'n," but simply "he": somebody from whom one never heard a word that was not either an order or a reprimand; or received a glance that came from man to man, but only those looks that meant surveillance or emphasized the demand for some required effort. Lhévéder, the sailor in charge of stores, had summed it up in three words one evening as he watched Rolland, with his curt step, pacing the deck: "He's all hard knots." That could be said of him as of gouty people who no longer have any play in their joints.

If Rolland had known of the phrase, he would have been forced to accept it, as he accepted Gicquel's cold precision, and that sort of absence into which the junior officer withdrew at the least suspicion of a friendly attention. "All hard knots," exactly; no other reflex than a stiffening; feeling within himself only shrunken and shriveled things. . . .

But were they all imagining that he found this amusing; that he would not have preferred to be different—one of those "good captains," expansive, friendly, bright-eyed and ruddy-skinned, joyfully obeyed, and presented with bouquets of paper flowers by their crews on their saint's day? Since one has to take oneself as he is, others can only take him as he is, also.

Rancors were lulled to sleep, however, during two weeks of the trade winds' easy monotony. Since the captain had no more demands to make of them, it was possible to ignore him. France, drawing nearer, was making all their burdens lighter. Only Gicquel had not relinquished the attitude of tacit reproach in which he had been immured since Bourgoin's fall, and Rolland had never tried to break through it.

One evening Lhévéder, going into the crew's quarters where the heat was like an oven, announced. "We don't sing on this accursed ship, but we're going to sing tomorrow, and it'll be a fine song, I'm telling you, called 'Brace and brace and brace some more!' "

After days and days of limpid blueness the sky, in fact, was darkening. Heavy clouds were lifting blunt heads on the northern horizon. The breeze was commencing to sputter: sometimes it would haul abaft, sometimes ahead; then it would suddenly fall; then it would return to its first direction with driving force, and one would think one had found the trade wind again. That would last for an hour, sometimes two, with so many miles gained on the northbound course. Then, flic, flac, the sails would be beating against the masts, and the ship, with no wind to bear it up any longer, would be rolling from side to side.

One morning, at daybreak, they were lying in a dead calm cut into by rain squalls, on a sea that was quite motionless except for slow undulations, folds of still water that would swell and flatten again without apparent cause. The fo'c'sle bell sounded one stroke: ship to starboard. Then two short strokes announced another vessel on the port side. A little later, four more sailing-ships were discovered, their bowsprits turned in directions as divergent as they were involuntary: colleagues becalmed like the *Argonaute* but sunk more deeply in the "pitch-pot" of the Doldrums.

Rolland, on the poop, examined his new companions through the binoculars.

"The three-master to starboard, that has no royals, is a Rouen ship. Run up the flag and the number."

A few minutes later the vessel addressed hoisted the French colors and her own insignia: she was the *Croisset,* of Rouen, belonging to the firm of Prentout, Leblond, and Boniface. Gicquel, who with Courtier, was also on the poop, had been looking aport meanwhile and now called attention to a four-master, rather close to the *Argonaute* on the port side, which had just run up her number under the British standard.

"He is addressing us, without any doubt," he said. "We are the nearest to him."

Rolland looked, too.

"You are right," he said. "Reply, and hoist our number again."

The English craft at once hauled down its signal and ran up two flags. But the breeze had suddenly dropped, they hung slack, and it was impossible to distinguish their colors.

"Hoist 'We do not understand,' and send it up flying," Rolland directed.

This last was the order to place the flags horizontally under the peak of the spanker, so that they could be displayed in their entirety and could be read in the still air.

The English ship performed the same movement, and the men on the *Argonaute* made out the letters Y O. Roland leafed through the international code book.

"Urgent signal," he said. "Ah, here it is! 'Y O'—'We need provisions at once.' Hoist word that they are to send a boat."

He looked at the four-master through the telescope for a long time. Her wales must have been painted in stripes, but all the paint had been eaten away by rust.

"What days at sea they must have had!" he murmured.

His voice was softened by respect and a vague pity for the exhausted ship. Gicquel looked at him in surprise.

The English crew had launched a boat. The men on the *Argonaute* saw it pull away from the stern of the four-master. For a moment it would disappear in the lazy swell, then would come in sight again on the summit. A little flurry of wind sprang up on the starboard side.

"Brace everywhere, and be quick about it," Rolland called out, "so we can take advantage of this breeze and meet them."

The men dashed off to their task. Ten minutes later, the ship and the boat came together. It was not necessary to lie to; the breeze was so weak! The bos'n threw a line to the boat. And the men of the *Argonaute* gazed as if hypnotized at the emaciated faces of the British sailors, and at the enormous eyes circled with dark smudges that they lifted toward them.

The officer who was steering the boat climbed slowly and weightily aboard the ship. It was obvious to everyone that he was bracing himself for an effort. Rolland was waiting for him at the top of the pilot's ladder. He shook hands with him and led him to the cabin, where the cabin boy, who had had his orders, was bustling about with plates. Before this, however, the captain had beckoned to Gicquel.

"Have the boat's crew brought aboard and see that they are taken care of," he said. "Send two of our men to shove off the boat."

When the order had been carried out, and the British sailors had been seated in the fo'c'sle with opened cans of food and bottles of wine, Gicquel returned to the cabin. The officer was eating, great avid mouthfuls. He had started to talk, but Rolland had interrupted him.

"Have your lunch first."

He was serving him abundantly. Four pairs of eyes were watching him take his fill: Rolland, Gicquel, Courtier, and the cabin boy, who remained standing at the pantry door. But Gicquel would sometimes take his eyes off the guest to cast a glance at the captain. He had never seen him with this relaxed, almost affable, countenance. . . .

It was after refilling his guest's glass for the second time that Rolland finally asked, "Where do you come from?"

"We left Puget Sound on the 22nd of last September, for Falmouth for orders."

"The 22nd of September!"

"Yes, Captain. And as this is the 15th of April, that makes two hundred and five days that we have been at sea."

The figure fell upon the three listeners with all its crushing force and struck them motionless: they were counting up exactly what it meant; yet they had only to look at the officer, all skin and bone, his cheeks hollow, his skin gray. . . . He was Scottish, first mate of the four-master *Flying Fish*, of Glasgow. His strong, highly etched features had a dried-up look. It was impossible to guess his age, because of the wrinkles that slashed his face all over, and the indrawing of his sunken mouth, like a toothless old man's. Two hundred and five days at sea—that meant at least fifty days of famine. He explained: weeks of calm in the Pacific; then at Cape Horn the *Flying Fish* had encountered nothing but storms from the east, instead of the customary west winds that had driven the *Argonaute* along at such speed that the men had said, "Well, aren't we on parade! You'd think all the girls in Le Havre were pulling on the tow-line!" After that, in the South Atlantic, the British craft had had only calm and a head wind.

"The hull is so fouled that even with a good wind we can't reach five knots," he said. "The storerooms are empty. For eight weeks we have been on half-rations, and we have hardly enough provisions left to last ten days. Fortunately, the water tanks are full. It has rained so much!"

He smiled, a miserable smile over white gums, as he added that the captain, "a rough Scotchman," would have thought himself dishonored to go into port at Saint Helena or elsewhere, and that he had had a hard time persuading him to ask for provisions.

Rolland was nodding his head in sympathy with every sentence of this recital. Gicquel noticed that. Usually, the captain gave evidence of his attention only by his immobility. Then Rolland called Courtier, and, turning aside and speaking in a low voice while the Scot was drinking his scalding coffee, he instructed him to bring out, from the large store, casks of salt pork and flour, cases of canned meat, bags of beans, sugar, and coffee, and two casks of wine and brandy. The second mate, appalled by the amounts, murmured, "After that, Captain, we shall have barely enough for ourselves!"

"We will take in our belts if we have to," Rolland answered. "We can do it."

When Rolland had given him a translation of the list, the Scottish officer sat still for several seconds, not moving and not speaking; then he rose, reached his hand across the table, and seized Rolland's in a long hard grasp. He had brought a purse full of dollars, and he proposed paying at once. Rolland refused. That would not be "regular." He and the Scot would sign duplicate lists of the provisions delivered; the British officer would take one away with him, the other would be left on board.

"My ship-owners, when I get in, will send yours a bill for what is due them," he said, "and all will be for the best." He got up. "I am happy to have been of service to you," he added, "and, who knows . . . one good turn deserves another. . . ."

"God preserve you from that!" the Scotchman responded gravely.

They went out on the deck together. The *Argonaute's* men, under Courtier's direction, had loaded and packed the provisions on their colleague's boat. The foreign officer embarked after brief farewells.

But when they had gone a few strokes from the ship, his men lifted their oars from the water, while he stood up and bared his head.

"Three cheers for the *Argonaute* and her crew!" he cried, in his own language.

The Scottish sailors shouted out the three Hurrahs. The French crew, lined up at the rail, responded. And as if the echo of these acclamations had reached the shabby and rusted four-master, they saw her flag lowered three times. Rolland's face had taken on its everyday expression once more.

"They are fortunate, even so," he said to Gicquel, "not to have had either scurvy or beri-beri. But these English always take quantities of lemon juice aboard, and they are right."

"Captain," said Gicquel, as if he were replying to this observation, "my younger sister is to be married in May. The news reached me in Frisco. Will you give us the pleasure of your company at the wedding?"

XXX

HE HAD BACKED UP against the oak sideboard, and was holding his glass of white wine in his right hand. Men in their Sunday clothes were standing all around the room, each with his full glass. Rolland had recognized the men of the sea at a glance, because they held themselves erect without effort, and their bodies fell in a straight line, without hollows or bumps. Life at sea develops a man equally. The businessmen, and those who had retired from business, had bulging stomachs, while the farmers were bent in the back and at the knees.

The parlor-dining-room had had its straight chairs and red-upholstered armchairs—not enough to be of use on this occasion—pushed back into the corners. Meticulously painted, running free on the blue water, the four ships that Gicquel's father had commanded spread their sails upon the walls. Beneath them, in black frames with lines of gold, the general officers of the great sailing-ships folded

343

their arms below their heavy mustaches. Little ebony elephants from Ceylon marched in procession across the sideboard, and above the fireplace rose a Fujiyama in white and pink, bordered by Japanese girls with parasols.

Gicquel, now busy with his duties as best man, had presented Rolland to his mother when they arrived. Madame Gicquel had been sitting on the floor, for a hasty bit of stitching, before a tall girl in a blue tulle dress. She had got up, confused and blushing, to stammer out a few words of welcome.

"Hasn't Geneviève come down?" Gicquel had asked.

"No. She is arranging the veil."

"Geneviève is my older sister, who will be your partner," Gicquel had explained as he led Rolland into this room, where he had just been given a glass filled to the brim with white wine—no doubt to keep him from stirring. As he did not like to remain long impeded, he raised his glass:

"To the health of the bride and bridegroom!"

They all approved of this initiative and drank off half their glasses, which gave them a relative sense of ease. They could now move about, and some of them began to talk in an undertone. As for the women, they had gathered in the spacious kitchen, on the other side of the entrance hall from which the stairs led up to the second story. Pink, blue, and mauve dresses were going up and coming down this staircase, entering and leaving the kitchen. Rolland caught glimpses of them through the wide-open door, but not one of them ventured into the room reserved for the men. He spoke to his neighbor, a stocky little man tightly buttoned into a frock coat. "What is the bridegroom's profession?"

"He has just received his license as naval pharmacist. A very nice boy. He comes from here."

"The younger sister is being married before the older?"

"Geneviève? Yes. That is not because she has not had suitors; but she is hard to please. She was educated at a boarding-school."

"Then she is 'grand,' " Rolland finished the sentence.

"Grand," that meant "haughty," and he was already uneasy at the thought of being tied for the whole day to a pretentious shrew. But the man he was talking with protested. "Oh, not at all! On the contrary. Only, she won't find anyone here who comes up to her. She is my goddaughter," he added.

He seemed disposed to go on talking, but someone near the door announced, "Ah, there is the bride."

Everybody leaned forward at the same time.

They saw her only in profile as she stepped across the space of the open door. She was proceeding cautiously, half-blinded by her veil,

344

held in check by her train. But her coming downstairs was a sign that everything was beginning. The men emptied their glasses with one gulp and looked around for some place to put them. Rolland, who was nearest to the sideboard, lifted a beckoning finger and got rid of them with a few quick movements. A gentleman with a gold watch chain spoke to him, as a gesture of politeness: "At this season, Saint Cast is still not very agreeable. You ought to see it two months from now."

Then he found a way to let Rolland know that he was a member of the Municipal Council, and that he was working hard to double the number of bathing cabins on the beach.

At this moment Gicquel appeared between the two doors, with a list in his hand.

"Mademoiselle Françoise Gicquel, Monsieur Frostin," he called.

The stout man in the frock coat who had answered Rolland's questions made his way between the shoulders about him, to offer his arm to the bride.

"Who is he?" Rolland asked the city councillor.

"The bride's uncle, her mother's brother, who will give her away. Her father is dead."

"Yes, I know," Rolland said.

"Madame Le Clézio, Monsieur Yves Le Clézio."

Rolland caught sight of a gaunt youth, in the uniform of a naval officer, leaning over to give his arm to a short lady in a flame-colored dress. As he held out that left arm Rolland noticed the band of green velvet on his sleeve, the insignia of the pharmacy service.

"Madame Gicquel, Monsieur Francis Le Clézio."

Rolland recognized the lady who had welcomed him, now in a dress of black Chantilly, her countenance gently resigned, her smile absent-minded. As for the bridegroom's father, he was the broad-shouldered, well-set-up type of businessman, with a heavy mustache whose ends had been curled with a little iron.

"Go on out into the yard," Rolland's junior officer ordered the couples already formed. Then he went back to his list:

"Mademoiselle Renée Le Clézio, with me."

He called to his side a girl in a mauve dress, the bridegroom's sister.

"Mademoiselle Geneviève Gicquel, Captain Rolland."

Rolland, in his turn, stepped out from the men's company. Gicquel interrupted his roll-call to make the introduction:

"My sister Geneviève."

Rolland stood motionless before her for a second: time for that attentive glance he could never help giving to those people—men or women—who seemed to be worth attention. This time his glance was met by another, gray-blue, penetrating, precisely like his own in its alert curiosity.

"She looks like her brother," he said to himself, at once.

She did look like him, but it was a lighter replica. A little dimple softened the resolute chin, the firm lines of the mouth expanded in a smile of welcome. Her fresh and lovely color glowed under the broad tulle hat, and her flounced faille dress did not stiffen the movement of her slender body.

She is good-looking, and she is distinguished, Rolland thought.

They were two words which he had not often had occasion to apply, both together, to women he met.

"Will you permit me?" he said.

She was vainly trying, with her left hand, to button the long suède glove that reached above her elbow. As for him, he still had the agile fingers of the topman. He fastened the pearl buttons adroitly and swiftly.

Gicquel was finishing his list. But the tail-end of the procession he was forming was not lining up well. Already there was a steady chattering, a calling back and forth from one couple to another. The last guests had come to enjoy themselves, and they were starting right in.

Geneviève Gicquel had turned around toward this hearty disorder, and was observing it with an air of amusement.

"They ought to be yelled at a little," she remarked, "but André never yells."

That was true. Aboardship Rolland had never heard the junior officer raise his voice.

"You wouldn't yell either," she added.

She had turned again toward her partner and seemed to be scrutinizing him, with a half-smile.

"What makes you think that?"

"André told me."

He laughed with her, surprised at the facility with which she extricated herself from that personal interchange in which each one seeks to fill the silence, and always as cheaply as possible. She accepted the first idea that came to her, and it was precisely the one which could best make them feel natural with each other.

The procession set off at last. Even in the courtyard they were hit and harassed by the gusty wind. They had to walk bent over, the men hanging on to their hats with their right hands, the women using their free hand to keep down the billowing of their full skirts. The bride's veil flew out, sometimes almost straight up in the air, and her friends—their very words slashed by the wind—were la-

346

menting, "She's going to have it blown right off!" The train of her dress was whipping around, too, and she was trying to master that.

"Please excuse me. . . ."

Geneviève dropped Rolland's arm to run to the head of the procession and catch up her sister's veil, which was pulling her head backward. She remained beside her while the wedding party made its way over the dike, along the broad sea beach, and past the empty hotels. Rolland looked out at the water. It was a yellow-green color, with a haze of spray above it, and it broke in enormous waves on the sand.

When they reached their port of call, at the mayor's office, Geneviève came back to sit down beside him.

"Sails to be furled," she apologized.

The mayor made an amiable speech, in which he reminded his hearers that the marine service was honored by this marriage, insomuch as the daughter of a sea captain in the foreign trade, whom all Saint Cast remembered and who was as much esteemed by his fellow-townsmen as he had been loved by his crews, was being united to an officer who was putting his scientific knowledge and his personal devotion at the service of sick or injured seamen. Rolland held back a smile at the evocation of those pharmacists at military ports or arsenals with whom he had come in contact during his government service, and who had done little more than hand out licorice, ipecac, copaiba, and tincture of iodine. This title of pharmacist continued nevertheless to make its impression upon him.

The wind ceased tormenting them when they attacked the steep winding streets that led up to the church. The procession halted a moment before crossing the portico, however, for the women insisted on adjusting their broad-brimmed hats for the solemn march up the nave. When he reached his seat, Rolland cast an approving glance at the altar, piled high with arum lilies and white azaleas around the candlesticks. Then he folded his arms and listened, at first with attention, to the address, imbedded as it was in the ritual, which the priest was delivering to the couple seated behind their red velvet *prie-dieu*.

It was not long, however, before he began to be bored by the starched formulas, the vagueness, in which the exhortations lost themselves. The code said, "Fidelity, assistance; the wife must follow her husband." And these things, at least, were clear. But here an old priest with spectacles was reading in a monotonous voice, "We are the children of saints, the young Tobias said to his spouse in former days, and we must not live like those who do not know the Lord." Children of saints? Children of good honest people, probably, but no more than that.

347

Here are people, his thoughts went on, most of whom they see only three times in their lives: at their first communion, their marriage, a baby's baptism. And they bore them to death with phrases out of a book. It's as if I were to read my men the Nautical Instructions!

So then he stopped listening. His eyes, wandering about at random, encountered a dusty three-master hanging from the vaulted ceiling, and he examined it attentively. It was manifestly the work of a seaman, for no detail of construction was lacking. Cobwebs stretched a gray-toned rigging over the masts and yards.

It certainly is becalmed! he thought.

The polite immobility of the congregation came to a brisk end with the final words, "To arrive together at the same goal, which is heaven." People were stirring about, straining their heads forward or turning them to one side, so as to hear the two voices say, "Yes," and not to miss the exchange of rings. Rolland bent over slightly to look at his neighbor, and saw her set and tense, waiting for the moment of the marriage benediction, the sign of the cross above the clasped hands. He had attended the nuptial Mass of more than one colleague, before this, and he had remarked the attraction which the ritual gestures of the sacrament exercised upon girls, their quivering attention, as if they were observing an extraordinary metamorphosis that was ready to touch them, too. But when the rings had been exchanged, Geneviève turned toward him with a somewhat twisted smile, and clouded eyes. That she should thus have spontaneously offered her emotion to him was something that filled his mind until the end of the Mass.

The hotel at which the reception was held fronted the beach with a long salon, its ocean side all glass, where tables had been set in a horseshoe formation. Some of the guests went at once to the windows: these were the inland people, many of whom had never seen a stormy sea and were now gazing at it, both curious and as if reproving in the face of the waves' frenzied charge. As for the seafaring men themselves, they merely flung a glance at the water in order to judge the force of the wind. That done, they turned their backs. The heavy weather was none of their affair this time! They were the first to make the tour of the tables to find the cards which would indicate their place.

Rolland, seating himself at the table of honor, caught sight of the tumultuous line of the water, on the level with the windows opposite.

"Mama and I would have preferred a garden," Geneviève declared, as she unfolded the bishop's hat of her napkin. She made a motion of her chin toward the greenish chaos, streaked all over with

348

spray, that spread out beyond the windows. He had just been thinking that this hotel, "with a view of the sea," had been selected in honor of the marine service, and that really that was not necessary. . . . "But, you see," she went on, "we had no choice. All the hotels with a possible salon of that kind are closed."

"Are you afraid of seasickness?" he asked.

"Oh, frightfully! But, after all, not here! Only, Mama and I were thinking of André, and all our captain friends, even of you, who would perhaps have preferred to lunch with a different outlook."

"Don't you know yet," he demanded, with pretended severity, "that the sailor cannot do without the sea: that he misses something when he isn't seeing it?"

She shook her head.

"Ah, no! I am the daughter of a sea captain. And when Papa came back from a voyage he had only one idea: to get into the country. At least, for the first days. . . . You aren't like that?"

"Oh, me, the country—I very soon get bored by it," he had to confess. And he kept himself from adding, "For that matter, I get bored everywhere."

"Perhaps you don't open your eyes wide enough," she suggested, "and only look inside yourself or at the ground under your feet. So you see nothing but the dust, and it ends by getting inside you."

He thought this over.

"Perhaps that is true," he admitted.

"Certainly it is true!" she said.

He was amazed by the singular turn taken quite naturally, and also quickly, in a conversation which he had anticipated as the last word in banality.

"And how did you learn that?" he asked.

"Undoubtedly, by walking around."

He laughed again, and remembered that he had not laughed for months. As she was interesting him more and more, he undertook to question her about her likes and dislikes, her life at Saint Cast. She responded with the same easy vivacity, and he was conscious of that sense of solace that his ships gave him when they were running with the wind in fair weather. He nodded his head toward the newly-weds opposite them, and ventured to ask, "And when will it be your turn?"

"I am not in a hurry, you know," she replied.

"Yes, I know already that you are hard to please."

This time she looked at him gravely. "Am I wrong in that?"

"Certainly not! I do not like to pay compliments, but it is not a compliment to say that you have a right to be exacting. All the same—how do you see him, the husband of your dreams?"

"Ah, now you are too inquisitive!"

She was shutting herself up with the suddenness of a shellfish, terrified because, if she replied, she would now have to reply, "Since this morning, he has been like you." Her confusion was increased by the fear that Rolland might have noticed it. She recovered herself, however, and in a low voice advised him, "You should talk a little with your neighbor on the other side. She is Françoise's godmother," she added. "Her husband was a captain in the coastal trade."

He turned to the lady without too good grace, and for something to say, remarked, "Mademoiselle Geneviève has just told me that you are the bride's godmother, Madame."

Then he gave a semblance of listening to a recital of the relations between the two families for the past twenty years, and a lament that the bride had been so buffeted by the wind on the way to the mayor's office. At the first moment of silence he introduced his other association: "Your husband was a coastal captain?"

This recital was even longer: the entire career of a "crab-crusher," two shipwrecks, and the praises of the ship-owners—"not employers . . . friends." Then, in order to be polite, the bride's godmother asked, "And you, Captain, you were commander of the ship on which André was the mate?"

An earnest, though rapid, eulogy of Gicquel followed, and then Rolland went back to Geneviève, whose attention was still lingering with an uncle of the bridegroom.

"Mission accomplished," he announced in an undertone.

She beckoned to a waitress and had his wine glass refilled.

"In that case, you have a right to the double ration," she said.

But at the end of the table a young man leaned forward to speak to her:

"You were born on the Pacific Ocean, weren't you, Geneviève?"

She, also, leaned forward, to nod in assurance that this was certainly true. The young man turned back toward his partner. "I told you so!" he said.

Now Rolland echoed, "You were born on the Pacific?"

"Of course I was! So, you see, in priority of sailing, I'm away ahead of you!"

He was no longer joking. "Your mother went to sea?"

"Yes, she made five voyages with my father. It was on the third one that I was born. Papa hoped to get to San Francisco in time, but I was there ten days early. I have always loathed being late."

"You say that your mother made five voyages?" he echoed.

"Yes, five. One of them lasted eighteen months, and she went around Cape Horn four times."

He could not believe it. This shy and retiring woman, so easily upset when he had found her taken up with her mending that morning, and whom he was now looking at across the table: silent, reflective, hardly ever raising her concerned and over-sensitive eyes. . . . She, more than any of the others, was the one he would have imagined as confined to her home, subject to the routine of housekeeping, resigned to absences and patient waiting. Instead of that, four voyages around the Horn, and a baby born on the Pacific!

"One would never suspect it," he said. "She has such a gentle air." And to himself he added, "So weak, so defenseless. . . ."

Geneviève looked at him in astonishment.

"But that is no obstacle!" she said. "It is a question of figures. She reckoned it up: if she had not gone to sea, she would have lived with Papa only four years out of twenty. It was we children who made it necessary for her to give it up, when there came to be three of us."

"And your father never raised any objections to taking her with him?"

"But Papa was as devoted to her as she was to him."

"No doubt; but a wife aboardship always complicates the situation for a captain, with the officers, the crew, the ship's owners."

She shook her head.

"On the contrary, I believe that it can simplify it. The shipping firm does not allow a woman to be taken on a voyage unless they are sure of her, and of her husband. When she keeps to her place, the crew respects and esteems her. The men realize, you see, that life aboard is not gay for her. To remain cloistered for months, not even on the ship but in the stern of the ship, without ever going out on deck . . . sewing, embroidering, reading. . . . Mama has told us how one evening, off the Cape of Good Hope, when a hurricane was blowing up, the helmsman said to her, 'You certainly would be better off this evening in your house at Saint Cast than with us, Madame Gicquel. Well, the fellows have sent me to tell you that you mustn't worry: they're going to bring you out of this bad blow, as they have out of the others.' They understood, I assure you."

She was becoming very animated, leaning toward him to meet his unyielding gaze.

"But in a hurricane, precisely, nothing would disturb her husband more than her being there," he said.

"Why? Because he would be fighting for her, as well as for his ship and his men? I am quite certain, on the contrary, that this would double his courage. Disturb him? In a bad storm, when Papa ordered, 'Everyone up on duty, you go below,' she would obey just as promptly as the men who leaped into the shrouds. And she would stay shut up for days without seeing him again, until the danger was over and the damage had been repaired."

Rolland looked at Madame Gicquel again. She was peeling an orange, carefully. He tried to imagine her shut up alone, in the depths of a ship assaulted by storm: thrown against the partition walls, beset by the furious blows the sea was striking above her head, under her feet, against each side. He did not succeed in imagining it; but since it had happened, he had to admit it. To go from that to accepting it—

"And during this time your father, up there, could not keep from thinking, If we don't get out of this, I shall have killed her."

She retorted quickly, "Up there, as below, they were thinking the same thing: Our lives are united: we save them or lose them together."

He refrained from replying, "That does not come from your mother: it comes from you, and it comes from romance." He merely put to one side what seemed to him to be only a phrase and said, "The captain should live better than the men, in the matter of food, lodging, attendance: better, but not differently. His officers and his crew should not be able to say, 'Why does he have his wife with him, when we don't? He is at the service of the ship, like everyone else.' "

She flung back at him, her face rosy with indignation, "But who is telling you that the service of the ship loses? Everything depends on the wife. When Mama left the *Chanard,* there were men who cried."

"I don't doubt it. But, you see, sentiment and navigation don't go together." And he was amazed to hear himself adding, "Unfortunately. . . ."

The bridal couple, each holding a glass of champagne, had started on the tour of the tables. The bride had just torn up her veil and was giving everyone a little piece of it. The women were fastening theirs to their corsage, the men were putting theirs through their buttonhole. Françoise had reached her sister, and as they held each other in a long embrace Rolland saw on Geneviève's face the same smile close to tears with which she had entrusted him in the church. In a hearty good-fellow's tone which he did not recognize, he pointed out, "She is not lost. *She* isn't sailing. . . ."

Geneviève thanked him with a glance for closing the debate in this fashion, but she answered him back: "Do you think so? Marriage is always a sailing, and for a long voyage."

After this, it was time for singing. The songs ranged from "Golden Grain" to "When I Follow the Horses." A big red-faced man was a great hit with "The Farmer's Automobile." Some girls, choking over the last syllables, sang "Good Evening, Madame Moon," and

"If God Gave the Flowers Speech." When from spicy suggestions the songs veered into broad ambiguities, Rolland thought it his duty to murmur, "They are going it rather strong!"

"Yes," she replied, with tranquil indulgence, "but without that it wouldn't be a real wedding party."

They spent the last part of the afternoon dancing, and began again after dinner. Rolland, like all sailors, danced well; but from the first polka, the supple body he was leading gave him a surprise. He knew women allowed themselves to be carried along, passive, fitting themselves to their partner and following him without even thinking about it; and he considered them the best. He had also, at wedding parties like this one, had to dance with stiff-bodied girls who held back from him, and with stupid ones who, having learned a step, are unwilling to relinquish it and are set against all imagination. He had never encountered this harmony, in which the woman he was dancing with remained herself, yet obeyed his movements so willingly and so quickly that the least directions were followed almost before they were guessed. They were not talking, simply enjoying themselves wholly.

He did speak, however, as they passed one of the broad bay-windows, now lashed with rain by the storm.

"Listen how it's blowing," he said.

"Yes," she responded. "It's nice in here."

She spoke with a certain happy relish, and for the first time he wondered if he himself counted for anything in her delight. This led him to the realization that she alone had counted for him since morning, and that it seemed to him that he knew her well, from this day.

"For once, I am lucky," he declared, as he sat down beside her after a waltz.

The look she gave him was somewhat embarrassed, because she had guessed what he was going to say.

"Yes, I am lucky," he repeated, "in having been given you, and no one else, as a partner."

She blushed.

"But I am lucky, too," she said in a low voice, and then: "Oh, here is a skating step! You know it?"

This dance was no longer, like the polkas, mazurkas and waltzes, a dance of separate couples, but a line that would glide from one side to the other when the music of the mechanical piano broke its rhythm and turned into a round: a slow promenade, side by side, the couples merely holding each other by the hand. Rolland was not enthusiastic about this march in file.

"It's a procession," he said.

"Yes, but it is very restful," she responded.

Just then a servant came in, walked to the center of the room—left empty by the low swaying line of dancers—and sought out someone in the company. When she discovered him—a clean-shaven man with graying hair, in a tight black coat, who was attacking his side steps with a thrust of his shoulders as if he were trying to break in a door—she beckoned. He left the line, taking his partner with him, listened with an air of vexation to what the maid was saying, questioned her briefly, and then stood planted in the middle of the room, in what seemed to be a state of indecision. Geneviève had turned around, and was keeping her eyes fixed on him.

"He is the master of the life-boat," she said. "They have come to get him. There is certainly some vessel in danger."

"You have a life-boat here?"

"Yes: one of the boats of the Breton Rescue and Hospital Association."

Rolland was looking with a sincere commiseration at the man standing there, his brow wrinkled with annoyance as he waited for the end of the dance before speaking.

"I can understand that he is not enjoying this," he averred.

As soon as the piano stopped, everyone rushed up to the life-boat master and asked questions. He knew nothing but what he had just been told: a boat had sent up distress flares in the offing beyond Fort La Latte; the signal station had given the alarm to the life-boat crew and relayed word on to him, the master. With a shrug of his shoulders, he concluded, "I must go and see."

Regrets were pouring out all around him, and he responded to them with an air of disillusionment: "It is always like that!"

Quite naturally, it was the guest forced to leave the party that they felt sorry for. The sailors, especially, were putting themselves in his place.

"They ought to have been able to choose another day," one of them declared. And continued, "To be sure, they had no choice!"

The women were silent. The thought of the boat lost in the darkness had perhaps crossed some of their minds. For the first time that evening they were hearing the muffled booming of the waves. But most of them, in their hearts, were deploring the chill which the news had thrown upon the party. They were afraid it might spoil the pleasure that was left between now and daybreak. Their feeling was one of unseemliness; and when the boat's master went away, after pressing several hands and with a last shrug of his shoulders, they had a sense of deliverance, as if he had taken with him this misfortune which, for them, was no more than inopportune. The men, however, felt obliged to station themselves along the windows,

354

their foreheads against the black panes. They could not see anything, and they knew it; but this was a sort of polite gesture.

"The boat can't even be launched," someone said.

This futility of all succor seemed to absolve them from the sin of enjoying themselves. For decency's sake the floor was left empty for three-quarters of the player piano cylinder, then two dancers stepped out. In the mazurka that followed, couples came back to the floor one by one, and the ball was soon under way as gaily as before.

Rolland had not suggested to Geneviève that they join the rest. For his own part, he would not have seen any impropriety in it. His thought, like that of all the seafaring men present, was that nothing could be done, that everything possible had been done already; but he felt from his first glance at her that his partner was still, so to speak, paralyzed by the intrusion of the shipwrecked men into the celebration. Even though for all the other guests they had just been dissolved into the night, they continued to weigh upon her. He found this attitude more acceptable when she explained:

"Seven years ago, when the *Hilda* was lost on the Portes, the dead were washed in on the beach for two days. One morning the men who were looking for them brought one body to our house, while they waited for the wagon that was taking them to the town hall. It was a young man, and his eyes were open."

An emotion of sensitive youth, which was sweeping over her again, as vivid as ever, tonight, and which she could not control.

He tried to reassure her. "You know flares—that may say everything or nothing. It all depends on the man who sends them off. Some men get panicky and call for help when they could perfectly well get out of it by themselves."

"And we can't know anything!"

He realized that she would not be free, now, of the thought of the unknown men fighting for their lives on the other side of that dark window. She was one of those rare persons whom the misfortunes of others fix to and hold fast. But as for knowing whether she should be congratulated or pitied on that account—! More out of consideration for her anxiety than for any actual interest in the men tossing on the wrecked ship, he suggested, "Suppose we try to get some information? Will you come with me?"

They left the ball-room, crossed a corridor, passed through the hotel entrance hall, and came out on the veranda above the stoop. The rain had stopped, but a raging wind hit them in the face and flung them back against the glass-paned door, which Rolland had already had a hard time opening. The glow from the lighted windows showed them two women in white aprons standing at the

355

farther end of the veranda, beside a man in boots and yellow oilskins that gleamed in the light. They went up to the group, and Rolland asked, "Do they know who it is?"

Put on the alert by the sharp voice, the man turned around.

"No. It was from the signal station that they saw the flares, about an hour ago. There were three of them sent up. They must have been half a mile east of the Cape." He turned again to the women. "That would put them not far from the Banc de l'Etendrée," he said.

They bowed their heads in agreement. The man went back to Rolland.

"That is a shelf that runs along for a mile, east of Fréhel. They have a verse about it here: it's a bad place to get by when there's a strong wind."

"Will the life-boat be able to get out?" Rolland asked.

"If it hasn't gone, it's because it couldn't."

The two women corroborated this, with the same air of concern.

"Anyway," the man concluded, "we shan't know anything until daylight." He shuffled his feet. "Now that I've done my errand, I'll go back."

"It's kept you rushing," one of the women said.

"And there's nothing doing with a bicycle in weather like this; it just makes it worse," the man commented. "Well then, good evening. Or rather, good morning." It was three o'clock. "And thank you," he added, as he went down the steps.

They must have given him a good ballast in the kitchen.

When he reached the street, he turned toward Rolland and Geneviève and put a finger to his cap; then he took his bicycle, which he had left at the foot of the steps, and went off with it in tow. When he had vanished around the corner of the hotel, the two maids went inside.

Rolland took Geneviève's arm gently. "Don't stay here: you'll be frozen." He led her to the other end of the portico, where the jutting of a wall made a sheltered angle. "You know," he said, "they may be peacefully anchored now in Fresnaye Bay. The tide would carry them there."

Then he took her hands, which had grown very cold.

"Aren't you ashamed to be so nervous—you who are twice the daughter of Cape Horn veterans?" he said. "Wait at least until you are sure there are casualties."

"I know," she answered. "I always have to torment myself beforehand."

He let go of her hands, but only to seize her shoulders and give her a friendly shake.

356

"That *is* clever, isn't it? What a lecture I'd give you, if I had the right!"

"You may. I know that I am very silly sometimes," she confessed.

"If it is only sometimes!" he echoed. Then his voice changed. "Anyway, what I can predict for you is that you will never marry a sailor."

But she replied to this briskly, "Why not? Because I worry about them? But you, you never worry, do you?"

That was true. Danger tightened his nerves and muscles, fortified him, sometimes irritated him so much that it drove him to distraction; but it never worried him. He was no longer so sure that this was a quality of strength.

"No," he had to agree. "Not enough."

"And I, too much," she said.

"That would make an average, don't you think?"

He had asked the question in a low voice, and gravely. He did not dare hope for a reply. But she murmured, "No—because with you, you see, I am not afraid any more."

He took her arm and held her against him with a pressure which he was forcing himself not to make too strong, though there was a buzzing in his temples, and he would have liked to crush her close. She did not resist him until they were breast against shoulder, and her hair was touching his cheek. Then she said, in a low voice, "Let us go in. They will think we have been carried away by the squall."

But she caught hold of his wrist as she freed herself, and only let it go as they re-entered the ball-room.

Madame Gicquel caught sight of them and came forward.

"Your sister is waiting to say goodbye to you. You will excuse her, Captain?"

She dragged Geneviève after her toward the end of the salon, cutting across the couples who were still dancing. They disappeared through the door of the anteroom where the bride and the bridegroom must be waiting, impatient to slip away.

To feel yourself alone—he knew what that meant. But to find yourself alone again—he realized to his dismay that that was still worse. . . . At the same time, he was oppressed by the forlorn ennui of the tail-end of a party, the dull lassitude of those bad hours of early morning that are always the most difficult on watch.

He hardly saw her again before he left. When she and her mother returned to the party they were monopolized by others, who were about to leave. All she could do was send him a smile of apology from a distance. The Saint Cast guests all left together, to get a few hours' sleep. The country relatives wanted to be home by daybreak,

357

"for the animals." There remained only a small group standing about idly, those whom the Gicquel family was obliged still to be responsible for, in view of the next day. Rolland, himself, asked Gicquel about a carriage that could take him to Matignon, where he could make connections for Nantes. The second mate went to find out, and came back to say, "Our cousins from Hénanbihen have a place, Captain, and they will drop you off; but they are ready to leave now."

Rolland stood stock still where he was. Gicquel, receiving no answer, was looking at him in surprise, which was intensified when he saw suddenly on his face that concentrated expression that used to hold his features taut before venturing upon a dangerous maneuver.

"Your sister is not thinking of marrying, is she, Gicquel?" he blurted out.

The second mate also let some time go by before he responded.

"She has been sought in marriage several times," he said at last. "Up to now, she has refused. She will only have a man who absolutely pleases her."

Rolland registered this with a movement of his head. He was keeping his eyes on the squares of the parquet floor. When he spoke, it was slowly. "She pleases me very much: even absolutely, as you say. Will you take it in hand to tell her that?"

Gicquel contented himself with bowing his head, as he used to do on the poop when he received an unforeseen and surprising order. Rolland raised his eyes, and looked at him.

"She does not know me; but you do. You will say to her what you think ought to be said. I know that you are just."

There was an uncertain smile on the junior officer's face.

"What I might be able to say to her—it isn't that! She will decide for herself, and by herself. Be that as it may, I will speak to her this very day."

"Thank you. Then write me. You have my address."

They shook hands. Rolland went to get his overcoat, then came back to make his farewells. He thanked Madame Gicquel "for the delightful day," and assured Geneviève of his "pleasure in making her acquaintance." She replied that "all the pleasure had been hers," and he went out, to find the carriage in the street and the horse, head down, tapping the ground with its right hoof at what Rolland recognized as almost equal intervals.

The maid looked around the room and walked straight up to the master of the lifeboat. "They are asking for you, Monsieur Taillefer."

358

Rolland turned, as if he had been hit on the shoulder.

"Oh no," he said. "That isn't beginning again!"

"Not at all," Geneviève assured him. "It's his bottled cider he wants to give us a taste of. He sent the boy to get the bottles. This is just to let him know that they have come."

"That suits me better!" Rolland said.

"Does it all seem to you too much the same?" she asked, with an anxious smile.

"Yes, a little," he confessed.

"It doesn't to me," she reflected. "I know very well that one might think we had gone back to six weeks ago. But for me that is not possible. I have come too long a way since."

Everything had happened with the haste usual to sailors ashore: so much so that it was really as if someone had said to Rolland at the end of the first wedding dinner, "Change four chairs around, we're beginning again." He would then have found himself where he now was, in the seat of the bridegroom.

For actually it had been the same thing again: Gicquel summoning the guests, in the hallway; young Tobias in the church; the luncheon in the same hotel salon. The very fact that there was a change in the menu was evidence of someone's saying, "Look out! At least don't give them exactly the same things to eat!" So Marenne oysters were replacing lobster. Rolland stepped back into reality, this evening, only when he looked at "his wife." Why was that not enough to make him forget the rest and find everything different, as she did?

At Nantes, two days after the wedding party, he had received Gicquel's reply to his proposal: one page in which the writer was unable to conceal his surprise, almost embarrassment, over having to transmit so prompt an acceptance. He, too, had felt suddenly chilled by the ease of his victory. All his distrust had risen to the surface again, with the fear of having stumbled without looking into an open trap, of having fallen—as at Val André—into the arms of a girl who was only too glad to rush up at the first beckoning signal. He had sent word that he would come to Saint Cast—that was a matter of course; but he had said to himself, "It's to take another look."

She herself had opened the door. And with his first glance at her he had told himself, "No; it was a mistake."

In her simple dress, and with her everyday coiffure, she was, to be sure, less pretty than he remembered her; but what disturbed him especially was that anxious, helpless air she had, like Barquet on the deck of the *Galatée* years before. It made him hard now, as it had then. It was only when she had turned around to lead him into the house that he had been touched, ever so lightly, by a feeling of remorse.

In the dining room the constraint had at once become unbearable. Gicquel, already warned by the reserved tone of Rolland's letter, had grasped the situation from the first moment and, almost scornfully, had thrown him a buoy.

"I have got the papers ready that you asked me for, Captain. But I could have sent them to you, without your putting yourself out."

That was to say: "You now have a pretext for having come. Make use of it to get away." He was, indeed, adding, "I will go and get them for you."

He rose to go up to his room, from which he would soon have to come down with a bunch of folders. But at this point Madame Gicquel intervened, with that slow-moving sweetness which must have been her real defense. She explained that she was trying to sell her husband's cutter.

"The only thing is, André and I don't agree about the price we should ask. I think he is putting it too high. If you would be willing just to glance at it, Captain, and give us your opinion, you would be doing us a service. Geneviève could take you to see it."

This was cornering him, to have it out. He realized that, and got up.

"I shall be very glad, Madame. . . ."

He was going to make an end of it, to use the sentence he had all ready: "I have thought it over. I am afraid that I could not make you happy." And then he would go away. It was always that instinct in him, of the fish that circles around the bait and swims off as soon as it suspects the hard curve of the hook beneath it.

Then they went out, and Geneviève spoke. "It was I who told Mama that tale of the cutter. From the tone of your letter, I understood; and when you came in, I could no longer believe that my reading between the lines might have been mistaken. But what I want to know is what has happened between your speaking to André and now. . . ."

This was no longer either the tone or the attitude of helplessness which he had felt on his arrival. She was not merely resigning herself. He would not be pulling himself out through a loophole. There would be conflict. She was clinging to him already, in all those dreams of a life together which well-behaved girls are so quick to spin from the moment of the first advances. Even more than at the wedding and the ball, she was finding him handsome to look at; his athlete's body, as he stood upright in the full sunshine, cast a spell upon her. Her questions had taken on the trenchant brevity of the orders which Rolland, or her own father, would fling out from the poop, under the threat of a hurricane.

"Has somebody told you some story about me?"

He had thought he might be listening to the sewing-girls at Saint-Sylvère, and he had indicated that, rather rudely.

"I know everything that can be invented, but I do not know what you are capable of believing," she had replied. "Is there someone else, whom you do not want to, or cannot, leave?"

"Of course not!"

He had been reassured by seeing her make a false start in this way, and he did not realize that she was clearing the ground for the attack.

"Then you have been mistaken in me and in yourself."

"How is that?"

"About me, it is quite simple. The moment you came in, you said to yourself, 'That's all it is!' Oh, yes! As for yourself, you have been mistaken because you took a passing whim for a real emotion."

She was walking along beside him, keeping step, but this time she was not raising her head, as she had recommended his doing on his country strolls. Her eyes were on the pebbles under their feet. And she continued:

"When André spoke to me—and he did that as soon as you had gone —I said to him, as I am saying to you, 'He is mistaken, about me and about himself.' 'Then it is No,' André said. And I answered, 'It is Yes. If it doesn't come off, what do I risk? A hurt to my vanity? Sorrow? It hasn't gone very far yet.' Then André said, 'And if it should come off, do you realize that what you are risking is your whole life? Because I warn you, with the captain, the game wouldn't be played out on the wedding night.' You see, I am telling you everything. And I answered, 'That is why I am saying Yes. If it were that sort of game, would it be worth the trouble?' "

He had been listening to her, set blinking by the clear light she was throwing on herself and on him: a light that would tolerate no shadow. While he, the man, was about to involve himself in tortuous phrases about life and happiness, she was cutting right to the quick, averring that a future with him would be hazardous and that she was drawn by that risk. But what he had got from this was only the opportunity to introduce the sentence he had been going over in his mind since he left Nantes:

"Since your brother has warned you, I can only repeat his warning —and that is why I came. I do not feel that I am capable of making a woman happy."

She had smiled; but the eyes she fixed upon him made him turn away his own.

"That is what has to be brought up at all costs: it makes it possible for men to keep their fine roles, and for silly women to believe themselves so precious that one daren't touch them. Only, the men who really think that think it once for all, and do not make demands. Don't you agree?"

She was driving him out from under cover, sternly. He said nothing, but his face had hardened, as it did whenever he was put in the wrong. She continued, this time for herself:

"What you have just said, what a man says to free himself from an engagement or to avoid entering into one, I have never believed in. Happiness is not something a woman takes ready-made from her husband; it does not drop down like the monthly pay. Happiness is something to be conquered, to be deserved and defended. Otherwise it is the happiness of the feeding-trough. You don't believe in that kind of happiness either. No, that is not the reason. . . ."

"And what is the reason, according to you?"

She hesitated, and he insisted: "Well?"

"It is that you have always been alone, and you do not feel capable of living any other way."

The repercussion of the words, within him, had been like the shock of a collision. For a moment he had hoped that they were only words, that she had not actually penetrated to such a depth. He had answered, rather jeeringly, "It seems to me, on the contrary, that that would be a reason for trying to live differently."

She had shaken her head emphatically. "No. You have got the habit of it, and then, there is pride in it; you shudder at it, too, at certain moments, but perhaps fundamentally you need it. That would be your misfortune."

Every word was striking home, and this instinctive awareness terrified him. Who was she, this mere girl who had never lived at all, to decipher, as in an open book, what he himself hardly discerned and had never been willing to acknowledge? He remembered Madame Gicquel, her mother, who behind that tranquil forehead and those dreamy eyes was turning over the memories of hurricanes; and he recalled Gicquel's silences aboardship, and their resonance.

"In that case," he said, almost with violence, "if it is incurable, if you thought that—"

"I should have tried to join you. You would only have known it if I had succeeded, by perceiving that you were no longer alone. You see, I had plenty of self-confidence!"

It was impossible to treat this as romantic dreaming. For him, it was as clear and precise as a route traced out on a map. Gicquel's sister knew exactly where she wanted to go; she had indicated the position with a sureness that staggered him. He suddenly remembered the time in Mother Girard's café in Thio when, after examining his unresponsive countenance in a mirror and inspecting it as if it were a stranger's, he had concluded that he could only actually attract those women that liked difficulty. But were there any such women, he had asked himself? Well, there was at least one!

"I wasn't worth the trouble that you would have brought upon yourself," he said.

It was what he was really thinking as he looked at her walking along beside him, so slender, her face bent down: that face which nevertheless had given in to nothing, neither to regret nor to bitterness, but which kept its balance of gentleness and firmness; the face which her mother must have presented, in the old days, to the hurricanes of Cape Horn.

"No," he had repeated with emphasis. "I wasn't worth it. I did not know that a little while ago. I am sure of it now."

She had looked at him with eyes that had the same expression as his own when someone was trying to trespass upon his domains or dispute his decisions.

"That," she said, "was my affair." Then her head had drooped again, and her voice had fallen in discouragement, as she concluded: "At bottom, it is much more simple. I attracted you one evening. I do not attract you any more. There is nothing you can do about that!"

This was no longer true. He was going to say so, when he would have straightened out all the contradictions that were jostling against one another inside his stubborn skull. He realized that every second of silence was an insulting confirmation of that repudiation which she was attributing to him, and which had long since been left behind. But how to explain it? What to seize hold of in this whirlpool, among these fears, regrets, desires, these leaps and these recoils?

But she was speaking again, in a thin voice which seemed already weakened by distance. "Then, when we go in, I will say, 'We have not been to see the cutter, but we have talked together frankly and we realize that we are not suited to each other.' That will be best."

He had had the sense of seeing her move away from him, grow smaller on the road; and he had been submerged by panic, the first emotion in his life that went beyond his control. If his ship had been sinking under him, he would not have stretched out his hands toward a vanishing succor with such despair. He had caught her by both arms, and drawn her back to him so violently that he had seen a momentary gleam of fear in her eyes; and his voice had been choking as he enjoined her:

"Stay with me!"

They had taken refuge in a window embrasure, tired of these dances in which they had been joining inattentively, as a matter of convention. He was keeping his gaze upon her, a gaze which, when he fixed her with it like this, seemed to isolate the man and woman who shared it from all the rest of the world. Such looks as this were what she had had from him—these and a few words—during the swift weeks of their engagement. The words were not words of love, but of astonishment: surprise at feeling himself no longer the same, at watching the slow raising up of a new man; a free man, but one who still moved cautiously, not yet able to convince himself that everything that weighed upon him and constricted him had been lightened and relaxed. He was no longer "all hard knots," as his men used to say. With her, near her, he was savoring a sense of felicitous ease, still interrupted by suspicions and harshnesses which she would perceive at the first indication and would arrest with a tender or whimsical word. She would leave him, after this, aghast at having sunk into the void, and astonished, too, at being controlled so simply.

"I cannot believe that a month ago I did not know you," he said, as he had said before. "It seems to me that you have always been there."

"There should be a name for that," she responded.

His only reply was to seize her hand in a pressure so hard that it bruised the delicate fingers, and so long that he did not let her go until he saw her nostrils contract, her clear eyes fixed in their gaze. And once again he murmured the appeal that swept her off her feet more completely than any cry of passion:

"Stay with me!"

"You can leave now, you know. . . ."

They turned around. Madame Gicquel repeated, "You can leave now. It is one o'clock."

They waited for the beginning of a polka which launched the entire wedding party once more upon the dancing floor, and then the three slipped away in single file, Geneviève ahead; they passed the row of chairs and disappeared behind the pantry door. There, trestle tables were piled high with dirty dishes, and they had to watch their step so as not to upset the empty bottles on the floor. Madame Gicquel stopped them in front of a set of shelves heaped up with white napkins.

"You haven't forgotten anything?" she asked.

"I don't think so," Geneviève answered.

"I've put your tailored suit in the big bag."

"Yes."

"Goodbye, then."

Mother and daughter kissed, but the mother's tone had dictated what the kiss was to be: they were to remain within the framework of every day, of the simple and the ordinary. They were three people who detested effusiveness, who felt its emptiness and sensed the impropriety of sentimental tears.

"Goodbye, Mama," Rolland said, in his turn.

"Goodbye, Pierre."

They kissed each other three times, as was the custom in Brittany. A maidservant was waiting for them, a stout woman whose own eyes were moist. She went ahead of them through the corridors. They were to spend the rest of the night at the hotel before taking the little trolley, very early in the morning, for Plancoët. There they would board the train for Paris, a city which seemed to Rolland more distant and more exotic than all the great seaports of the world.

There was a pleasant blaze in the fireplace of their room, and Geneviève went up to it. "That's a good idea," she said, "having a fire."

"Yes, the nights are not always warm in May."

They remained standing side by side for a moment, looking at the leaping flame. Then quietly, without saying anything and as if she had been alone, Geneviève moved away toward the other end of the room. Rolland turned around, saw her hands going to the neck of her white corsage, beginning to unfasten the hooks. His eyes went back to the logs in the fireplace.

Under his feet he heard a sort of cadenced rumble, which was the steps of the dancers, interspersed with the crash of cymbals. These outbursts were all that came to him from the grand piano, whose sound was decanted, so to speak, through the ceilings in between. After the long-drawn-out pageant and the prolonged meals, he was still feeling only the lassitude of the end of a watch. But he knew himself, and he remained on guard so as not to let himself be surprised and carried away by a bit of flesh dimly glimpsed. He had too much experience with those crashing storms that would fling him bestially upon a woman as a ship is dashed upon the belly of the sea. What was the use of having knocked about so much, if he were not to be master of himself when the time came? All those other women had paid the price for this one, that with her it might be different. . . .

He did not turn around until he heard her getting into bed: a canopied bed hung with faded rep curtains. She was waiting for him, lying back in the pillows, motionless, her hands resting on the cool sheet. He controlled himself to the point of merely taking one of those hands and holding it for a moment between his own, as he

365

stood leaning over her. But with a sudden movement she freed herself, flung her bare arms about his neck, and drew him to her with a force that astonished him.

"But come," she whispered, in a voice vibrant with impatience. "Come. . . . I love you. . . ."

XXXI

"NOW REALLY, Captain, this has got hold of you like a cramp!"

Monsieur Hamon, the manager for the shipping firm, was striding around his office, his hands behind his back, his heels pounding on the floor. He was a ruddy-faced man, with the shoulders of a bos'n, and anger had the effect of puffing him up. He had stopped in his march to blurt out his comment. Now he started walking again.

"I know of at least three, you understand, who have broken their husband's careers. The first—a damn pretty woman she was, too, with hair that came down to her heels—she got bored, and so she took to drinking. Then he would beat her. And when she would show up with a bump on her face he would explain, to the men as well as to the officers, 'A sudden roll; the door hit her over the eye.' But she, behind him, would call out, 'A door! It was that dirty swine there!' What do you say to that for a trick? There were others who were more accommodating. One I had business with used to give the sailors an extra wine ration as a bonus for picking up his wife in all the corners of the ship. The men ended up by stretching ropes in front of her feet, when she was drunk, so she would fall; then they would set her on her keel again and collect their double ration. The third case was worse. She would have shaved an egg; and she forced the captain to cut down on food until the men revolted."

As if the demonstration had precluded further debate, Monsieur Hamon paused once more and fixed his heavy gaze upon Rolland. He met an expression of such complete scorn that he apologized, but with an obviously irritated effort.

"Naturally, there is no question that any of that could have the slightest connection with Madame Rolland. What I have said is merely to show you that the companies may sometimes have peculiar reasons for not liking to have women sailing on their ships. But—"

His steps followed the rhythm of his speech again, as if to attest his determination to regain the ground he had lost.

"But quite aside from these incidents, which, I know as well as you do, are exceptions," he continued, "a woman aboard, as discreet and tactful as you will, is always out of place. You know the old rule: 'The captain owes his ship all his time and all his moments.' It has not changed." He repeated, stressing it, the deliberate pleonasm of the old text: "All his time and all his moments, so as to proceed steadily and swiftly. You know captains, as I do, who, with their wives aboard, lay to whenever the wind gets fresh, so as to keep things calm. Why does the Bordes firm not want any women on their new ships? Because a woman cuts down speed more than a fouled hull."

Rolland interrupted at this point, dryly: "In the matter of speed, it seems to me that up to now I have served you rather well. This might be a good time not to forget it."

Monsieur Hamon moved his jaws to swallow this morsel.

"Exactly! You have always made excellent crossings. We have been so far from forgetting it that you are now in command of the company's finest four-master. It is that which makes me fear—"

"That I will come in at the tail end of the line because I take my wife with me? Listen, Monsieur Hamon: what I am going to say is not for the purpose of wringing an authorization from you, since you will give me that in any case—" He interrupted himself long enough to nod in response to the sudden right-about turn of the shipping agent, who was scrutinizing him closely. "Yes, you will give it to me," he repeated. "So it is not that which I am concerned with now, but with my next visit here, to your office, when I come back from this voyage. There is one thing, then, which you will not be able to say to me, no matter how much you may want to fling it in my face. You will not be able to say to me, 'Well, wasn't I right? This is your longest crossing since you have been a captain.' Or, if you do say it to me, it will be because the ship will not be worth much when I turn her back to you. That I swear to you, Monsieur Hamon." He rose. "Now you can rest easy. And I ask you, so, for your answer."

The ship-owners' representative was reflecting. "Rest easy," yes, he could do that. He had just set a terrific personal pride in motion, and that was a success. After such words, spoken in such a tone, there was no likelihood that the presence of a young woman would jeopardize the best interests of the voyage. Knowing his man, he would have been tempted to say, "On the contrary." As a matter of principle, however, and in order not to seem to give in on the spot, he replied in a voice which had again become composed and official:

"I am not refusing you my confidence. I am about to refer the matter, by telegram, to the Company."

"In that case, tell them it is either the authorization or my resignation," Rolland said.

This time, Monsieur Hamon plunged both his hands deep into his pockets, because he was too strongly tempted to brandish a fist in the rebel's face.

"Do you know what that is called, an ultimatum like that, just as the ship is about to sail?" he sputtered.

Rolland gave a curt nod.

"It is called knowing what one wants, and saying so," he said.

Under this cold insolence, Monsieur Hamon choked.

"Be that as it may, you have not always known! You waited until the very moment of departure to become aware that you could not get along without your wife. Unless you did it to force our hand. . . . In whichever case, it is not called either knowing what one wants or, perhaps, doing it. . . . Since you tell us to take it or leave it, very well. Let Madame Rolland sail with you. I suppose that you have already made the necessary preparations. As for me, I will inform the company." He opened the door wide. "Upon that, I say *Bon Voyage*. You understand, Captain, a *good voyage!*"

"For everything that depends on me, it will be good," Rolland assured him as he stepped over the threshold. "After what you have just said, Monsieur Hamon, it could not be otherwise."

"Very well—I hope so," the head of the shipping office bellowed, before slamming the door with a bang that set the glass panes quivering.

By the time he was in the street Rolland found himself perilously denuded of both scorn and anger. He felt nothing but the shame of having been told to his face the thing he was hiding away within himself, in one of those obscure corners of consciousness into which one pushes back everything that is disturbing, as a lazy sweeper pushes the dust into a dark corner of the room. He had just been treated—he, Rolland!—as a man who was irresolute, capricious; and it was true: he was. . . . The reproach was spreading through him like a poison in the blood, with the constriction, the frozen paralysis, which such poison brings.

He had been married for three weeks—twenty-two days, to be exact—and when Geneviève had drawn him to her in the hotel bedroom he had sworn to fill those days and those nights so full that they would make up, to both of them, for the ten empty months that lay ahead. That night, as he held her to him, he had felt again all the fever and excitement of his early ports of call, their surge and upspring, but without the brutality with which his twenty-five years used to stigmatize the women whose appeal was solely of the flesh. He was ten years older now, and he had a wife: a wife whom he would set to one side when he sailed, only to come back to on his return; she was not to be seized and plundered, like a port prostitute whom he would never see again.

They had gone to Paris, where, during a fortnight, he had made a considerable hole in the savings accumulated through the years and noted in his savings-bank book. He was not willing to give a thought to that. Nothing was too fine or too expensive for that pride of all seafaring men, from common sailors to captains, in wanting their wives to be showered with everything good, and to overwhelm with envy all those friends and neighbors who have their husbands with them throughout the year! Everything in a great and grand swoop, everything at once!

Geneviève had immediately given up trying to dam this flow of expenditure; she contented herself with directing it, adroitly, toward purchases for their home—bedroom and dining-room furniture, dishes. She had had no trouble in awakening in him the bourgeois vanity in regard to comfort. He was only surprised by her choices, which would go straight to what he had not noticed at all, to what, according to him, "made no effect." He was soothed, however, by the price: what she choose was always just as dear as what had seized his fancy. He had quickly observed, too, that the shop people's attitude became noticeably deferential as soon as she let her tastes be known. He felt proud of her. So, when she consulted him, it would be no effort for him to reply, "You know better than I. You attend to it."

"But it must at least please you," she would say.

And he would promise, "It will please me."

Then she would laugh, and say, "We'll take it."

But it was only in the shops that he handed over control. As soon as they were outside he would take the helm again and set the course for the restaurants, cafés, music-halls, moving-picture houses with full orchestra, amusing night spots. He was briefed on Paris, as he was on all the big seaports, by the recitals of colleagues; he knew the places where one got good food, the places where one had a good time, and everything that one must not go away without seeing. Geneviève would let him guide her, steer her, push her through the whirlpool, and sometimes, bewildered, she would catch hold of his arm; sometimes, too, she would press both hands to her forehead, as on the down-plunge of the scenic railway.

"My head is turned upside down," she would say then.

"Here, that is the right position," he would reply, with approval and pleasure. And, for his own part, he would confess: "With you, I've become a youngster again: more of a youngster than I ever was when I was a youngster!"

From Paris, they had gone back to Saint Cast for their final week. They had unpacked their furniture and fitted up the ground-floor apartment which Madame Gicquel had set aside for them in a villa she rented for the summer. On his arrival, Rolland had learned that his brother-in-law had asked to change his ship and was sailing as first mate on the *Prométhée*. André Gicquel's face had held the half-smile of fair-weather days as he made the announcement, and as he explained, "The family is one thing, the service is another."

And Rolland could only agree.

It was two nights before he was to sail that, as he lay down beside her, Geneviève had seized the hands that were searching for her, as they did every night, and had said, "You are going to leave me?"

She had never yet alluded to his departure, and he was grateful to her for that. He had thought, now, This had to come. But he was a little put out, for he considered that it was coming at least twenty-four hours too soon. Then at once, she had added, "Take me with you. . . ."

That had reassured him. He was expecting a fit of weeping, and he found himself face to face with a preposterous demand. All he had to do was point out its absurdity. He had undertaken this task— much easier than that of consolation!—and had talked for a long time, very gently. She was half sitting up against the pillow as she listened, her eyes looking straight ahead of her, her hand lying inert in his.

"Take me with you!"

He had often been up against pig-headed men who, too, would burst out with, and then repeat, "I want to beat it out of here!" With the repetition, he would understand the situation and would stop trying to break in the wall. When reason is not listened to, force must have the word. He would simply grab hold of the men, or have the bos'n grab hold of them. This time, again, he had abruptly changed tone and method.

"I have told you it was impossible," he said.

"Oh, that's too easy!"

She jerked her hand away and, her whole body thrust forward, had reeled off names upon names: the names of all his fellow-captains who had taken their wives with them on their long voyages, who were taking them still. They were just as good captains as the others, and just as successful. For them it was not "impossible." On the contrary, it seemed to them very simple. They did not invent obstacles to throw in the way!

"Then don't say, 'I cannot do it,' " she cried. "You would be the only one who could not do it. Say 'I do not want to.' "

"Very well: I do not want to."

"Good. But then you must tell me why. Since none of the reasons you have given me is worth anything, you must tell me the real one. Or, if you haven't the courage, I will tell it to you."

In a fury, one shoulder escaping from her nightgown, she had entrenched herself in the depths of the bed, against the wall.

"And that is?"

"Fear! You are afraid, afraid of everything and everybody: of your ship-owners, your fellow-captains, your officers, your men; of words, smiles, looks, silences; afraid of everything! Captain Rolland—become like everyone else! Clinging to his wife, wanting her beside him—that would be to return to the ranks. . . . It is your pride that is at stake: your pride and nothing else."

"And afterward?" he had growled. "Does it follow that because your mother sailed—?"

She had looked straight at him as she had answered, in a calm and almost conciliatory voice, "You are mistaken. I have not spoken of Mama. But if one must speak of anyone, it is not of her! it is of Papa. It was he who wanted to take her with him—and he would be able to tell you why, if he were still here. And that would all be contained in three words: he loved her."

She fell back on the pillows, shaken with sobs. He was not mollified. He was thinking that she too was returning to the ranks, as she would say. For this was what women were: asking for the moon, refusing to listen to explanations, crying when you don't give it to them. An obscure satisfaction was mingled with his disappointment at discovering her to be like the others—unfair, capricious, clinging stubbornly to what was preposterous. He felt reassured, now, that in this scene she should have conformed so closely to his notions about women. All the superiority in reason and self-mastery remained securely his.

But she had turned back toward him, with a swift movement of her back like the leap of a dorado, to say, "Perhaps you will let me go with you as far as Le Havre?"

"Of course, if you want to."

He had stretched out his arm to grasp her to him again, but when he touched her she had flung herself back against the wall. He had seen nothing but a child's spitefulness in that.

Yet it was her body as it had been that night, turned away from him in bitterness and grief, that came back to him now in the trolley car which was taking him from the shipping office to the docks. Whatever Hamon might say, the old crab, it was he, Rolland, and he alone, who had decided to take his wife with him, without her having had a word to say. It was less than two hours ago; but since when had he had to ponder for days and days over his actions?

They had arrived in Le Havre, he and she, that morning. He had found his new ship, the *Atalante,* anchored in the roads: Hamon had had it taken out by the mate. The pilot-boat had brought them out to her, and Geneviève had gone over the ship with an abstracted gaze, saying nothing at all. As for him, he had restrained his amazement in her presence. They had gone ashore again for luncheon, and in the restaurant, finding it impossible to meet her eyes, he had asked, "Well, are you going to pull a face like that until the end?"

From the look she gave him, he had realized at once that she was not "pulling a face": that she was prostrated by a desperate sadness. He knew that he had no chart for these sea depths, so he had navigated cautiously, with long silences in which from time to time he would hazard a few words of encouragement, like soundings.

He left her in the afternoon to do his last errands. When he joined her again at the café where she was to wait for him, he said, "I am going to take you to the station. I have time: just so I am on board by six o'clock."

"No," she said. "I would rather say goodbye to you here."

"As you like."

He cast an anxious sidelong glance at her; he had never seen that look of a somnambulist in anyone.

"You are to go home feeling quite at peace," he said. "You will be reasonable. And the time will pass quickly—you'll see."

"Yes."

"I mustn't make you late for your train."

He got up, and put his arms around her; but it was not a long kiss on her cold lips, because she was begging him, "Go; go now."

He had seen this at other sailings, on the docks, where seafaring men dash away in flight before a crushing despair as before a shattering squall. It was his turn to go through it. . . . He went away without turning around and strode off to the port. There, he jumped into the pilot-boat, and as soon as he was aboard his ship he shut himself up in his cabin.

The trolley car turned and twisted, ringing the changes on a long-drawn-out grinding noise. The shrill sound seemed to emphasize a recognition which he had dimly glimpsed in his cabin, and which had continued to hold first place in his mind: if he had gone away after those miserable farewells in which nothing had been said that ought to have been said, he would have found her, on his return, settled down in his absence like so many others; she would have arranged a life for herself, and he would figure in it only as a passing guest. A woman so avid to give herself takes herself back when she appears to be rejected.

It was at six o'clock that this fear struck him. He had just looked at his watch, and thought, She has started; she is getting toward Rennes."

He had gone into his office: he would write to her. He would tell her that for the first time in his life he felt that a whole part of himself had been amputated, the best part, which remained bound up in her: "I do not want you to keep the bad impression of our farewell in the café. I am very anxious to tell you that I shall miss you very much all through this voyage, and that I am already thinking of the happiness of coming back to you."

There! He had said everything, and it took five lines! As stiff and dry as the wood of his penholder. . . . He had torn up the page in a fury and taken another, knowing in advance that it would be useless. And at this moment someone had knocked on his door: his new first mate, Loisel.

His thought lingered for a moment on this young man, who interested him. Neither the officers' staff nor the crew had been, this time, of his choosing. He was taking over, at a moment's notice, the command of a captain whose son had been lost on the last crossing and who, for that reason, had refused to go to sea again. The officers were those who had served with the former master. Hamon had assured the new captain, at the time of his first visit, that he could not have wished him any better. He himself was reserving judgment until he saw them at work.

Loisel, at any rate, was not the ordinary type of second-in-command, with mustaches and the shoulders of a policeman, rough and conscientious overseers. He was a very fair-skinned youth, with an open countenance, alert and intelligent eyes, and a small mustache curled at the ends. Rolland had classified him at first glance as of the "genus liner-officer," a type which was becoming frequent now that the sons of captains, ship-owners, and even businessmen were graduating from the colleges into the merchant marine. They altered the environment. But it did not displease Rolland that these young men should now be wearing officers' caps, with two or three gold stripes: he saw in it a sign of increased prestige for the commercial marine service. The Prentout firm had just launched its *France II,* a five-master of eight thousand tons, the largest sailing-ship in the world. On the *Atalante* the comfort, even the luxury, of the living quarters had surprised the new captain. And he gladly admitted that such craft demanded officers of more distinction than the former strong-arms of the foreign trade.

"Captain," Loisel had said, "Madame Rolland is here."

The trolley was jolting him, in a long and jerky descent, and he caught hold of the platform rail because he wanted to be quiet to look clearly again at what had happened; it was worth the effort of recalling. *Madame Rolland*—for a second he really had not taken it in: he had read the name on envelopes, but he had never heard it spoken. And, besides, it was a kind of phantasmagoria, that she should be here at the very moment when he had been thinking of her with such intensity. Aboardship—and he was aboardship—his first reaction was always to reject the extraordinary.

But Loisel had added, "She is hurt."

With that, the news had at once become concrete and beyond dispute. This species of apparition, which the mate was announcing, was incarnated at one stroke. A physical hurt—nothing could more clearly emphasize a body, attest an actual presence. He had immediately assumed the worst: a serious accident, perhaps a train wreck; they were bringing her to him. . . . Loisel had caught his expression, as he rose, and hastened to explain. "It was as she climbed aboard, Captain. She crushed her finger between the ladder and the hull."

He had found her in the galley, with her hand plunged into a basin of cold water. David the cook and Hervy the second mate were standing one on each side of her. She had turned still more pale when he came in with the first mate.

She took her hand out of the reddened water. The first phalanx of her thumb was crushed, and the nail torn off. He turned again to Loisel. "Tell the pilot-boat to wait."

As he crossed the deck he had caught sight of the little steamboat that had brought her, lying beside the ship.

"Come with me," he said.

He led her to his cabin, supporting her as they went, and she explained: "I learned at the office of the *Abeilles* that you were not sailing until tomorrow morning. I could not let you go as you had gone. . . ."

As he dabbed the wound with iodine, he grumbled, "And you may be going to lose a finger!"

"Does that matter, when I am going to lose you for a year?" Then

374

she half whimpered: "You had the pilot-boat wait: you are sending me back? I had hoped we might have the night together."

He had not answered as he finished winding the gauze band around the wounded finger. When he had tied on the dressing she had repeated, in the same pitiful voice, "Then you are going to send me back?"

He had caught her in his arms and held her with all his might against him. It still seemed to him that another being, stronger than himself, had spoken across and through him. "No! I am keeping you here. . . ."

She had looked at him with immense eyes, her mouth half-open, not daring to understand.

"I am keeping you here tonight, tomorrow, all the days. I am taking you with me."

She went slack in his arms, as she had not done with the pain of her injury. He laid her on the sofa, snatched a bottle out of a cupboard, filled a glass with rum—spilling it on the floor as he did so—and forced her to drink it, holding her mouth shut on the scalding alcohol. Her eyelids flickered, and she sat up again.

"Can you stand on your feet? Try. That's good," he said. "Now, then, hop it! There's no time to lose."

On deck, he signaled to the first sailor he saw.

"Cozic, come with me," he said. Then he jumped to the deck of the pilot-boat. "Be good enough to make your best speed," he said.

During the short run he said to her, "Here is some money. Buy everything you need: a coat, dresses, underwear. Cozic will carry your packages. Stop at a pharmacy to have your finger looked at. It is ten minutes after six. Everything closes at seven. You have three-quarters of an hour."

"That is more than I need," she replied.

It was twenty minutes after seven now; she must be on the quay, with the sailor, waiting for him. In ten minutes he would be taking her back with him, in spite of—

His thought slipped ahead, drew back harshly; and when he got down at the end of the line it was the ferocious "A good voyage!" of old Hamon that he found driven into his brain.

She was indeed waiting for him, with Cozic, in front of the pilots' landing-place. The sailor had just taken her packages aboard the little steamer, which put off as soon as Rolland—the last of its three passengers—had stepped aboard.

"You have done all your errands?" he asked.

375

From the curtness of his voice she realized that he had just been having a fight.

"Yes. And you?" she said.

"It's all settled. Your finger?"

"The pharmacist gave me what I needed."

They did not speak again during the short passage. When they came alongside, Cozic handed the packages up to the men who were standing by the rail. Rolland guided her so that she could take hold of the ladder at the right moment, and he went up behind her, supporting her firmly under the armpits.

"Don't do it again," he advised, in the same curt tone.

The mate Loisel, standing at the gang-port, held out his arms to assist her in stepping aboard. Rolland pointed out the cardboard boxes to two of the men:

"Take all that to the saloon."

He led Geneviève there. It was a spacious room with bulkheads of polished rosewood, in the stern of the ship under the poop. A large mahogany table, with a red cloth cover, was screwed down in the middle of the cabin, eight swivel chairs around it. A sofa upholstered in red plush stood against the wall beside the door. At the other end was a marble fireplace, and a painting had been set in the central panel of the wall above the mantel: against a background of mountains, a rosy-fleshed woman with naked thighs and one breast escaping from her tunic was seen running—Atalanta. . . . The sailors who had caught a glimpse of it said, "There's a tart who's on the run." And the supposed motives for this flight were supplying material for jokes to the fo'c'sle. Rolland knew that it was a painting of a woman who was a champion in foot-racing; the ship that was named for her had been built with an eye to speed, the speed that was now the dominant concern of the shipping companies, their defense against steam.

Geneviève cast a glance at the picture as she entered the saloon. The niggardly gleam that was falling from the skylight, filtered through the broad bars of a brass grating, gave the Arcadian girl's springing pace an air of ghostly flight. She tried, not too successfully, to keep from being disturbed by the picture as she asked, in a voice she was endeavoring to make casual, "What is she escaping from?"

"She is not escaping; she is running a race," he said.

"Did she win it?"

"Oh, that—" After reflection, however, he added: "Probably. Otherwise they wouldn't have put her here."

Geneviève turned her back to look at the bundles piled up on the table.

"Now it's for you to escape," she ordered. "I've made you waste

376

enough time. I'm going to be busy on my own, putting all this stuff away."

Alone in the spacious saloon, already growing dim in the twilight, she began to untie the strings of her packages. The dry rustle of the wrapping-paper was the only sound she heard. The ship seemed deserted. She interrupted her task for some seconds to listen, and she found herself hedged about with silence; a thick and featureless silence, the silence of snow. The austere and frigid atmosphere of the "grand salon" was having its effect upon her: she felt an intruder here, a petty invader, at once over-bold and absurd; this room "of state" was setting its emptiness and fixed immobility against her. She could change nothing, move nothing: the chairs, table and sofa were all riveted to the floor.

She was swept by a flood of agonizing distress, like the panic of a child lost in the oncoming night. This was the time when her mother would be receiving the telegram that announced her departure, she thought: *Pierre has decided to take me with him. I am going as you did. You will understand. Do not grieve.*

"Do not grieve"—that was only said to those who had reason for grief. But, "I am going as you did"—was that true? Would her mother be able to believe that her daughter was continuing the magnificent adventure? Did she believe it herself? Oh, the fear of having made a mistake; the fear that this husband, whom she still knew far too little, would not be prepared to supersede everything else in her life, now that she was reduced to having nothing, any more, but him!

"You can't see."

He had come back. But she knew at once that he had not let down his defenses, that in memory he was still fighting against the person, or persons, who must have opposed her impromptu embarkation. She knew, too, that a day would come when he would make her bear the weight of the reprimands and reproaches which she had brought upon him. For the moment, she was still the woman for whom a man has just been fighting, and whom he is snatching away; so she still had her price.

"Dinner is served. If you want to come—"

She was tempted to reply that she was not hungry, that her finger was hurting her so much that she could not swallow a mouthful. But he was already going on ahead of her, and she followed him.

The officers' staff was waiting for them in the saloon—the first mate, Loisel, and the three officers. Hervy the second mate was a tall dark-haired man, bearded like a missionary, sturdy in shoulders and in face; he must have been in his thirties, and he had a cordial air. Monsieur Foulon, the second of the junior officers, was third mate, younger, and more gaunt in build. His gray eyes fixed themselves upon the young woman with a kind of dazed astonishment; he turned them away, but the clean-shaven and severely modeled face still showed a little line, as of resentment. Pléneau, the "lieutenant of the chicken-coop," the last of the officers, opened his heavy eyes too wide in his peasant face, for a tactless inspection of the new arrival.

They had already been speaking of her in low tones, keeping their eyes on the door, before she came in. When she returned from shore, the packages and cartons brought aboard had made them think she would be sailing with them. They had had no further doubt of that when Cozic, the sailor-porter, was heard to relate in a loud voice, on the deck, how he had just made a damn good tack into the shirt shops; the little woman there knew what she wanted, he had added, and she wouldn't go veering around for hours before setting the course for a pair of pants.

They themselves, the officers, found it impossible to get over this embarkation "on the run." They were acquainted, naturally, with the fame of their new captain, and he was the last man they would ever have thought of as bringing his wife along! There was only one thing which seemed to them to fit in with the idea they had of him: the swiftness and unexpectedness of his decision. That was indeed in his recognized manner of not wanting to do anything like anyone else.

"I'd have paid for an apéritif for my whole watch, to have seen old Hamon's face!" Hervy had just been saying, as the two of them came into the wardroom.

Rolland made the introductions quickly; then he looked in perplexity at the settee of red imitation leather, backed up against the mahogany paneling, and the swivel chairs, none of which anyone was making up his mind to occupy.

"Well, let's see," he said.

Frowning, he studied the allotment of places. For already Geneviève's arrival was disarranging the immutable order: the first mate at his right, the second mate at his left, the other two officers across the table.

But the young woman, quite simply, swung the chair opposite her husband toward herself.

"Monsieur Loisel. . . ."

She indicated the place on her right.

"Monsieur Hervy. . . ."

She called the second mate to the chair on her left.

"And these gentlemen next to you," she said to Rolland.

Foulon and Pléneau went obediently to flank the captain on the settee.

She sat down. The cabin boy—a washed-out blond youngster of fifteen, with too-long arms and a face so dotted over with freckles that the officers had nicknamed him "the archipelago"—stood open-mouthed in the face of this swift revolution. A quick glance from Hervy sent him back to his galley. The officers had grasped the situation and summed it up in their own minds: "She is doing what she would do in her own home." The mate obviously approved. Hervy, a big rough man, was not attaching much importance to it. Foulon, drawn back within himself, seemed to have adopted the course of no longer seeing her. Pléneau, on the contrary, was still staring at her with undiminished astonishment.

"And your finger, Madame?" Loisel asked, as he took his seat.

"For the moment, it is numb; but so is my whole arm. It will be all right soon."

With the first spoonfuls of too-greasy soup which she forced herself to swallow, she remembered that this, too, was something she would have to conquer: this food for men, designed only for nourishment—food which was made to fill their big bodies with solid things, and which they absorbed as an engine absorbs its fuel. She had known it by heart since her childhood, the menu of the sailing-ships. Her father had often recited it when, at home, he had exclaimed over a jugged hare, or even a mutton chop. Monday and Wednesday, salt pork and potatoes in their jackets; Tuesday and Friday, salt codfish and boiled potatoes; Thursday and Sunday, canned meat stew and fried potatoes. In addition, the officers had a right to another canned dish—vegetables, fish, or meat—at each meal. She knew, too, that the potatoes would not last through the voyage, and that in a few days, as soon as the fresh provisions were exhausted, the "sea menu" would begin. Nevertheless, she refused the beef-and-carrots with which they were filling their plates.

"Thank you, I am not hungry. I have a little fever, from my finger."

"You ought to eat though," replied Rolland, who was cutting his meat. "Because you know, gentlemen, that we are going to have a passenger."

No one uttered a word. Only Loisel, the second-in-command, looked at her and inclined his head.

"Yes indeed, and an unexpected passenger," she said. "I was consigned to shore. I disobeyed, and I have been punished. But that has won me hospitalization aboardship."

"Nobody will complain of that," the mate assured her pleasantly.

And big Hervy added, in his sonorous voice, "You will not be the first, or the only, one. I was on the *Michelet* for two trips with the captain's wife aboard. She made at least six voyages."

"Madame Condroyer made nine, on the *Suzanne*." It was Loisel who put forth this figure, like a bid at an auction.

"Mama made five," Geneviève said.

"That explains everything," said the mate, and added:

> *"Southern Cross, Northern Star,*
> *And a woman aboard,*
> *Guide the ship to a good harbor."*

She thanked him with a smile. At least two of them had just accepted her, accorded her that spontaneous sympathy of seafaring men, which they give or refuse at first sight. First there was Loisel the mate, whose more cultivated upbringing, and whose alert and open mind, she had at once sensed. It was plain that he was congratulating himself upon her sailing, as an unhoped-for piece of good luck. He was looking forward to the different atmosphere, to conversations, everything that a woman's presence brings to a cabin in times of relaxation: everything in the way of stimulation, unconscious coquetry, attention to behavior, manners, dress. His father had said to him, long ago, that "a woman makes life smoother for everyone. Even the men are more courteous, more self-controlled." And he would say, further, "Her tact can do as much as the captain's authority to assure order and a good understanding." Then Hervy, the second mate, had accepted her just as sincerely, for the simple reason that he liked her kind, that she was neither bold and impudent nor a poseur. There remained, thus, the two younger officers, who were sitting opposite her. Foulon was pretending he didn't know she was there, perhaps because he was an earnest and austere lad and such youths are apt to be intolerant of what they believe to be a weakness on the part of a skipper. As for Pléneau, he simply had the air of not having grasped the situation: when he thought he was not being observed, he would fix on her the round eye of a cowherd on guard against some alien creature at the gate of his field. Rolland himself was eating his dinner, between the two junior officers, in silence.

"The tug will take us off at ten o'clock tomorrow morning," he said at last.

"It can," said Loisel. "Everything is ready."

"Will it be possible for them to deliver a letter?" Geneviève asked.

"Certainly," Hervy assured her. He looked at the bandage that made her injured thumb big and clumsy. "The difficulty won't be in delivering it; it's more likely to be in writing it," he said.

"Oh, I have four fingers left, after all," she answered.

The dinner was finished, and Rolland rose.

"Monsieur Loisel, I have some things to ask you." If there had not been a woman aboard, he would have added, "Will you come to my cabin?" Instead, he snapped his fingers to call the cabin boy. "Hurry and clean the table," he said. Then he turned to Geneviève. "I will join you presently."

The officers said good night and went out. They all addressed the captain first, and their "Good night, Madame" remained cautious. They seemed to be once more in the throes of their first embarrassment, which Rolland had done nothing to dissipate. It might have been thought that they did not feel authorized to accept her fully. As she herself was leaving, she turned in the wrong direction, and it was Hervy, seeing this, who guided her.

"Have you matches?" he asked. "The cabin boy would certainly not have thought of lighting your lamp."

She had none. He handed out a box, after shaking it to make sure there were some inside. Then he wished her a good night.

She went into the cabin and struck a match. With her bad hand, in which pain was now shooting into all the fingers, she had a hard time lighting the hanging lamp, especially in replacing the chimney. But the white-painted cabin had a neatness without coldness which seemed to her welcoming. The bunk, covered with a white wool blanket, was wide, as if in acknowledgment that sometime two people might sleep together there. As a matter of fact, this extra width was merely in accordance with the principle that granted the captain more space, more "rations," more leisure, than the others. Under this bed were two large drawers. A sofa was screwed down under the porthole, and the floor was covered with brown linoleum, waxed.

She opened a little door: here was a tiny "bathroom," with tub, washstand, nickel-plated faucets, and an enameled medicine chest. Another door opened into the captain's office. She went in; the light from the bedroom, shining through the door she had left open, was enough to enable her to make a tour of the room, without bumping into the corners of the furniture or the back of the swivel chair. She stopped before a glass case, listened to the ticking of the chronometers there. In its cubical glass frame the self-registering barometer seemed dead, its cylinder inert.

When she had completed this inventory, she went back to the bedroom. She was keeping her right arm bent and raised, and this position seemed to quiet the twinges of pain and drain away the burning weight, like molten lead, from her hand. The dull ache that was left was not enough to keep her from thinking, though it occupied her sufficiently to leave her no longer upset by all that was unbelievable and disquieting in the miracle of her sailing. Standing under the lamp now, she gazed attentively at the soft roll of the bandage: was it not actually to it that she owed her presence here? One of those overwhelming moods of tenderness that seize upon hard men in the face of a woman's injury, and that Pierre was regretting already? She had been brought here by surprise, installed by accident. But had it not always been so, since she had known her husband? She had the feeling, with him, of finding herself in front of a wall; and suddenly a breach would open in it, and she would pass through. The play of his sudden revulsions was in her favor. Were they to be explained at all, if not as evidence of the imperceptible labor of her love, already eating into his armor?

She looked around her, savored the close and intimate atmosphere of the room, the virile innocence of the white bed with its severely folded sheets, the vigilance of the portholes—round eyes, lidless. A sense of assuagement emanated from all this, and she surrendered herself to it. For the first time, she was feeling at home on this ship; and little by little that was indeed taking on the proportions of a miracle!

She ventured, then, to begin undressing, which was a long and difficult process, especially trying to unhook her corset with her left hand. At last she slipped in between the cool sheets and settled herself close against the wall, leaving a wide space to the edge of the bunk. Her arm, stretched out along her body, seemed quieted, too, by her recumbent position; she only felt the blood throbbing in her finger like the ticking of a big watch. Before climbing into the bunk, she had turned down the lamp to its lowest point. But at regular intervals a porthole would be lighted up, a glow would pass and repass across her face: the oscillating beam from a lighthouse. She lost that sense of risking an unbounded adventure, which had overwhelmed her in the empty saloon under Atalanta arrested by the artist in full flight. To share a life, like a fruit of which one may take one half or the other indifferently, because both are equal; to create a presence, a wholeness of being-there, without distinguishing between what one contributes and what one enjoys—this was what she had come to try to do. She knew that her own possessiveness would forever charge her husband's departures with being desertions of her; and, from that, all that was best in her would be running the risk of becoming like the mortified flesh of her finger, which, when the injury had been scarred over, would remain deformed and half-numb.

This danger, she was thinking, had been averted. She would now have to win forgiveness of her victory, forgetfulness of it. That would be the first task. She thought that it would be just so much the easier in that he was picturing himself as having pledged precious things to it: his reputation, his prestige. All that would remain to his credit, and she would see him once more with that astonished face which she used to watch for, when, after leading him around an obstacle without his suspecting it, she would bring him out into a clear field.

It seemed to her that she heard a door open somewhere: he would be coming back. There must be no encounter between them this evening, when he would still be feeling some rancor, undoubtedly, after having had to do battle for her. . . . She nestled as close as possible against the wall. He came in, and she listened to him undressing, heard him blow out the lamp. Then, as he lay down beside her, he asked, in an undertone, "Are you asleep?"

Tense as she was, she endeavored to keep her breathing regular. She knew very well that he would be thinking, She hasn't taken long to get used to it! and that this would hurt his feelings. But anything was better than to speak. At one moment she felt his hand passing lightly over her back and down her side; and she forced herself to remain inert, in spite of her wild desire to turn in one single movement and fling herself into his arms. That embrace might take too dangerous a direction.

He went to sleep long before she did. When she heard the rhythmic beat of his breathing she turned over and, resting on the arm that was hurting her, looked at him as he slept. She saw his face only as it appeared and disappeared, swept by the gleam from the lighthouse. It was as if he were being given to her a hundred different times, a thousand times. All she thought was, He is here! And the sky was growing pale before she had exhausted her wonder over this presence which sleep was surrendering to her at last.

XXXII

HE WAS no longer beside her when she awoke. The morning light was coming in through the portholes. It was the shattering noise of the anchor chains being drawn up on the windlass that had snatched her out of sleep: a rumbling and clanging, a monstrous rattling which, iron banging on iron, set the whole ship vibrating. This uproar, however, was no longer threatening her. . . .

She remembered the captain's wife, a friend of her mother's who, like herself, had wanted to spend a last night with her husband aboardship. That was at Rotterdam. At four o'clock in the morning the tug-boat had arrived, although it was not expected before seven. And, suddenly, the wife was no more than an intruder, almost a stowaway, to whom her husband called out, as he rushed off to work his vessel, "Get out of the way! Throw your stuff on the dock!" On that dock she had sat on her suitcase, waiting, from four o'clock till six. Then the milkmen who were going by, with their carts drawn by big dogs, had taken pity on her and carried her luggage to the ferry-boat. . . .

Geneviève made up her mind, in the first place, that she would not be a curious onlooker at the sailing. She knew how disagreeable it is, for men who are working hard, to serve as a spectacle. She got up and went to look out of the porthole. The sea was as dazzling as a tub of mercury. A steamship lay fixed in the very center of the sunlight. And that light had an exquisite freshness. The nearby coast rose, fair and white, behind the thin wash of the sun-drenched mist. The silver flashes that were sea-gulls glistened in the gray-blue sky— one of those spring skies, so fragile that she almost held her breath for fear of spoiling the weather.

She stayed there at the porthole for a long time, letting the clarity of the early morning sink into her very soul. At the end, she was no longer able to make out whether this radiance came from herself or from the objects outside her. It was the thought of the letter she must write her mother that pulled her away from the porthole at last. She got dressed, went into the office, sat down at the mahogany desk, and by the necessity of holding the pen between her first and middle fingers, was at once recalled to this factual present which she must explain and justify in black and white.

It surely would be easy! All she had to do was allow the certainties that filled her mind and heart to overflow onto the paper: "You know that my place is beside him. If I had not taken that place, I should have lost it. If I do not become something he needs, I can only be a kind of extra in his life, and that I do not want at any price. At bottom, the real reason is that I cannot endure his not being beside me any more. I can no longer imagine myself apart from him. You have often put me on guard against that 'too much' that I used to expect of life. Well, without trying to, without knowing it, he has already given me infinitely more than I should ever have dared to hope for. All that force of longing that frightened me when I first became conscious of it, those indignant refusals to accept a humdrum everyday life, that taste for risk and combat which I used to try to hide from you and which you guessed—since you would say to me, 'There is your underseas volcano again!'—you see, this has riveted me to him. . . ."

She did not write one word of all that. She realized perfectly that it was the light of this clear fresh morning that was permeating her spirit and transfiguring everything. And perhaps the burning fever in her hand had its part, too, in this exaltation. She forbade herself none of her dreams, but she was able to judge them.

For there was in her a sound practical girl, too, who knew what a "situation" was and had taken account of it in making up her mind; an adventurous girl, whose curiosity about the world had been aroused by her father's recitals and who had seized the opportunity to satisfy it; a hot-blooded girl, of whom marriage had made a woman that waited impatiently for the night. She was not fretting over finding herself, in all this, so like other women. Pierre would not have liked an idle dreamer, any more than her mother would have liked a chatterbox.

She contented herself, therefore, with retracing, in large clumsy letters, the events of the evening before: the accident, her husband's decision, the raids upon the shops, her embarkation. She explained it in, so to speak, two words: *You know Pierre: what he wants, he wants right away, and completely.* But as her mother had indirect connections with one of the ship-owners, she commissioned her, also, to mitigate the effects of that rash act: *Put it all on me. Say that he only gave in because he saw that I was desperate. It won't be lying, to say that.*

As she sealed the letter, she could not keep her thought from going back to the dining room at Saint Cast, where it would be read. Yet her face brightened, and she smiled. Why, just at this moment, was it not her mother whom she was discovering there but a visitor, the wife of a sea-captain? Already gray-haired, but brisk and amusing, she never spoke of her husband except as "my phenomenon." And she would explain: "It is very simple: for thirty years, with him, I have felt as if I were always drunk." Yes, that was it: a persistent intoxication; the sensation of being whirled around and around in strong arms, arms that never let one go—since she was here. . . .

The *Atalante*, in tow, was gliding over the smooth sea now in a movement in which one felt all the water's gentle elasticity. Geneviève was hearing the ripple along the side of the ship, as she would have heard the cool murmur of a brook. She went back to the porthole and watched the coast of Normandy growing pale. Before she had been able to guess what emotions this flight was going to instill into her, the door burst open. She turned around. The cabin boy, transfixed and gaping, was standing in the doorway.

It was true that his elongated countenance was dotted over like an archipelago. That was the first thing Geneviève noticed, because a ray from the still low sun struck him full in the face, emphasizing the russet tone of the freckles, outlining their islands scattered over the pallid skin.

"Can I do the room?"

He made the demand ungraciously, plainly shocked by this extraordinary presence that he had forgotten all about. She realized at once that this one was not to be tamed, because he was at the age when one scorns women in order to play the man. A sloping skull, ears that stuck out, a loutish stare—it was important that she should make him afraid of her, and at once!

"No," she said. "Not now. You are to go to the galley and get some coffee and some bread. You will find butter in the pantry. Bring it all to me, here. Then you will tell the cook that he is to get a large jug of hot water ready for me. Do you know what that is, *hot* water?"

"They've had their coffee already."

"Who are 'they'? 'Can't you say the captain and the officers?' I know that they have had their breakfast. But I shall have mine here. Now go."

This time, the muddy gray eyes turned away, subjugated, and the boy went out. He was back in five minutes, carrying a broad tin-plated iron dish which did duty as a tray, and which held a coffee-pot, an opened can of condensed milk, several slices of bread on a plate, an empty bowl on another plate, and, in two saucers, a square of butter and six lumps of sugar. A clean napkin was folded under the plate that held the bowl. Looking at this lay-out, Geneviève realized at once that someone who was not an officer had decided from the first morning to treat her as the captain's wife and a lady.

"Was it the cook who arranged this?"

"Yes."

She saw again, in her mind's eye, the stout man with a chubby shining face, and rolling goggle eyes that popped out still farther as he watched her bleeding into his basin.

"Tell him that it is very well set up, and that I am much obliged. Tell him also that the pitcher of hot water is to bathe my arm."

The boy's gaze slid lightly over the bandage; then he announced, "The cook said that the jug would be sea water."

She stared at him, with an exaggerated air of surprise.

"I should think so! He can't be giving anyone a jug of fresh water out of the ten quarts he's allowed for his cooking!"

The lad's respectful amazement told her that her knowledge of ship's rations had attained the desired result; and, alone again, she was enjoying it as she unwound her bandage. When he brought

386

the hot water, she had him put the pitcher on the folding shelf at the head of the bunk, and plunged first her hand, and then her arm up to the elbow, into it. The swelling had gone down somewhat, but the crushed thumb was still black, the color of a storm cloud.

From where she was, she could look through the porthole and see the ripple of the sea.

"Well, you've treated yourself to a nap!"

The voice was cordial. Rolland was leaving the poop, where he had just been seeing something that pleased him: a helmsman who steered delicately, had the feeling of the ship, anticipated the tensions and slackenings of the tow-line. The captain had also remarked that on the deck every preparation had been made for getting under sail without any need for intervention on his part, as if things went ahead on their own: the halyards were ready to be fitted to the windlass, the pressure was up in the little steam boiler. He cast a glance, now, at the breakfast tray, and the attention did not escape him, either.

"By George, the cook is taking care of you as if you were in a palace! Let me have a look at your finger." He examined it closely and said, "It's getting all right."

Her look was half-serious, half-teasing.

"Too much 'all right'! You are going to be sorry you let yourself be moved by such a little thing."

He sat down on the sofa.

"There is no question of that," he declared. "I am not in the habit of going back on a decision; I would not go back on that one, above all. Only, I have come down to talk to you, so that everything will be quite clear."

She realized that having left everything in order on deck, checked everything up above, he was now resolved to do the same below. She bowed her head docilely.

"All right, then," he began. "Naturally, you are never to talk to the men. You are to know them only by what you hear others say of them. I remember a fellow-captain who stretched a tarpaulin along the whole length of the poop. The men going to the wheel would pass only on one side of the canvas, the side where his wife wasn't. Yes, I know, that was carrying it rather far, but what I mean to say is, you must act as if the tarpaulin were there."

She acquiesced again with a nod, a little too emphatic. But he did not see it, and went on. "You will have to find your occupation only in my cabin. A woman who concerns herself with the conduct of the men, or with seamanship, is a misfortune all round. With the officers, except at mealtime, it will be, 'Good morning, sir. Good evening, sir.' If a woman talks with one more than with another, it makes gossip right away."

She was listening gravely, repressing the smile that sprang to her lips on hearing him decree, with so much conviction, the code of behavior for a woman aboardship. It was a code which she knew better than he did, and which she would have been easily able to complete. When she thought he had finished, she spoke to reassure him. "Everything will work out very well—you'll see."

But he still had something important to say.

"Naturally, this does not mean that you are to be kept shut up in the living quarters. You can come to the poop. Only, be careful not to show yourself around too much. All you need do is make yourself comfortable forward of the chart-house."

"Yes, but not this morning. I haven't unpacked yet. Everything is still in the saloon. I want to set your things to rights a little, too."

He got up, satisfied. "Just as you like."

"When do you expect to cast off the tow-line?"

"Around two this afternoon."

"Very well, I will come on deck then, to see the ship take sail."

He nodded in approval. She could not fail to be interested in such a beautiful spectacle, and at that solemn moment of the real departure her presence could seem no more than natural.

On reflection, the appropriateness of the reply struck him, and from the doorway he offered her her reward.

"Now to hell with old Hamon!" he said, before he turned and went out.

At a quarter past eleven, at the noon meal—for the officers were eating before the men so that the captain might be free for a rest before sailing—the mate remarked, "I told you that you would bring us good luck, Madame. One couldn't dream of nicer weather."

"But there is a straight head wind," Foulon reminded him, in his colorless voice, and without raising his eyes.

It was Rolland who objected to this, a little curtly.

"The ship has two sides, hasn't she? And besides, the barometer is rising. We shall have land breezes before long."

A little before two, the cabin boy knocked at Geneviève's door.

"The captain said that you should send your letter to the saloon, and that you should come up on deck."

When she stepped out on the poop, she was dazzled by the full sunlight. She paused for an instant at the threshold of the chart-house, staggered by space.

"Let out the jibs; the stays'ls!"

Behind her, on the other side of the heavy block of teakwood,

Rolland was calling out the first order which would bring the inert craft to life. She had never heard his voice as master: it sounded strong and full, without unnecessary harshness, but so decisive and authoritative that one felt it creating force. The young wife was swept by a wave of pride: "This is the best captain on the coast. This is my husband!"

She did not turn toward the bow, where the sails were being run up, nor toward the tugboat, which she heard puffing as it came closer. She was seeking, first, for a place on the poop where she might settle herself, from which she could see "without showing herself too much." She found it quickly, on the port side aft, at the end of the saloon's high skylight, and she took a folding chair there. Seated, she had her back turned to the man at the wheel. The projection of the skylight, which came up to her shoulders, hid her, while forward the chart-house served as a screen. From the main deck one would have been hard put to it to make out, in the angle formed by the poop-rail, the gray splash of the scarf knotted over her hair.

She saw the *Abeille* draw close alongside, a rare achievement, and possible only in a sea as calm as this. The tugboat was coming to have the towing voucher signed and take off the last mail. When it shoved off, she heard its captain call out, "A good voyage, all!" Then there were the salutes of the flag, the three blasts of the whistle in response, and the water widened in separation between the two vessels.

The piece of embroidery she had brought with her had fallen on her lap, and without giving a thought now to the tug that was growing smaller to the south, she was watching the rest of the canvas being run up. Its smacking swiftness made her think of the little toy reed-pipes children blow into, unrolling a spiral of paper and swelling it out with a single breath.

"The leaves have come out on the trees again."

It was the helmsman, at her back, who was speaking aloud and evidently wishing her to hear him. She half turned around. The man, standing behind his wheel on a sort of little platform, had his eyes raised to the upper sails. He lowered them to meet the young woman's glance and smile, responded to them with a slight movement of his head, and then returned to his contemplation of the canvas.

Until evening she stayed there on the poop, bent over her embroidery, which she would drop from time to time to look out toward the open sea. She was not thinking of anything, a little intoxicated by the vigorous air and the even sweep of the breeze, lulled by the ship's gliding motion and the gentle lament of the blocks. She felt that she was being carried away, easily, without jar: she had only to surrender herself.

"What, are you here?" Rolland, coming aft to the chart-house, had literally stumbled into her chair. "I thought you hadn't come up," he added. "I hadn't seen you."

She raised her eyes and smiled: that teasing smile he used to love, because he had the satisfaction of understanding at once that she was poking fun at him. This time, again, he translated: it meant, "Wasn't that what you wanted?"

"You've certainly known how to hunt out a fine corner," he said approvingly. "Then you saw us putting on sail?"

"Yes. And it was beautiful."

"Eight knots on the log, with those winds! And they are going to change; I stick to what I said about that. We'll have a good breeze tomorrow to get out of the Channel." He rubbed his hands together. "To get out of the Channel tomorrow—do you realize what that means? When I think that it once took me a month to go from Start Point to Saint Nazaire! That really could be called having it hard!" He dropped his voice, because the helmsman was listening. "It's enough to make one think that Loisel is right, and that you are bringing us good luck!"

"But of course I am," she responded calmly.

"Why are you so sure? Have you been saying prayers?"

"That, too. . . ."

After dinner he warned her, "Don't think about me. As long as we are in the Channel, I shan't leave the poop. I'll sleep in the chart-house."

"Come in and say good night to me, won't you?"

But he was in the cabin almost as soon as she was.

"Come and see," he said.

She followed him to the poop. A mother-of-pearl wake stretched out behind the ship, all sparkling in the moonlight. The twin beams of Barfleur-Cotteville were splashing into the pure darkness of the night. In the offing, a liner was driving toward Le Havre with its three tiers of brilliant illumination. And almost everywhere, on the water around them, glimmered the white signal lights of the fishing-boats that were dragging their broad nets in the sea. She raised her head; above her, the airy sails were filling, so light that one might have called them transparent.

"How beautiful!" she said again.

But she held her voice in, because Foulon, whose watch it was, had just paused abruptly in the stroll that would have brought him close to them. He was leaning over the poop-rail now as if there were something he must keep his eyes on below. For her, that stubborn and, she knew, hostile back lay like a heavy weight on the ship and the sea. Rolland turned around.

"Well, are things going as you wish, Monsieur Foulon?"

The third mate straightened up.

"We are doing almost nine knots, Captain. But it must be said that the keel is clean, and the sea calm."

Why must it be said? To let it be understood that heavy seas were coming, and then warm seas in which the hull would drag along a fleece of sea-weeds and colonies of parasites, to drain away the ship's speed?

"Let us take advantage of this while it is given us," Rolland replied, in the somewhat dry voice that he was adopting with this junior officer. "When it is a matter of getting out of the Channel, nine knots are worth twelve. I will see you presently." He turned to his wife. "You are coming?"

Foulon raised his soft cap with its two gold stripes: "Good night, Madame."

When Rolland had led her back to their cabin, she flung her left arm around his neck.

"Thank you," she said, "for this beautiful first day."

"But I haven't had much time to pay attention to you."

"What of that?" she protested. "You haven't been ten yards away!"

He caught her close to him. When he pressed too hard against her injured arm, she was not quick enough to keep from wincing.

"Did I hurt you?" he cried.

She thrust her hand behind her back with a little girl's fury.

"Oh, this silly thing! *No!* But run away now. Monsieur Foulon is waiting for you, and I don't want him to have to wait. We shall have so many nights. . . ."

It was he who brought her coffee to her next morning, before she was up.

"That will be more convenient," he explained. "This way, you can stay in bed all morning. All the same, I can't have the cabin boy bringing your breakfast. Oh, and after this it will be the novice who takes care of your room. The Archipelago is too stupid; and I caught him taking a nip out of your can of condensed milk. . . . When you are dressed, come on deck and see England."

He seemed very happy to have it to offer her, like this, as she woke up. Yet when he had kissed her, he remained standing beside the bunk. She drew him to her with her good arm. He submitted no more, his own hands supine by the edge of the mattress. If he were to touch her, he would not go back to the deck immediately; and it was the hour when he should be there. She guessed this, and sat up.

"This is a real wedding trip," she exclaimed, as she took the tray he handed her.

"When I see you here, I wonder if it is really true," he confessed.

"Do you think you will be able to get used to it?"

"I will try," he promised, in the same tone.

When she reached the poop, the tall cliffs of the Isle of Wight were looming up before the boom. The sun, still low, was picking out the roofs of cottages, glittering on windows, emphasizing the checkerboard pattern of paddocks and hedged fields. Quite close to shore a number of steamboats were sending forth streamers of smoke that mingled as they rose into the quiet sky. She heard Rolland say to Hervy, the second mate, "Decidedly, the wind is dropping, more and more."

The sails that she had seen so rounded under the moon were falling back in long folds along the masts.

"You might as well be turning a wheel at the lottery!" the man at the helm growled.

She felt the last breaths of the wind dying down around her. The ripples were wiped out on the transparent sea. It was a "blue calm." Yet on the ship thus checked in her course, the watch on duty was only hurrying the faster to complete the labors begun the evening before. When they reached deep water, everything must be ready.

When Geneviève went back to the cabin, she found a tall boy there, humming as he turned the mattress.

"Oh, excuse me, Madame!" He took off his beret and introduced himself without embarrassment. "I am François, the novice. The captain has told me to look after the living-quarters."

He had an air of intelligence, and seemed likable. Only one thing troubled Geneviève: he had presented himself under his first name. That is never done aboardship, where a man's first name is a gift not to be squandered.

"What is your family name?" she asked.

He broke into a laugh. "It is François, Madame. My name is Robert François."

She asked him about his home. He was from Plancoët, and he let her know, rather skillfully, that he had gone as far as the second year of high school at the Cordeliers in Dinan.

"I am sure that we shall get on very well together," she said.

"I will do my best, Madame," he answered.

In the afternoon she went back to the poop, to her place against the skylight. Toward four o'clock, the surface of the water on the land side became glazed over, so to speak, with little flakes of ripples. She heard a man on the deck say, "Have a look at the cat's piddle."

That was, most likely, the forerunner of a breeze. And in fact it was soon possible, under the tall pale cliffs of the Isle of Wight, to distinguish a dark line that was growing wider, making headway toward the open sea, and approaching the *Atalante,* which was still on the port tack but turned toward the west by the wind's capricious flurries. Geneviève saw the veering of the sails as they were trimmed for the wind from starboard. The breeze reached the ship. The canvas quivered, there was a sudden beating of wings that were smoothing themselves out, and then the sails filled, and the murmur of a mountain stream ran along the side of the vessel once more. The wind was feeble, however, and it was only very slowly that the cliffs of the island slipped away to starboard.

"We're not making five knots yet. But five knots on a good course is better than ten tacking."

Again, this was said for her; and, as on the day before, she turned around. It was a different helmsman: this one was gaunt and loose-jointed, with tremendous hands. He received the same smile and the same discreet gesture of approval. That evening in the crew's quarters he was to say, "She acts very pleasant, and doesn't put on airs."

The wind remained steady in the north all night: a night which Rolland spent, as he had spent the others, on the poop and in the chart-house. Geneviève saw him for only a few minutes, when he brought her breakfast coffee. The sea was in fact becoming considerably more populated, and about two in the morning a freighter had cut dangerously across their course.

"They must have been asleep," Rolland said. "I wanted to get hold of my gun and send a broadside through the glass on their bridge, to teach them manners."

When Geneviève went on deck, about ten o'clock, there was a busy criss-cross of steamships and sailing-ships of all types on the level sea. Their diverse routes gave the onlooker that sense of incoherence which, on indeterminate reaches, is imparted by directions as precise as they are unknown. Hervy was just going into the chart-house to note the ship's speed in the log-book, and he paused to speak to her:

"You ought to get your eyes full of this, Madame Rolland, before we are out on the open sea. Meeting one other ship will be an event, there."

When he came out again, the second mate spied a large fishing-smack to leeward, which had just run the French colors up to its masthead.

"That is for us," he said, and turned back to the helmsman. "Bear away!"

The fishing-smack's sail carried the symbol C 531, and long pink gob-lines could be made out on her black hull.

"Come and see, Madame."

Geneviève followed the junior officer to the poop-rail, where Rolland also had his eyes on the French boat.

"She is from Port-en-Bessin or Grand-Camp; she has come to fish in Torbay waters." He was speaking to Geneviève now, as much as to his officers. Then he turned forward, to give the order, "Bouse the mains'l tacks and sheets. Square the yards aft."

The *Atalante* was brought to.

The fishing-craft's big pot-bellied boat was already putting off. Handled by two sturdy bareheaded lads and steered by the bark's skipper, she soon came alongside the large sailing-ship, and the three men climbed aboard. In this weather they did not have to be afraid of damaging each other's paint! Rolland welcomed them on deck.

"Excuse me, Captain," the skipper said, touching his cap with his finger and speaking in a broad patois, "but it's a week that we've been at sea, and we'd like to have a pinch of tobacco for our pipes, and some salt pork for our kettle, and some hardtack, too, for we've hardly any bread aboard."

As he spoke, the sunburned Norman, whose broad shoulders had brought a smile to the officers' faces, was pointing to the bottom of his craft, all wriggling with ray-fish, red mullet, even sole and brill.

"To even things up, I'll dip you out a bit of fish from our last catch, to make you a *matelote*." *

Hervy, standing behind Geneviève, commented in amusement, "A bit, he calls it! There's enough there to feed to the whole crew for four days!"

The men had come over to the port rail, so as to be present at this interview. Geneviève heard one of them calling to the skipper, "A good swap—bananas for pineapples!" †

"Right you are, my boy!" the Norman called back, in the direction from which the voice came, "and nobody's the loser!"

Rolland was already giving his orders to the steward. "You will add a dozen cans of meat, ten quarts of wine, and two bottles of brandy."

But the first mate addressed the fishing-smack skipper with his most serious air. "If you have been at sea for a week, I'm thinking you must be short of drinking water. Do you want some?"

The Norman's big laugh filled the whole ship and convulsed the crew.

* A dish of fish cooked with wine and onions. Tr.

† A delightful remark, whose charm is lost in translation: *"Troqui, troqua: bananes, ananas."*

"Well, I'll tell you, sir: we aren't in the habit of having much truck with that liquid, which is only good to wash your face with. We've got our cider aboard, and there's water enough in that, I'm telling you!"

The exchange was being concluded. The fishermen—not a hurried race—would gladly have remained longer aboard the big sailing-ship, however, to admire her rigging as connoisseurs, if Rolland had not intervened.

"Come along, boys—a cup of coffee before you leave, and then we're off. I've got the voyage to Frisco still ahead of me."

The coffee, served on the tarpaulin cover of the small after-hatch, was swallowed at once.

"Don't you worry, Captain," the skipper counseled, as he wiped his mouth. "You'll have a good east wind by noon. It's me that's telling you. Watch the land if it gets foggy."

Then, disdaining the pilot's ladder, the fishermen jumped down into their craft and made off.

"A good voyage, Captain—to you and your lady and all the crew!" the skipper called. "There'll be another good *matelote* for you, if we see you coming back!"

Geneviève's eyes were blurred as she listened to this farewell. She did not even understand the crew's hearty laughter when the Normans, uncorking a quart of brandy, poured the liquor down their throats without touching their lips to the bottle. Her emotion was exaggerating a chance phrase out of all reason. His mention of her in his good wishes took on the proportions of an adoption. After the sea with its smiles, the worthy folk who peopled it were now accepting her, offering her their welcome. Hervy, who had noticed her emotion, was mistaken as to its cause.

"Those are the last Frenchmen we shall see for a long time," he thought it his duty to say to her. "It's like when the tug lets you go: you feel more alone."

As the Norman skipper had predicted, the breeze veered to the northeast around noon and became considerably fresher. The sea, sheltered by the land masses, was still flat, but the ship's speed increased immediately.

"We shan't be long getting out of the Channel," Rolland said to Foulon. "We have come abreast of Start Point already. A hundred and eight miles more, and we'll be south of the Bishop."

"We are certainly having unhoped-for weather," Foulon had to admit. "You were right about the wind, Captain."

There were the sharp strokes of a bell, from the patent log.

"We've gone beyond thirteen knots," the lieutenant announced.

At dinner that evening, Rolland repeated, "We shan't be long in passing the Lizard. This is a magnificent speeder that we have under our feet!"

The compliment was intended for the officers, who had been on the *Atalante* longer than he. They talked, now, of Lizard Point, which for them marked the end of the land. All of them had stories to tell of ships which, as Rolland would say, had had it hard, either getting out of the English Channel or coming into it. They bandied memories back and forth, of contrary winds, dead calms, gales, fog. They recalled the Channel shipwrecks, as numerous as those of Cape Horn; the collisions and groundings that had become famous.

Geneviève, who had listened in silence to this litany of disaster, said, at last, "But you are sending shivers down my back, when I think of all that might happen to us."

Loisel answered her, laughing: "That's just the point, Madame. We are only talking of things that are past, because this time we are going through the Channel as if we were on parade."

And Hervy added, in confirmation, "It is always a good sign when seafaring men tell terrible tales. It is because they are sure that none of that will happen to them."

Foulon, who up to this time had said nothing, put in a word of amendment. "At least this time. . . ." Then he added, with that air he had of speaking as if he did not see anyone around him but was simply pursuing a thought of his own; "I went to Lizard Point when we were at Falmouth with the *Cassiopée*. It is twelve-odd miles away. There are extraordinary rocks, and caves such as I have never seen anywhere else, with veins of rare stones."

"You must have had the sun in your eyes, Monsieur Foulon," declared Rolland, for whom the Lizard had never been anything but a dark headland or a lighthouse.

"No, Captain. All the jewelers in Cornwall were coming there to get supplies of rock crystal and ophite."

Geneviève looked at him with an astonishment that was tinged with a hesitant fellow-feeling. Then he was capable, this man, of getting away from the printed map, of going twelve miles to look at rocks and caves? But the third mate had plunged now into his old depths of indifference and was entirely absorbed in the paring of an apple. After dinner, however, as he was standing aside to let the young woman pass, at the doorway of the saloon, he suggested, "I have a few books with me, Madame. If they might interest you they are at your disposal."

Geneviève thanked him.

"Sailing so suddenly, I had not time to bring a single book with me," she said, "and that is something I shall miss very much." The simple desire to appear kind and courteous made her add, "Are you married, Monsieur Foulon?"

"Yes, Madame."

The melancholy face had suddenly contracted. The young officer had answered her with a restrained violence that left her amazed and dismayed. What hidden sore had she touched? Suddenly, she caught his arm. The vessel's first broad roll had taken her unaware and sent her staggering. Foulon, recovering himself, announced, "We have passed the last land."

When Rolland returned, after picking up the Bishop Rock lighthouse, the last European beacon, he cried out, as he flung his cap on the sofa, "Here we are, out of the Channel, and in two days! That never happened to me before!" Then he went into the office and looked at the barometer. "It is going down, but hardly any. The voyage promises well with such a beginning, anyway. She's a speeder, the *Atalante!* And you can be sure I'll throw them down his throat, that damn old Hamon's backhanded compliments!"

He came back into the bedroom. Geneviève, as on the first night, had settled herself on the farther side of the bunk, her face against the wall. He put his hand on her shoulder, somewhat surprised that she should have made no reply, that she should not even have turned toward him when he came in.

"You aren't asleep already?" he asked.

She turned her head ponderously. He saw her pallid face, her mouth half-open, the dew of cold sweat that was gluing a lock of hair to her forehead.

"What's the matter? Are you sick?"

"It was when she began to roll," she groaned.

He was disappointed, but he was even more taken aback.

"But she's hardly moving at all!" he exclaimed. "What are you going to say when she starts to roll in earnest?"

Standing there at the head of the bed, his hands behind his back, he was surveying her with a dissatisfied and ill humored air. But her desolate and suppliant gaze did not succeed in finding his. He was fixing his eyes on a fold of the sheet now, instead.

"My poor darling," she apologized, in a broken voice, "look what you find when you come below to bed! And the first night that you have come. . . . But I shall get used to it, I promise you."

397

XXXIII

"HOW IS Madame Rolland?"

It was Loisel, enfolded in his streaming oilskins, who was calling to Rolland as the latter appeared on the poop. The captain shrugged his shoulders.

"Still just the same."

"That's bound to be, in this weather."

The rain was lashing them in horizontal scuds, spat out by northwest squalls. The *Atalante* was just running close to the wind, after furling her small sails. The ship was keeping her nose ahead. Rolland wanted to beat off as much as possible into the west, so as to pass at a good distance from Finisterre, in case the winds should have veered forward again. But in this Gulf of Gascony, which was always choppy, the sea was attacking the vessel across the bow, lifting her up, and then, swiftly gaining the stern, delivering a brutal upthrust there from which she took a long time to recover. The danger came from the confusion of the waters, from those waves thrown back by the nearby shores, which were tumbling in all directions like a panicky herd of animals driven to bay against a mountain wall. They were striking the ship on the flank, pounding at the hull and heeling it over, hitting the rail down to the level of the water. Sometimes, too, they would charge heavily on the port side and there would be a perilous lurch toward the bed of the wind, the risk of being taken aback and dismasted. Rolland had sent two men to the wheel, and they were laboring hard—sticking to the spokes for dear life—to keep the vessel on her course and break her sudden swerves in time.

The *Atalante* was responding to the sea's incoherence by a kind of disjointed agitation that was neither pitching nor rolling but, rather, a monstrous and convulsive churning. What they were still calling the course was no more than a series of twistings and jerkings, abortive upward movements that became downward tumbles, and then would be swerved again by the push of a swell. A profound contortion of the waves would put the ship gunnel under for several seconds, to end with a violent uprearing under the violent thrust of a misshapen roller coming up abreast.

Geneviève was lying prostrate in the havoc of her bunk.

When she had gone back to her cabin after exchangiing the few words with Foulon, she had at first been merely surprised to feel the hitherto motionless deck planking springing to activity beneath her. Nothing seemed changed in the cozy cabin. Everything appeared to be just as horizontal or vertical as it had been before. It was her own involuntary steps, her abrupt advances, her stoppings and recoils, that had first provoked an uneasy astonishment, which had been followed by a contraction of her whole being, the inner anticipation of a menace whose nature was not clear. This distress had mounted with the sea; and then her head had begun to feel squeezed and empty, an emptiness which had spread almost immediately to her body and her soul. Strength and courage, together, were being drained from her. She was at the same time tormented and exhausted, limp all over, wanting nothing but to lie flat and close her eyes, to escape from this dreadful distress by losing consciousness.

It was only by sitting wedged into a corner of the sofa that she succeeded in taking off her clothes. Yet she was growing drowsy when Rolland came in, stepping down from another world, the world from which she had just been so roughly expelled. She had scarcely promised to "get used to it" when an abrupt seizure drove her from the bunk, her teeth clenched.

A period of calm followed this first attack of vomiting, and Rolland had taken advantage of it to talk to her: to talk a great deal, to say odious things, like the counsels a rich man gives a poverty-stricken mortal to induce him to "brace up" and swim against the current.

"The whole point is not to think you *can* be sick, not to suggest it to yourself," he said. "Seasickness is more than three-quarters imagination."

She had merely murmured, "If I could get to sleep—"

But a new contortion in her stomach had sent her rushing from the bunk again, tottering on her bare feet.

It was then that he said, none too graciously, "I will make myself a bed on the sofa for tonight."

Overcome by the weariness of three nights on watch, he had fallen asleep immediately, and Geneviève had found some solace in this slumber. Not to have to listen any longer, or to answer; to be able to stumble to the other end of the room without being seen, when her empty stomach seemed to turn inside out like the finger of a glove, in order to spit out a few threads of bilious and horribly bitter liquid. . . . Then even that movement back and forth had become impossible; she could do no more than drag herself on her hands and knees to the sofa, catch at her husband's arm, and beg him for a basin.

Waking up, he had looked about him, bewildered, until he caught sight of her collapsed on the floor, her chin on her breast. It had taken him several seconds to remember that she was on the ship, and to realize what she wanted.

"Then you really are not well?" he said.

He had had to take her under the armpits to lift her back onto the bed, and he had thought of the man who was crushed, on the *Antonine*. The same slack body, the same legs like rags. . . .

He had brought her, not a basin, but a broad empty meat tin, and he had watched her exhausting herself above it, in excruciating and futile efforts that were interrupted by gasps, as of a fish hauled up on dry land. This time he was plainly disturbed as he repeated, "If you are sick when the ship is hardly budging, what will you do when she really begins to dance?"

Worn out by the dreadful night, she was asleep when he left the room, at dawn. But he had come back again, at the time when he usually brought her coffee, with nothing in his hand this morning but a plate of sea-biscuits which he had had the cook break into small pieces. She had opened her eyes when he came in.

"Well, now, you feel better?"

She had not had the strength even to shake her head. He had stood there for a moment looking at the waxen face all shiny with sweat, the pinched nostrils, the white lips; but, never having seen a woman ill, he hesitated over the meaning to ascribe to these symptoms. Above all, with the stubbornness of a bee butting against a pain of glass, he continued to stumble against his own logic, his clear visualization of cause and effect. The breeze had freshened with the morning, but the speed of the *Atalante* in a heavy sea had delighted him. In spite of a cargo of cast iron, one of the worst for rolling, she was rising on the surge with the sinewy flexibility of a great racing craft, clinging tight to the swell in a steady glide, so that the speed itself gave the pitching a long stretch that kept it from being troublesome. It seemed almost scandalous that a run so easy and rhythmic should be able to cause such a collapse!

He spoke, now, with determination: "You must eat! One must always eat after vomiting. It is vomiting from an empty stomach that makes you sick. I have not brought any coffee: liquids take the rolling inside you, running around in your stomach. You are to nibble at these little crumbs of biscuit. The sickness will wear off. It always does. Meanwhile, I'm going to strap you."

He had made her sit up, and she remained so, with her back bent and her head fallen forward. He had strapped her with a flannel band, tightly, from the groins to above the breasts. Then she had

400

dropped back on the bunk again, and he had left her, promising, "You're going to be better now; you'll see."

When he got back to the poop, the wind was showing a tendency to veer to the north. *Backing wind, bad sign,* he had thought. Then in the afternoon the breeze had slackened, shifting, at the same time, still more. It had begun to rain, and, after sunset, a calm had fallen upon a harsh and choppy sea. The *Atalante,* no longer borne up by so much as a teardrop of wind, had taken on the roll of a buoy—a big and heavy object without directing intelligence.

This hip-thrust movement altered the form of Geneviève's torment. Up to now, she had suffered only from the vessel's shiftings, its hesitations, its dashes forward. The balance of her being was destroyed by that inconsistency, which seemed to confuse everything inside her, set all her organs to swimming together in a nauseating mess. But with the violent rolling of the becalmed ship, all the brutality of the mass had been let loose to bruise and break her from without. It had started like a surly awakening of inanimate objects: banging doors; pots and pans in the pantry tumbling down with a hurly-burly that reached her in her bed; in the office next to her, something heavy that had fallen and was rolling back and forth on the floor. Then, in a more abrupt crash, a drawer directly under her bunk had flown open and spat out underwear, cakes of soap, a box of face powder. The bathroom door, which she had not closed tight, was slamming wildly. The chair Rolland had brought in as an extra, on which, overcome with nausea as she was, she had laid out her day's clothing the evening before, had upset, scattering her dress, her chemise, her corsets, her stockings, and keeping only her ruffled underdrawers hanging grotesquely to one of its arms.

When the meat can that Rolland had placed beside her on the shelf-table had also gone over, upside down, the very magnitude of the disaster had restored some of her strength. She had got up, bumping against all the corners of the furniture, and, dropping to her knees, had crawled about on the polished linoleum, trying, with hands like cotton wadding, to collect all the things that were lying there. With enormous effort, she had succeeded in gathering up the underwear and the other clothing, but she had not the strength to put back the drawer. The chair she had set on its feet capsized again; the round can went on rolling, soiling everything it touched. Desperate, she gave up the attempt at salvage, with no other idea than to pick herself up again.

A deep lurch of the vessel to port had thrown her back halfway across the bunk, on which she tried to hoist herself; but the bed fought against her, like a horse that will not let itself be mounted,

401

and the blanket kept slipping away from her clutching fingers. A door was opened and closed again, very close to her own, and this filled her with panic. Someone might knock, might come in: the novice, who would find her prostrate, in her nightgown, on the floor beside this bed. The thought of that shame had jerked her upright; she had succeeded in flinging herself on the bunk and pulling a fold of the sheet over her body.

As he felt the sailing-ship rolling heavily under his feet, Rolland, on the poop, was thinking of her, and his thought was both anxious and fair. He admitted, now, that she could be, that she must be, ill. He had just had the sails furled, heavy with rain; he had even had the mains'l fitted with robands, to receive the blow which he foresaw behind this calm, and for which, standing beside the helmsman, he was waiting. There could be no question of his leaving this post, even for five minutes, to go down and reassure her. Then whom could he send? Not an officer. . . . The novice? A mere boy. . . . He called the officer on watch. "Monsieur Hervy, will you have the carpenter come up here?"

The carpenter, François Huchet, had been nicknamed "My Pension" by the men, because, at forty-four, he was approaching the age for a pension, and he used to speak of it in every connection: he never undertook any piece of work without muttering something about getting his pension soon! He boasted, further, of being the only grandfather in the crew, thanks to a daughter who had married at eighteen. It was all this that had decided Rolland: since there was no one else's wife to send to his own, an "old man" would do.

"Huchet, you are to go to my cabin and put the side plank on the bunk. With anyone as seasick as my wife is, this rolling is enough to make her fall out of bed."

Huchet went down. He knocked, heard no response, and went in. This time everything was on the floor: the mattress, the woman, and a whole kit of bureau drawers and their contents trotting all over the place! He stood aghast on the doorstep for a moment, then he, too, said, "You aren't well?"

Crumpled up beside the bunk, helpless as a sawdust doll against the ship's tossings, she had not seen the newcomer until her head was thrown back by the *Atalante's* downward swoop. Huchet seized her beneath the arms, lifted her to the sofa, and then remade the bed, watching her out of the corner of his eye for fear she would begin to slide. After that, he fastened the side plank to the bunk; then came back and leaned down toward her.

"Put your arm around my neck," he said.

She tried, but her arm fell back.

Then he took her up, his own arms under her knees and her back, and laid her in the bed, all limp, like a woman who has fainted. His mind now at peace, he put back the drawers that had fallen out, and locked them. He made a pile of the soiled linen and bundled it under his arm, recovered the tinned-meat can and stopped it up with a napkin, and tied the chair to the bunk with one of the bits of string that were always lying around at the bottom of his pockets. This completed his housework, and he turned back to her.

"It will wear off," he assured her. "The body gets used to the motion. But it takes time. Never mind, we're on the way to the good spots."

She gathered all her forces, to screw her face into a smile. He stood beside the bed, looking at her with sympathy.

"It's tearing you to bits," he said. "You'd rather be thrown over-board than have to budge an inch. I sailed on the *Solidor* two years ago, with Captain Hardouin and his wife, and she was like you: no worse, but just as bad. It lasted a week, with her; a week when she couldn't swallow a mouthful. And then she got the best of it, and even off Cape Horn she never turned a hair! It's like the toothache: people laugh at it, but it makes you mighty sick." He saw her closing her eyes, and finished: "The best thing is to try to sleep."

He put the extra pillow against the side plank, as a padding, and went out.

"It lasted a week. . . ." All that was still alive in her had em-braced that figure as if it were a pillar of support. But her aching head, that felt as if nails were being driven into it, had to give up counting those days, adding those she had already lived through in the depths of the pit, subtracting these, and finding the sum still due. Time had its limits now only in a few halts for sleep, from which she would be dragged by brutal attacks of nausea. And she was so cold, in spite of the double blankets; so thirsty, in spite of the milk-and-water that came up as soon as it was swallowed. There was the day with the horizon turning upside down beyond the portholes; and there was the night with its sense of endlessness, the feeling that it was invading you and turning everything to darkness within you, and that this was still the night—this forlorn hopeless-ness, this dreadful indifference to everything.

Her husband brought her only one solace: the certainty that everything would be all right when they got into the trade winds, into the good weather those breezes brought. There had been a gust from the southwest, after the calm, off the Gulf of Gascony, and a rough sea along the coast of Portugal. Today the wind was shifting to the north as it grew stronger, and the sea was higher—it was a heavy sea. But the *Atalante* was whipping along with a carrying wind and all sails set, toward the sun, and the warmth and tranquillity of the tropics.

"Only, you've got to have nourishment! It's a full week since you swallowed a mouthful. You can't stick it out on that diet! Come now, make yourself eat!"

How would he have guessed that he was adding all his weight to the ship's rolling, to aggravate it, or that a man's serene incomprehension is an insult and a torture for a sick woman? It is a sure instinct that leads a woman to hide her sufferings and distresses from her husband, because she realizes how incapable he is of sympathizing with them, even of visualizing them. Geneviève was the only woman—and a sick woman—among healthy and robust men, the healthiest and the most robust of whom was her husband. And her sickness was not dangerous, not an ailment that could be taken seriously. "They laugh at it," the carpenter had reminded her. They called it "counting your shirts," and "feeding the fishes." Seafaring men scoffed at it, as a tribute the sea would exact from those who were not at home there, a practical joke for novices.

"In another week, you won't even be thinking about it."

"A week!" she moaned.

That was the limit the carpenter had fixed, four days ago. . . . Would someone or other be coming back every week, then, to say, "One week more"?

"It will never be over," she said.

"You are crazy!" he retorted. "We are beyond the parallel of Gibraltar. At this rate, we shall pass Madeira day after tomorrow, and the Canary Islands at the end of the week."

He refrained from adding, "No voyage ever started out so well as this one," and from telling her how pleased he was. It irritated him to be obliged to conceal that satisfaction from her. He would have liked to talk to her about his work, his good work, like all those men who came home to their wives in the evening. Now that he had a wife of his own, he had a great desire to talk, to set forth and explain those impressions and reactions which he had so easily kept to himself in the old days. And besides, had she not got him accustomed to feeling himself understood, forestalled in understanding? First reticently, then with the swiftness that was characteristic of him in everything, he had formed the habit of confiding in her. And look how he was finding her now: apathetic, unresponsive, all taken up with the writhings of her viscera! It was just his luck!

Yet he had things to say, and they were important things—about the ship, the officers, the men, and, especially, himself!

The ship was the largest, the most beautiful, the fastest, that he had ever commanded. He had not yet exhausted the pride that the magnificent four-master conferred upon him, from this "bathroom" here to the fifteen knots which the *Atalante* attained with such ease in a good wind. Her delicate lines, he had just learned, had been inspired by the famous English clipper, *Jenny Lightbody— "Jenny au corps léger"*—which was so renowned for its swift sailing.

Then there were the officers. . . . Loisel, who had passed the written examinations at the Naval College and flunked on his oral tests, had tacked his course toward the merchant marine. Foulon, a balking horse whose doctor-father had made him start medical studies, had run away from the university to go to sea as an apprentice. Of the three, only Hervy had come up like himself, Rolland, from the common sailors' ranks.

At the beginning, the new captain had been distrustful of this first mate who was always smiling and well-groomed, this junior officer whose silence could so easily pass for disdain. One evening, in the saloon, Hervy had told a story about one of his sailings when all the crew had been so drunk that the second mate had had a world of trouble finding two men who were capable of launching a boat and rowing to the jetty to get the captain. *"Rari nantes,"* Loisel had murmured, as he passed around the wine. Foulon had smiled quickly. Hervy, abashed, had fallen silent. As for Rolland, he had had the feeling that those two, the two who were better educated, were talking over the heads of the seamen-officers. He had not liked it, and he caught it up.

"Do you speak Chinese?" he asked.

"Alas, no, Captain. It would have served me well at Frisco."

And with perfect naturalness Loisel had launched upon a very lively adventure that had befallen him in San Francisco's Chinatown.

The captain had observed his first mate at close hand during difficult hours, to start with, just as he had done with Gicquel on the voyage before. Loisel had shown himself to be polite—Rolland could find nothing but that idiotic and extraordinary word to sum up his impressions. Drenched, knocked about, in the water up to his middle, Loisel remained polite. He continued to express himself like a gentleman, without swearing, without screaming, but with an exactness in his orders which the new captain had quickly appreciated. He had never encountered such agility of mind in any officer. There was no "dead time" with Loisel: those few seconds they would all take to understand and accept a sudden menace, before calling out the order that must meet it. Loisel saw the whole thing on the instant: the man who was going to be swept off his feet, and what he would hang onto; the block on the point of jamming; the wave that would cause a lurch. Then there would be a word, a gesture, sometimes a mere glance, which the men grasped at once—for one realized that they were broken in to his ways. Rolland, who was not given to paying compliments, had sought for a compliment to pay him and had found it. After a tack carried out in record time, as Loisel, streaming with sea-water, was returning to the poop, he had said to him, "That was beautiful work, Monsieur Loisel. You made me think of an orchestra leader."

The mate's face had lighted up. His first response was a look that was surprised, and then happy.

"Nothing could give me more pleasure, Cap'n," he declared.

Since that day, Rolland had felt, on the mate's part, a regard which was addressed to him more as the man than as the ship's master. He himself had even indulged in a bit of friendly teasing, the time he had seen his second-in-command flung by a crashing wave against the freshly tarred shrouds, and pulling out his pocket mirror as he carefully wiped his face.

With Foulon, it was quite different. He was like a composite of Monnard and Gicquel. His coldness could be sensed as something deliberate, something he was laced into like a suit of armor. Along with this, he had a taste for contradiction and paradox. That he should have become a sailor, and the sailor he was, gave evidence already of that. He came from Moulins, and he had never seen the ocean when he made up his mind to go to sea. When he caught sight of it for the first time, at the end of a narrow street in Dieppe, he had said calmly, "Well, well, mountains!"

When he had told about this, in the saloon, Rolland had cried out upon it as a big piece of spoofing, but Foulon, in his sharp-edged voice, had averred, "In the half-mist, that evening, it did look like mountains."

His special worth lay in an omnipresent attention to detail, so punctilious that Rolland had never, in his morning inspections, found anything that could be improved upon. Yet the men did not seem to be irritated by the constant effort the second mate demanded of them, in everything that concerned the ship's appearance. At the end of a squall, and when another was threatening, when there was just time to straighten out the tangle of rigging on the deck, Rolland had seen Foulon make a sailor undo a hastily coiled line and twist it again in regular spirals, merely by saying, "Come, come, give it a little style!"

When the work was done over, and done well, the officer gave an approving little nod and passed on to something else.

Rolland knew how much these scrupulously thorough officers can exasperate the men. But among the *Atalante's* crew he had observed nothing but a prompt and easy obedience, sometimes punctuated by the boyish smile of someone who thought he was hiding a piece of negligence and was unresentfully amused on seeing it discovered.

One morning when the captain was standing on the poop he saw Foulon, who was walking up and down the ship's deck below him, pause before a copper rod, call a seaman on the running watch, and point out to him Rolland did not know what, probably a spot of verdigris. And the wind had carried the beginning of a sentence: "When a man is a sailor on the *Atalante*—"

He had realized, then, that this second mate had succeeded in giving the men a personal pride in their ship. Nothing is more difficult, or requires more tact. He remembered what Berlot, at Kanala, had said of Captain Thirard: "His two watches would break their necks seeing which one could make her side the best-looking." It was something which he, Rolland, had never obtained except by demanding it.

Of Hervy and Pléneau, there was nothing to say. The first was a conscientious giant, a good fellow who worked well at his trade after the fashion of the old sailing-ship officers, bawling and roaring in thunderous blasts, and laughing with the same gusto. Pléneau was a sort of young farmer in his Sunday clothes, who had strayed onto a ship; he was absorbed in his chickens and pigs, but he held his own in the steward's cabin with the sharpness of a peasant at market.

There was still another officer on the *Atalante*, whose presence Rolland felt more and more, though he noted nothing on board which fully explained it: his predecessor, Captain Belin. He had commanded the vessel since her launching, three years before; and the *Atalante* was the "admiral ship" of the company. That was enough to classify her commander. In the merchant marine, when the choice of a captain is in question, neither favoritism nor intrigue has any part to play, since the ship-owners would pay for an undeserved promotion out of their own pockets. For the best ship they seek the best man; and Rolland would never have commanded the *Atalante* if Belin had not resigned his post. He had succeeded other captains before this, but now he felt himself to be indeed a successor, with all that that word carries over from the past. He had taken the place of a man who had set a strong and significant stamp upon that place, and even at his taking over he had read in all eyes, and in all the silences, the comparison with the chief who had preceded him.

He had run across Belin two or three times, in various ports. He remembered him as an affable man in his forties who listened, smiling, more than he talked, and who would fix a gaze upon you that was at first benevolent but quickly became incisive. With his full round face, his tact, his measured words, the quiet authority that emanated from him, what Rolland thought of, strange as it might seem, was a bishop. And he had not regarded that association as so absurd after he had been put in command of the *Atalante* and ascertained, almost every day, the veneration in which the former captain was held.

Rolland's first command had been of a new ship; he had commanded others, since then, in which what was needed was a regaining of control. His ship-owners knew that he was a man to set things to rights, and to obtain the maximum output; so he had most often replaced captains who were tired or old. This time, he had to equal his predecessor before hoping to surpass him. The new atmosphere which he found here had been created by Belin, and his former officers were preserving it jealously: the care for elegance which was maintained by Foulon, as on a racing yacht; Loisel's courteous good will. Now, Rolland had a principle: to everyone his own method if it is a good one. These were.

When he had become convinced of that, it was himself that he kept an eye on, too sagacious, too proud also, to cast himself in the role of the narrow-minded new chief who changes everything, so that all will be different from what it was before he came. He must make his own impression, certainly; but first of all by proving that he, the captain come up from the ranks, regarded as altogether natural that spirit of the "admiral ship"—almost like a warship— that held sway from the wardroom to the fo'c'sle.

He had very quickly realized the help that Geneviève could be to him. She was truly made for her, this ship of which the comfort, on his first visit, had almost intimidated him. When she had seated herself in the officers' quarters, with its rosewood paneling, in front of the spacious plate-glass mirror that was redoubling the light, and when she had indicated the places at table with such sophisticated ease, the impression she had produced upon the officers had been by no means lost upon him. He had felt that he himself was profiting by having chosen a wife of this category, and being loved by her so much that she had come running to the ship in spite of his orders and had climbed the dangerous ladder in order to spend a few hours with him.

They all asked about her every morning. As for him, he could only repeat, "We are moving very fast toward good weather. The sickness will pass of itself when we get there."

The bell had just sounded six strokes, and he went below to the noon meal. The cabin boy brought in an omelette. This was due to Pléneau's vigilance, to the padlocked doors of his hen-coop. He was not one whom a pilfering cook would have been able to take in about an egg! He received the others' compliments with a hearty laugh of pleasure, that thrust out his shiny cheeks like two big apples. Then Loisel suggested, "Shall we keep some of it for Madame Rolland? I am sure she would let herself be tempted."

"There are some more eggs," declared Pléneau. "I thought of that."

Foulon raised his eyes.

"Is she taking a little nourishment?"

"Not enough to amount to anything," Rolland had to confess. "A few crumbs of biscuit—when they stay down."

"Then she must be very weak," Foulon commented, in his colorless voice. "It is ten days now. . . ."

"That is what I was just saying to her. She ought to make herself eat."

Hervy shook his head. "Yes, but when the stomach doesn't cooperate—"

"Ah, there it is!"

They fell silent. They knew from experience, as he did, that there was nothing to do but wait.

Rolland was to remember later that it was just at this moment that he had said, "There is one thing I should like to ask you, about Captain Belin. How did it happen, the—the accident to his son?"

The question brought a frozen look to all their faces, such as follows an impropriety. Rolland realized at once that he should have questioned one of them by himself, and at a favorable moment; at the end of a watch, for example, when one talks more freely. And it should have been in good weather, not now when the wine was whirling around at the bottom of their glasses in the *Atalante's* present intolerable frying-pan dance. He thought of this too late, and he would have been hard put to it to account for the compelling and sudden curiosity that had made him speak.

Loisel at last brought himself to answer, in a tone which he tried to make unconcerned: "It happened on the 6th of September, on the return voyage, when we were barely past Cape Horn. There was a raging sea, but most of all there were continual abrupt shifts of the wind, northwest-southwest, such as often occur, as you know, Captain, at the end of the southern winter. It was when we were fleeing before it, at about five o'clock that evening, that an enormous wave swept over the ship from one end to the other, as we were clewing up the main upper tops'l. It washed the crew all the way under the quarter-deck, wounded three men, and carried the captain's son overboard. He was serving as cabin boy. Captain Belin had wanted him to start at the bottom of the ladder. He had taken him out of school for that voyage."

Everything seemed to have been said; nothing had been said as yet.

"Did Captain Belin not authorize you to put out a boat?" Rolland asked, in a deliberately restrained voice.

The mate's only reply was to shake his head. It was Hervy who answered: "With the weather what it was, that would have been to lose seven men in order not to save one."

"But weren't there volunteers?"

This time it was Foulon's clear voice that stated, "There were more than ten."

"And who begged to be allowed to go!" said Hervy. And he added, in a lower tone, "Monsieur Loisel has not told you that the captain was obliged to forbid him, officially, to launch the life-boat."

. . . That life-boat of which the mate would have taken immediate command. . . .

Loisel gave a slight shrug of his shoulders: that was something it was unnecessary to recall.

"Obviously, Belin was doing his duty," Rolland concluded, after some reflection.

He himself remembered having lost a man in almost the same circumstances, and in an equally rough sea.

He did not recount this memory. It would have seemed a mockery to the four men who had lived through the *Atalante's* tragedy and were living through it again. As for him, he could do no more, and no less, than imagine it: both watches, in the midst of clewing up the main upper tops'l, all at once swept off their feet by the wave and flung, in a tangle of arms and legs, against the quarter-deck; then the cry, when they had picked themselves up, "Man overboard!"—the first, and only, time that the poor youngster had been taken as a "man." Then, in Rolland's ears, rang another cry, a choking cry, "It's the cap'n's son!" Then Loisel shouting, "Put off the life-boat!" and, dashing to the deck, immediately stopped by the voice that said, "No." The mate, then, turning back, raising his head toward the poop-rail, pleading. . . . Rolland was picturing it all so clearly, what his face must have been at that minute. . . . And behind him ten sailors, more than ten, calling out to the man who was being crucified, "Let us go, Cap'n!" And Belin, his hands clenched on the rail, shaking his head to tell them no, and then finding his voice again—and what a voice it must have been!—to bring out, "I forbid it, Monsieur Loisel."

What Rolland would have liked to know was what Loisel had

done at that moment. Had he made another plea, had he flung himself into action in the ship's movement, or had he gone, with leaden feet, to the poop, to find and support the father? Rolland's mind was lingering on that frightful moment, but the others had already left it behind.

"The worst came afterward," Hervy explained, in a low voice, "the nearer we got to France. Madame Belin had not wanted the little fellow to sail. One might have said she had a presentiment."

The stillness of the four officers made it plain that their thought had taken them back to the company of the man who was ticking off the days like someone condemned to death; who, as he marked the ship's position on the chart every day at noon, was seeing the distance lessen between him and the utter shipwreck that awaited him at the dock. Loisel was recalling the day when he had found Captain Belin sitting at his desk before his open prayer-book. He knew that the captain was very faithful in his religious observances, and he had been glad to think of the solace he must find in prayer. But it was a drawn and distorted face that Belin had raised from the little red-edged book. "Listen to this, Monsieur Loisel. . . ." And he had read to him, in French, a strophe from the *Dies Irae:* "*What terror will grip me, when the Judge comes to demand my accounting. . . . What shall I say then, unhappy wretch that I am?*" Then, as he closed the book, he had added, "I do not know what the Last Judgment will be, but it cannot be worse than what is waiting for me at home."

Loisel had pleaded with him, passionately. Before she was a mother, Madame Belin was his wife. She knew him; she was proud of him. She would understand that he had done his whole duty, a terrible duty.

"She will be worthy of you, Captain," the mate had declared.

But Belin had fixed a gaze of appalling lucidity upon him: "My dear Loisel, would you dare to tell her that I had forbidden you to launch the life-boat, that I had kept you from trying to do anything?"

Loisel, crushed, had been silent. The shadow of a heartbreaking smile had appeared on the captain's face.

"You see. . . . And you see, too, it was not seven lives for one; it was seven lives for three: his own, his mother's, mine. I knew that, from the first moment. But it made no difference."

Hervy, who had remained more on the outside of the tragedy, went on with the story: "The flag was at half-mast. But when a steamship came astern of us off Rio, the captain had it run up to full staff again. He did not want to give any notice of the disaster. He was determined that his wife should only learn of it from him."

Rolland was picturing that return now, but in his own way: the frenzied reproaches of the mother whose child had been drowned, the mad refusal to understand what was perfectly clear, the furious indictment of the man who had not cried out, as she would have done, "Save him!" There would have been only one chance, as he saw it, of Belin's silencing her: if he had said, "I sent Loisel and six men to look for him; they did not come back." Failing this criminal action, he stood condemned.

Now that his inquiry was finished, he felt almost scornful of Belin for having remained ashore, to begin again, indefinitely, the same futile argument, or to submit in silence, chained to a woman who would not forgive him the pain of having done his duty—that duty of a sea captain, which every woman refuses to understand.

Not for one second did it occur to him that the woman who was suffering for him, a few steps away, would have been able to understand, to join him, if need be, at the summit of such a calvary, and to suffer in his anguish first of all.

"If I had been in Belin's place," he asserted, "I might have changed my ship, but I should have gone back to sea."

XXXIV

THEY HAD PASSED Madeira without seeing it. For several days the sea had been blue beneath a pale sky, and the swells had lengthened out and, on their passage, lifted the *Atalante* with the rhythm of a tranquil breath. Then the winds abated when they were southwest of the Canaries; senseless flurries from one side or the other made it necessary to be continually bracing the yards; and the men were already working half-naked, streaming with perspiration, with the Sahara to port. At last, one afternoon, the northeast trade winds announced their presence, timidly at first but with a good brisk breeze by nightfall. This time it was really fine weather! The *Atalante* would pursue her regular course like a steamship now, without a line ever having to be touched; and the men would sleep on the level deck, under the stars, for eight hours without interruption.

In the cabin, Geneviève was stifling, in spite of the open portholes. Since the *Atalante* had begun rising and descending almost imperceptibly, in long and gentle undulations, she had very slowly come back to the surface of existence. She was not suffering any more,

412

but the exhaustion of her long-drawn-out torment had literally paralyzed her. It was a paralysis, a negation, that was both in and around her; everything seemed to be mingled together in a torpor to which the heat, as of a steam-bath, was now adding its weight. The only thought left to her was that she must be careful not to move, so as to avoid waking the entrails that were now sleeping like a bunch of snakes; the festoons the ship was tracing, its outstretchings and slack relaxations, were keeping the sense of insecurity alive in her, the feeling that the cessation of conscious distress was undependable and still menaced: just not to stir!

Rolland, in the face of this period of quiet, had been only too tempted to meet his wife's seasickness with a stony, and logical, lack of sympathy. Among sailors, seasickness is combated by action. It is treated by methods which are brutal and unfailingly efficacious. One drags a Barquet from his bunk, kicks him up on deck, fastens him with a rope around his feet, and has him slapped and doused by the breakers. Those icy shocks, the fear of being washed overboard, the frantic search for something to hold fast to—all this serves very quickly to supplant the discomfort of an upset stomach. The instinct of self-preservation, thus awakened, is in full play, and from the moment that enters the game it is the only thing of which the sick person is conscious. He still vomits, but, so to speak, with discretion; the whole being is concentrated on the threat of death, which is given brutal significance by the sea washing over the deck, ready to gather up and carry away all that abandons itself to it.

Obviously there could be no question of this heroic treatment with a woman; but was he not right, thenceforth, in repeating to her all day long, "You ought to fight against it; you ought to brace up."?

This morning he had come to the cabin with a piece of chicken, white meat, which the cook had put on a warmed plate and deluged with melted butter. Geneviève had rejected it as if it were a poison, pushing the plate away with frantic hands. And he, beside himself, had cried out, "But, in God's name, try!"

Then, frowning, he had sat her up in the bunk, all spineless, yielding pitifully to the motion of the ship as it shifted her head to right and left like the bubble in a spirit-level. When he had her propped up among the pillows, which he pushed back with his fist, he cut the tender meat into very small morsels and thrust them, in a little spoon, against her closed mouth.

"Come now, you must do it. Keep swallowing. If you can't keep it down, then we'll see."

She turned her head away with a grimace of disgust, like a child threatened with a spoonful of cod-liver oil.

413

"Put it on the table," she said. "I'll try it by myself."

"You promise?"

"Yes."

When he came back, an hour later, she had pecked away, bit by bit, until she had eaten about half of what was on the plate.

"You see, you are better," he said, in triumph. "I told you so!"

She did not answer, or open her eyes. He stood looking at her for some time, in silence. He was becoming aware that in these disturbances the balance had been reversed. He was finding himself at the top, and Geneviève at the bottom. He had accepted, and sought after, in her, that superiority which he was proud to recognize wherever he encountered it—in Monnard, in Monnard's brother the priest, in Thirard, in Belin. Before he met her, his experience with women had been confined to the girls in the ports of call, more or less artificially dolled up, and the plump and serene spouses of his fellow-officers, absorbed in looking after their well-upholstered homes and bringing up their children in the father's absence. There was nothing to get excited over, in any of that.

But with Geneviève he had had the sense of new directions which she was discovering for him with every word; of mysterious zones which she inhabited, and into which she could retire, without his knowing any too well how to find her again. It was precisely what he had sensed for the first time years ago in Dunkerque, when he had seen an unknown girl coming down the steps from a theater: the certitude that another world existed, a new world of intuitions and thoughts in which certain beings were at home, while he went roaming about its edges.

From these domains Geneviève had been driven by this grotesque and degrading malady. No ailment, so long as it lasted, could be more profoundly destructive of mind and spirit, or surrender the entire self more completely to merely animal nature. To see her now, besotted by misery like any beggar woman, like the wretched creatures of whom he had encountered so many in the nooks and crannies of the ports—that was to despoil her of all prestige. He knew himself: he would never forget any fall from high estate, even if it were as involuntary, as undeserved, as this.

It might not have needed much pressure to make him confess that in his heart of hearts he was not wholly dissatisfied to have his wife reduced to a strictly physical presence on this ship. She was occupying merely those few feet of bunk that he had given over to her; for he had installed himself, definitively, in the chart-house. In this way, he did not have to be divided in spirit, or to reproach himself for the despotic interest with which this ship inspired him—the most beautiful ship of his career, and, without any doubt, the last. . . .

For he was realizing with force, here at the bedside of this woman who was being tormented by an absurd ailment, that the real menace, the one that was weighing upon his life, was elsewhere. Shipping under sail was, little by little, vanishing. Already the Bordes Company was setting up auxiliary motors on its vessels. The latest sailing-ships built, such as the *Atalante,* attained perfection; but she was like the end-piece of a fireworks display. No more were coming from the shipyards. This one was only three years old, which meant that a fine career still lay ahead of her. And Rolland would guide her to the end, since he was now, following Belin's withdrawal, the best captain in the Company. That made a kind of marriage with the *Atalante,* after the short-lived affairs with other craft. It followed, from that, that a wife would be missed less on this ship than on any other, because this was a ship that demanded all there was in a man. It was the former captain of the *Andromède,* the *Marie-Laurentine,* the *Saint Sever,* the *Argonaute,* who had kept Geneviève aboard, not the commander of the *Atalante.* The last-named was almost astonished that he had for one moment believed it necessary.

"Go away. Leave me alone."

For an instant he actually imagined that he had been thinking out loud, and that she was exiling him for treason: one of those divinations that had so often amazed him. But she added, "I don't want you to look at me."

His alarm dispelled, he recovered himself and began to laugh. "You're getting your vanity back; that's a good sign!" he said.

He did not suspect that she had followed his unguarded course of reflection from beginning to end, that she had felt all the dreadfulness of his implacable scrutiny. He was merely thinking that if she was worrying about her appearance everything must be beginning to be all right. . . .

He felt even more assured of that when he went up again to the poop. The *Atalante* had found her own climate now. For all ships, the localities of the trade winds are easy and agreeable; but this one, with her elegance and her patrician quality, seemed made for this sparkling sea and this radiant sky.

"A ship ahead to starboard, on the same course."

A topman on the mainm'st had just called this out, very high above his head.

He trained his binoculars on the horizon at once, but from the deck it was impossible to see anything. On the yard of the main tops'l where he was working, the sailor could only make out the top of the other ship's masts.

"If the wind doesn't die down, we'll pass her before dark," Loisel averred.

The mate spoke with calm certainty, though he did not know whether or not their fellow-craft was going to sheet and haul taut, so as not to let itself be overtaken.

"Before dark?" Rolland repeated doubtfully.

"That's the schedule, Captain: eight to ten hours to catch up with a ship, from the moment she is signaled. Once, with Captain Belin, we held the *Potasi* astern for thirty-two hours before we let her pass us."

The *Potasi*, that great German five-master, the fastest sailing-ship in the world!

Rolland did not ask to hear the story of this prowess. He had suddenly become aware that the *Atalante* was running on a sea that was as level as a pond. Her gliding movement was now perfectly horizontal. He was surprised at himself for noticing it; to him, as to all seafaring men, the motion of the ship, starting from a certain degree of calm, was something of which he was unconscious. He felt it no more than a man walking feels little roughnesses in the road. Yet something in him had just put him on the alert.

"If you put a billiard ball on the deck it wouldn't budge an inch, as they say," he remarked. "There can't be any more question of seasickness!"

"Some people have it even on a train," Loisel reminded him. Then he added, at once: "But it is not like that with Madame Rolland. She was so well before we got out of the Channel. And there is less motion today than the day we sailed! She ought to be able to come out into the air."

"That is what I have been telling her over and over for the last two days," exclaimed Rolland. "You ought to go and tell it to her."

From the tone in which he made the suggestion, this could pass for a mere sally. As a matter of fact, if Loisel had said, "At your service, Captain," Rolland would have led him without hesitation to his cabin. But the mate contented himself with a brief smile and then made a suggestion of his own:

"We ought to have a kind of nook fixed up, on the poop, with two or three tarpaulins, where she would be sheltered from the sun and as quiet as in her own cabin. Would you like me to attend to it, Captain? I believe that might persuade her."

Rolland agreed, and Loisel called out, "Thomas, Menu!"

He went off toward the stern with the two men from the running watch. Rolland continued his stroll on the deck, his hands behind his back. But as the rest of the rust-chippers, interested in this unfamiliar task for two of their number, remained with their heads turned and their tools in the air, he paused to look at them; they went back to their work immediately.

"Well, here we are, Captain. . . ."

With pieces of sail-cloth stretched in the shrouds, Loisel had had a tent constructed on the poop, closed on three sides and open only toward the stern. It was reached directly from the chart-house. In it the mate had placed a chaise-longue, with a pillow. "As quiet as in her own room," he had said; and Rolland observed that the woman lying there would not, indeed, be seen by anyone, either the men on the deck, the helmsman, or the officer of the watch. And she herself would have no sight of the sea: nothing but the sails and the sky, fixed and steady. He went below to the cabin.

"You are going up on deck. They have put a chaise-longue up there for you. You must get out in the air. You won't gain any strength as long as you are stuck down here."

This time he had found her with her eyes open, staring at the low ceiling with its stripes of light wood that seemed intended not to confuse her dulled mind. The perfect evenness of the ship's forward movement, the absence of any pitching or tossing whatever, had brought her only the stupefaction of someone stunned after an interminable fall. She was lying at the bottom of the crevasse, with only the instinct of immobility and the fear of a thought whose awakening would do no more than measure the height from which she had been flung. He, meanwhile, was bustling about the room, gathering up her clothing, and she realized that this time he would not go away without her.

"Give me a mirror," she said at last.

She gazed at herself for some time, and then murmured, "I look like a corpse."

"You are to get dressed and go up on deck," he repeated.

Her reply was almost a scream: "No, no! I should be too ashamed! I should make you too ashamed!"

He seized her under the armpits, to make her sit up.

"Come now, don't be silly! What do you want? A comb?"

He brought her one, from the "bathroom." With an arm that kept falling, she began to try to get the tangles out of her hair. The comb was like a leaden weight in her hand, and her head dropped on her shoulder to meet it. He stood in the middle of the cabin and watched her exhausting labor.

"I can never do it alone," she moaned.

"And what kind of hairdresser do you think I am?" he retorted.

He took the comb, nevertheless, and began to attack her lusterless hair; he only really applied himself to the task after he had run into

417

a bad tangle and made her jump, but at last the mop became normal tresses whose suppleness and smoothness brought back to him a little of the woman she had been, and made him gentler.

"Now shall I braid it?" he asked.

That, he knew how to do! How many yards of hemp he had braided since his days as a cabin boy! He was almost disappointed when she refused!

"No. Just gather it together in the back and fasten it at my neck."

"Fasten it, with what? A ribbon?"

"You won't find any."

He took out his knife, cut off the end of her corset lace, twisted her hair in his hand, and tied it at the nape of her neck, like a horse's tail. Drawn back like this, it made her face look still smaller. Then he sat down beside her, swinging his legs over the raised edge of the bunk, and helped her dress. The work went swiftly. But when he hooked up the corsets that hung so loosely on her, he exclaimed, "Well, bless me, you haven't got any fatter! Now for the stockings. . . ."

He pulled them straight up on her legs with a single movement. Then he slipped her skirt over her head and got her into her lawn blouse, which plagued him because there were too many little pearl buttons to insert into the buttonholes. Finally he leaned down, picked up her shoes, and put them on her feet.

"There, you're in sailing order," he said.

The seaman's phrase meant simply "ready," and she knew it; but it seemed a mockery to her none the less. Her flaccid fingers attempted to pull her blouse into better shape.

"Find me a scarf—in the lower drawer."

He turned it inside out to discover a green silk scarf, which he handed to her. She looked at it in dismay. The one color that would most accentuate the waxen pallor of her face! She did not dare ask him to hunt for another, and she tried to tie it in a bandanna knot. But there was always that weight of her arms, falling back again as soon as she raised them.

"You only have to fix it the way country women do."

He took the scarf from her, folded it in a triangle on his knee, and knotted it kerchief style under her chin.

"And there you are!"

He took her arm.

"Give me a handkerchief and a bottle of cologne," she demanded.

She passed the handkerchief, soaked in the alcohol of the eau-de-cologne, over her face that was all shiny with perspiration.

"A cat's toilet," he remarked.

But before he corked the bottle he poured a generous amount on another, folded, handkerchief, which he handed to her.

"And now, off we go!"

He had taken hold of her under the right shoulder, and pulled her to her feet; but he felt that she was escaping from him, sinking down on the other side. He came to a quick decision and picked her up in his arms. The narrow corridor was empty, and he carried her through it, and up the companionway which opened onto the charthouse. She had put her arm around his neck, and as they went up the stairs she leaned her cheek against his, to mark the gesture of force with a little sweetness. He took her out on the poop and placed her, skillfully, on the chaise-longue. Her look showed that she, too, appreciated the perfect isolation of the place arranged for her.

"You see, you'll be comfortable here. Up here, you're going to get strong again." He was entrusting her to what had given him his muscles: the pure air, the sun, the tonic breeze. "Now rest," he said.

He gave her a gay little wink before he went away. Then he abandoned her to her lassitude, which little by little, however, was being filled with a sense of well being. She went to sleep. . . .

"Come, swallow this for me."

He was returning with two eggs, one in each hand. That was a windfall, the gift of the tongue-tied Pléneau. When he left his chicken-coop, which was always kept like one in an agricultural fair, he had said to Rolland, "I have some fresh eggs, Cap'n. Madame Rolland ought to suck them. They always go down."

He said "suck" for "swallow," but Rolland was immediately attracted by the idea: food that was quick, fresh, and easy; to be eaten by drinking. He made two little holes in each one, and while Geneviève was taking them he announced, "You will have two more presently. That will soon get you built up again."

At noon it was David, the cook, who appeared between the iron stanchions of his galley door and said, "You must have a bottle of beef extract given to me, Cap'n, to put in Madame Rolland's bouillon."

The stout master of the kitchen, too, had at once had the idea of an easy and efficacious form of nourishment, extract of meat. Rolland had thought of meat only to regret the lack of it: "If we could only give her a good rare beefsteak!"

Summer days, when the eyes drank in the sky, when the invigorating trade wind lingered over face and hands with its mild caress, when the vessel's smooth progress brought the appeasement of the open sea, and its profound relaxation. . . . Hours like this were slipping by for Geneviève in a happy lethargy, like that of a baby never tired of contemplating the ceiling when it wakes up. She did not feel any resurgence of energy, nothing that would be like water gushing from the depths and bubbling forth on the surface; her convalescence resembled, rather, the spreading of a spot of oil. She understood only that everything was coming back from very far away, and very slowly: the force still stagnant deep within her and not yet reaching her limbs; the thoughts that could still form no relationship with one another; the feelings that could vanish away after an instant's brightness and warmth, like heat lightning. After the mere look that was at first her only way of response and speech, she was now rediscovering a smile as a means of expression; there were as yet no words.

The life of the ship came to her only by fits and starts, in fragmentary images. This afternoon, there had been a cry from the helmsman: "To the line!"

The men had heard the tic-toc of the warning toggle struck on the deck. Geneviève saw silhouettes appearing swiftly on the poop, rushing toward the stern. Then there was Loisel's voice: "Hand over hand, and gently!"

The men were looking into the ship's wake, where a large fish was running at the end of the line.

"Haul it up gently, boys. It's going to tire itself out. It's a tuna— and what a size!"

Rolland's voice was raised now. "We are going too fast. Bear away before the wind. Take care that the spanker doesn't jibe."

Not stirring, only hearing orders, she was sensing the big catch coming close.

"Pass the line out beyond the shrouds. When we've got him straight up, we'll send out a running bow-line to hook him by the tail."

At last the bos'n called out, "Haul up your ox!"

There were squealings from the block, cadenced grunts, then hard slaps, wet and furious, on the after deck.

"He weighs a hundred and fifty pounds, I'm telling you!"

"You can call it two hundred!"

They dragged the creature along right beneath the chaise-longue, so that the captain's wife could admire it. She had to lift herself up to get a look at the giant tuna, with a torpedo body, and gills palpitating in a mechanical and brutal rhythm. She made a polite movement of her head, to express her admiration. The men had ceased to contemplate their capture: it was at her that they were looking, these men who had not seen her since the day she came

420

aboard, and they were dumbfounded to find her so changed. As they went down the companionway, they were telling each other in an undertone, "She's in a bad way, the skipper's wife!"

"It would have been better to leave her on the dock," averred Cozio, the sailor who had gone ashore with her at Le Havre.

"She won't have been much use to him," said Legris, a seaman from Normandy. He winked as he spoke, but, appearances to the contrary notwithstanding, he was not inviting his comrades to a broad jest. With a nod in the direction of the captain, he concluded: "And with that gentleman, when you're of no use any longer, you'd better not hang on his neck!"

Rolland had the tuna divided between the fo'c'sle and the chart-house. Yet Geneviève, that evening, could not swallow a single mouthful of the solid meat.

"But it's fresh fish!"

For him, the only difference between tuna and sole was in the taste.

The officers were eating outdoors now, at a table set on the poop. There was no question of Geneviève's being able to join them. The slightest swaying of the ship, a stronger flurry of wind that would give it a little tilt, would turn her inside-out again. She felt sickness rearing up in her, at such times, like an awakened beast. And she would escape from it, as one escapes from an animal, only by playing dead: remaining stretched out without stirring, almost without breathing, until it had gone back to sleep.

After meals, the officers would come to greet her and ask how she was. She would drag out a few words for them, always the same: "Still not very robust," or, "I wouldn't have believed it would take so long to get over." But she always added firmly, "The air is doing me good." And they would agree, repeating, also, the same phrases about the even breeze and the cloudless sky.

Yet each of them, in his own mind, was worried about the slowness of her recovery. They knew that every day of this good weather ought to count for two, insomuch as she not only had to catch up on what she had lost, but must make a solid advance for the bad weeks that were coming.

One evening after dinner, for which the cabin boy had brought her an egg flip and some biscuit to pick at, she ventured to ask the mate, "Is this weather going to last long?"

"It is the regular weather for the trade winds, Madame," Loisel replied. "And when the northeast trade winds have dropped us, we shall find those from the southeast, on the other side of the Equator."

She knew that as well as they did. She had been acquainted with the ship run since childhood.

"Yes," she said, "but between the two there will be the Doldrums, and at the end of the southeast trade winds there will be Cape Horn."

"There will be enough good weather for the present to get you inured to the sea," Hervy declared.

He spoke with a heartening laugh, but when he had returned to the foreward end of the poop, with Loisel and Foulon, he was very serious: "If she goes on eating like a sparrow, she'll never stick it out!" The first mate shook his head. "And yet this is exceptional weather, even for the trade winds," he pointed out. "Not the slightest gust; I have never known the breeze to be so steady."

Foulon remarked, in his impersonal voice, "I don't believe the captain understands—"

"She has been badly shaken up," Loisel said.

"She isn't starting a baby, by any chance?" Hervy asked, in a still lower tone. "That would explain everything."

"It would settle nothing," Foulon retorted. "On the contrary. . . ."

They had to agree on that.

Every evening, now, the sun was going down in splendor: the fixation, in their fall, of vermilion cascades; an aerial smithy where the clouds, like ingots, blazed forth in the insupportable brilliance of their smelting. It was the only spectacle that Geneviève could bear. The level sea, scarcely roughened by the waves' brief periods of harshness, might spread all its dazzling radiance before her, and her eyes would turn away in flight.

"Come see the goldfish."

Since she had begun to take a few steps on the poop, Rolland had never failed to bring all the attractions of the tropical waters to her notice: the flying-fish, the bonito's merry-go-round, the dorado—"goldfish"—that would swim along by the ship so close as to graze the hull, outdistance it, and then reappear under the bowsprit, where the fishermen would throw out hooks garnished with bits of raveled cloth, to dance on the water and gain their attention. She was leaning out over that transparent water now, but she scarcely noticed the big fish with their threshing fins. It was the tumultuous upheaval of this calm sea which she was imagining, to the point of dizziness.

When darkness fell, and the great round stars would be suspended in the velvet-black sky, life would be stilled aboardship. On the deck, the men would be talking, sitting on the small hatch after gulping down a great swig at the water-butt. The officer of the watch would be pacing the poop with measured steps. Sometimes Geneviève would hear a harsh smack on the deck, and then the clatter of boots: a flying fish had just knocked itself senseless against the deck-houses and the men were rushing to pick it up. They had tried in vain to make her eat them. . . . This was the hour when she could almost forget where she was, in the center of the vast circle of water which pressed upon her all day. Rolland had quickly left her alone. She had asked him to do that. "Above all, you are not to pay any attention to me. I am always tired in the evening."

He did not insist. Besides, what was he to say? There is a way of talking to sick women which only women know. The best thing was to wait until she had got the best of it. A Barquet, years ago, had weathered it well.

For he had reached the point, now, of drawing a parallel between the *Galatée's* apprentice and his wife: two people who had gone mistakenly to sea. He did not even suspect that the placid scorn he still felt for the one might, in some sort, be carried over to the other. Since he had learned of Barquet's appointment as co-director of the Shipping Association at Cherbourg, he had made him serve, again, as a whipping-boy for the Companies, those famous Companies that old Hamon was so full of. . . . In any case, since such a milksop had come through it, in the old days, his wife would come through it, too.

Geneviève came through it, actually, only on the morning when, arriving on the poop after the passage which she now made alone, one step at a time, she caught sight of Santa Antão Island, in the Cape Verde archipelago, off the starboard bow. There were summits six thousand feet high, which lifted abrupt and arid ridges into the dazzling sky; and all morning she kept looking at those mountains, leaning her elbows on the hand-rail for the first time, above the sea, as if the proximity of land had dispersed the evil spell of the waters.

As for Rolland, he was giving his entire attention to the wind. Since they struck the trade winds, the breeze had remained at north-northeast, even shifting to north at moments; and here it was showing a tendency to back and die down! With the binoculars to his eyes, he was exploring the sea ahead; and Geneviève heard his order: "To the port braces! Trim for a beam wind!"

When the two sails were braced, he had the ship steered so as to get away from the land as quickly as possible, for he had noticed that a zone of calm was reaching out rather far toward the open sea. What he was saying to the first mate reached Geneviève's ears:

"We shall have had to make a little more of a turn, but I wanted good bearings in order to check the chronometers. After these islands, we shan't see any more land before Staten."

The word made her shudder: Staten, the island that marked the infernal threshold of Cape Horn, that made way for the onslaught of the Cape's monstrous tempests! . . .

The *Atalante* was drawing perceptibly away from the coast now, from those gilded peaks that dropped straight down to the dazzling water. But the breeze was slackening more and more, and soon the sails began to flap noisily against the masts.

"It's caught us! Everybody ready to work ship!"

Struck by the hardness and fury of the voice, Geneviève turned toward him and saw a face she did not know, with harshly pinched lips and angry eyes. And that for a possible few hours of lying motionless!

His wife's gaze left him very soon, however, to return to the contemplation of the island. It upreared itself, rocky and parched, beneath the Pao de Assucar, its Sugar Loaf, the volcanic cone of which reached its summit seventy-five hundred feet above the sea. It was only a convict island, and circled over by the flights of vultures, but the exaltation of the tropic morning drenched its cliffs in tawny gold, filled the fissures in its rocks with blue shadow, and rained down in full splendor upon its peaks, as on mountains of transfiguration. Its stronghold steepness bore witness to its fixity, its unshakable stability, on the moving sea. And, although she was not conscious of it, this firmness of basalt rock was what hypnotized Genevèive, riveting her eyes to its proud and reassuring immobility.

Rolland, behind her, was endeavoring only to rediscover the inconstant wind and the perfidious sea. When a slight flurry sprang up astern, he called out, "Square the yards everywhere!"

This would no sooner have been done than a breath of wind from the port side would force them to trim to get closer, until another flurry, coming unexpectedly from somewhere else, would make it necessary to change the tack.

The heat was gradually becoming stifling. The tar melted and stuck to the sailors' bare feet. The men were streaming with sweat, as they heaved on the braces starboard and port. Geneviève's own interest was concentrated, violently, on this tall land which seemed, at a distance, to be keeping the ship at its feet. When the men's oaths underscored the failure of their work, she was conscious of a stealthy contentment.

Rolland, nervous, was smoking one cigarette after another. Beside him the bos'n, in old-time fashion, was whistling gently, to recall the vanished wind. But all he got were false flurries that died

424

away almost as soon as they were perceived. In the entire day of workings, the *Atalante* only succeeded in getting halfway around the island and coming under its northern point. About six in the evening there came a dead calm. There was not a ripple on the water. The ship was not steering any longer, and it was in vain that Rolland blew the smoke of his cigarette into the warm air in the hope of seeing it drift; it rose as straight as a cloud of incense in a church.

That evening, for the first time since the beginning of the voyage, Geneviève sat down once more at the officers' table. They congratulated her on this, and even more on the fact that, on this ship that was as if nailed to the still water and as steady as at the quay, she was at last able to eat. As for the captain, he was swallowing his food sullenly and with vituperations, between every two mouthfuls, against this calm that was biting into a record passage. He blamed himself for not having gone farther out to sea, for having hugged the land too closely—and needlessly, since it had only served to verify the chronometers' accuracy. He got up before the dessert.

"Take your time, since there's nothing we can do but wait," he said.

When he had gone, she ventured to question the officers about the island. They knew very little about it, as about all the shores which they passed without thought of calling, and which for them were only empty outlines on the marine chart. Hervy declared that Santo Antão had nothing but bad roadsteads. Foulon knew, however, that it was the most populous island of the archipelago, with thirty thousand inhabitants in four towns, while São Thiago, the largest island and the capital, where the Portuguese Governor had his residence, counted a population of only twenty thousand. He believed that settlers and convicts, miscellaneously, grew cotton and tobacco, and that the mountains abounded in roebuck and monkeys. The Atlantic steamships often put in at Porto Grande, on the island of São Vicente, on the way to and from Brazil.

When he had said that, he stopped short, as if he had been struck with a sudden idea, and it was in a slower voice that he added, "From there, they go direct to Lisbon."

But Geneviève was only interested in giving a more present reality to this land from which she was scarcely taking her eyes away. It was only about Santo Antão that she wished to be informed. Foulon was obliged to confess his ignorance.

It was dark when they rose from the table. The great somber silhouette of the island seemed nearer than during the day. Lights—they, too, fixed—shone in tiers above an inlet: a town! Foulon gave her the name: Ribera-Brava. Sometimes the phosphorescent sea would rise up a very little, with an undulation as slight as a sigh. The sky was all studded with stars, but the young woman leaning with her elbows on the hand-rail had eyes only for the placid lights of the shore: they were windows! Behind them she was imagining, seeing, people seated, women bending forward under the lamp. . . . Withdrawn from her by two steps, Foulon was gazing at her steadily. Silence, a sullen silence of disappointment, hardly broken by the flap of a sail, the whine of a block, weighed over the entire ship. The junior officer walked away, without Geneviève's seeing him. Loisel was waiting beside the wheel, which was useless now but to which the helmsman's fists were still holding. Foulon touched his arm, to motion him to one side.

"Don't you agree with me that the captain ought to take advantage of this calm to put his wife ashore?"

The first mate objected. "It is not a very convenient port of call, and, after all, she is better."

"That is just it. . . ."

A few steps away from them, at the forward end of the poop, Rolland was lighting another cigarette. They saw him holding out the lighted match, observing it: the flame was dipping almost imperceptibly toward the bow.

Foulon spoke again, in a low and hurried voice: "I assure you that he ought to put her ashore."

At that moment, behind them, the man at the wheel, the Norman Legris, cried out: "Here comes the breeze, Cap'n! Here comes the breeze!"

Off to their right, Geneviève had suddenly stood straight up, as if the cry had struck her full in the face.

Rolland was already giving the order: "Head to the west-south-west! We'll see if the ship steers."

Slowly, the *Atalante* obeyed the rudder.

"The breeze is at the top," Hervy's voice called. "It's the royals that are getting us out."

But, in their turn, first the to'gants'ls and then the lower tops'ls filled and rounded. The murmur of the wake rolled back from the ship with its sound of crumpling silk. The land seemed to sway into distance. Loisel and Foulon looked at each other. The first mate, longer at sea and more fatalistic, gave a slight shrug of his shoulders. Rolland was already on his way toward them.

"As soon as the helmsman strikes eight bells, we will go and drink a toast to the good wind," he announced, in the voice that belonged to the finest weather.

XXXV

THERE HAD COME a morning when Rolland, after a sullen glance at the flat and oily sea, the limp sails, the sky blocked up with masses of darkness, groaned, in so low a tone that Loisel, close by, did not hear him, "Here we are in the sewer!"

Geneviève, in the Doldrums as off Santo Antão, had at first felt nothing but the absolute immobility of the ship. But she had been quickly overpowered by the suffocating heat, and she could not swallow the slightest bit of food in that steam bath which drenches the whole body, even to one's lips. Then a sudden downpour had driven her from the poop, wet through and through, while the eddying storm was bewildering her with its thunder-claps, and the ship was listing so much that she might have been flung overboard if Hervey had not caught hold of her.

There had been the exhausting alternation of torrid calms and storms that were almost enough to spring the masts. The *Atalante* would only rouse from her prostration to writhe in the epileptic fits of the storm, and with every one of those convulsions, Geneviève would fall back on her bunk as if she had been stabbed.

There had been the crossing of the Line, the baptism on a ship that was pitching, though indeed very little. A sailor had sprinkled her forehead with a few drops of water, explaining, "For your lady, Cap'n, that will do." And the interminable celebration at which she had to be present, with a mist of dizziness before her eyes; the sack race, when she staggered as if her own legs had been tied up in a bag; the thread to be cut blindfolded, when her own eyes no longer made out anything clearly on the deck.

A few days' truce had followed, in the southeast trade winds, in spite of the jolting speed of the ship running close to the wind. But the work of defense that was energetically carried on during those days had underscored their quality of mere reprieve. The rigging was inspected, inch by inch. The new sails were attached to the yards. The hatches were reinforced. They were getting ready for the worst everywhere, and the importance given to the precautions was forewarning of the violence of the expected assault. Hervy had assured her that they would be going around the Cape at the best

427

moment. Loisel had told her that Madame Rosé, on the *Michelet*, had remained seated on the deck as they passed it. The two officers were endeavoring to stay her up before the ordeal, just as was being done to the ship.

As for Rolland, since she had been able more or less to stand on her own feet, he had entirely deserted her for the *Atalante*, which he kept examining with the meticulousnes of a near-sighted man. He was checking everything, no longer trusting anyone but himself. That sort of proxy which he had given to his officers at the beginning of the voyage seemed now to be revoked. Neither Loisel nor Foulon was much concerned about this. They realized that it was not real distrust, but a kind of compulsion. Had he not gone so far as to cut new sails himself, a lower to'gants'l and a main lower tops'l?

The days of regular breezes and a sun-bathed sea were frightful! Geneviève had struggled with all her force to come close to her husband again. She knew that she was about to fall back into the same horrible prostration, that it was a question of the last hours of living with him, before the pit of darkness opened, from which she might never return. But he was a very busy captain, who, with a wife on board, could neglect her, because he could always find her again. What an outburst of laughter there would have been if she had said to him, "Stay near me. Give me these hours. Will there be any others?" At the table, when he noticed that she was scarcely eating at all, his only response was a shake of the head, which grew daily more absent-minded: he was becoming habituated to seeing her go without food. He himself, moreover, would hurry through his meals, so as to return more quickly to his meticulous inspections.

She was the only one who guessed that this absorbing attention to detail came neither from a scrupulous sense of responsibility nor from the arrogance of a skipper who relies on no one but himself. It was to his pleasure that he was rushing away, to the delight of tuning the superb instrument on which, as a virtuoso, he was about to play. For Cape Horn, the mere approach to which was making her faint, would be for him, this time, the bravura piece which, as he was now getting ready to attack it, he would carry off with a dash and brilliancy that would capture the admiration of everyone: his officers, his crew, his fellow-captains, his ship-owners, even his wife, insomuch as she would be there to applaud him when he made his bow of triumph. She remembered what he had said to her, one afternoon when she was feeling her mouth fill again with saliva: "With this ship, that hugs the wind closer than a yacht, we ought to run by the Cape near enough to scratch our paint on it! You won't have time to be seasick!"

428

She had looked at him as if they had been, the one and the other, on opposite sides of a river so wide that she no longer had even the courage to hold out her arms to him.

There was only one victory in those hateful days, a victory which she knew to be her most crushing defeat: to have again become, for him, a body; nothing but a body, which he would find there at night, and of which he would possess himself after a well-filled day. . . .

Then there had been that day, already chilly, when a white dot had loomed up on the southern horizon and put the whole ship in a flutter: the first albatross. The bird had swiftly approached the ship, made a tour of the masts, and then paused, wings outstretched and rigid, above the poop. Its head bent down, it had fixed its untamed eyes in contemplation upon the men and the woman who were watching it, and then, its examination completed, it had flown off like an arrow toward the cold regions from which it came.

Geneviève had heard a sailor grumbling: "When those dirty bastards come so far north, you've got to think things aren't a bit good at the Cape, and they need to rest a little."

Foulon had taken pains to correct this, and Geneviève knew that he was doing it for her.

"It's a sign, especially, that they are finding more fish in the north than in the south," he said.

There were ten days after that, during which Rolland, when asked for news of his wife, had had to answer, "This is not the weather for her." And he would add: "But I find that she is not suffering so much as the first time."

One evening, in the saloon, Loisel had paused in his own dinner to say, "The disturbing thing is that she has not got used to it. The body generally does that, after a longer or shorter time, and then there is no more to be said. But has Madame Rolland eaten one real meal since we left Cape Verde?"

"What goes down best at the present moment is hardtack crumbled in white wine," Rolland answered. "The wine keeps her up."

"But it doesn't nourish her," big Hervy objected.

"I know. . . . So, the sooner we get around the Cape and into the Pacific . . . At this rate, it won't take long. I've never seen the trade winds come down so far!"

The sea continued to be sullen, but what was most striking was the quality of the light, as the day grew shorter with the passing miles. It was dark at five in the afternoon now, and a dirty dawn had hardly made its appearance by eight next morning. They were coming into winter, but as one comes into it when it is a question of space and not of time. They were coming into it by their own movement, not waiting for the earth to turn; it developed, then, very quickly. In a few weeks they had passed through three seasons: the French spring in which they had sailed, the summer in the tropics, the brief autumn along Brazil. And now, having passed the Plata, they were already, with Argentina, on the threshold of the southern winter.

Cold, rain, snow, had become the daily schedule. The fog penetrated the men's thick sweaters; and the stoves that were kept stuffed with coal night and day in the crew's quarters were not enough to dry out the plankings: coming in with their boots and oilskins streaming, the men brought with them all the wet from outdoors.

The little porcelain stove in the captain's cabin had been the first to be lighted.

"I am freezing," Geneviève had moaned, one afternoon.

"It might be the cold that is making you sick," Rolland had answered. "We don't feel it, we are always moving about."

He had had a fire made in the stove at once. She had turned her head on the pillow and looked at the flame dancing on the other side of the isinglass.

"You see, things are better already," he said.

"It makes company," she murmured.

Rolland ascertained that she was not vomiting so much. She was lying all day flat on her stomach, her head buried in the pillow, as if she felt the need of becoming one with the bed. And, yes, in return for this immobility, this blindness, this semi-asphyxiation, it was true that she was vomiting less. It was movement, the mere fact of raising her head or lifting herself on one elbow, that brought on the attacks of nausea. He had noticed that; and now, when he came into the room, he would counsel her, "Don't budge!"

So what he would oftenest see of her, through a whole day, was only a ball of disheveled hair and a pale neck with conspicuous tendons.

One morning in a fog, a glacial fog which had come on with sunrise and was so thick that from the stern not half the deck could be distinguished, Rolland had the line got ready for deep soundings. According to his reckoning, the *Atalante* ought to be on the Malouine Banks by ten o'clock, if the wind did not change either its force or its direction.

At nine, they hove to.

The tallowed lead was cast into the sea. The men, stationed at regular intervals along the windward-rail, were running their coils of line and repeating the regulation "Stand by!" The man standing abreast of the main shrouds cried, *"Bottom!"*

He quickly made a knot in the line which his comrades at once pulled in.

"Sixty fathoms," the bos'n announced, as he took the captain the sample of the sea-bottom, which had stuck to the tallow.

"Sand and broken shells. That is in accordance with the position," Rolland stated. And, turning toward Foulon, he added: "Our chronometers are exactly right. Good business!"

Just then Loisel came up on the poop, obviously preoccupied. He had gone off to rest after his watch, and the officers used sometimes to tease him about his appetite for sleep and the hubbub the cabin boy was instructed to make, pounding on his door. Rolland and Foulon watched him walking toward them now, rather surprised to see him again so soon.

"Captain, there has been a little accident in Madame Rolland's room," he said. "When the novice was putting more coal in the stove he did not close the door tight. It came open with the ship's rolling, and a live coal fell out on the floor. Madame Rolland knocked on my wall, to call for help, and I heard her, fortunately, and put it out." As if he had had to bring his mind to it, he added: "But the linoleum is burned."

Rolland, who had kept his sounding lead in his hand, said, "Thank you, Monsieur Loisel. Send the novice to me, so that I can give him a piece of my mind."

But the mate still stood there. His forehead was wrinkled, and his eyes were fixed on the planking of the deck. When he spoke, it was in the same restrained voice in which he had told of the accident:

"It is almost two weeks since I last saw Madame Rolland. I have found her very much changed, and extremely weak. She had tried to get up, and had fallen. She could only just drag herself as far as the partition wall to pound on it with the poker."

Rolland shook his head, this time with an obvious anxiety.

"Weak, how could she help being weak?" he said.

He was surprised, however, that Loisel remained planted in front of him, with that air at once stubborn and hesitant which he had seen in certain sailors determined to blurt out some enormity: they would not go away without saying it, and they could not make up their minds to say it. With them, he would bring the conversation to an end and ask, as he asked Loisel now, "Well?" But, because it was his wife who was at issue, he added: "What can I do?"

Since there was nothing he could do but wait, this was in fact to close the incident. The captain was already turning away, so as to make it plain that everything had been said; but this time Loisel

431

raised his head, and Rolland, put on the alert by his resolute gaze, had to face him.

"You see Madame Rolland every day, Captain, and her condition cannot strike you as it does someone who has not seen her for some time. . . ."

"But, I repeat, what can I do about it?"

"Put into port."

Rolland wheeled about, in a single movement. The unbelievable words had come from behind him, and it was Foulon, in his dry voice, who had just shot them out. With an emphatic nod of his head, Loisel testified that this was exactly his thought.

Rolland looked from one to the other in stupefaction and repeated, as if indeed he could not believe his ears, "Put into port!"

Loisel was explaining already: "From Montevideo, Captain, she could reach Rio by train, after resting, and go from there to Europe."

Rolland interrupted. "Since you have forgotten the Instructions, I remind you of them: *Any putting into port is forbidden unless the navigation of the vessel is absolutely impossible.* Is that the case?"

"There can be other risks than that of navigation," replied Loisel, unsubdued.

"Then, that would be a personal risk, to be taken by me. The ship itself is not running any risk. I have not the right to put into port."

He took two steps, to mark the end of the argument. But he changed his mind and turned back to the officers.

"We are too far south to go back. We should lose an enormous amount of time in returning to Montevideo. We shall go up the coast, yes, but on the other side, and it won't be long until then! We are about to pass the Cape, and once that is behind us everything will be better."

"It sometimes happens that a ship is held up for weeks off Cape Horn," Foulon's impersonal voice reminded him.

"That should not happen with a fast ship like this," Rolland answered. "Trust me not to go to sleep off the Cape!"

Loisel bowed his head.

"I apologize, Captain, for having brought up this question which has nothing to do with the service, but I believed it to be my duty."

"And mine is to sail the ship which has been entrusted to me as fast and as well as possible, without taking account of my personal interests if they should come to be at stake. Having said that, I may add that I am sure that the question does not arise, and that you have got yourself into a panic."

"I hope so, Captain."

The two officers went away and Rolland, his hands behind his back, began to pace up and down the narrow space of the poop. He regretted only one word, the last he had spoken. For it was not panic with which he had to reproach Loisel. Panic is the dislocation of the entire man, a general agitation. It quiets down under a kick or the slap of a sharp word. But those imaginations that invent danger, and refine it at leisure—that is a malady of educated men, too much habituated to handling ideas, and piling them up in structures that are knocked down by the mere breath of facts. It was that, and perhaps the memory of Belin's son, continuing to haunt them, which inclined them to the fear of returning misfortune. The thing to do, then, as in the case of the *Argonaute's* cat, was not to discuss it; to ignore it; and, when the time came, and everything had turned out successfully, to say, "And just think, if I had listened to you . . ."

With this persistent fog the wind had almost died down, and the sea had flattened. Although the *Atalante* had all canvas up, it was slipping along at barely three knots, the cautious progress of a blind man. If Rolland thought of the respite which this gentle and even pace must give the sick woman, it was to conclude that the weather was beginning to side with him. He went down to her cabin.

This time, he did not find his wife stretched out on the bunk as if something had crushed her. She was lying on her back, and her eyes were open. He went over to the green porcelain stove and tried the nickel-plated catch with the tips of his fingers.

"So that idiot François left this open?" He noticed the wide black burn in the linoleum. "Well, he's made a nice mess!"

He was vain about this neat cabin, which the novice's carelessness had smudged up, and he had to make an effort to turn his eyes away from the scorched spot and back to his wife. He scrutinized her for a long time, and more closely than Loisel had done. Certainly she was emaciated, with blue circles about the too-wide sunken eyes; her cheeks and forehead were wrinkled, shriveled up: granted. All this might well strike an oversensitive young man, discovering a woman collapsed on a floor that was catching fire. But, good God, all one had to do was use one's mind! A face like that on a really sick woman, with some filthy disease that attacks from within, gnaws at the lungs or the stomach—yes, that would have meant something. But here there was nothing at all! All the organs were perfectly sound. It was only an indisposition, then, that was lasting a long time, to be sure, and making her very weak, as one does become weak when one isn't eating, but that would dis-

433

appear as it had disappeared once already; a surface distress, the distress of a ship that is gray with salt and needs fresh paint after days of heavy weather, but is not seriously damaged; nothing vital touched. A baby on the way? Not very far, in any case. . . .

"You are to take advantage of the sea's not being bumpy, and swallow a little something," he said. "What would you like?"

"Nothing."

He went up to her and pressed against the bunk's side plank, as if he were trying to dominate her at close quarters.

"You know that cannot, must not, go on," he said. "I am going to have them bring you a milk flip. It will stay down or it will not stay down, but you will swallow it."

He was astounded to hear her murmur, "What is it you're saying?"

She had not even listened to him!

He understood why, when she went on to assert, in a strange voice, tranquil and sure, "I shall never get over it."

"Have you seen many people die of seasickness?" he demanded. And a suspicion at once struck him. "Did you say that to Loisel?"

That would have explained everything.

She shook her head disconsolately. "I didn't even thank him."

"Do you know what he has just advised me to do? Go back to Montevideo, to put you ashore! You can see old Hamon's face, from here!"

He had the feeling that he was committing a crime. It was all that was worst in him, speaking: the monstrous will to assault weakness and silence, a murderous fury surging up from his most murky depths; the fury that on the *Galatée* had made him dirty a girl's photograph and drive a Barquet into the waves of Cape Horn, that had made him torture a Father Monnard on his deathbed. . . . He was seized, just now, with a cold rage against this Loisel, who had presumed to pride himself on setting a higher value on his wife than he did.

"What do you say to that, eh?"

He was not trying to make her deny her champion; only to make her move, speak, say whatever she wanted to, blurt out reproaches if she had any. He would force her out of this muteness, this resignation in which the weak entrenched themselves, and in which they became so strong—stronger than he.

"That is for you to decide."

She had barely murmured the words, yet they resounded like thunderclaps in his brain: "for you to decide. . . ." It could mean everything, or nothing. What did she expect? That he would take her in his arms, that he would say to her—in those accents in which

434

he had once cried, "Stay with me!"—"I am not willing to see you suffer any longer. In a few days you will be on land, well-cared-for, resting, and, beyond everything else, happy in what I have sacrificed for you." Was that it? The thought was only a lightning flash, one of those sudden flashes, too swift, that are blinding.

"We haven't got to that point, thank God," he assured her, with a rather tremulous little chuckle. After all, had she not simply meant to say, "Act for the best"?

With his shame and remorse over having told her of the mate's application, something of gentleness was coming back to him. He put his hand on her shoulder. The skin was as if kneaded beneath his fingers: skin too loose for the flesh on which it seemed no longer to have a hold. You might think it was a dog's skin, he reflected: one of those skins that one takes hold of, and that fill the hand like some thick glossy fabric. . . .

"Come now, rest," he said.

In the afternoon the fog dissolved, gradually and then more and more rapidly, as the welcome wind from the northwest became more brisk. Before long, the horizon was clear. Three ships were in sight, then, off the bow to the south: a square-rigged three-master and two four-masters. The three-master, of which they could distinguish the long black hull, attracted Rolland's attention particularly because of her elegant lines, her irreproachable spread of canvas. He took up the telescope.

"A German boat, one of the P—— ships from Hamburg, and two of the Bordes craft," he announced to Hervy. "We mustn't drag along after them. Have the mains'l set for me, and the royals, and the stays'ls."

The other vessels, which, like his own, had lessened sail when the wind rose as the fog was lifting, were also unfurling their canvas. The exciting game was beginning, one of those spontaneous sailing races which would be run for the ships' honor, whenever two vessels caught sight of one another on the same course. The men were as thrilled over them as the officers, and showed it more. The boredom of the unbroken sea, interrupted by these encounters, had something to do with it, of course; but, above all, it was the fighting instinct which was awakened in the breasts of these Bretons, Normans, Flemings—brawlers, speeders, experts in fine maneuvers, and attached to the home ship, and the yard that built her, by ties whose strength was revealed in these combats. It was there, in the midst of action, that they would feel that the ship belonged to them, much more than to the shipping men, who had only known her lying passive along a quay; even more than to the officers, whose

435

intimacy was limited to looking and speaking, without rude physical contact with the racing craft.

From time to time the captain would take a compass bearing of the position of the three ships, then he would return to the poop.

"The three-master is gaining on us sharply," he said to Hervy. "I'll wager she is the famous *Pampa*, from the Laëstz Company of Hamburg."

The movement of Hervy's beard registered agreement that this might be so. Loisel and Foulon, listening a little to one side, guessed the captain's excitement from the liveliness of his voice: an excitement aroused by the mere notion of a competition with the celebrated German ship. The *Pampa* had made the crossing from Cuxhaven to Valparaiso in sixty-one days.

"It never took more than eighty days for the Europe-Chile passage," Rolland recalled.

"All the P—— ships are speeders," remarked Hervy, in corroboration.

As if they had been given a signal, the there vessels were running up their colors and their numbers.

The two four-masters from the Bordes Company were the *Madeleine* and the *Wulfram-Puget*. The number of the German ship could be made out perfectly, but the *Atalante* did not possess the list of foreign numberings, and they could not know if they were really racing with the *Pampa*. The *Atalante* was almost neck to neck with the *Madeleine* now, and seemed to be gaining a little on the *Wulfram-Puget*.

"Take a good look at them, Monsieur Hervy," Rolland suddenly counseled, in a changed voice. "Take a look at them, because we shan't be seeing them long. The machine is destroying them, one by one. And then what is to become of us? Shall we sign up on a steamship and go back to the bottom of the ladder, or shall we plant our cabbages?"

Hervy raised his broad shoulders. "They will last our time," he said.

Rolland shook his head. "I don't think so. I have counted those that are being dismantled and those that are being built: ten, against two! At that rate, they'll not hold out for ten years. So, everything that can still be done with fine navigation we ought to make the most of, in God's name!"

His voice, at the last words, was filled with such wrath and bitterness that Hervy gazed at him in dumb amazement. But he had already turned his back and returned to the compass bearings.

These verified the fact that the German was gaining little by little on her rivals. At twilight, the big rotunda of her poop was

436

beginning to sink beneath the horizon. After dinner Rolland searched the sea with his binoculars, vainly; no signal light was to be seen. He spent a part of the night on deck, for the wind had slackened and shifted to the west, then to the south-southwest. Finally, at three in the morning, it had veered again and returned to the west. Rolland had responded to each shuffled with an immediate tacking of the ship. He had taken the helm himself so as to manage the vessel at the very moment when it was required. At dawn, after a brief rest, he was once more on deck, with the binoculars at his eyes.

The German three-master had fallen back on her advance. Her hull was higher on the water. One of the four-masters, having made a too-prolonged tack to the southeast, was finding herself considerably blanketed. The other Bordes ship, left behind, was shortening sail three miles astern of the *Atalante*. Two competitors outdistanced, another—and what another, perhaps!—half caught up with, thanks to the unceasing operations through the night! There was a fixed, almost fanatical, smile on Rolland's face, that lingered for a long time.

He did not leave the poop all day: feeling out the wind, responding with a working to its slightest variation. The weather was fairly clear, but at moments there would be a drifting mist, blotting out the outlines of the vessels that kept their distances until darkness fell.

They spent that night in the channel of the Malouines, three hundred miles between the Falkland Islands and the Virgin's Cape, which bends back like a fishhook at the entrance to the Strait of Magellan. The gray and surly dawn, across which tatters of fog were trailing, found Rolland standing beside the wheel. The two Bordes ships had come close to each other, astern. The German was near enough, now, for its name to be read through the telescope: "*Pampa*, Hamburg."

"What did I tell you?" Rolland cried to Hervy, the only one of the officers with whom he had felt like talking for the past two days. "She isn't gaining any longer. This isn't her kind of wind."

He had scarcely turned around to cast a glance at the *Madeleine* and the *Wulfram-Puget*. Those two no longer mattered. The whole game was between him and the unknown commander of the famous courser. Once again, that radical simplification of the game was asserting itself in him, as in all sportsmen: nothing existed, any more, except that ephemeral goal that must be reached and passed. Only his eyes kept contact with the *Pampa:* his mind was soaring above the ship, in the wind itself, attentive to its slightest deviations, ready to call out an order, a figure, as soon as they were perceived.

437

In the afternoon two other ships came in sight, nearer the mainland: a three-masted Norwegian barque, bulky in the bow, loaded almost to the point of foundering; and an elegant square-rigged three-master which was drawing close to the group of competitors, steering with the wind on the quarter, and on the port tack. When she was well within view she ran up her standard and her number.

"An Italian," a sailor said. "Look at the tobacco jar she has in the white stripe of her flag."

He meant the shield of Savoy, topped with the crown as with a lid.

Rolland spent the following night, again, on deck, ready to work ship. When daylight came, stagnant as a swamp, they had their first sight of the high snowy mountains of Tierra del Fuego. The cold light was creeping over them as if from an air-vent. It seemed to be held back by the summits; and the sea was left in a misty twilight, splotched with gleams of light that were like puddles on a pavement after rain.

When this light from limbo at last reached Rolland's eyes, he descried Staten Island ahead: a high rocky streak laid out from east to west, hacked and jagged as a heap of slag. Together with the warped point of the South American continent, it created a zigzag trench, Le Maire Strait. This channel, Rolland had decided to enter: first, because it was shorter than making the turn around Staten Island, and also to keep to a level sea for a longer time. He was thinking again of his wife, but in connection, now, with the ship's course. In the Strait, sheltered by the land on each side, it would be possible still to make headway before encountering the blast of the west wind, that torrent of air which has charged across from time immemorial from the Pacific to the Atlantic, and seems to have raveled out all this end of the continent into islands.

There was a risk to be run: not of the whirlpools that the Nautical Instructions taught mariners to fear, but of a calm. With a calm and the current in the Strait, one would be caught, and would run aground. But a calm is rare in these regions!

The sickly gleam that was dragging over the water was finally bringing the other ships to view. Rolland pursed his lips: the two Bordes craft and the Italian were clearly left behind in the north, but the *Pampa* had recovered her advance, and, quite near the shore, was obviously preparing also to make the entrance into the Strait, with a free wind and on the port tack. She had triumphed. There was nothing to do now but follow her.

Hervy, coming up to the poop, turned to look with satisfaction at the ships that were outdistanced.

"Three of them behind us," he said.

"And one ahead!"

"Oh, yes, but that one! . . ."

Rolland jerked his head, by no means resigned to admitting that "that one" was unbeatable. Then he took up his binoculars to look at her again. He saw her coming along to starboard, fronting the entrance of the Strait, directly in the middle, between the escarpments of Tierra del Fuego, rising beneath the saw-tooth ridge of the sierras, and the low point of Staten Island. He ceased his observation only when the masts had disappeared behind an outjutting cliff. And it was then that he felt the fatigue of three sleepless nights dropping upon his head, with the weight of his defeat. I'll go below, he thought.

Go below to his cabin, to which for the past three days he had made only hurried visits, like a conductor checking tickets, to see a sick woman who was not actually ill. . . . He was making his way toward the chart-house when the helmsman's voice stopped him.

"Look, what's happened to the Boche? Didn't he get his bill of health?"

Rolland turned around. The man was making a gesture with his chin toward the entrance to the Strait. The *Pampa* was moving slowly back from it, against the wind that was veering to the north, sailing close-hauled and making so little headway that she seemed driven in between the unmoving points. Rolland's thought came in a lightning flash: She has been caught aback by the gusts that are coming from the mountain, and she is working to regain the open sea. And he yelled, "Brace everywhere for the wind abeam!"

It was obvious that he was abandoning the idea of the Strait in which the other ship's way had been blocked. He was going to go around Staten Island, and with all the lead given by the German's delay. With her new trim, the *Atalante* began to cut into the course again. The cabin boy, coming up to announce the noon meal, was brusquely sent back. Rolland was taking bearings. The wind was growing stronger, and off to the north the Bordes vessels could be seen taking in their small sails. The men who had gone off watch at eight o'clock were refusing to go to bed, gripped now by the excitement of the game's last round. Rolland went into the chart-house for a moment, to mark his position on the chart. When he came out he called, in a voice which had grown young again, and with which no one near him was familiar, "Bear away, boys! We've beaten them!"

They passed Cape Saint John, the western point of Staten Island. The waters of Cape Horn were opening before them, and Rolland was the first to enter them!

Grasping the hand-rail of the poop, he leaned over to call, in the

439

same tune, to the crew, who, all bursting with pride, had just braced the yards in the twinkling of an eye: "Double wine ration for everyone!"

Foulon had watched the race, for the past three days, with the same attention but also the same impassiveness as if a professor at the Hydrographic Institute had been explaining it to him at the blackboard. He turned around, now, to say to Loisel, in an implacable voice, "For everyone . . . except his wife. . . ."

XXXVI

"FURL THE MAIN upper tops'l!"

He had just called out the order, stiffening himself against the binnacle, body to body with the two helmsmen who were clinging with both hands to the wheel. He had called it out in bitter aversion, knowing he had the knife at his throat, at the moment when he felt everything was about to break to pieces. How would Loisel, Foulon, Hervy, Pléneau, with the two watches, with the mechanic, the carpenter, the cook, the novice, all the men they would be able to get together—how would they succeed in mastering this sail which he had kept up beyond the point of folly, which had held in this raging tempest beyond the point of any likelihood? But what did they matter to him? Let them turn back their fingernails, let them crawl on their knees, on their bellies, let them bite into the sail with their teeth if they wanted to, they would have less suffering to choke them than he had had, in dragging out of his throat the order to take in canvas, to knuckle under on the course.

. . . Snow, rain, hail, a wind from the world's end, and a sea of rock—a sea that was no longer water, but a mass of blocks against which the boat struck with the force of collision; nights of dreadful spoliation, which left a man neither eyes, blindfolded by the darkness, nor ears, stuffed to deafness with explosive noises, nor the will to accept what was happening. Within Rolland himself there were only two things fixed, hammered into his brain: one thought— *Geneviève, below, in this weather!* and one figure—*Fifteen days!*

Fifteen days since the *Atalante* had rounded Cape Horn. . . .

With the first abrupt dip of the great swell and the first heavy pitch of the vessel, as soon as the point of Staten Island had been

440

laid down in the north, Rolland had declared, "The race is over. Now, to make for the west!"

There was a song about that: to make for the west meant a hard time for ship and crew.

The waters off Cape Horn were a rallying ground for "speeders," those captains who refused to go farther south to gather up the ends of the east wind, on a less monstrous sea. Like the others—and more than the others, with such a ship as this, and with a sick wife to be succored—Rolland intended now to force the coastwise passage, to take advantage of the eternal tempest's three-part time: three beats, with two of them helping the ship on her way. The direction of the hurricanes made a design on the compass card like a crescent moon. From the northwest the storm would move down, at the end of a day or two, to the west, then to the southwest, growing still stronger. For several days it would pour out all its rage there; then it would abate, only to jump back to the northwest and start its journey all over again. So the two ends of the crescent would permit an advance to the ships that had not been damaged by the high point of the storm's fury. But this meant to work ship, to work—especially when that no longer seemed possible.

It had very quickly become apparent, however, that the old Cape would not kick up a rumpus this time. April and May were its good months, a kind of Indian summer. In spite of the gigantic roll of the swells, the *Atalante* had run on the surface, all sails set. And Hervy had remarked, "It's unusual to see the sun and clear weather with north winds."

Yes, it was extravagant weather for this locality. In the afternoon the wind had slackened and the ship's speed had dropped to five or six knots, but Rolland was still steering so as to pass within sight of the Horn. The *Pampa* and the Bordes ships had also doubled Staten Island, but at present they were hardly to be seen.

The next day at noon, the *Atalante* had the Cape to the north and south.

Most of the men had never had a sight of it. Only in such extraordinary weather was it possible to hug the shore as close as this. What they were looking at was an island, the most southerly of the archipelago, a dark and rugged point accented with puffs of spray.

"It doesn't even stand high," said a man from Saint Malo. "It looks like the Conchée."

This is a tiny island off Saint Malo, fortified by Vauban.

Rolland was leaning over the poop-rail. "Now the men who had never gone around the Horn have a right to spit in the wind, like the veterans," he declared.

441

A pig had been slaughtered the evening before. That meant a succulent meal for the fo'c'sle as well as for the chart-house, and it was moistened by a double ration of wine for the crew's quarters and vintage burgundy in the saloon. Rolland, pouring it out, refrained from any boasting.

"What is won is won," was all he said.

Loisel, always spontaneous, raised his glass. "I wish nothing so much as to continue to be wrong, Captain," he said.

The phrase spared the officer's dignity, but it put things on a good footing again, and Rolland nodded in acceptance of this. In return, while there had been nothing said about his wife, in the saloon, since the mate's exhortation, he announced, "She has been able to eat a little fresh ham."

Once more, he got up before the end of the meal, but this time it was to hurry to her room.

"You know we have just passed Cape Horn?" he cried.

The extensive pitching in the powerful swells seemed to trouble her less than Rolland had feared. She looked at him now, incredulous.

"Is that true?"

The Cape, which for weeks past had loomed before her as the murderous ordeal of which as a child she had heard such frightful stories, and which she was awaiting as she would await the bottom of a whirlpool of ice in which she would be broken to bits—they had passed the Cape! Rolland had seen the life venturing back, still uncertain and hesitant, to her face.

"So here you are in the Pacific," he said. "Where we are now, it still doesn't deserve its name, but that is coming, hour by hour. I have gone around the Cape eleven times; this is the first time I have seen it so close. Don't you say that you aren't bringing us good luck!"

He had dared to use that phrase consciously, at the risk of her thinking it the stupid blunder of a clumsy brute. But he was trying to take advantage of their unbelievable achievement to instill some optimism into her, because it was the most effective way he knew. And in fact she half accepted it.

"Oh, good luck, for the others. . . ."

"What do you mean, 'the others'? On a ship, good luck isn't divided up. When it is there for all, it is there for one. Tomorrow we shall be sailing into the north. You will be starting on the up-grade, getting well again; and this time it will all come right!"

He was seized with an inspiration, and yielded to it on the impulse:

"Listen—when we get to Frisco, you will have a good month's

442

rest; but I shall not take you back on the ship. Even if the return voyage is less hard than the voyage out, there are bound to be some bad days, and you have had more than your share of those, my poor darling. So then, when we are ready to sail and you are entirely recovered, you will take the train for New York; and from there, by steamship, you will be in France in a week."

"That will be horribly expensive," she said.

The objection was the best possible proof that she was taking an interest in things again, and was beginning once more to reckon with the future.

"If it cost twice as much, we wouldn't dispute it." He took her cold hands in his. "I am in love with you, you know."

She raised her eyes to meet his, but her gaze was measuring all the lost road between herself, who had really fallen to the very bottom of the world, and the man who stood there, bigger and broader than ever in the sweater and heavy jacket that he wore against the severe cold. She had come to sea to conquer him, force his defenses one by one. She had brought him nothing but a responsibility and a burden. And here he was, going back to his voice of the finest sailing weather, to say to her, "You understand, when I get home I want to find a beautiful wife again, instead of my poor little skin-and-bones darling. Otherwise, I shall have been cheated."

"Yes, you have been cheated."

He was laughing.

"I'm never cheated for long, you know. I see to it that it's handed back to me. You will go through it like the others, and you will pay the arrears; I will force you to it. Don't you think I am capable of that?"

She pressed his hands as she murmured, with the old fervor, "Yes, I think you are capable of it." Then she added, "You did right to keep me."

For this miracle of a benevolent Cape Horn was freeing her from a frightful thought, the thought that had been tormenting her ever since he had said what he did about putting into port, and that she had kept repeating to herself: "He has sacrificed me to his pride." Now, her response made him suddenly serious.

"I believe that," he said. "But, to be sure of it, I am going back now."

He put his arms around her and kissed her, tenderly and cautiously, and smiled at her again from the door. He was always at his best when he had put himself in the right. . . . On the poop, he found the wan sun again in its place in the fragile sky, and the ship, under full sail, cutting her way into the west, grazing the crooked heel of the South American continent.

A little before four o'clock, just as the sun was slipping toward the horizon, Rolland had noticed a great white cloud-bank in the west, which was taking possession of what had become an ashen sky.

"Bad business," he had said to the mate, in a changed voice. "The White Arch* is showing its face to us."

"The barometer?" Loisel had asked.

"It doesn't predict anything. It is low, with the north winds, which is normal. But the sea is taking it upon itself to warn us. Look at its curlicues!"

In spite of the lax wind, the wave crests were already breaking into white flounces. Rolland had had the royals and to'gants'ls furled. The wind was shifting forward little by little without growing any stronger, and the *Atalante*, almost athwart the waves, was rolling gunnel under.

"We're going to have a filthy blow," Hervy declared at dinner, performing prodigious feats of balance as he spoke, in keeping the contents of his plate from capsizing on the oilcloth. "Every time you get away with one of them, the place pulls another storm out of its belly."

Then, a little later, there was the bos'n calling through the door of the chart-house: "Cap'n, the winds are changing to west, and the weather's getting a dirty look."

They had left the dinner unfinished. As soon as he reached the poop, Rolland gave the order, "Haul in the fore lower tops'l. Everybody up!"

The two watch crews, working together, had scarcely finished spilling the sail when a roar had resounded through the rigging. The savage storm from the west, dormant for a few hours, was charging down upon them.

That was fifteen days ago: fifteen days of frenzied movements, by men whose wrists were cut by the friction of the oilskins they never took off now; a crew to which Rolland was allowing no sleep, who were warming themselves up with wine and brandy. On the third night, Loisel had said to them, "We've got to make it! There is a woman caught in this, and if we don't bring her through it, it means throwing her overboard."

But on this sixteenth night, out on the threshing yard-arm, hanging onto the canvas that was as hard as iron, some of them, with no more strength left, and no more kindness, were growling, "Good God, let her die—and let him heave to!"

He himself knew that in spite of the superhuman efforts he had dragged out of their very entrails, his ship had fallen back here in

* English term in the original. Tr.

444

the west; that she had first returned to the meridian of Cape Horn, then had been pushed beyond it; that everything was to be done over, and that he had no more time. That main lower tops'l that he had had run up again an hour ago—now he had to have it taken in. And it had been like that for fifteen days! At the slightest suspicion of a lull, he would put on canvas, only to have it trussed up again when it was hardly in place, just before the hurricane would have torn it away. And, every time, there was all that heap of men piled up under the weather-cloth, who had to be wakened, roused, driven back to the torrential drenching of the deck:

"Get up! You don't think you're going to take a nap, do you? Am I asleep, me?"

When he had succeeded, once again, in starting them off, he could rest easy about them: the instinct of survival would have come to the rescue and taken the men in charge. Threatened with death by the wave that would carry them away, the sail that would struggle against them and fling them down, they would hang on, spill the sail, come down again, and crouch at his feet for an hour, until they got the next order.

But below, in the cabin, that saving instinct was dead. He had tried hard to keep it alive. As soon as the canvas was clewed up, the first evening, he had gone down again, to find her racked and retching.

"It is nothing, just a bad blow. It was bound to happen; but it won't last. We've doubled the Cape." But he knew as he spoke that he was losing. "I swear that I will get you out of it, and quickly," he added.

And then he had fled, so as no longer to see the heart-rending anguish of that gaze which, only a little while ago, had been fixed upon a miracle. . . .

Since then he had escaped more than twenty times a day, between workings, to go to her bunk, as one might go to look at a leak. The water was rising, slowly and silently, with seethings of nausea from time to time. In spite of the stove, kept hot enough to come near cracking its enamel, and the hot-water bottle which the novice filled in the galley three times a day, the cold was gaining over the prostrate body, from which the most violent lurches of the ship no longer drew even a moan.

He would reach the cabin by a series of wide steps from side to side, to balance the rolling of the ship. First he had to open, and then close, the door, which, like all the ship's doors, would escape from one's hands to open and close itself with the brutal movement of a sprung trap. One long stride would take him from the doorway to the side of the bed, and he would hold onto the stanchions and

445

look at her, always with the stunned amazement of finding an unknown creature there. Every day, this illness—which he was ashamed
to have so long called seasickness—was effacing some feature of the
wife he had chosen. It was making a sort of substitution, in this
alcove of varnished boards, which filled him less with compassion
than with the dread of an evil spell. And it was an effort to speak to
this fleshless and inert stranger as if she were really his wife.

He did speak to her, but it was with the restrained violence of an
exorcist, to call her back, by force, to this body from which she was
withdrawing.

"You must hold out! You must not let go! This won't last. You
are very uncomfortable, and very much shaken up: that is because
we are fighting to get through it, so that you will be well!"

Did she hear him? Sometimes, with the slow movement of exhausting labor, she would raise her purple eyelids, streaked with
little red veins like those of very old women, and look at him. But it
was as if he too were a stranger, met by chance, whose features she
was trying to recall.

One morning, after a terrible night, she had gazed for a long
time at his weary face, his eyes sunken by long watches, his unshaven
cheeks crusted over with salt; and she had murmured, "What a state
you are in!"

He had clenched his teeth on a sob, and fled.

But yesterday, when he leaned over her, she had moaned, "I
don't see you any more. It's all blurred."

The sixteenth day dawned. As soon as the tops'l was in position
again, Rolland had flung himself down, still in his boots and
armored in his sou'wester, on the chart-house sofa: three hours,
perhaps four, of unconsciousness. . . . When he went back on deck,
he found the *Atalante* hove to, under the lower tops'ls and the fore
stays'l, head to wind and dropping again eastward: orders from the
mate.

There was nothing he could say. Loisel explained that he had
been obliged to have the fores'l furled, because of the abnormal
weather. The men of his watch had been knocked over three times
in the fore-and-aft gangway; one sailor had a gash in his head, another had a dislocated shoulder, and the others were done in.

Rolland looked at his second-in-command. These fifteen days had
left their mark on him, too: an unkempt beard, the leaden skin of
fatigue, hollow features—but, as happens with the firm skin of
youth, less hollowed than slashed with wrinkles as fine as if made
with a knife blade. Loisel had not once balked at the charging orders
that the captain had poured forth in such numbers during the past

446

fifteen days, to hurry the passage. He had repeated them all with an energy which made it plain that he accepted responsibility for them, and the twentieth time as much as the first. Rolland was convinced that he, too, was fighting for Geneviève; from pity, from chivalrous valor, perhaps also because he found her intelligent and charming. Then, if he had hove to, if he had given up trying to make headway, it was because he had to.

The sea, moreover, was there to prove him right: the Cape Horn sea, no more terrible than he had seen it ten times over, but just as bad. In the squalid light, it was nothing but a turmoil of waves flung one upon the other, and so high as to take the wind out of the lower sails. Snowy craters, in which the vessel struggled, with a sharp grinding of overtaxed iron plates; lithe maelstroms which would whirl for an instant before breaking up in the clashing of masses of water: through this, the *Atalante*, like a passer-by caught in the convulsions of a surging crowd, was pulling herself up almost vertically, as if to cut into the low sky with her bowsprit, and then falling back precipitately and plunging into the pit where the great blows were awaiting her. Yes, it was a sea to take off one's tops'ls to! Loisel had been right to close-reef.

Lying hove-to meant leisure for everyone. Rolland went below to his cabin. He returned again, to knock at the mate's door. The officer had just come off watch.

"Monsieur Loisel, I would like you to come here a minute."

Propping themselves against the swaying partitions as they went, they reached the cabin. Geneviève, white as the sheet itself, with blanched lips, was lying there in a terrifying immobility.

"Her heart hasn't failed, has it?" Rolland asked.

His dreadful ignorance, once again, of all forms of weakness. . . .

Loisel picked up the wrist that lay limp along the bed; and Rolland realized that his more delicate fingers would perceive what life might be left in that body. The mate laid the arm back on the bedclothes.

"The pulse is faint, but regular," he said. "It is a case of prostration."

"And what is to be done? Some people who are sick in bed and hardly take any nourishment hold out for months; and she is not sick. . . ."

"There is this constant vomiting."

"She has not vomited for the last two days. You don't think we ought to wake her?"

The mate shook his head. "While she sleeps she is not suffering," he said.

Rolland's eyes were on the emaciated throat, where the feeble

447

breath was throbbing with an almost imperceptible movement which he at last made out.

"Ah, if I had only listened to you!" he murmured. "But now? Sail before the wind and go back to Montevideo?"

Loisel, standing motionless, did not reply.

"Yes, the time has gone by. . . . We will make for the west then, since that is our trade. I thank you, Monsieur Loisel. Now go and rest."

Left alone, he leaned over the closed lips, his hear bent to listen. A light hissing breath was reaching him now. Suppose that meant that she, also, was hove to, that she was sparing every movement in order to hold out? And, on his own part, there was nothing to be done! All the more reason, perhaps, for him to sleep, so as to be ready if the wind shifted. . . .

He went out, climbed heavily up the companionway to the chart-house, stumbling against more than one step, and called Foulon. "The moment it calms down, put the sails up. I am relying on you. . . . And send the carpenter to the cabin every half-hour, to put coal on the fire and see if my wife needs anything."

He tumbled onto the imitation-leather sofa.

At noon, Loisel came to take the watch.

"We should let him sleep," he said. "He will eat later."

Still benumbed by his almost trancelike slumber, Rolland came out of the chart-house in the afternoon. Loisel had run up the tops'ls again, and gone back to the course through the chaos. For a moment Rolland stared at the *Atalante*, struggling under the blasts that were coming from all directions, gaining the west a little across the precipitous fall and explosive rise of the sea. He gave the mate a nod of approval, and then hurried below.

The uproar in the cabin was such that he stopped on the threshold, wedging the door with his shoulder, almost not daring to go in. The poop, above, was only a deck, where the water swooped over and then ran off; but here the sea was pounding from all directions. He listened to its crashes over his head, on the side, under his feet, in blows there was no escaping. The ship's plates were groaning as if they had been shaken loose from their rivets. It could not be sleep, then, that was keeping her pressed so close against the mattress, shutting her eyes so tight. . . . He held onto the bunk's side plank, to lean over her and take her hand. She murmured something in a whisper, without opening her eyes, and he heard her with the same clarity that had astounded him on the night of the cyclone, when the whisper from Captain Thirard dominated a Witches' Sabbath such as this:

"You must marry again. . . . It was too soon. . . ."

448

He screamed at her, "You are mad!"

Only the advice had registered in his mind; the rest seemed to him already to be a part of delirium. He cried out those things that he no longer believed, the same old things: that he was going to save her, that she must stick it out, that it would end soon, that she would be well. He did not cry out that he loved her, because that would have sounded like a farewell. But there was no response to anything, either because she considered it not worth the effort, or because she was completely prostrate again.

It was during the night watch, when he had hove to again under a redoubled assault from the storm, that he came back, ruminating, to the two sentences.

With even more anger than horror, he went over that scandalous command: to marry again! It was as if she had betrayed him, insulted him, scratched out their past with a single word; brief and meager as it was, it was worth something more than that! But, above all, she had brought him face to face with tomorrow: he who like a child had been clinging for the past two weeks to the present moment, unwilling to be aware of anything except the immediate instant when the wind might change, when the sea might calm down, when the ship might hoist full sail with her head toward the northwest: a child, yes, a little beast of a youngster who would go, from time to time, to visit the cage where he had shut up a bird that refused to eat, and who would cry out in complete contentment, "It is still alive!"

Remorse sent him unconsciously to thinking of those other words she had spoken, which had seemed to him incoherent.

"It was too soon. . . ." What did she mean, "too soon"? Too soon for him to marry, at the age of thirty-five? Suddenly the meaning struck him with its lightning flash: one of those things she used to say, so penetrating that he only understood them afterward. Too soon. . . . Yes: too soon to have a wife who would be a real wife to him, to whom a man owed all that he had not given her, a wife whom he defended against herself, against life, against him. . . .

He understood it now; thanks perhaps to the very chaos of the sinister night, which was in accordance with his own overthrow. Waves, remorse, squalls, frantic reproaches, panic fits of anguish, and the icy blows of the sea, everything was confusedly blended in this aimless drifting of the ship and the man, in which the man could not even protect himself, as the ship did, by the backwash of recoil. After he had sent Loisel and Hervy off to sleep he stayed there where he was, because only the hurricane was capable of offering a balance to the torment of his soul.

"Ship lights to windward!"

The two signal lights at the same time, red and green. . . . It was a sailing-ship running down from the west, from Chile or Frisco, with a full wind astern. At moments the lights would be eclipsed in the hollows of the gigantic swells, then they would leap up anew in the high ranges of the night, before plunging back into the waves' trough. They were cutting across the *Atalante's* route at full speed, and they were drawing closer.

"The torch," Rolland demanded, not raising his voice.

The crew on watch, massed to windward, was showing signs of panic:

"They're going to run into us!"

"They're coming right on top of us!"

Rolland flung three words at them: "Shut your mouths!"

He seized the torch that a sailor had just lighted with a great deal of difficulty, in the chart-house, and scattered gleams of flame over the whole poop. The sailing-ship perceived them, and passed at a bare hundred yards from the *Atalante*.

"A hell of a trade this is," a sailor growled. "A little more, and we both would have gone to the bottom."

Rolland turned around.

"Are you through sniveling?" he called into the darkness. "Instead of squatting on your fannies under the weather-cloth, you'd better be keeping watch, the whole lot of you!"

The encounter put him in the saddle again. He, too, was going on watch. Moreover, the weather was no longer something that could possibly allow itself to be forgotten: it was getting worse from minute to minute. The west wind, charging on them at more than a hundred miles an hour—enough to peel the skin off your cheeks—clamped all the consciousness a man had left to the swollen curve of the sails, which were still holding but were ready to split.

"Clew up the fores'l!"

This time his thought did not leave the men as they moved toward the bow, a file of slow and staggering shadows on the flying bridge. They were ploughing their way through the icy water on the fore-and-aft gangway, in a temperature far below freezing point, to get at the lines that refused to turn in the chunks of ice that were the blocks. Now they were out on the yard, seamen and officers, in hand-to-hand battle with the sail, hard as a wall, which was struggling in its clew-lines, bloodying the fingers that were numb with cold. Their mouths were full of snow, their beards were hung with gleaming icicles. It was the first time he had felt their hardships with this force; the first time he had been aware, beyond the polar cold that held him rigid, beyond the anxiety that tortured him, of this fraternal warmth within himself. He had sent word to

450

the cook to have boiling-hot tea ready for them, with the order to fortify it strongly with alcohol. He would add tinned meat, and sea-biscuit. . . .

When they came down again, after an hour and a half of super-human efforts which had succeeded in saving the major sail, they drank and ate without uttering a word. Their faces had the dulled look of paralytics, and their eyes were vacant. They collapsed in a heap together under the weather-cloth, heads and boots dovetailed.

"Everybody up, to tack!"

They had scarcely sunk into the depths of a heavy sleep, when they were hit by the order called out above their massed bodies. Rolland had just observed that the storm had taken a sudden jump to north-northwest. They extricated themselves laboriously and went off again, with the jerky movements of automatons.

"To the port braces! Up helm! Brace!"

Taking a firm stance over the rope, as over a deep root they were trying to pull out, they were not succeeding in disengaging the yards, conquering the oblique thrust of the hurricane. Rolland plunged into it beside them.

"Yank it out for me, my lads!"

It was a phrase no sailor had ever heard from him, and it tightened all their muscles. The yards turned. The ship, moving into the wind, took on a nightmare speed. The tall breakers were rising to the height of the top cross-trees. The threatening approach of their great mass could be made out by everyone, in spite of the darkness.

The stern of the ship suddenly reared itself up to a prodigious height; the bow plunged down as straight as a diver, and with a rapidity akin to suicide. The engulfing flood swept up to the level of the poop-rail, washing over the entire deck. The men, taking refuge on the flying bridge and the deck-houses, were waiting for the moment to rush on the braces.

Shaking itself from side to side like a wet dog, the *Atalante* got rid of the crushing load. In quick succession, a second wave, less powerful, then a third, filled the well-deck. Rolland, who was having the ship running before the sea and was not taking his eyes off the water, let out a strident whistle which cut like a sword through the uproar. The men moved off to trim the fores'l sharp and stiffen the weather braces. The *Atalante* cleared the dangerous position without damage, and its speed died down.

Rolland spoke to Loisel, again standing near him, in the voice of the vanquished: "We will continue the southern tack as far as the ice-field, if necessary. There is nothing doing to the north."

This was to recognize defeat, to accept the southbound course of cautious men, in order to circumvent the Horn's defenses. It meant slipping down to the very extremity of the harrow of the storms, between its last teeth and the ice of the Antarctic. He, too, was about to make a wide detour, where he had dreamed of a direct and swift progress.

As he dragged his way heavily toward his cabin, he was under no illusion: he knew that this new route might carry them to a point from which his wife would never return.

XXXVII

COULD SHE KEEP afloat, in these waves, long enough for him to reach and save her? It was the third day of the southbound course. He was hardly leaving the cabin now; minute by minute he watched for that possible sinking, just as he had watched for that of the *Antonine,* glutted with the sea, those years ago. Now, as then, there was a shore to be reached, with this wreck that was a woman, half submerged. Now, as then, there was nothing to be done, except to look on, to spy out the advances and the delays in this slow absorption. Sometimes he would force a few drops of milk, in a teaspoon, between her dry lips: a superficial aid only, as much a mockery as that which the sailors of the *Antonine* had brought to their ship that was broken in its depths, when they stopped up the little holes on the deck with tow. But, as he had been then, so he was now possessed by the stubborn hope of keeping the wreck above water long enough to reach the dock, to make repairs. He had never felt his will so taut and firm, even to the point of a physical pain within his skull. Could that will not go out from him, like a virtue, to pass into her, and keep her on the surface of the engulfing sea?

Last night, in a stupor of sleep on the sofa, he had been awakened by her moans: her legs were being tortured by cramp. He massaged them for a long time, without any result, and heated cloths on the stove, to wrap them in; then he had the idea of flexing her knees, bending them and stretching them out again.

"Doesn't that ease you?" he asked. "Are you still suffering so much?"

Her only reply was the same little whimper, brief and rhythmic.

452

He straightened up, pulled the covers over her again, and remained standing, motionless. As impotent below decks as above. . . . Not even Thirard's morphine. . . .

He had never had time to look at suffering. When a man is felled by the crashing of a yard or shattered by a fall from the rigging, it is always at a time when the captain must be keeping watch over his imperiled ship. So he would leave the victim to others, after the quick first-aid. And as a sailor himself he had been too busy for contemplation. Now he took a chair, sat down beside the sick woman, and tried to listen to her moans, as was his duty. But in a few minutes he was sound asleep again.

When he opened his eyes, the whimpering had ceased, but he noticed that her breathing had taken on an unusual cadence, in three equal beats: an intake of breath, a period of suspension, an outbreathing. Even that harsh regularity reassured, rather than worried, him: it seemed a move toward the sparing of her strength.

In the morning, when he went back on deck, the men were in the midst of fishing for albatross. He found one hung up under the quarterdeck, already gutted, doused with vinegar, and sprinkled with salt. Six others were flat on the planks, one wing tipped over the other, mouths gaping, eyes half-closed: they, too, a prey to the horrors of seasickness. The men were amusing themselves by setting the ship's bull-dog on them, a vicious beast that could be approached by no one but the carpenter. He was dashing frantically around the birds, dodging their beaks the while, and he had already succeeded in strangling two by jumping on their backs, when Rolland ordered curtly, "Come now, stop it."

Ordinarily, he would let the men take their fill of sport with the carrion creatures.

"In three or four days we'll make a fine pot-pie of them," declared David, the cook, as he cut their throats.

When Rolland pushed the cabin door ajar, that afternoon, he stopped short in amazement: there was talking inside. Geneviève had found her voice again, and was apparently answering someone calmly: "No, I assure you, he is not here."

He opened the door. There was no one else in the room. She was speaking in a tranquil delirium, her eyes closed. There was no contour to anything she said. At first he thought that the hallucination had to do with an absence, for she kept repeating, "He is not here; he could not come." Was this meant to refer to him? But she continued, in a tone of despair: "It is the other, the other one who is running."

453

She went back to the exhausted voice of the very ill, from whom words demanded so much effort that she confined them to the essential, as she demanded, "Drink."

He lifted her up and held a glass of sweetened milk, diluted with Vichy, to her lips. As soon as she felt it against her mouth she began to drink eagerly, and without opening her eyes she swallowed it to the last drop. If she were only commencing to take some nourishment he thought.

As he left the room he ran into Loisel, who was hurrying toward him.

"Captain, the winds are shifting to the southeast!"

The mate explained that Hervy, who was on watch, had just had the yards squared abaft when he had noticed that the main lower tops'l was shivering to starboard, in a swift fluttering of the blanketed canvas.

Winds from the southeast! The winds that Rolland had come all this way to seek, and that were driving straight toward the Pacific! He followed the mate hurriedly to the companionway. When he came out on the poop, Hervy had already had the lower to'gants'ls run up, and everything braced for the wind on the quarter port tack.

The swell was not abating; and the good winds, too feeble, gave little support to the sailing-ship, whose rolling was accentuated when the direction was changed. The deck was sheeted over with a thick covering of ice, on which the rolling watch was scattering shovelfuls of cinders. Foulon, who was responsible for the oceanographic observations, had taken a bucket of water from over the side and plunged his thermometer into it; the bucket was upset by the roll of the ship, and the water was solidified immediately in broad spits of ice.

"Let out the royals, the flying jib, the tops'l!"

It was just so much the worse that the enormous swell was rushing at the bow like a tidal wave, and was about to set the ship a-quiver up to the trucks of the masts. Rolland was running up all the old linen again, and the high sails covered with ice that gave less speed than shock, and loaded the ship from above so as to risk the masts' breaking. A crazy engineer who opened his throttle on an unriveted track. . . . Loisel, launching his men into the shrouds, looked at Foulon. The junior officer raised his shoulders imperceptibly.

"He is doing what he knows how to do," he murmured.

What he knew how to do, what he had done so much of: risking a dismasting to gain one knot. He had done it on the *Antonine* when he was fleeing before the cyclone with an insensate amount of sail. This time it was death he was trying to shake off to the south.

He remained standing there against the wheel until darkness fell, until he had at last got the best of the storm and the swell was gradually diminishing. As always when he was on watch, he had sent the carpenter to his cabin every hour to re-stoke the narrow little stove which he was keeping red-hot and to report on the sick woman's condition. All afternoon the man had been coming back to say, "She is still just the same, Cap'n." Once, even, he had added, "She doesn't complain."

Rolland spent the night on the poop, keeping watch on the wind. He had the feeling that if he were to relax this surveillance the breeze would take advantage of it to die down and veer forward. He had never had such notions before. He accepted this one, nevertheless, without recognizing it as one of those sailors' superstitions which had always irritated him so much. He escaped from his post, during the night, only for a few swift runs to his cabin. He would push the door ajar, cast a glance inside, listen to that curious breathing, cut like the crenelations of a medieval fortress—one full, one empty, one full—and then go back to the deck. Up there, he would hear the play of that beat, again.

In the morning, with the good winds persisting, the men began to talk once more. The best sign that they felt themselves already free of the Cape was that they dared to speak of it. At Rolland's back an old seaman, Papa Sergent, was making a reckoning: "If we are getting hold of good weather at last, it will make three weeks of having things hard. That's neither too good nor too bad. Me, I was stuck off the Cape fifty-five days once, in the *Trois Soeurs.*"

Rolland knew he was right: an ordinary voyage. . . . Twenty days to get around the Horn, and without tearing so much as a handkerchief's width of canvas—there was nothing there either to exult in or to complain of. Even with all the lead they had gained since leaving France, the passage would remain merely a good passage, but with no incidents: in short, the very type of voyage that put the ship-owners in a good humor. Its only threat was of costing him his wife. . . .

That afternoon, in the midst of snow flurries, they passed Desolation Island, at the western entrance to the Strait of Magellan.

"If the winds don't change we shall have Chiloé to the south of us by day after tomorrow," Loisel said.

This was the last island of the austral ocean. After that would come the beginning of the stern coast-line of Chile; but that coast was cut into by bays, and at the head of the bays there were towns, and in the towns there were hospitals. Divia was the first town: a good port on a river that descended from the Cordillera of the

Andes, with a railroad to Santiago and Valparaiso. In the chart-house, Rolland looked for long minutes at the circle at the end of a bayonet stroke that was its mark on the map.

Toward five in the evening, the carpenter came again to the poop.

"She seems to me to be breathing queerly, Cap'n," he said.

. . . When Rolland entered the room, he was roughly met by the noisy snoring of a drunken sailor, the kind that makes the men break into laughter in the crew's quarters. He had only this memory to compare it with, because he had never heard the death rattle before. But he went out and called the mate.

Loisel examined the waxen face, the pinched nostrils.

"The kidneys have been blocked since day before yesterday," Rolland avowed. "That is what is poisoning her."

Loisel spoke very gently. "You might try to make her take a little champagne, Captain."

Rolland stared at him with wide eyes: it was champagne they gave to the dying; he knew that.

"Do you think so?" he asked.

Gravely, Loisel bowed his head.

All night, he moistened her lips with it. The contents of the spoon would run along the corners of her mouth, and fall in driblets over the shrunken chin. He thought up a plan of dipping a clean handkerchief in the glass, and wringing it out over the lips that were not only parched but as if roasted. He soaked another hand-kerchief generously in eau-de-cologne, to dab her forehead and cheeks. He was forcing back, as he did it, all emotion, all fondness: to yield to that would have meant to accept. . . . And he had never accepted: not one ship that was on fire, not another that was sink-ing under him. He had never made the gesture of surrender. . . .

As dawn approached he was persuaded that, now again, he had won. By degrees, the rumbling breath had quieted down, resolved itself into a quiet respiration, really the respiration of a placid sleep, with lips closed. He thought he was recognizing that improve-ment which so often comes to sick people in the morning, after the struggles of the night. He stood beside her for a moment, listening to that light breath, then he went over and sat down again on the sofa, with the feeling that his bad watch was finished. He leaned his head back and settled down to get an hour's sleep before return-ing to the poop.

For how long a time did he lose consciousness? Five minutes? A quarter of an hour? He never knew. He found himself sitting up again, dismayed, wide-eyed, as after a nightmare. But he had not dreamed any of this: the blow that had struck him with alarm had come from outside. In two steps, he was back at the bunk.

The oscillations of the hanging lamp sent their shadows back and forth over a rigid face, the mouth open, the features as if congealed in a stupefaction of shock. For death is a shock, the shock of a body cast off, empty, and left behind. . . . He leaned down, his ear level with the gaping mouth, and listened with all his might, sure that he would hear the slightest breath in spite of the pounding of the sea against the ship's hull. When he got up again, he spoke aloud:

"It can't be!"

It was not yet the refusal to accept the loss of her. It was merely the refusal to accept having been so misused, in her going away on tiptoe, taking advantage of a moment's unconsciousness to slip away from him, when he had watched over her all night.

"It isn't possible!" he said again.

This seemed to have happened in a world that was parallel to the world he knew, but alien to it, a world in which he could neither see nor live: another element.

He went out, made his way to the poop with the step of an automaton, and was surprised to find himself in the cold and the wind, as if he had left all that a long time ago. He paused for a moment on the threshold of the chart-house, to convince himself of the reality of familiar things. There was a distrust awakening in him, of all that seemed ordinary and perhaps was not.

Foulon, his coat-collar turned up, his throat muffled to his chin, his hands in his pockets, was pacing the deck, smoking. Rolland went up to him.

"My wife has just died," he said.

The officer took his cigarette out of his mouth. For a moment he stood motionless, and without speaking. Then he asked, "Did she suffer?"

"No."

Almost with curiosity, Rolland observed the other's saddened composure, which held not the slightest trace of surprise. And he could not keep from remarking, "You were prepared for it; I wasn't."

Meeting the overwhelming naïveté of this avowal, Foulon threw a sharp glance at his captain. It was all he could do to refrain from retorting, "That is just what we reproach you for!" But he realized immediately that Rolland was sincere, terribly sincere. There were certain elementary things that no one had taught him; what everybody knows by instinct and he did not know at all. . . . On a sailing-ship a sick person is on principle a slacker. Give him an emetic and a purgative and cut off his wine ration. . . . And this man's experience of life was confined to sailing-ships.

The evening before, in his own cabin, the third mate had re-read

457

the third volume of *Toilers of the Sea*. He would frequently give himself the luxury of recitals of hurricanes, when the waves and the wind would underscore the text, with a pride in reflecting that such reading conditions were rare. Now he was recalling the sentence: "The cave of the winds is more monstrous than the den of lions." The unbending man who stood before him had been thrown into that cave almost as a child. It had developed in him only his strength for survival; it had given him the muscles and the soul of a tamer of wild beasts. And he had scarcely come out of it when he had been entrusted with a woman, a real woman, and fragile. And how unknown!

Then had he, Foulon, a son of the comfortable middle class, the right to condemn him? He was acquitted on the ground that he acted without discrimination or understanding. But could Foulon go on from that to stifle his own revolt against the senseless forfeit? That was impossible, because of a face which the dead woman's had kept him thinking of, since the ship sailed, with yearning; and he had been first irritated and then anxious.

"No one will forget Madame Rolland, Captain. You have my deep sympathy," he said.

They buried her at sea, the next day.

They had been much perplexed at first. A dead woman, a captain's wife who had died—here was something altogether unusual aboardship. There was no tradition that could be applied to such a situation. Loisel had decided that there must be, as a matter of course, a service resembling ordinary funerals; but it was "My Pension," the carpenter, who first thought of practical essentials. He considered her a part of his duty, in death as in illness, and as soon as the news became known, he had approached the mate.

"Has the captain thought about laying her out? Would he like me to attend to that? I was a bell-ringer in my village, and I used to lend a hand in dressing the dead."

Rolland, when this was suggested to him, had nodded in agreement, and the carpenter went below. He came up again at the end of half-an-hour.

"Everything is ready, Cap'n. She was not hard to arrange."

Loisel and Foulon accompanied Rolland to the cabin. They found her dressed in her black frock, with shoes on her feet, and a scarf knotted like a chin strap to close her lips; her hands were clasped on a rosary. A candle was burning on the shelf-table, and an albatross feather was in a glass of water nearby.

The three men remained standing for a minute, then Loisel and

Foulon, after the sign of the cross and an aspersion, went out. Rolland drew up a chair and sat down.

Geneviève's face was returning from the past with the swiftness of hallucination. The relaxation of the first hours of death was restoring the features, even though much thinner, of the young girl; that visage which had attracted the Gicquel's wedding guest from the moment he caught sight of it. Then the delicate features grew almost childlike; the slender body seemed to become smaller still. The watcher was stricken by the evidence of her fragility. This was what he had done to it. "They let themselves be broken, my poor Pierre, and afterward it is irreparable. . . ." Father Monnard had foretold this. . . .

When the watch changed, Hervy and Pléneau visited the cabin. Then Loisel came to say that the crew was asking to see her. The men came down by watches, taking off their caps as they arrived. They looked at her, and then went out again, after little signs of the cross which only touched their foreheads and ended in the air.

The mechanic and the carpenter had put their heads together to construct a coffin for her, a real one. They were far from willing simply to lash her skillfully to a plank, as they did a sailor. They made a coffin of heavy sheet-iron, so that it would sink in one block, spelling each other in sawing, filing, bolting, all night. Then they screwed a zinc cross on the lid. Loisel, on his own responsibility, had a piece of new canvas handed over, to make an ample shroud.

In the morning, when she had been placed on her bier, he had the dead woman carried into the saloon.

Rolland had seated himself beside the coffin, which was covered with a white cloth. When he raised his eyes, after a long minute, they fell on the picture, Atalanta's immutable race, and the symbolism of that lambent image struck him for the first time: this was the speed of which he had made a murderous law.

"She is what I sacrificed her to," he reflected, staring with abhorrence at the motionless racer as if she were a living creature. "I am going to cast my wife, *my wife*, into the sea; the woman they have installed here will remain. It is she whom I shall take back with me."

A thought cut through him like a knife: before him, long before him, Geneviève had known that she would die so that the woman set up there would not have failed, so that the ship would continue to be worthy of its name. He was hearing her moan, in her delirium, "It is the other, the other one who is running." He was sure now that she had been struggling against this wretched mess of a painting, on that day. And he was seeing his dead wife again, that first

459

evening, in this saloon. She, too, had looked at the picture for a long time. "Did she win?" she had asked.

Yes, she had won!

The door opened. Loisel, his cap in his hand, came in. Four men were following him.

They had brought the ship to, and had placed the heavy coffin in the fore-and-aft gangway, after ballasting it further with pieces of pig-iron. The thaw had set in. Thick candle-lengths of ice were detaching themselves from the masting and crashing on the deck. A block of it fell on the coffin and bounced back in a burst of crystal. Papa Sergent, the "dean" of the sailors, stepped forward and brushed the lid clean with the back of his hand, while Loisel was reading the De Profundis aloud.

The vessel was still rolling heavily; but as she was wedged in there between the high steel rail and the large hatch, surrounded by bareheaded seamen who had put on coats and rigged themselves with neckties, she seemed at last protected, more at home on this ship than she had ever been when she was alive. When the prayer was finished four men, with great effort, lifted the coffin and balanced it on the rail.

They did not have to push it at all: it was the *Atalante*, casting to starboard, which discharged her burden in one swift glide.

They waited a moment until the eddy had disappeared, then, one by one, they put on their hats again; for nothing embarrassed them more than to remain for a long time bareheaded. Rolland was standing in the front row, rigid and impenetrable. He, too, covered his head again and went away, with slow steps, toward the poop-rail.

Loisel was already giving orders to continue the course. As he had prophesied, they passed Chiloé the next day and ran into good weather. The officers had the hatches opened, the doors of the deck-houses unsealed, the quarters washed out.

"Our hard time is leaving us, like a rat's tail," declared Cozic, as he went on watch at noon. "If we had had a good wind a week earlier, the poor woman would have got over it."

Then the nights became shorter, and the sun shed a little of its true warmth in the middle of the day. One morning, Pléneau's pigs and chickens saw the doors of their prison open, after being caged up so long; and the black cat, that had cowered for weeks in the galley, ventured a cautious paw on deck.

The thought of the dead woman continued to force itself upon the men, because the captain never left the deck any more, day or night. He had not returned to his cabin at all, and he was only sleeping for a few hours in the chart-house. The best of the men

said, as the men of the *Antonine* had said of the furious promenades of Captain Thirard, "He is wearing out his trouble by walking." The others, lashed by some reproach that was scarcely just,
by some too-harsh word that underscored a negligence, growled behind his back: "We have to foam at the mouth, because that's what
he's doing. When he's bawling us out, he isn't thinking any more
how he shoved her into the water. For you can say that he did shove
her in."

The officers had at once realized that he meant to wall himself up
in his official duties, and that distances must be, more than ever,
rigorously kept. Loisel, more expansive, might easily have regretted
this, but Foulon, with a certain respect, had declared: "It is better
that way. It simplifies everything."

For him, the widower, the loss of his wife was only beginning,
and he knew that the adjustment would take a long time. He was,
in fact, capsizing, but slowly, hour by hour. Once the complete turn
was made, he would find again on the bottom what had always been
on top; after that, he would have to sail keel up.

He had a service held for her at Frisco, but it was an Irish priest,
with a terrible accent, so that the prayers, shorn of their customary
sound, did not seem to have to do with her any longer.

One evening when he went into the saloon, he found Pléneau and
his three colleagues examining some photographs that were spread
out on the table. The "chicken-coop lieutenant," seeing him come
in, blushed like a fiery coal and made a move to sweep up the pile.
Rolland leaned over.

"It's some photos I've just had developed in town," Pléneau
stammered.

He had taken them at the time of the Equator celebration, and
in two of the prints Geneviève, in a light dress, but already terribly
thin, was smiling at the sailors' masquerade. Rolland took one in
each hand and looked at them for a long time.

"Could you let me have them, or have other prints made for me?"
he asked.

"Of course, Captain."

"She was already ill, that day," Hervy recalled, in his deep voice,
"and it took courage to stay up."

"She had courage, to the end," Rolland averred; and, as if to
himself, he added, "Too much."

On the return voyage, the *Atalante* performed prodigies of speed,
to which he gave no thought this time. It was one of those fantasti-
cally lucky crossings, when the wind veered with the ship at every
change of its course; always running free with the wind astern. . . .
The officers and the crew, their sporting instincts aroused again,

would not tear themselves away from the deck, the log, the compass. He himself had only the feeling of retracing the course of time. He discovered her again, dying, off Cape Horn. Next came the latitude where she had moaned, "It was too soon!" Then there was the parallel of Montevideo, where he could have saved her; and the Equator, where he looked at Pléneau's photographs for hours on end. In the Doldrums, which they rushed through in thirty hours, he again saw her fleeing from the poop, with her dress plastered to her body by the sudden pelting showers. In the trade winds, he pictured the tent and the chaise-longue to which he had abandoned her. The pilgrimage was the more cruel for being made through the emptiness of the sea and the hours. For memory found only the map's co-ordinates to attach itself to. Wherever he went, back over the course, he would find her only in odd bits, because he had been, on the voyage out, so indifferent to her. The ship had separated them more widely than two oceans could have done. So the loneliness to which he had condemned her was turning back upon him, and deepening from mile to mile.

Yet he knew that he would only touch bottom when he was cast ashore, at the spot where she would have been waiting for him.

She became once more really actual and living, in fact, when the *Atalante* had drawn fairly close to the coast of France. There had been so little of the material left to her when she died, she had already become so transparent, that she seemed ready to become a phantom. But he was not one whose eyes caught sight of white ladies running along the deck at night. What he was seeing now, with a terrible intensity, was her visits to the officers' quarters, the dinners of the first evenings, which she transfigured with her presence and her smile. He had allowed her to dissolve upon the sea. In revenge, she was recovering vigor and force, an increased corporeal density, in the approach to her home. The woman who lay dying was slipping far away, there in the south. In her place was rising up, alive, animated, full of all sensuous response, the Geneviéve of the embarkation and of the land. That image was sinking deeper within him, like a hollow mold whose contours would grow more precise with every day, opening up a yawning void in his inmost being; that void, all that remained of her, he would at least know how to keep. "He will make his life over again," big Hervy had said to Foulon one evening, when they were talking with their backs against the chart-house, without any suspicion that he was shut up inside. . . . *No!*

It was to Le Havre that they were going. It was there that she awaited him, with her poor crushed finger. But he would never have imagined such an abominable shock as he received there, when he saw her standing on the dock where the men were making fast the hawsers. Her head was thrown back, her eyes were ranging over the ship; they fell upon him, passed on indifferently, searched farther. . . .

"My wife, Captain."

Close to, the resemblance faded, enough to dissipate his panic and make it possible for him to remain standing upright before this strange woman, slack and as if broken in two as his body was. More pronounced features, darker hair, especially eyes which were only looking outward: a replica of Geneviève, at once accentuated and superficial. . . .

Yet this explained why Foulon, those first days, should have been chilled by a presence which was bringing back under his eyes, at all hours, this young wife whom he had just left; and then why he should have defended Geneviève with a violence that manifests itself only when someone precious is threatened, even if in a double, and by a kind of proxy. All the same, that did not justify the cruelty of this presentation. The junior officer should have taken his wife aside, should have told her. . . .

"My apologies, Captain, but my wife tells me that the order for general mobilization has been posted," Foulon said.

For a young man, a piece of news like that would be more important than everything else put together! Foulon had been intent upon having it verified, on the spot, by the woman who had just read the first white placards, with their little flags, as she waited for him on this summer day in 1914.

XXXVIII

THE CORVETTE CAPTAIN, President of the War Council, looked up from the sheaf of papers he was holding in both hands and fixed his cold eyes on those of Rolland, who was standing before him.

"Captain, I have read your affidavit as ship-master. It makes it plain that you abandoned your ship, the *Caldera,* taking with you your entire crew, following an attack by submarine, and this without having fired a shot at the German submersible. But less than three weeks before, right here in Cherbourg, two naval guns of ninety millimeters had been installed on your ship, and you had been given a leading seaman, with four bluejackets, to take charge of them. The matter is all the more regrettable in that we have just been informed that two other large sailing-ships, in the same localities, have been sunk, and probably by the same submarine. But they defended themselves, in such fashion that the first had more than half its crew on the casualty list, whether killed or wounded, and there were two killed and six wounded on the second ship. What have you to say in your defense?

Rolland had listened, his arms folded across his chest. The three gold stripes that marked his rank were gleaming on the sleeves of his navy-blue pea-jacket, itself crumpled and soiled both by the days endured in the life-boats at sea after the *Caldera* sank, and by the interminable voyage getting back to France. Commander of a vessel of more than twenty-five hundred gross tons, he had been granted a commission as auxiliary lieutenant-commander; and he had put on his dress uniform for the correct reception of the German officer and the seizure party that accompanied him. He replied now in the curt voice which his officers and crews had learned to know and fear.

"Monsieur President, I merely confirm what I stated in my report: the enemy was at no moment within range of my guns, either in direction or in distance."

"What time was it when you caught sight of the submarine, and what was your speed at that instant?"

"It was four forty-five A.M. The *Caldera* was running free, on the port tack, under a faint breeze from north to east. The speed was almost nothing; only just enough for us to keep the vessel answering the helm."

"Your report indicates that you recalled your men to combat posts. At that moment, then, it was your intention to fight?"

"Neither more nor less at that moment than at any other time. To the end, it was my intention to fight."

"It is unfortunate that this intention should have led to no result."

Rolland unfolded his arms for a brief gesture with his right hand.

"I think," he said, "that we do not understand the same thing by the word 'fight.' There is a fight when the adversaries can exchange blows. There is not, and there cannot be, when one of the two is solely in a position to receive them, without being able to deliver any in return."

The corvette captain leaned back in his chair.

"What, then, would you call the action of your fellow-commander, the captain of the *Mathilde*, who fired more than two hundred shells before abandoning his ship, which was on fire?"

"Leaving eight dead and taking with him ten wounded, all civilian sailors. . . . As not one of those two hundred shells could reach the submarine, since in the case of the *Mathilde,* as in my case, the enemy remained constantly out of range, I call that useless slaughter."

"The tribunal compliments itself on not sharing your opinion. A heroic defense is never useless."

Looking to right and left, the officer noted four nods of agreement from his fellow-members of the court.

"As to whether there was heroism, you are certainly good judges, gentlemen," Rolland replied, "but I maintain that there was not a defense. To defend oneself is to repulse force with force. To return to what concerns me: I have specified in my report that the submarine was abeam of us at a distance of at least eleven thousand yards when it fired its first shell. The range of our guns was no more than nine thousand yards; in practice, according to the master gunner, they would not even reach that far. It was impossible for me, therefore, to engage in an action from which I could have hoped for any result whatever."

He left time for the figures to sink in; then he continued, with equal dryness, and in the tone of a blackboard demonstration, "Moreover—I have also called attention to this in my report—the wind had by that time completely died down. I was becalmed, and I could neither approach the enemy nor move my ship. I had only one chance of coming to grips: precisely by *not* firing back rashly, so that the enemy, believing me unarmed, would come closer, with the object of saving his ammunition. But I learned, from the officer in command of the prize crew, that he was perfectly informed. As a matter of fact, the submarine discharged three other shells at me, one of which went through my canvas, but it still kept itself out of my range. And when it drew up, to send the officer and his men aboard, it only did so by remaining always on my bow and on the vessel's axis, which would obviously make it unfeasible for me to fire."

"But, after all, you are not going to make me believe that there was nothing else to be tried, that you were obliged to let yourself be taken without resistance!"

A gleam was coming into the eyes that Rolland kept fixed upon the president. That gentleman, to all evidence, had not too much knowledge of what a sailing-ship was!

"I have already said, and written," he reminded him, with exasperation, "that I was immobilized in a calm. Then, what ought I to have done? Put off in the dinghy with the cabin boy and try

465

to swing the vessel around, towing it from the bow, so as to bring my guns at last into firing position?"

Four of the looks bent upon Rolland were frozen still further by this sarcasm. Only one of the officers, a lieutenant-commander in the Reserve, already with graying hair, who probably came from the commerce and sailing administration, had an amused light in his eyes, and regarded Rolland with more sympathy.

As for the president, he closed the report that had lain open before him on the table, and concluded: "I suppose that comes back to saying that you did not believe that you ought even to attempt a gesture of defense before surrendering your ship. We agree on this?"

Rolland bowed his head, and replied in a different voice, the gravity of which stilled his judges to attention, "A gesture, exactly. . . . It is because I did not make this gesture that since the beginning of this session you have been reproaching me—though without wishing to say so expressly—with having failed in my duty. If I had fired, with the certainty of only making a noise and some holes in the water, if I had made the 'gesture,' I should be here only to receive your congratulations. I should not have saved my ship, I should not even have scratched the enemy's paint, but I should have had some members of my crew slaughtered. That, I was not willing to do. You are at liberty to blame me for this, gentlemen, if you believe that you ought to do so."

The president felt that this time everything had been said. He questioned the four judges with a look. As none of them moved a muscle, he turned back to Rolland:

"You need not stay longer, Captain. But do not go far away while the inquiry is in progress."

Rolland wheeled about. Behind him, the room had filled up: he found himself now facing a small crowd: his officers, his crew. He did not know them well. Since the *Atalante,* he had asked to change his ship with almost every voyage. These men here had been under his orders for barely two weeks when they had the encounter with the submarine. On that morning all his officers, with one voice, had approved his decision: there was nothing to be done, therefore do nothing. To them, as to himself, that seemed a matter of course. And in the life-boats they had behaved extremely well. Four hundred miles to get over, eight days packed in the boats like sardines, in heat that was like molten lead, before they reached the first land, Santa Cruz de la Palma, in the Canaries. . . . The first mate's life-boat had leaked like a wicker basket. Two of his men bailed day and night, but when Rolland, worried, questioned him, he had replied. "We're keeping up a rate of thirty buckets a minute, Cap'n. Everything's all right."

The men? As always, they acted like kids. At Santa Cruz they had hardly sobered up at all: the little "cooked wine," akin to Madeira. . . . Getting them onto the steamship which was to repatriate them was the same story as at the sailings from Dunkerque or Le Havre, minus the "square-braces." They had all arrived flanked by women they had picked up on the island.

Rolland had to split their ranks, now, to get outside. As they could not catch his eye, they at least showed their deference and approbation by the alacrity with which they made way for him.

Beyond their group, there were curious spectators, perspiring in the stifling-hot room. One of them signaled to him as he went out. He recognized the man: a captain who had been stopped three months earlier by the German corsair *Felix Count Luckner,* which had sacked his ship, flung his spare sails overboard, and sawed off his to'gants'l masts before removing the three-hundred-odd prisoners he was carrying. He, too, knew that one does not always do as one wishes. . . .

Rolland went out and began to walk up and down the courtyard, under the scraggy lime trees, while the inquiry was being continued inside, through the questioning of the officers and men. They would be at it for hours! When the investigators had heard all the others repeat what he himself had repeated over and over—that a cannon is not made to shoot more than two thousand yards beyond its range, and that unless it is bent it will not shoot lengthwise if it is so fixed as to be able to shoot only crosswise—they would end up by understanding. They would ratify the report, without venturing to go as far as reprimand, or even "regret." They would console themselves for his not having nailed his standard to the mainmast, as in the time of the kings, and gone down crying, "Long live Poincaré!"

What he had done was more difficult.

He would never forget what he had felt, that morning, when his second-in-command had wakened him.

"Captain, there is something rather peculiar across our port bow. I have been observing it for more than a quarter of an hour, and I am sure it is a submarine."

He had been getting into his clothes, in feverish haste, as he replied, "You are seeing things. We have been out of their territory for a long time."

He had been refusing to believe in such a piece of luck, reckoned with on every voyage. And when he reached the poop, leaping up the stairs four at a time, there had been that constriction in his throat, from joy, when through the binoculars he made out the periscope and two "masts" of a submarine that had come to the surface.

If he had not, on the instant, opened up his two guns and fired first, it was, as he had said, because the target was out of reach, and he was awaiting the right moment to expose his artillery. It was the old reflex, once more active, of the Saint Malo privateers, disguised as merchant ships, which would never fire their broadsides until they were within a good range, when the volleys would be murderous. Yet, when it had become evident that the enemy knew he was armed and intended to demolish him without danger to himself, how his spirit had sprung toward his guns! To uncover them, spit out their shells like insults, and, since he could not hit his target, to bawl out—at least to bawl out—to the Boche, with his cannon fire, "You'll have to kill me to silence me!"

And the judges, just now, who were wondering if he would have been able to do that! And colleagues who would be whispering to one another behind his back, "If there was one man from whom a combat of honor was to be expected—"

He had been stopped short, nailed to the planks of the deck. At this instant, from the innermost depths of himself, the others had risen up, all together, to block him. He did not know they were there. . . . The others, his men, who were looking at him fixedly to find out what he was going to do with their lives; and the cabin boy, who was fifteen years old and who put up a brave show because his name was Yves Monnard, and because Rolland had said to him, when he signed him on, "I am taking you with me to make you such a man as your father was. . . ." He had paid with his wife's life—and what a wife!—for the ribbon of fine voyages. That was enough! These men here should not have to pay him with their flesh, uselessly, for a swashbuckler's medal.

And there it was! He had not seized the opportunity to blow up everything, and himself with it, because he was not alone in the business, and because, after all, he had realized that. Not alone, that time; but alone afterward, as before! . . .

"Captain Rolland?"

This unknown man, very well-groomed, in a gray suit, had just come out of the room where the judges were still sitting, and after a brief hesitation he had stepped up to Rolland and stopped him. Without waiting for an answer, he introduced himself: "Jean Barquet."

For a moment Rolland wondered whether this man, too, had not been called for the inquiry. Then he remembered: Monsieur Barquet, junior, was manager of his company, in Cherbourg. The former apprentice had come as a spectator. Perhaps, if he held a lasting spite, he had not been ill-pleased to see him affronted and stung, in his turn: a jesuitical fashion of settling old accounts. . . .

"I should not have recognized you," he remarked.

He was speaking with complete detachment. This was a ghost, returning—but from such a distant past, from a world that was indeed dead! That "Débarqué" should have succeeded in life had once made him wild with rage, but it had no importance whatever, any more.

"Will you permit me to congratulate you?"

Well, yes, quite so: this was really Barquet! He was remembering: that way the apprentice had had, at once timid and obstinate, of following out his own thought, without paying any attention to what had just been said or not said. . . . Rolland went back to the sarcastic tone of the topman on the *Galatée*, to ask, "Do you really think congratulations are called for?"

If this man was not sticking up for "heroic defense," he was thinking, sardonically, then goodbye to France!

"You said, a while ago," Barquet went on, "that you had placed the lives of your men ahead of everything else. That was what was so good!"

"It surprised you, eh?"

"Oh, no!"

He had almost cried out the words, and Rolland was not able to restrain the twitching of his lips which showed him to be deeply and unexpectedly moved. The look that the former apprentice was now fixing upon him made it impossible for him to doubt the meaning that his testimony was meant to convey: the testimony of all the weak, whom he, Rolland, had trampled upon, who had detested and cursed his hard-heartedness, but who had never ceased to appeal from it to the man he had become, the man who had been able to remain motionless and mute on the deck of the *Caldera*. From the *Galatée* to the *Caldera*—the course could be measured so. Since Monnard the priest, Thirard, Geneviève, were all dead, there was only this man left who could do it.

"You make me very happy," he said.

But then, caught up at once by his old distrust of exaggeration, his hatred of sentimentality, he flung out, "Yet you didn't come just on purpose to tell me that."

"I came also," Jean Barquet replied composedly, "to make you a proposition. The government has asked for two of our ships, to be fitted out as decoy-ships. It would be possible for us to have you given the command of one of them. Do you want to take it? You have a right to your revenge."

469

The decoy-ships: submarine chasers, camouflaged, powerfully armed, with picked crews. . . . They had to seek every opportunity to get themselves attacked by the enemy. . . .

"I thank you," Rolland said. "I accept."

He held out his hand, and surprised himself by its firm and swift pressure.

"Afterward," Barquet added, "once the war is over, the Company will be able to offer you—"

Rolland interrupted him, with a half-smile.

"Oh, the 'afterward,' on those ships, even in the ordinary line of duty—there can't be one for everybody," he said.